Adam Smith, Joseph Black

Essays on I. Moral sentiments; II. Astronomical inquiries; III.

Formation of languages

Adam Smith, Joseph Black

Essays on I. Moral sentiments; II. Astronomical inquiries; III. Formation of languages

ISBN/EAN: 9783337204471

Printed in Europe, USA, Canada, Australia, Japan

Cover: Foto ©Andreas Hilbeck / pixelio.de

More available books at **www.hansebooks.com**

THE

ESSAYS

OF

ADAM SMITH.

.

ESSAYS

ON

I. MORAL SENTIMENTS;
II. ASTRONOMICAL INQUIRIES;
III. FORMATION OF LANGUAGES;
IV. HISTORY OF ANCIENT PHYSICS;
V. ANCIENT LOGIC AND METAPHYSICS;
VI. THE IMITATIVE ARTS;
VII. MUSIC, DANCING, POETRY;
VIII. THE EXTERNAL SENSES;
IX. ENGLISH AND ITALIAN VERSES.

BY

ADAM SMITH, LL.D. F.R.S.,

Author of the 'Inquiry into the Nature and Causes of the Wealth of Nations.'

———◆◆———

LONDON:
ALEX. MURRAY & CO., 30, QUEEN SQUARE, W.C.
1872.

LONDON:
BRADBURY, EVANS, AND CO., PRINTERS, WHITEFRIARS.

BIOGRAPHICAL NOTICE.

ADAM SMITH, the author of these Essays and of the 'Inquiry into the Nature and Causes of the Wealth of Nations,' was born at Kirkaldy, June 5, 1723, a few months after the death of his father. He was a sickly child, and indulged by his mother, who was the object of his filial gratitude for sixty years. When about three years old, and at the house of Douglass of Strathenry, his mother's brother, he was carried off by tinkers or gipsies, but soon recovered from them. At the burgh school of his native town he made rapid progress, and soon attracted notice by his passion for books, and by the extraordinary powers of his memory. His weakness of body prevented him joining in athletic sports, but his generous and friendly temperament made him a favourite with his schoolmates; and he was noted then, as through after life, for absence in company and a habit of speaking to himself when alone. From the grammar school of Kirkaldy, he was sent, in 1737, to the University of Glasgow, whence, in 1740, he went to Baliol College, Oxford, enjoying an exhibition on the Snell foundation. When at Glasgow College, his favourite studies were mathematics and natural philosophy, but that did not long divert his mind from pursuits more congenial to him, more particularly the political history of mankind, which gave scope to the power of his comprehensive genius, and gratified his ruling passion of contributing to the happiness and the improvement of society. To his early taste for Greek generally, may be due the clearness and fulness with which he states his political reasonings. At Oxford he employed himself frequently in the practice of translation, with a view to the improvement of his own style, and used to commend such exercises to all who cultivate the art of composition. He also cultivated with the greatest care the study of languages; and his knowledge of them led him to a peculiar experience in everything that could illustrate the institutions, the manners, and the ideas of different ages and nations.

After a residence at Oxford of seven years, he returned to Kirkaldy, and lived two years with his mother, engaged in studies, but without any fixed plan for his future life. He had been originally destined for the Church of England; but not finding the ecclesiastical profession suitable to his taste, he took chance of obtaining some of those moderate preferments, to which literary attainments lead in Scotland. Removing to Edinburgh in 1748, he read lectures on rhetoric and belles lettres, under the patronage of Lord Kames; and when in Edinburgh became intimate with David Hume.

In 1751 he was elected Professor of Logic in the University of Glasgow; and, the year following, he became Professor of Moral Philosophy there; a situation he held for thirteen years, and used to look back on as the most useful and happy of his life; and, though but a narrow scene for his ambition, may have led to the future eminence of his literary character. In delivering his lectures, Mr. Smith trusted

almost entirely to extemporary elocution. His manner, though not
graceful, was plain and unaffected, and he never failed to interest his
hearers.   Each discourse consisted commonly of several distinct propositions, which he successively endeavoured to prove and illustrate.
At first he often appeared to speak with hesitation; but, as he advanced,
the matter seemed to crowd upon him, his manner became warm and
animated, and his expression easy and fluent.   His reputation as a
philosopher attracted a multitude of students from a great distance to
the University ; and those branches of science which he taught became
fashionable, and his opinions were the chief topics of discussion in the
clubs and literary societies of Glasgow.   While Adam Smith became
thus eminent as a public lecturer, he was gradually laying the foundation of a more extensive reputation by preparing for the press his
System of Morals; and the first edition of his Essays appeared in
1757, under the title of THE THEORY OF MORAL SENTIMENTS.

Of this essay, Dugald Stewart remarks, 'that whatever opinion we
may entertain of the justness of its conclusions, it must be allowed to
be a singular effort of invention, ingenuity, and subtilty; that it contains a large mixture of important truth, and has had the merit of
directing the attention of philosophers to a view of human nature,
which had formerly in a great measure escaped their notice ; and no
work, undoubtedly, can be mentioned, ancient or modern, which exhibits so complete a view of those facts with respect to our moral perceptions, which it is one great object of this branch of science to refer
to their general laws ; and well deserves the careful study of all whose
taste leads them to prosecute similar enquiries.   These facts are presented in the most happy and beautiful lights ; and when the subject
leads him to address the imagination and the heart, the variety and
felicity of his illustrations, the richness and fluency of his eloquence ;
and the skill with which he wins the attention and commands the passions of his readers, leave him, among our English moralists, without a
rival.   Towards the close of 1763, Mr. Smith arranged to visit the
continent with the Duke of Buccleugh, returning to London in 1766.
For the next ten years he lived quietly with his mother at Kirkaldy ;
and in 1776, accounted to the world for his long retreat, by the publication of his 'INQUIRY INTO THE NATURE AND CAUSES OF THE
WEALTH OF NATIONS.'   In 1778, Mr. Smith was appointed a Com-
missioner of Customs in Scotland, the pecuniary emoluments of which
were considerable.   In 1784, he lost his mother.   In 1788, his cousin,
Miss Douglass, died, to whom he had been strongly attached ; and in
July, 1790, he died, having, a short while before, in conversation with
his friend Riddell, regretted that 'HE HAD DONE SO LITTLE.'

[Above biographic notes and literary opinions have been abridged from a paper on 'The
Life and Writings of Adam Smith,' by Professor Dugald Stewart, of Edinburgh. 1793.—A. M.]

ADVERTISEMENT
TO THE SIXTH EDITION.

———

SINCE the first publication of the THEORY OF MORAL SENTIMENTS, which was in the beginning of the year 1759, several corrections, and a good many illustrations of the doctrines contained in it, have occurred to me. But the various occupations in which the different accidents of my life necessarily involved me, have till now prevented me from revising this work with the care and attention which I always intended. The reader will find the principal alterations which I have made in this New Edition, in the last Chapter of the third Section of Part First; and in the four first Chapters of Part Third. Part Sixth, as it stands in this New Edition, is altogether new. In Part Seventh, I have brought together the greater part of the different passages concerning the Stoical Philosophy, which, in the former Editions, had been scattered about in different parts of the work. I have likewise endeavoured to explain more fully, and examine more distinctly, some of the doctrines of that famous sect. In the fourth and last Section of the same Part, I have thrown together a few additional observations concerning the duty and the principle of veracity. There are, besides, in other parts of the work, a few other alterations and corrections of no great moment.

In the last paragraph of the first Edition of the present work, I said that I should in another discourse endeavour to give an account of the general principles of law and government, and of the different revolutions which they had undergone in the different ages and periods of society; not only in what concerns justice, but in what concerns police, revenue, and arms, and whatever else is the object of law. In the *Inquiry concerning the Nature and Causes of the Wealth of Nations*, I have partly executed this promise; at least so far as concerns police, revenue, and arms. What remains, the theory of jurisprudence, which I have long projected, I have hitherto been hindered from executing, by the same occupations which had till now prevented me from revising the present work. Though my very advanced age leaves me, I acknowledge, very little expectation of ever being able to execute this great work to my own satisfaction; yet, as I have not altogether abandoned the design, and as I wish still to continue under the obligation of doing what I can, I have allowed the paragraph to remain as it was published more than thirty years ago, when I entertained no doubt of being able to execute every thing which it announced.

ESSAYS BY ADAM SMITH

ON

PHILOSOPHICAL SUBJECTS.

ADVERTISEMENT BY THE EDITORS.

THE much lamented author of these Essays left them in the hands of his friends to be disposed of as they thought proper, having immediately before his death destroyed many other manuscripts which he thought unfit for being made public. When these were inspected, the greater number of them appeared to be parts of a plan he once had formed, for giving a connected history of the liberal sciences and elegant arts. It is long since he found it necessary to abandon that plan as far too extensive ; and these parts of it lay beside him neglected until his death. His friends are persuaded, however, that the reader will find in them that happy connection, that full and accurate expression, and that clear illustration which are conspicuous in the rest of his works ; and that though it is difficult to add much to the great fame he so justly acquired by his other writings, these will be read with satisfaction and pleasure.

JOSEPH BLACK.
JAMES HUTTON.

CONTENTS.

THE THEORY OF MORAL SENTIMENTS.

PART I.

OF THE PROPRIETY OF ACTIONS.

PART II.

OF MERIT AND DEMERIT ; OR, OF THE OBJECTS OF REWARD AND PUNISHMENT.

PART III.

OF THE FOUNDATION OF OUR JUDGMENTS CONCERNING OUR OWN SENTI-
MENTS AND CONDUCT, AND OF THE SENSE OF DUTY.

PART IV.

OF THE EFFECT OF UTILITY UPON THE SENTIMENT OF APPROBATION.

THEORY

OF

MORAL SENTIMENTS.

Part I.—*Of the Propriety of Action.*

SEC. I.—OF THE SENSE OF PROPRIETY.

CHAP. I.—*Of Sympathy.*

HOW selfish soever man may be supposed, there are evidently some principles in his nature, which interest him in the fortune of others, and render their happiness necessary to him, though he derives nothing from it except the pleasure of seeing it. Of this kind is pity or compassion, the emotion which we feel for the misery of others, when we either see it, or are made to conceive it in a very lively manner. That we often derive sorrow from the sorrow of others, is a matter of fact too obvious to require any instances to prove it; for this sentiment, like all the other original passions of human nature, is by no means confined to the virtuous and humane, though they perhaps may feel it with the most exquisite sensibility. The greatest ruffian, the most hardened violator of the laws of society, is not altogether without it.

As we have no immediate experience of what other men feel, we can form no idea of the manner in which they are affected, but by conceiving what we ourselves should feel in the like situation. Though our brother is upon the rack, as long as we ourselves are at our ease, our senses will never inform us of what he suffers. They never did, and never can, carry us beyond our own person, and it is by the imagination only that we can form any conception of what are his sensations. Neither can that faculty help us to this any other way, than by representing to us what would be our own, if we were in his case. It is the impressions of our own senses only, not those of his, which our imaginations copy. By the imagination we place ourselves in his situation, we conceive ourselves enduring all the same torments, we enter as it were into his body, and become in some measure the same person with him, and thence form some idea of his sensations, and even feel something which, though weaker in degree, is not altogether unlike them. His agonies, when they are thus brought home to ourselves, when we have thus adopted and made them our own, begin at last to affect us, and we then tremble and shudder at the thought of what he feels. For as to be in pain or distress of any kind excites the most excessive sorrow, so to conceive or to imagine that we are in it, excites some degree of the same emotion, in proportion to the vivacity or dulness of the conception.

That this is the source of our fellow-feeling for the misery of others, that it is by changing places in fancy with the sufferer, that we come either to conceive or to be affected by what he feels, may be demonstrated by many obvious observations, if it should not be thought sufficiently evident of itself. When we see a stroke aimed and just ready to fall upon the leg or arm of another person, we naturally shrink and draw back our own leg or our own arm; and when it does fall, we feel it in some measure, and are hurt by it as well as the sufferer. The mob, when they are gazing at a dancer on the slack rope, naturally writhe and twist and balance their own bodies, as they see him do, and as they feel that they themselves must do if in his situation. Persons of delicate fibres and a weak constitution of body complain, that in looking on the sores and ulcers which are exposed by beggars in the streets, they are apt to feel an itching or uneasy sensation in the corresponding part of their own bodies. The horror which they conceive at the misery of those wretches affects that particular part in themselves more than any other; because that horror arises from conceiving what they themselves would suffer, if they really were the wretches whom they are looking upon, and if that particular part in themselves was actually affected in the same miserable manner. The very force of this conception is sufficient, in their feeble frames, to produce that itching or uneasy sensation complained of. Men of the most robust make, observe that in looking upon sore eyes they often feel a very sensible soreness in their own, which proceeds from the same reason; that organ being in the strongest man more delicate, than any other part of the body is in the weakest.

Neither is it those circumstances only, which create pain or sorrow, that call forth our fellow-feeling. Whatever is the passion which arises from any object in the person principally concerned, an analogous emotion springs up, at the thought of his situation, in the breast of every attentive spectator. Our joy for the deliverance of those heroes of tragedy or romance who interest us, is as sincere as our grief for their distress, and our fellow-feeling with their misery is not more real than that with their happiness. We enter into their gratitude towards those faithful friends who did not desert them in their difficulties; and we heartily go along with their resentment against those perfidious traitors who injured, abandoned, or deceived them. In every passion of which the mind of man is susceptible, the emotions of the by-stander always correspond to what, by bringing the case home to himself, he imagines should be the sentiments of the sufferer.

Pity and compassion are words appropriated to signify our fellow-feeling with the sorrow of others. Sympathy, though its meaning was, perhaps, originally the same, may now, however, without much impropriety, be made use of to denote our fellow-feeling with any passion whatever.

Upon some occasions sympathy may seem to arise merely from the view of a certain emotion in another person. The passions, upon some occasions, may seem to be transfused from one man to another, instantaneously, and antecedent to any knowledge of what excited them in the person principally concerned. Grief and joy, for example, strongly expressed in the look and gestures of any one, at once affect the spectator with some degree of a like painful or agreeable emotion. A smiling face is, to everybody that sees it, a cheerful object; as a sorrowful countenance, on the other hand, is a melancholy one.

This, however, does not hold universally, or with regard to every passion. There are some passions of which the expressions excite no sort of sympathy, but before we are acquainted with what gave occasion to them, serve rather to disgust and provoke us against them. The furious behaviour of an angry man is more likely to exasperate us against himself than against his enemies. As we are unacquainted with his provocation, we cannot bring his case home to ourselves, nor conceive anything like the passions which it excites. But we plainly see what is the situation of those with whom he is angry, and to what violence they may be exposed from so enraged an adversary. We readily, therefore, sympathise with their fear or resentment, and are immediately disposed to take part against the man from whom they appear to be in so much danger.

If the very appearances of grief and joy inspire us with some degree of the like emotions, it is because they suggest to us the general idea of some good or bad fortune that has befallen the person in whom we observe them: and in these passions this is sufficient to have some little influence upon us. The effects of grief and joy terminate in the person who feels those emotions, of which the expressions do not, like those of resentment, suggest to us the idea of any other person for whom we are concerned, and whose interests are opposite to his. The general idea of good or bad fortune, therefore, creates some concern for the person who has met with it, but the general idea of provocation excites no sympathy with the anger of the man who has received it. Nature, it seems, teaches us to be more averse to enter into this passion, and, till informed of its cause, to be disposed rather to take part against it.

Even our sympathy with the grief or joy of another, before we are informed of the cause of either, is always extremely imperfect. General lamentations, which express nothing but the anguish of the sufferer, create rather a curiosity to inquire into his situation, along with some

2 o

disposition to sympathize with him, than any actual sympathy that is very sensible. The first question which we ask is, What has befallen you? Till this be answered, though we are uneasy both from the vague idea of his misfortune, and still more from torturing ourselves with con-jectures about what it may be, yet our fellow-feeling is not very considerable.

Sympathy, therefore, does not arise so much from the view of the passion, as from that of the situation which excites it. We sometimes feel for another, a passion of which he himself seems to be altogether incapable; because, when we put ourselves in his case, that passion arises in our breast from the imagination, though it does not in his from the reality. We blush for the impudence and rudeness of another, though he himself appears to have no sense of the impropriety of his own behaviour; because we cannot help feeling with what confusion we ourselves should be covered, had we behaved in so absurd a manner.

Of all the calamities to which the condition of mortality exposes mankind, the loss of reason appears, to those who have the least spark of humanity, by far the most dreadful, and they behold that last stage of human wretchedness, with deeper commiseration than any other. But the poor wretch, who is in it, laughs and sings perhaps, and is altogether insensible of his own misery. The anguish which humanity feels, therefore, at the sight of such an object cannot be the reflection of any sentiment of the sufferer. The compassion of the spectator must arise altogether from the consideration of what he himself would feel if he was reduced to the same unhappy situation, and, what perhaps is impossible, was at the same time able to regard it with his present reason and judgment.

What are the pangs of a mother, when she hears the moanings of her infant that during the agony of disease cannot express what it feels? In her idea of what it suffers, she joins, to its real helplessness, her own consciousness of that helplessness, and her own terrors for the unknown consequences of its disorder; and out of all these, forms, for her own sorrow, the most complete image of misery and distress. The infant, however, feels only the uneasiness of the present instant, which can never be great. With regard to the future, it is perfectly secure, and in its thoughtlessness and want of foresight, possesses an antidote against fear and anxiety, the great tormentors of the human breast, from which, reason and philosophy will, in vain, attempt to defend it when it grows up to a man.

We sympathize even with the dead, and overlooking what is of real importance in their situation, that awful futurity which awaits them, we are chiefly affected by those circumstances which strike our senses, but can have no influence upon their happiness. It is miserable, we think, to be deprived of the light of the sun; to be shut out from life and conversation; to be laid in the cold grave, a prey to corruption and the reptiles of the earth; to be no more thought of in this world, but to be obliterated, in a little time, from the affections, and almost from the memory, of their dearest friends and relations. Surely, we imagine, we can never feel too much for those who have suffered so dreadful a calamity. The tribute of our fellow-feeling seems doubly due to them now, when they are in danger of being forgot by every body; and, by the vain honours which we pay to their memory, we endeavour, for our own misery, artificially to keep alive our melancholy remembrance of their misfortune. That our sympathy can afford them no consolation seems to be an addition to their calamity; and to think that all we can do is unavailing, and that, what alleviates all other distress, the regret, the love, and the lamentations of their friends, can yield no comfort to them, serves only to exasperate our sense of their misery. The happiness of the dead, however, most assuredly, is affected by none of these circumstances; nor is it the thought of these things which can ever disturb the profound security of their repose. The idea of that dreary and endless melancholy, which the fancy naturally ascribes to their condition, arises altogether from our joining to the change which has been produced upon them, our own consciousness of that change, from our putting ourselves in their situation, and from our lodging, if I may be allowed to say so, our own living souls in their inanimated bodies, and thence conceiving what would be our emotions in this case. It is from this very illusion of the imagination, that the foresight of our own dissolution is so terrible to us, and that the idea of those circumstances, which undoubtedly can give us no pain when we are dead, makes us miserable while we are alive. And from thence arises one of the most important principles in human nature, the dread of death, the great poison to the happiness, but the great restraint upon the injustice of mankind, which, while it afflicts and mortifies the individual, guards and protects the society.

CHAP. II.—*Of the Pleasure of mutual Sympathy.*

BUT whatever may be the cause of sympathy, or however it may be excited, nothing pleases us more than to observe in other men a fellow-feeling with all the emotions of our own breast; nor are we ever so much shocked as by the appearance of the contrary. Those who are fond of deducing all our sentiments from certain refinements of self-love, think themselves at no loss to account, according to their own principles, both for this pleasure and this pain. Man, say they, conscious of his own weakness, and of the need which he has for the assistance of others, rejoices whenever he observes that they adopt his own passions, because he is then assured of that assistance; and grieves whenever he observes the contrary, because he is then assured of their opposition.   But both the pleasure and the pain are always felt so instantaneously, and often upon such frivolous occasions, that it seems evident that neither of them can be derived from any such self-interested consideration.   A man is mortified when, after having endeavoured to divert the company, he looks round and sees that nobody laughs at his jests but himself.   On the contrary, the mirth of the company is highly agreeable to him, and he regards this correspondence of their sentiments with his own as the greatest applause.

Neither does his pleasure seem to arise altogether from the additional vivacity which his mirth may receive from sympathy with theirs, nor his pain from the disappointment he meets with when he misses this pleasure ; though both the one and the other, no doubt, do in some measure.   When we have read a book or poem so often that we can no longer find any amusement in reading it by ourselves, we can still take pleasure in reading it to a companion.   To him it has all the graces of novelty ; we enter into the surprise and admiration which it naturally excites in him, but which it is no longer capable of exciting in us ; we consider all the ideas which it presents rather in the light in which they appear to him, than in that in which they appear to ourselves, and we are amused by sympathy with his amusement which thus enlivens our own.   On the contrary, we should be vexed if he did not seem to be entertained with it, and we could no longer take any pleasure in reading it to him.   It is the same case here.   The mirth of the company, no doubt, enlivens our own mirth, and their silence, no doubt, disappoints us.   But though this may contribute both to the pleasure which we derive from the one, and to the pain which we feel from the other, it is by no means the sole cause of either ; and this correspondence of the sentiments of others with our own appears to be a cause of pleasure, and the want of it a cause of pain, which cannot be accounted for in this manner.   The sympathy, which my friends express with my joy, might, indeed, give me pleasure by enlivening that joy : but that which they express with my grief could give me none, if it served only to enliven that grief.   Sympathy, however, enlivens joy and alleviates grief.   It enlivens joy by presenting another source of satisfaction ; and it alleviates grief by insinuating into the heart almost the only agreeable sensation which it is at that time capable of receiving.

It is to be observed accordingly, that we are still more anxious to communicate to our friends our disagreeable than our agreeable passions, that we derive still more satisfaction from their sympathy with the former than from that with the latter, and that we are still more shocked by the want of it.

How are the unfortunate relieved when they have found out a person to whom they can communicate the cause of their sorrow ?   Upon his sympathy they seem to disburthen themselves of a part of their distress : he is not improperly said to share it with them.   He not only feels a sorrow of the same kind with that which they feel, but, as if he had derived a part of it to himself, what he feels seems to alleviate the weight of what they feel.   Yet by relating their misfortunes they in some measure renew their grief.   They awaken in their memory the remembrance of those circumstances which occasion their affliction.   Their tears accordingly flow faster than before, and they are apt to abandon themselves to all the weakness of sorrow.   They take pleasure, however, in all this, and, it is evident, are sensibly relieved by it ; because the sweetness of his sympathy more than compensates the bitterness of that sorrow, which, in order to excite this sympathy, they had thus enlivened and renewed.   The cruellest insult, on the contrary, which can be offered to the unfortunate, is to appear to make light of their calamities.   To seem not to be affected with the joy of our companions is but want of politeness; but not to wear a serious countenance when they tell us their afflictions, is real and gross inhumanity.

Love is an agreeable, resentment a disagreeable, passion ; and accordingly we are not half so anxious that our friends should adopt our friendships, as that they should enter into our resentments.   We can forgive them though they seem to be little affected with the favours which we may have received, but lose all patience if they seem indifferent about the injuries which may have been done to us : nor are we half so angry with them for not entering into our gratitude, as for not sympathizing with our resentment.   They can easily avoid being friends to our friends, but can hardly avoid being enemies to those with whom we are at variance.   We seldom resent their being at enmity with the first, though upon that account we may sometimes affect to make an awkward quarrel with them ; but we quarrel with them in good earnest if they live in friendship with the last.   The agreeable passions of love and joy can satisfy and support the heart without any auxiliary pleasure.   The bitter and painful emotions of grief and resentment more strongly require the healing consolation of sympathy.

As the person who is principally interested in any event is pleased with our sympathy, and hurt by the want of it, so we, too, seem to be pleased when we are able to sympathize with him, and to be hurt when we are unable to do so.   We run not only to congratulate the successful, but to condole with the afflicted ; and the pleasure which we find in the conversation of one whom in all the passions of his heart we can entirely sympathize with, seems to do more than compensate the painfulness of that sorrow with which the view of his situation affects us.   On the contrary, it is always disagreeable to feel that we cannot sympathize with him, and instead of being pleased with this exemption from sympathetic pain, it hurts us to find that we cannot share his uneasiness.   If we hear a person loudly lamenting his misfortunes, which however, upon bringing the case home to ourselves, we feel, can produce no such violent effect upon us, we are shocked at his grief ; and, because we cannot enter into it, call it pusillanimity and weakness.   It gives us the spleen, on the other hand, to see another too happy or too much elevated, as we call it, with any little piece of good fortune.   We are disobliged even with his joy; and, because we cannot go along with it, call it levity and folly.   We are even put out of humour if our companion laughs louder or longer at a joke than we think it deserves ; that is, than we feel that we ourselves could laugh at it.

CHAP. III.—*Of the Manner in which we judge of the Propriety or Impropriety of the Affections of other Men, by their Concord or Dissonance with our own.*

WHEN the original passions of the person principally concerned are in perfect concord with the sympathetic emotions of the spectator, they necessarily appear to this last just and proper, and suitable to their objects ; and, on the contrary, when, upon bringing the case home to himself, he finds that they do not coincide with what he feels, they necessarily appear to him unjust and improper, and unsuitable to the causes which excite them.   To approve of the passions of another, therefore, as suitable to their objects, is the same thing as to observe that we entirely sympathize with them ; and not to approve of them as such, is the same thing as to observe that we do not entirely sympathize with them.   The man who resents the injuries that have been done to me, and observes that I resent them precisely as he does, necessarily approves of my resentment.   The man whose sympathy keeps time to my grief, cannot but admit the reasonableness of my sorrow.   He who admires the same poem, or the same picture, and admires them exactly as I do, must surely allow the justness of my admiration.   He who laughs at the same joke, and laughs along with me, cannot well deny the propriety of my laughter.   On the contrary, the person who, upon these different occasions, either feels no such emotion as that which I feel, or feels none that bears any proportion to mine, cannot avoid disapproving my sentiments on account of their dissonance with his own.   If my animosity goes beyond what the indignation of my friend can correspond to ; if my grief exceeds what his most tender compassion can go along with; if my admiration is either too high or too low to tally with his own; if I laugh loud and heartily when he only smiles, or, on the contrary, only smile when he laughs loud and heartily; in all these cases, as soon as he comes from considering the object, to observe how I am affected by it, according as there is more or less disproportion between his sentiments and mine, I must incur a greater or less degree of his disapprobation : and upon all occasions his own sentiments are the standards and measures by which he judges of mine.

To approve of another man's opinions is to adopt those opinions, and to adopt them is to approve of them. If the same arguments which convince you convince me likewise, I necessarily approve of your conviction; and if they do not, I necessarily disapprove of it: neither can I possibly conceive that I should do the one without the other. To approve or disapprove, therefore, of the opinions of others is acknowledged, by every body, to mean no more than to observe their agreement or disagreement with our own. But this is equally the case with regard to our approbation or disapprobation of the sentiments or passions of others.

There are, indeed, some cases in which we seem to approve without any sympathy or correspondence of sentiments, and in which, consequently, the sentiment of approbation would seem to be different from the perception of this coincidence. A little attention, however, will convince us that even in these cases our approbation is ultimately founded upon a sympathy or correspondence of this kind. I shall give an instance in things of a very frivolous nature, because in them the judgments of mankind are less apt to be perverted by wrong systems. We may often approve of a jest, and think the laughter of the company quite just and proper, though we ourselves do not laugh, because, perhaps, we are in a grave humour, or happen to have our attention engaged with other objects. We have learned, however, from experience, what sort of pleasantry is upon most occasions capable of making us laugh, and we observe that this is one of that kind. We approve, therefore, of the laughter of the company, and feel that it is natural and suitable to its object; because, though in our present mode we cannot easily enter into it, we are sensible that upon most occasions we should very heartily join in it.

The same thing often happens with regard to all the other passions. A stranger passes by us in the street with all the marks of the deepest affliction; and we are immediately told that he has just received the news of the death of his father. It is impossible that, in this case, we should not approve of his grief. Yet it may often happen, without any defect of humanity on our part, that, so far from entering into the violence of his sorrow, we should scarce conceive the first movements of concern upon his account. Both he and his father, perhaps, are entirely unknown to us, or we happen to be employed about other things, and do not take time to picture out in our imagination the different circumstances of distress which must occur to him. We have learned, however, from experience, that such a misfortune naturally excites such a degree of sorrow, and we know that if we took time to consider his situation, fully in all its parts, we should, without doubt, most sincerely sympathize with him. It is upon the consciousness of this conditional sympathy, that our approbation of his sorrow is founded, even in those cases in which that sympathy does not actually take place;

and the general rules derived from our preceding experience of what our sentiments would commonly correspond with, correct upon this, as upon many other occasions, the impropriety of our present emotions.

The sentiment or affection of the heart from which any action proceeds, and upon which its whole virtue or vice must ultimately depend, may be considered under two different aspects, or in two different relations ; first, in relation to the cause which excites it, or the motive which gives occasion to it ; and secondly, in relation to the end which it proposes, or the effect which it tends to produce.

In the suitableness or unsuitableness, in the proportion or disproportion which the affection seems to bear to the cause or object which excites it, consists the propriety or impropriety, the decency or ungracefulness of the consequent action.

In the beneficial or hurtful nature of the effects which the affection aims at, or tends to produce, consists the merit or demerit of the action, the qualities by which it is entitled to reward, or is deserving of punishment.

Philosophers have, of late years, considered chiefly the tendency of affections, and have given little attention to the relation which they stand in to the cause which excites them. In common life, however, when we judge of any person's conduct, and of the sentiments which directed it, we constantly consider them under both these aspects. When we blame in another man the excesses of love, of grief, of resentment, we not only consider the ruinous effect which they tend to produce, but the little occasion which was given for them. The merit of his favourite, we say, is not so great, his misfortune is not so dreadful, his provocation is not so extraordinary, as to justify so violent a passion. We should have indulged, we say, perhaps, have approved of the violence of his emotion, had the cause been in any respect proportioned to it.

When we judge in this manner of any affection as proportioned or disproportioned to the cause which excites it, it is scarce possible that we should make use of any other rule or canon but the correspondent affection in ourselves. If, upon bringing the case home to our own breast, we find that the sentiments which it gives occasion to, coincide and tally with our own, we necessarily approve of them as proportioned and suitable to their objects ; if otherwise, we necessarily disapprove of them, as extravagant and out of proportion.

Every faculty in one man is the measure by which he judges of the like faculty in another. I judge of your sight by my sight, of your ear by my ear, of your reason by my reason, of your resentment by my resentment, of your love by my love. I neither have, nor can have, any other way of judging about them.

CHAP. IV.—*The same Subject continued.*

WE may judge of the propriety or impropriety of the sentiments of another person by their correspondence or disagreement with our own, upon two different occasions; either, first, when the objects which excite them are considered without any peculiar relation, either to ourselves or to the person whose sentiments we judge of; or, secondly, when they are considered as peculiarly affecting one or other of us.

1. With regard to those objects which are considered without any peculiar relation either to ourselves or to the person whose sentiments we judge of; wherever his sentiments entirely correspond with our own, we ascribe to him the qualities of taste and good judgment. The beauty of a plain, the greatness of a mountain, the ornaments of a building, the expression of a picture, the composition of a discourse, the conduct of a third person, the proportions of different quantities and numbers, the various appearances which the great machine of the universe is perpetually exhibiting, with the secret wheels and springs which produce them; all the general subjects of science and taste, are what we and our companions regard as having no peculiar relation to either of us. We both look at them from the same point of view, and we have no occasion for sympathy, or for that imaginary change of situations from which it arises, in order to produce, with regard to these, the most perfect harmony of sentiments and affections. If, notwithstanding, we are often differently affected, it arises either from the different degrees of attention, which our different habits of life allow us to give easily to the several parts of those complex objects, or from the different degrees of natural acuteness in the faculty of the mind to which they are addressed.

When the sentiments of our companion coincide with our own in things of this kind, which are obvious and easy, and in which, perhaps, we never found a single person who differed from us, though we, no doubt, must approve of them, yet he seems to deserve no praise or admiration on account of them. But when they not only coincide with our own, but lead and direct our own; when in forming them he appears to have attended to many things which we had overlooked, and to have adjusted them to all the various circumstances of their objects; we not only approve of them, but wonder and are surprised at their uncommon and unexpected acuteness and comprehensiveness, and he appears to deserve a very high degree of admiration and applause. For approbation heightened by wonder and surprise, constitutes the sentiment which is properly called admiration, and of which applause is the natural expression. The decision of the man who judges that exquisite beauty is preferable to the grossest deformity, or that twice two are equal to four, must certainly be approved of by all the world, but will not, surely, be much admired. It is the acute and delicate discernment of the man of taste, who distinguishes the minute, and scarce perceptible differences of beauty and deformity; it is the comprehensive accuracy of the experienced mathematician, who unravels, with ease, the most intricate and perplexed proportions; it is the great leader in science and taste, the man who directs and conducts our own sentiments, the extent. and superior justness of whose talents astonish us with wonder and surprise, who excites our admiration, and seems to deserve our applause; and upon this foundation is grounded the greater part of the praise which is bestowed upon what are called the intellectual virtues.

The utility of those qualities, it may be thought, is what first recommends them to us; and, no doubt, the consideration of this, when we come to attend to it, gives them a new value. Originally, however, we approve of another man's judgment, not as something useful, but as right, as accurate, as agreeable to truth and reality: and it is evident we attribute those qualities to it for no other reason but because we find that it agrees with our own. Taste, in the same manner, is originally approved of, not as useful, but as just, as delicate, and as precisely suited to its object. The idea of the utility of all qualities of this kind, is plainly an afterthought, and not what first recommends them to our approbation.

2. With regard to those objects, which affect in a particular manner either ourselves or the person whose sentiments we judge of, it is at once more difficult to preserve this harmony and correspondence, and at the same time, vastly more important. My companion does not naturally look at the misfortune that has befallen me, or the injury that has been done me, from the same point of view in which I consider them. They affect me much more nearly. We do not view them from the same station, as we do a picture, or a poem, or a system of philosophy, and are, therefore, apt to be very differently affected by them. But I can much more easily overlook the want of this correspondence of sentiments with regard to such indifferent objects as concern neither me nor my companion, than with regard to what interests me so much as the misfortune that has befallen me, or the injury that has been done me. Though you despise that picture, or that poem, or even that system of philosophy, which I admire, there is little danger of our quarrelling upon that account. Neither of us can reasonably be much interested about them. They ought all of them to be matters of great indifference to us both; so that, though our opinions may be opposite, our affections may still be very nearly the same. But it is quite otherwise with regard to those objects by which either you or I are particularly affected. Though your judgments in matters of speculation, though your sentiments in matters of taste, are quite opposite to mine, I can easily overlook this opposition; and if I

have any degree of temper, I may still find some entertainment in your conversation, even upon those very subjects. But if you have either no fellow-feeling for the misfortunes I have met with, or none that bears any proportion to the grief which distracts me; or if you have either no indignation at the injuries I have suffered, or none that bears any proportion to the resentment which transports me, we can no longer converse upon these subjects. We become intolerable to one another. I can neither support your company, nor you mine. You are confounded at my violence and passion, and I am enraged at your cold insensibility and want of feeling.

In all such cases, that there may be some correspondence of sentiments between the spectator and the person principally concerned, the spectator must, first of all, endeavour, as much as he can, to put himself in the situation of the other, and to bring home to himself every little circumstance of distress which can possibly occur to the sufferer. He must adopt the whole case of his companion with all its minutest incidents; and strive to render as perfect as possible, that imaginary change of situation upon which his sympathy is founded.

After all this, however, the emotions of the spectator will still be very apt to fall short of the violence of what is felt by the sufferer. Mankind, though naturally sympathetic, never conceive, for what has befallen another, that degree of passion which naturally animates the person principally concerned. That imaginary change of situation, upon which their sympathy is founded, is but momentary. The thought of their own safety, the thought that they themselves are not really the sufferers, continually intrudes itself upon them; and though it does not hinder them from conceiving a passion somewhat analogous to what is felt by the sufferer, hinders them from conceiving any thing that approaches to the same degree of violence. The person principally concerned is sensible of this, and at the same time passionately desires a more complete sympathy. He longs for that relief which nothing can afford him but the entire concord of the affections of the spectators with his own. To see the emotions of their hearts, in every respect, beat time to his own, in the violent and disagreeable passions, constitutes his sole consolation. But he can only hope to obtain this by lowering his passion to that pitch, in which the spectators are capable of going along with him. He must flatten, if I may be allowed to say so, the sharpness of its natural tone, in order to reduce it to harmony and concord with the emotions of those who are about him. What they feel, will, indeed, always be, in some respects, different from what he feels, and compassion can never be exactly the same with original sorrow; because the secret consciousness that the change of situations, from which the sympathetic sentiment arises, is but imaginary, not only lowers it in degree, but, in some measure, varies it in kind, and gives it a quite different modification. These two sentiments, however, may, it is evident, have such a correspondence with one another, as is sufficient for the harmony of society. Though they will never be unisons, they may be concords, and this is all that is wanted or required.

In order to produce this concord, as nature teaches the spectators to assume the circumstance of the person principally concerned, so she teaches this last in some measure to assume those of the spectators. As they are continually placing themselves in his situation, and thence conceiving emotions similar to what he feels ; so he is as constantly placing himself in theirs, and thence conceiving some degree of that coolness about his own fortune, with which he is sensible that they will view it. As they are constantly considering what they themselves would feel, if they actually were the sufferers, so he is as constantly led to imagine in what manner he would be affected if he was only one of the spectators of his own situation. As their sympathy makes them look at it, in some measure, with his eyes, so his sympathy makes him look at it, in some measure, with theirs, especially when in their presence and acting under their observation : and as the reflected passion, which he thus conceives, is much weaker than the original one, it necessarily abates the violence of what he felt before he came into their presence, before he began to recollect in what manner they would be affected by it, and to view his situation in this candid and impartial light.

The mind, therefore, is rarely so disturbed, but that the company of a friend will restore it to some degree of tranquillity and sedateness. The breast is, in some measure, calmed and composed the moment we come into his presence. We are immediately put in mind of the light in which he will view our situation, and we begin to view it ourselves in the same light ; for the effect of sympathy is instantaneous. We expect less sympathy from a common acquaintance than from a friend : we cannot open to the former all those little circumstances which we can unfold to the latter : we assume, therefore, more tranquillity before him, and endeavour to fix our thoughts upon those general outlines of our situation which he is willing to consider. We expect still less sympathy from an assembly of strangers, and we assume, therefore, still more tranquillity before them, and always endeavour to bring down our passion to that pitch, which the particular company we are in may be expected to go along with. Nor is this only an assumed appearance : for if we are at all masters of ourselves, the presence of a mere acquaintance will really compose us, still more than that of a friend ; and that of an assembly of strangers still more than that of an acquaintance.

Society and conversation, therefore, are the most powerful remedies for restoring the mind to its tranquillity, if, at any time, it has unfortunately lost it ; as well as the best preservatives of that equal and happy temper, which is so necessary to self-satisfaction and enjoyment Men of retirement and speculation, who are apt to sit brooding at home over either grief or resentment, though they may often have more humanity, more generosity, and a nicer sense of honour, yet seldom possess that equality of temper which is so common among men of the world.

CHAP. V.—*Of the amiable and respectable Virtues.*

UPON these two different efforts, upon that of the spectator to enter into the sentiments of the person principally concerned, and upon that of the person principally concerned to bring down his emotions to what the spectator can go along with, are founded two different sets of virtues. The soft, the gentle, the amiable virtues, the virtues of candid condescension and indulgent humanity, are founded upon the one: the great, the awful and respectable, the virtues of self-denial, of self-government, of that command of the passions which subjects all the movements of our nature to what our own dignity and honour, and the propriety of our own conduct require, take their origin from the other.

How amiable does he appear to be, whose sympathetic heart seems to re-echo all the sentiments of those with whom he converses, who grieves for their calamities, who resents their injuries, and who rejoices at their good fortune! When we bring home to ourselves the situation of his companions, we enter into their gratitude, and feel what consolation they must derive from the tender sympathy of so affectionate a friend. And for a contrary reason, how disagreeable does he appear to be, whose hard and obdurate heart feels for himself only, but is altogether insensible to the happiness or misery of others! We enter, in this case, too, into the pain which his presence must give to every mortal with whom he converses, to those especially with whom we are most apt to sympathize, the unfortunate and the injured.

On the other hand, what noble propriety and grace do we feel in the conduct of those who, in their own case, exert that recollection and self-command which constitute the dignity of every passion, and which bring it down to what others can enter into? We are disgusted with that clamorous grief, which, without any delicacy, calls upon our compassion with sighs and tears and importunate lamentations. But we reverence that reserved, that silent and majestic sorrow, which discovers itself only in the swelling of the eyes, in the quivering of the lips and cheeks, and in the distant, but affecting, coldness of the whole behaviour. It imposes the like silence upon us. We regard it with respectful attention, and watch with anxious concern over our whole behaviour, lest by any impropriety we should disturb that concerted tranquillity, which it requires so great an effort to support.

The insolence and brutality of anger, in the same manner, when we indulge its fury without check or restraint, is of all objects the most detestable. But we admire that noble and generous resentment which governs its pursuit of the greatest injuries, not by the rage which they are apt to excite in the breast of the sufferer, but by the indignation which they naturally call forth in that part of the impartial spectator ; which allows no word, no gesture, to escape it beyond what this more equitable sentiment would dictate ; which never, even in thought, attempts any greater vengeance, nor desires to inflict any greater punishment, than what every indifferent person would rejoice to see executed.

And hence it is, that to feel much for others and little for ourselves, that to restrain our selfish, and to indulge our benevolent affections, constitutes the perfection of human nature ; and can alone produce among mankind that harmony of sentiments and passions in which consists their whole grace and propriety. As to love our neighbour as we love ourselves is the great law of Christianity, so it is the great precept of nature to love ourselves only as we love our neighbour, or what comes to the same thing, as our neighbour is found capable of loving us.

As taste and good judgment, when they are considered as qualities which deserve praise and admiration, are supposed to imply a delicacy of sentiment and an acuteness of understanding not commonly to be met with ; so the virtues of sensibility and self-command are not appre- hended to consist in the ordinary, but in the uncommon degrees of those qualities. The amiable virtue of humanity requires, surely, a sensibility much beyond what is possessed by the rude vulgar of man- kind. The great and exalted virtue of magnanimity undoubtedly demands much more than that degree of self-command, which the weakest of mortals is capable of exerting. As in the common degree of the intellectual qualities, there is no ability ; so in the common degree of the moral, there is no virtue. Virtue is excellence, some- thing uncommonly great and beautiful, which rises far above what is vulgar and ordinary. The amiable virtues consist in that degree of sensibility which surprises by its exquisite and unexpected delicacy and tenderness. The awful and respectable, in that degree of self-com- mand which astonishes by its amazing superiority over the most un- governable passions of human nature.

There is, in this respect, a considerable difference between virtue and mere propriety ; between those qualities and actions which deserve to be admired and celebrated, and those which simply deserve to be approved of. Upon many occasions, to act with the most perfect pro- priety, requires no more than that common and ordinary degree of sensibility or self-command which the most worthless of mankind are possest of, and sometimes even that degree is not necessary. Thus, to give a very low instance, to eat when we are hungry, is certainly, upon ordinary occasions, perfectly right and proper, and cannot miss being approved of as such by every body. Nothing, however, could be more absurd than to say it was virtuous.

On the contrary, there may frequently be a considerable degree of virtue in those actions which fall short of the most perfect propriety ; because they may still approach nearer to perfection than could well be expected upon occasions in which it was so extremely difficult to attain it : and this is very often the case upon those occasions which require the greatest exertions of self-command. There are some situations which bear so hard upon human nature, that the greatest degree of self-government, which can belong to so imperfect a creature as man, is not able to stifle altogether the voice of human weakness, or reduce the violence of the passions to that pitch of moderation, in which the impartial spectator can entirely enter into them. Though in those cases, therefore, the behaviour of the sufferer fall short of the most perfect propriety, it may still deserve some applause, and even in a certain sense may be denominated virtuous. It may still manifest an effort of generosity and magnanimity of which the greater part of men are wholly incapable ; and though it fails of absolute perfection, it may be a much nearer approximation towards perfection, than what, upon such trying occasions, is commonly either to be found or to be expected.

In cases of this kind, when we are determining the degree of blame or applause which seems due to any action, we very frequently make use of two different standards. The first is the idea of complete propriety and perfection, which, in those difficult situations, no human conduct ever did, or ever can come up to ; and in comparison with which the actions of all men must for ever appear blamable and imperfect. The second is the idea of that degree of proximity or distance from this complete perfection, which the actions of the greater part of men commonly arrive at. Whatever goes beyond this degree, how far soever it may be removed from absolute perfection, seems to deserve applause ; and whatever falls short of it, to deserve blame.

It is in the same manner that we judge of the productions of all the arts which address themselves to the imagination. When a critic examines the work of any of the great masters in poetry or painting, he may sometimes examine it by an idea of perfection, in his own mind, which neither that nor any other human work will ever come up to ; and as long as he compares it with this standard, he can see nothing in it but faults and imperfections. But when he comes to consider the rank which it ought to hold among other works of the same kind, he necessarily compares it with a very different standard, the common degree of excellence which is usually attained in this particular art ; and when he judges of it by this new measure, it may often appear to deserve the highest applause, upon account of its approaching much nearer to perfection than the greater part of those works which can be brought into competition with it.

Sec. II.—Of the Degrees of the Different Passions which are Consistent with Propriety.

Introduction.—The propriety of every passion excited by objects peculiarly related to ourselves, the pitch which the spectator can go along with, must lie, it is evident, in a certain mediocrity. If the passion is too high, or if it is too low, he cannot enter into it. Grief and resentment for private misfortunes and injuries may easily, for example, be too high, and in the greater part of mankind they are so. They may likewise, though this more rarely happens, be too low. We denominate the excess weakness and fury : and we call the defect stupidity, insensibility, and want of spirit. We can enter into neither of them, but are astonished and confounded to see them.

This mediocrity, however, in which the point of propriety consists, is different in different passions. It is high in some, and low in others. There are some passions which it is indecent to express very strongly, even upon those occasions, in which it is acknowledged that we cannot avoid feeling them in the highest degree. And there are others of which the strongest expressions are upon many occasions extremely graceful, even though the passions themselves do not, perhaps, arise so necessarily. The first are those passions with which, for certain reasons, there is little or no sympathy : the second are those with which, for other reasons, there is the greatest. And if we consider all the different passions of human nature, we shall find that they are regarded as decent, or indecent, just in proportion as mankind are more or less disposed to sympathize with them.

Chap. I.—*Of the Passions which take their Origin from the Body.*

1. It is indecent to express any strong degree of those passions which arise from a certain situation or disposition of the body ; because the company, not being in the same disposition, cannot be expected to sympathize with them. Violent hunger, for example, though upon many occasions not only natural, but unavoidable, is always indecent, and to eat voraciously is universally regarded as a piece of ill manners. There is, however, some degree of sympathy, even with hunger. It is agreeable to see our companions eat with a good appetite, and all expressions of loathing are offensive. The disposition of body which is habitual to a man in health, makes his stomach easily keep time, if I may be allowed so coarse an expression, with the one, and not with the other.

We can sympathize with the distress which excessive hunger occasions when we read the description of it in the journal of a siege, or of a sea voyage. We imagine ourselves in the situation of the sufferers, and thence readily conceive the grief, the fear, and consternation, which must necessarily distract them. We feel, ourselves, some degree of those passions, and therefore sympathize with them : but as we do not grow hungry by reading the description, we cannot properly, even in this case, be said to sympathize with their hunger.

It is the same case with the passion by which Nature unites the two sexes. Though naturally the most furious of all the passions, all strong expressions of it are upon every occasion indecent, even between persons in whom its most complete indulgence is acknowledged by all laws, both human and divine, to be perfectly innocent. There seems, however, to be some degree of sympathy even with this passion. To talk to a woman as we should to a man is improper : it is expected that their company should inspire us with more gaiety, more pleasantry, and more attention ; and an entire insensibility to the fair sex, renders a man contemptible in some measure even to the men.

Such is our aversion for all the appetites which take their origin from the body ; all strong expressions of them are loathsome and disagreeable. According to some ancient philosophers, these are the passions which we share in common with the brutes, and which, having no connexion with the characteristical qualities of human nature, are upon that account beneath its dignity. But there are many other passions which we share in common with the brutes, such as resentment, natural affection, even gratitude, which do not, upon that account, appear to be so brutal. The true cause of the peculiar disgust which we conceive for the appetites of the body when we see them in other men, is that we cannot enter into them. To the person himself who feels them, as soon as they are gratified, the object that excited them ceases to be agreeable : even its presence often becomes offensive to him ; he looks round to no purpose for the charm which transported him the moment before, and he can now as little enter into his own passion as another person. When we have dined, we order the covers to be removed ; and we should treat in the same manner the objects of the most ardent and passionate desires, if they were the objects of no other passions but those which take their origin from the body.

In the command of those appetites of the body consists that virtue which is properly called temperance. To restrain them within those bounds which regard to health and fortune prescribes, is the part of prudence. But to confine them within those limits which grace, which propriety, which delicacy, and which modesty, require, is the office of temperance.

2. It is for the same reason that to cry out with bodily pain, how intolerable soever, appears always unmanly and unbecoming. There

3 *

is, however, a good deal of sympathy even with bodily pain. If, as has
already been observed, I see a stroke aimed, and just ready to fall upon
the leg, or arm, of another person, I naturally shrink and draw back
my own leg, or my own arm: and when it does fall, I feel it in some
measure, and am hurt by it as well as the sufferer. My hurt, however,
is, no doubt, excessively slight, and, upon that account, if he makes
any violent outcry, as I cannot go along with him, I never fail to despise him. And this is the case of all the passions which take their
origin from the body: they excite either no sympathy at all, or such a
degree of it, as is altogether disproportioned to the violence of what is
felt by the sufferer.

It is quite otherwise with those passions which take their origin from
the imagination. The frame of my body can be but little affected by
the alterations which are brought about upon that of my companion:
but my imagination is more ductile, and more readily assumes, if I may
say so, the shape and configuration of the imaginations of those with
whom I am familiar. A disappointment in love, or ambition, will,
upon this account, call forth more sympathy than the greatest bodily
evil. Those passions arise altogether from the imagination. The
person who has lost his whole fortune, if he is in health, feels nothing
in his body. What he suffers is from the imagination only, which
represents to him the loss of his dignity, neglect from his friends, contempt from his enemies, dependence, want, and misery, coming fast
upon him; and we sympathize with him the more strongly upon this
account, because our imaginations can the more readily mould themselves upon his imagination, than our bodies can mould themselves
upon his body.

The loss of a leg may generally be regarded as a more real calamity
than the loss of a mistress. It would be a ridiculous tragedy, however,
of which the catastrophe was to turn upon a loss of that kind. A misfortune of the other kind, how frivolous soever it may appear to be, has
given occasion to many a fine one.

Nothing is so soon forgot as pain. The moment it is gone the whole
agony of it is over, and the thought of it can no longer give us any sort
of disturbance. We ourselves cannot then enter into the anxiety and
anguish which we had before conceived. An unguarded word from a
friend will occasion a more durable uneasiness. The agony which this
creates is by no means over with the word. What at first disturbs us
is not the object of the senses, but the idea of the imagination. As it
is an idea, therefore, which occasions our uneasiness, till time and other
accidents have in some measure effaced it from our memory, the imagination continues to fret and rankle within, from the thought of it.

Pain never calls forth any very lively sympathy unless it is accompanied with danger. We sympathize with the fear, though not with the
agony of the sufferer. Fear, however, is a passion derived altogether

from the imagination, which represents, with an uncertainty and fluctuation that increases our anxiety, not what we really feel, but what we may hereafter possibly suffer. The gout or the tooth-ache, though exquisitely painful, excite very little sympathy; more dangerous diseases, though accompanied with very little pain, excite the highest.

Some people faint and grow sick at the sight of a chirurgical operation, and that bodily pain which is occasioned by tearing the flesh, seems, in them, to excite the most excessive sympathy. We conceive in a much more lively and distinct manner the pain which proceeds from an external cause, than we do that which arises from an internal disorder. I can scarce form an idea of the agonies of my neighbour when he is tortured with the gout, or the stone; but I have the clearest conception of what he must suffer from an incision, a wound, or a fracture. The chief cause, however, why such objects produce such violent effects upon us, is their novelty. One who has been witness to a dozen dissections, and as many amputations, sees, ever after, all operations of this kind with great indifference, and often with perfect insensibility. Though we have read or seen represented more than five hundred tragedies, we shall seldom feel so entire an abatement of our sensibility to the objects which they represent to us.

In some of the Greek tragedies there is an attempt to excite compassion, by the representation of the agonies of bodily pain. Philoctetes cries out and faints from the extremity of his sufferings. Hippolytus and Hercules are both introduced as expiring under the severest tortures, which, it seems, even the fortitude of Hercules was incapable of supporting. In all these cases, however, it is not the pain which interests us, but some other circumstance. It is not the sore foot, but the solitude, of Philoctetes which affects us, and diffuses over that charming tragedy, that romantic wildness, which is so agreeable to the imagination. The agonies of Hercules and Hippolytus are interesting only because we foresee that death is to be the consequence. If those heroes were to recover, we should think the representation of their sufferings perfectly ridiculous. What a tragedy would that be of which the distress consisted in a colic! Yet no pain is more exquisite. These attempts to excite compassion by the representation of bodily pain, may be regarded as among the greatest breaches of decorum of which the Greek theatre has set the example.

The little sympathy which we feel with bodily pain, is the foundation of the propriety of constancy and patience in enduring it. The man, who under the severest tortures allows no weakness to escape him, vents no groan, gives way to no passion which we do not entirely enter into, commands our highest admiration. His firmness enables him to keep time with our indifference and insensibility. We admire and entirely go along with the magnanimous effort which he makes for this purpose. We approve of his behaviour, and from our experience of the common weakness of human nature, we are surprised, and wonder how he should be able to act so as to deserve approbation. Approbation, mixed and animated by wonder and surprise, constitutes the sentiment which is properly called admiration, of which, applause is the natural expression, as has already been observed.

CHAP. II.—*Of those Passions which take their Origin from a particular Turn or Habit of the Imagination.*

EVEN of the passions derived from the imagination, those which take their origin from a peculiar turn or habit it has acquired, though they may be acknowledged to be perfectly natural, are, however, but little sympathized with. The imaginations of mankind, not having acquired that particular turn, cannot enter into them; and such passions, though they may be allowed to be almost unavoidable in some part of life, are always, in some measure, ridiculous. This is the case with that strong attachment which naturally grows up between two persons of different sexes, who have long fixed their thoughts upon one another. Our imagination not having run in the same channel with that of the lover, we cannot enter into the eagerness of his emotions. If our friend has been injured, we readily sympathize with his resentment, and grow angry with the very person with whom he is angry. If he has received a benefit, we readily enter into his gratitude, and have a very high sense of the merit of his benefactor. But if he is in love, though we may think his passion just as reasonable as any of the kind, yet we never think ourselves bound to conceive a passion of the same kind, and for the same person for whom he has conceived it. The passion appears to every body, but the man who feels it, entirely disproportioned to the value of the object; and love, though it is pardoned in a certain age because we know it is natural, is always laughed at, because we cannot enter into it. All serious and strong expressions of it appear ridiculous to a third person; and though a lover may be good company to his mistress, he is so to nobody else. He himself is sensible of this; and as long as he continues in his sober senses, endeavours to treat his own passion with raillery and ridicule. It is the only style in which we care to hear of it; because it is the only style in which we ourselves are disposed to talk of it. We grow weary of the grave, pedantic, and long-sentenced love of Cowley and Petrarca, who never have done with exaggerating the violence of their attachments; but the gaiety of Ovid, and the gallantry of Horace, are always agreeable.

But though we feel no proper sympathy with an attachment of this kind, though we never approach even in imagination towards conceiving a passion for that particular person, yet as we either have conceived, or may be disposed to conceive, passions of the same kind, we readily enter into those high hopes of happiness which are proposed from its gratification, as well as into that exquisite distress which is feared from its disappointment. It interests us not as a passion, but as a situation. that gives occasion to other passions which interest us; to hope, to fear, and to distress of every kind: in the same manner as in a description of a sea voyage, it is not the hunger which interests us, but the distress which that hunger occasions. Though we do not properly enter into the attachment of the lover, we readily go along with those expectations of romantic happiness which he derives from it. We feel how natural it is for the mind, in a certain situation, relaxed with indolence, and fatigued with the violence of desire, to long for serenity and quiet, to hope to find them in the gratification of that passion which distracts it, and to frame to itself the idea of that life of pastoral tranquillity and retirement which the elegant, the tender, and the passionate Tibullus takes so much pleasure in describing; a life like what the poets describe in the Fortunate Islands, a life of friendship, liberty, and repose; free from labour, and from care, and from all the turbulent passions which attend them. Even scenes of this kind interest us most, when they are painted rather as what is hoped, than as what is enjoyed. The grossness of that passion, which mixes with, and is, perhaps, the foundation of love, disappears when its gratification is far off and at a distance; but renders the whole offensive, when described as what is immediately possessed. The happy passion, upon this account, interests us much less than the fearful and the melancholy. We tremble for whatever can disappoint such natural and agreeable hopes: and thus enter into all the anxiety, and concern, and distress of the lover.

Hence it is, that, in some modern tragedies and romances, this passion appears so wonderfully interesting. It is not so much the love of Castalio and Monimia which attaches us in the orphan, as the distress which that love occasions. The author who should introduce two lovers, in a scene of perfect security, expressing their mutual fondness for one another, would excite laughter, and not sympathy. If a scene of this kind is ever admitted into a tragedy, it is always, in some measure, improper, and is endured, not from any sympathy with the passion that is expressed in it, but from concern for the dangers and difficulties with which the audience foresee that its gratification is likely to be attended.

The reserve which the laws of society impose upon the fair sex, with regard to this weakness, renders it more peculiarly distressful in them, and, upon that very account, more deeply interesting. We are charmed with the love of Phædra, as it is expressed in the French tragedy of that name, notwithstanding all the extravagance and guilt which attend it. That very extravagance and guilt may be said, in some measure, to recommend it to us. Her fear, her shame, her remorse, her horror, her despair, become thereby more natural and interesting. All the secondary passions, if I may be allowed to call them so, which arise from the situation of love, become necessarily more furious and violent; and it is with these secondary passions only that we can properly be said to sympathize.

Of all the passions, however, which are so extravagantly disproportioned to the value of their objects, love is the only one that appears, even to the weakest minds, to have any thing in it that is either graceful or agreeable.   In itself, first of all, though it may be ridiculous, it is not naturally odious ; and though its consequences are often fatal and dreadful, its intentions are seldom mischievous.   And then, though there is little propriety in the passion itself, there is a good deal in some of those which always accompany it.   There is in love a strong mixture of humanity, generosity, kindness, friendship, esteem ; passions with which, of all others, for reasons which shall be explained immediately, we have the greatest propensity to sympathize, even notwithstanding we are sensible that they are, in some measure, excessive. The sympathy which we feel with them, renders the passion which they accompany less disagreeable, and supports it in our imagination, notwithstanding all the vices which commonly go along with it ; though in the one sex it necessarily leads to the last ruin and infamy ; and though in the other, where it is apprehended to be least fatal, it is almost always attended with an incapacity for labour, a neglect of duty, a contempt of fame, and even of common reputation.   Notwithstanding all this, the degree of sensibility and generosity with which it is supposed to be accompanied, renders it to many the object of vanity ; and they are fond of appearing capable of feeling what would do them no honour if they had really felt it.

It is for a reason of the same kind, that a certain reserve is necessary when we talk of our own friends, our own studies, our own professions. All these are objects which we cannot expect should interest our companions in the same degree in which they interest us.   And it is for want of this reserve, that the one half of mankind make bad company to the other.   A philosopher is company to a philosopher only ; the member of a club, to his own little knot of companions.

CHAP. III.—*Of the unsocial Passions.*

THERE is another set of passions, which, though derived from the imagination, yet before we can enter into them, or regard them as graceful or becoming, must always be brought down to a pitch much lower than that to which undisciplined nature would raise them.   These are, hatred and resentment, with all their different modifications.   With regard to all such passions, our sympathy is divided between the person who feels them, and the person who is the object of them.   The interests of these two are directly opposite. What our sympathy with the person who feels them would prompt us to wish for, our fellow-feeling with the other would lead us to fear. As they are both men, we are concerned for both, and our fear for what the one may suffer, damps our resentment for what the other has suffered. Our sympathy, therefore, with the man who has received the provocation, necessarily falls short of the passion which naturally animates him, not only upon account of those general causes which render all sympathetic passions inferior to the original ones, but upon account of that particular cause which is peculiar to itself, our opposite sympathy with another person. Before resentment, therefore, can become graceful and agreeable, it must be more humbled and brought down below that pitch to which it would naturally rise, than almost any other passion.

Mankind, at the same time, have a very strong sense of the injuries that are done to another. The villain, in a tragedy or romance, is as much the object of our indignation, as the hero is that of our sympathy and affection. We detest Iago as much as we esteem Othello ; and delight as much in the punishment of the one, as we are grieved at the distress of the other. But though mankind have so strong a fellow-feeling with the injuries that are done to their brethren, they do not always resent them the more that the sufferer appears to resent them. Upon most occasions, the greater his patience, his mildness, his humanity, provided it does not appear that he wants spirit, or that fear was the motive of his forbearance, the higher the resentment against the person who injured him. The amiableness of the character exasperates their sense of the atrocity of the injury.

These passions, however, are regarded as necessary parts of the character of human nature. A person becomes contemptible who tamely sits still, and submits to insults, without attempting either to repel or to revenge them. We cannot enter into his indifference and insensibility : we call his behaviour mean-spiritedness, and are as really provoked by it as by the insolence of his adversary. Even the mob are enraged to see any man submit patiently to affronts and ill usage. They desire to see this insolence resented, and resented by the person who suffers from it. They cry to him with fury, to defend or to revenge himself. If his indignation rouses at last, they heartily applaud, and sympathize with it. It enlivens their own indignation against his enemy, whom they rejoice to see him attack in turn, and are as really gratified By his revenge, provided it is not immoderate, as if the injury had been done to themselves.

But though the utility of those passions to the individual, by rendering it dangerous to insult or to injure him, be acknowledged ; and though their utility to the public, as the guardians of justice, and of the equality of its administration, be not less considerable, as shall be shewn hereafter ; yet there is still something disagreeable in the passions themselves, which makes the appearance of them in other men the natural object of our aversion. The expression of anger towards any body present, if it exceeds a bare intimation that we are sensible of his ill usage, is regarded not only as an insult to that particular person, but as a rudeness to the whole company. Respect for them ought to have restrained us from giving way to so boisterous and offensive an emotion. It is the remote effects of these passions which are agreeable; the immediate effects are mischief to the person against whom they are directed. But it is the immediate, and not the remote effects of objects which render them agreeable or disagreeable to the imagination. A prison is certainly more useful to the public than a palace; and the person who founds the one is generally directed by a much juster spirit of patriotism, than he who builds the other. But the immediate effects of a prison, the confinement of the wretches shut up in it, are disagreeable; and the imagination either does not take time to trace out the remote ones, or sees them at too great a distance to be much affected by them. A prison, therefore, will always be a disagreeable object; and the fitter it is for the purpose for which it was intended, it will be the more so. A palace, on the contrary, will always be agreeable; yet its remote effects may often be inconvenient to the public. It may serve to promote luxury, and set the example of the dissolution of manners. Its immediate effects, however, the conveniency, the pleasure, and the gaiety of the people who live in it, being all agreeable, and suggesting to the imagination a thousand agreeable ideas, that faculty generally rests upon them, and seldom goes further in tracing its more distant consequences. Trophies of the instruments of music or of agriculture, imitated in painting or in stucco, make a common and an agreeable ornament of our halls and dining rooms. A trophy of the same kind, composed of the instruments of surgery, of dissecting and amputation-knives, of saws for cutting the bones, of trepanning instruments, &c., would be absurd and shocking. Instruments of surgery, however, are always more finely polished, and generally more nicely adapted to the purposes for which they are intended, than instruments of agriculture. The remote effects of them too, the health of the patient, is agreeable; yet as the immediate effect of them is pain and suffering, the sight of them always displeases us. Instruments of war are agreeable, though their immediate effect may seem to be in the same manner pain and suffering. But then it is the pain and suffering of our enemies, with whom we have no sympathy. With regard to us, they are immediately connected with the agreeable ideas of courage, victory, and honour. They are themselves, therefore, supposed to make one of the noblest parts of dress, and the imitation of them one of the finest ornaments of architecture. It is the same case with the qualities of the mind. The ancient stoics were of opinion, that as the world was governed by the

all-ruling providence of a wise, powerful, and good God, every single
event ought to be regarded, as making a necessary part of the plan of
the universe, and as tending to promote the general order and happiness of the whole : that the vices and follies of mankind, therefore,
made as necessary a part of this plan as their wisdom or their virtue ;
and by that eternal art which educes good from ill, were made to tend
equally to the prosperity and perfection of the great system of nature.
No speculation of this kind, however, how deeply soever it might be
rooted in the mind, could diminish our natural abhorrence for vice,
whose immediate effects are so destructive, and whose remote ones are
too distant to be traced by the imagination.

It is the same case with those passions we have been just now considering. Their immediate effects are so disagreeable, that even when
they are most justly provoked, there is still something about them
which disgusts us. These, therefore, are the only passions of which
the expressions, as I formerly observed, do not dispose and prepare us
to sympathize with them, before we are informed of the cause which
excites them. The plaintive voice of misery, when heard at a distance,
will not allow us to be indifferent about the person from whom it comes.
As soon as it strikes our ear, it interests us in his fortune, and, if continued, forces us almost involuntarily to fly to his assistance. The sight
of a smiling countenance, in the same manner, elevates even the pen-
sive into that gay and airy mood, which disposes him to sympathize
with, and share the joy which it expresses ; and he feels his heart,
which with thought and care was before that shrunk and depressed, instantly expanded and elated. But it is quite otherwise with the expressions of hatred and resentment. The hoarse, boisterous, and discordant
voice of anger, when heard at a distance, inspires us either with fear or
aversion. We do not fly towards it, as to one who cries out with pain
and agony. Women, and men of weak nerves, tremble and are overcome with fear, though sensible that themselves are not the objects of
the anger. They conceive fear, however, by putting themselves in the
situation of the person who is so. Even those of stouter hearts are
disturbed ; not indeed enough to make them afraid, but enough to make
them angry ; for anger is the passion which they would feel in the situation of the other person. It is the same case with hatred. Mere
expressions of spite inspire it against nobody, but the man who uses
them. Both these passions are by nature the objects of our aversion.
Their disagreeable and boisterous appearance never excites, never
prepares, and often disturbs our sympathy. Grief does not more power-
fully engage and attract us to the person in whom we observe it, than
these, while we are ignorant of their cause, disgust and detach us from
him. It was, it seems, the intention of Nature, that those rougher and
more unamiable emotions, which drive men from one another, should
be less easily and more rarely communicated.

When music imitates the modulations of grief or joy, it either actually inspires us with those passions, or at least puts us in the mood which disposes us to conceive them. But when it imitates the notes of anger, it inspires us with fear. Joy, grief, love, admiration, devotion, are all of them passions which are naturally musical. Their natural tones are all soft, clear, and melodious ; and they naturally express themselves in periods which are distinguished by regular pauses, and which upon that account are easily adapted to the regular returns of the correspondent airs of a tune. The voice of anger, on the contrary, and of all the passions which are akin to it, is harsh and discordant. Its periods too are all irregular, sometimes very long, and sometimes very short, and distinguished by no regular pauses. It is with difficulty therefore, that music can imitate any of those passions ; and the music which does imitate them is not the most agreeable. A whole entertainment may consist, without any impropriety, of the imitation of the social and agreeable passions. It would be a strange entertainment which consisted altogether of the imitations of hatred and resentment.

If those passions are disagreeable to the spectator, they are not less so to the person who feels them. Hatred and anger are the greatest poison to the happiness of a good mind. There is, in the very feeling of those passions, something harsh, jarring, and convulsive, something that tears and distracts the breast, and is altogether destructive of that composure and tranquillity of mind which is so necessary to happiness, and which is best promoted by the contrary passions of gratitude and love. It is not the value of what they lose by the perfidy and ingratitude of those they live with, which the generous and humane are most apt to regret. Whatever they may have lost, they can generally be very happy without it. What most disturbs them is the idea of perfidy and ingratitude exercised towards themselves ; and the discordant and disagreeable passions which this excites, constitute, in their own opinion, the chief part of the injury which they suffer.

How many things are requisite to render the gratification of resentment completely agreeable, and to make the spectator thoroughly sympathize with our revenge? The provocation must first of all be such that we should become contemptible, and be exposed to perpetual insults, if we did not, in some measure, resent it. Smaller offences are always better neglected ; nor is there any thing more despicable than that froward and captious humour which takes fire upon every slight occasion of quarrel. We should resent more from a sense of the propriety of resentment, from a sense that mankind expect and require it of us, than because we feel in ourselves the furies of that disagreeable passion. There is no passion, of which the human mind is capable, concerning whose justness we ought to be so doubtful, concerning whose indulgence we ought so carefully to consult our natural sense of propriety, or so diligently to consider what will be the sentiments of the cool and impartial spectator. Magnanimity, or a regard to maintain our own rank and dignity in society, is the only motive which can ennoble the expressions of this disagreeable passion. This motive must characterize our whole style and deportment. These must be plain, open, and direct ; determined without positiveness, and elevated without insolence ; not only free from petulance and low scurrility, but generous, candid, and full of all proper regards, even for the person who has offended us. It must appear, in short, from our whole manner, without our labouring affectedly to express it, that passion has not extinguished our humanity ; and that if we yield to the dictates of revenge, it is with reluctance, from necessity, and in consequence of great and repeated provocations. When resentment is guarded and qualified in this manner, it may be admitted to be even generous and noble.

CHAP. IV.—*Of the Social Passions.*

As it is a divided sympathy which renders the whole set of passions just now mentioned, upon most occasions, so ungraceful and disagreeable : so there is another set opposite to these, which a redoubled sympathy renders almost always peculiarly agreeable and becoming. Generosity, humanity, kindness, compassion, mutual friendship and esteem, all the social and benevolent affections, when expressed in the countenance or behaviour, even towards those who are not peculiarly connected with ourselves, please the indifferent spectator upon almost every occasion. His sympathy with the person who feels those passions, exactly coincides with his concern for the person who is the object of them. The interest, which, as a man, he is obliged to take in the happiness of this last, enlivens his fellow-feeling with the sentiments of the other, whose emotions are employed about the same object. We have always, therefore, the strongest disposition to sympathize with the benevolent affections. They appear in every respect agreeable to us. We enter into the satisfaction both of the person who feels them, and of the person who is the object of them. For as to be the object of hatred and indignation gives more pain than all the evil which a brave man can fear from his enemies : so there is a satisfaction in the consciousness of being beloved, which, to a person of delicacy and sensibility, is of more importance to happiness, than all the advantage which he can expect to derive from it. What character is so detestable as that of one who takes pleasure to sow dissention among friends, and to turn their most tender love into mortal hatred ? Yet wherein does the atrocity of this so much abhorred injury consist ? Is it in depriving them of the frivolous good offices, which, had their friendship continued, they might have expected from one another ? It is in depriving them of that friendship itself, in robbing them of each other's affections, from which both derived so much satisfaction ; it is in disturbing the harmony of their hearts, and putting an end to that happy commerce which had before subsisted between them. These affections, that harmony, this commerce, are felt, not only by the tender and the delicate, but by the rudest vulgar of mankind, to be of more importance to happiness than all the little services which could be expected to flow from them.

The sentiment of love is, in itself, agreeable to the person who feels it. It soothes and composes the breast, seems to favour the vital motions, and to promote the healthful state of the human constitution ; and it is rendered still more delightful by the consciousness of the gratitude and satisfaction which it must excite in him who is the object of it. Their mutual regard renders them happy in one another, and sympathy, with this mutual regard, makes them agreeable to every other person. With what pleasure do we look upon a family, through the whole of which reign mutual love and esteem, where the parents and children are companious for one another, without any other difference than what is made by respectful affection on the one side, and kind indulgence on the other; where freedom and fondness, mutual raillery and mutual kindness, show that no opposition of interest divides the brothers, nor any rivalship of favour sets the sisters at variance, and where every thing presents us with the idea of peace, cheerfulness, harmony, and contentment? On the contrary, how uneasy are we made when we go into a house in which jarring contention sets one half of those who dwell in it against the other; where, amidst affected smoothness and complaisance, suspicious looks and sudden starts of passion betray the mutual jealousies which burn within them, and which are every moment ready to burst out through all the restraints which the presence of the company imposes?

Those amiable passions, even when they are acknowledged to be excessive, are never regarded with aversion. There is something agreeable even in the weakness of friendship and humanity. The too tender mother, the too indulgent father, the too generous and affectionate friend, may sometimes, perhaps, on account of the softness of their natures, be looked upon with a species of pity, in which, however, there is a mixture of love, but can never be regarded with hatred and aversion, nor even with contempt, unless by the most brutal and worthless of mankind. It is always with concern, with sympathy and kindness, that we blame them for the extravagance of their attachment. There is a helplessness in the character of extreme humanity which more than any thing interests our pity. There is nothing in itself which renders it either ungraceful or disagreeable. We only regret that it is unfit for the world, because the world is unworthy of it, and because it must expose the person who is endowed with it as a prey to the perfidy and ingratitude of insinuating falsehood, and to a thousand pains and uneasinesses, which, of all men, he the least deserves to feel, and which generally too he is, of all men, the least capable of supporting. It is quite otherwise with hatred and resentment. Too violent a propensity to those detestable passions, renders a person the object of universal dread and abhorrence, who, like a wild beast, ought, we think, to be hunted out of all civil society.

CHAP. V.—*Of the Selfish Passions.*

BESIDES those two opposite sets of passions, the social and unsocial, there is another which holds a sort of middle place between them; is never either so graceful as is sometimes the one set, nor is ever so odious as is sometimes the other. Grief and joy, when conceived upon account of our own private good or bad fortune, constitute this third set of passions. Even when excessive, they are never so disagreeable as excessive resentment, because no opposite sympathy can ever interest us against them: and when most suitable to their objects, they are never so agreeable as impartial humanity and just benevolence; because no double sympathy can ever interest us for them. There is, however, this difference between grief and joy, that we are generally most disposed to sympathize with small joys and great sorrows. The man who, by some sudden revolution of fortune, is lifted up all at once into a condition of life, greatly above what he had formerly lived in, may be assured that the congratulations of his best friends are not all of them perfectly sincere. An upstart, though of the greatest merit, is generally disagreeable, and a sentiment of envy commonly prevents us from heartily sympathizing with his joy. If he has any judgment, he is sensible of this, and instead of appearing to be elated with his good fortune, he endeavours, as much as he can, to smother his joy, and keep down that elevation of mind with which his new circumstances naturally inspire him. He affects the same plainness of dress, and the same modesty of behaviour, which became him in his former station. He redoubles his attention to his old friends, and endeavours more than ever to be humble, assiduous, and complaisant. And this is the behaviour which in his situation we most approve of; because we expect, it seems, that he should have more sympathy with our envy and aversion to his happiness, than we have with his happiness. It is seldom that with all this he succeeds. We suspect the sincerity of his humility, and he grows weary of this constraint. In a little time, therefore, he generally leaves all his old friends behind him, some of the meanest of them excepted, who may, perhaps, condescend to become his dependents: nor does he always acquire any new ones; the pride of his new connections is as much affronted at finding him their equal, as that of his old ones had been by his becoming their superior; and it requires the most obstinate and persevering modesty to atone for this modification to either. He generally grows weary too soon, and is provoked, by the sullen and suspicious pride of the one, and by the saucy contempt of the other, to treat the first with neglect, and the second with petulance, till at last he grows habitually insolent, and forfeits the esteem of all. If the chief part of human happiness arises from the consciousness of being beloved, as I believe it does, those sudden changes of fortune seldom contribute much to happiness. He is happiest who advances more gradually to greatness, whom the public destines to every step of his preferment long before he arrives at it, in whom, upon that account, when it comes, it can excite no extravagant joy, and with regard to whom it cannot reasonably create either any jealousy in those he overtakes, or envy in those he leaves behind.

Mankind, however, more readily sympathize with those smaller joys which flow from less important causes. It is decent to be humble amidst great prosperity; but we can scarce express too much satisfaction in all the little occurrences of common life, in the company with which we spent the evening last night, in the entertainment that was set before us, in what was said and what was done, in all the little incidents of the present conversation, and in all those frivolous nothings which fill up the void of human life. Nothing is more graceful than habitual cheerfulness, which is always founded upon a peculiar relish for all the little pleasures which common occurrences afford. We readily sympathize with it: it inspires us with the same joy, and makes every trifle turn up to us in the same agreeable aspect in which it presents itself to the person endowed with this happy disposition. Hence it is that youth, the season of gaiety, so easily engages our affections. That propensity to joy which seems even to animate the bloom, and to sparkle from the eyes of youth and beauty, though in a person of the same sex, exalts, even the aged, to a more joyous mood than ordinary. They forget, for a time, their infirmities, and abandon themselves to those agreeable ideas and emotions to which they have long been strangers, but which, when the presence of so much happiness recalls them to their breast, take their place there, like old acquaintance, from whom they are sorry to have ever been parted, and whom they embrace more heartily upon account of this long separation.

It is quite otherwise with grief. Small vexations excite no sympathy, but deep affliction calls forth the greatest. The man who is made uneasy by every little disagreeable incident, who is hurt if either the cook or the butler have failed in the least article of their duty, who feels every defect in the highest ceremonial of politeness, whether it be shown to himself or to any other person, who takes it amiss that his intimate friend did not bid him good-morrow when they met in the forenoon, and that his brother hummed a tune all the time he himself was telling a story; who is put out of humour by the badness of the weather when in the country, by the badness of the roads when upon a journey, and by the want of company and dulness of all public diversions when in town; such a person, I say, though he should have some reason, will seldom meet with much sympathy. Joy is a pleasant emotion, and we gladly abandon ourselves to it upon the slightest occasion. We readily, therefore, sympathize with it in others, whenever we are not prejudiced by envy. But grief is painful, and the mind, even when it is our own misfortune, naturally resists and recoils from it. We would endeavour either not to conceive it at all, or to shake it off as soon as we have conceived it. Our aversion to grief will not, indeed, always hinder us from conceiving it in our own case upon very trifling occasions, but it constantly prevents us from sympathizing with it in others when excited by the like frivolous causes: for our sympathetic passions are always less irresistible than our original ones. There is, besides, a malice in mankind, which not only prevents all sympathy with little uneasinesses, but renders them in some measure diverting. Hence the delight which we all take in raillery, and in the small vexation which we observe in our companion, when he is pushed, and urged, and teased upon all sides. Men of the most ordinary good-breeding dissemble the pain which any little incident may give them; and those who are more thoroughly formed to society, turn of their own accord, all such incidents into raillery, as they know their companions will do for them. The habit which a man, who lives in the world, has acquired of considering how every thing that concerns himself will appear to others, makes those frivolous calamities turn up in the same ridiculous light to him, in which he knows they will certainly be considered by them.

Our sympathy, on the contrary, with deep distress, is very strong and very sincere. It is unnecessary to give an instance. We weep even at the feigned representation of a tragedy. If you labour, therefore, under any signal calamity, if by some extraordinary misfortune you are fallen into poverty, into diseases, into disgrace and disappointment; even though your own fault may have been, in part, the occasion, yet you may generally depend upon the sincerest sympathy of all your friends, and, as far as interest and honour will permit, upon their kindest assistance too. But if your misfortune is not of this dreadful kind, if you have only been a little baulked in your ambition, if you have only been jilted by your mistress, or are only hen-pecked by your wife, lay your account with the raillery of all your acquaintance.

SEC. III.—OF THE EFFECTS OF PROSPERITY AND ADVERSITY UPON THE JUDGMENT OF MANKIND WITH REGARD TO THE PROPRIETY OF ACTION; AND WHY IT IS MORE EASY TO OBTAIN THEIR APPROBATION IN THE ONE STATE THAN IN THE OTHER.

CHAP. I.—*That though our Sympathy with Sorrow is generally a more lively Sensation than our Sympathy with Joy, it commonly falls much more Short of the Violence of what is naturally felt by the Person principally concerned.*

OUR sympathy with sorrow, though not more real, has been more taken notice of than our sympathy with joy. The word sympathy, in its most proper and primitive signification, denotes our fellow-feeling with the sufferings, not that with the enjoyments, of others. A late ingenious and subtile philosopher thought it necessary to prove, by arguments, that we had a real sympathy with joy, and that congratulation was a principle of human nature. Nobody, I believe, ever thought it necessary to prove that compassion was such.

First of all, our sympathy with sorrow is, in some sense, more universal than that with joy. Though sorrow is excessive, we may still have some fellow-feeling with it. What we feel does not, indeed, in this case, amount to that complete sympathy, to that perfect harmony and correspondence of sentiments, which constitutes approbation. We do not weep, and exclaim, and lament, with the sufferer. We are sensible, on the contrary, of his weakness and of the extravagance of his passion, and yet often feel a very sensible concern upon his account. But if we do not entirely enter into, and go along with, the joy of another, we have no sort of regard or fellow feeling for it. The man who skips and dances about with that intemperate and senseless joy which we cannot accompany him in, is the object of our contempt and indignation.

Pain besides, whether of mind or body, is a more pungent sensation than pleasure, and our sympathy with pain, though it falls greatly short of what is naturally felt by the sufferer, is generally a more lively and distinct perception than our sympathy with pleasure, though this last often approaches more nearly, as I shall show immediately, to the natural vivacity of the original passion.

Over and above all this, we often struggle to keep down our sympathy with the sorrow of others. Whenever we are not under the observation of the sufferer, we endeavour, for our own sake, to suppress it as much as we can, and we are not always successful. The opposition which we make to it, and the reluctance with which we yield to it, necessarily oblige us to take more particular notice of it. But we never have occasion to make this opposition to our sympathy with joy.

If there is any envy in the case, we never feel the least propensity towards it ; and if there is none, we give way to it without any reluctance. On the contrary, as we are always ashamed of our own envy, we often pretend, and sometimes really wish to sympathize with the joy of others, when by that disagreeable sentiment we are disqualified from doing so. We are glad, we say, on account of our neighbour's good fortune, when in our hearts, perhaps, we are really sorry. We often feel a sympathy with sorrow when we would wish to be rid of it ; and we often miss that with joy when we would be glad to have it. The obvious observation, therefore, which it naturally falls in our way to make, is, that our propensity to sympathize with sorrow must be very strong, and our inclination to sympathize with joy very weak.

Notwithstanding this prejudice, however, I will venture to affirm, that, when there is no envy in the case, our propensity to sympathize with joy is much stronger than our propensity to sympathize with sorrow; and that our fellow-feeling for the agreeable emotion approaches much more nearly to the vivacity of what is naturally felt by the persons principally concerned, than that which we conceive for the painful one.

We have some indulgence for that excessive grief which we cannot entirely go along with. We know what a prodigious effort is requisite before the sufferer can bring down his emotions to complete harmony and concord with those of the spectator. Though he fails, therefore, we easily pardon him. But we have no such indulgence for the intemperance of joy; because we are not conscious that any such vast effort is requisite to bring it down to what we can entirely enter into. The man who, under the greatest calamities, can command his sorrow, seems worthy of the highest admiration ; but he who, in the fulness of prosperity, can in the same manner master his joy, seems hardly to deserve any praise. We are sensible that there is a much wider interval in the one case than in the other, between what is naturally felt by the person principally concerned, and what the spectator can entirely go along with.

What can be added to the happiness of the man who is in health, who is out of debt, and has a clear conscience ? To one in this situation, all accessions of fortune may properly be said to be superfluous ; and if he is much elevated on account of them, it must be the effect of the most frivolous levity. This situation, however, may very well be called the natural and ordinary state of mankind. Notwithstanding the present misery and depravity of the world, so justly lamented, this really is the state of the greater part of men. The greater part of men, therefore, cannot find any great difficulty in elevating themselves to all the joy which any accession to this situation can well excite in their companion.

But though little can be added to this state, much may be taken from it. Though between this condition and the highest pitch of human prosperity, the interval is but a trifle ; between it and the lowest depth of misery the distance is immense and prodigious. Adversity, on this account, necessarily depresses the mind of the sufferer much more below its natural state, than prosperity can elevate him above it. The spectator, therefore, must find it much more difficult to sympathize entirely, and keep perfect time, with his sorrow, than thoroughly to enter into his joy, and must depart much further from his own natural and ordinary temper of mind in the one case than in the other. It is on this account, that though our sympathy with sorrow is often a more pungent sensation than our sympathy with joy, it always falls much more short of the violence of what is naturally felt by the person principally concerned.

It is agreeable to sympathize with joy ; and wherever envy does not oppose it, our heart abandons itself with satisfaction to the highest transports of that delightful sentiment. But it is painful to go along with grief, and we always enter into it with reluctance.* When we attend to the representation of a tragedy, we struggle against that sympathetic sorrow which the entertainment inspires as long as we can, and we give way to it at last only when we can no longer avoid it ; we even then endeavour to cover our concern from the company. If we shed any tears, we carefully conceal them, and are afraid, lest the spectators, not entering into this excessive tenderness, should regard it as effeminacy and weakness. The wretch whose misfortunes call upon our compassion feels with what reluctance we are likely to enter into his sorrow, and therefore proposes his grief to us with fear and hesitation : he even smothers the half of it, and is ashamed, upon account of this hard-heartedness of mankind, to give vent to the fulness of his affliction. It is otherwise with the man who riots in joy and success. Wherever envy does not interest us against him, he expects our completest sympathy. He does not fear, therefore, to announce himself with shouts of exultation, in full confidence that we are heartily disposed to go along with him.

Why should we be more ashamed to weep than to laugh before company ? We may often have as real occasion to do the one as to do the other ; but we always feel that the spectators are more likely to go along with us in the agreeable, than in the painful emotion. It is

---

* It has been objected to me that as I found the sentiment of approbation, which is always agreeable, upon sympathy, it is inconsistent with my system to admit any disagreeable sympathy. I answer, that in the sentiment of approbation there are two things to be taken notice of ; first, the sympathetic passion of the spectator ; and secondly, the emotion which arises from his observing the perfect coincidence between this sympathetic passion in himself, and the original passion in the person principally concerned. This last emotion, in which the sentiment of approbation properly consists, is always agreeable and delightful. The other may either be agreeable or disagreeable, according to the nature of the original passion, whose features it must always, in some measure, retain.

always miserable to complain, even when we are oppressed by the most dreadful calamities. But the triumph of victory is not always ungraceful. Prudence, indeed, would often advise us to bear our prosperity with more moderation ; because prudence would teach us to avoid that envy which this very triumph is, more than any thing, apt to excite.

How hearty are the acclamations of the mob, who never bear any envy to their superiors, at a triumph or a public entry ? And how sedate and moderate is commonly their grief at an execution ? Our sorrow at a funeral generally amounts to no more than an affected gravity ; but our mirth at a christening or a marriage, is always from the heart, and without any affectation. Upon these, and all such joyous occasions, our satisfaction, though not so durable, is often as lively as that of the persons principally concerned. Whenever we cordially congratulate our friends, which, however, to the disgrace of human nature, we do but seldom, their joy literally becomes our joy : we are, for the moment, as happy as they are : our heart swells and overflows with real pleasure : joy and complacency sparkle from our eyes, and animate every feature of our countenance, and every gesture of our body.

But on the contrary, when we condole with our friends in their afflictions, how little do we feel, in comparison of what they feel? We sit down by them, we look at them, and while they relate to us the circumstances of their misfortune, we listen to them with gravity and attention. But while their narration is every moment interrupted by those natural bursts of passion which often seem almost to choke them in the midst of it ; how far are the languid emotions of our hearts from keeping time to the transports of theirs ? We may be sensible, at the same time, that their passion is natural, and no greater than what we ourselves might feel upon the like occasion. We may even inwardly reproach ourselves with our own want of sensibility, and perhaps, on that account, work ourselves up into an artificial sympathy, which however, when it is raised, is always the slightest and most transitory imaginable ; and generally, as soon as we have left the room, vanishes, and is gone for ever. Nature, it seems, when she loaded us with our own sorrows, thought they were enough, and therefore did not command us to take any further share in those of others, than what was necessary to prompt us to relieve them.

It is on account of this dull sensibility to the afflictions of others, that magnanimity amidst great distress appears always so divinely graceful. His behaviour is genteel and agreeable who can maintain his cheerfulness amidst a number of frivolous disasters. But he appears to be more than mortal who can support in the same manner the most dreadful calamities. We feel what an immense effort is requisite to silence those violent emotions which naturally agitate and distract those in his situation. We are amazed to find that he can command himself so entirely. His firmness at the same time, perfectly coincides with our insensibility. He makes no demand upon us for that more exquisite degree of sensibility which we find, and which we are mortified to find, that we do not possess. There is the most perfect correspondence between his sentiments and ours, and on that account the most perfect propriety in his behaviour. It is a propriety too, which, from our experience of the usual weakness of human nature, we could not reasonably have expected he should be able to maintain. We wonder with surprise and astonishment at that strength of mind which is capable of so noble and generous an effort. The sentiment of complete sympathy and approbation, mixed and animated with wonder and surprise, constitutes what is properly called admiration, as has already been more than once take notice of. Cato, surrounded on all sides by his enemies, unable to resist them, disdaining to submit to them, and reduced, by the proud maxims of that age, to the necessity of destroying himself; yet never shrinking from his misfortunes, never supplicating with the lamentable voice of wretchedness, those miserable sympathetic tears which we are always so unwilling to give; but on the contrary, arming himself with manly fortitude, and the moment before he executes his fatal resolution, giving, with his usual tranquillity, all necessary orders for the safety of his friends; appears to Seneca, that great preacher of insensibility, a spectacle which even the gods themselves might behold with pleasure and admiration.

Whenever we meet, in common life, with any examples of such heroic magnanimity, we are always extremely affected. We are more apt to weep and shed tears for such as, in this manner, seem to feel nothing for themselves, than for those who give way to all the weakness of sorrow· and in this particular case, the sympathetic grief of the spectator appears to go beyond the original passion in the person principally concerned. The friends of Socrates all wept when he drank the last potion, while he himself expressed the gayest and most cheerful tranquillity. Upon all such occasions the spectator makes no effort, and has no occasion to make any, in order to conquer his sympathetic sorrow. He is under no fear that it will transport him to any thing that is extravagant and improper; he is rather pleased with the sensibility of his own heart, and gives way to it with complacence and self-approbation. He gladly indulges, therefore, the most melancholy views which can naturally occur to him, concerning the calamity of his friend, for whom, perhaps, he never felt so exquisitely before, the tender and tearful passion of love. But it is quite otherwise with the person principally concerned. He is obliged, as much as possible, to turn away his eyes from whatever is either naturally terrible or disagreeable in his situation. Too serious an attention to those circumstances, he fears, might make so violent an impression upon him, that he could no longer keep within the bounds of moderation, or render himself the object of the complete sympathy and approbation of the spectators.

He fixes his thoughts, therefore, upon those only which are agreeable, the applause and admiration which he is about to deserve by the heroic magnanimity of his behaviour. To feel that he is capable of so noble and generous an effort, to feel that in this dreadful situation he can still act as he would desire to act, animates and transports him with joy, and enables him to support that triumphant gaiety which seems to exult in the victory he thus gains over his misfortunes.

On the contrary, he always appears, in some measure, mean and despicable, who is sunk in sorrow and dejection upon account of any calamity of his own. We cannot bring ourselves to feel for him what he feels for himself, and what, perhaps, we should feel for ourselves if in his situation : we, therefore, despise him ; unjustly perhaps, if any sentiment could be regarded as unjust, to which we are by nature irresistibly determined. The weakness of sorrow never appears in any respect agreeable, except when it arises from what we feel for ourselves. A son, upon the death of an indulgent and respectable father, may give way to it without much blame. His sorrow is chiefly founded upon a sort of sympathy with his departed parent ; and we readily enter into his humane emotion. But if he should indulge the same weakness upon account of any misfortune which affected himself only, he would no longer meet with any such indulgence. If he should be reduced to beggary and ruin, if he should be exposed to the most dreadful dangers, if he should even be led out to a public execution, and there shed one single tear upon the scaffold, he would disgrace himself for ever in the opinion of all the gallant and generous part of mankind. Their compassion for him, however, would be very strong, and very sincere ; but as it would still fall short of this excessive weakness, they would have no pardon for the man who could thus expose himself in the eyes of the world. His behaviour would affect them with shame rather than with sorrow ; and the dishonour which he had thus brought upon himself would appear to them the most lamentable circumstance in his misfortune. How did it disgrace the memory of the intrepid Duke of Biron, who had so often braved death in the field, that he wept upon the scaffold, when he beheld the state to which he was fallen, and remembered the favour and the glory from which his own rashness had so unfortunately thrown him ?

CHAP. II.—*Of the Origin of Ambition, and of the Distinction of Ranks.*

IT is because mankind are disposed to sympathize more entirely with our joy than with our sorrow, that we make parade of our riches, and conceal our poverty. Nothing is so mortifying as to be obliged to expose our distress to the view of the public, and to feel, that though our situation is open to the eyes of all mankind, no mortal conceives for us the half of what we suffer. Nay, it is chiefly from this regard to the sentiments of mankind, that we pursue riches and avoid poverty. For to what purpose is all the toil and bustle of this world? what is the end of avarice and ambition, of the pursuit of wealth, of power, and pre-eminence? Is it to supply the necessities of nature? The wages of the meanest labourer can supply them. We see that they can afford him food and clothing, the comfort of a house and of a family. If we examine his œconomy with rigour, we should find that he spends a great part of them upon conveniences, which may be regarded as superfluities, and that, upon extraordinary occasions, he can give something even to vanity and distinction. What then is the cause of our aversion to his situation, and why should those who have been educated in the higher ranks of life, regard it as worse than death, to be reduced to live, even without labour, upon the same simple fare with him, to dwell under the same lowly roof, and to be clothed in the same humble attire? Do they imagine that their stomach is better or their sleep sounder in a palace than in a cottage? The contrary has been so often observed, and, indeed, is so very obvious, though it had never been observed, that there is nobody ignorant of it. From whence, then arises that emulation which runs through all the different ranks of men, and what are the advantages which we propose by the great purpose of human life which we call bettering our condition? To be observed, to be attended to, to be taken notice of with sympathy, complacency, and approbation, are all the advantages which we can propose to derive from it. It is the vanity, not the ease or the pleasure, which interests us. But vanity is always founded upon the belief of our being the object of attention and approbation. The rich man glories in his riches, because he feels that they naturally draw upon him the attention of the world, and that mankind are disposed to go along with him in all those agreeable emotions with which the advantages of his situation so readily inspire him. At the thought of this, his heart seems to swell and dilate itself within him, and he is fonder of his wealth upon this account, than for all the other advantages it procures him. The poor man, on the contrary, is ashamed of his poverty. He feels that it either places him out of the sight of mankind, or, that if they take any notice of him, they have, however, scarce any fellow-feeling with the misery and distress which he suffers. He is mortified upon both accounts; for though to be overlooked, and to be disapproved of, are things entirely different, yet as obscurity covers us from the daylight of honour and approbation, to feel that we are taken no notice of, necessarily damps the most agreeable hope, and disappoints the most ardent desire, of human nature. The poor man goes out and comes in unheeded, and when in the midst of a crowd is in the same obscurity as if shut up in his own hovel. Those humble

cares and painful attentions which occupy those in his situation, afford
no amusement to the dissipated and the gay.   They turn away their
their eyes from him, if the extremity of his distress forces them to look
at him, it is only to spurn so disagreeable an object from among them.
The fortunate and the proud wonder at the insolence of human
wretchedness, that it should dare to present itself before them, and
with the loathsome aspect of its misery presume to disturb the serenity
of their happiness.   The man of rank and distinction, on the contrary,
is observed by all the world.   Every body is eager to look at him, and
to conceive, at least by sympathy, that joy and exultation with which
his circumstances naturally inspire him.   His actions are the objects
of the public care.   Scarce a word, scarce a gesture, can fall from him
that is altogether neglected.   In a great assembly he is the person
upon whom all direct their eyes ; it is upon him that their passions
seem to wait with expectation, in order to receive that movement and
direction which he shall impress upon them ; and if his behaviour is
not altogether absurd, he has, every moment, an opportunity of
interesting mankind, and of rendering himself the object of the observation and fellow feeling of every body about him.   It is this, which,
notwithstanding the restraint it imposes, notwithstanding the loss of
liberty with which it is attended, renders greatness the object of envy,
and compensates, in the opinion of mankind, all that toil, all that
anxiety, all those mortifications which must be undergone in the pursuit of it ; and what is of yet more consequence, all that leisure, all
that ease, all that careless security, which are forfeited for ever by the
acquisition.

When we consider the condition of the great, in those delusive
colours in which the imagination is apt to paint it, it seems to be almost
the abstract idea of a perfect and happy state.   It is the very state
which, in all our waking dreams and idle reveries, we had sketched
out to ourselves as the final object of our desires.   We feel, therefore, a
peculiar sympathy with the satisfaction of those who are in it.   We
favour all their inclinations, and forward all their wishes.   What pity, we
think, that any thing should spoil and corrupt so agreeable a situation.
We could even wish them immortal ; and it seems hard to us, that
death should at last put an end to such perfect enjoyment.   It is cruel,
we think, in Nature to compel them from their exalted stations to that
humble, but hospitable home, which she has provided for all her children.   Great king, live for ever ! is the compliment which, after the
manner of eastern adulation, we should readily make them, if experience did not teach us its absurdity.   Every calamity that befals them,
every injury that is done them, excites in the breast of the spectator
ten times more compassion and resentment than he would have felt,
had the same things happened to other men.   It is the misfortune of
kings only which afford the proper subjects for tragedy.   They resemble

in this respect, the misfortunes of lovers. Those two situations are the chief which interest us upon the theatre; because, in spite of all that reason and experience can tell us to the contrary, the prejudices of the imagination attach to these two states a happiness superior to any other. To disturb, or to put an end to such perfect enjoyment, seems to be the most atrocious of all injuries. The traitor who conspires against the life of his monarch, is thought a greater monster than any other murderer. All the innocent blood that was shed in the civil wars provoked less indignation than the death of Charles I. A stranger to human nature, who saw the indifference of men about the misery of their inferiors, and the regret and indignation which they feel for the misfortunes and sufferings of those above them, would be apt to imagine, that pain must be more agonizing, and the convulsions of death more terrible to persons of higher rank, than they are to those of meaner stations.

Upon this disposition of mankind, to go along with all the passions of the rich and the powerful, is founded the distinction of ranks, and the order of society. Our obsequiousness to our superiors more frequently arises from our admiration for the advantages of their situation, than from any private expectations of benefit from their goodwill. Their benefits can extend but to a few; but their fortunes interest almost every body. We are eager to assist them in completing a system of happiness that approaches so near to perfection; and we desire to serve them for their own sake, without any recompense but the vanity or the honour of obliging them. Neither is our deference to the inclinations founded chiefly, or altogether, upon a regard to the utility of such submission, and to the order of society, which is best supported by it. Even when the order of society seems to require that we should oppose them, we can hardly bring ourselves to do it. That kings are servants of the people, to be obeyed, resisted, deposed, or punished, as the public conveniency may require, is the doctrine of reason and philosophy; but it is not the doctrine of nature. Nature would teach us to submit to them for their own sake, to tremble and bow down before their exalted station, to regard their smile as a reward sufficient to compensate any services, and to dread their displeasure, though no other evil were to follow from it, as the severest of all mortifications. To treat them in any respect as men, to reason and dispute with them upon ordinary occasions, requires such resolution, that there are few men whose magnanimity can support them in it, unless they are likewise assisted by similarity and acquaintance. The strongest motives, the most furious passions, fear, hatred, and resentment, are scarce sufficient to balance this natural disposition to respect them: and their conduct must, either justly or unjustly, have excited the highest degree of those passions, before the bulk of the people can be brought to oppose them with violence, or to desire to see them either punished or deposed. Even when the people have been brought this length, they are apt to relent every moment, and easily relapse into their habitual state of deference to those whom they have been accustomed to look upon as their natural superiors. They cannot stand the mortification of their monarch. Compassion soon takes the place of resentment, they forget all past provocations, their old principles of loyalty revive, and they run to re-establish the ruined authority of their old masters, with the same violence with which they had opposed it. The death of Charles I. brought about the restoration of the royal family. Compassion for James II., when he was seized by the populace in making his escape on ship-board, had almost prevented the Revolution, and made it go on more heavily than before.

Do the great seem insensible of the easy price at which they may acquire the public admiration; or do they seem to imagine that to them, as to other men, it must be the purchase either of sweat or of blood? By what important accomplishments is the young nobleman instructed to support the dignity of his rank, and to render himself worthy of that superiority over his fellow citizens, to which the virtue of his ancestors had raised them: Is it by knowledge, by industry, by patience, by self-denial, or by virtue of any kind? As all his words, as all his motions are attended to, he learns an habitual regard to every circumstance of ordinary behaviour, and studies to perform all those small duties with the most exact propriety. As he is conscious how much he is observed, and how much mankind are disposed to favour all his inclinations, he acts, upon the most indifferent occasions, with that freedom and elevation which the thought of this naturally inspires. His air, his manner, his deportment, all mark that elegant and graceful sense of his own superiority, which those who are born to inferior stations can hardly ever arrive at. These are the arts by which he proposes to make mankind more easily submit to his authority, and to govern their inclinations according to his own pleasure: and in this he is seldom disappointed. These arts, supported by rank and pre-eminence, are, upon ordinary occasions, sufficient to govern the world. Lewis XIV. during the greater part of his reign, was regarded, not only in France, but over all Europe, as the most perfect model of a great prince. But what were the talents and virtues by which he acquired this great reputation? Was it by the scrupulous and inflexible justice of all his undertakings, by the immense dangers and difficulties with which they were attended, or by the unwearied and unrelenting application with which he pursued them? Was it by his extensive knowledge, by his exquisite judgment, or by his heroic valour? It was by none of these qualities. But he was, first of all, the most powerful prince in Europe, and consequently held the highest rank among kings; and then says his historian, 'he surpassed all his courtiers in the grace- 'fulness of his shape, and the majestic beauty of his features. The

'sound of his voice, noble and affecting, gained those hearts which his
'presence intimidated.   He had a step and a deportment which could
'suit only him and his rank, and which would have been ridiculous in
'any other person.   The embarrassment which he occasioned to those
'who spoke to him, flattered that secret satisfaction with which he felt
'his own superiority.   The old officer, who was confounded and fal-
'tered in asking him a favour, and not being able to conclude his dis-
'course, said to him : " Sir, your majesty, I hope, will believe that I do
'not tremble thus before your enemies :" had no difficulty to obtain what
'he demanded.'   These frivolous accomplishments, supported by his
rank, and, no doubt too, by a degree of other talents and virtues, which
seems, however, not to have been much above mediocrity, established
this prince in the esteem of his own age, and have drawn, even from
posterity, a good deal of respect for his memory.   Compared with these,
in his own times, and in his own presence, no other virtue, it seems,
appeared to have any merit.   Knowledge, industry, valour, and beneficence trembled, were abashed, and lost all dignity before them.

But it is not by accomplishments of this kind, that the man of inferior
rank must hope to distinguish himself.   Politeness is so much the virtue
of the great, that it will do little honour to any body but themselves.
The coxcomb, who imitates their manner, and affects to be eminent by
the superior propriety of his ordinary behaviour, is rewarded with a
double share of contempt for his folly and presumption.   Why should
the man, whom nobody thinks it worth while to look at, be very anxious
about the manner in which he holds up his head, or disposes of his
arms while he walks through a room ?   He is occupied surely with a
very superfluous attention, and with an attention too that marks a sense
of his own importance, which no other mortal can go along with.   The
most perfect modesty and plainness, joined to as much negligence as is
consistent with the respect due to the company, ought to be the chief
characteristics of the behaviour of a private man.   If ever he hopes to
distinguish himself, it must be by more important virtues.   He must
acquire dependants to balance the dependants of the great, and he has
no other fund to pay them from, but the labour of his body and the
activity of his mind.   He must cultivate these therefore : he must
acquire superior knowledge in his profession and superior industry in
the exercise of it.   He must be patient in labour, resolute in danger,
and firm in distress.   These talents he must bring into public view, by
the difficulty, importance, and at the same time, good judgment of his
undertakings, and by the severe and unrelenting application, with which
he pursues them.   Probity and prudence, generosity and frankness,
must characterize his behaviour upon all ordinary occasions; and he
must, at the same time, be forward to engage in all those situations, in
which it requires the greatest talents and virtues to act with propriety,
but in which the greatest applause is to be acquired by those who can

acquit themselves with honour.   With what impatience does the man of spirit and ambition, who is depressed by his situation, look round for some great opportunity to distinguish himself?   No circumstances, which can afford this, appear to him undesirable.   He even looks forward with satisfaction to the prospect of foreign war or civil dissension; and, with secret transport and delight, sees through all the confusion and bloodshed which attend them, the probability of those wished-for occasions presenting themselves, in which he may draw upon himself the attention and admiration of mankind.   The man of rank and distinction, on the contrary, whose whole glory consists in the propriety of his ordinary behaviour, who is contented with the humble renown which this can afford him, and has no talents to acquire any other, is unwilling to embarrass himself with what can be attended either with difficulty or distress.   To figure at a ball is his great triumph, and to succeed in an intrigue of gallantry, his highest exploit.   He has an aversion to all public confusions, not from the love of mankind, for the great never look upon their inferiors as their fellow-creatures; nor yet from want of courage, for in that he is seldom defective; but from a consciousness that he possesses none of the virtues which are required in such situations, and that the public attention will certainly be drawn away from him by others.   He may be willing to expose himself to some little danger, and to make a campaign when it happens to be the fashion.   But he shudders with horror at the thought of any situation which demands the continual and long exertion of patience, industry, fortitude, and application of thought.   These virtues are hardly ever to be met with in men who are born to those high stations.   In all governments, accordingly, even in monarchies, the highest offices are generally possessed, and the whole detail of the administration conducted, by men who were educated in the middle and inferior ranks of life, who have been carried forward by their own industry and abilities, though loaded with the jealousy, and opposed by the resentment, of all those who were born their superiors, and to whom the great, after having regarded them first with contempt, and afterwards with envy, are at last contented to truckle with the same abject meanness with which they desire that the rest of mankind should behave to themselves.

It is the loss of this easy empire over the affections of mankind which renders the fall from greatness so insupportable.   When the family of the king of Macedon was led in triumph by Paulus Æmilius, their misfortunes, it is said, made them divide with their conqueror the attention of the Roman people.   The sight of the royal children, whose tender age rendered them insensible of their situation, struck the spectators, amidst the public rejoicings and prosperity, with the tenderest sorrow and compassion.   The king appeared next in the procession; and seemed like one confounded and astonished, and bereft of all sentiment, by the greatness of his calamities. His friends and ministers followed after him. As they moved along, they often cast their eyes upon their fallen sovereign, and always burst into tears at the sight; their whole behaviour demonstrating that they thought not of their own misfortunes, but were occupied entirely by the superior greatness of his. The generous Romans, on the contrary, beheld him with disdain and indignation, and regarded as unworthy of all compassion the man who could be so mean-spirited as to bear to live under such calamities. Yet what did those calamities amount to? According to the greater part of historians, he was to spend the remainder of his days, under the protection of a powerful and humane people, in a state which in itself should seem worthy of envy, a state of plenty, ease, leisure, and security, from which it was impossible for him even by his own folly to fall. But he was no longer to be surrounded by that admiring mob of fools, flatterers, and dependants, who had formerly been accustomed to attend upon all his motions. He was no longer to be gazed upon by multitudes, nor to have it in his power to render himself the object of their respect, their gratitude, their love, their admiration. The passions of nations were no longer to mould themselves upon his inclinations. This was that insupportable calamity which bereaved the king of all sentiment; which made his friends forget their own misfortunes; and which the Roman magnanimity could scarce conceive how any man could be so mean-spirited as to bear to survive.

'Love,' says my Lord Rochefaucault, 'is commonly succeeded by 'ambition; but ambition is hardly ever succeeded by love.' That passion, when once it has got entire possession of the breast, will admit neither a rival nor a successor. To those who have been accustomed to the possession, or even to the hope of public admiration, all other pleasures sicken and decay. Of all the discarded statesmen who for their own ease have studied to get the better of ambition, and to despise those honours which they could no longer arrive at, how few have been able to succeed? The greater part have spent their time in the most listless and insipid indolence, chagrined at the thoughts of their own insignificancy, incapable of being interested in the occupations of private life, without enjoyment except when they talked of their former greatness, and without satisfaction except when they were employed in some vain project to recover it. Are you in earnest resolved never to barter your liberty for the lordly servitude of a court, but to live free, fearless, and independent? There seems to be one way to continue in that virtuous resolution; and perhaps but one. Never enter the place from whence so few have been able to return; never come within the circle of ambition; nor ever bring yourself into comparison with those masters of the earth who have already engrossed the attention of half mankind before you.

Of such mighty importance does it appear to be, in the imaginations

of men, to stand in that situation which sets them most in the view of
general sympathy and attention. And thus, place, that great object
which divides the wives of aldermen, is the end of half the labours of
human life; and is the cause of all the tumult and bustle, all the rapine
and injustice, which avarice and ambition have introduced into this
world. People of sense, it is said, indeed despise place; that is, they
despise sitting at the head of the table, and are indifferent who it is
that is pointed out to the company by that frivolous circumstance, which
the smallest advantange is capable of overbalancing. But rank, distinction, pre-eminence, no man despises, unless he is either raised very
much above, or sunk very much below, the ordinary standard of human
nature; unless he is either so confirmed in wisdom and real philosophy,
as to be satisfied that, while the propriety of his conduct renders him
the just object of approbation, it is of little consequence though he be
neither attended to, nor approved of; or so habituated to the idea of
his own meanness, so sunk in slothful and sottish indifference, as
entirely to have forgot the desire and almost the very wish for superiority over his fellows.

As to become the natural object of the joyous congratulations and
sympathetic attentions of mankind is, in this manner, the circumstance
which gives to prosperity all its dazzling splendour; so nothing darkens
so much the gloom of adversity as to feel that our misfortunes are the
objects, not of the fellow-feeling, but of the contempt and aversion of
our brethren. It is upon this account that the most dreadful calamities
are not always those which it is most difficult to support. It is often
more mortifying to appear in public under small disasters, than under
great misfortunes. The first excite no sympathy; but the second,
though they may excite none that approaches to the anguish of the
sufferer, call forth, however, a very lively compassion. The sentiments
of the spectators are, in this last case, less wide of those of the sufferer, and their imperfect fellow-feeling lends him some assistance in
supporting his misery. Before a gay assembly, a gentleman would be
more mortified to appear covered with filth and rags than with blood
and wounds. This last situation would interest their pity; the other
would provoke their laughter. The judge who orders a criminal to be
set in the pillory, dishonours him more than if he had condemned him
to the scaffold. The great prince, who, some years ago, caned a general officer at the head of his army, disgraced him irrecoverably. The
punishment would have been much less had he shot him through his
body. By the laws of honour, to strike with a cane dishonours, to
strike with a sword does not, for an obvious reason. Those slighter
punishments, when inflicted on a gentleman, to whom dishonour is the
greatest of all evils, come to be regarded among a humane and generous people, as the most dreadful of any. With regard to persons of
that rank, therefore, they are universally laid aside, and the law, while

it takes their life upon many occasions, respects their honour upon almost all. To scourge a person of quality, or to set him in the pillory, upon account of any crime whatever, is a brutality of which no European government, except that of Russia, is capable.

A brave man is not rendered contemptible by being brought to the scaffold; he is, by being set in the pillory. His behaviour in the one situation may gain him universal esteem and admiration. No behaviour in the other can render him agreeable. The sympathy of the spectators supports him in the one case, and saves him from that shame, that consciousness that his misery is felt by himself only, which is of all sentiments the most unsupportable. There is no sympathy in the other; or, if there is any, it is not with his pain, which is a trifle, but with his consciousness of the want of sympathy with which this pain is attended. It is with his shame, not with his sorrow. Those who pity him, blush and hang down their heads for him. He droops in the same manner, and feels himself irrecoverably degraded by the punishment, though not by the crime. The man, on the contrary, who dies with resolution, as he is naturally regarded with the erect aspect of esteem and approbation, so he wears himself the same undaunted countenance; and, if the crime does not deprive him of the respect of others, the punishment never will. He has no suspicion that his situation is the object of contempt or derision to any body, and he can, with propriety, assume the air, not only of perfect serenity, but of triumph and exultation.

'Great dangers,' says the Cardinal de Retz, 'have their charms, 'because there is some glory to be got, even when we miscarry. But 'moderate dangers have nothing but what is horrible, because the loss 'of reputation always attends the want of success.' His maxim has the same foundation with what we have been just now observing with regard to punishments.

Human virtue is superior to pain, to poverty, to danger, and to death; nor does it even require its utmost efforts to despise them. But to have its misery exposed to insult and derision, to be led in triumph, to be set up for the hand of scorn to point at, is a situation in which its constancy is much more apt to fail. Compared with the contempt of mankind, all other external evils are easily supported.

CHAP. III.—*Of the Corruption of our Moral Sentiments, which is occasioned by this Disposition to admire the Rich and the Great, and to despise or neglect Persons of poor and mean Condition.*

THIS disposition to admire, and almost to worship, the rich and the powerful, and to despise or, at least, to neglect persons of poor and mean condition, though necessary both to establish and to maintain the distinction of ranks and the order of society, is, at the same time, the great and most universal cause of the corruption of our moral sentiments. That wealth and greatness are often regarded with the respect and admiration which are due only to wisdom and virtue; and that the contempt, of which vice and folly are the only proper objects, is often most unjustly bestowed upon poverty and weakness, has been the complaint of moralists in all ages.

We desire both to be respectable and to be respected. We dread both to be contemptible and to be contemned. But, upon coming into the world, we soon find that wisdom and virtue are by no means the sole objects of respect; nor vice and folly, of contempt. We frequently see the respectful attentions of the world more strongly directed towards the rich and the great, than towards the wise and the virtuous. We see frequently the vices and follies of the powerful much less despised than the poverty and weakness of the innocent. To deserve, to acquire, and to enjoy the respect and admiration of mankind, are the great objects of ambition and emulation. Two different roads are presented to us, equally leading to the attainment of this so much desired object; the one, by the study of wisdom and the practice of virtue; the other, by the acquisition of wealth and greatness. Two different characters are presented to our emulation; the one, of proud ambition and ostentatious avidity; the other, of humble modesty and equitable justice.. Two different models, two different pictures, are held out to us, according to which we may fashion our own character and behaviour; the one more gaudy and glittering in its colouring; the other more correct and more exquisitely beautiful in its outline: the one forcing itself upon , the notice of every wandering eye; the other, attracting the attention of scarce any body but the most studious and careful observer. They are the wise and the virtuous chiefly, a select, though, I am afraid, but a small party, who are the real and steady admirers of wisdom and virtue. The great mob of mankind are the admirers and worshippers, and, what may seem more extraordinary, most frequently the disinterested admirers and worshippers, of wealth and greatness.

The respect which we feel for wisdom and virtue is, no doubt, different from that which we conceive for wealth and greatness; and it requires no very nice discernment to distinguish the difference. But, notwithstanding this difference, those sentiments bear a very considerable resemblance to one another. In some particular features they are, no doubt, different, but, in the general air of the countenance, they seem to be so very nearly the same, that inattentive observers are very apt to mistake the one for the other.

In equal degrees of merit there is scarce any man who does not respect more the rich and the great, than the poor and the humble. With most men the presumption and vanity of the former are much more admired, than the real and solid merit of the latter. It is scarce agreeable to good morals, or even to good language, perhaps, to say, that mere wealth and greatness, abstracted from merit and virtue, deserve our respect. We must acknowledge, however, that they almost constantly obtain it; and that they may, therefore, be considered as, in some respects, the natural objects of it. Those exalted stations may, no doubt, be completely degraded by vice and folly. But, the vice and folly must be very great, before they can operate this complete degradation. The profligacy of a man of fashion is looked upon with much less contempt and aversion, than that of a man of meaner condition. In the latter, a single transgression of the rules of temperance and propriety, is commonly more resented, than the constant and avowed contempt of them ever is in the former.

In the middling and inferior stations of life, the road to virtue and that to fortune, to such fortune, at least, as men in such stations can reasonably expect to acquire, are, happily, in most cases, very nearly the same. In all the middling and inferior professions, real and solid professional abilities, joined to prudent, just, firm, and temperate conduct, can very seldom fail of success. Abilities will even sometimes prevail where the conduct is by no means correct. Either habitual imprudence, however, or injustice, or weakness, or profligacy, will always cloud, and sometimes depress altogether, the most splendid professional abilities. Men in the inferior and middling stations of life, besides, can never be great enough to be above the law, which must generally overawe them into some sort of respect for, at least, the more important rules of justice. The success of such people, too, almost always depends upon the favour and good opinion of their neighbours and equals; and without a tolerably regular conduct these can very seldom be obtained. The good old proverb, therefore, that honesty is the best policy, holds, in such situations, almost always perfectly true. In such situations, therefore, we may generally expect a considerable degree of virtue; and, fortunately for the good morals of society, these are the situations of the greater part of mankind.

In the superior stations of life the case is unhappily not always the same. In the courts of princes, in the drawing-rooms of the great, where success and preferment depend, not upon the esteem of intelligent and well-informed equals, but upon the fanciful and foolish favour of ignorant, presumptuous, and proud superiors; flattery and falsehood too often prevail over merit and abilities. In such societies the abilities to please, are more regarded than the abilities to serve. In quiet and peaceable times, when the storm is at a distance, the prince, or great man, wishes only to be amused, and is even apt to fancy that he has scarce any occasion for the service of any body, or that those who amuse him are sufficiently able to serve him. The external graces, the frivolous accomplishments of that impertinent and foolish thing called a man of fashion, are commonly more admired than the solid and masculine virtues of a warrior, a statesman, a philosopher, or a legislator. All the great and awful virtues, all the virtues which can fit, either for the council, the senate, or the field, are, by the insolent and insignificant flatterers, who commonly figure the most in such corrupted societies, held in the utmost contempt and derision. When the Duke of Sully was called upon by Louis the Thirteenth, to give his advice in some great emergency, he observed the favourites and courtiers whispering to one another, and smiling at his unfashionable appearance. 'Whenever your Majesty's father,' said the old warrior and statesman, 'did me the honour to consult me, he ordered the buffoons of the court 'to retire into the antechamber.'

It is from our disposition to admire, and consequently to imitate, the rich and the great, that they are enabled to set, or to lead, what is called the fashion. Their dress is the fashionable dress; the language of their conversation, the fashionable style; their air and deportment, the fashionable behaviour. Even their vices and follies are fashionable; and the greater part of men are proud to imitate and resemble them in the very qualities which dishonour and degrade them. Vain men often give themselves airs of a fashionable profligacy, which, in their hearts, they do not approve of, and of which, perhaps, they are really not guilty. They desire to be praised for what they themselves do not think praiseworthy, and are ashamed of unfashionable virtues which they sometimes practise in secret, and for which they have secretly some degree of real veneration. There are hypocrites of wealth and greatness, as well as of religion and virtue; and a vain man is as apt to pretend to be what he is not, in the one way, as a cunning man is in the other. He assumes the equipage and splendid way of living of his superiors, without considering that whatever may be praiseworthy in any of these, derives its whole merit and propriety from its suitableness to that situation and fortune which both require and can easily support the expense. Many a poor man places his glory in being thought rich, without considering that the duties (if one may call such follies by so venerable a name) which that reputation imposes upon him, must soon reduce him to beggary, and render his situation still more unlike that of those whom he admires and imitates, than it had been originally.

To attain to this envied situation, the candidates for fortune too frequently abandon the paths of virtue; for unhappily, the road which leads to the one, and that which leads to the other, lie sometimes in very opposite directions. But the ambitious man flatters himself that, in the splendid situation to which he advances, he will have so many means of commanding the respect and admiration of mankind, and will be enabled to act with such superior propriety and grace, that the lustre of his future conduct will entirely cover, or efface, the foulness of the steps by which he arrived at that elevation. In many governments the candidates for the highest stations are above the law; and, if they

5 *

can attain the object of their ambition, they have no fear of being called to account for the means by which they acquired it. They often endeavour, therefore, not only by fraud and falsehood, the ordinary and vulgar arts of intrigue and cabal; but sometimes by the perpetration of the most enormous crimes, by murder and assassination, by rebellion and civil war, to supplant and destroy those who oppose or stand in the way of their greatness. They more frequently miscarry than succeed; and commonly gain nothing but the disgraceful punishment which is due to their crimes. But, though they should be so lucky as to attain that wished-for greatness, they are always most miserably disappointed in the happiness which they expect to enjoy in it. It is not ease or pleasure, but always honour, of one kind or another, though frequently an honour very ill understood, that the ambitious man really pursues. But the honour of his exalted station appears, both in his own eyes and in those of other people, polluted and defiled by the baseness of the means through which he rose to it. Though by the profusion of every liberal expense; though by excessive indulgence in every profligate pleasure, the wretched, but usual, resource of ruined characters; though by the hurry of public business, or by the prouder and more dazzling tumult of war, he may endeavour to efface, both from his own memory and from that of other people, the remembrance of what he has done; that remembrance never fails to pursue him. He invokes in vain the dark and dismal powers of forgetfulness and oblivion. He remembers himself what he has done, and that remembrance tells him that other people must likewise remember it. Amidst all the gaudy pomp of the most ostentatious greatness; amidst the venal and vile adulation of the great and of the learned; amidst the more innocent, though more foolish, acclamations of the common people; amidst all the pride of conquest and the triumph of successful war, he is still secretly pursued by the avenging furies of shame and remorse; and, while glory seems to surround him on all sides, he himself, in his own imagination, sees black and foul infamy fast pursuing him, and every moment ready to overtake him from behind. Even the great Cæsar, though he had the magnanimity to dismiss his guards, could not dismiss his suspicions. The remembrance of Pharsalia still haunted and pursued him. When, at the request of the senate, he had the generosity to pardon Marcellus, he told that assembly, that he was not unaware of the designs which were carrying on against his life; but that, as he had lived long enough both for nature and for glory, he was contented to die, and therefore despised all conspiracies. He had, perhaps, lived long enough for nature. But the man who felt himself the object of such deadly resentment from those whose favour he wished to gain, and whom he still wished to consider as his friends, had certainly lived too long for real glory; or for all the happiness which he could ever hope to enjoy in the love and esteem of his equals.

Part II.—*Of Merit and Demerit; or, of the Objects of Reward and Punishment.*

SEC. I.—OF THE SENSE OF MERIT AND DEMERIT.

INTRODUCTION.—There is another set of qualities ascribed to the actions and conduct of mankind, distinct from their propriety or impropriety, their decency or ungracefulness, and which are the objects of a distinct species of approbation and disapprobation. These are Merit and Demerit, the qualities of deserving reward and of deserving punishment.

It has already been observed, that the sentiment or affection of the heart, from which any action proceeds, and upon which its whole virtue or vice depends, may be considered under two different aspects, or in two different relations: first, in relation to the cause or object which excites it; and, secondly, in relation to the end which it proposes, or to the effect which it tends to produce: that upon the suitableness or unsuitableness, upon the proportion or disproportion, which the affection seems to bear to the cause or object which excites it, depends the propriety or impropriety, the decency or ungracefulness of the consequent action; and that upon the beneficial or hurtful effects which the affection proposes or tends to produce, depends the merit or demerit, the good or ill desert of the action to which it gives occasion. Wherein consists our sense of the propriety or impropriety of actions, has been explained in the former part of this discourse. We come now to consider, wherein consists that of their good or ill desert.

CHAP. I.—*That whatever appears to be the proper Object of Gratitude, appears to deserve Reward; and that, in the same Manner, whatever appears to be the proper Object of Resentment, appears to deserve Punishment.*

To us, therefore, that action must appear to deserve reward, which appears to be the proper and approved object of that sentiment, which most immediately and directly prompts us to reward, or to do good to another. And in the same manner, that action must appear to deserve punishment, which appears to be the proper and approved object of that sentiment which most immediately and directly prompts us to punish, or to inflict evil upon another.

The sentiment which most immediately and directly prompts us to reward, is gratitude; that which most immediately and directly prompts us to punish, is resentment.

To us, therefore, that action must appear to deserve reward, which appears to be the proper and approved object of gratitude; as, on the other hand, that action must appear to deserve punishment, which appears to be the proper and approved object of resentment.

To reward, is to recompense, to remunerate, to return good for good received. To punish, too, is to recompense, to remunerate, though in a different manner; it is to return evil for evil that has been done.

There are some other passions, besides gratitude and resentment, which interest us in the happiness or misery of others; but there are none which so directly excite us as to be instruments of either. The love and esteem which grow upon acquaintance and habitual approbation, necessarily lead us to be pleased with the good fortune of the man who is the object of such agreeable emotions, and consequently to be willing to lend a hand to promote it. Our love, however, is fully satisfied, though his good fortune should be brought about without our assistance. All that this passion desires is to see him happy, without regarding who was the author of his prosperity. But gratitude is not to be satisfied in this manner. If the person to whom we owe many obligations, is made happy without our assistance, though it pleases our love, it does not content our gratitude. Till we have recompensed him, till we ourselves have been instrumental in promoting his happiness, we feel ourselves still loaded with that debt which his past services have laid upon us.

The hatred and dislike, in the same manner, which grow upon the habitual disapprobation, would often lead us to take a malicious pleasure in the misfortune of the man whose conduct and character excite so painful a passion. But though dislike and hatred harden us against all sympathy, and sometimes dispose us even to rejoice at the distress of another, yet, if there is no resentment in the case, if neither we nor our friends have received any great personal provocation, these passions would not naturally lead us to wish to be instrumental in bringing it about. Though we could fear no punishment in consequence of our having had some hand in it, we would rather that it should happen by other means. To one under the dominion of violent hatred it would be agreeable, perhaps, to hear, that the person whom he abhorred and detested was killed by some accident. But if he had the least spark of justice, which, though this passion is not very favourable to virtue, he might still have, it would hurt him excessively to have been himself, even without design, the occasion of this misfortune. Much more would the very thought of voluntarily contributing to it shock him beyond all measure. He would reject with horror even the imagination of so execrable a design; and if he could imagine himself capable of such an enormity, he would begin to regard to himself in the same odious light in which he had considered the person who was the object his dislike. But it is quite otherwise with resentment: if the person who had done us some great injury, who had murdered our father or our brother, for example, should soon afterwards die of a fever, or even be brought to the scaffold upon account of some other crime, though it might soothe our hatred, it would not fully gratify our resentment. Resentment would prompt us to desire, not only that he should be punished, but that he should be punished by our means, and upon account of that particular injury which he had done to us. Resentment cannot be fully gratified, unless the offender is not only made to grieve in his turn, but to grieve for that particular wrong which we have suffered from him. He must be made to repent and be sorry for this very action, that others, through fear of the like punishment, may be terrified from being guilty of the like offence. The natural gratification of this passion tends, of its own accord, to produce all the political ends of punishment ; the correction of the criminal, and example to the public.

Gratitude and resentment, therefore, are the sentiments which most immediately and directly prompt to reward and to punish. To us, therefore, he must appear to deserve reward, who appears to be the proper and approved object of gratitude ; and he to deserve punishment, who appears to be that of resentment.

CHAP. II.—*Of the proper Objects of Gratitude and Resentment.*

To be the proper and approved object either of gratitude or resentment, can mean nothing but to be the object of that gratitude and of that resentment which naturally seems proper, and is approved of.

But these, as well as all the other passions of human nature, seem proper and are approved of, when the heart of every impartial spectator entirely sympathizes with them, when every indifferent by-stander entirely enters into and goes along with them.

He, therefore, appears to deserve reward, who, to some person or persons, is the natural object of a gratitude which every human heart is disposed to beat time to, and thereby applaud: and he, on the other hand, appears to deserve punishment, who in the same manner is to some person or persons the natural object of a resentment which the breast of every reasonable man is ready to adopt and sympathize with. To us, surely, that action must appear to deserve reward, which every body who knows of it would wish to reward, and therefore delights to see rewarded: and that action must as surely appear to deserve punishment, which every body who hears of it is angry with, and upon that account rejoices to see punished.

1. As we sympathize with the joy of our companions, when in prosperity, so we join with them in the complacency and satisfaction with which they naturally regard whatever is the cause of their good fortune.

We enter into the love and affection which they conceive for it, and begin to love it too. We should be sorry for their sakes if it was destroyed, or even if it was placed at too great a distance from them, and out of the reach of their care and protection, though they should lose nothing by its absence except the pleasure of seeing it. If it is man who has thus been the fortunate instrument of the happiness of his brethren, this is still more peculiarly the case. When we see one man assisted, protected, relieved by another, our sympathy with the joy of the person who receives the benefit serves only to animate our fellow-feeling with his gratitude towards him who bestows it. When we look upon the person who is the cause of his pleasure with the eyes with which we imagine he must look upon him, his benefactor seems to stand before us in the most engaging and amiable light. We readily therefore sympathize with the grateful affection which he conceives for a person to whom he has been so much obliged ; and consequently applaud the returns which he is disposed to make for the good offices conferred upon him. As we entirely enter into the affection from which these returns proceed, they necessarily seem every way proper and suitable to their object.

2. In the same manner, as we sympathize with the sorrow of our fellow-creature whenever we see his distress, so we likewise enter into his abhorrence and aversion for whatever has given occasion to it. Our heart, as it adopts and beats time to his grief, so is it likewise animated with that spirit by which he endeavours to drive away or destroy the cause of it. The indolent and passive fellow-feeling, by which we accompany him in his sufferings, readily gives way to that more vigorous and active sentiment by which we go along with him in the effort he makes, either to repeal them, or to gratify his aversion to what has given occasion to them. This is still more peculiarly the case, when it is man who has caused them. When we see one man oppressed or injured by another, the sympathy which we feel with the distress of the sufferer seems to serve only to animate our fellow-feeling with his resentment against the offender. We are rejoiced to see him attack his adversary in his turn, and are eager and ready to assist him whenever he exerts himself for defence, or even for vengeance within a certain degree. If the injured should perish in the quarrel, we not only sympathize with the real resentment of his friends and relations, but with the imaginary resentment which in fancy we lend to the dead, who is no longer capable of feeling that or any other human sentiment. But as we put ourselves in his situation, as we enter, as it were, into his body, and in our imaginations, in some measure, animate anew the deformed and mangled carcass of the slain, when we bring home in this manner his case to our own bosoms, we feel upon this, as upon many other occasions, an emotion which the person principally concerned is incapable of feeling, and which yet we feel by an illusive

sympathy with him.   The sympathetic tears which we shed for that
immense and irretrievable loss, which in our fancy he appears to have
sustained, seem to be but a small part of the duty which we owe him.
The injury which he has suffered demands, we think, a principal part
of our attention.   We feel that resentment which we imagine he ought
to feel, and which he would feel, if in his cold and lifeless body there
remained any consciousness of what passes upon earth.   His blood,
we think, calls aloud for vengeance.   The very ashes of the dead seem
to be disturbed at the thought that his injuries are to pass unrevenged.
The horrors which are supposed to haunt the bed of the murderer, the
ghosts which superstition imagines rise from their graves to demand
vengeance upon those who brought them to an untimely end, all take
their origin from this natural sympathy with the imaginary resentment
of the slain.   And with regard, at least, to this most dreadful of all
crimes, Nature, antecedent to all reflection upon the utility of punishment, has in this manner stamped upon the human heart, in the
strongest and most indelible characters, an immediate and instinctive
approbation of the sacred and necessary law of retaliation.

CHAP. III.—*That where there is no Approbation of the Conduct
of the Person who confers the Benefit, there is little Sympathy with the
Gratitude of him who receives it: and that, on the Contrary, where
there is no Disapprobation of the Motives of the Person who does
the Mischief, there is no Sort of Sympathy with the Resentment of
him who suffers it.*

IT is to be observed, however, that, how beneficial soever on the one
hand, or hurtful soever on the other, the actions or intentions of the
person who acts may have been to the person who is, if I may say so,
acted upon, yet if in the one case there appears to have been no propriety in the motives of the agent, if we cannot enter into the affections which influenced his conduct, we have little sympathy with the
gratitude of the person who receives the benefit : or if, in the other
case, there appears to have been no impropriety in the motives of the
agent, if, on the contrary, the affections which influenced his conduct
are such as we must necessarily enter into, we can have no sort of
sympathy with the resentment of the person who suffers.   Little
gratitude seems due in the one case, and all sort of resentment seems
unjust in the other.   The one action seems to merit little reward, the
other to deserve no punishment.

1. First, I say, that wherever we cannot sympathize with the affections of the agent, wherever there seems to be no propriety in the motives
which influenced his conduct, we are less disposed to enter into the

gratitude of the person who received the benefit of his actions. A very small return seems due to that foolish and profuse generosity which confers the greatest benefits from the most trivial motives, and gives an estate to a man merely because his name and surname happen to be the same with those of the giver. Such services do not seem to demand any proportionable recompense. Our contempt for the folly of the agent hinders us from thoroughly entering into the gratitude of the person to whom the good office has been done. His benefactor seems unworthy of it. As when we place ourselves in the situation of the person obliged, we feel that we could conceive no great reverence for such a benefactor, we easily absolve him from a great deal of that submissive veneration and esteem which we should think due to a more respectable character ; and provided he always treats his weak friend with kindness and humanity, we are willing to excuse him from many attentions and regards which we should demand to a worthier patron. Those princes who have heaped, with the greatest profusion, wealth, power and honours, upon their favourites, have seldom excited that degree of attachment to their persons which has often been experienced by those who were more frugal of their favours. The well-natured, but injudicious prodigality of James the First of Great Britain seems to have attached nobody to his person ; and that prince, notwithstanding his social and harmless disposition, appears to have lived and died without a friend. The whole gentry and nobility of England exposed their lives and fortunes in the cause of Charles I., his more frugal and distinguishing son, notwithstanding the coldness and distant severity of his ordinary deportment.

2. Secondly, I say, That wherever the conduct of the agent appears to have been entirely directed by motives and affections which we thoroughly enter into and approve of, we can have no sort of sympathy with the resentment of the sufferer, how great soever the mischief which may have been done to him. When two people quarrel, if we take part with, and entirely adopt the resentment of one of them, it is impossible that we should enter into that of the other. Our sympathy with the person whose motives we go along with, and whom therefore we look upon as in the right, cannot but harden us against all fellow-feeling with the other, whom we necessarily regard as in the wrong. Whatever this last, therefore, may have suffered, while it is no more than what we ourselves should have wished him to suffer, while it is no more than what our own sympathetic indignation would have prompted us to inflict upon him, it cannot either displease or provoke us. When an inhuman murderer is brought to the scaffold, though we have some compassion for his misery, we can have no sort of fellow-feeling with his resentment, if he should be so absurd as to express any against either his prosecutor or his judge. The natural tendency of their just indignation against so vile a criminal is indeed the most fatal and

ruinous to him. But it is impossible that we should be displeased with the tendency of a sentiment, which, when we bring the case home to ourselves, we feel that we cannot avoid adopting.

CHAP. IV.—*Recapitulation of the foregoing Chapters.*

1. WE do not therefore thoroughly and heartily sympathize with the gratitude of one man towards another, merely because this other has been the cause of his good fortune, unless he has been the cause of it from motives which we entirely go along with. Our heart must adopt the principles of the agent, and go along with all the affections which influenced his conduct, before it can entirely sympathize with and beat time to, the gratitude of the person who has been benefited by his actions. If in the conduct of the benefactor there appears to have been no propriety, how beneficial soever its effects, it does not seem to demand, or necessarily to require, any proportionable recompense.

But when to the beneficent tendency of the action is joined the propriety of the affection from which it proceeds, when we entirely sympathize and go along with the motives of the agent, the love which we conceive for him upon his own account enhances and enlivens our fellow-feeling with the gratitude of those who owe their prosperity to his good conduct. His actions seem then to demand, and, if I may say so, to call aloud for a proportionable recompense. We then entirely enter into that gratitude which prompts to bestow it. The benefactor seems then to be the proper object of reward, when we thus entirely sympathize with, and approve of, that sentiment which prompts to reward him. When we approve of, and go along with, the affection from which the action proceeds, we must necessarily approve of the action, and regard the person towards whom it is directed, as its proper and suitable object.

2. In the same manner, we cannot at all sympathize with the resentment of one man against another, merely because this other has been the cause of his misfortune, unless he has been the cause of it from motives which we cannot enter into. Before we can adopt the resentment of the sufferer, we must disapprove of the motives of the agent, and feel that our heart renounces all sympathy with the affections which influenced his conduct. If there appears to have been no impropriety in these, how fatal soever the tendency of the action which proceeds from them to those against whom it is directed, it does not seem to deserve any punishment, or to be the proper object of any resentment.

But when to the hurtfulness of the action is joined the impropriety of the affection from whence it proceeds, when our heart rejects with abhorrence all fellow-feeling with the motives of the agent, we then heartily and entirely sympathize with the resentment of the sufferer. Such actions seem then to deserve, and, if I may say so, to call aloud for, a proportionable punishment; and we entirely enter into, and thereby approve of, that resentment which prompts to inflict it. The offender necessarily seems then to be the proper object of punishment, when we thus entirely sympathize with, and thereby approve of, that sentiment which prompts to punish. In this case too, when we approve, and go along with, the affection from which the action proceeds, we must necessarily approve the action, and regard the person against whom it is directed, as its proper and suitable object.

―――――

CHAP. V.—*The Analysis of the Sense of Merit and Demerit.*

1. AS our sense, therefore, of the propriety of conduct arises from what I shall call a direct sympathy with the affections and motives of the person who acts, so our sense of its merit arises from what I shall call an indirect sympathy with the gratitude of the person who is, if I may say so, acted upon.

As we cannot indeed enter thoroughly into the gratitude of the person who receives the benefit, unless we beforehand approve of the motives of the benefactor, so, upon this account, the sense of merit seems to be a compounded sentiment, and to be made up of two distinct emotions ; a direct sympathy with the sentiments of the agents, and an indirect sympathy with the gratitude of those who receive the benefit of his actions.

We may, upon many different occasions, plainly distinguish those two different emotions combining and uniting together in our sense of the good desert of a particular character or action. When we read in history concerning actions of proper and beneficent greatness of mind, how eagerly do we enter into such designs? How much are we animated by that high-spirited generosity which directs them? How keen are we for their success? How grieved at their disappointment? In imagination we become the very person whose actions are represented to us : we transport ourselves in fancy to the scenes of those distant and forgotten adventures, and imagine ourselves acting the part of a Scipio or a Camillus, a Timoleon or an Aristides. So far our sentiments are founded upon the direct sympathy with the person who acts. Nor is the indirect sympathy with those who receive the benefit of such actions less sensibly felt. Whenever we place ourselves in the situation of these last, with what warm and affectionate fellow-feeling do we enter into their gratitude towards those who served them so essentially? We embrace, as it were, their benefactor along with them. Our heart

readily sympathizes with the highest transports of their grateful affection.   No honours, no rewards, we think, can be too great for them to
bestow upon him.   When they make this proper return for his services,
we heartily applaud and go along with them ; but are shocked beyond
all measure, if by their conduct they appear to have little sense of the
obligations conferred upon them.   Our whole sense, in short, of the
merit and good desert of such actions, of the propriety and fitness of
recompensing them, and making the person who performed them
rejoice in his turn, arises from the sympathetic emotions of gratitude
and love, with which, when we bring home to our own breast the situation of those principally concerned, we feel ourselves naturally transported towards the man who could act with such proper and noble
beneficence.

2. In the same manner as our sense of the impropriety of conduct
arises from a want of sympathy, or from a direct antipathy to the
affections and motives of the agent, so our sense of its demerit arises
from what I shall here too call an indirect sympathy with the resentment of the sufferer.

As we cannot indeed enter into the resentment of the sufferer, unless
our heart beforehand disapproves the motives of the agent, and
renounces all fellow-feeling with them ; so upon this account the sense
of demerit, as well as that of merit, seems to be a compounded sentiment, and to be made up of two distinct emotions; a direct antipathy
to the sentiments of the agent, and an indirect sympathy with the resentment of the sufferer.

We may here too, upon many different occasions, plainly distinguish
those two different emotions combining and uniting together in our
sense of the ill desert of a particular character or action.   When we
read in history concerning the perfidy and cruelty of a Borgia or a
Nero, our heart rises up against the detestable sentiments which influenced their conduct, and renounces with horror and abomination all
fellow-feeling with such execrable motives.   So far our sentiments are
founded upon the direct antipathy to the affections of the agent : and
the indirect sympathy with the resentment of the sufferers is still more
sensibly felt.   When we bring home to ourselves the situation of the
persons whom those scourges of mankind insulted, murdered, or betrayed, what indignation do we not feel against such insolent and inhuman oppressors of the earth?   Our sympathy with the unavoidable
distress of the innocent sufferers is not more real nor more lively, than
our fellow-feeling with their just and natural resentment.   The former
sentiment only heightens the latter, and the idea of their distress serves
only to inflame and blow up our animosity against those who occasioned it.   When we think of the anguish of the sufferers, we take part
with them more earnestly against their oppressors ; we enter with more
eagerness into all their schemes of vengeance, and feel ourselves every

moment wreaking, in imagination, upon such violators of the laws of
society, that punishment which our sympathetic indignation tells us is
due to their crimes.   Our sense of the horror and dreadful atrocity of
such conduct, the delight which we take in hearing that it was properly
punished, the indignation which we feel when it escapes this due retaliation, our whole sense and feeling, in short, of its ill desert, of the propriety and fitness of inflicting evil upon the person who is guilty of it,
and of making him grieve in his turn, arises from the sympathetic indignation which naturally boils up in the breast of the spectator,
whenever he thoroughly brings home to himself the case of the
sufferer.*

SECT. II.—OF JUSTICE AND BENEFICENCE.

CHAP. I.—*Comparison of those two Virtues.*

ACTIONS of a beneficent tendency, which proceed from proper motives,
seem alone to require reward; because such alone are the approved
objects of gratitude, or excite the sympathetic gratitude of the spectator.

Actions of a hurtful tendency, which proceed from improper motives,
seem alone to deserve punishment; because such alone are the approved objects of resentment, or excite the sympathetic resentment of
the spectator.

Beneficence is always free, it cannot be extorted by force, the mere

* To ascribe in this manner our natural sense of the ill desert of human actions to a sympathy
with the resentment of the sufferer, may seem, to the greater part of the people, to be a degradation of that sentiment. Resentment is commonly regarded as so odious a passion, that they
will be apt to think it impossible that so laudable a principle, as the sense of the ill desert
of vice, should in any respect be founded upon it.   They will be more willing, perhaps, to admit that our sense of the merit of good actions is founded upon a sympathy with
the gratitude of the persons who receive the benefit of them : because gratitude, as well as all
the other benevolent passions, is regarded as an amiable principle, which can take nothing
from the worth of whatever is founded upon it. Gratitude and resentment, however, are in
every respect, it is evident, counterparts to one another; and if our sense of merit arises from
a sympathy with the one, our sense of demerit can scarce miss to proceed from a fellow-feeling
with the other.
Let it be considered, too, that resentment, though in the degree in which we too often see it,
the most odious, perhaps, of all the passions, is not disapproved of when properly humbled and
entirely brought down to the level of the sympathetic indignation of the spectator. When we
who are the bystanders, feel that our own animosity entirely corresponds with that of the
sufferer, when the resentment of this last does not in any respect go beyond our own, when no
word, no gesture, escapes him that denotes an emotion more violent than what we can keep
time to, and when he never aims at inflicting any punishment beyond what we should
rejoice to see inflicted, or what we ourselves would upon this account even desire to be the
instruments of inflicting, it is impossible that we should not entirely approve of his sentiment.
Our own emotion in this case must, in our eyes, undoubtedly justify his. And as experience
teaches us how much the greater part of mankind are incapable of this moderation, and how
great an effort must be made in order to bring down the rude and undisciplined impulse of
resentment to this suitable temper, we cannot avoid conceiving a considerable degree of esteem

want of it exposes to no punishment; because the mere want of beneficence tends to do no real positive evil. It may disappoint of the

and admiration for one who appears capable of exerting so much self-command over one of the
most ungovernable passions of his nature. When indeed the animosity of the sufferer exceeds,
as it almost always does, that we can go along with, as we cannot enter into it, we necessarily
disapprove of it. We even disapprove of it more than we should of an equal excess of almost
any other passion derived from the imagination. And this too violent resentment, instead of
carrying us along with it becomes itself the object of our resentment and indignation. We
enter into the opposite resentment of the person who is the object of this unjust emotion, and
who is in danger of suffering from it. Revenge, therefore, the excess of resentment, appears
to be the most detestable of all the passions, and is the object of the horror and indignation of
every body. And as in the way in which this passion commonly discovers itself among mankind, it is excessive a hundred times for once that it is immoderate, we are very apt to consider
it as altogether odious and detestable, because in its most ordinary appearances it is so. Nature, however, even in the present depraved state of mankind, does not seem to have dealt so
unkindly with us, as to have endowed us with any principle which is wholly and in every
respect evil, or which, in no degree and in no direction, can be the proper object of praise and
approbation. Upon some occasions we are sensible that this passion, which is generally too
strong, may likewise be too weak. We sometimes complain that a particular person shows
too little spirit, and has too little sense of the injuries that have been done to him; and we are
as ready to despise him for the defect, as to hate him for the excess of this passion.

The inspired writers would not surely have talked so frequently or so strongly of the wrath
and anger of God, if they had regarded every degree of those passions as vicious and evil, even
in so weak and imperfect a creature as man.

Let it be considered too, that the present inquiry is not concerning a matter of right, if I may
say so, but concerning a matter of fact. We are not at present examining upon what principles a perfect being would approve of the punishment of bad actions; but upon what principles so weak and imperfect a creature as man actually and in fact approves of it. The principles which I have just now mentioned, it is evident, have a very great effect upon his sentiments; and it seems wisely ordered that it should be so. The very existence of society requires
that unmerited and unprovoked malice should be restrained by proper punishments; and consequently, that to inflict those punishments should be regarded as a proper and laudable action.
Though man, therefore, be naturally endowed with a desire of the welfare and preservation of
society, yet the Author of nature has not entrusted it to his reason to find out that a certain
application of punishments is the proper means of attaining this end; but has endowed him
with an immediate and instinctive approbation of that very application which is most proper to
attain it. The œconomy of nature is in this respect exactly of a piece with what it is upon
many other occasions. With regard to all those ends which, upon account of their peculiar
importance, may be regarded, if such an expression is allowable, as the favourite ends of nature,
she has constantly in this manner not only endowed mankind with an appetite for the end
which she proposes, but likewise with an appetite for the means by which alone this end can be
brought about, for their own sakes, and independent of their tendency to produce it. Thus
self-preservation, and the propagation of the species, are the great ends which Nature seems
to have proposed in the formation of all animals. Mankind are endowed with a desire of those
ends, and an aversion to the contrary; with a love of life, and a dread of dissolution; with a
desire of the continuance and perpetuity of the species, and with an aversion to the thoughts
of its entire extinction. But though we are in this manner endowed with a very strong desire
of those ends, it has not been intrusted to the slow and uncertain determinations of our reason
to find out the proper means of bringing them about. Nature has directed us to the greater
part of these by original and immediate instincts. Hunger, thirst, the passion which unites
the two sexes, the love of pleasure, and the dread of pain, prompt us to apply those means for
their own sakes, and without any consideration of their tendency to those beneficent ends
which the great Director of nature intended to produce by them.

Before I conclude this note, I must take notice of a difference between the approbation of
propriety and that of merit or beneficence. Before we approve of the sentiments of any person
as proper and suitable to their objects, we must not only be affected in the same manner
as he is, but we must perceive this harmony and correspondence of sentiments between him
and ourselves. Thus, though upon hearing of a misfortune that had befallen my friend, I should

good which might reasonably have been expected, and upon that account it may justly excite dislike and disapprobation: it cannot, however, provoke any resentment which mankind will go along with. The man who does not recompense his benefactor, when he has it in his power, and when his benefactor needs his assistance, is, no doubt, guilty of the blackest ingratitude. The heart of every impartial spectator rejects all fellow-feeling with the selfishness of his motives, and he is the proper object of the highest disapprobation. But still he does no positive hurt to any body. He only does not do that good which in propriety he ought to have done. He is the object of hatred, a passion which is naturally excited by impropriety of sentiment and behaviour; not of resentment, a passion which is never properly called forth but by actions which tend to do real and positive hurt to some particular persons. His want of gratitude, therefore, cannot be punished. To oblige him by force to perform, what in gratitude he ought to perform, and what every impartial spectator would approve of him for performing, would, if possible, be still more improper than his neglecting to perform it. His benefactor would dishonour himself if he attempted by violence to constrain him to gratitude, and it would be impertinent for any third person, who was not the superior of either, to intermeddle. But of all the duties of beneficence, those which gratitude recommends to us approach nearest to what is called a perfect and complete obligation. What friendship, what generosity, what charity, would prompt us to do with universal approbation, is still more free, and can still less be extorted by force than the duties of gratitude. We talk of the debt of gratitude, not of charity, or generosity, nor even of friendship, when friendship is mere esteem, and has not been enhanced and complicated with gratitude for good offices.

Resentment seems to have been given us by nature for defence, and for defence only. It is the safeguard of justice and the security of innocence. It prompts us to beat off the mischief which is attempted to be done to us, and to retaliate that which is already done; that the

---

conceive precisely that degree of concern which he gives way to ; yet till I am informed of the manner in which he behaves, till I perceive the harmony between his emotions and mine, I cannot be said to approve of the sentiments which influence his behaviour. The approbation of propriety therefore requires, not only that we should entirely sympathize with the person who acts, but that we should perceive this perfect concord between his sentiments and our own. On the contrary, when I hear of a benefit that has been bestowed upon another person, let him who has received it be affected in what manner he pleases, if, by bringing his case home to myself, I feel gratitude arise in my own breast, I necessarily approve of the conduct of his benefactor, and regard it as meritorious, and the proper object of reward. Whether the person who has received the benefit conceives gratitude or not, cannot, it is evident, in any degree alter our sentiments with regard to the merit of him who has bestowed it. No actual correspondence of sentiments, therefore, is here required. It is sufficient that if he was grateful, they would correspond ; and our sense of merit is often founded upon one of those illusive sympathies, by which, when we bring home to ourselves the case of another, we are often affected in a manner in which the person principally concerned is incapable of being affected. There is a similar difference between our disapprobation of demerit, and that of impropriety

offender may be made to repent of his injustice, and that others, through fear of the like punishment, may be terrified from being guilty of the like offence.   It must be reserved therefore for these purposes, nor can the spectator ever go along with it when it is exerted for any other. But the mere want of the beneficent virtues, though it may disappoint us of the good which might reasonably be expected, neither does, nor attempts to do, any mischief from which we can have occasion to defend ourselves.

There is however another virtue, of which the observance is not left to the freedom of our own wills, which may be extorted by force, and of which the violation exposes to resentment, and consequently to punishment.   This virtue is justice: the violation of justice is injury: it does real and positive hurt to some particular persons, from motives which are naturally disapproved of.   It is, therefore, the proper object of resentment, and of punishment, which is the natural consequence of resentment.   As mankind go along with and approve of the violence employed to avenge the hurt which is done by injustice, so they much more go along with, and approve of, that which is employed to prevent and beat off the injury, and to restrain the offender from hurting his neighbours.   The person himself who meditates an injustice is sensible of this, and feels that force may, with the utmost propriety, be made use of, both by the person whom he is about to injure, and by others, either to obstruct the execution of his crime, or to punish him when he has executed it.   And upon this is founded that remarkable distinction between justice and all the other social virtues, which has of late been particularly insisted upon by an author of very great and original genius, that we feel ourselves to be under a stricter obligation to act according to justice, than agreeably to friendship, charity, or generosity; that the practice of these last mentioned virtues seems to be left in some mea- sure to our own choice, but that, somehow or other, we feel ourselves to be in a peculiar manner tied, bound, and obliged to the observation of justice.   We feel, that is to say, that force may, with the utmost propriety, and with the approbation of all mankind, be made use of to constrain us to observe the rules of the one, but not to follow the pre- cepts of the other.

We must always, however, carefully distinguish what is only blam- able, or the proper object of disapprobation, from what force may be employed either to punish or to prevent.   That seems blamable which falls short of that ordinary degree of proper beneficence which experi- ence teaches us to expect of every body; and on the contrary, that seems praise-worthy which goes beyond it.   The ordinary degree itself seems neither blamable nor praise-worthy.   A father, a son, a brother, who behaves to the correspondent relation neither better nor worse than the greater part of men commonly do, seems properly to deserve neither praise nor blame.   He who surprises us by extraordinary and

6

unexpected, though still proper and suitable kindness, or on the contrary, by extraordinary and unexpected as well as unsuitable unkindness, seems praise-worthy in the one case, and blamable in the other.

Even the most ordinary degree of kindness or beneficence, however, cannot among equals, be extorted by force. Among equals each individual is naturally, and antecedent to the institution of civil government, regarded as having a right both to defend himself from injuries, and to exact a certain degree of punishment for those which have been done to him. Every generous spectator not only approves of his conduct when he does this, but enters so far into his sentiments as often to be willing to assist him. When one man attacks, or robs, or attempts to murder another, all the neighbours take the alarm, and think that they do right when they run, either to revenge the person who has been injured, or to defend him who is in danger of being so. But when a father fails in the ordinary degree of parental affection towards a son; when a son seems to want that filial reverence which might be expected to his father; when brothers are without the usual degree of brotherly affection; when a man shuts his breast against compassion, and refuses to relieve the misery of his fellow-creatures, when he can with the greatest ease; in all these cases, though every body blames the conduct, nobody imagines that those who might have reason, perhaps, to expect more kindness, have any right to extort it by force. The sufferer can only complain, and the spectator can intermeddle no other way than by advice and persuasion. Upon all such occasions, for equals to use force against one another, would be thought the highest degree of insolence and presumption.

A superior may, indeed, sometimes, with universal approbation, oblige those under his jurisdiction to behave, in this respect, with a certain degree of propriety to one another. The laws of all civilized nations oblige parents to maintain their children, and children to maintain their parents, and impose upon men many other duties of beneficence. The civil magistrate is entrusted with the power not only of preserving the public peace by restraining injustice, but of promoting the prosperity of the commonwealth, by establishing good discipline, and by discouraging every sort of vice and impropriety; he may prescribe rules, therefore, which not only prohibit mutual injuries among fellow-citizens, but command mutual good offices to a certain degree. When the sovereign commands what is merely indifferent, and what, antecedent to his orders, might have been omitted without any blame, it becomes not only blamable but punishable to disobey him. When he commands, therefore, what, antecedent to any such order, could not have been omitted without the greatest blame, it surely becomes much more punishable to be wanting in obedience. Of all the duties of a lawgiver, however, this perhaps is that which it requires the greatest delicacy and reserve to execute with propriety and judgment. To

neglect it altogether exposes the commonwealth to many gross disorders and shocking enormities, and to push it too far is destructive of
all liberty, security, and justice.

Though the mere want of beneficence seems to merit no punishment
from equals, the greater exertions of that virtue appear to deserve the
highest reward. By being productive of the greatest good, they are
the natural and approved objects of the liveliest gratitude. Though
the breach of justice, on the contrary, exposes to punishment, the
observance of the rules of that virtue seems scarce to deserve any
reward. There is, no doubt, a propriety in the practice of justice, and
it merits, upon that account, all the approbation which is due to propriety. But as it does no real positive good, it is entitled to very little
gratitude. Mere justice is, upon most occasions, but a negative virtue,
and only hinders us from hurting our neighbour. The man who barely
abstains from violating either the person, or the estate, or the reputation of his neighbours, has surely very little positive merit. He fulfils,
however, all the rules of what is peculiarly called justice, and does every
thing which his equals can with propriety force him to do, or which
they can punish him for not doing. We may often fulfil all the rules
of justice by sitting still and doing nothing.

As every man doth, so shall it be done to him, and retaliation seems
to be the great law which is dictated to us by Nature. Beneficence and
generosity we think due to the generous and beneficent. Those whose
hearts never open to the feelings of humanity, should, we think, be shut
out in the same manner, from the affections of all their fellow-creatures,
and be allowed to live in the midst of society, as in a great desert where
there is nobody to care for them, or to inquire after them. The violator
of the laws of justice ought to be made to feel himself that evil which
he has done to another; and since no regard to the sufferings of his
brethren is capable of restraining him, he ought to be over-awed by
the fear of his own. The man who is barely innocent, who only observes the laws of justice with regard to others, and merely abstains
from hurting his neighbours, can merit only that his neighbours in their
turn should respect his innocence, and that the same laws should be
religiously observed with regard to him.

———

CHAP. II.—*Of the Sense of Justice, of Remorse, and of the Conscious-ness of Merit.*

THERE can be no proper motive for hurting our neighbour, there can
be no incitement to do evil to another, which mankind will go along
with, except just indignation for evil which that other has done to us.
To disturb his happiness merely because it stands in the way of our
own, to take from him what is of real use to him merely because it

6 *

may be of equal or of more use to us, or to indulge, in this manner, at the expense of other people, the natural preference which every man has for his own happiness above that of other people, is what no impartial spectator can go along with. Every man is, no doubt, by nature, first and principally recommended to his own care; and as he is fitter to take care of himself than of any other person, it is fit and right that it should be so. Every man, therefore, is much more deeply interested in whatever immediately concerns himself, than in what concerns any other man: and to hear, perhaps, of the death of another person, with whom we have no particular connexion, will give us less concern, will spoil our stomach or break our rest much less, than a very insignificant disaster which has befallen ourselves. But though the ruin of our neighbour may affect us much less than a very small misfortune of our own, we must not ruin him to prevent that small misfortune, nor even to prevent our own ruin. We must, here, as in all other cases, view ourselves not so much according to that light in which we may naturally appear to ourselves, as according to that in which we naturally appear to others. Though every man may, according to the proverb, be the whole world to himself, to the rest of mankind he is a most insignificant part of it. Though his own happiness may be of more importance to him than that of all the world besides, to every other person it is of no more consequence than that of any other man. Though it may be true, therefore, that every individual, in his own breast, naturally prefers himself to all mankind, yet he dares not look mankind in the face, and avow that he acts according to this principle. He feels that in this preference they can never go along with him, and that how natural soever it may be to him, it must always appear excessive and extravagant to them. When he views himself in the light in which he is conscious that others will view him, he sees that to them he is but one of the multitude in no respect better than any other in it. If he would act so as that the impartial spectator may enter into the principles of his conduct, which is what of all things he has the greatest desire to do, he must, upon this, as upon all other occasions, humble the arrogance of his self-love, and bring it down to something which other men can go along with. They will indulge it so far as to allow him to be more anxious about, and to pursue with more earnest assiduity, his own happiness than that of any other person. Thus far, whenever they place themselves in his situation, they will readily go along with him. In the race for wealth, for honours, and preferments, he may run as hard as he can, and strain every nerve and every muscle, in order to outstrip all his competitors. But if he should justle, or throw down any of them, the indulgence of the spectators is entirely at an end. It is a violation of fair play, which they cannot admit of. This man is to them, in every respect, as good as he: they do not enter into that self-love by which he prefers himself so much to this other, and cannot go along with the motive from which he hurt him. They readily, therefore, sympathize with the natural resentment of the injured, and the offender becomes the object of their hatred and indignation. He is sensible that he becomes so, and feels that those sentiments are ready to burst out against him.

As the greater and more irreparable the evil that is done, the resentment of the sufferer runs naturally the higher; so does likewise the sympathetic indignation of the spectator, as well as the sense of guilt in the agent. Death is the greatest evil which one man can inflict upon another, and excites the highest degree of resentment in those who are immediately connected with the slain. Murder, therefore, is the most atrocious of all crimes which affect individuals only, in the sight both of mankind, and of the person who has committed it. To be deprived of that which we are possessed of, is a greater evil than to be disappointed of what we have only the expectation. Breach of property, therefore, theft and robbery, which take from us what we are possessed of, are greater crimes than breach of contract, which only disappoints us of what we expected. The most sacred laws of justice, therefore, those whose violation seems to call loudest for vengeance and punishment, are the laws which guard the life and person of our neighbour; the next are those which guard his property and possessions; and last of all come those which guard what are called his personal rights, or what is due to him from the promises of others.

The violator of the more sacred laws of justice can never reflect on the sentiments which mankind must entertain with regard to him, without seeing all the agonies of shame, and horror, and consternation. When his passion is gratified, and he begins coolly to reflect on his past conduct, he can enter into none of the motives which influenced it. They appear now as detestable to him as they did always to other people. By sympathizing with the hatred and abhorrence which other men must entertain for him, he becomes in some measure the object of his own hatred and abhorrence. The situation of the person, who suffered by his injustice, now calls upon his pity. He is grieved at the thought of it; regrets the unhappy effects of his own conduct, and feels at the same time that they have rendered him the proper object of the resentment and indignation of mankind, and of what is the natural consequence of resentment, vengeance and punishment. The thought of this perpetually haunts him, and fills him with terror and amazement. He dares no longer look society in the face, but imagines himself as it were rejected, and thrown out from the affections of all mankind. He cannot hope for the consolation of sympathy in this his greatest and most dreadful distress. The remembrance of his crimes has shut out all fellow-feeling with him from the hearts of his fellow-creatures. The sentiments which they entertain with regard to him, are the very thing which he is most afraid of. Every thing seems hostile, and he would be glad to fly to some inhospitable desert, where he might never more behold the face of a human creature, nor read in the countenance of mankind the condemnation of his crimes. But solitude is still more dreadful than society. His own thoughts can present him with nothing but what is black, unfortunate, and disastrous, the melancholy forebodings of incomprehensible misery and ruin. The horror of solitude drives him back into society, and he comes again into the presence of mankind, astonished to appear before them, loaded with shame and distracted with fear, in order to supplicate some little protection from the countenance of those very judges, who he knows have already all unanimously condemned him. Such is the nature of that sentiment, which is properly called remorse; of all the sentiments which can enter the human heart the most dreadful. It is made up of shame from the sense of the impropriety of past conduct; of grief for the effects of it; of pity for those who suffer by it; and of the dread and terror of punishment from the consciousness of the justly provoked resentment of all rational creatures.

The opposite behaviour naturally inspires the opposite sentiment. The man who, not from frivolous fancy, but from proper motives, has performed a generous action, when he looks forward to those whom he has served, feels himself to be the natural object of their love and gratitude, and, by sympathy with them, of the esteem and approbation of all mankind. And when he looks backward to the motive from which he acted, and surveys it in the light in which the indifferent spectator will survey it, he still continues to enter into it, and applauds himself by sympathy with the approbation of this supposed impartial judge. In both these points of view his own conduct appears to him every way agreeable. His mind, at the thought of it, is filled with cheerfulness, serenity, and composure. He is in friendship and harmony with all mankind, and looks upon his fellow-creatures with confidence and benevolent satisfaction, secure that he has rendered himself worthy of their most favourable regards. In the combination of all these sentiments consists the consciousness of merit, or of deserved reward.

CHAP. III.—*Of the Utility of this Constitution of Nature.*

IT is thus that man, who can subsist only in society, was fitted by nature to that situation for which he was made. All the members of human society stand in need of each others assistance, and are likewise exposed to mutual injuries. Where the necessary assistance is reciprocally afforded from love, from gratitude, from friendship, and esteem, the society flourishes and is happy. All the different members of it are bound together by the agreeable bands of love and affection, and are, as it were, thereby drawn to one common centre of mutual good offices.

But though the necessary assistance should not be afforded from such generous and disinterested motives, though among the different members of the society there should be no mutual love and affection, the society, though less happy and agreeable, will not necessarily be dissolved. Society may subsist among different men, as among different merchants, from a sense of its utility, without any mutual love or affection; and though no man in it should owe any obligation, or be bound in gratitude to any other, it may still be upheld by a mercenary exchange of good offices according to an agreed valuation.

Society, however, cannot subsist among those who are at all times ready to hurt and injure one another. The moment that injury begins, the moment that mutual resentment and animosity take place, all the bands of it are broke asunder, and the different members of which it consisted are, as it were, dissipated and scattered abroad by the violence and opposition of their discordant affections. If there is any society among robbers and murderers, they must at least, according to the trite observation, abstain from robbing and murdering one another. Beneficence, therefore, is less essential to the existence of society than justice. Society may subsist, though not in the most comfortable state, without beneficence; but the prevalence of injustice must utterly destroy it.

Though Nature, therefore, exhorts mankind to acts of beneficence, by the pleasing consciousness of deserved reward, she has not thought it necessary to guard and enforce the practice of it by the terrors of merited punishment in case it should be neglected. It is the ornament which embellishes, not the foundation which supports, the building, and which it was, therefore, sufficient to recommend, but by no means necessary to impose. Justice, on the contrary, is the main pillar that upholds the whole edifice. If it is removed, the great, the immense fabric of human society, that fabric which to raise and support seems in this world, if I may say so, to have been the peculiar and darling care of Nature, must in a moment crumble into atoms. In order to enforce the observation of justice, therefore, Nature has implanted in the human breast that consciousness of ill-desert, those terrors of merited punishment which attend upon its violation, as the great safeguards of the association of mankind, to protect the weak, to curb the violent, and to chastise the guilty. Men, though naturally sympathetic, feel so little for another, with whom they have no particular connexion, in comparison of what they feel for themselves; the misery of one, who is merely their fellow-creature, is of so little importance to them in comparison even of a small conveniency of their own; they have it so much in their power to hurt him, and may have so many temptations to do so, that if this principle did not stand up within them in his defence, and overawe them into a respect for his innocence, they would, like wild beasts, be at all times ready to fly upon him; and a man would enter an assembly of men as he enters a den of lions.

In every part of the universe we observe means adjusted with the nicest artifice to the ends which they are intended to produce; and in the mechanism of a plant, or animal body, admire how every thing is contrived for advancing the two great purposes of nature, the support of the individual, and the propagation of the species. But in these, and in all such objects, we still distinguish the efficient from the final cause of their several motions and organizations. The digestion of the food, the circulation of the blood, and the secretion of the several juices which are drawn from it, are operations all of them necessary for the great purposes of animal life. Yet we never endeavour to account for them from those purposes as from their efficient causes, nor imagine that the blood circulates, or that the food digests of its own accord, and with a view or intention to the purposes of circulation or digestion. The wheels of the watch are all admirably adjusted to the end for which it was made, the pointing of the hour. All their various motions conspire in the nicest manner to produce this effect. If they were endowed with a desire and intention to produce it, they could not do it better. Yet we never ascribe any such desire or intention to them, but to the watch-maker, and we know that they are put into motion by a spring, which intends the effect it produces as little as they do. But though, in accounting for the operations of bodies, we never fail to distinguish in this manner the efficient from the final cause, in accounting for those of the mind we are very apt to confound these two different things with one another. When by natural principles we are led to advance those ends which a refined and enlightened reason would recommend to us, we are very apt to impute to that reason, as to their efficient cause, the sentiments and actions by which we advance those ends, and to imagine that to be the wisdom of man, which in reality is the wisdom of God. Upon a superficial view, this cause seems sufficient to produce the effects which are ascribed to it; and the system of human nature seems to be more simple and agreeable when all its different operations are thus deduced from a single principle.

As society cannot subsist unless the laws of justice are tolerably observed, as no social intercourse can take place among men who do not generally abstain from injuring one another; the consideration of this necessity, it has been thought, was the ground upon which we approved of the enforcement of the laws of justice by the punishment of those who violated them. Man, it has been said, has a natural love for society, and desires that the union of mankind should be preserved for its own sake, and though he himself was to derive no benefit from it. The orderly and flourishing state of society is agreeable to him, and he takes delight in contemplating it. Its disorder and confusion, on the

contrary, is the object of his aversion, and he is chagrined at whatever
tends to produce it. He is sensible too that his own interest is connected with the prosperity of society, and that the happiness, perhaps
the preservation of his existence, depends upon its preservation. Upon
every account, therefore, he has an abhorrence at whatever can tend
to destroy society, and is willing to make use of every means, which
can hinder so hated and so dreadful an event. Injustice necessarily
tends to destroy it. Every appearance of injustice, therefore, alarms
him, and he runs (if I may say so), to stop the progress of what, if
allowed to go on, would quickly put an end to every thing that is dear
to him. If he cannot restrain it by gentle and fair means, he must bear
it down by force and violence, and at any rate must put a stop to its
further progress. Hence it is, they say, that he often approves of the
enforcement of the laws of justice even by the capital punishment of
those who violate them. The disturber of the public peace is hereby
removed out of the world, and others are terrified by his fate from
imitating his example.

Such is the account commonly given of our approbation of the
punishment of injustice. And so far this account is undoubtedly true,
that we frequently have occasion to confirm our natural sense of the
propriety and fitness of punishment, by reflecting how necessary it is
for preserving the order of society. When the guilty is about to suffer
that just retaliation, which the natural indignation of mankind tells
them is due to his crimes; when the insolence of his injustice is broken
and humbled by the terror of his approaching punishment; when he
ceases to be an object of fear, with the generous and humane he begins
to be an object of pity. The thought of what he is about to suffer
extinguishes their resentment for the sufferings of others to which he
has given occasion. They are disposed to pardon and forgive him,
and to save him from that punishment, which in all their cool hours
they had considered as the retribution due to such crimes. Here,
therefore, they have occasion to call to their assistance the consideration of the general interest of society. They counterbalance the impulse of this weak and partial humanity by the dictates of a humanity
that is more generous and comprehensive. They reflect that mercy to
the guilty is cruelty to the innocent, and oppose to the emotions of
compassion which they feel for a particular person, a more enlarged
compassion which they feel for mankind.

Sometimes too we have occasion to defend the propriety of observing the general rules of justice by the consideration of their necessity
to the support of society. We frequently hear the young and the
licentious ridiculing the most sacred rules of morality, and professing,
sometimes from the corruption, but more frequently from the vanity of
their hearts, the most abominable maxims of conduct. Our indignation rouses, and we are eager to refute and expose such detestable

principles. But though it is their intrinsic hatefulness and detestableness, which originally inflames us against them, we are unwilling to assign this as the sole reason why we condemn them, or to pretend that it is merely because we ourselves hate and detest them. The reason, we think, would not appear to be conclusive. Yet why should it not, if we hate and detest them because they are the natural and proper objects of hatred and detestation? But when they are asked why we should not act in such or such a manner, the very question seems to suppose that, to those who ask it, this manner of acting does not appear to be for its own sake the natural and proper object of those sentiments. We must show them, therefore, that it ought to be so for the sake of something else. Upon this account we generally cast about for other arguments, and the consideration which first occurs to us, is the disorder and confusion of society which would result from the universal prevalence of such practices. We seldom fail, therefore, to insist upon this topic.

But though it commonly requires no great discernment to see the destructive tendency of all licentious practices to the welfare of society, it is seldom this consideration which first animates us against them. All men, even the most stupid and unthinking, abhor fraud, perfidy and injustice, and delight to see them punished. But few men have reflected upon the necessity of justice to the existence of society, how obvious soever that necessity may appear to be.

That it is not a regard to the preservation of society, which originally interests us in the punishment of crimes committed against individuals, may be demonstrated by many obvious considerations. The concern which we take in the fortune and happiness of individuals does not, in common cases, arise from that which we take in the fortune and happiness of society. We are no more concerned for the destruction or loss of a single man, because this man is a member or part of society, and because we should be concerned for the destruction of society, than we are concerned for the loss of a single guinea, because this guinea is a part of a thousand guineas, and because we should be concerned for the loss of the whole sum. In neither case does our regard for the individuals arise from our regard for the multitude : but in both cases our regard for the multitude is compounded and made up of the particular regards which we feel for the different individuals of which it is composed. As when a small sum is unjustly taken from us, we do not so much prosecute the injury from a regard to the preservation of our whole fortune, as from a regard to that particular sum which we have lost ; so when a single man is injured or destroyed, we demand the punishment of the wrong that has been done to him, not so much from a concern for the general interest of society, as from a concern for that very individual who has been injured. It is to be observed, however, that this concern does not necessarily include in it any degree of those exquisite sentiments which are commonly called love, esteem, and affection, and by which we distinguish our particular friends and acquaintance. The concern which is requisite for this, is no more than the general fellow-feeling which we have with every man merely because he is our fellow-creature. We enter into the resentment even of an odious person, when he is injured by those to whom he has given no provocation. Our disapprobation of his ordinary character and conduct does not in this case altogether prevent our fellow-feeling with his natural indignation; though with those who are not either extremely candid, or who have not been accustomed to correct and regulate their natural sentiments by general rules, it is very apt to damp it.

Upon some occasions, indeed, we both punish and approve of punishment, merely from a view to the general interest of society, which, we imagine, cannot otherwise be secured. Of this kind are all the punishments inflicted for breaches of what is called either civil police, or military discipline. Such crimes do not immediately or directly hurt any particular person; but their remote consequences, it is supposed, do produce, or might produce, either a considerable inconveniency, or a great disorder in the society. A sentinel, for example, who falls asleep upon his watch, suffers death by the laws of war, because such carelessness might endanger the whole army. This severity may, upon many occasions, appear necessary, and, for that reason, just and proper. When the preservation of an individual is inconsistent with the safety of a multitude, nothing can be more just than that the many should be preferred to the one. Yet this punishment, how necessary soever, always appears to be excessively severe. The natural atrocity of the crime seems to be so little, and the punishment so great, that it is with great difficulty that our heart can reconcile itself to it. Though such carelessness appears very blamable, yet the thought of this crime does not naturally excite any such resentment as would prompt us to take such dreadful revenge. A man of humanity must recollect himself, must make an effort, and exert his whole firmness and resolution, before he can bring himself either to inflict it, or to go along with it when it is inflicted by others. It is not, however, in this manner, that he looks upon the just punishment of an ungrateful murderer or parricide. His heart, in this case, applauds with ardour, and even with transport, the just retaliation which seems due to such detestable crimes, and which, if, by any accident, they should happen to escape, he would be highly enraged and disappointed. The very different sentiments with which the spectator views those different punishments, is a proof that his approbation of the one is far from being founded upon the same principles with that of the other. He looks upon the sentinel as an unfortunate victim, who, indeed, must, and ought to be, devoted to the safety of numbers, but whom still, in his heart, he would be glad to save ; and he is only sorry, that the interest of the many should oppose it. But if the murderer should escape from punishment, it would excite his highest indignation, and he would call upon God to avenge, in another world, that crime which the injustice of mankind had neglected to chastise upon earth.

For it well deserves to be taken notice of, that we are so far from imagining that injustice ought to be punished in this life, merely on account of the order of society, which cannot otherwise be maintained, that Nature teaches us to hope, and religion, we suppose, authorises us to expect, that it will be punished, even in a life to come. Our sense of its ill desert pursues it, if I may say so, even beyond the grave, though the example of its punishment there cannot serve to deter the rest of mankind, who see it not, who know it not, from being guilty of the like practices here. The justice of God, however, we think, still requires, that he should hereafter avenge the injuries of the widow and the fatherless, who are here so often insulted with impunity. In every religion, and in every superstition that the world has ever beheld, accordingly, there has been a Tartarus as well as an Elysium ; a place provided for the punishment of the wicked, as well as one for the reward of the just.

SECT. III.—OF THE INFLUENCE OF FORTUNE UPON THE SENTI-MENTS OF MANKIND, WITH REGARD TO THE MERIT OR DEMERIT OF THEIR ACTIONS.

INTRODUCTION.—Whatever praise or blame can be due to any action, must belong either, first, to the intention or affection of the heart, from which it proceeds, or, secondly, to the external action or movement of the body, which this affection gives occasion to ; or, lastly, to the good or bad consequences, which actually, and in fact, proceed from it. These three different things constitute the whole nature and circumstances of the action, and must be the foundation of whatever quality can belong to it.

That the two last of these three circumstances cannot be the foundation of any praise or blame, is abundantly evident ; nor has the contrary ever been asserted by any body. The external action or movement of the body is often the same in the most innocent and in the most blamable actions. He who shoots a bird, and he who shoots a man, both of them perform the same external movement : each of them draws the trigger of a gun. The consequences which actually, and in fact, happen to proceed from any action, are, if possible, still more indifferent either to praise or blame, than even the external movement of the body. As they depend, not upon the agent, but upon fortune, they cannot be the proper foundation for any sentiment, of which his character and conduct are the objects.

The only consequences for which he can be answerable, or by which he can deserve either approbation or disapprobation of any kind, are those which were some way or other intended, or those which, at least, show some agreeable or disagreeable quality in the intention of the heart, from which he acted. To the intention or affection of the heart, therefore, to the propriety or impropriety, to the beneficence or hurtfulness of the design, all praise or blame, all approbation or disapprobation, of any kind, which can justly be bestowed upon any action must ultimately belong.

When this maxim is thus proposed, in abstract and general terms, there is nobody who does not agree to it. Its self-evident justice is acknowledged by all the world, and there is not a dissenting voice among all mankind. Every body allows, that how different soever the accidental, the unintended and unforeseen consequences of different actions, yet, if the intentions or affections from which they arose were, on the one hand, equally proper and equally beneficent, or, on the other, equally improper and equally malevolent, the merit or demerit of the actions is still the same, and the agent is equally the suitable object either of gratitude or of resentment.

But how well soever we may seem to be persuaded of the truth of this equitable maxim, when we consider it after this manner, in abstract, yet when we come to particular cases, the actual consequences which happen to proceed from any action, have a very great effect upon our sentiments concerning its merit or demerit, and almost always either enhance or diminish our sense of both. Scarce, in any one instance, perhaps, will our sentiments be found, after examination, to be entirely regulated by this rule, which we all acknowledge ought entirely to regulate them.

This irregularity of sentiment, which every body feels, which scarce any body is sufficiently aware of, and which nobody is willing to acknowledge, I proceed now to explain; and I shall consider, first, the cause which gives occasion to it, or the mechanism by which Nature produces it; secondly, the extent of its influence; and, last of all, the end which it answers, or the purpose which the Author of nature seems to have intended by it.

CHAP. I.—*Of the Causes of this Influence of Fortune.*

THE causes of pain and pleasure, whatever they are, or however they operate, seem to be the objects, which, in all animals, immediately excite those two passions of gratitude and resentment. They are excited by inanimated, as well as by animated objects. We are angry, for a moment, even at the stone that hurts us.   A child beats it, a dog barks at it, a choleric man is apt to curse it.   The least reflection, indeed, corrects this sentiment, and we soon become sensible, that what has no feeling is a very improper object of revenge.   When the mischief, however, is very great, the object which caused it becomes disagreeable to us ever after, and we take pleasure to burn or destroy it.   We should treat, in this manner, the instrument which had accidentally been the cause of the death of a friend, and we should often think ourselves guilty of a sort of inhumanity, if we neglected to vent this absurd sort of vengeance upon it.

We conceive, in the same manner, a sort of gratitude for those inanimated objects, which have been the causes of great or frequent pleasure to us.   The sailor, who, as soon as he got ashore, should mend his fire with the plank upon which he had just escaped from a shipwreck, would seem to be guilty of an unnatural action.   We should expect that he would rather preserve it with care and affection, as a monument that was, in some measure, dear to him.   A man grows fond of a snuffbox, of a pen-knife, of a staff which he has long made use of, and conceives something like a real love and affection for them.   If he breaks or loses them, he is vexed out of all proportion to the value of the damage.   The house which we have long lived in, the tree, whose verdure and shade we have long enjoyed, are both looked upon with a sort of respect that seems due to such benefactors.   The decay of the one, or the ruin of the other, affects us with a kind of melancholy, though we should sustain no loss by it.   The Dryads and the Lares of the ancients, a sort of genii of trees and houses, were probably first suggested by this sort of affection, which the authors of those superstitions felt for such objects, and which seemed unreasonable, if there was nothing animated about them.

But, before any thing can be the proper object of gratitude or resentment, it must not only be the cause of pleasure or pain, it must likewise be capable of feeling them.   Without this other quality, those passions cannot vent themselves with any sort of satisfaction upon it. As they are excited by the causes of pleasure and pain, so their gratification consists in retaliating those sensations upon what gave occasion to them ; which it is to no purpose to attempt upon what has no sensibility.   Animals, therefore, are less improper objects of gratitude and resentment than animated objects.   The dog that bites, the ox that gores, are both of them punished.   If they have been the causes of the death of any person, neither the public, nor the relations of the slain, can be satisfied, unless they are put to death in their turn : nor is this merely for the security of the living, but, in some measure, to revenge the injury of the dead.   Those animals, on the contrary, that have been remarkably serviceable to their masters, become the objects of a very lively gratitude.   We are shocked at the brutality of that officer, mentioned in the Turkish Spy, who stabbed the horse that had carried him across an arm of the sea, lest that animal should afterwards distinguish some other person by a similar adventure.

But, though animals are not only the causes of pleasure and pain, but are also capable of feeling those sensations, they are still far from being complete and perfect objects, either of gratitude or resentment ; and those passions still feel, that there is something wanting to their entire gratification.   What gratitude chiefly desires, is not only to make the benefactor feel pleasure in his turn, but to make him conscious that he meets with this reward on account of his past conduct, to make him pleased with that conduct, and to satisfy him that the person upon whom he bestowed his good offices was not unworthy of them.   What most of all charms us in our benefactor, is the concord between his sentiments and our own, with regard to what interests us so nearly as the worth of our own character, and the esteem that is due to us.   We are delighted to find a person who values us as we value ourselves, and distinguishes us from the rest of mankind, with an attention not unlike that with which we distinguish ourselves.   To maintain in him these agreeable and flattering sentiments, is one of the chief ends proposed by the returns we are disposed to make to him.   A generous mind often disdains the interested thought of extorting new favours from its bene-factor, by what may be called the importunities of its gratitude.   But to preserve and to increase his esteem, is an interest which the greatest mind does not think unworthy of its attention.   And this is the founda-tion of what I formerly observed, and when we cannot enter into the motives of our benefactor, when his conduct and character appear un-worthy of our approbation, let his services have been ever so great, our gratitude is always sensibly diminished.   We are less flattered by the distinction ; and to preserve the esteem of so weak, or so worthless a patron, seems to be an object which does not deserve to be pursued for its own sake.

The object, on the contrary, which resentment is chiefly intent upon, is not so much to make our enemy feel pain in his turn, as to make him conscious that he feels it upon account of his past conduct, to make him repent of that conduct, and to make him sensible, that the person whom he injured did not deserve to be treated in that manner.   What chiefly enrages us against the man who injures or insults us, is the little account which he seems to make of us, the unreasonable preference which he gives to himself above us, and that absurd self-love, by which he seems to imagine, that other people may be sacrificed at any time, to his con-veniency or his humour.   The glaring impropriety of his conduct, the gross insolence and injustice which it seems to involve in it, often shock and exasperate us more than all the mischief which we have suffered. To bring him back to a more just sense of what is due to other people, to make him sensible of what he owes us, and of the wrong that he has done to us, is frequently the principal end proposed in our revenge, which is always imperfect when it cannot acomplish this. When our enemy appears to have done us no injury, when we are sensible that he acted quite properly, that, in his situation, we should have done the same thing, and that we deserved from him all the mischief we met with ; in that case, if we have the least spark either of candour or justice, we can entertain no sort of resentment.

Before any thing, therefore, can be the complete and proper object, either of gratitude or resentment, it must possess three different qualifications. First, it must be the cause of pleasure in the one case, and of pain in the other. Secondly, it must be capable of feeling those sensations. And, thirdly, it must not only have produced those sensations, but it must have produced them from design, and from a design that is approved of in the one case, and disapproved of in the other. It is by the first qualification, that any object is capable of exciting those passions : it is by the second, that it is in any respect capable of gratifying them : the third qualification is not only necessary for their complete satisfaction, but as it gives a pleasure or pain that is both exquisite and peculiar, it is likewise an additional exciting cause of those passions.

As what gives pleasure or pain, therefore, either in one way or another, is the sole exciting cause of gratitude and resentment ; though the intentions of any person should be ever so proper and beneficent, on the one hand, or ever so improper and malevolent on the other; yet, if he has failed in producing either the good or the evil which he intended, as one of the exciting causes is wanting in both cases, less gratitude seems due to him in the one, and less resentment in the other. And, on the contrary, though in the intentions of any person, there was either no laudable degree of benevolence on the one hand, or no blamable degree of malice on the other ; yet, if his actions should produce either great good or great evil, as one of the exciting causes takes place upon both these occasions, some gratitude is apt to arise towards him in the one, and some resentment in the other. A shadow of merit seems to fall upon him in the first, a shadow of demerit in the second. And, as the consequences of actions are altogether under the empire of Fortune, hence arises her influence upon the sentiments of mankind with regard to merit and demerit.

CHAP. II.—*Of the Extent of this Influence of Fortune.*

THE effect of this influence of fortune is, first, to diminish our sense of the merit or demerit of those actions which arose from the most laudable or blamable intentions, when they fail of producing their proposed effects : and, secondly, to increase our sense of the merit or demerit of actions, beyond what is due to the motives or affections from which they proceed, when they accidentally give occasion either to extraordinary pleasure or pain.

1. First, I say, though the intentions of any person should be ever so proper and beneficent, on the one hand, or ever so improper and malevolent, on the other, yet, if they fail in producing their effects, his merit seems imperfect in the one case, and his demerit incomplete in the other. Nor is this irregularity of sentiment felt only by those who are immediately affected by the consequence of any action. It is felt, in some measure, even by the impartial spectator. The man who solicits an office for another, without obtaining it, is regarded as his friend, and seems to deserve his love and affection. But the man who not only solicits, but procures it, is more peculiarly considered as his patron and benefactor, and is entitled to his respect and gratitude. The person obliged, we are apt to think, may, with some justice, imagine himself on a level with the first . but we cannot enter into his sentiments, if he does not feel himself inferior to the second. It is common indeed to say, that we are equally obliged to the man who has endeavoured to serve, as to him who actually did so. It is the speech which we constantly make upon every unsuccessful attempt of this kind ; but which, like all other fine speeches, must be understood with a grain of allowance. The sentiments which a man of generosity entertains for the friend who fails, may often indeed be nearly the same with those which he conceives for him who succeeds : and the more generous he is, the more nearly will those sentiments approach to an exact level. With the truly generous, to be beloved, to be esteemed by those whom they themselves think worthy of esteem, gives more pleasure, and thereby excites more gratitude, than all the advantages which they can ever expect from those sentiments. When they lose those advantages therefore, they seem to lose but a trifle, which is scarce worth regarding. They still however lose something. Their pleasure therefore, and consequently their gratitude, is not perfectly complete : and accordingly if, between the friend who fails and the friend who succeeds, all other circumstances are equal, there will, even in the noblest and best mind, be some little difference of affection in favour of him who succeeds. Nay, so unjust are mankind in this respect, that though the intended benefit should be procured, yet if it is not procured by the means of a particular benefactor, they are apt to think that less gratitude is due to the man, who with the best intentions in the world could do no more than help it a little forward. As their gratitude is in this case divided among the different persons who contributed to their pleasure, a smaller share of it seems due to any one. Such a person, we hear men commonly say, intended no doubt to serve us ; and we really believe exerted himself to the utmost of his abilities for that purpose. We are not, however, obliged to him for this benefit;

7

since, had it not been for the concurrence of others, all that he could have done would never have brought it about. This consideration, they imagine, should, even in the eyes of the impartial spectator, diminish the debt which they owe to him. The person himself who has unsuccessfully endeavoured to confer a benefit, has by no means the same dependency upon the gratitude of the man whom he meant to oblige, nor the same sense of his own merit towards him, which he would have had in the case of success.

Even the merit of talents and abilities which some accident has hindered from producing their effects, seems in some measure imperfect, even to those who are fully convinced of their capacity to produce them. The general who has been hindered by the envy of ministers from gaining some great advantage over the enemies of his country, regrets the loss of the opportunity for ever after. Nor is it only upon account of the public that he regrets it. He laments that he was hindered from performing an action which would have added a new lustre to his character in his own eyes, as well as in those of every other person. It satisfies neither himself nor others to reflect that the plan or design was all that depended on him, that no greater capacity was required to execute it than what was necessary to concert it : that he was allowed to be every way capable of executing it, and that had he been permitted to go on, success was infallible. He still did not execute it ; and though he might deserve all the approbation which is due to a magnanimous and great design, he still wanted the actual merit of having performed a great action. To take the management of any affair of public concern from the man who has almost brought it to a conclusion, is regarded as the most invidious injustice. As he had done so much, he should, we think, have been allowed to acquire the complete merit of putting an end to it. It was objected to Pompey, that he came in upon the victories of Lucullus, and gathered those laurels which were due to the fortune and valour of another. The glory of Lucullus, it seems, was less complete even in the opinion of his own friends, when he was not permitted to finish that conquest which his conduct and courage had put in the power of almost any man to finish. It mortifies an architect when his plans are either not executed at all, or when they are so far altered as to spoil the effect of the building. The plan, however, is all that depends upon the architect. The whole of his genius is, to good judges, as completely discovered in that as in the actual execution. But a plan does not, even to the most intelligent, give the same pleasure as a noble and magnificent building. They may discover as much both of taste and genius in the one as in the other. But their effects are still vastly different, and the amusement derived from the first, never approaches to the wonder and admiration which are sometimes excited by the second. We may believe of many men, that their talents are superior to those of Cæsar and Alexander; and that in the same situations they would perform still greater actions. In the mean time, however, we do not behold them with that astonishment and admiration with which those two heroes have been regarded in all ages and nations. The calm judgments of the mind may approve of them more, but they want the splendour of great actions to dazzle and transport it. The superiority of virtues and talents has not, even upon those who acknowledge that superiority, the same effect with the superiority of achievements.

As the merit of an unsuccessful attempt to do good seems thus, in the eyes of ungrateful mankind, to be diminished by the miscarriage, so does likewise the demerit of an unsuccessful attempt to do evil. The design to commit a crime, how clearly soever it may be proved, is scarce ever punished with the same severity as the actual commission of it. The case of treason is perhaps the only exception. That crime immediately affecting the being of the government itself, the government is naturally more jealous of it than of any other. In the punishment of treason, the sovereign resents the injuries which are immediately done to himself: in the punishment of other crimes he resents those which are done to other men. It is his own resentment which he indulges in the one case; it is that of his subjects which by sympathy he enters into in the other. In the first case, therefore, as he judges in his own cause, he is very apt to be more violent and sanguinary in his punishments than the impartial spectator can approve of. His resentment too rises here upon smaller occasions, and does not always, as in other cases, wait for the perpetration of the crime, or even for the attempt to commit it. A treasonable concert, though nothing has been done, or even attempted in consequence of it, nay, a treasonable conversation, is in many countries punished in the same manner as the actual commission of treason. With regard to all other crimes, the mere design, upon which no attempt has followed, is seldom punished at all, and is never punished severely. A criminal design, and a criminal action, it may be said indeed, do not necessarily suppose the same degree of depravity, and ought not therefore to be subjected to the same punishment. We are capable, it may be said, of resolving, and even of taking measures to execute, many things which, when it comes to the point, we feel ourselves altogether incapable of executing. But this reason can have no place when the design has been carried the length of the last attempt. The man, however, who fires a pistol at his enemy but misses him, is punished with death by the laws of scarce any country. By the old law of Scotland, though he should wound him, yet, unless death ensues within a certain time, the assassin is not liable to the last punishment. The resentment of mankind, however, runs so high against this crime, their terror for the man who shows himself capable of committing it is so great, that the mere attempt to commit it ought in all countries to be capital. The attempt to commit smaller crimes is almost always punished very lightly, and sometimes is not punished at all. The thief, whose hand has been caught in his neighbour's pocket before he had taken any thing out of it, is punished with ignominy only. If he had got time to take away an handkerchief, he might have been put to death. The house-breaker, who has been found setting a ladder to his neighbour's window, but had not got into it, is not exposed to the capital punishment. The attempt to ravish is not punished as a rape. The attempt to seduce a married woman is not punished at all, though seduction is punished severely. Our resentment against the person who only attempted to do a mischief, is seldom so strong as to bear us out in inflicting the same punishment upon him, which we should have thought due if he had actually done it. In the one case, the joy of our deliverance alleviates our sense of the atrocity of his conduct; in the other, the grief of our misfortune increases it. His real demerit, however, is undoubtedly the same in both cases, since his intentions were equally criminal; and there is in this respect, therefore an irregularity in the sentiments of all men, and a consequent relaxation of discipline in the laws of, I believe, all nations of the most civilized, as well as of the most barbarous. The humanity of a civilized people disposes them either to dispense with, or to mitigate punishments, wherever their natural indignation is not goaded on by the consequences of the crime. Barbarians, on the other hand, when no actual consequence has happened from any action, are not apt to be very delicate or inquisitive about the motives.

The person himself who either from passion, or from the influence of bad company, has resolved, and perhaps taken measures to perpetrate some crime, but who has fortunately been prevented by an accident which put it out of his power, is sure, if he has any remains of conscience, to regard this event all his life after as a great and signal deliverance. He can never think of it without returning thanks to Heaven, for having been thus graciously pleased to save him from the guilt in which he was just ready to plunge himself, and to hinder him from rendering all the rest of his life a scene of horror, remorse, and repentance. But though his hands are innocent, he is conscious that his heart is equally guilty as if he had actually executed what he was so fully resolved upon. It gives great ease to his conscience, however, to consider that the crime was not executed, though he knows that the failure arose from no virtue in him. He still considers himself as less deserving of punishment and resentment; and this good fortune either diminishes, or takes away altogether, all sense of guilt. To remember how much he was resolved upon it, has no other effect than to make him regard his escape as the greater and more miraculous: for he still fancies that he has escaped, and he looks back upon the danger to which his peace of mind was exposed, with that terror, with which one who is in safety may sometimes remember the hazard he was in of falling over a precipice, and shudder with horror at the thought.

2. The second effect of this influence of fortune, is to increase our sense of the merit or demerit of actions beyond what is due to the motives or affection from which they proceed, when they happen to give occasion to extraordinary pleasure or pain. The agreeable or disagreeable effects of the action often throw a shadow of merit or demerit upon the agent, though in his intention there was nothing that deserved either praise or blame, or at least that deserved them in the degree in which we are apt to bestow them. Thus, even the messenger of bad news is disagreeable to us, and, on the contrary, we feel a sort of gratitude for the man who brings us good tidings. For a moment we look upon them both as the authors, the one of our good, the other of our bad fortune, and regard them in some measure as if they had really brought about the events which they only give an account of. The first author of our joy is naturally the object of a transitory gratitude: we embrace him with warmth and affection, and should be glad, during the instant of our prosperity, to reward him as for some signal service. By the custom of all courts, the officer, who brings the news of a victory, is entitled to considerable preferments, and the general always chooses one of his principal favourites to go upon so agreeable an errand. The first author of our sorrow is, on the contrary, just as naturally the object of a transitory resentment. We can scarce avoid looking upon him with chagrin and uneasiness; and the rude and brutal are apt to vent upon him that spleen which his intelligence gives occasion to. Tigranes, King of Armenia, struck off the head of the man who brought him the first account of the approach of a formidable enemy. To punish in this manner the author of bad tidings, seems barbarous and inhuman: yet, to reward the messenger of good news, is not disagreeable to us; we think it suitable to the bounty of kings. But why do we make this difference, since, if there is no fault in the one, neither is there any merit in the other? It is because any sort of reason seems sufficient to authorize the exertion of the social and benevolent affections; but it requires the most solid and substantial to make us enter into that of the unsocial and malevolent.

But though in general we are averse to enter into the unsocial and malevolent affections, though we lay it down for a rule that we ought never to approve of their gratification, unless so far as the malicious and unjust intention of the person, against whom they are directed, renders him their proper object; yet, upon some occasions, we relax of this severity. When the negligence of one man has occasioned some unintended damage to another, we generally enter so far into the resentment of the sufferer, as to approve of his inflicting a punishment upon the offender much beyond what the offence would have appeared to deserve, had no such unlucky consequence followed from it.

There is a degree of negligence, which would appear to deserve some chastisement though it should occasion no damage to any body. Thus, if a person should throw a large stone over a wall into a public street without giving warning to those who might be passing by, and without regarding where it was likely to fall, he would undoubtedly deserve some chastisement. A very accurate police would punish so absurd an action, even though it had done no mischief. The person who has been guilty of it, shows an insolent contempt of the happiness and safety of others. There is real injustice in his conduct. He wantonly exposes his neighbour to what no man in his senses would choose to expose himself, and evidently wants that sense of what is due to his fellow-creatures, which is the basis of justice and of society. Gross negligence therefore is, in the law, said to be almost equal to malicious design. (Lata culpa prope dolum est.) When any unlucky consequences happen from such carelessness, the person who has been guilty of it, is often punished as if he had really intended those consequences; and his conduct, which was only thoughtless and insolent, and what deserved some chastisement, is considered as atrocious, and as liable to the severest punishment. Thus if, by the imprudent action above-mentioned, he should accidentally kill a man, he is, by the laws of many countries, particularly by the old law of Scotland, liable to the last punishment. And though this is no doubt excessively severe, it is not altogether inconsistent with our natural sentiments. Our just indignation against the folly and inhumanity of his conduct is exasperated by our sympathy with the unfortunate sufferer. Nothing, however, would appear more shocking to our natural sense of equity, than to bring a man to the scaffold merely for having thrown a stone carelessly into the street without hurting any body. The folly and inhumanity of his conduct, however, would in this case be the same; but still our sentiments would be very different. The consideration of this difference may satisfy us how much the indignation, even of the spectator, is apt to be animated by the actual consequences of the action. In cases of this kind there will, if I am not mistaken, be found a great degree of severity in the laws of almost all nations; as I have already observed that in those of an opposite kind there was a very general relaxation of discipline.

There is another degree of negligence which does not involve in it any sort of injustice. The person who is guilty of it treats his neighbour as he treats himself, means no harm to any body, and is far from entertaining any insolent contempt for the safety and happiness of others. He is not, however, so careful and circumspect in his conduct as he ought to be, and deserves upon this account some degree of blame and censure, but no sort of punishment. Yet if, by a negligence (Culpa levis) of this kind he should occasion some damage to another person, he is by the laws of, I believe, all countries, obliged to compensate it.

And though this is, no doubt, a real punishment, and what no mortal would have thought of inflicting upon him, had it not been for the unlucky accident which his conduct gave occasion to; yet this decision of the law is approved of by the natural sentiments of all mankind. Nothing, we think, can be more just than that one man should not suffer by the carelessness of another; and that the damage occasioned by blamable negligence, should be made up by the person who was guilty of it.

There is another species of negligence (Culpa levissima), which consists merely in a want of the most anxious timidity and circumspection, with regard to all the possible consequences of our actions. The want of this painful attention, when no bad consequences follow from it, is so far from being regarded as blamable, that the contrary quality is rather considered as such. That timid circumspection which is afraid of every thing, is never regarded as a virtue, but as a quality which more than any other incapacitates for action and business. Yet when, from a want of this excessive care, a person happens to occasion some damage to another, he is often by the law obliged to compensate it. Thus, by the Aquilian law, the man, who not being able to manage a horse that had accidentally taken fright, should happen to ride down his neighbour's slave, is obliged to compensate the damage. When an accident of this kind happens, we are apt to think that he ought not to have rode such a horse, and to regard his attempting it as an unpardonable levity; though without this accident we should not only have made no such reflection, but should have regarded his refusing it as the effect of timid weakness, and of an anxiety about merely possible events, which it is to no purpose to be aware of. The person himself, who by an accident even of this kind has involuntarily hurt another, seems to have some sense of his own ill desert, with regard to him. He naturally runs up to the sufferer to express his concern for what has happened, and to make every acknowledgment in his power. If he has any sensibility, he necessarily desires to compensate the damage, and to do every thing he can to appease that animal resentment which he is sensible will be apt to arise in the breast of the sufferer. To make no apology, to offer no atonement, is regarded as the highest brutality. Yet why should he make an apology more than any other person? Why should he, since he was equally innocent with any other by-stander, be thus singled out from among all mankind, to make up for the bad fortune of another? This task would surely never be imposed upon him, did not even the impartial spectator feel some indulgence for what may be regarded as the unjust resentment of that other.

CHAP. III.—*Of the final Cause of this Irregularity of Sentiments.*

SUCH is the effect of the good or bad consequence of actions upon the sentiments both of the person who performs them, and of others; and thus, Fortune, which governs the world, has some influence where we should be least willing to allow her any, and directs in some measure the sentiments of mankind, with regard to the character and conduct both of themselves and others. That the world judges by the event, and not by the design, has been in all ages the complaint, and is the great discouragement of virtue. Every body agrees to the general maxim, that as the event does not depend on the agent, it ought to have no influence upon our sentiments, with regard to the merit or propriety of his conduct. But when we come to particulars, we find that our sentiments are scarce in any one instance exactly conformable to what this equitable maxim would direct. The happy or unprosperous event of any action, is not only apt to give us a good or bad opinion of the prudence with which it was conducted, but almost always too animates our gratitude or resentment, our sense of the merit or demerit of the design.

Nature, however, when she implanted the seeds of this irregularity in the human breast, seems, as upon all other occasions, to have intended the happiness and perfection of the species. If the hurtfulness of the design, if the malevolence of the affection, were alone the causes which excited our resentment, we should feel all the furies of that passion against any person in whose breast we suspected or believed such designs or affections were harboured, though they had never broke out into any actions. Sentiments, thoughts, intentions, would become the objects of punishment; and if the indignation of mankind run as high against them as against actions; if the baseness of the thought which had given birth to no action, seemed in the eyes of the world as much to call aloud for vengeance as the baseness of the action, every court of judicature would become a real inquisition. There would be no safety for the most innocent and circumspect conduct. Bad wishes, bad views, bad designs, might still be suspected: and while these excited the same indignation with bad conduct, while bad intentions were as much resented as bad actions, they would equally expose the person to punishment and resentment. Actions, therefore, which either produce actual evil, or attempt to produce it, and thereby put us in the immediate fear of it, are by the Author of nature rendered the only proper and approved objects of human punishment and resentment. Sentiments, designs, affections, though it is from these that according to cool reason human actions derive their whole merit or demerit, are placed by the great Judge of hearts beyond the limits of every human jurisdiction, and are reserved for the cognisance of his own unerring tribunal. That necessary rule of justice, therefore, that men in this life are liable to punishment for their actions only, not for their designs and intentions, is founded upon this salutary and useful irregularity in human sentiments concerning merit or demerit, which at first sight appears so absurd and unaccountable. But every part of nature, when attentively surveyed, equally demonstrates the providential care of its Author, and we may admire the wisdom and goodness of God even in the weakness and folly of men.

Nor is that irregularity of sentiments altogether without its utility, by which the merit of an unsuccessful attempt to serve, and much more that of mere good inclinations and kind wishes, appears to be imperfect. Man was made for action, and to promote by the exertion of his faculties such changes in the external circumstances both of himself and others, as may seem most favourable to the happiness of all. He must not be satisfied with indolent benevolence, nor fancy himself the friend of mankind, because in his heart he wishes well to the prosperity of the world. That he may call forth the whole vigour of his soul, and strain every nerve, in order to produce those ends which it is the purpose of his being to advance, Nature has taught him, that neither himself nor mankind can be fully satisfied with his conduct, nor bestow upon it the full measure of applause, unless he has actually produced them. He is made to know, that the praise of good intentions, without the merit of good offices, will be but of little avail to excite either the loudest acclamations of the world, or even the highest degree of self applause. The man who has performed no single action of importance, but whose whole conversation and deportment express the justest, the noblest, and most generous sentiments, can be entitled to demand no very high reward, even though his inutility should be owing to nothing but the want of an opportunity to serve. We can still refuse it him without blame. We can still ask him, What have you done? What actual service can you produce, to entitle you to so great a recompense? We esteem you, and love you; but we owe you nothing. To reward indeed that latent virtue which has been useless only for want of an opportunity to serve, to bestow upon it those honours and preferments, which, though in some measure it may be said to deserve them, it could not with propriety have insisted upon, is the effect of the most divine benevolence. To punish, on the contrary, for the affections of the heart only, where no crime has been committed, is the most insolent and barbarous tyranny. The benevolent affections seem to deserve most praise, when they do not wait till it becomes almost a crime for them not to exert themselves. The malevolent, on the contrary, can scarce be too tardy, too slow, or deliberate.

It is even of considerable importance, that the evil which is done without design should be regarded as a misfortune to the doer as well as to the sufferer. Man is thereby taught to reverence the happiness of his brethren, to tremble lest he should, even unknowingly, do any thing that can hurt them, and to dread that animal resentment which, he feels, is ready to burst out against him, if he should, without design, be the unhappy instrument of their calamity. As in the ancient heathen religion, that holy ground which had been consecrated to some god, was not to be trod upon but upon solemn and necessary occasions, and the man who had even ignorantly violated it, became piacular from that moment, and, until proper atonement should be made, incurred the vengeance of that powerful and invisible being to whom it had been set apart ; so by the wisdom of nature, the happiness of every innocent man is, in the same manner, rendered holy, consecrated, and hedged round against the approach of every other man ; not to be wantonly trod upon, not even to be, in any respect, ignorantly and involuntarily violated, without requiring some expiation, some atonement in proportion to the greatness of such undesigned violation. A man of humanity, who accidentally, and without the smallest degree of blamable negligence, has been the cause of the death of another man, feels himself piacular, though not guilty. During his whole life he considers this accident as one of the greatest misfortunes that could have befallen him. If the family of the slain is poor, and he himself in tolerable circumstances, he immediately takes them under his protection, and, without any other merit, thinks them entitled to every degree of favour and kindness. If they are in better circumstances, he endeavours by every submission, by every expression of sorrow, by rendering them every good office which he can devise or they accept of, to atone for what has happened, and to propitiate, as much as possible, their, perhaps natural, though no doubt most unjust resentment, for the great, though involuntary, offence which he has given unto them.

The distress which an innocent person feels, who, by some accident, has been led to do something which, if it had been done with knowledge and design, would have justly exposed him to the deepest reproach, has given occasion to some of the finest and most interesting scenes both of the ancient and of the modern drama. It is this fallacious sense of guilt, if I may call it so, which constitutes the whole distress of Oedipus and Jocasta upon the Greek, of Monimia and Isabella upon the English, theatre. They are all in the highest degree piacular, though not one of them is in the smallest degree guilty.

Notwithstanding, however, all these seeming irregularities of sentiment, if man should unfortunately either give occasion to those evils which he did not intend, or fail in producing that good which he intended, Nature has not left his innocence altogether without consolation, nor his virtue altogether without reward. He then calls to his assistance that just and equitable maxim, That those events which did not depend upon our conduct, ought not to diminish the esteem that is due to us. He summons up his whole magnanimity and firmness of soul, and strives to regard himself, not in the light in which he at present appears, but in that in which he ought to appear, in which he would have appeared had his generous designs been crowned with success, and in which he would still appear, notwithstanding their miscarriage, if the sentiments of mankind were either altogether candid and equitable, or even perfectly consistent with themselves. The more candid and humane part of mankind entirely go along with the efforts which he thus makes to support himself in his own opinion. They exert their whole generosity and greatness of mind, to correct in themselves this irregularity of human nature, and endeavour to regard his unfortunate magnanimity in the same light in which, had it been successful, they would, without any such generous exertion, have naturally been disposed to consider it.

Part III.—Of the Foundation of our Judgments concerning our own Sentiments and Conduct, and of the Sense of Duty.

CHAP. I.—*Of the Principle of Self-approbation and of Self-disapprobation.*

IN the two foregoing parts of this discourse, I have chiefly considered the origin and foundation of our judgments concerning the sentiments and conduct of others. I come now to consider more particularly the origin of those concerning our own.

The principle by which we naturally either approve or disapprove of our own conduct, seems to be altogether the same with that by which we exercise the like judgments concerning the conduct of other people. We either approve or disapprove of the conduct of another man according as we feel that, when we bring his case home to ourselves, we either can or cannot entirely sympathize with the sentiments and motives which directed it. And, in the same manner, we either approve or disapprove of our own conduct, according as we feel that, when we place ourselves in the situation of another man, and view it, as it were, with his eyes and from his station, we either can or cannot entirely enter into and sympathize with the sentiments and motives which influenced it. We can never survey our own sentiments and motives, we can never form any judgment concerning them ; unless we remove ourselves, as it were, from our own natural station, and endeavour to view them as at a certain distance from us. But we can do this in no other way than by endeavouring to view them with the eyes of other people, or as other people are likely to view them. Whatever judgment we can form concerning them, accordingly, must always bear some secret reference, either to what are, or to what, upon a certain condition, would be, or to what, we imagine, ought to be the judgment of others. We endeavour to examine our own conduct as we imagine any other fair and impartial spectator would examine it. If, upon placing ourselves in his situation, we thoroughly enter into all the passions and motives which influenced it, we approve of it, by sympathy with the approbation of this supposed equitable judge. If otherwise, we enter into his disapprobation, and condemn it.

Were it possible that a human creature could grow up to manhood in some solitary place, without any communication with his own species, he could no more think of his own character, of the propriety or demerit of his own sentiments and conduct, of the beauty or deformity of his own mind, than of the beauty or deformity of his own face. All these are objects which he cannot easily see, which naturally he does not look at, and with regard to which he is provided with no mirror which can present them to his view. Bring him into society, and he is immediately provided with the mirror which he wanted before. It is placed in the countenance and behaviour of those he lives with, which always mark when they enter into, and when they disapprove of his sentiments ; and it is here that he first views the propriety and impropriety of his own passions, the beauty and deformity of his own mind. To a man who from his birth was a stranger to society, the objects of his passions, the external bodies which either pleased or hurt him, would occupy his whole attention. The passions themselves, the desires or aversions, the joys or sorrows, which those objects excited, though of all things the most immediately present to him, could scarce ever be the objects of his thoughts. The idea of them could never interest him so much as to call upon his attentive consideration. The consideration of his joy could in him excite no new joy, nor that of his sorrow any new sorrow, though the consideration of the causes of those passions might often excite both. Bring him into society and all his own passions will immediately become the causes of new passions. He will observe that mankind approve of some of them, and are disgusted by others. He will be elevated in the one case, and cast down in the other ; his desires and aversions, his joys and sorrows, will now often become the causes of new desires and new aversions, new joys and new sorrows : they will now, therefore, interest him deeply, and often call upon his most attentive consideration.

Our first ideas of personal beauty and deformity, are drawn from the shape and appearance of others, not from our own. We soon become sensible, however, that others exercise the same criticism upon us. We are pleased when they approve of our figure, and are disobliged when they seem to be disgusted. We become anxious to know how far our appearance deserves either their blame or approbation. We examine our persons limb by limb, and by placing ourselves before a looking-glass, or by some such expedient, endeavour as much as pos-

sible, to view ourselves at the distance and with the eyes of other people. If, after this examination, we are satisfied with our own appearance, we can more easily support the most disadvantageous judgments
of others. If, on the contrary, we are sensible that we are the natural
objects of distaste, every appearance of their disapprobation mortifies us
beyond all measure. A man who is tolerably handsome, will allow you to
laugh at any little irregularity in his person; but all such jokes are
commonly unsupportable to one who is really deformed. It is evident,
however, that we are anxious about our own beauty and deformity,
only upon account of its effect upon others. If we had no connexion
with society, we should be altogether indifferent about either.

In the same manner our first moral criticisms are exercised upon the
characters and conduct of other people; and we are all very forward
to observe how each of these affects us. But we soon learn, that other
people are equally frank with regard to our own. We become anxious
to know how far we deserve their censure or applause, and whether to
them we must necessarily appear those agreeable or disagreeable creatures which they represent us. We begin, upon this account, to examine our own passions and conduct, and to consider how these must
appear to them; by considering how they would appear to us if
in their situation. We suppose ourselves the spectators of our own
behaviour, and endeavour to imagine what effect it would, in this light,
produce upon us. This is the only looking-glass by which we can, in
some measure, with the eyes of other people, scrutinize the propriety of
our own conduct. If in this view it pleases us, we are tolerably satisfied. We can be more indifferent about the applause, and, in some
measure, despise the censure of the world; secure that, however misunderstood or misrepresented, we are the natural and proper objects of
approbation. On the contrary, if we are doubtful about it, we are often,
upon that very account, more anxious to gain their approbation, and,
provided we have not already, as they say, shaken hands with infamy,
we are altogether distracted at the thoughts of their censure, which
then strikes us with double severity.

When I endeavour to examine my own conduct, when I endeavour
to pass sentence upon it, and either to approve or condemn it, it is
evident that, in all such cases, I divide myself, as it were, into two persons; and that I, the examiner and judge, represent a different character from that other I, the person whose conduct is examined into
and judged of. The first is the spectator, whose sentiments with regard to my own conduct I endeavour to enter into, by placing myself
in his situation, and by considering how it would appear to me, when
seen from that particular point of view. The second is the agent, the
person whom I properly call myself, and of whose conduct, under the
character of a spectator, I was endeavouring to form some opinion.
The first is the judge; the second the person judged of. But that the

judge should, in every respect, be the same with the person judged of, is as impossible, as that the cause should, in every respect, be the same with the effect.

To be amiable and to be meritorious; that is, to deserve love and to deserve reward, are the great characters of virtue; and to be odious and punishable, of vice. But all these characters have an immediate reference to the sentiments of others. Virtue is not said to be amiable, or to be meritorious, because it is the object of its own love, or of its own gratitude; but because it excites those sentiments in other men. The consciousness that it is the object of such favourable regards, is the source of that inward tranquillity and self-satisfaction with which it is naturally attended, as the suspicion of the contrary gives occasion to the torments of vice. What so great happiness as to be beloved, and to know that we deserve to be beloved? What so great misery as to be hated, and to know that we deserve to be hated?

CHAP. II.—*Of the Love of Praise, and of that of Praise-worthiness; and of the dread of Blame, and of that of Blame-worthiness.*

MAN naturally desires, not only to be loved, but to be lovely; or to be that thing which is the natural and proper object of love. He naturally dreads, not only to be hated, but to be hateful; or to be that thing which is the natural and proper object of hatred. He desires, not only praise, but praise-worthiness; or to be that thing which, though it should be praised by nobody, is, however, the natural and proper object of praise. He dreads, not only blame, but blame-worthiness; or to be that thing which, though it should be blamed by nobody, is, however, the natural and proper object of blame.

The love of praise-worthiness is by no means derived altogether from the love of praise. Those two principles, though they resemble one another, though they are connected, and often blended with one another, are yet, in many respects, distinct and independent of one another.

The love and admiration which we naturally conceive for those whose character and conduct we approve of, necessarily dispose us to desire to become ourselves the objects of the like agreeable sentiments, and to be as amiable and as admirable as those whom we love and admire the most. Emulation, the anxious desire that we ourselves should excel, is originally founded in our admiration of the excellence of others. Neither can we be satisfied with being merely admired for what other people are admired. We must at least believe ourselves to be admirable for what they are admirable. But, in order to attain this satisfaction, we must become the impartial spectators of our own character and conduct. We must endeavour to view them with the eyes of other people, or as other people are likely to view them. When seen in this light, if they appear to us as we wish, we are happy and contented. But it greatly confirms this happiness and contentment when we find that other people, viewing them with those very eyes with which we, in imagination only, were endeavouring to view them, see them precisely in the same light in which we ourselves had seen them. Their approbation necessarily confirms our own self-approbation. Their praise necessarily strengthens our own sense of our own praise-worthiness. In this case, so far is the love of praise-worthiness from being derived altogether from that of praise; that the love of praise seems, at least in a great measure, to be derived from that of praise-worthiness.

The most sincere praise can give little pleasure when it cannot be considered as some sort of proof of praise-worthiness. It is by no means sufficient that, from ignorance or mistake, esteem and admiration should, in some way or other, be bestowed upon us. If we are conscious that we do not deserve to be so favourably thought of, and that if the truth were known, we should be regarded with very different sentiments, our satisfaction is far from being complete. The man who applauds us either for actions which we did not perform, or for motives which had no sort of influence upon our conduct, applauds not us, but another person. We can derive no sort of satisfaction from his praises. To us they should be more mortifying than any censure, and should perpetually call to our minds, the most humbling of all reflections, the reflection of what we ought to be, but what we are not. A woman who paints, could derive, one should imagine, but little vanity from the compliments that are paid to her complexion. These, we should expect, ought rather to put her in mind of the sentiments which her real complexion would excite, and mortify her the more by the contrast. To be pleased with such groundless applause is a proof of the most superficial levity and weakness. It is what is properly called vanity, and is the foundation of the most ridiculous and contemptible vices, the vices of affectation and common lying; follies which, if experience did not teach us how common they are, one should imagine the least spark of common sense would save us from. The foolish liar, who endeavours to excite the admiration of the company by the relation of adventures which never had any existence; the important coxcomb, who gives himself airs of rank and distinction which he well knows he has no just pretensions to; are both of them, no doubt, pleased with the applause which they fancy they meet with. But their vanity arises from so gross an illusion of the imagination, that it is difficult to conceive how any rational creature should be imposed upon by it. When they place themselves in the situation of those whom they fancy they have deceived, they are struck with the highest admiration for their own persons. They look upon themselves, not in that light in which, they know, they ought to appear to their companions, but in that in which they believe their

companions actually look upon them. Their superficial weakness and
trivial folly hinder them from ever turning their eyes inwards, or from
seeing themselves in that despicable point of view in which their own
consciences must tell them that they would appear to every body, if the
real truth should ever come to be known.

As ignorant and groundless praise can give no solid joy, no satisfaction that will bear any serious examination, so, on the contrary, it often
gives real comfort to reflect, that though no praise should actually be
bestowed upon us, our conduct, however, has been such as to deserve
it, and has been in every respect suitable to those measures and rules
by which praise and approbation are naturally and commonly bestowed.
We are pleased, not only with praise, but with having done what is
praise-worthy. We are pleased to think that we have rendered ourselves the natural objects of approbation, though no approbation should
ever actually be bestowed upon us : and we are mortified to reflect that
we have justly merited the blame of those we live with, though that
sentiment should never actually be exerted against us. The man who
is conscious to himself that he has exactly observed those measures of
conduct which experience informs him are generally agreeable, reflects
with satisfaction on the propriety of his own behaviour. When he
views it in the light in which the impartial spectator would view it, he
thoroughly enters into all the motives which influenced it. He looks
back upon every part of it with pleasure and approbation, and though
mankind should never be acquainted with what he has done, he regards
himself, not so much according to the light in which they actually regard him, as according to that in which they would regard him if they
were better informed. He anticipates the applause and admiration
which in this case would be bestowed upon him, and he applauds and
admires himself by sympathy with sentiments, which do not indeed actually take place, but which the ignorance of the public alone hinders
from taking place, which he knows are the natural and ordinary effects
of such conduct, which his imagination strongly connects with it, and
which he has acquired a habit of conceiving as something that naturally
and in propriety ought to follow from it. Men have voluntarily thrown
away life to acquire after death a renown which they could no longer
enjoy. Their imagination, in the mean time, anticipated that fame
which was in future times to be bestowed upon them. Those applauses
which they were never to hear rung in their ears ; the thoughts of that
admiration, whose effects they were never to feel, played about their
hearts, banished from their breasts the strongest of all natural fears,
and transported them to perform actions which seem almost beyond
the reach of human nature. But in point of reality there is surely no
great difference between that approbation which is not to be bestowed
till we can no longer enjoy it, and that which, indeed, is never to be
bestowed, but which would be bestowed, if the world was ever made to

understand properly the real circumstances of our behaviour. If the one often produces such violent effects, we cannot wonder that the other should always be highly regarded.

Nature, when she formed man for society, endowed him with an original desire to please, and an original aversion to offend his brethren. She taught him to feel pleasure in their favourable, and pain in their unfavourable regard. She rendered their approbation most flattering and most agreeable to him for its own sake ; and their disapprobation most mortifying and most offensive.

But this desire of the approbation, and this aversion to the disapprobation of his brethren, would not alone have rendered him fit for that society for which he was made. Nature, accordingly, has endowed him, not only with a desire of being approved of, but with a desire of being what ought to be approved of ; or of being what he himself approves of in other men. The first desire could only have made him wish to appear to be fit for society. The second was necessary in order to render him anxious to be really fit. The first could only have prompted him to the affectation of virtue, and to the concealment of vice. The second was necessary in order to inspire him with the real love of virtue, and with the real abhorrence of vice. In every well-formed mind this second desire seems to be the strongest of the two. It is only the weakest and most superficial of mankind who can be much delighted with that praise which they themselves know to be altogether unmerited. A weak man may sometimes be pleased with it, but a wise man rejects it upon all occasions. But, though a wise man feels little pleasure from praise where he knows there is no praise-worthiness, he often feels the highest in doing what he knows to be praise-worthy, though he knows equally well that no praise is ever to be bestowed upon it. To obtain the approbation of mankind, where no approbation is due, can never be an object of any importance to him. To obtain that approbation where it is really due, may sometimes be an object of no great importance to him. But to be that thing which deserves approbation, must always be an object of the highest.

To desire, or even to accept of praise, where no praise is due, can be the effect only of the most contemptible vanity. To desire it where it is really due is to desire no more than that a most essential act of justice should be done to us. The love of just fame, of true glory, even for its own sake, and independent of any advantage which he can derive from it, is not unworthy even of a wise man. He sometimes, however, neglects, and even despises it ; and he is never more apt to do so than when he has the most perfect assurance of the perfect propriety of every part of his own conduct. His self-approbation, in this case, stands in need of no confirmation from the approbation of other men. It is alone sufficient, and he is contented with it. This self-approbation, if not the only, is at least the principal object, about which he can or ought to be anxious.   The love of it is the love of virtue.

As the love and admiration which we naturally conceive for some characters, dispose us to wish to become ourselves the proper objects of such agreeable sentiments ; so the hatred and contempt which we as naturally conceive for others, dispose us, perhaps still more strongly, to dread the very thought of resembling them in any respect.   Neither is it, in this case, too, so much the thought of being hated and despised that we are afraid of, as that of being hateful and despicable.   We dread the thought of doing any thing which can render us the just and proper objects of the hatred and contempt of our fellow-creatures ; even though we had the most perfect security that those sentiments were never actually to be exerted against us.   The man who has broke through all those measures of conduct, which can alone render him agreeable to mankind, though he should have the most perfect assurance that what he had done was for ever to be concealed from every human eye, it is all to no purpose.   When he looks back upon it, and views it in the light in which the impartial spectator would view it, he finds that he can enter into none of the motives which influenced it. He is abashed and confounded at the thoughts of it, and necessarily feels a very high degree of that shame which he would be exposed to, if his actions should ever come to be generally known.   His imagination, in this case too, anticipates the contempt and derision from which nothing saves him but the ignorance of those he lives with.   He still feels that he is the natural object of these sentiments, and still trembles at the thought of what he would suffer, if they were ever actually exerted against him.   But if what he had been guilty of was not merely one of those improprieties which are the objects of simple disapprobation, but one of those enormous crimes which excite detestation and resentme it, he could never think of it, as long as he had any sensibility left, without feeling all the agony of horror and remorse ; and though he could be assured that no man was ever to know it, and could even bring himself to believe that there was no God to revenge it, he would still feel enough of both these sentiments to embitter the whole of his life : he would still regard himself as the natural object of the hatred and indignation of all his fellow-creatures ; and, if his heart was not grown callous by the habit of crimes, he could not think without terror and astonishment even of the manner in which mankind would look upon him, of what would be the expression of their countenance and of their eyes, if the dreadful truth should ever come to be known. These natural pangs of an affrighted conscience are the dæmons, the avenging furies, which, in this life, haunt the guilty, which allow them neither quiet nor repose, which often drive them to despair and distraction, from which no assurance of secrecy can protect them, from which no principles of irreligion can entirely deliver them, and from which nothing can free them but the vilest and most abject of all states, a complete insensibility to honour and infamy, to vice and virtue.   Men of the most detestable characters, who, in the execution of the most dreadful crimes, had taken their measures so coolly as to avoid even the suspicion of guilt, have sometimes been driven, by the horror of their situation, to discover, of their own accord, what no human sagacity could ever have investigated. By acknowledging their guilt, by submitting themselves to the resentment of their offended fellow-citizens, and, by thus satiating that vengeance of which they were sensible that they had become the proper objects, they hoped, by their death to reconcile themselves, at least in their own imagination, to the natural sentiments of mankind ; to be able to consider themselves as less worthy of hatred and resentment ; to atone, in some measure, for their crimes, and, by thus becoming the objects rather of compassion than of horror, if possible, to die in peace and with the forgiveness of all their fellow-creatures. Compared to what they felt before the discovery, even the thought of this, it seems was happiness.

In such cases, the horror of blame-worthiness seems, even in persons who cannot be suspected of any extraordinary delicacy or sensibility of character, completely to conquer the dread of blame. In order to allay that horror, in order to pacify, in some degree, the remorse of their own consciences, they voluntarily submitted themselves both to the reproach and to the punishment which they knew were due to their crimes, but which, at the same time, they might easily have avoided.

They are the most frivolous and superficial of mankind only who can be much delighted with that praise which they themselves know to be altogether unmerited.   Unmerited reproach, however, is frequently capable of mortifying very severely even men of more than ordinary constancy.   Men of the most ordinary constancy, indeed, easily learn to despise those foolish tales which are so frequently circulated in society, and which, from their own absurdity and falsehood, never fail to die away in the course of a few weeks, or of a few days.   But an innocent man, though of more than ordinary constancy, is often, not only shocked, but most severely mortified by the serious, though false, imputation of a crime ; especially when that imputation happens unfortunately to be supported by some circumstances which gave it an air of probability.   He is humbled to find that any body should think so meanly of his character as to suppose him capable of being guilty of it. Though perfectly conscious of his own innocence, the very imputation seems often, even in his own imagination, to throw a shadow of disgrace and dishonour upon his character.   His just indignation, too, at so very gross an injury, which, however, it may frequently be improper and sometimes even impossible to revenge, is itself a very painful sensation.   There is no greater tormentor of the human breast than violent resentment which cannot be gratified.   An innocent man, brought to the scaffold by the false imputation of an infamous or odious crime, suffers the most cruel misfortune which it is possible for innocence to suffer. The agony of his mind may, in this case, frequently be greater than that of those who suffer for the like crimes, of which they have been actually guilty. Profligate criminals, such as common thieves and highwaymen, have frequently little sense of the baseness of their own conduct, and consequently no remorse. Without troubling themselves about the justice or injustice of the punishment, they have always been accustomed to look upon the gibbet as a lot very likely to fall to them. When it does fall to them, therefore, they consider themselves only as not quite so lucky as some of their companions, and submit to their fortune, without any other uneasiness than what may arise from the fear of death; a fear which, even by such worthless wretches, we frequently see, can be so easily, and so very completely conquered. The innocent man, on the contrary, over and above the uneasiness which this fear may occasion, is tormented by his own indignation at the injustice which has been done to him. He is struck with horror at the thoughts of the infamy which the punishment may shed upon his memory, and foresees, with the most exquisite anguish, that he is hereafter to be remembered by his dearest friends and relations, not with regret and affection, but with shame, and even with horror for his supposed disgraceful conduct: and the shades of death appear to close round him with a darker and more melancholy gloom than naturally belongs to them. Such fatal accidents, for the tranquillity of mankind, it is to be hoped, happen very rarely in any country; but they happen sometimes in all countries, even in those where justice is in general very well administered. The unfortunate Calas, a man of much more than ordinary constancy (broke upon the wheel and burnt at Tholouse for the supposed murder of his own son, of which he was perfectly innocent), seemed, with his last breath, to deprecate, not so much the cruelty of the punishment, as the disgrace which the imputation might bring upon his memory. After he had been broke, and was just going to be thrown into the fire, the monk, who attended the execution, exhorted him to confess the crime for which he had been condemned. 'My father,' said Calas, 'can you yourself bring yourself ' to believe that I am guilty?'

To persons in such unfortunate circumstances, that humble philosophy which confines its views to this life, can afford, perhaps, but little consolation. Every thing that could render either life or death respectable is taken from them. They are condemned to death and to everlasting infamy. Religion can alone afford them any effectual comfort. She alone can tell them that it is of little importance what man may think of their conduct, while the all-seeing Judge of the world approves of it. She alone can present to them the view of another world; a world of more candour, humanity, and justice, than the present; where their innocence is in due time to be declared, and their virtue to be finally rewarded : and the same great principle which can alone strike terror into triumphant vice, affords the only effectual consolation to disgraced and insulted innocence.

In smaller offences, as well as in greater crimes, it frequently happens that a person of sensibility is much more hurt by the unjust imputation, than the real criminal is by the actual guilt. A woman of gallantry laughs even at the well-founded surmises which are circulated concerning her conduct. The worst founded surmise of the same kind is a mortal stab to an innocent virgin. The person who is deliberately guilty of a disgraceful action, we may lay it down, I believe, as a general rule, can seldom have much sense of the disgrace; and the person who is habitually guilty of it, can scarce ever have any.

When every man, even of middling understanding, so readily despises unmerited applause, how it comes to pass that unmerited reproach should often be capable of mortifying so severely men of the soundest and best judgment, may, perhaps, deserve some consideration.

Pain, I have already had occasion to observe, is, in almost all cases, a more pungent sensation than the opposite and correspondent pleasure. The one, almost always, depresses us much more below the ordinary, or what may be called the natural, state of our happiness, than the other ever raises us above it. A man of sensibility is apt to be more humiliated by just censure than he is ever elevated by just applause. Unmerited applause a wise man rejects with contempt upon all occasions ; but he often feels very severely the injustice of unmerited censure. By suffering himself to be applauded for what he has not performed, by assuming a merit which does not belong to him, he feels that he is guilty of a mean falsehood, and deserves, not the admiration, but the contempt of those very persons who, by mistake, had been led to admire him. It may, perhaps, give him some well-founded pleasure to find that he has been, by many people, thought capable of performing what he did not perform. But, though he may be obliged to his friends for their good opinion, he would think himself guilty of the greatest baseness if he did not immediately undeceive them. It gives him little pleasure to look upon himself in the light in which other people actually look upon him, when he is conscious that, if they knew the truth, they would look upon him in a very different light. A weak man, however, is often much delighted with viewing himself in this false and delusive light. He assumes the merit of every laudable action that is ascribed to him, and pretends to that of many which nobody ever thought of ascribing to him. He pretends to have done what he never did, to have written what another wrote, to have invented what another discovered ; and is led into all the miserable vices of plagiarism and common lying. But though no man of middling good sense can derive much pleasure from the imputation of a laudable action which he never performed, yet a wise man may suffer great pain from the serious imputation of a crime which he never committed. Nature, in this case, has rendered the pain, not only more pungent than the opposite and correspondent pleasure, but she has rendered it so in a much greater than the ordinary degree. A denial rids a man at once of the foolish and ridiculous pleasure ; but it will not always rid him of the pain. When he refuses the merit which is ascribed to him, nobody doubts his veracity. It may be doubted when he denies the crime which he is accused of. He is at once enraged at the falsehood of the imputation, and mortified to find that any credit should be given to it. He feels that his character is not sufficient to protect him. He feels that his brethren, far from looking upon him in that light in which he anxiously desires to be viewed by them, think him capable of being guilty of what he is accused of. He knows perfectly that he has not been guilty. He knows perfectly what he has done; but, perhaps, scarce any man can know perfectly what he himself is capable of doing. What the peculiar constitution of his own mind may or may not admit of, is, perhaps, more or less a matter of doubt to every man. The trust and good opinion of his friends and neighbours, tends more than any thing to relieve him from this most disagreeable doubt ; their distrust and unfavourable opinion to increase it. He may think himself very confident that their unfavourable judgment is wrong : but this confidence can seldom be so great as to hinder that judgment from making some impression upon him ; and the greater his sensibility, the greater his delicacy, the greater his worth in short, this impression is likely to be the greater.

The agreement or disagreement both of the sentiments and judgments of other people with our own, is, in all cases, it must be observed, of more or less importance to us, exactly in proportion as we ourselves are more or less uncertain about the propriety of our own sentiments, about the accuracy of our own judgments.

A man of sensibility may sometimes feel great uneasiness lest he should have yielded too much even to what may be called an honourable passion ; to his just indignation, perhaps, at the injury which may have been done either to himself or to his friend. He is anxiously afraid lest, meaning only to act with spirit, and to do justice, he may, from the too great vehemence of his emotion, have done a real injury to some other person ; who, though not innocent, may not have been altogether so guilty as he at first apprehended. The opinion of other people becomes, in this case, of the utmost importance to him. Their approbation is the most healing balsam ; their disapprobation, the bitterest and most tormenting poison that can be poured into his uneasy mind. When he is perfectly satisfied with every part of his own conduct, the judgment of other people is often of less importance to him.

There are some very noble and beautiful arts, in which the degree of excellence can be determined only by a certain nicety of taste, of which the decisions, however, appear always, in some measure, uncertain. There are others, in which the success admits, either of clear demonstration, or very satisfactory proof. Among the candidates for excellence in those different arts, the anxiety about the public opinion is always much greater in the former than in the latter.

The beauty of poetry is a matter of such nicety, that a young beginner can scarce ever be certain that he has attained it. Nothing delights him so much, therefore, as the favourable judgments of his friends and of the public ; and nothing mortifies him so severely as the contrary. The one establishes, the other shakes, the good opinion which he is anxious to entertain concerning his own performances. Experience and success may in time give him a little more confidence in his own judgment. He is at all times, however, liable to be most severely mortified by the unfavourable judgments of the public. Racine was so disgusted by the indifferent success of his Phædra, the finest tragedy, perhaps, that is extant in any language, that, though in the vigour of his life, and at the height of his abilities, he resolved to write no more for the stage. That great poet used frequently to tell his son, that the most paltry and impertinent criticism had always given him more pain than the highest and justest eulogy had ever given him pleasure. The extreme sensibility of Voltaire to the slightest censure of the same kind is well known to every body. The Dunciad of Mr. Pope is an everlasting monument of how much the most correct, as well as the most elegant and harmonious of all the English poets, had been hurt by the criticisms of the lowest and most contemptible authors. Gray (who joins to the sublimity of Milton the elegance and harmony of Pope, and to whom nothing is wanting to render him, perhaps, the first poet in the English language, but to have written a little more) is said to have been so much hurt by a foolish and impertinent parody of two of his finest odes, that he never afterwards attempted any considerable work. Those men of letters who value themselves upon what is called fine writing in prose, approach somewhat to the sensibility of poets.

Mathematicians, on the contrary, who may have the most perfect assurance, both of the truth and of the importance of their discoveries, are frequently very indifferent about the reception which they may meet with from the public. The two greatest mathematicians that I ever had the honour to be known to, and I believe, the two greatest that have lived in my time, Dr. Robert Simpson of Glasgow, and Dr. Matthew Stewart of Edinburgh, never seemed to feel even the slightest uneasiness from the neglect with which the ignorance of the public received some of their most valuable works. The great work of Sir Isaac Newton, *his Mathematical Principles of Natural Philosophy*, I have been told, was for several years neglected by the public. The tranquillity of that great man, it is probable, never suffered, upon that account, the interruption of a single quarter of an hour. Natural philosophers, in their independency upon the public opinion, approach nearly to mathematicians, and, in their judgments concerning the merit of their own discoveries and observations, enjoy some degree of the same security and tranquillity.

The morals of those different classes of men of letters are, perhaps, sometimes somewhat affected by this very great difference in their situation with regard to the public.

Mathematicians and natural philosophers, from their independency upon the public opinion, have little temptation to form themselves into factions and cabals, either for the support of their own reputation, or for the depression of that of their rivals. They are almost always men of the most amiable simplicity of manners, who live in good harmony with one another, are the friends of one another's reputation, enter into no intrigue in order to secure the public applause, but are pleased when their works are approved of, without being either much vexed or very angry when they are neglected.

It is not always the same case with poets, or with those who value themselves upon what is called fine writing. They are very apt to divide themselves into a sort of literary faction ; each cabal being often avowedly, and almost always secretly, the mortal enemy of the reputation of every other, and employing all the mean arts of intrigue and solicitation to pre-occupy the public opinion in favour of the works of its own members, and against those of its enemies and rivals. In France, Despreaux and Racine did not think it below them to set themselves at the head of a literary cabal, in order to depress the reputation, first of Quinault and Perreault, and afterwards of Fontenelle and La Motte, and even to treat the good La Fontaine with a species of most disrespectful kindness. In England, the amiable Mr. Addison did not think it unworthy of his gentle and modest character to set himself at the head of a little cabal of the same kind, in order to keep down the rising reputation of Mr. Pope. Mr. Fontenelle, in writing the lives and characters of the members of the academy of sciences, a society of mathematicians and natural philosophers, has frequent opportunities of celebrating the amiable simplicity of their manners ; a quality which, he observes, was so universal among them as to be characteristical, rather of that whole class of men of letters, than of any individual. Mr. D'Alembert, in writing the lives and characters of the members of the French Academy, a society of poets and fine writers, or of those who are supposed to be such, seems not to have had such frequent opportunities of making any remark of this kind, and no where pretends to represent this amiable quality as characteristical of that class of men of letters whom he celebrates.

Our uncertainty concerning our own merit, and our anxiety to think favourably of it, should together naturally enough make us desirous to know the opinion of other people concerning it ; to be more than ordinarily elevated when that opinion is favourable, and to be more than ordinarily mortified when it is otherwise : but they should not make us desirous either of obtaining the favourable, or of avoiding the unfavourable opinion, by intrigue and cabal. When a man has bribed all the judges, the most unanimous decision of the court, though it may gain him his law-suit, cannot give him any assurance that he was in the right : and had he carried on his law-suit merely to satisfy himself that he was in the right, he never would have bribed the judges. But though he wished to find himself in the right, he wished likewise to gain his law-suit ; and therefore he bribed the judges. If praise were of no consequence to us, but as a proof of our own praise-worthiness, we never should endeavour to obtain it by unfair means. But, though to wise men it is, at least in doubtful cases, of principal consequence upon this account ; it is likewise of some consequence upon its own account : and therefore (we cannot, indeed, upon such occasions, call them wise men), but men very much above the common level have sometimes attempted both to obtain praise, and to avoid blame, by very unfair means.

Praise and blame express what actually are, praise-worthiness and blame-worthiness what naturally ought to be, the sentiments of other people with regard to our character and conduct. The love of praise is the desire of obtaining the favourable sentiments of our brethren. The love of praise-worthiness is the desire of rendering ourselves the proper objects of those sentiments. So far those two principles resemble and are akin to one another. The like affinity and resemblance take place between dread of blame and that of blame-worthiness.

The man who desires to do, or who actually does, a praise-worthy action, may likewise desire the praise which is due to it, and sometimes, perhaps, more than is due to it. The two principles are in this case blended together. How far his conduct may have been influenced by the one, and how far by the other, may frequently be unknown even to himself. It must almost always be so to other people. They who are disposed to lessen the merit of his conduct, impute it chiefly or altogether to the mere love of praise, or to what they call mere vanity. They who are disposed to think more favourably of it, impute it chiefly or altogether to the love of praise-worthiness ; to the love of what is really honourable and noble in human conduct ; to the desire, not merely of obtaining, but of deserving the approbation and applause of his brethren. The imagination of the spectator throws upon it either the one colour or the other, according either to his habits of thinking, or to the favour or dislike which he may bear to the person whose conduct he is considering.

Some splenetic philosophers, in judging of human nature, have done as peevish individuals are apt to do in judging of the conduct of one another, and have imputed to the love of praise, or to what they call vanity, every action which ought to be ascribed to that of praise-worthiness. I shall hereafter have occasion to give an account of some of their systems, and shall not at present stop to examine them.

Very few men can be satisfied with their own private consciousness that they have attained those qualities, or performed those actions, which they admire and think praise-worthy in other people ; unless it is, at the same time, generally acknowledged that they possess the one, or have performed the other ; or, in other words, unless they have actually obtained that praise which they think due both to the one and to the other. In this respect, however, men differ considerably from one another. Some seem indifferent about the praise, when, in their own minds, they are perfectly satisfied that they have attained the praise-worthiness. Others appear much less anxious about the praise-worthiness than about the praise.

No man can be completely, or even tolerably satisfied, with having avoided every thing blame-worthy in his conduct, unless he has like-wise avoided the blame or the reproach. A wise man may frequently neglect praise, even when he has best deserved it ; but, in all matters of serious consequence, he will most carefully endeavour so to regulate his conduct as to avoid, not only blame-worthiness, but, as much as possible, every probable imputation of blame. He will never, indeed, avoid blame by doing any thing which he judges blame-worthy; by omitting any part of his duty, or by neglecting any opportunity of doing any thing which he judges to be really and greatly praise-worthy. But, with these modifications, he will most anxiously and carefully avoid it. To show much anxiety about praise, even for praise-worthy actions, is seldom a mark of great wisdom, but generally of some degree of weak-ness. But, in being anxious to avoid the shadow of blame or reproach, there may be no weakness, but frequently there may be the most praise-worthy prudence.

' Many people,' says Cicero, ' despise glory, who are yet most ' severely mortified by unjust reproach ; and that most inconsistently.' This inconsistency, however, seems to be founded in the unalterable principles of human nature.

The all-wise Author of Nature has, in this manner, taught man to respect the sentiments and judgments of his brethren ; to be more or less pleased when they approve of his conduct, and to be more or less hurt when they disapprove of it. He has made man, if I may say so, the immediate judge of mankind ; and has, in this respect, as in many others, created him after his own image, and appointed him his vice-gerent upon earth, to superintend the behaviour of his brethren. They are taught by nature, to acknowledge that power and jurisdiction which

has thus been conferred upon him, to be more or less humbled and
mortified when they have incurred his censure, and to be more or less
elated when they have obtained his applause.

But though man has, in this manner, been rendered the immediate
judge of mankind, he has been rendered so only in the first instance ;
and an appeal lies from his sentence to a much higher tribunal, to
the tribunal of their own consciences, to that of the supposed impartial and well-informed spectator, to that of the man within the
breast, the great judge and arbiter of their conduct. The jurisdictions
of those two tribunals are founded upon principles which, though in
some respects resembling and akin, are, however, in reality different and
distinct. The jurisdiction of the man without, is founded altogether in
the desire of actual praise, and in the aversion to actual blame. The
jurisdiction of the man within, is founded altogether in the desire of
praise-worthiness, and in the aversion to blame-worthiness ; in the
desire of possessing those qualities, and performing those actions,
which we love and admire in other people ; and in the dread of possessing those qualities, and performing those actions, which we hate
and despise in other people. If the man without should applaud us, either
for actions which we have not performed, or for motives which had no
influence upon us ; the man within can immediately humble that pride
and elevation of mind which such groundless acclamations might otherwise occasion, by telling us, that as we know that we do not deserve
them, we render ourselves despicable by accepting them. If, on the
contrary, the man without should reproach us, either for actions which
we never performed, or for motives which had no influence upon those
which we may have performed, the man within may immediately
correct this false judgment, and assure us, that we are by no means
the proper objects of that censure which has so unjustly been bestowed upon us. But in this and in some other cases, the man within seems sometimes, as it were, astonished and confounded by the
vehemence and clamour of the man without. The violence and loudness with which blame is sometimes poured out upon us, seems to
stupify and benumb our natural sense of praise-worthiness and blame-
worthiness ; and the judgments of the man within, though not, perhaps,
absolutely altered or perverted, are, however, so much shaken in the
steadiness and firmness of their decision, that their natural effect, in
securing the tranquillity of the mind, is frequently in a great measure
destroyed. We scarce dare to absolve ourselves, when all our brethren
appear loudly to condemn us. The supposed impartial spectator of
our conduct seems to give his opinion in our favour with fear and hesitation ; when that of all the real spectators, when that of all those with
whose eyes and from whose station he endeavours to consider it, is
unanimously and violently against us. In such cases, this demigod
within the breast appears, like the demigods of the poets, though

partly of immortal, yet partly too of mortal extraction. When his judgments are steadily and firmly directed by the sense of praise-worthiness and blame-worthiness, he seems to act suitably to his divine extraction : but when he suffers himself to be astonished and confounded by the judgments of ignorant and weak man, he discovers his connexion with mortality, and appears to act suitably, rather to the human, than to the divine, part of his origin.

In such cases, the only effectual consolation of humbled and afflicted man lies in an appeal to a still higher tribunal, to that of the all-seeing Judge of the world, whose eye can never be deceived, and whose judgments can never be perverted. A firm confidence in the unerring rectitude of this great tribunal, before which his innocence is in due time to be declared, and his virtue to be finally rewarded, can alone support him under the weakness and despondency of his own mind, under the perturbation and astonishment of the man within the breast, whom nature has set up as, in this life, the great guardian, not only of his innocence, but of his tranquillity. Our happiness in this life is thus, upon many occasions, dependent upon the humble hope and expectation of a life to come: a hope and expectation deeply rooted in human nature; which can alone support its lofty ideas of its own dignity; can alone illumine the dreary prospect of its continually approaching mortality, and maintain its cheerfulness under all the heaviest calamities to which, from the disorders of this life, it may sometimes be exposed. That there is a world to come, where exact justice will be done to every man, where every man will be ranked with those who, in the moral and intellectual qualities, are really his equals; where the owner of those humble talents and virtues which, from being depressed by fortunes, had, in this life, no opportunity of displaying themselves; which were unknown, not only to the public, but which he himself could scarce be sure that he possessed, and for which even the man within the breast could scarce venture to afford him any distinct and clear testimony; where that modest, silent, and unknown merit, will be placed upon a level, and sometimes above those who, in this world, had enjoyed the highest reputation, and who, from the advantage of their situation, had been enabled to perform the most splendid and dazzling actions; is a doctrine, in every respect so venerable, so comfortable to the weakness, so flattering to the grandeur of human nature, that the virtuous man who has the misfortune to doubt of it, cannot possibly avoid wishing most earnestly and anxiously to believe it. It could never have been exposed to the derision of the scoffer, had not the distribution of rewards and punishments, which some of its most zealous assertors have taught us was to be made in that world to come, been too frequently in direct opposition to all our moral sentiments. .

That the assiduous courtier is often more favoured than the faithful and active servant; that attendance and adulation are often shorter and surer roads to preferment than merit or service; and that a campaign at Versailles or St. James's is often worth two either in Germany or Flanders, is a complaint which we have all heard from many a venerable, but discontented, old officer.   But what is considered as the greatest reproach even to the weakness of earthly sovereigns, has been ascribed, as an act of justice, to divine perfection; and the duties of devotion, the public and private worship of the Deity, have been represented, even by men of virtue and abilities, as the sole virtues which can either entitle to reward or exempt from punishment in the life to come.   They were the virtues perhaps, most suitable to their station, and in which they themselves chiefly excelled; and we are all naturally disposed to over-rate the excellencies of our own characters.   In the discourse which the eloquent and philosophical Massillon pronounced, on giving his benediction to the standards of the regiment of Catinat, there is the following address to the officers: 'What is most deplorable 'in your situation, gentlemen, is, that in a life hard and painful, in 'which the services and the duties sometimes go beyond the rigour and 'severity of the most austere cloisters; you suffer always in vain for 'the life to come, and frequently even for this life.   Alas! the solitary 'monk in his cell, obliged to mortify the flesh and to subject it to the 'spirit, is supported by the hope of an assured recompense, and by the 'secret unction of that grace which softens the yoke of the Lord.   But 'you, on the bed of death, can you dare to represent to Him your 'fatigues and the daily hardships of your employment? can you dare 'to solicit Him for any recompense? and in all the exertions that you 'have made, in all the violences that you have done to yourselves, what 'is there that He ought to place to His own account?   The best days 'of your life, however, have been sacrificed to your profession, and ten 'years' service has more worn out your body, than would, perhaps, have 'done a whole life of repentance and mortification.   Alas! my brother, 'one single day of those sufferings, consecrated to the Lord, would, 'perhaps, have obtained you an eternal happiness.   One single action, 'painful to nature, and offered up to Him, would, perhaps, have secured 'to you the inheritance of the saints.   And you have done all this, and 'in vain, for this world.'

To compare, in this manner, the futile mortifications of a monastery, to the ennobling hardships and hazards of war; to suppose that one day, or one hour, employed in the former should, in the eye of the great Judge of the world, have more merit than a whole life spent honourably in the latter, is surely contrary to all our moral sentiments: to all the principles by which nature has taught us to regulate our contempt or admiration.   It is this spirit, however, which, while it has reserved the celestial regions for monks and friars, or for those whose conduct and conversation resembled those of monks and friars, has condemned to the infernal all the heroes, all the statesmen and lawgivers, all the poets and philosophers of former ages; all those who have invented, improved, or excelled in the arts, which contribute to the subsistence, to the conveniency, or to the ornament of human life; all the great protectors, instructors, and benefactors of mankind; all those to whom our natural sense of praise-worthiness forces us to ascribe the highest merit and most exalted virtue. Can we wonder that so strange an application of this most respectable doctrine should sometimes have exposed it to contempt and derision; with those at least who had themselves, perhaps, no great taste or turn for the devout and contemplative virtues?*

CHAP. III.—*Of the Influence and Authority of Conscience.*

BUT though the approbation of his own conscience can scarce, upon some extraordinary occasions, content the weakness of man; though the testimony of the supposed impartial spectator of the great inmate of the breast, cannot always alone support him; yet the influence and authority of this principle is, upon all occasions, very great; and it is only by consulting this judge within, that we can ever see what relates to ourselves in its proper shape and dimensions; or that we can ever make any proper comparison between our own interests and those of other people.

As to the eye of the body, objects appear great or small, not so much according to their real dimensions, as according to the nearness or distance of their situation; so do they likewise to what may be called the natural eye of the mind: and we remedy the defects of both these organs pretty much in the same manner. In my present situation an immense landscape of lawns, and woods, and distant mountains, seems to do no more than cover the little window which I write by, and to be out of all proportion less than the chamber in which I am sitting. I can form a just comparison between those great objects and the little objects around me, in no other way, than by transporting myself, at least in fancy, to a different station, from whence I can survey both at nearly equal distances, and thereby form some judgment of their real proportions. Habit and experience have taught me to do this so easily and so readily, that I am scarce sensible that I do it; and a man must be, in some measure, acquainted with the philosophy of vision, before he can be thoroughly convinced, how little those distant objects would appear to the eye, if the imagination, from a knowledge of their real magnitudes, did not swell and dilate them.

In the same manner, to the selfish and original passions of human nature, the loss or gain of a very small interest of our own, appears to be of vastly more importance, excites a much more passionate joy or

* Vous y grillez sage et docte Platon,
  Divin Homere, eloquent Ciceron, etc.—*See* Voltaire.

sorrow, a much more ardent desire or aversion, than the greatest concern of another with whom we have no particular connexion. His interests, as long as they are surveyed from this station, can never be put into the balance with our own, can never restrain us from doing whatever may tend to promote our own, how ruinous so ever to him. Before we can make any proper comparison of those opposite interests, we must change our position. We must view them, neither from our own place nor yet from his, neither with our own eyes nor yet with his, but from the place and with the eyes of a third person, who has no particular connexion with either, and who judges with impartiality between us. Here, too, habit and experience have taught us to do this so easily and so readily, that we are scarce sensible that we do it; and it requires, in this case too, some degree of reflection, and even of philosophy, to convince us, how little interest we should take in the greatest concerns of our neighbour, how little we should be affected by whatever relates to him, if the sense of propriety and justice did not correct the otherwise natural inequality of our sentiments.

Let us suppose that the great empire of China, with all its myriads of inhabitants, was suddenly swallowed up by an earthquake, and let us consider how a man of humanity in Europe, who had no sort of connexion with that part of the world, would be affected upon receiving intelligence of this dreadful calamity. He would, I imagine, first of all, express very strongly his sorrow for the misfortune of that unhappy people, he would make many melancholy reflections upon the precariousness of human life, and the vanity of all the labours of man, which could thus be annihilated in a moment. He would, too, perhaps, if he was a man of speculation, enter into many reasonings concerning the effects which this disaster might produce upon the commerce of Europe, and the trade and business of the world in general. And when all this fine philosophy was over, when all these humane sentiments had been once fairly expressed, he would pursue his business or his pleasure, take his repose or his diversion, with the same ease and tranquillity, as if no such accident had happened. The most frivolous disaster which could befal himself would occasion a more real disturbance. If he was to lose his little finger to-morrow, he would not sleep to-night; but, provided he never saw them, he will snore with the most profound security over the ruin of a hundred millions of his brethren, and the destruction of that immense multitude seems plainly an object less interesting to him, than this paltry misfortune of his own. To prevent, therefore, this paltry misfortune to himself, would a man of humanity be willing to sacrifice the lives of a hundred millions of his brethren, provided he had never seen them? Human nature startles with horror at the thought, and the world, in its greatest depravity and corruption, never produced such a villain as could be capable of entertaining it. But what makes this difference? When our passive feelings are almost always so sordid and so selfish, how comes it that our active principles should often be so generous and so noble? When we are always so much more deeply affected by whatever concerns ourselves than by whatever concerns other men, what is it which prompts the generous, upon all occasions, and the mean upon many, to sacrifice their own interests to the greater interests of others? It is not the soft power of humanity, it is not that feeble spark of benevolence which Nature has lighted up in the human heart, that is thus capable of counteracting the strongest impulses of self-love. It is a stronger power, a more forcible motive, which exerts itself upon such occasions. It is reason, principle, conscience, the inhabitant of the breast, the man within, the great judge and arbiter of our conduct. It is he who, whenever we are about to act so as to affect the happiness of others, calls to us, with a voice capable of astonishing the most presumptuous of our passions, that we are but one of the multitude, in no respect better than any other in it; and when we prefer ourselves so shamefully and so blindly to others, we become the proper objects of resentment, abhorrence, and execration. It is from him only that we learn the real littleness of ourselves, and of whatever relates to ourselves, and the natural misrepresentations of self-love can be corrected only by the eye of this impartial spectator. It is he who shows us the propriety of generosity and the deformity of injustice; the propriety of resigning the greatest interests of our own, for the yet greater interests of others, and the deformity of doing the smallest injury to another, in order to obtain the greatest benefit to ourselves. It is not the love of our neighbour, it is not the love of mankind, which upon many occasions prompts us to the practice of those divine virtues. It is a stronger love, a more powerful affection, which generally takes place upon such occasions; the love of what is honourable and noble, of the grandeur, and dignity, and superiority of our own characters.

When the happiness or misery of others depends in any respect upon our conduct, we dare not, as self-love might suggest to us, prefer the interest of one to that of many. The man within immediately calls to us, that we value ourselves too much and other people too little, and that, by doing so, we render ourselves the proper object of the contempt and indignation of our brethren. Neither is this sentiment confined to men of extraordinary magnanimity and virtue. It is deeply impressed upon every tolerably good soldier, who feels that he would become the scorn of his companions, if he could be supposed capable of shrinking from danger, or of hesitating, either to expose or to throw away his life, when the good of the service required it.

One individual must never prefer himself so much even to any other individual, as to hurt or injure that other, in order to benefit himself, though the benefit to the one should be much greater than the hurt or injury to the other.   The poor man must neither defraud nor steal from the rich, though the acquisition might be much more beneficial to the one than the loss could be hurtful to the other.   The man within immediately calls to him in this case too, that he is no better than his neighbour, and that by his unjust preference he renders himself the proper object of the contempt and indignation of mankind; as well as of the punishment which that contempt and indignation must naturally dispose them to inflict, for having thus violated one of those sacred rules, upon the tolerable observation of which depend the whole security and peace of human society.   There is no commonly honest man who does not more dread the inward disgrace of such an action, the indelible stain which it would for ever stamp upon his own mind, than the greatest external calamity which, without any fault of his own, could possibly befal him; and who does not inwardly feel the truth of that great stoical maxim, that for one man to deprive another unjustly of any thing, or unjustly to promote his own advantage by the loss or disadvantage of another, is more contrary to nature, than death, than poverty, than pain, than all the misfortunes which can affect him, either in his body, or in his external circumstances.

When the happiness or misery of others, indeed, in no respect depends upon our conduct, when our interests are altogether separated and detached from theirs, so that there is neither connexion nor competition between them, we do not always think it so necessary to restrain, either our natural and, perhaps, improper anxiety about our own affairs, or our natural and, perhaps, equally improper indifference about those of other men.   The most vulgar education teaches us to act, upon all important occasions, with some sort of impartiality between ourselves and others, and even the ordinary commerce of the world is capable of adjusting our active principles to some degree of propriety.   But it is the most artificial and refined education only, it has been said, which can correct the inequalities of our passive feelings; and we must for this purpose, it has been pretended, have recourse to the severest, as well as to the profoundest philosophy.

Two different sets of philosophers have attempted to teach us this hardest of all the lessons of morality.   One set have laboured to increase our sensibility to the interests of others; another, to diminish that to our own.   The first would have us feel for others as we naturally feel for ourselves.   The second would have us feel for ourselves as we naturally feel for others.   Both, perhaps, have carried their doctrines a good deal beyond the just standard of nature and propriety.

The first are those whining and melancholy moralists, who are perpetually reproaching us with our happiness, while so many of our brethren are in misery,[1] who regard as impious the natural joy of

---

[1] " Ah ! little think the gay licentious proud," &c. See Thomson's Seasons, Winter. See also Pascal.

prosperity, which does not think of the many wretches that are at every instant labouring under all sorts of calamities, in the languor of poverty, in the agony of disease, in the horrors of death, under the insults and oppressions of their enemies. Commiseration for those miseries which we never saw, which we never heard of, but which we may be assured are at all times infesting such numbers of our fellow-creatures, ought, they think, to damp the pleasures of the fortunate, and to render a certain melancholy dejection habitual to all men. But first of all, this extreme sympathy with misfortunes which we know nothing about, seems altogether absurd and unreasonable. Take the whole earth at an average, for one man who suffers pain or misery, you will find twenty in prosperity and joy, or at least in tolerable circumstances. No reason, surely, can be assigned why we should rather weep with the one than rejoice with the twenty. This artificial commiseration, besides, is not only absurd, but seems altogether unattainable; and those who affect this character have commonly nothing but a certain affected and sentimental sadness, which, without reaching the heart, serves only to render the countenance and conversation impertinently dismal and disagreeable. And last of all, this disposition of mind, though it could be attained, would be perfectly useless, and could serve no other purpose than to render miserable the person who possessed it. Whatever interest we take in the fortune of those with whom we have no acquaintance or connexion, and who are placed altogether out of the sphere of our activity, can produce only anxiety to ourselves without any manner of advantage to them. To what purpose should we trouble ourselves about the world in the moon? All men, even those at the greatest distance, are no doubt entitled to our good wishes, and our good wishes we naturally give them. But if, notwithstanding, they should be unfortunate, to give ourselves any anxiety upon that account, seems to be no part of our duty. That we should be but little interested, therefore, in the fortune of those whom we can neither serve nor hurt, and who are in every respect so very remote from us, seems wisely ordered by nature; and if it were possible to alter in this respect the original constitution of our frame, we could yet gain nothing by the change.

It is never objected to us that we have too little fellow-feeling with the joy of success. Wherever envy does not prevent it, the favour which we bear to prosperity is rather apt to be too great; and the same moralists who blame us for want of sufficient sympathy with the miserable, reproach us for the levity with which we are too apt to admire and almost to worship the fortunate and the powerful.

Among the moralists who endeavour to correct the natural inequality of our passive feelings by diminishing our sensibility to what peculiarly concerns ourselves, we may count all the ancient sects of philosophers, but particularly the ancient Stoics. Man, according to the Stoics, ought to regard himself, not as something separated and detached, but as a citizen of the world, a member of the vast commonwealth of nature. To the interest of this great community, he ought at all times to be willing that his own little interest should be sacrificed. Whatever concerns himself, ought to affect him no more than whatever concerns any other equally important part of this immense system. We should view ourselves, not in the light in which our own selfish passions are apt to place us, but in the light in which any other citizen of the world would view us. What befalls ourselves we should regard as what befalls our neighbour, or, what comes to the same thing, as our neighbour regards what befalls us. 'When our neighbour,' says Epictetus, 'loses his wife, or his son, there is nobody who is not 'sensible that this is a human calamity, a natural event altogether 'according to the ordinary course of things; but when the same thing 'happens to ourselves, then we cry out, as if we had suffered the most 'dreadful misfortune. We ought, however, to remember how we were 'affected when this accident happened to another, and such as we 'were in his case, such ought we to be in our own.'

Those private misfortunes, for which our feelings are apt to go beyond the bounds of propriety, are of two different kinds. They are either such as affect us only indirectly, by affecting, in the first place, some other persons who are particularly dear to us; such as our parents, our children, our brothers and sisters, our intimate friends; or they are such as affect ourselves immediately and directly, either in our body, in our fortune, or in our reputation; such as pain, sickness, approaching death, poverty, disgrace, etc.

In misfortunes of the first kind, our emotions may, no doubt, go very much beyond what exact propriety will admit of; but they may likewise fall short of it, and they frequently do so. The man who should feel no more for the death or distress of his own father, or son, than for those of any other man's father or son, would appear neither a good son nor a good father. Such unnatural indifference, far from exciting our applause, would incur our highest disapprobation. Of these domestic affections, however, some are most apt to offend by their excess, and others by their defect. Nature, for the wisest purposes, has rendered, in most men, perhaps in all men, parental tenderness a much stronger affection than filial piety. The continuance and propagation of the species depend altogether upon the former, and not upon the latter. In ordinary cases, the existence and preservation of the child depend altogether upon the care of the parents. Those of the parents seldom depend upon that of the child. Nature, therefore, has rendered the former affection so strong, that it generally requires not to be excited, but to be moderated; and moralists seldom endeavour to teach us how to indulge, but generally how to restrain our fondness, our excessive attachment, the unjust preference which we

9 *

are disposed to give to our own children above those of other people. They exhort us, on the contrary, to an affectionate attention to our parents, and to make a proper return to them, in their old age, for the kindness which they had shown to us in our infancy and youth. In the Decalogue we are commanded to honour our fathers and mothers. No mention is made of the love of our children. Nature has sufficiently prepared us for the performance of this latter duty. Men are seldom accused of affecting to be fonder of their children than they really are. They have sometimes been suspected of displaying their piety to their parents with too much ostentation. The ostentatious sorrow of widows has, for a like reason, been suspected of insincerity. We should respect, could we believe it sincere, even the excess of such kind affections; and though we might not perfectly approve, we should not severely condemn it. That it appears praise-worthy, at least in the eyes of those who affect it, the very affectation is a proof.

Even the excess of those kind affections which are most apt to offend by their excess, though it may appear blamable, never appears odious. We blame the excessive fondness and anxiety of a parent, as something which may, in the end, prove hurtful to the child, and which, in the mean time, is excessively inconvenient to the parent; but we easily pardon it, and never regard it with hatred and detestation. But the defect of this usually excessive affection appears always peculiarly odious. The man who appears to feel nothing for his own children, but who treats them upon all occasions with unmerited severity and harshness, seems of all brutes the most detestable. The sense of propriety, so far from requiring us to eradicate altogether that extra. ordinary sensibility which we naturally feel for the misfortunes of our nearest connections, is always much more offended by the defect, than it ever is by the excess of that sensibility. The stoical apathy is, in such cases, never agreeable, and all the metaphysical sophism by which it is supported can seldom serve any other purpose than to blow up the hard insensibility of a coxcomb to ten times its native impertinence. The poets and romance writers, who best paint the refinements and delicacies of love and friendship, and of all other private and domestic affections, Racine and Voltaire; Richardson, Maurivaux, and Ricco-boni; are, in such cases, much better instructors than the philosophers Zeno, Chrysippus, or Epictetus.

That moderated sensibility to the misfortunes of others, which does not disqualify us for the performance of any duty; the melancholy and affectionate remembrance of our departed friends; *the pang*, as Gray says, *to secret sorrow dear;* are by no means undelicious sensations. Though they outwardly wear the features of pain and grief, they are all inwardly stamped with the ennobling characters of virtue and of self-approbation.

It is otherwise in the misfortunes which affect ourselves immediately and directly, either in our body, in our fortune, or in our reputation. The sense of propriety is much more apt to be offended by the excess, than by the defect of our sensibility, and there are but few cases in which we can approach too near to the stoical apathy and indifference.

That we have very little fellow-feeling with any of the passions which take their origin from the body, has already been observed. That pain which is occasioned by an evident cause; such as, the cutting or tearing of the flesh; is, perhaps, the affection of the body with which the spectator feels the most lively sympathy. The approaching death of his neighbour, too, seldom fails to affect him a good deal. In both cases, however, he feels so very little in comparison of what the person principally concerned feels, that the latter can scarce ever offend the former by appearing to suffer with too much ease.

The mere want of fortune, mere poverty, excites little compassion. Its complaints are too apt to be the objects rather of contempt than of fellow-feeling. We despise a beggar; and, though his importunities may extort an alms from us, he is scarce ever the object of any serious commiseration. The fall from riches to poverty, as it commonly occasions the most real distress to the sufferer, so it seldom fails to excite the most sincere commiseration in the spectator. Though, in the present state of society, this misfortune can seldom happen without some misconduct, and some very considerable misconduct too, in the sufferer; yet he is almost always so much pitied that he is scarce ever allowed to fall into the lowest state of poverty; but by the means of his friends, frequently by the indulgence of those very creditors who have much reason to complain of his imprudence, is almost always supported in some degree of decent, though humble, mediocrity. To persons under such misfortunes, we could, perhaps, easily pardon some degree of weakness; but at the same time, they who carry the firmest countenance, who accommodate themselves with the greatest ease to their new situation, who seem to feel no humiliation from the change, but to rest their rank in the society, not upon their fortune, but upon their character and conduct, are always the most approved of, and command our highest and most affectionate admiration.

As, of all the external misfortunes which can affect an innocent man immediately and directly, the undeserved loss of reputation is certainly the greatest; so a considerable degree of sensibility to whatever can bring on so great a calamity, does not always appear ungraceful or disagreeable. We often esteem a young man the more, when he resents, though with some degree of violence, any unjust reproach that may have been thrown upon his character or his honour. The affliction of an innocent young lady, on account of the groundless surmises which may have been circulated concerning her conduct, appears often perfectly amiable. Persons of an advanced age, whom long experience of the folly and injustice of the world has taught to pay little regard, either to its censure or to its applause, neglect and despise obloquy, and do not even deign to honour its futile authors with any serious resentment. This indifference, which is founded altogether on a firm confidence in their own well-tried and well-established characters, would be disagreeable in young people, who neither can nor ought to have any such confidence. It might in them be supposed to forebode, in their advancing years, a most improper insensibility to real honour and infamy of character.

In all other private misfortunes which affect ourselves immediately and directly, we can very seldom offend by appearing to be too little affected. We frequently remember our sensibility to the misfortunes of others with pleasure and satisfaction. We can seldom remember that to our own, without some degree of shame and humiliation.

If we examine the different shades and gradations of weakness and self-command, as we meet with them in common life, we shall very easily satisfy ourselves that this control of our passive feeling must be acquired, not from the abstruse syllogisms of a quibbling dialectic, but from that great discipline which Nature has established for the acquisition of this and of every other virtue; a regard to the sentiments of the real or supposed spectator of our conduct.

A very young child has no self-command; but, whatever are its emotions, whether fear, or grief, or anger, it endeavours always, by the violence of his outcries, to alarm, as much as it can, the attention of its nurse or of its parents. While it remains under the custody of such partial protectors, its anger is the first and, perhaps, the only passion which it is taught to moderate. By noise and threatening they are, for their own ease, often obliged to frighten it into good temper; and the passion which incites it to attack, is restrained by that which teaches it to attend to its own safety. When it is old enough to go to school, or to mix with its equals, it soon finds that they have no such indulgent partiality. It naturally wishes to gain their favour, and to avoid their hatred or contempt. Regard even to its own safety teaches it to do so; and it soon finds that it can do so in no other way than by moderating not only its anger, but all its other passions, to the degree which its play-fellows and companions are likely to be pleased with. It thus enters into the great school of self-command, it studies to be more and more master of itself, and begins to exercise over its own feelings a discipline which the practice of the longest life is very seldom sufficient to bring to complete perfection.

In all private misfortunes, in pain, in sickness, in sorrow, the weakest man, when his friend, and still more when a stranger visits him, is immediately impressed with the view in which they are likely to look upon his situation. Their view calls off his attention from his own view; and his breast is, in some measure, becalmed the moment they come into his presence. This effect is produced instantaneously and,

as it were, mechanically ; but, with a weak man, it is not of long continuance. His own view of his situation immediately recurs upon him.
He abandons himself, as before, to sighs and tears and lamentations ;
and endeavours, like a child that has not yet gone to school, to produce
some sort of harmony between his own grief and the compassion of
the spectator, not by moderating the former, but by importunately
calling upon the latter.

With a man of a little more firmness, the effect is somewhat more
permanent. He endeavours, as much as he can, to fix his attention
upon the view which the company are likely to take of his situation.
He feels, at the same time, the esteem and approbation which they
naturally conceive for him when he thus preserves his tranquillity ; and,
though under the pressure of some recent and great calamity, appears
to feel for himself no more than what they really feel for him. He approves and applauds himself by sympathy with their approbation, and
the pleasure which he derives from this sentiment supports and enables
him more easily to continue this generous effort. In most cases he
avoids mentioning his own misfortune ; and his company, if they are
tolerably well bred, are careful to say nothing which can put him in
mind of it. He endeavours to entertain them, in his usual way, upon
indifferent subjects, or, if he feels himself strong enough to venture to
mention his misfortune, he endeavours to talk of it as, he thinks, they
are capable of talking of it, and even to feel it no further than they are
capable of feeling it. If he has not, however, been well inured to the
hard discipline of self-command, he soon grows weary of this restraint.
A long visit fatigues him ; and, towards the end of it, he is constantly
in danger of doing, what he never fails to do the moment it is over, of
abandoning himself to all the weakness of excessive sorrow. Modern
good manners, which are extremely indulgent to human weakness, for-
bid, for some time, the visits of strangers to persons under great family
distress, and permit those only of the nearest relations and most intimate friends. The presence of the latter, it is thought, will impose less
restraint than that of the former ; and the sufferers can more easily
accommodate themselves to the feelings of those, from whom they have
reason to expect a more indulgent sympathy. Secret enemies, who
fancy that they are not known to be such, are frequently fond of
making those charitable visits as early as the most intimate friends.
The weakest man in the world, in this case, endeavours to support his
manly countenance, and, from indignation and contempt of their malice
to behave with as much gaiety and ease as he can.

The man of real constancy and firmness, the wise and just man who
has been thoroughly bred in the great school of self-command, in the
bustle and business of the world, exposed, perhaps, to the violence and
injustice of faction, and to the hardships and hazards of war, maintains
this control of his passive feelings upon all occasions ; and whether in

solitude or in society, wears nearly the same countenance, and is affected very nearly in the same manner.   In success and in disappointment, in prosperity and in adversity, before friends and before enemies,
he has often been under the necessity of supporting this manhood. He
has never dared to forget for one moment the judgment which the impartial spectator would pass upon his sentiments and conduct. He has
never dared to suffer the man within his breast to be absent one
moment from his attention.   With the eyes of this great inmate he has
always been accustomed to regard whatever relates to himself.   This
habit has become perfectly familiar to him.   He has been in the constant practice, and, indeed, under the constant necessity, of modelling,
or of endeavouring to model, not only his outward conduct and behaviour, but, as much as he can, even his inward sentiments and feelings,
according to those of this awful and respectable judge.   He does not
merely affect the sentiments of the impartial spectator.   He really
adopts them.   He almost identifies himself with, he almost becomes
himself that impartial spectator, and scarce even feels but as that great
arbiter of his conduct directs him to feel.

The degree of the self-approbation with which every man, upon such
occasions, surveys his own conduct, is higher or lower, exactly in proportion to the degree of self-command which is necessary in order to
obtain that self-approbation.   Where little self-command is necessary,
little self-approbation is due.   The man who has only scratched his
finger, cannot much applaud himself, though he should immediately
appear to have forgot this paltry misfortune.   The man who has lost
his leg by a cannon shot, and who, the moment after, speaks and acts
with his usual coolness and tranquillity, as he exerts a much higher
degree of self-command, so he naturally feels a much higher degree of
self-approbation.   With most men, upon such an accident, their own
natural view of their own misfortune would force itself upon them with
such a vivacity and strength of colouring, as would entirely efface all
thought of every other view.   They would feel nothing, they could attend to nothing, but their own pain and their own fear ; and not only
the judgment of the ideal man within the breast, but that of the real
spectators who might happen to be present, would be entirely overlooked and disregarded.

The reward which Nature bestows upon good behaviour under misfortune, is thus exactly proportioned to the degree of that good behaviour.   The only compensation she could possibly make for the bitterness of pain and distress is thus, too, in equal degrees of good behaviour,
exactly proportioned to the degree of that pain and distress. ·In proportion to the degree of self-command which is necessary in order to
conquer our natural sensibility, the pleasure and pride of the conquest
are so much the greater ; and this pleasure and pride are so great that
no man can be altogether unhappy who completely enjoys them. Misery

and wretchedness can never enter the breast in which dwells complete self-satisfaction ; and though it may be too much, perhaps, to say, with the Stoics, that, under such an accident as that above mentioned, the happiness of a wise man is in every respect equal to what it could have been under any other circumstances ; yet it must be acknowledged, at least, that this complete enjoyment of his own self-applause, though it may not altogether extinguish, must certainly very much alleviate his sense of his own sufferings.

In such paroxysms of distress, if I may be allowed to call them so, the wisest and firmest man, in order to preserve his equanimity, is obliged, I imagine, to make a considerable, and even a painful exertion. His own natural feeling of his own distress, his own natural view of his own situation, presses hard upon him, and he cannot, without a very great effort, fix his attention upon that of the impartial spectator. Both views present themselves to him at the same time.   His sense of honour, his regard to his own dignity, directs him to fix his whole attention upon the one view.   His natural, his untaught, and undisciplined feelings, are continually calling it off to the other.   He does not, in this case, perfectly identify himself with the ideal man within the breast, he does not become himself the impartial spectator of his own conduct. The different views of both characters exist in his mind separate and distinct from one another, and each directing him to a behaviour different from that to which the other directs him.   When he follows that view which honour and dignity point out to him, Nature does not, indeed, leave him without a recompense.   He enjoys his own complete self-approbation, and the applause of every candid and impartial spectator.   By her unalterable laws, however, he still suffers ; and the recompense which she bestows, though very considerable, is not sufficient completely to compensate the sufferings which those laws inflict. Neither is it fit that it should.   If it did completely compensate them, he could, from self-interest, have no motive for avoiding an accident which must necessarily diminish his utility both to himself and to society ; and Nature, from her parental care of both, meant that he should anxiously avoid all such accidents.   He suffers, therefore; and though in the agony of the paroxysm, he maintains, not only the manhood of his countenance, but sedateness and sobriety of judgment, it requires his utmost and most fatiguing exertions to do so.

By the constitution of human nature, however, agony can never be permanent ; and, if he survives the paroxysm, he soon comes, without any effort, to enjoy his ordinary tranquillity.   A man with a wooden leg suffers, no doubt, and foresees that he must continue to suffer during the remainder of his life, a very considerable inconveniency. He soon comes to view it, however, exactly as every impartial spectator views it ; as an inconveniency under which he can enjoy all the ordinary pleasures both of solitude and of society.   He soon identifies himself with the ideal man within the breast, he soon becomes himself the impartial spectator of his own situation. He no longer weeps, he no longer laments, he no longer grieves over it, as a weak man may sometimes do in the beginning. The view of the impartial spectator becomes so perfectly habitual to him, that, without effort, without exertion, he never thinks of surveying his misfortune in any other view.

The never-failing certainty with which all men, sooner or later, accommodate themselves to whatever becomes their permanent situation, may, perhaps, induce us to think that the Stoics were, at least, thus far very nearly in the right; that, between one permanent situation and another, there was, with regard to real happiness, no essential difference: or that, if there were any difference, it was no more than just sufficient to render some of them the objects of simple choice or preference; but not of any earnest or anxious desire: and others, of simple rejection, as being fit to be set aside or avoided; but not of any earnest or anxious aversion. Happiness consists in tranquillity and enjoyment. Without tranquillity there can be no enjoyment; and where there is perfect tranquillity there is scarce any thing which is not capable of amusing. But in every permanent situation, where there is no expectation of change, the mind of every man, in a longer or shorter time, returns to its natural and usual state of tranquillity. In prosperity, after a certain time, it falls back to that state; in adversity, after a certain time, it rises up to it. In the confinement and solitude of the Bastile, after a certain time, the fashionable and frivolous Count de Lauzun recovered tranquillity enough to be capable of amusing himself with feeding a spider. A mind better furnished would, perhaps, have both sooner recovered its tranquillity, and sooner found, in its own thoughts, a much better amusement.

The great source of both the misery and disorders of human life, seems to arise from over-rating the difference between one permanent situation and another. Avarice over-rates the difference between poverty and riches: ambition, that between a private and a public station: vain-glory, that between obscurity and extensive reputation. The person under the influence of any of those extravagant passions, is not only miserable in his actual situation, but is often disposed to disturb the peace of society, in order to arrive at that which he so foolishly admires. The slightest observation, however, might satisfy him, that, in all the ordinary situations of human life, a well-disposed mind may be equally calm, equally cheerful, and equally contented. Some of those situations may, no doubt, deserve to be preferred to others: but none of them can deserve to be pursued with that passionate ardour which drives us to violate the rules either of prudence or of justice; or to corrupt the future tranquillity of our minds, either by shame from the remembrance of our own folly, or by remorse from the horror of our own injustice. Wherever prudence does not direct, wherever justice does not permit, the attempt to change our situation, the man who does attempt it, plays at the most unequal of all games of hazard, and stakes every thing against scarce any thing. What the favourite of the King of Epirus said to his master, may be applied to men in all the ordinary situations of human life. When the king had recounted to him, in their proper order, all the conquests which he proposed to make, and had come to the last of them; And what does your Majesty propose to do then? said the favourite:—I propose then, said the king, to enjoy myself with my friends, and endeavour to be good company over a bottle.—And what hinders your Majesty from doing so now? replied the favourite. In the most glittering and exalted situation that our idle fancy can hold out to us, the pleasures from which we propose to derive our real happiness, are almost always the same with those which, in our actual, though humble station, we have at all times at hand, and in our power. Except the frivolous pleasures of vanity and superiority, we may find, in the most humble station, where there is only personal liberty, every other which the most exalted can afford ; and the pleasures of vanity and superiority are seldom consistent with perfect tranquillity, the principle and foundation of all real and satisfactory enjoyment. Neither is it always certain that, in the splendid situation which we aim at, those real and satisfactory pleasures can be enjoyed with the same security as in the humble one which we are so very eager to abandon. Examine the records of history, recollect what has happened within the circle of your own experience, consider with attention what has been the conduct of almost all the greatly unfortunate, either in private or public life, whom you may have either read of, or heard of, or remember; and you will find that the misfortunes of by far the greater part of them have arisen from their not knowing when they were well, when it was proper for them to sit still and to be contented. The inscription upon the tomb-stone of the man who had endeavoured to mend a tolerable constitution by taking physic; *'I was well; I wished to be better; here I am;'* may generally be applied with great justness to the distress of disappointed avarice and ambition.

It may be thought a singular, but I believe it to be a just, observation, that, in the misfortunes which admit of some remedy, the greater part of men do not either so readily or so universally recover their natural and usual tranquillity, as in those which plainly admit of none. In misfortunes of the latter kind, it is chiefly in what may be called the paroxysm, or in the first attack, that we can discover any sensible difference between the sentiments and behaviour of the wise and those of the weak man. In the end, Time, the great and universal comforter, gradually composes the weak man to the same degree of tranquillity which a regard to his own dignity, which manhood teaches the wise man to assume in the beginning. The case of the man with the wooden leg is an obvious example of this. In the irreparable misfortunes occasioned by the death of children, or of friends and relations, even a wise man may for some time indulge himself in some degree of moderated sorrow. An affectionate, but weak woman, is often, upon such occasions, almost perfectly distracted. Time, however, in a longer or shorter period, never fails to compose the weakest woman to the same degree of tranquillity as the strongest man. In all the irreparable calamities which affect himself immediately and directly, a wise man endeavours, from the beginning, to anticipate and to enjoy before-hand, that tranquillity which he foresees the course of a few months, or a few years, will certainly restore to him in the end.

In the misfortunes for which the nature of things admits, or seems to admit, of a remedy, but in which the means of applying that remedy are not within the reach of the sufferer, his vain and fruitless attempts to restore himself to his former situation, his continual anxiety for their success, his repeated disappointments upon their miscarriage, are what chiefly hinder him from resuming his natural tranquillity, and frequently render miserable, during the whole of his life, a man to whom a greater misfortune, but which plainly admitted of no remedy, would not have given a fortnight's disturbance. In the fall from royal favour to disgrace, from power to insignificancy, from riches to poverty, from liberty to confinement, from strong health to some lingering, chronical, and perhaps incurable disease, the man who struggles the least, who most easily and readily acquiesces in the fortune which has fallen to him, very soon recovers his usual and natural tranquillity, and surveys the most disagreeable circumstances of his actual situation in the same light, or, perhaps, in a much less unfavourable light, than that in which the most indifferent spectator is disposed to survey them. Faction, intrigue, and cabal, disturb the quiet of the unfortunate statesman. Extravagant projects, visions of gold mines, interrupt the repose of the ruined bankrupt. The prisoner, who is continually plotting to escape from his confinement, cannot enjoy that careless security which even a prison can afford him. The medicines of the physician are often the greatest torment of the incurable patient. The monk who, in order to comfort Joanna of Castile, upon the death of her husband Philip, told her of a king, who, fourteen years after his decease, had been restored to life again, by the prayers of his afflicted queen, was not likely, by his legendary tale, to restore sedateness to the distempered mind of that unhappy princess. She endeavoured to repeat the same experiment in hopes of the same success; resisted for a long time the burial of her husband, soon after raised his body from the grave, attended it almost constantly herself, and watched, with all the impatient anxiety of frantic expectation, the happy moment when her wishes were to be gratified by the revival of her beloved Philip.*

* See Robertson's Charles V. vol. ii. pp. 14 and 15, first edit.

Our sensibility to the feelings of others, so far from being incon-sistent with the manhood of self-command, is the very principle upon which that manhood is founded.   The very same principle or instinct which, in the misfortune of our neighbour, prompts us to compassionate his sorrow ; in our own misfortune, prompts us to restrain the abject and miserable lamentations of our own sorrow.   The same principle or instinct which, in his prosperity and success, prompts us to congratu-late his joy ; in our own prosperity and success, prompts us to restrain the levity and intemperance of our own joy.   In both cases, the pro-priety of our own sentiments and feelings seems to be exactly in pro-portion to the vivacity and force with which we enter into and conceive his sentiments and feelings.

The man of the most perfect virtue, the man whom we naturally love and revere the most, is he who joins, to the most perfect command of his own original and selfish feelings, the most exquisite sensibility both to the original and sympathetic feelings of others.   The man who, to all the soft, the amiable, and the gentle virtues, joins all the great, the awful, and the respectable, must surely be the natural and proper object of our highest love and admiration.

The person best fitted by nature for acquiring the former of those two sets of virtues, is likewise necessarily best fitted for acquiring the latter.   The man who feels the most for the joys and sorrows of others, is best fitted for acquiring the most complete control of his own joys and sorrows.   The man of the most exquisite humanity, is naturally the most capable of acquiring the highest degree of self-command. He may not, however, always have acquired it ; and it very frequently happens that he has not.   He may have lived too much in ease and tranquillity.   He may have never been exposed to the violence of faction, or to the hardships and hazards of war.   He may have never experienced the insolence of his superiors, the jealous and malignant envy of his equals, or the pilfering injustice of his inferiors.   When, in an advanced age, some accidental change of fortune exposes him to all these, they all make too great an impression upon him.   He has the disposition which fits him for acquiring the most perfect self-command ; but he has never had the opportunity of acquiring it.   Exercise and practice have been wanting ; and without these no habit can ever be tolerably established.   Hardships, dangers, injuries, misfortunes, are the only masters under whom we can learn the exercise of this virtue. But these are all masters to whom nobody willingly puts himself to school.

The situations in which the gentle virtue of humanity can be most happily cultivated, are by no means the same with those which are best fitted for forming the austere virtue of self-command.   The man who is himself at ease can best attend to the distress of others.   The man who is himself exposed to hardships is most immediately called upon to attend to, and to control his own feelings. In the mild sun-shine of undisturbed tranquillity, in the calm retirement of undissipated and philosophical leisure, the soft virtue of humanity flourishes the most, and is capable of the highest improvement. But, in such situa-tions, the greatest and noblest exertions of self-command have little exercise. Under the boisterous and stormy sky of war and faction, of public tumult and confusion, the sturdy severity of self-command pros-pers the most, and can be the most successfully cultivated. But, in such situations, the strongest suggestions of humanity must frequently be stifled or neglected; and every such neglect necessarily tends to weaken the principle of humanity. As it may frequently be the duty of a soldier not to take, so it may sometimes be his duty not to give quarter; and the humanity of the man who has been several times under the necessity of submitting to this disagreeable duty, can scarce fail to suffer a considerable diminution. For his own ease, he is too apt to learn to make light of the misfortunes which he is so often under the necessity of occasioning; and the situations which call forth the noblest exertions of self-command, by imposing the necessity of violat-ing sometimes the property, and sometimes the life of our neighbour, always tend to diminish, and too often to extinguish altogether, that sacred regard to both, which is the foundation of justice and humanity. It is upon this account, that we so frequently find in the world men of great humanity who have little self-command, but who are indolent and irresolute, and easily disheartened, either by difficulty or danger, from the most honourable pursuits; and, on the contrary, men of the most perfect self-command, whom no difficulty can discourage, no danger appal, and who are at all times ready for the most daring and desperate enterprises, but who, at the same time, seem to be hardened against all sense either of justice or humanity.

In solitude, we are apt to feel too strongly whatever relates to our-selves: we are apt to over-rate the good offices we may have done, and the injuries we may have suffered: we are apt to be too much elated by our own good, and too much dejected by our own bad for-tune. The conversation of a friend brings us to a better, that of a stranger to a still better, temper. The man within the breast, the abstract and ideal spectator of our sentiments and conduct, requires often to be awakened and put in mind of his duty, by the presence of the real spectator: and it is always from that spectator, from whom we can expect the least sympathy and indulgence, that we are likely to learn the most complete lesson of self-command.

Are you in adversity? Do not mourn in the darkness of solitude, do not regulate your sorrow according to the indulgent sympathy of your intimate friends; return, as soon as possible, to the daylight of the world and of society. Live with strangers, with those who know nothing, or care nothing about your misfortune; do not even shun the

company of enemies; but give yourself the pleasure of mortifying their
malignant joy, by making them feel how little you are affected by your
calamity, and how much you are above it.

Are you in prosperity? Do not confine the enjoyment of your good
fortune to your own house, to the company of your own friends, perhaps of your flatterers, of those who build upon your fortune the hopes
of mending their own ; frequent those who are independent of you,
who can value you only for your character and conduct, and not for
your fortune.   Neither seek nor shun, neither intrude yourself into nor
run away from the society of those who were once your superiors, and
who may be hurt at finding you their equal, or, perhaps, even their
superior.   The impertinence of their pride may, perhaps, render their
company too disagreeable : but if it should not, be assured that it is
the best company you can possibly keep ; and if, by the simplicity of
your unassuming demeanour, you can gain their favour and kindness,
you may rest satisfied that you are modest enough, and that your head
has been in no respect turned by your good fortune.

The propriety of our moral sentiments is never so apt to be corrupted, as when the indulgent and partial spectator is at hand, while
the indifferent and impartial one is at a great distance.

Of the conduct of one independent nation towards another, neutral
nations are the only indifferent and impartial spectators. But they
are placed at so great a distance that they are almost quite out of
sight. When two nations are at variance, the citizen of each pays
little regard to the sentiments which foreign nations may entertain
concerning his conduct. His whole ambition is to obtain the approbation of his own fellow-citizens ; and as they are all animated by the
same hostile passions which animate himself, he can never please them
so much as by enraging and offending their enemies. The partial
spectator is at hand : the impartial one at a great distance. In war
and negotiation, therefore, the laws of justice are very seldom observed.
Truth and fair dealing are almost totally disregarded. Treaties are
violated ; and the violation, if some advantage is gained by it, sheds
scarce any dishonour upon the violator. The ambassador who dupes
the minister of a foreign nation, is admired and applauded. The just
man who disdains either to take or to give any advantage, but who
would think it less dishonourable to give than to take one ; the man
who, in all private transactions, would be the most beloved and the
most esteemed ; in those public transactions is regarded as a fool and
an idiot, who does not understand his business ; and he incurs always
the contempt, and sometimes even the detestation of his fellow-citizens.
In war, not only what are called the laws of nations, are frequently violated, without bringing (among his own fellow-citizens, whose judgments he only regards) any considerable dishonour upon the violator ;
but those laws themselves are, the greater part of them, laid down with

very little regard to the plainest and most obvious rules of justice. That the innocent, though they may have some connexion or dependency upon the guilty (which, perhaps, they themselves cannot help), should not, upon that account, suffer or be punished for the guilty, is one of the plainest and most obvious rules of justice. In the most unjust war, however, it is commonly the sovereign or the rulers only who are guilty. The subjects are almost always perfectly innocent. Whenever it suits the conveniency of a public enemy, however, the goods of the peaceable citizens are seized both at land and at sea; their lands are laid waste, their houses are burnt, and they themselves, if they presume to make any resistance, are murdered or led into captivity; and all this in the most perfect conformity to what are called the laws of nations.

The animosity of hostile factions, whether civil or ecclesiastical, is often still more furious than that of hostile nations; and their conduct towards one another is often still more atrocious. What may be called the laws of faction have often been laid down by grave authors with still less regard to the rules of justice than what are called the laws of nations. The most ferocious patriot never stated it as a serious question, Whether faith ought to be kept with public enemies?—Whether faith ought to be kept with rebels? Whether faith ought to be kept with heretics? are questions which have been often furiously agitated by celebrated doctors both civil and ecclesiastical. It is needless to observe, I presume, that both rebels and heretics are those unlucky persons, who, when things have come to a certain degree of violence, have the misfortune to be of the weaker party. In a nation distracted by faction, there are, no doubt, always a few, though commonly but a very few, who preserve their judgment untainted by the general contagion. They seldom amount to more than, here and there, a solitary individual, without any influence, excluded, by his own candour, from the confidence of either party, and who, though he may be one of the wisest, is necessarily, upon that very account, one of the most insignificant men in the society. All such people are held in contempt and derision, frequently in detestation, by the zealots of both parties.

A true party-man hates and despises candour; and, in reality, there is no vice which could so effectually disqualify him for the trade of a party-man as that single virtue. The real, revered, and impartial spectator, therefore, is, upon no occasion, at a greater distance than amidst the violence and rage of contending parties. To them, it may be said, that such a spectator scarce exists any where in the universe. Even to the great Judge of the universe, they impute all their own prejudices, and often view that Divine Being as animated by all their own vindictive and implacable passions. Of all the corrupters of moral sentiments, therefore, faction and fanaticism have always been by far the greatest.

Concerning the subject of self-command, I shall only observe further, that our admiration for the man who, under the heaviest and most un-expected misfortunes, continues to behave with fortitude and firmness, always supposes that his sensibility to those misfortunes is very great, and such as it requires a very great effort to conquer or command. The man who was altogether insensible to bodily pain, could deserve no applause from enduring the torture with the most perfect patience and equanimity. The man who had been created without the natural fear of death, could claim no merit from preserving his coolness and presence of mind in the midst of the most dreadful dangers. It is one of the extravagancies of Seneca, that the Stoical wise man was, in this respect, superior even to a god ; that the security of the god was altogether the benefit of nature, which had exempted him from suffering ; but that the security of the wise man was his own benefit, and derived altogether from himself and from his own exertions.

The sensibility of some men, however, to some of the objects which immediately affect themselves, is sometimes so strong as to render all self-command impossible. No sense of honour can control the fears of the man who is weak enough to faint, or to fall into convulsions, upon the approach of danger. Whether such weakness of nerves, as it has been called, may not, by gradual exercise and proper discipline, admit of some cure, may, perhaps, be doubtful. It seems certain that it ought never to be trusted or employed.

CHAP. IV.—*Of the Nature of Self-deceit, and of the Origin and Use of general Rules.*

IN order to pervert the rectitude of our own judgments concerning the propriety of our own conduct, it is not always necessary that the real and impartial spectator should be at a great distance. When he is at hand, when he is present, the violence and injustice of our own selfish passions are sometimes sufficient to induce the man within the breast to make a report very different from what the real circumstances of the case are capable of authorising.

There are two different occasions upon which we examine our own conduct, and endeavour to view it in the light in which the impartial spectator would view it : first, when we are about to act ; and secondly, after we have acted. Our views are apt to be very partial in both cases ; but they are apt to be most partial when it is of most import-ance that they should be otherwise.

When we are about to act, the eagerness of passion will seldom allow us to consider what we are doing, with the candour of an indifferent person. The violent emotions which at that time agitate us, discolour our views of things, even when we are endeavouring to place ourselves in the situation of another, and to regard the objects that interest us in the light in which they will naturally appear to him.   The fury of our own passions constantly calls us back to our own place, where every thing appears magnified and misrepresented by self-love.   Of the manner in which those objects would appear to another, of the view which he would take of them, we can obtain, if I may say so, but instantaneous glimpses, which vanish in a moment, and which, even while they last, are not altogether just.   We cannot even for that moment divest ourselves entirely of the heat and keenness with which our peculiar situation inspires us, nor consider what we are about to do with the complete impartiality of an equitable judge.   The passions, upon this account, as Father Malebranche says, all justify themselves, and seem reasonable and proportioned to their objects, as long as we continue to feel them.

When the action is over, indeed, and the passions which prompted it have subsided, we can enter more coolly into the sentiments of the indifferent spectator.   What before interested us is now become almost as indifferent to us as it always was to him, and we can now examine our own conduct with his candour and impartiality.   The man of to-day is no longer agitated by the same passions which distracted the man of yesterday : and when the paroxysm of emotion, in the same manner as when the paroxysm of distress, is fairly over, we can identify ourselves, as it were, with the ideal man within the breast, and, in our own character, view, as in the one case, our own situation, so in the other, our own conduct, with the severe eyes of the most impartial spectator.   But our judgments now are often of little importance in comparison of what they were before ; and can frequently produce nothing but vain regret and unavailing repentance ; without always securing us from the like errors in time to come.   It is seldom, however, that they are quite candid even in this case.   The opinion which we entertain of our own character depends entirely on our judgment concerning our past conduct.   It is so disagreeable to think ill of ourselves, that we often purposely turn away our view from those circumstances which might render that judgment unfavourable.   He is a bold surgeon, they say, whose hand does not tremble when he performs an operation upon his own person ; and he is often equally bold who does not hesitate to pull off the mysterious veil of self-delusion, which covers from his view the deformities of his own conduct.   Rather than see our own behaviour under so disagreeable an aspect, we too often, foolishly and weakly, endeavour to exasperate anew those unjust passions which had formerly misled us ; we endeavour by artifice to awaken our old hatreds, and irritate afresh our almost forgotten resentments : we even exert ourselves for this miserable purpose, and thus persevere in injustice, merely because we once were unjust, and because we are ashamed and afraid to see that we were so.

So partial are the views of mankind with regard to the propriety of their own conduct, both at the time of action and after it ; and so difficult is it for them to view it in the light in which any indifferent spectator would consider it. But if it was by a peculiar faculty, such as the moral sense is supposed to be, that they judged of their own conduct, if they were endued with a particular power of perception which distinguished the beauty or deformity of passions and affections ; as their passions would be more immediately exposed to the view of this faculty, it would judge more accurately concerning them, than concerning those of other men, of which it had only a more distant prospect.

This self-deceit, this fatal weakness of mankind, is the source of half the disorders of human life. If we saw ourselves in the light in which others see us, or in which they would see us if they knew all, a reformation would generally be unavoidable. We could not otherwise endure the sight exposed to us.

Nature, however, has not left this weakness, which is of so much importance, altogether without a remedy ; nor has she abandoned us entirely to the delusions of self-love. Our continual observations upon the conduct of others, insensibly lead us to form to ourselves certain general rules concerning what is fit and proper either to be done or to be avoided. Some of their actions shock all our natural sentiments. We hear every body about us express the like detestation against them. This still further confirms, and even exasperates our natural sense of their deformity. It satisfies us that we view them in the proper light, when we see other people view them in the same light. We resolve never to be guilty of the like, nor ever, upon any account, to render ourselves in this manner the objects of universal disapprobation. We thus naturally lay down to ourselves a general rule, that all such actions are to be avoided, as tending to render us odious, contemptible, or punishable, the objects of all those sentiments for which we have the greatest dread and aversion. Other actions, on the contrary, call forth our approbation, and we hear every body around us express the same favourable opinion concerning them. Every body is eager to honour and reward them. They excite all those sentiments for which we have by nature the strongest desire ; the love, the gratitude, the admiration of mankind. We become ambitious of performing the like ; and thus naturally lay down to ourselves a rule of another kind, that every opportunity of acting in this manner is to be sought after.

It is thus that the general rules of morality are formed. They are ultimately founded upon experience of what, in particular instances, our moral faculties, our natural sense of merit and propriety, approve, or disapprove of. We do not originally approve or condemn particular actions ; because, upon examination, they appear to be agreeable or inconsistent with a certain general rule. The general rule, on the contrary, is formed, by finding from experience, that all actions of a cer-

10 *

tain kind, or circumstanced in a certain manner, are approved or disapproved of. To the man who first saw an inhuman murder, committed
from avarice, envy, or unjust resentment, and upon one too that loved
and trusted the murderer, who beheld the last agonies of the dying person, who heard him, with his expiring breath, complain more of the
perfidy and ingratitude of his false friend, than of the violence which
had been done to him, there could be no occasion, in order to conceive
how horrible such an action was, that he should reflect, that one of the
most sacred rules of conduct was what prohibited the taking away the
life of an innocent person, that this was a plain violation of that rule,
and consequently a very blamable action. His detestation of this crime,
it is evident, would arise instantaneously and antecedent to his having
formed to himself any such general rule. The general rule, on the contrary, which he might afterwards form, would be founded upon the detestation which he felt necessarily arise in his own breast, at the thought
of this and every other particular action of the same kind.

When we read in history or romance, the account of actions either
of generosity or of baseness, the admiration which we conceive for the
one, and the contempt which we feel for the other, neither of them
arise from reflecting that there are certain general rules which declare
all actions of the one kind admirable, and all actions of the other contemptible. Those general rules, on the contrary, are all formed from
the experience we have had of the effects which actions of all different
kinds naturally produce upon us.

An amiable action, a respectable action, an horrid action, are all of
them actions which naturally excite for the person who performs them,
the love, the respect, or the horror of the spectator. The general rules
which determine what actions are, and what are not, the objects of
each of those sentiments, can be formed no other way than by observing what actions actually and in fact excite them.

When these general rules, indeed, have been formed, when they are
universally acknowledged and established, by the concurring sentiments of mankind, we frequently appeal to them as to the standards of
judgment, in debating concerning the degree of praise or blame that
is due to certain actions of a complicated and dubious nature. They
are upon these occasions commonly cited as the ultimate foundations
of what is just and unjust in human conduct; and this circumstance
seems to have misled several very eminent authors, to draw up their
systems in such a manner, as if they had supposed that the original
judgments of mankind with regard to right and wrong, were formed
like the decisions of a court of judicatory, by considering first the
general rule, and then, secondly, whether the particular action under
consideration fell properly within its comprehension.

Those general rules of conduct, when they have been fixed in our
mind by habitual reflection, are of great use in correcting the misrepre-

sentations of self-love concerning what is fit and proper to be done in our particular situation. The man of furious resentment, if he was to listen to the dictates of that passion, would perhaps regard the death of his enemy, as but a small compensation for the wrong, he imagines, he has received; which, however, may be no more than a very slight provocation. But his observations upon the conduct of others, have taught him how horrible all such sanguinary revenges appear. Unless his education has been very singular, he has laid it down to himself as an inviolable rule, to abstain from them upon all occasions. This rule preserves its authority with him, and renders him incapable of being guilty of such a violence. Yet the fury of his own temper may be such, that had this been the first time in which he considered such an action, he would undoubtedly have determined it to be quite just and proper, and what every impartial spectator would approve of. But that reverence for the rule which past experience has impressed upon him, checks the impetuosity of his passion, and helps him to correct the too partial views which self-love might otherwise suggest, of what was proper to be done in his situation. If he should allow himself to be so far transported by passion as to violate this rule, yet, even in this case, he cannot throw off altogether the awe and respect with which he has been accustomed to regard it. At the very time of acting, at the moment in which passion mounts the highest, he hesitates and trembles at the thought of what he is about to do: he is secretly conscious to himself that he is breaking through those measures of conduct which, in all his cool hours, he had resolved never to infringe, which he had never seen infringed by others without the highest disapprobation, and of which the infringement, his own mind forebodes, must soon render him the object of the same disagreeable sentiments. Before he can take the last fatal resolution, he is tormented with all the agonies of doubt and uncertainty; he is terrified at the thought of violating so sacred a rule, and at the same time is urged and goaded on by the fury of his desires to violate it. He changes his purpose every moment; sometimes he resolves to adhere to his principle, and not indulge a passion which may corrupt the remaining part of his life with the horrors of shame and repentance; and a momentary calm takes possession of his breast, from the prospect of that security and tranquillity which he will enjoy when he thus determines not to expose himself to the hazard of a contrary conduct. But immediately the passion rouses anew, and with fresh fury drives him on to commit what he had the instant before resolved to abstain from. Wearied and distracted with those continual irresolutions, he at length, from a sort of despair, makes the last fatal and irrecoverable step; but with that terror and amazement with which one flying from an enemy, throws himself over a precipice, where he is sure of meeting with more certain destruction than from any thing that pursues him from behind. Such are his sentiments even at the time of acting; though he is then, no doubt, less sensible of the impropriety of his own conduct than afterwards, when his passion being gratified and palled, he begins to view what he has done in the light in which others are apt to view it; and actually feels, what he had only foreseen very imperfectly before, the stings of remorse and repentance begin to agitate and torment him.

CHAP. V.—*Of the Influence and Authority of the general Rules of Morality, and that they are justly regarded as the Laws of the Deity.*

THE regard of those general rules of conduct, is what is properly called a sense of duty, a principle of the greatest consequence in human life, and the only principle by which the bulk of mankind are capable of directing their actions.   Many men behave very decently, and through the whole of their lives avoid any considerable degree of blame, who yet, perhaps, never felt the sentiment upon the propriety of which we found our approbation of their conduct, but acted merely from a regard to what they saw were the established rules of behaviour.   The man who has received great benefits from another person, may, by the natural coldness of his temper, feel but a very small degree of the sentiment of gratitude.   If he has been virtuously educated, however, he will often have been made to observe how odious those actions appear which denote a want of this sentiment, and how amiable the contrary.   Though his heart therefore is not warmed with any grateful affection, he will strive to act as if it was, and will endeavour to pay all those regards and attentions to his patron which the liveliest gratitude could suggest.   He will visit him regularly; he will behave to him respectfully; he will never talk of him but with expressions of the highest esteem, and of the many obligations which he owes to him.   And what is more, he will carefully embrace every opportunity of making a proper return for past services.   He may do all this too without any hypocrisy or blamable dissimulation, without any selfish intention of obtaining new favours, and without any design of imposing either upon his benefactor or the public.   The motive of his actions may be no other than a reverence for the established rule of duty, a serious and earnest desire of acting, in every respect, according to the law of gratitude.   A wife, in the same manner, may sometimes not feel that tender regard for her husband which is suitable to the relation that subsists between them. If she has been virtuously educated, however, she will endeavour to act as if she felt it, to be careful, officious, faithful, and sincere, and to be deficient in none of those attentions which the sentiment of conjugal affection could have prompted her to perform.   Such a friend, and such a wife, are neither of them, undoubtedly, the very best of their kinds; and though both of them may have the most serious and earnest desire to fulfil every part of their duty, yet they will fail in many nice and delicate regards, they will miss many opportunities of obliging, which they could never have overlooked if they had possessed the sentiment that is proper to their situation. Though not the very first of their kinds, however, they are perhaps the second; and if the regard to the general rules of conduct has been very strongly impressed upon them, neither of them will fail in any very essential part of their duty. None but those of the happiest mould are capable of suiting, with exact justness, their sentiments and behaviour to the smallest difference of situation, and of acting upon all occasions with the most delicate and accurate propriety. The coarse clay of which the bulk of mankind are formed, cannot be wrought up to such perfection. There is scarce any man, however, who by discipline, education, and example, may not be so impressed with a regard to general rules, as to act upon almost every occasion with tolerable decency, and through the whole of his life to avoid any considerable degree of blame.

Without this sacred regard to general rules, there is no man whose conduct can be much depended upon. It is this which constitutes the most essential difference between a man of principle and honour and a worthless fellow. The one adheres, on all occasions, steadily and resolutely to his maxims, and preserves through the whole of his life one even tenor of conduct. The other, acts variously and accidentally, as humour, inclination, or interest chance to be uppermost. Nay, such are the inequalities of humour to which all men are subject, that without this principle, the man who, in all his cool hours, had the most delicate sensibility to the propriety of conduct, might often be led to act absurdly upon the most frivolous occasions, and when it was scarce possible to assign any serious motive for his behaving in this manner. Your friend makes you a visit when you happen to be in a humour which makes it disagreeable to receive him: in your present mood his civility is very apt to appear an impertinent intrusion; and if you were to give way to the views of things which at this time occur, though civil in your temper, you would behave to him with coldness and contempt. What renders you incapable of such a rudeness, is nothing but a regard to the general rules of civility and hospitality, which prohibit it. That habitual reverence which your former experience has taught you for these, enables you to act, upon all such occasions, with nearly equal propriety, and hinders those inequalities of temper, to which all men are subject, from influencing your conduct in any very sensible degree. But if without regard to these general rules, even the duties of politeness, which are so easily observed, and which one can scarce have any serious motive to violate, would yet be so frequently violated, what would become of the duties of justice, of truth, of chastity, of fidelity, which it is often so difficult to observe, and which there may be so many strong motives to violate? But upon the tolerable observance of these duties depends the very existence of human society, which would crumble into nothing if mankind were not generally impressed with a reverence for those important rules of conduct.

This reverence is still further enhanced by an opinion which is first impressed by nature, and afterwards confirmed by reasoning and philosophy, that those important rules of morality are the commands and laws of the Deity, who will finally reward the obedient and punish the transgressors of their duty.

This opinion or apprehension, I say, seems first to be impressed by nature. Men are naturally led to ascribe to those mysterious beings, whatever they are, which happen, in any country to be the objects of religious fear, all their own sentiments and passions. They have no other, they can conceive no other to ascribe to them. Those unknown intelligences which they imagine but see not, must necessarily be formed with some sort of resemblance to those intelligences of which they have experience. During the ignorance and darkness of pagan superstition, mankind seem to have formed the ideas of their divinities with so little delicacy, that they ascribed to them, indiscriminately, all the passions of human nature, those not excepted which do the least honour to our species, such as lust, hunger, avarice, envy, revenge. They could not fail, therefore, to ascribe to those beings, for the excellence of whose nature they still conceived the highest admiration, those sentiments and qualities which are the great ornaments of humanity, and which seem to raise it to a resemblance of divine perfection, the love of virtue and beneficence, and the abhorrence of vice and injustice. The man who was injured, called upon Jupiter to be witness of the wrong that was done to him, and could not doubt, but that divine being would behold it with the same indignation which would animate the meanest of mankind, who looked on when injustice was committed. The man who did the injury, felt himself to be the proper object of the detestation and resentment of mankind ; and his natural fears led him to impute the same sentiments to those awful beings, whose presence he could not avoid, and whose power he could not resist. These natural hopes, and fears, and suspicions, were propagated by sympathy, and confirmed by education; and the gods were universally represented and believed to be the rewarders of humanity and mercy, and the avengers of perfidy and injustice. And thus religion, even in its rudest form, gave a sanction to the rules of morality, long before the age of artificial reasoning and philosophy. That the terrors of religion should thus enforce the natural sense of duty, was of too much importance to the happiness of mankind, for nature to leave it dependent upon the slowness and uncertainty of philosophical researches.

These researches, however, when they came to take place, confirmed those original anticipations of nature. Upon whatever we suppose that moral faculties are founded, whether upon a certain modification of reason, upon an original instinct, called a moral sense, or upon some other principle of our nature, it cannot be doubted, that they were given us for the direction of our conduct in this life. They carry along with them the most evident badges of this authority, which denote that they were set up within us to be the supreme arbiters of all our actions, to superintend all our senses, passions, and appetites, and to judge how each of them was either to be indulged or restrained. Our moral faculties are by no means, as some have pretended, upon a level in this respect with the other faculties and appetites of our nature, endowed with no more right to restrain these last, than these last are to restrain them. No other faculty or principle of action judges of any other. Love does not judge of resentment, nor resentment of love. Those two passions may be opposite to one another, but cannot, with any propriety, be said to approve or disapprove of one another. But it is the peculiar office of those faculties now under our consideration to judge, to bestow censure or applause upon all the other principles of our nature. They may be considered as a sort of senses of which those principles are the objects. Every sense is supreme over its own objects. There is no appeal from the eye with regard to the beauty of colours, nor from the ear with regard to the harmony of sounds, nor from the taste with regard to the agreeableness of flavours. Each of those senses judges in the last resort of its own objects. Whatever gratifies the taste is sweet, whatever pleases the eye is beautiful, whatever soothes the ear is harmonious. The very essence of each of those qualities consists in its being fitted to please the sense to which it is addressed. It belongs to our moral faculties, in the same manner to determine when the ear ought to be soothed, when the eye ought to be indulged, when the taste ought to be gratified, when and how far every other principle of our nature ought either to be indulged or restrained. What is agreeable to our moral faculties, is fit, and right, and proper to be done; the contrary wrong, unfit, and improper. The sentiments which they approve of, are graceful and becoming : the contrary, ungraceful and unbecoming. The very words, right, wrong, fit, improper, graceful, unbecoming, mean only what pleases or displeases those faculties.

Since these, therefore, were plainly intended to be the governing principles of human nature, the rules which they prescribe are to be regarded as the commands and laws of the Deity, promulgated by those vicegerents which he has thus set up within us. All general rules are commonly denominated laws : thus the general rules which bodies observe in the communication of motion, are called the laws of motion. But those general rules which our moral faculties observe in approving or condemning whatever sentiment or action is subjected to their examination, may much more justly be denominated such. They have a much greater resemblance to what are properly called laws, those general rules which the sovereign lays down to direct the conduct of his subjects. Like them they are rules to direct the free actions of men: they are prescribed most surely by a lawful superior, and are attended too with the sanction of rewards and punishments. Those vicegerents of God within us, never fail to punish the violation of them, by the torments of inward shame, and self-condemnation ; and on the contrary, always reward obedience with tranquillity of mind, with full contentment and self-satisfaction.

There are innumerable other considerations which serve to confirm the same conclusion. The happiness of mankind, as well as of all other rational creatures, seems to have been the original purpose intended by the Author of nature, when he brought them into existence. No other end seems worthy of that supreme wisdom and divine benignity which we necessarily ascribe to him ; and this opinion, which we are led to by the abstract consideration of his infinite perfections, is still more confirmed by the examination of the works of nature, which seem all intended to promote happiness, and to guard against misery. But by acting accordingly to the dictates of our moral faculties, we necessarily pursue the most effectual means for promoting the happiness of mankind, and may therefore be said, in some sense, to co-operate with the Deity, and to advance as far as in our power the plan of Providence. By acting otherwise, on the contrary, we seem to obstruct, in some measure, the scheme which the Author of nature has established for the happiness and perfection of the world, and to declare ourselves, if I may say so, in some measure the enemies of God. Hence we are naturally encouraged to hope for his extraordinary favour and reward in the one case, and to dread his sure vengeance and punishment in the other.

There are besides many other reasons, and many other natural principles, which all tend to confirm and inculcate the same salutary doctrine. If we consider the general rules by which external prosperity and adversity are commonly distributed in this life, we shall find, that notwithstanding the disorder in which all things appear to be in this world, yet even here every virtue naturally meets with its proper reward, with the recompense which is most fit to encourage and promote it ; and this too so surely, that it requires a very extraordinary concurrence of circumstances entirely to disappoint it. What is the reward most proper for encouraging industry, prudence, and circumspection ? Success in every sort of business. And is it possible that in the whole of life these virtues should fail of attaining it ? Wealth and external honours are their proper recompense, and the recompense which they can seldom fail of acquiring. What reward is most proper for promoting the practice of truth, justice, and humanity ? The confidence, the esteem, the love of those we live with. Humanity does not desire to be great, but to be beloved. It is not in being rich that truth and justice would rejoice, but in being trusted and believed, recompenses which those virtues must almost always acquire.   By some very extraordinary and unlucky circumstance, a good man may come to be suspected of a crime of which he was altogether incapable, and upon that account be most unjustly exposed for the remaining part of his life to the horror and aversion of mankind.   By an accident of this kind he may be said to lose his all, notwithstanding his integrity and justice ; in the same manner as a cautious man, notwithstanding his utmost circumspection, may be ruined by an earthquake or an inundation.   Accidents of the first kind, however, are perhaps still more rare, and still more contrary to the common course of things than those of the second ; and it still remains true, that the practice of truth, justice, and humanity is a certain and almost infallible method of acquiring what these virtues chiefly aim at, the confidence and love of those we live with.   A person may be very easily misrepresented with regard to a particular action ; but it is scarce possible that he should be so with regard to the general tenor of his conduct.   An innocent man may be believed to have done wrong : this, however, will rarely happen.   On the contrary, the established opinion of the innocence of his manners, will often lead us to absolve him where he has really been in the fault, notwithstanding very strong presumptions.   A knave, in the same manner, may escape censure, or even meet with applause, for a particular knavery, in which his conduct is not understood.   But no man was ever habitually such, without being almost universally known to be so, and without being even frequently suspected of guilt, when he was in reality perfectly innocent.   And so far as vice and virtue can be either punished or rewarded by the sentiments and opinions of mankind, they both, according to the common course of things meet even here with something more than exact and impartial justice.

But though the general rules by which prosperity and adversity are commonly distributed, when considered in this cool and philosophical light, appear to be perfectly suited to the situation of mankind in this life, yet they are by no means suited to some of our natural sentiments. Our natural love and admiration for some virtues is such, that we should wish to bestow on them all sorts of honours and rewards, even those which we must acknowledge to be the proper recompenses of other qualities, with which those virtues are not always accompanied. Our detestation, on the contrary, for some vices is such, that we should desire to heap upon them every sort of disgrace and disaster, those not excepted which are the natural consequences of very different qualities.   Magnanimity, generosity, and justice, command so high a degree of admiration, that we desire to see them crowned with wealth, and power, and honours of every kind, the natural consequences of prudence, industry, and application ; qualities with which those virtues are not inseparably connected.   Fraud, falsehood, brutality, and violence, on the other hand, excite in every human breast such scorn and abhorrence, that our indignation rouses to see them possess those advantages which they may in some sense be said to have merited, by the diligence and industry with which they are sometimes attended. The industrious knave cultivates the soil, the indolent man leaves it uncultivated. Who ought to reap the harvest? Who starve, and who live in plenty? The natural course of things decides it in favour of the knave : the natural sentiments of mankind in favour of the man of virtue. Man judges, that the good qualities of the one are greatly over-recompensed by those advantages which they tend to procure him, and that the omissions of the other are by far too severely punished by the distress which they naturally bring upon him ; and human laws, the consequences of human sentiments, forfeit the life and the estate of the industrious and cautious traitor, and reward, by extraordinary recompenses, the fidelity and public spirit of the improvident and careless good citizen. Thus man is by Nature directed to correct, in some measure, that distribution of things which she herself would otherwise have made. The rules which for this purpose she prompts him to follow, are different from those which she herself observes. She bestows upon every virtue, and upon every vice, that precise reward or punishment which is best fitted to encourage the one, or to restrain the other. She is directed by this sole consideration, and pays little regard to the different degrees of merit and demerit, which they may seem to possess in the sentiments and passions of man. Man, on the contrary, pays regard to this only, and would endeavour to render the state of every virtue precisely proportioned to that degree of love and esteem, and of every vice to that degree of contempt and abhorrence, which he himself conceives for it. The rules which she follows are fit for her, as, those which he follows are for him : but both are calculated to promote the same great end, the order of the world, and the perfection and happiness of human nature.

But though man is thus employed to alter that distribution of things which natural events would make, if left to themselves ; though, like the gods of the poets, he is perpetually interposing, by extraordinary means, in favour of virtue, and in opposition to vice, and, like them, endeavours to turn away the arrow that is aimed at the head of the righteous, but to accelerate the sword of destruction that is lifted up against the wicked ; yet he is by no means able to render the fortune of either quite suitable to his own sentiments and wishes. The natural course of things cannot be entirely controlled by the impotent endeavours of man : the current is too rapid and too strong for him to stop it ; and though the rules which direct it appear to have been established for the wisest and best purposes, they sometimes produce effects which shock all his natural sentiments. That a great combination of men should prevail over a small one ; that those who engage in an enterprise with forethought and all necessary preparation, should prevail over such as oppose them without any ; and that every end should be acquired by those means only which nature has established for acquiring it, seems to be a rule not only necessary and unavoidable in itself, but even useful and proper for rousing the industry and attention of mankind.　Yet, when, in consequence of this rule, violence and artifice prevail over sincerity and justice, what indignation does it not excite in the breast of every human spectator ?　What sorrow and compassion for the sufferings of the innocent, and what furious resentment against the success of the oppressor ?　We are equally grieved and enraged at the wrong that is done, but often find it altogether out of our power to redress it.　When we thus despair of finding any force upon earth which can check the triumph of injustice, we naturally appeal to heaven, and hope that the great Author of our nature will himself execute hereafter what all the principles which he has given us for the direction of our conduct prompt us to attempt even here ; that he will complete the plan which he himself has thus taught us to begin ; and will, in a life to come, render to every one according to the works which he has performed in this world.　And thus we are led to the belief of a future state, not only by the weaknesses, by the hopes and fears of human nature, but by the noblest and best principles which belong to it, by the love of virtue, and by the abhorrence of vice and injustice.

' Does it suit the greatness of God,' says the eloquent and philosophical bishop of Clermont, with that passionate and exaggerating force of imagination, which seems sometimes to exceed the bounds of decorum; 'does it suit the greatness of God, to leave the world which he has 'created in so universal a disorder ?　To see the wicked prevail almost 'always over the just ; the innocent dethroned by the usurper ; the 'father become the victim of the ambition of an unnatural son ; the 'husband expiring under the stroke of a barbarous and faithless wife ? 'From the height of his greatness ought God to behold those melan-'choly events as a fantastical amusement, without taking any share in 'them?　Because he is great, should he be weak, or unjust, or barba-'rous?　Because men are little, ought they to be allowed either to be 'dissolute without punishment or virtuous without reward?　O God ! 'if this is the character of your Supreme Being ; if it is you whom we 'adore under such dreadful ideas ; I can no longer acknowledge you for 'my father, for my protector, for the comforter of my sorrow, the sup-'port of my weakness, the rewarder of my fidelity.　You would then be 'no more than an indolent and fantastical tyrant, who sacrifices man-'kind to his vanity, and who has brought them out of nothing only to 'make them serve for the sport of his leisure and of his caprice.'

When the general rules which determine the merit and demerit of actions, come thus to be regarded as the laws of an all-powerful Being, who watches over our conduct and, who, in a life to come, will reward the observance, and punish the breach of them ; they necessarily acquire a new sacredness from this consideration. That our regard to the will of the Deity ought to be the supreme rule of our conduct, can be doubted of by nobody who believes his existence. The very thought of disobedience appears to involve in it the most shocking impropriety. How vain, how absurd would it be for man, either to oppose or to neglect the commands that were laid upon him by Infinite Wisdom, and Infinite Power! How unnatural, how impiously ungrateful, not to reverence the precepts that were prescribed to him by the infinite goodness of his Creator, even though no punishment was to follow their violation. The sense of propriety too is here well supported by the strongest motives of self-interest. The idea that, however we may escape the observation of man, or be placed above the reach of human punishment, yet we are always acting under the eye, and exposed to the punishment of God, the great avenger of injustice, is a motive capable of restraining the most headstrong passions, with those at least who, by constant reflection, have rendered it familiar to them.

It is in this manner that religion enforces the natural sense of duty : and hence it is, that mankind are generally disposed to place great confidence in the probity of those who seem deeply impressed with religious sentiments. Such persons, they imagine, act under an additional tie, besides those which regulate the conduct of other men. The regard to the propriety of action, as well as to reputation, the regard to the applause of his own breast, as well as to that of others, are motives which they suppose have the influence over the religious man, as over the man of the world. But the former lies under another restraint, and never acts deliberately but as in the presence of that Great Superior who is finally to recompense him according to his deeds. A greater trust is reposed, upon this account, in the regularity and exactness of his conduct. And wherever the natural principles of religion are not corrupted by the factious and party zeal of some worthless cabal ; wherever the first duty which it requires, is to fulfil all the obligations of morality ; wherever men are not taught to regard frivolous observances, as more immediate duties of religion than acts of justice and beneficence ; and to imagine, that by sacrifices, and ceremonies, and vain supplications, they can bargain with the Deity for fraud, and perfidy, and violence, the world undoubtedly judges right in this respect, and justly places a double confidence in the rectitude of the religious man's behaviour.

CHAP. VI.—*In what Cases the Sense of Duty ought to be the sole Principle of our Conduct ; and in what Cases it ought to concur with other Motives.*

RELIGION affords such strong motives to the practice of virtue, and guards us by such powerful restraints from the temptations of vice, that many have been led to suppose, that religious principles were the sole laudable motives of action. We ought neither, they said, to reward from gratitude, nor punish from resentment ; we ought neither to protect the helplessness of our children, nor afford support to the infirmities of our parents, from natural affection. All affections for particular objects, ought to be extinguished in our breast, and one great affection take the place of all others, the love of the Deity, the desire of rendering ourselves agreeable to him, and of directing our conduct, in every respect, according to his will. We ought not to be grateful from gratitude, we ought not to be charitable from humanity, we ought not to be public-spirited from the love of our country, nor generous and just from the love of mankind. The sole principle and motive of our conduct in the performance of all those different duties, ought to be a sense that God has commanded us to perform them. I shall not at present take time to examine this opinion particularly ; I shall only observe, that we should not have expected to have found it entertained by any sect, who professed themselves of a religion in which, as it is the first precept to love the Lord our God with all our heart, with all our soul, and with all our strength, so it is the second to love our neighbour as we love ourselves ; and we love ourselves surely for our own sakes, and not merely because we are commanded to do so. That the sense of duty should be the sole principle of our conduct, is no where the precept of Christianity ; but that it should be the ruling and the governing one, as philosophy, and as, indeed, common sense directs. It may be a question, however, in what cases our actions ought to arise chiefly or entirely from a sense of duty, or from a regard to general rules ; and in what cases some other sentiment or affection ought to concur, and have a principal influence on our conduct.

The decision of this question, which cannot, perhaps, be given with any very great accuracy, will depend upon two different circumstances ; first, upon the natural agreeableness or deformity of the sentiment or affection which would prompt us to any action independent of all regard to general rules ; and, secondly, upon the precision and exactness, or the looseness and inaccuracy, of the rules themselves.

I. First, I say, it will depend upon the natural agreeableness or deformity of the affection itself, how far our actions ought to arise from it, or entirely proceed from a regard to the general rule.

All those graceful and admired actions, to which the benevolent affections would prompt us, ought to proceed as much from the passions themselves, as from any regard to the general rules of conduct. A benefactor thinks himself but ill requited, if the person upon whom he has bestowed his good offices, repays them merely from a cold sense of duty, and without any affection to his person. A husband is dissatisfied with the most obedient wife, when he imagines her conduct is animated

by no other principle besides her regard to what the relation she stands
in requires.   Though a son should fail in none of the offices of filial
duty, yet if he wants that affectionate reverence which it so well
becomes him to feel, the parent may justly complain of his indifference.
Nor could a son be quite satisfied with a parent who, though he performed all the duties of his situation, had nothing of that fatherly fondness which might have been expected from him.   With regard to all
such benevolent and social affections, it is agreeable to see the sense of
duty employed rather to restrain than to enliven them, rather to hinder
us from doing too much, than to prompt us to do what we ought.   It
gives us pleasure to see a father obliged to check his own fondness for
his children, a friend obliged to set bounds to his natural generosity, a
person who has received a benefit, obliged to restrain the too sanguine
gratitude of his own temper.

The contrary maxim takes place with regard to the malevolent and
unsocial passions.   We ought to reward from the gratitude and generosity of our own hearts, without any reluctance, and without being
obliged to reflect how great the propriety of rewarding: but we ought
always to punish with reluctance, and more from a sense of the propriety of punishing, than from any savage disposition to revenge.
Nothing is more graceful than the behaviour of the man who appears
to resent the greatest injuries, more from a sense that they deserve, and
are the proper objects of resentment, than from feeling himself the
furies of that disagreeable passion; who, like a judge, considers only
the general rule, which determines what vengeance is due for each particular offence; who, in executing that rule, feels less for what himself
has suffered, than for what the offender is about to suffer; who, though
in wrath, does ever remember mercy, and is disposed to interpret the
rule in the most gentle and favourable manner, and to allow all the
alleviations which the most candid humanity could, consistently with
good sense, admit of.

As the selfish passions, according to what has formerly been observed,
hold, in other respects, a sort of middle place, between the social and
unsocial affections, so do they likewise in this.   The pursuit of the
objects of private interest, in all common, little, and ordinary cases,
ought to flow rather from a regard to the general rules which prescribe
such conduct, than from any passion for the objects themselves; but
upon more important and extraordinary occasions, we should be awkward, insipid, and ungraceful, if the objects themselves did not appear
to animate us with a considerable degree of passion.   To be anxious,
or to be laying a plot either to gain or to save a single shilling, would
degrade the most vulgar tradesman in the opinion of all his neighbours.
Let his circumstances be ever so mean, no attention to any such small
matters, for the sake of the things themselves, must appear in his conduct.   His situation may require the most severe œconomy and the

most exact assiduity: but each particular exertion of that œconomy and assiduity must proceed, not so much from a regard for that particular saving or gain, as for the general rule which to him prescribes, with the utmost rigour, such a tenor of conduct.   His parsimony to-day must not arise from a desire of the particular three-pence which he will save by it, nor his attendance in his shop from a passion for the particular ten-pence which he will acquire by it: both the one and the other ought to proceed solely from a regard to the general rule, which prescribes, with the most unrelenting severity, this plan of conduct to all persons in his way of life.   In this consists the difference between the character of a miser and that of a person of exact œconomy and assiduity.   The one is anxious about small matters for their own sake ; the other attends to them only in consequence of the scheme of life which he has laid down to himself.

It is quite otherwise with regard to the more extraordinary and important objects of self-interest.   A person appears mean-spirited, who does not pursue these with some degree of earnestness for their own sake.   We should despise a prince who was not anxious about conquering or defending a province.   We should have little respect for a private gentleman who did not exert himself to gain an estate, or even a considerable office, when he could acquire them without either meanness or injustice.   A member of parliament who shews no keenness about his own election, is abandoned by his friends, as altogether unworthy of their attachment.   Even a tradesman is thought a poor-spirited fellow among his neighbours, who does not bestir himself to get what they call an extraordinary job, or some uncommon advantage. This spirit and keenness constitutes the difference between the man of enterprise and the man of dull regularity.   Those great objects of self-interest, of which the loss or acquisition quite changes the rank of the person, are the objects of the passion properly called ambition; a passion, which when it keeps within the bounds of prudence and justice, is always admired in the world, and has even sometimes a certain irregular greatness, which dazzles the imagination, when it passes the limits of both these virtues, and is not only unjust but extravagant.   Hence the general admiration for heroes and conquerors, and even for statesmen, whose projects have been very daring and extensive though altogether devoid of justice, such as those of the Cardinals of Richlieu and of Retz.   The objects of avarice and ambition differ only in their greatness.   A miser is as furious about a half-penny, as a man of ambition about the conquest of a kingdom.

II. Secondly, I say, it will depend partly upon the precision and upon the exactness, or the looseness and the inaccuracy of the general rules themselves, how far our conduct ought to proceed entirely from a regard to them.

The general rules of almost all the virtues, the general rules which determine what are the offices of prudence, of charity, of generosity, of gratitude, of friendship, are in many respects loose and inaccurate, admit of many exceptions, and require so many modifications, that it is scarce possible to regulate our conduct entirely by a regard to them. The common proverbial maxims of prudence, being founded in universal experience, are perhaps the best general rules which can be given about it. To affect, however, a very strict and literal adherence to them would evidently be the most absurd and ridiculous pedantry. Of all the virtues I have just now mentioned, gratitude is that, perhaps, of which the rules are the most precise, and admit of the fewest exceptions. That as soon as we can we should make a return of equal, and if possible of superior, value to the services we have received, would seem to be a pretty plain rule, and one which admitted of scarce any exceptions. Upon the most superficial examination, however, this rule will appear to be in the highest degree loose and inaccurate, and to admit of ten thousand exceptions. If your benefactor attended you in your sickness, ought you to attend him in his? or can you fulfil the obligation of gratitude, by making a return of a different kind? If you ought to attend him, how long ought you to attend him? The same time which he attended you, or longer, and how much longer? If your friend lent you money in your distress, ought you to lend him money in his? How much ought you to lend him? When ought you to lend him? Now, or to-morrow, or next month? And for how long a time? It is evident, that no general rule can be laid down, by which a precise answer can, in all cases, be given to any of these questions. The difference between his character and yours, between his circumstances and yours, may be such, that you may be perfectly grateful, and justly refuse to lend him a half-penny: and, on the contrary, you may be willing to lend, or even to give him ten times the sum which he lent you, and yet justly be accused of the blackest ingratitude, and of not having fulfilled the hundredth part of the obligation you lie under. As the duties of gratitude, however, are perhaps the most sacred of all those which the beneficent virtues prescribe to us, so the general rules which determine them are, as I said before, the most accurate. Those which ascertain the actions required by friendship, humanity, hospitality, generosity, are still more vague and indeterminate.

There is, however, one virtue of which the general rules determine with the greatest exactness every external action which it requires. This virtue is justice. The rules of justice are accurate in the highest degree, and admit of no exceptions or modifications, but such as may be ascertained as accurately as the rules themselves, and which generally, indeed, flow from the very same principles with them. If I owe a man ten pounds, justice requires that I should precisely pay him ten pounds, either at the time agreed upon, or when he demands it. What I ought to perform, how much I ought to perform, when and where I

ought to perform it, the whole nature and circumstances of the action
prescribed, are all of them precisely fixed and determined.   Though it
may be awkward and pedantic, therefore, to affect too strict an adherence to the common rules of prudence or generosity, there is no
pedantry in sticking fast by the rules of justice.   On the contrary, the
most sacred regard is due to them; and the actions which this virtue
requires are never so properly performed, as when the chief motive for
performing them is a reverential and religious regard to those general
rules which require them.   In the practice of the other virtues, our
conduct should rather be directed by a certain idea of propriety, by a
certain taste for a particular tenor of conduct, than by any regard to a
precise maxim or rule; and we should consider the end and foundation
of the rule, more than the rule itself.   But it is otherwise with regard
to justice: the man who in that refines the least, and adheres with the
most obstinate steadfastness to the general rules themselves, is the most
commendable, and the most to be depended upon.   Though the end of
the rules of justice be, to hinder us from hurting our neighbour, it may
frequently be a crime to violate them, though we could pretend with
some pretext of reason, that this particular violation could do no hurt.
A man often becomes a villain the moment he begins, even in his own
heart, to chicane in this manner.   The moment he thinks of departing
from the most staunch and positive adherence to what those inviolable
precepts prescribe to him, he is no longer to be trusted, and no man
can say what degree of guilt he may not arrive at.   The thief imagines
he does no evil, when he steals from the rich, what he supposes they
may easily want, and what possibly they may never even know has
been stolen from them.   The adulterer imagines he does no evil, when
he corrupts the wife of his friend, provided he covers his intrigue from
the suspicion of the husband, and does not disturb the peace of the
family.   When once we begin to give way to such refinements, there is
no enormity so gross of which we may not be capable.

The rules of justice may be compared to the rules of grammar; the
rules of the other virtues, to the rules which critics lay down for the
attainment of what is sublime and elegant in composition.   The one,
are precise, accurate, and indispensable.   The other, are loose, vague,
and indeterminate, and present us rather with a general idea of the
perfection we ought to aim at, than afford us any certain and infallible
directions for acquiring it.   A man may learn to write grammatically
by rule, with the most absolute infallibility; and so, perhaps, he may
be taught to act justly.   But there are no rules whose observance will
infallibly lead us to the attainment of elegance or sublimity in writing;
though there are some which may help us, in some measure, to correct,
and ascertain the vague ideas which we might otherwise have entertained of those perfections.   And there are no rules by the knowledge
of which we can infallibly be taught to act upon all occasions with pru-

dence, with just magnanimity, or proper beneficence : though there are some which may enable us to correct and ascertain, in several respects, the imperfect ideas which we might otherwise have entertained of those virtues—the rules of justice.

It may sometimes happen, that with the most serious and earnest desire of acting so as to deserve approbation, we may mistake the proper rules of conduct, and thus be misled by that very principle which ought to direct us. It is in vain to expect, that in this case mankind should entirely approve of our behaviour. They cannot enter into that absurd idea of duty which influenced us, nor go along with any of the actions which follow from it. There is still, however, something respectable in the character and behaviour of one who is thus betrayed into vice, by a wrong sense of duty, or by what is called an erroneous conscience. How fatally soever he may be misled by it, he is still, with the generous and humane, more the object of commiseration than of hatred or resentment. They lament the weakness of human nature, which exposes us to such unhappy delusions, even while we are most sincerely labouring after perfection, and endeavouring to act according to the best principle which can possibly direct us. False notions of religion are almost the only causes which can occasion any very gross perversion of our natural sentiments in this way ; and that principle which gives the greatest authority to the rules of duty, is alone capable of distorting our ideas of them in any considerable degree. In all other cases, common sense is sufficient to direct us, if not to the most exquisite propriety of conduct, yet to something which is not very far from it ; and provided we are in earnest desirous to do well, our behaviour will always, upon the whole, be praiseworthy. That to obey the will of the Deity, is the first rule of duty, all men are agreed. But concerning the particular commandments which that will may impose upon us, they differ widely from one another. In this, therefore, the greatest mutual forbearance and toleration is due ; and though the defence of society requires that crimes should be punished, from whatever motives they proceed, yet a good man will always punish them with reluctance, when they evidently proceed from false notions of religious duty. He will never feel against those who commit them that indignation which he feels against other criminals, but will rather regret, and sometimes even admire their unfortunate firmness and magnanimity, at the very time that he punishes their crime. In the tragedy of Mahomet, one of the finest of Mr. Voltaire's, it is well represented, what ought to be our sentiments for crimes which proceed from such motives. In that tragedy, two young people of different sexes, of the most innocent and virtuous dispositions, and without any other weakness except what endears them the more to us, a mutual fondness for one another, are instigated by the strongest motives of a false religion, to commit a horrid murder, that shocks all the principles of human nature. A venerable old man, who had expressed the most tender affection for them both, for whom, notwithstanding he was the avowed enemy of their religion, they had both conceived the highest reverence and esteem, and who was in reality their father, though they did not know him to be such, is pointed out to them as a sacrifice which God had expressly required at their hands, and they are commanded to kill him. While about executing this crime, they are tortured with all the agonies which can arise from the struggle between the idea of the indispensable-ness of religious duty on the one side, and compassion, gratitude, reverence for the age, and love for the humanity and virtue of the person whom they are going to destroy, on the other. The representation of this exhibits one of the most interesting, and perhaps the most in-structive spectacle that was ever introduced upon any theatre. The sense of duty, however, at last prevails over all the amiable weaknesses of human nature. They execute the crime imposed upon them ; but immediately discover their error, and the fraud which had deceived them, and are distracted with horror, remorse, and resentment. Such as are our sentiments for the unhappy Seid and Palmira, such ought we to feel for every person who is in this manner misled by religion, when we are sure that it is really religion which misleads him, and not the pretence of it, which is made too often a cover to some of the worst of human passions.

As a person may act wrong by following a wrong sense of duty, so nature may sometimes prevail, and lead him to act right in opposition to it. We cannot in this case be displeased to see that motive prevail, which we think ought to prevail though the person himself is so weak as to think otherwise. As his conduct, however, is the effect of weakness, not principle, we are far from bestowing upon it any thing that approaches to complete approbation. A bigoted Roman Catholic, who, during the massacre of St. Bartholomew, had been so overcome by compassion, as to save some unhappy Protestants, whom he thought it his duty to de-stroy, would not seem to be entitled to that high applause which we should have bestowed upon him, had he exerted the same generosity with com-plete self-approbation. We might be pleased with the humanity of his temper, but we should still regard him with a sort of pity which is altogether inconsistent with the admiration that is due to perfect virtue. It is the same case with all the other passions. We do not dislike to see them exert themselves properly, even when a false notion of duty would direct the person to restrain them. A very devout Quaker, who upon being struck upon one cheek, instead of turning up the other, should so far forget his literal interpretation of our Saviour's precept, as to bestow some good discipline upon the brute that insulted him, would not be disagreeable to us. We should laugh and be diverted with his spirit, and rather like him the better for it. But we should by no means regard him with that respect and esteem which would seem due to one who, upon a like occasion, had acted properly from a just sense of what was proper to be done.   No action can properly be called virtuous, which is not accompanied with the sentiment of self-approbation.

————

Part IV.—Of the Effect of Utility upon the Sentiment of Approbation.

CHAP. I.—*Of the Beauty which the Appearance of Utility bestows upon all the Productions of Art, and of the extensive Influence of this Species of Beauty.*

THAT utility is one of the principal sources of beauty has been observed by every body, who has considered with any attention what constitutes the nature of beauty.   The conveniency of a house gives pleasure to the spectator as well as its regularity, and he is as much hurt when he observes the contrary defect, as when he sees the correspondent windows of different forms, or the door not placed exactly in the middle of the building.   That the fitness of any system or machine to produce the end for which it was intended, bestows a certain propriety and beauty upon the whole, and renders the very thought and contemplation of it agreeable, is so obvious that nobody has over-looked it.

The cause too, why utility pleases, has of late been assigned by an ingenious and agreeable philosopher, who joins the greatest depth of thought to the greatest elegance of expression, and possesses the singular and happy talent of treating the abstrusest subjects not only with the most perfect perspicuity, but with the most lively eloquence.   The utility of any object, according to him, pleases the master by perpetually suggesting to him the pleasure or conveniency which it is fitted to promote.   Every time he looks at it, he is put in mind of this pleasure ; and the object in this manner becomes a source of perpetual satisfaction and enjoyment.   The spectator enters by sympathy into the sentiments of the master, and necessarily views the object under the same agreeable aspect.   When we visit the palaces of the great, we cannot help conceiving the satisfaction we should enjoy if we ourselves were the masters, and were possessed of so much artful and ingeniously contrived accommodation. A similar account is given why the appearance of inconveniency should render any object disagreeable both to the owner and to the spectator.

But that this fitness, this happy contrivance of any production of art, should often be more valued, than the very end for which it was intended ; and that the exact adjustment of the means for attaining any conveniency or pleasure, should frequently be more regarded, than that very conveniency or pleasure, in the attainment of which their whole merit would seem to consist, has not, so far as I know, been yet taken notice of by any body.   That this, however, is very frequently the case, may be observed in a thousand instances, both in the most frivolous and in the most important concerns of human life.

When a person comes into his chamber, and finds the chairs all standing in the middle of the room, he is angry with his servant, and rather than see them continue in that disorder, perhaps takes the trouble himself to set them all in their places with their backs to the wall. The whole propriety of this new situation arises from its superior conveniency in leaving the floor free and disengaged.   To attain this conveniency he voluntarily puts himself to more trouble than all he could have suffered from the want of it ; since nothing was more easy, than to have set himself down upon one of them, which is probably what he does when his labour is over.   What he wanted, therefore, it seems, was not so much this conveniency, as that arrangement of things which promotes it.   Yet it is this conveniency alone which may ultimately recommend that arrangement, and bestows upon it the whole of its propriety and beauty.

A watch, in the same manner, that falls behind above two minutes in a day, is despised by one curious in watches.   He sells it perhaps for a couple of guineas, and purchases another at fifty, which will not lose above a minute in a fortnight.   The sole use of watches, however, is to tell us what o'clock it is, and to hinder us from breaking any engagement, or suffering any other inconveniency by our ignorance in that particular point.   But the person so nice with regard to this machine, will not always be found either more scrupulously punctual than other men, or more anxiously concerned upon any other account, to know precisely what time of day it is.   What interests him is not so much the attainment of this piece of knowledge, as the perfection of the machine which enables him to attain it.

How many people ruin themselves by laying out money on trinkets of frivolous utility ?   What pleases these lovers of toys is not so much the utility, as the aptness of the machines which are fitted to promote it.   All their pockets are stuffed with little conveniences.   They contrive new pockets, unknown in the clothes of other people, in order to carry a greater number.   They walk about loaded with a multitude of baubles, in weight and sometimes in value not inferior to an ordinary Jew's-box, some of which may sometimes be of some little use, but all of which might at all times be very well spared, and of which the whole utility is not worth the fatigue of bearing the burden.   :

Nor is it only with regard to such frivolous objects that our conduct is influenced by this principle; it is often the secret motive of the most serious and important pursuits of both private and public life.

The poor man's son, whom Heaven in its anger has visited with ambition, when he begins to look around him, admires the condition of the rich.   He finds the cottage of his father too small for his accommodation, and fancies he should be lodged more at his ease in a palace. He is displeased with being obliged to walk a-foot, or to endure the fatigue of riding on horseback. He sees his superiors carried about in machines, and imagines that in one of these he could travel with less inconveniency. He feels himself naturally indolent, and willing to serve himself with his own hands as little as possible; and judges, that a numerous retinue of servants would save him from a great deal of trouble. He thinks if he had attained all these, he would sit still contentedly, and be quiet, enjoying himself in the thought of the happiness and tranquillity of his situation. He is enchanted with the distant idea of this felicity. It appears in his fancy like the life of some superior rank of beings, and, in order to arrive at it, he devotes himself for ever to the pursuit of wealth and greatness. To obtain the conveniences which these afford, he submits in the first year, nay, in the first month of his application, to more fatigue of body and more uneasiness of mind than he could have suffered through the whole of his life from the want of them. He studies to distinguish himself in some laborious profession. With the most unrelenting industry he labours night and day to acquire talents superior to all his competitors. He endeavours next to bring those talents into public view, and with equal assiduity solicits every opportunity of employment. For this purpose he makes his court to all mankind; he serves those whom he hates, and is obsequious to those whom he despises. Through the whole of his life he pursues the idea of a certain artificial and elegant repose which he may never arrive at, for which he sacrifices a real tranquillity that is at all times in his power, and which, if in the extremity of old age he should at last attain to it, he will find to be in no respect preferable to that humble security and contentment which he had abandoned for it. It is then, in the last dregs of life, his body wasted with toil and diseases, his mind galled and ruffled by the memory of a thousand injuries and disappointments which he imagines he has met with from the injustice of his enemies, or from the perfidy and ingratitude of his friends, that he begins at last to find that wealth and greatness are mere trinkets of frivolous utility, no more adapted for procuring ease of body or tranquillity of mind than the tweezer-cases of the lover of toys; and, like them too, more troublesome to the person who carries them about with him than all the advantages they can afford him are commodious. There is no other real difference between them, except that the conveniences of the one are somewhat more observable than those of the other. The palaces, the gardens, the equipage, the retinue of the great, are objects of which the obvious conveniency strikes every body. They do not require that their masters should point out to us wherein consists their utility. Of our own accord we readily enter into it, and by sympathy enjoy and thereby applaud the satisfaction which they are fitted to afford him. But the curiosity of a tooth-pick, of an ear-picker, of a machine for cutting the nails, or of any other trinket of the same kind, is not so obvious. Their conveniency may perhaps be equally great, but it is not so striking, and we do not so readily enter into the satisfaction of the man who possesses them. They are therefore less reasonable subjects of vanity than the magnificence of wealth and greatness; and in this consists the sole advantage of these last. They more effectually gratify that love of distinction so natural to man. To one who was to live alone in a desolate island it might be a matter of doubt, perhaps, whether a palace, or a collection of such small conveniencies as are commonly contained in a tweezer-case, would contribute most to his happiness and enjoyment. If he is to live in society, indeed, there can be no comparison, because in this, as in all other cases, we constantly pay more regard to the sentiments of the spectator, than to those of the person principally concerned, and consider rather how his situation will appear to other people, than how it will appear to himself. If we examine, however, why the spectator distinguishes with such admiration the condition of the rich and the great, we shall find that is is not so much upon account of the superior ease or pleasure which they are supposed to enjoy, as of the numberless artificial and elegant contrivances for promoting this ease or pleasure. He does not even imagine that they are really happier than other people: but he imagines that they possess more means of happiness. And it is the ingenious and artful adjustment of those means to the end for which they were intended, that is the principal source of his admiration. But in the languor of disease and the weariness of old age, the pleasures of the vain and empty distinctions of greatness disappear. To one, in this situation, they are no longer capable of recommending those toilsome pursuits in which they had formerly engaged him. In his heart he curses ambition, and vainly regrets the ease and the indolence of youth, pleasures which are fled for ever, and which he has foolishly sacrificed for what, when he has got it, can afford him no real satisfaction. In this miserable aspect does greatness appear to every man when reduced either by spleen or disease to observe with attention his own situation, and to consider what it is that is really wanting to his happiness. Power and riches appear then to be, what they are, enormous and operose machines contrived to produce a few trifling conveniencies to the body, consisting of springs the most nice and delicate, which must be kept in order with the most anxious attention, and which in spite of all our care are ready every moment to burst into pieces, and to crush in their ruins their unfortunate possessor. They are immense fabrics, which it requires the labour of a life to raise, which threaten every moment to overwhelm the person that dwells in them, and which while they stand, though they may save him from some smaller inconveniencies, can protect him from none of the severer inclemencies of the season. They keep off the summer shower, not the winter storm, but leave him always as much, and sometimes more, exposed than before, to anxiety, to fear, and to sorrow ; to diseases, to danger, and to death.

But though this splenetic philosophy, which in time of sickness or low spirits is familiar to every man, thus entirely depreciates those great objects of human desire, when in better health and in better humour, we never fail to regard them under a more agreeable aspect. Our imagination, which in pain and sorrow seems to be confined and cooped up within our own persons, in times of ease and prosperity expands itself to every thing around us. We are then charmed with the beauty of that accommodation which reigns in the palaces and œconomy of the great : and admire how every thing is adapted to promote their ease, to prevent their wants, to gratify their wishes, and to amuse and entertain their most frivolous desires. If we consider the real satisfaction which all these things are capable of affording, by itself and separated from the beauty of that arrangement which is fitted to promote it, it will always appear in the highest degree contemptible and trifling. But we rarely view it in this abstract and philosophical light. We naturally confound it in our imagination with the order, the regular and harmonious movement of the system, the machine or œconomy by means of which it is produced. The pleasures of wealth and greatness, when considered in this complex view, strike the imagination as something grand and beautiful and noble, of which the attainment is well worth all the toil and anxiety which we are so apt to bestow upon it.

And it is well that nature imposes upon us in this manner. It is this deception which rouses and keeps in continual motion the industry of mankind. It is this which first prompted them to cultivate the ground, to build houses, to found cities and commonwealths, and to invent and improve all the sciences and arts, which ennoble and embellish human life ; which have entirely changed the whole face of the globe, have turned the rude forests of nature into agreeable and fertile plains, and made the trackless and barren ocean a new fund of subsistence, and the great high road of communication to the different nations of the earth. The earth by these labours of mankind has been obliged to redouble her natural fertility, and to maintain a greater multitude of inhabitants. It is to no purpose, that the proud and unfeeling landlord views his extensive fields, and without a thought for the wants of his brethren, in imagination consumes himself the whole harvest that grows upon them. The homely and vulgar proverb, that the eye is larger than the belly, never was more fully verified than with regard to him. The capacity of his stomach bears no proportion to the immensity of his desires, and will receive no more than that of the meanest peasant. The rest he is obliged to distribute among those, who prepare, in the nicest manner, that little which he himself makes use of, among those who fit up the palace in which this little is to be consumed, among those who provide and keep in order all the different baubles and trinkets which are employed in the œconomy of greatness; all of whom thus derive from his luxury and caprice, that share of the necessaries of life, which they would in vain have expected from his humanity or his justice.   The produce of the soil maintains at all times nearly that number of inhabitants which it is capable of maintaining.   The rich only select from the heap what is most precious and agreeable.   They consume little more than the poor, and in spite of their natural selfishness and rapacity, though they mean only their own conveniency, though the sole end which they propose from the labours of all the thousands whom they employ, be the gratification of their own vain and insatiable desires, they divide with the poor the produce of all their improvements.   They are led by an invisible hand to make nearly the same distribution of the necessaries of life, which would have been made, had the earth been divided into equal portions among all its inhabitants, and thus without intending it, without knowing it, advance the interest of the society, and afford means to the multiplication of the species.   When Providence divided the earth among a few lordly masters, it neither forgot nor abandoned those who seemed to have been left out in the partition.   These last, too, enjoy their share of all that it produces.   In what constitutes the real happiness of human life, they are in no respect inferior to those who would seem so much above them.   In ease of the body and peace of the mind, all the different ranks of life are nearly upon a level, and the beggar, who suns himself by the side of the highway, possesses that security which kings are fighting for.

The same principle, the same love of system, the same regard to the beauty of order, of art and contrivance, frequently serves to recommend those institutions which tend to promote the public welfare.   When a patriot exerts himself for the improvement of any part of the public police, his conduct does not always arise from pure sympathy with the happiness of those who are to reap the benefit of it.   It is not commonly from a fellow-feeling with carriers and waggoners that a public-spirited man encourages the mending of high roads.   When the legislature establishes premiums and other encouragements to advance the linen or woollen manufactures, its conduct seldom proceeds from pure sympathy with the wearer of cheap or fine cloth, and much less from that with the manufacturer or merchant.   The perfection of police, the extension of trade and manufactures, are noble and magnificent objects.   The contemplation of them pleases us, and we are interested in whatever can tend to advance them.   They make part of the great system of government, and the wheels of the political machine seem to move with more harmony and ease by means of them.   We take pleasure in beholding the perfection of so beautiful and grand a system, and we are uneasy till we remove any obstruction that can in the least disturb or encumber the regularity of its motions.   All constitutions of government, however, are valued only in proportion as they tend to promote the happiness of those who live under them.   This is their sole use and end.   From a certain spirit of system, however, from a certain love of art and contrivance, we sometimes seem to value the means more than the end, and to be eager to promote the happiness of our fellow-creatures, rather from a view to perfect and improv a certain beautiful and orderly system, than from any immediate sense or feeling of what they either suffer or enjoy.   There have been men of the greatest public spirit, who have shown themselves in other respects not very sensible to the feelings of humanity.   And on the contrary, there have been men of the greatest humanity, who seem to have been entirely devoid of public spirit.   Every man may find in the circle of his acquaintance instances both of the one kind and the other.   Who had ever less humanity, or more public spirit, than the celebrated legislator of Muscovy ?   The social and well-natured James the First of Great Britain seems, on the contrary, to have had scarce any passion, either for the glory or the interest of his country.   Would you awaken the industry of the man who seems almost dead to ambition, it will often be to no purpose to describe to him the happiness of the rich and the great ; to tell him that they are generally sheltered from the sun and the rain, that they are seldom hungry, that they are seldom cold, and that they are rarely exposed to weariness, or to want of any kind.   The most eloquent exhortation of this kind will have little effect upon him.   If you would hope to succeed, you must describe to him the conveniency and arrangement of the different apartments in their palaces ; you must explain to him the propriety of their equipages, and point out to him the number, the order, and the different offices of all their attendants.   If any thing is capable of making impression upon him, this will.   Yet all these things tend only to keep off the sun and the rain, and save them from hunger and cold, from want and weariness.   In the same manner, if you would implant public virtue in the breast of him who seems heedless of the interest of his country, it will often be to no purpose to tell him, what superior advantages the subjects of a well-governed state enjoy ; that they are better lodged, that they are better clothed, that they are better fed.   These considerations will commonly make no great impression.   You will be more likely to persuade, if you describe the great system of public police which procures these advantages, if you explain the connexions and dependencies of its several parts, their mutual subordination to one another, and their general subserviency to the happiness of the society ; if you show how this system might be introduced into his own country, what it is that hinders it from taking place there at present, how those obstructions might be removed, and all the several wheels of the machine of government be made to move with more harmony and smoothness, without grating upon one another, or mutually retarding one another's motions. It is scarce possible that a man should listen to a discourse of this kind, and not feel himself animated to some degree of public spirit. He will, at least for a moment, feel some desire to remove those obstructions, and to put into motion so beautiful and so orderly a machine. Nothing tends so much to promote public spirit as the study of politics, of the several systems of civil government, their advantages and disadvantages, of the constitution of our own country, its situation, and interest with regard to foreign nations, its commerce, its defence, the disadvantages it labours under, the dangers to which it may be exposed, how to remove the one, and how to guard against the other. Upon this account political disquisition, if just and reasonable and practicable, are of all the works of speculation the most useful. Even the weakest and the worst of them are not altogether without their utility. They serve at least to animate the public passions of men, and rouse them to seek out the means of promoting the happiness of the society.

CHAP. II.—*Of the Beauty which the Appearance of Utility bestows upon the Characters and the Actions of Men; and how far the Perception of this Beauty may be regarded as one of the original Principles of Approbation.*

THE characters of men, as well as the contrivances of art, or the institutions of civil government, may be fitted either to promote or to disturb the happiness both of the individual and of the society. The prudent, the equitable, the active, resolute, and sober character promises prosperity and satisfaction, both to the person himself and to every one connected with him. The rash, the insolent, the slothful, effeminate, and voluptuous, on the contrary, forebodes ruin to the individual, and misfortune to all who have any thing to do with him. The first turn of mind has at least all the beauty which can belong to the most perfect machine that was ever invented for promoting the most agreeable purpose : and the second, all the deformity of the most awkward and clumsy contrivance. What institution of government could tend so much to promote the happiness of mankind as the general prevalence of wisdom and virtue? All government is but an imperfect remedy for the deficiency of these. Whatever beauty, therefore, can belong to civil government upon account of its utility, must in a far superior degree belong to these. On the contrary, what civil policy can be so ruinous and destructive as the vices of men? The fatal effects of bad government arise from nothing, but that it does not sufficiently guard against the mischiefs which human wickedness so often gives occasion to.

This beauty and deformity which characters appear to derive from their usefulness or inconveniency, are apt to strike, in a peculiar manner, those who consider, in an abstract and philosophical light, the actions and conduct of mankind. When a philosopher goes to examine why humanity is approved of, or cruelty condemned, he does not always form to himself, in a very clear and distinct manner, the conception of any one particular action either of cruelty or of humanity, but is commonly contented with the vague and indeterminate idea which the general names of those qualities suggest to him. But it is in particular instances only that the propriety or impropriety, the merit or demerit of actions is very obvious and discernible. It is only when particular examples are given that we perceive distinctly either the concord or disagreement between our two affections and those of the agent, or feel a social gratitude arise towards him in the one case, or a sympathetic resentment in the other. When we consider virtue and vice in an abstract and general manner, the qualities by which they excite these several sentiments seem in a great measure to disappear, and the sentiments themselves become less obvious and discernible. On the contrary, the happy effects of the one and the fatal consequences of the other seem then to rise up to the view, and as it were to stand out and distinguish themselves from all the other qualities of either.

The same ingenious and agreeable author who first explained why utility pleases, has been so struck with this view of things, as to resolve our whole approbation of virtue into a perception of this species of beauty which results from the appearance of utility. No qualities of the mind, he observes, are approved of as virtuous, but such as are useful or agreeable either to the person himself or to others; and no qualities are disapproved of as vicious but such as have a contrary tendency. And Nature, indeed, seems to have so happily adjusted our sentiments of approbation and disapprobation, to the conveniency both of the individual and of the society, that after the strictest examination it will be found, I believe, that this is universally the case. But still I affirm, that it is not the view of this utility or hurtfulness which is either the first or principal source of our approbation and disapprobation. These sentiments are no doubt enhanced and enlivened by the perception of the beauty or deformity which results from this utility or hurtfulness. But still, I say, that they were originally and essentially different from this perception.

For first of all, it seems impossible that the approbation of virtue should be a sentiment of the same kind with that by which we approve of a convenient and well-contrived building; or that we should have no other reason for praising a man than that for which we commend a chest of drawers.

And secondly, it will be found, upon examination, that the usefulness of any disposition of mind is seldom the first ground of our approbation ; and that the sentiment of approbation always involves in it a sense of propriety quite distinct from the perception of utility. We may observe this with regard to all the qualities which are approved of as virtuous, both those which, according to this system, are originally valued as useful to ourselves, as well as those which are esteemed on account of their usefulness to others.

The qualities most useful to ourselves are, first of all, superior reason and understanding, by which we are capable of discerning the remote consequences of all our actions, and of fore-seeing the advantage or detriment which is likely to result from them : and secondly, self-command, by which we are enabled to abstain from present pleasure or to endure present pain, in order to obtain a greater pleasure, or to avoid a greater pain in some future time. In the union of those two qualities consists the virtue of prudence, of all the virtues that which is the most useful to the individual.

With regard to the first of those qualities, it has been observed on a former occasion, that superior reason and understanding are originally approved of as just and right and accurate, and not merely as useful or advantageous. It is in the abstruser sciences, particularly in the higher parts of mathematics, that the greatest and most admired exertions of human reason have been displayed. But the utility of those sciences, either to the individual or to the public, is not very obvious, and to prove it, requires a discussion which is not always very easily comprehended. It was not, therefore, their utility which first recommended them to the public admiration. This quality was but little insisted upon, till it became necessary to make some reply to the reproaches of those, who, having themselves no taste for such sublime discoveries, endeavoured to depreciate them as useless.

That self-command, in the same manner, by which we restrain our present appetites, in order to gratify them more fully upon another occasion, is approved of, as much under the aspect of propriety, as under that of utility. When we act in this manner, the sentiments which influence our conduct seem exactly to coincide with those of the spectator. The spectator, however, does not feel the solicitations of our present appetites.

To him the pleasure which we are to enjoy a week hence, or a year hence, is just as interesting as that which we are to enjoy this moment. When for the sake of the present, therefore, we sacrifice the future, our conduct appears to him absurd and extravagant in the highest degree, and he cannot enter into the principles which influence it. On the contrary, when we abstain from present pleasure, in order to secure greater pleasure to come, when we act as if the remote object interested us as much as that which immediately presses upon the senses, as our affections exactly correspond with his own, he cannot fail to approve of our behaviour : and as he knows from experience, how few are capable of this self-command, he looks upon our conduct with a considerable degree of wonder and admiration. Hence arises that eminent esteem with which all men naturally regard a steady perseverance in the practice of frugality, industry, and application, though directed to no other purpose than the acquisition of fortune. The resolute firmness of the person who acts in this manner, and in order to obtain a great though remote advantage, not only gives up all present pleasures, but endures the greatest labour both of mind and body, necessarily commands our approbation. That view of his interest and happiness which appears to regulate his conduct, exactly tallies with the idea which we naturally form of it. There is the most perfect correspondence between his sentiments and our own, and at the same time, from our experience of the common weakness of human nature, it is a correspondence which we could not reasonably have expected. We not only approve, therefore, but in some measure admire his conduct, and think it worthy of a considerable degree of applause. It is the consciousness of this merited approbation and esteem which is alone capable of supporting the agent in this tenor of conduct. The pleasure which we are to enjoy ten years hence interests us so little in comparison with that which we may enjoy today, the passion which the first excites, is naturally so weak in comparison with that violent emotion which the second is apt to give occasion to, that the one could never be any balance to the other, unless it was supported by the sense of propriety, by the consciousness that we merited the esteem and approbation of every body, by acting in the one way, and that we became the proper objects of their contempt and derision by behaving in the other.

Humanity, justice, generosity, and public spirit, are the qualities most useful to others. Wherein consists the propriety of humanity and justice has been explained upon a former occasión, where it was shown how much our esteem and approbation of those qualities depended upon the concord between the affections of the agent and those of the spectators.

The propriety of generosity and public spirit is founded upon the same principle with that of justice. Generosity is different from humanity. Those two qualities, which at first sight seem so nearly allied, do not always belong to the same person. Humanity is the virtue of a woman, generosity of a man. The fair sex, who have commonly much more tenderness than ours, have seldom so much generosity. That women rarely make considerable donations, is an observation of the civil law.—(Raro mulieres donare solent.) Humanity consists merely in the exquisite fellow-feeling which the spectator entertains with the sentiments of the persons principally concerned, so as to grieve for their sufferings, to resent their injuries, and to rejoice at their good for-

tune. The most humane actions require no self-denial, no self-command, no great exertion of the sense of propriety. They consist only
in doing what this exquisite sympathy would of its own accord prompt
us to do.   But it is otherwise with generosity.   We never are generous
except when in some respect we prefer some other person to ourselves,
and sacrifice some great and important interest of our own to an equal
interest of a friend or of a superior.   The man who gives up his pretensions to an office that was the great object of his ambition, because
he imagines that the services of another are better entitled to it ; the
man who exposes his life to defend that of his friend, which he judges
to be of more importance, neither of them act from humanity, or because they feel more exquisitely what concerns that other person that
what concerns themselves.   They both consider those opposite interests, not in the light in which they naturally appear to themselves, but
in that in which they appear to others.   To every bystander, the success or preservation of this other person may justly be more interesting
than their own ; but it cannot be so to themselves.   When to the
interest of this other person, therefore, they sacrifice their own, they
accommodate themselves to the sentiments of the spectator, and by an
effort of magnanimity act according to those views of things which
they feel must naturally occur to any third person.   The soldier who
·throws away his life in order to defend that of his officer, would perhaps
be but little affected by the death of that officer, if it should happen
without any fault of his own ; and a very small disaster which had befallen himself might excite a much more lively sorrow.   But when he
endeavours to act so as to deserve applause, and to make the impartial
spectator enter into the principles of his conduct, he feels, that to every
body but himself, his own life is a trifle compared with that of his
officer, and that when he sacrifices the one to the other, he acts quite
properly and agreeably to what would be the natural apprehensions of
every impartial bystander.
     It is the same case with the greater exertions of public spirit. When
a young officer exposes his life to acquire some inconsiderable addition
to the dominions of his sovereign, it is not because the acquisition of
the new territory is, to himself, an object more desirable than the preservation of his own life.   To him his own life is of infinitely more
value than the conquest of a whole kingdom for the state which he
serves.   But when he compares those two objects with one another, he
does not view them in the light in which they naturally appear to himself, but in that in which they appear to the nation he fights for.   To
them the success of the war is of the highest importance ; the life of
a private person of scarce any consequence.   When he puts himself in
their situation, he immediately feels that he cannot be too prodigal of
his blood, if, by shedding it, he can promote so valuable a purpose.
In thus thwarting, from a sense of duty and propriety, the strongest of

all natural propensities, consists the heroism of his conduct.   There is many an honest Englishman, who, in his private station, would be more seriously disturbed by the loss of a guinea, than by the national loss of Minorca, who yet, had it been in his power to defend that fortress, would have sacrificed his life a thousand times rather than, through his fault, have let it fall into the hands of the enemy.   When the first Brutus led forth his own sons to a capital punishment, because they had conspired against the rising liberty of Rome, he sacrificed what, if he had consulted his own breast only, would appear to be the stronger to the weaker affection.   Brutus ought naturally to have felt much more for the death of his own sons, than for all that probably Rome could have suffered from the want of so great an example.   But he viewed them, not with the eyes of a father, but with those of a Roman citizen. He entered so thoroughly into the sentiments of this last character, that he paid no regard to that tie, by which he himself was connected with them ; and to a Roman citizen, the sons even of Brutus seemed contemptible, when put into the balance with the smallest interest of Rome.   In these and in all other cases of this kind, our admiration is not so much founded upon the utility, as upon the unexpected, and on that account the great, the noble, and exalted propriety of such actions. This utility, when we come to view it, bestows upon them, undoubtedly a new beauty, and upon that account still further recommends them to our approbation.   This new beauty, however, is chiefly perceived by men of reflection and speculation, and it is by no means the quality which first recommends such actions to the natural sentiments of the bulk of mankind.

It is to be observed, that so far as the sentiment of approbation arises from the perception of this beauty of utility, it has no reference of any kind to the sentiments of others.   If it was possible, therefore, that a person should grow up to manhood without any communication with society, his own actions might, notwithstanding, be agreeable or disagreeable to him on account of their tendency to his happiness or disadvantage.   He might perceive a beauty of this kind in prudence, temperance, and good conduct, and a deformity in the opposite beha-viour : he might view his own temper and character with that sort of satisfaction with which we consider a well-contrived machine, in the one case : or with that sort of distaste and dissatisfaction with which we regard a very awkward and clumsy contrivance, in the other.   As these perceptions, however, are merely a matter of taste, and have all the feebleness and delicacy of that species of perceptions, upon the justness of which what is properly called taste is founded, they proba-bly would not be much attended to by one in his solitary and miserable condition.   Even though they should occur to him, they would by no means have the same effect upon him, antecedent to his connexion with society, which they would have in consequence of that connexion.   He would not be cast down with inward shame at the thought of this deformity ; nor would he be elevated with secret triumph of mind from the consciousness of the contrary beauty.   He would not exult from the notion of deserving reward in the one case, nor tremble from the suspicion of meriting punishment in the other.   All such sentiments suppose the idea of some other being, who is the natural judge of the person that feels them ; and it is only by sympathy with the decisions of this arbiter of his conduct, that he can conceive, either the triumph of self-applause, or the shame of self-condemnation.

Part V.—Of the Influence of Custom and Fashion upon the Sentiments of Moral Approbation and Disapprobation.

CHAP. I.—Of the Influence of Custom and Fashion upon our notions of Beauty and Deformity.

THERE are other principles besides those already enumerated, which have a considerable influence upon the moral sentiments of mankind, and are the chief causes of the many irregular and discordant opinions which prevail in different ages and nations concerning what is blamable or praise-worthy.   These principles are custom and fashion, principles which extend their dominion over our judgments concerning beauty of every kind.

When two objects have frequently been seen together, the imagination acquires a habit of passing easily from the one to the other.   If the first appear, we lay our account that the second is to follow.   Of their own accord they put us in mind of one another, and the attention glides easily along them.   Though, independent of custom, there should be no real beauty in their union, yet when custom has thus connected them together, we feel an impropriety in their separation.   The one we think is awkward when it appears without its usual companion.   We miss something which we expected to find, and the habitual arrangement of our ideas is disturbed by the disappointment.   A suit of clothes, for example, seems to want something if they are without the most insignificant ornament which usually accompanies them, and we find a meanness or awkwardness in the absence even of a haunch button. When there is any natural propriety in the union, custom increases our sense of it, and makes a different arrangement appear still more disagreeable than it would otherwise seem to be.   Those who have been accustomed to see things in a good taste, are more disgusted by whatever is clumsy or awkward.   Where the conjunction is improper, custom either diminishes, or takes away altogether, our sense of the impropriety.   Those who have been accustomed to slovenly disorder lose all sense of neatness or elegance.   The modes of furniture or dress which seem ridiculous to strangers, give no offence to the people who have been used to them.

Fashion is different from custom, or rather is a particular species of it. That is not the fashion which every body wears, but which those wear who are of a high rank, or character. The graceful, the easy, and commanding manners of the great, joined to the usual richness and magnificence of their dress, give a grace to the very form which they happen to bestow upon it. As long as they continue to use this form, it is connected in our imaginations with the idea of something that is genteel and magnificent, and though in itself it should be indifferent, it seems, on account of this relation, to have something about it that is genteel and magnificent too. As soon as they drop it, it loses all the grace, which it had appeared to possess before, and being now used only by the inferior ranks of people, seems to have something of their meanness and their awkwardness.

Dress and furniture are allowed by all the world to be entirely under the dominion of custom and fashion. The influence of those principles, however, is by no means confined to so narrow a sphere, but extends itself to whatever is in any respect the object of taste, to music, to poetry, to architecture. The modes of dress and furniture are continually changing, and that fashion appearing ridiculous to-day which was admired five years ago, we are experimentally convinced that it owed its vogue chiefly or entirely to custom and fashion. Clothes and furniture are not made of very durable materials. A well-fancied coat is done in a twelve-month, and cannot continue longer to propagate, as the fashion, that form according to which it was made. The modes of furniture change less rapidly than those of dress; because furniture is commonly more durable. In five or six years, however, it generally undergoes an entire revolution, and every man in his own time sees the fashion in this respect change many different ways. The productions of the other arts are much more lasting, and, when happily imagined, may continue to propagate the fashion of their make for a much longer time. A well-contrived building may endure many centuries: a beautiful air may be delivered down by a sort of tradition, through many successive generations: a well-written poem may last as long as the world; and all of them continue for ages together, to give the vogue to that particular style, to that particular taste or manner, according to which each of them was composed. Few men have an opportunity of seeing in their own times the fashion in any of these arts change very considerably. Few men have so much experience and acquaintance with the different modes which have obtained in remote ages and nations, as to be thoroughly reconciled to them, or to judge with impartiality between them and what takes place in their own age and country. Few men therefore are willing to allow, that custom or fashion have much influence upon their judgments concerning what is beautiful or otherwise, in the productions of any of those arts; but imagine that all the rules, which they think ought to be observed in each of them, are founded upon reason and nature, not upon habit or prejudice. A very little attention may convince them of the contrary, and satisfy them, that the influence of custom and fashion over dress and furniture, is not more absolute than over architecture, poetry, and music.

Can any reason, for example, be assigned why the Doric capital should be appropriated to a pillar, whose height is equal to eight diameters; the Ionic volute to one of nine; and the Corinthian foliage to one of ten? The propriety of each of those appropriations can be founded upon nothing but habit and custom. The eye having been used to see a particular proportion connected with a particular ornament, would be offended if they were not joined together. Each of the five orders has its peculiar ornaments, which cannot be changed for any other, without giving offence to all those who know any thing of the rules of architecture. According to some architects, indeed, such is the exquisite judgment with which the ancients have assigned to each order its proper ornaments, that no others can be found which are equally suitable. It seems, however, a little difficult to be conceived that these forms, though, no doubt, extremely agreeable, should be the only forms which can suit those proportions, or that there should not be five hundred others which, antecedent to established custom, would have fitted them equally well. When custom, however, has established particular rules of building, provided they are not absolutely unreasonable, it is absurd to think of altering them for others which are only equally good, or even for others which, in point of elegance and beauty, have naturally some little advantage over them. A man would be ridiculous who should appear in public with a suit of clothes quite different from those which are commonly worn, though the new dress should in itself be ever so graceful or convenient. And there seems to be an absurdity of the same kind in ornamenting a house after a quite different manner from that which custom and fashion have prescribed; though the new ornaments should in themselves be somewhat superior to the common ones in use.

According to the ancient rhetoricians, a certain measure or verse was by nature appropriated to each particular species of writing, as being naturally expressive of that character, sentiment, or passion, which ought to predominate in it. One verse, they said, was fit for grave and another for gay works, which could not, they thought, be interchanged without the greatest impropriety. The experience of modern times, however, seems to contradict this principle, though in itself it would appear to be extremely probable. What is the burlesque verse in English, is the heroic verse in French. The tragedies of Racine and the Henriad of Voltaire, are nearly in the same verse with,

Let me have your advice in a weighty affair.

The burlesque verse in French, on the contrary, is pretty much the same with the heroic verse of ten syllables in English. Custom has made the one nation associate the ideas of gravity, sublimity, and seriousness, to that measure which the other has connected with whatever is gay, flippant, and ludicrous. Nothing would appear more absurd in English, than a tragedy written in the Alexandrine verses of the French; or in French, than a work of the same kind in hexametery, or verses of ten syllables.

An eminent artist will bring about a considerable change in the established modes of each of those arts, and introduce a new fashion of writing, music, or architecture. As the dress of an agreeable man of high rank recommends itself, and how peculiar and fantastical soever, comes soon to be admired and imitated; so the excellencies of an eminent master recommend his peculiarities, and his manner becomes the fashionable style in the art which he practises. The taste of the Italians in music and architecture has, within these fifty years, undergone a considerable change, from imitating the peculiarities of some eminent masters in each of those arts. Seneca is accused by Quintilian of having corrupted the taste of the Romans, and of having introduced a frivolous prettiness in the room of majestic reason and masculine eloquence. Sallust and Tacitus have by others been charged with the same accusation, though in a different manner. They gave reputation, it is pretended, to a style, which though in the highest degree concise, elegant, expressive, and even poetical, wanted, however, ease, simplicity, and nature, and was evidently the production of the most laboured and studied affectation. How many great qualities must that writer possess, who can thus render his very faults agreeable? After the praise of refining the taste of a nation, the highest eulogy, perhaps, which can be bestowed upon any author, is to say, that he corrupted it. In our own language, Mr. Pope and Dr. Swift have each of them introduced a manner different from what was practised before, into all works that are written in rhyme, the one in long verses, the other in short. The quaintness of Butler has given place to the plainness of Swift. The rambling freedom of Dryden, and the correct but often tedious and prosaic languor of Addison, are no longer the objects of imitation, but all long verses are now written after the manner of the nervous precision of Mr. Pope.

Neither is it only over the productions of the arts, that custom and fashion exert their dominion. They influence our judgments, in the same manner, with regard to the beauty of natural objects. What various and opposite forms are deemed beautiful in different species of things? The proportions which are admired in one animal, are altogether different from those which are esteemed in another. Every class of things has its own peculiar conformation, which is approved of, and has a beauty of its own, distinct from that of every other species.

It is upon this account that a learned Jesuit, Father Buffier, has determined that the beauty of every object consists in that form and colour, which is most usual among things of that particular sort to which it belongs. Thus, in the human form, the beauty of each feature lies in a certain middle, equally removed from a variety of other forms that are ugly. A beautiful nose, for example, is one that is neither very long, nor very short, neither very straight, nor very crooked, but a sort of middle among all these extremes, and less different from any one of them, than all of them are from one another. It is the form which nature seems to have aimed at in them all, which, however, she deviates from in a great variety of ways, and very seldom hits exactly; but to which all those deviations still bear a very strong resemblance. When a number of drawings are made after one pattern, though they may all miss it in some respects, yet they will all resemble it more than they resemble one another; the general character of the pattern will run through them all; the most singular and odd will be those which are most wide of it; and though very few will copy it exactly, yet the most accurate delineations will bear a greater resemblance to the most careless, than the careless ones will bear to one another. In the same manner, in each species of creatures, what is most beautiful bears the strongest characters of the general fabric of the species, and has the strongest resemblance to the greater part of the individuals with which it is classed. Monsters, on the contrary, or what is perfectly deformed, are always most singular and odd, and have the least resemblance to the generality of that species to which they belong. And thus the beauty of each species, though in one sense the rarest of all things, because few individuals hit this middle form exactly, yet in another, is the most common, because all the deviations from it resemble it more than they resemble one another. The most customary form, therefore, is in each species of things, according to him, the most beautiful. And hence it is that a certain practice and experience in contemplating each species of objects is requisite before we can judge of its beauty, or know wherein the middle and most usual form consists. The nicest judgment concerning the beauty of the human species will not help us to judge of that of flowers, or horses, or any other species of things. It is for the same reason that in different climates, and where different customs and ways of living take place, as the generality of any species receives a different conformation from those circumstances, so different ideas of its beauty prevail. The beauty of a Moorish is not exactly the same with that of an English horse. What different ideas are formed in different nations concerning the beauty of the human shape and countenance? A fair complexion is a shocking deformity upon the coast of Guinea. Thick lips and a flat nose are a beauty. In some nations long ears that hang down upon the shoulders are the objects of universal admiration. In China if a lady's foot is so large as to be fit to walk upon, she is regarded as a monster of ugliness. Some of the savage nations in North America tie four boards round the heads of their children, and thus squeeze them, while the bones are tender and gristly, into a form that is almost perfectly square. Europeans are astonished at the absurd barbarity of this practice, to which some missionaries have imputed the singular stupidity of those nations among whom it prevails. But when they condemn those savages, they do not reflect that the ladies in Europe had, till within these very few years, been endeavouring, for near a century past, to squeeze the beautiful roundness of their natural shape into a square form of the same kind. And that, notwithstanding the many distortions and diseases which this practice was known to occasion, custom had rendered it agreeable among some of the most civilized nations which, perhaps, the world has ever beheld.

Such is the system of this learned and ingenious father, concerning the nature of beauty; of which the whole charm, according to him, would thus seem to arise from its falling in with the habits which custom had impressed upon the imagination, with regard to things of each particular kind. I cannot, however, be induced to believe that our sense even of external beauty is founded altogether on custom. The utility of any form, its fitness for the useful purposes for which it was intended evidently recommends it, and renders it agreeable to us, independent of custom. Certain colours are more agreeable than others, and give more delight to the eye the first time it ever beholds them. A smooth surface is more agreeable than a rough one. Variety is more pleasing than a tedious undiversified uniformity. Connected variety, in which each new appearance seems to be introduced by what went before it, and in which all the adjoining parts seem to have some natural relation to one another, is more agreeable than a disjointed and disorderly assemblage of unconnected objects. But though I cannot admit that custom is the sole principle of beauty, yet I can so far allow the truth of this ingenious system as to grant, that there is scarce any one external form so beautiful as to please, if quite contrary to custom and unlike whatever we have ever been used to in that particular species of things : or so deformed as not to be agreeable, if custom uniformly supports it, and habituates us to see it in every single individual of the kind.

CHAP. II.—*Of the Influence of Custom and Fashion upon Moral Sentiments.*

SINCE our sentiments concerning beauty of every kind, are so much influenced by custom and fashion, it cannot be expected, that those, concerning the beauty of conduct, should be entirely exempted from the dominion of those principles. Their influence here, however, seems to be much less than it is every where else.   There is, perhaps, no form of external objects, how absurd and fantastical soever, to which custom will not reconcile us, or which fashion will not render even agreeable.   But the characters and conduct of a Nero, or a Claudius, are what no custom will ever reconcile us to, what no fashion will ever render agreeable; but the one will always be the object of dread and hatred ; the other of scorn and derision.   The principles of the imagination, upon which our sense of beauty depends, are of a very nice and delicate nature, and may easily be altered by habit and education : but the sentiments of moral approbation and disapprobation, are founded on the strongest and most vigorous passions of human nature ; and though they may be warped, cannot be entirely perverted.

But though the influence of custom and fashion upon moral sentiments, is not altogether so great, it is however perfectly similar to what it is every where else.   When custom and fashion coincide with the natural principles of right and wrong, they heighten the delicacy of our sentiments, and increase our abhorrence for every thing which approaches to evil.   Those who have been educated in what is really good company, not in what is commonly called such, who have been accustomed to see nothing in the persons whom they esteemed and lived with, but justice, modesty, humanity, and good order ; are more shocked with whatever seems to be inconsistent with the rules which those virtues prescribe.   Those, on the contrary, who have had the misfortune to be brought up amidst violence, licentiousness, falsehood, and injustice, lose, though not all sense of the impropriety of such conduct, yet all sense of its dreadful enormity, or of the vengeance and punishment due to it.   They have been familiarized with it from their infancy, custom has rendered it habitual to them, and they are very apt to regard it as, what is called, the way of the world, something which either may, or must be practised, to hinder us from being made the dupes of our own integrity.

Fashion, too, will sometimes give reputation to a certain degree of disorder, and, on the contrary, discountenance qualities which deserve esteem.   In the reign of Charles II. a degree of licentiousness was deemed the characteristic of a liberal education.   It was connected, according to the notions of those times, with generosity, sincerity, magnanimity, loyalty, and proved that the person who acted in this manner, was a gentleman, and not a puritan.   Severity of manners, and regularity of conduct, on the other hand, were altogether unfashionable, and were connected, in the imagination of that age, with cant, cunning, hypocrisy, and low manners.   To superficial minds, the vices of the great seem at all times agreeable.   They connect them, not only with the splendour of fortune, but with many superior virtues, which they ascribe to their superiors ; with the spirit of freedom and independency, with frankness, generosity, humanity, and politeness. The virtues of the inferior ranks of people, on the contrary, their parsimonious frugality, their painful industry, and rigid adherence to rules, seems to them mean and disagreeable. They connect them, both with the meanness of the station to which those qualities do commonly belong, and with many great vices which, they suppose, very usually accompany them; such as an abject, cowardly, ill-natured, lying, and pilfering disposition.

The objects with which men in the different professions and states of life are conversant, being very different, and habituating them to very different passions, naturally form in them very different characters and manners. We expect in each rank and profession, a degree of those manners, which, experience has taught us, belong to it. But as in each species of things, we are particularly pleased with the middle conformation, which, in every part and feature, agrees most exactly with the general standard which nature seems to have established for things of that kind ; so in each rank, or, if I may say so, in each species of men, we are particularly pleased, if they have neither too much, nor too little of the character which usually accompanies their particular condition and situation. A man, we say, should look like his trade and profession ; yet the pedantry of every profession is disagreeable. The different periods of life have, for the same reason, different manners assigned to them. We expect in old age, that gravity and sedateness which its infirmities, its long experience, and its worn-out sensibility seem to render both natural and respectable ; and we lay our account to find in youth that sensibility, that gaiety and sprightly vivacity which experience teaches us to expect from the lively impressions that all interesting objects are apt to make upon the tender and unpractised senses of that early period of life. Each of those two ages, however, may easily have too much of these peculiarities which belong to it. The flirting levity of youth, and the immovable insensibility of old age, are equally disagreeable. The young, according to the common saying, are most agreeable when in their behaviour there is something of the manners of the old, and the old, when they retain something of the gaiety of the young. Either of them, however, may easily have too much of the manners of the other. The extreme coldness, and the dull formality, which are pardoned in old age, make youth ridiculous. The levity, the carelessness, and the vanity, which are indulged in youth, will render old age contemptible.

The peculiar character and manners which we are led by custom to appropriate to each rank and profession, have sometimes perhaps a propriety independent of custom ; and are what we should approve of for their own sakes, if we took into consideration all the different circumstances which naturally affect those in each different state of life. The propriety of a person's behaviour, depends not upon its suitableness to any one circumstance of his situation, but to all the circumstances, which, when we bring his case home to ourselves, we feel, should naturally call upon his attention. If he appears to be so much occupied by any one of them, as entirely to neglect the rest, we disapprove of his conduct, as something which we cannot entirely go along with, because not properly adjusted to all the circumstances of his situation : yet, perhaps, the emotion he expresses for the object which principally interests him, does not exceed what we should entirely sympathize with, and approve of, in one whose attention was not required by any other thing. A parent in private life might, upon the loss of an only son, express without blame a degree of grief and tenderness, which would be unpardonable in a general at the head of an army, when glory, and the public safety, demanded so great a part of his attention. As different objects ought, upon common occasions, to occupy the attention of men of different professions, so different passions ought naturally to become habitual to them ; and when we bring home to ourselves their situation in this particular respect, we must be sensible, that every occurrence should naturally affect them more or less, according as the emotion which it excites, coincides or disagrees with the fixed habit and temper of their minds. We cannot expect the same sensibility to the gay pleasures and amusements of life in a clergyman, which we lay our account with in an officer. The man whose peculiar occupation it is to keep the world in mind of that awful futurity which awaits him, who is to announce what may be the fatal consequences of every deviation from the rules of duty, and who is himself to set the example of the most exact conformity, seems to be the messenger of tidings, which cannot, in propriety, be delivered either with levity or indifference. His mind is supposed to be continually occupied with what is too grand and solemn, to leave any room for the impressions of those frivolous objects, which fill up the attention of the dissipated and the gay. We readily feel therefore, that, independent of custom, there is a propriety in the manners which custom has allotted to this profession ; and that nothing can be more suitable to the character of a clergyman, than that grave, that austere and abstracted severity, which we are habituated to expect in his behaviour. These reflections are so very obvious, that there is scarce any man so inconsiderate, as not, at some time, to have made them, and to have accounted to himself in this manner for his approbation of the useful character of the clerical order.

The foundation of the customary character of some other professions is not so obvious, and our approbation of it is founded entirely in the habit, without being either confirmed or enlivened by any reflections of this kind. We are led by custom, for example, to annex the character of gaiety, levity, and sprightly freedom, as well as of some degree of dissipation, to the military profession. Yet, if we were to consider what mood or tone of temper would be most suitable to this situation, we should be apt to determine, perhaps, that the most serious and thoughtful turn of mind would best become those whose lives are continually exposed to uncommon danger, and who should therefore be more constantly occupied with the thoughts of death and its consequences than other men.   It is this very circumstance, however, which is not improbably the occasion why the contrary turn of mind prevails so much among men of this profession.   It requires so great an effort to conquer the fear of death, when we survey it with steadiness and attention, that those who are constantly exposed to it, find it easier to turn away their thoughts from it altogether, to wrap themselves up in careless security and indifference, and to plunge themselves, for this purpose, into every sort of amusement and dissipation. A camp is not the element of a thoughtful or a melancholy man : persons of that cast, indeed, are often abundantly determined, and are capable, by a great effort, of going on with inflexible resolution to the most unavoidable death.   But to be exposed to continual, though less imminent danger, to be obliged to exert, for a long time, a degree of this effort, exhausts and depresses the mind, and renders it incapable of all happiness and enjoyment.   The gay and careless, who have occasion to make no effort at all, who fairly resolve never to look before them, but to lose in continual pleasures and amusements all anxiety about their situation, more easily support such circumstances.   Whenever, by any peculiar circumstances, an officer has no reason to lay his account with being exposed to any uncommon danger, he is very apt to lose the gaiety and dissipated thoughtlessness of his character.   The captain of a city guard is commonly as sober, careful, and penurious an animal as the rest of his fellow-citizens.   A long peace is, for the same reason, very apt to diminish the difference between the civil and the military character.   The ordinary situation, however, of men of this profession, renders gaiety, and a degree of dissipation, so much their usual character ; and custom has, in our imagination, so strongly connected this character with this state of life, that we are very apt to despise any man, whose peculiar humour or situation renders him incapable of acquiring it.   We laugh at the grave and careful faces of a city guard, which so little resemble those of their profession.   They themselves seem often to be ashamed of the regularity of their own manners, and, not to be out of the fashion of their trade, are fond of affecting that levity, which is by no means natural to them.   Whatever is the deportment which we have been accustomed to see in a respectable order of men, it comes to be so associated in our imagination with that order, that whenever we see the one, we lay our account that we are to meet with the other, and when disappointed, miss something which we expected to find.   We are embarrassed, and put to a stand, and know not how to address ourselves to a character, which plainly affects to be of a different species from those with which we should have been disposed to class it.

The different situations of different ages and countries are apt, in the same manner, to give different characters to the generality of those who live in them, and their sentiments concerning the particular degree of each quality, that is either blamable or praise-worthy, vary according to that degree which is usual in their own country, and in their own times. That degree of politeness which would be highly esteemed, perhaps would be thought effeminate adulation, in Russia, would be regarded as rudeness and barbarism at the court of France. That degree of order and frugality, which, in a Polish nobleman, would be considered as excessive parsimony, would be regarded as extravagance in a citizen of Amsterdam. Every age and country look upon that degree of each quality, which is commonly to be met with in those who are esteemed among themselves, as the golden mean of that particular talent or virtue. And as this varies, according as their different circumstances render different qualities more or less habitual to them, their sentiments concerning the exact propriety of character and behaviour vary accordingly.

Among civilized nations, the virtues which are founded upon humanity, are more cultivated than those which are founded upon self-denial and the command of the passions. Among rude and barbarous nations, it is quite otherwise, the virtues of self-denial are more cultivated than those of humanity. The general security and happiness which prevail in ages of civility and politeness, afford little exercise to the contempt of danger, to patience in enduring labour, hunger, and pain. Poverty may easily be avoided, and the contempt of it therefore almost ceases to be a virtue. The abstinence from pleasure becomes less necessary, and the mind is more at liberty to unbend and to indulge its natural inclinations in all those particular respects.

Among savages and barbarians it is quite otherwise. Every savage undergoes a sort of Spartan discipline, and by the necessity of his situation is inured to every sort of hardship. He is in continual danger : he is often exposed to the greatest extremities of hunger, and frequently dies of pure want. His circumstances not only habituate him to every sort of distress, but teach him to give way to none of the passions which that distress is apt to excite. He can expect from his countrymen no sympathy or indulgence for such weakness. Before we can feel much for others, we must in some measure be at ease ourselves. If our own misery pinches us very severely, we have no leisure to attend to that of our neighbour : and all savages are too much occupied with their own wants and necessities, to give much attention to those of another person. A savage, therefore, whatever be the nature of his distress, expects no sympathy from those about him, and disdains, upon that account, to expose himself, by allowing the least weakness to escape him. His passions, how furious and violent soever, are never permitted to disturb the serenity of his countenance or the composure of his conduct and behaviour. The savages in North America, we are told, assume upon all occasions the greatest indifference, and would think themselves degraded if they should ever appear in any respect to be overcome, either by love, or grief, or resentment. Their magnanimity and self-command, in this respect, are almost beyond the conception of Europeans. In a country in which all men are upon a level, with regard to rank and fortune, it might be expected that the mutual inclinations of the two parties should be the only thing considered in marriages, and should be indulged without any sort of control. This, however, is the country in which all marriages, without exception, are made up by the parents, and in which a young man would think himself disgraced for ever, if he showed the least preference of one woman above another, or did not express the most complete indifference, both about the time when, and the person to whom, he was to be married. The weakness of love, which is so indulged in ages of humanity and politeness, is regarded among savages as the most unpardonable effeminacy. Even after the marriage, the two parties seem to be ashamed of a connexion which is founded upon so sordid a necessity. They do not live together. They see one another by stealth only. They both continue to dwell in the houses of their respective fathers, and the open cohabitation of the two sexes, which is permitted without blame in all other countries, is here considered as the most indecent and unmanly sensuality. Nor is it only over this agreeable passion that they exert this absolute self-command. They often bear, in the sight of all their countrymen, with injuries, reproach, and the grossest insults, with the appearance of the greatest insensibility, and without expressing the smallest resentment. When a savage is made prisoner of war, and receives, as is usual, the sentence of death from his conquerors, he hears it without expressing any emotion, and afterwards submits to the most dreadful torments, without ever bemoaning himself, or discovering any other passion but contempt of his enemies. While he is hung by the shoulders over a slow fire, he derides his tormentors, and tells them with how much more ingenuity he himself had tormented such of their countrymen as had fallen into his hands. After he has been scorched and burnt, and lacerated in all the most tender and sensible parts of his body for several hours together, he is often allowed, in order to prolong his misery, a short respite, and is taken down from the stake : he employs this interval in talking upon all indifferent subjects, inquires after the news of the country, and seems indifferent about nothing but his own situation. The spectators express the same insensibility ; the sight of so horrible an object seems to make no impression upon them ; they scarce look at the prisoner, except when they lend a hand to torment him. At other times they smoke tobacco, and amuse themselves with any common object, as if no such matter was going on. Every savage is said to prepare himself from his earliest youth for this dreadful end. He composes, for this purpose, what they call the song of death, a song which he is to sing when he has fallen into the hands of his enemies, and is expiring under the tortures which they inflict upon him. It consists of insults upon his tormentors, and expresses the highest contempt of death and pain. He sings this song upon all extraordinary occasions, when he goes out to war, when he meets his enemies in the field, or whenever he has a mind to show that he has familiarised his imagination to the most dreadful misfortunes, and that no human event can daunt his resolution or alter his purpose. The same contempt of death and torture prevails among all other savage nations. There is not a negro from the coast of Africa, who does not in this respect, possess a degree of magnanimity which the soul of his sordid master is too often scarce capable of conceiving. Fortune never exerted more cruelly her empire over mankind, than when she subjected those nations of heroes to the refuse of the jails of Europe, to wretches who possess the virtues neither of the countries which they come from, nor of those which they go to, and whose levity, brutality, and baseness, expose them to the contempt of the vanquished.

This heroic and unconquerable firmness, which the custom and education of his country demand of every savage, is not required of those who are brought up to live in civilized societies. If these last complain when they are in pain, if they grieve when they are in distress, if they allow themselves either to be overcome by love, or to be discomposed by anger, they are easily pardoned. Such weaknesses are not apprehended to affect the essential parts of their character. As long as they do not allow themselves to be transported to do anything contrary to justice or humanity, they lose but little reputation, though the serenity of their countenance, or the composure of their discourse and behaviour should be somewhat ruffled and disturbed. A humane and polished people, who have more sensibility to the passions of others, can more readily enter into an animated and passionate behaviour, and can more easily pardon some little excess. The person principally concerned is sensible of this ; and being assured of the equity of his judges, indulges himself in stronger expressions of passion, and is less afraid of exposing himself to their contempt by the violence of his emotions. We can venture to express more emotion in the presence of a friend than in that of a stranger, because we expect more indulgence from the one than from the other. And in the same manner the rules of decorum amongst civilized nations, admit of a more animated behaviour, than is approved of among barbarians. The first converse together with the openness of friends ; the second with the reserve of strangers. The emotion and vivacity with which the French and the Italians, the two most polished nations upon the continent, express themselves on occasions that are at all interesting, surprise at first those strangers who happen to be travelling among them, and who, having been educated among a people of duller sensibility, cannot enter into this passionate behaviour, of which they have never seen any example in their own country.   A young French nobleman will weep in the presence of the whole court upon being refused a regiment.   An Italian, says the Abbot Du Bos, expresses more emotion on being condemned in a fine of twenty shillings, than an Englishman on receiving the sentence of death.   Cicero, in the times of the highest Roman politeness, could, without degrading himself, weep with all the bitterness of sorrow in the sight of the whole senate and the whole people ; as it is evident he must have done in the end of almost every oration.   The orators of the earlier and ruder ages of Rome could not probably, consistent with the manners of the times, have expressed themselves with so much emotion.   It would have been regarded, I suppose, as a violation of nature and propriety in the Scipios, in the Leliuses, and in the elder Cato, to have exposed so much tenderness to the view of the public.   Those ancient warriors could express themselves with order, gravity, and good judgment : but are said to have been strangers to that sublime and passionate eloquence which was first introduced into Rome, not many years before the birth of Cicero, by the two Gracchi, by Crassus, and by Sulpitius.   This animated eloquence, which has been long practised, with or without success, both in France and Italy, is but just beginning to be introduced into England.   So wide is the difference between the degrees of self-command which are required in civilized and in barbarous nations, and by such different standards do they judge of the propriety of behaviour.

This difference gives occasion to many others that are not less essential. A polished people being accustomed to give way, in some measure, to the movements of nature, become frank, open, and sincere. Barbarians, on the contrary, being obliged to smother and conceal the appearance of every passion, necessarily acquire the habits of falsehood and dissimulation.   It is observed by all those who have been conversant with savage nations, whether in Asia, Africa, or America, that they are equally impenetrable, and that, when they have a mind to conceal the truth, no examination is capable of drawing it from them. They cannot be trepanned by the most artful questions.   The torture itself is incapable of making them confess any thing which they have no mind to tell.   The passions of a savage too, though they never express themselves by an outward emotion, but lie concealed in the breast of the sufferer, are, notwithstanding, all mounted to the highest pitch of fury.   Though he seldom shows any symptoms of anger, yet his vengeance, when he comes to give way to it, is always sanguinary and dreadful.   The least affront drives him to despair.   His countenance and discourse indeed, are still sober and composed, and express nothing but the most perfect tranquillity of mind : but his actions are often the most furious and violent. Among the North Americans it is not uncommon for persons of the tenderest age and more fearful sex to drown themselves upon receiving only a slight reprimand from their mothers, and this too without expressing any passion, or saying any thing, except, *you shall no longer have a daughter.* In civilized nations the passions of men are not commonly so furious or so desperate. They are often clamorous and noisy, but are seldom very hurtful; and seem frequently to aim at no other satisfaction, but that of convincing the spectator, that they are in the right to be so much moved, and of procuring his sympathy and approbation.

All these effects of custom and fashion, however, upon the moral sentiments of mankind, are inconsiderable, in comparison of those which they give occasion to in some other cases; and it is not concerning the general style of character and behaviour, that those principles produce the greatest perversion of judgment, but concerning the propriety or impropriety of particular usages.

The different manners which custom teaches us to approve of in the different professions and states of life, do not concern things of the greatest importance. We expect truth and justice from an old man as well as from a young, from a clergyman as well as from an officer; and it is in matters of small moment only that we look for the distinguishing marks of their respective characters. With regard to these, too, there is often some unobserved circumstance which, if it was attended to, would show us, that, independent of custom, there was a propriety in the character which custom had taught us to allot to each profession. We cannot complain, therefore, in this case, that the perversion of natural sentiment is very great. Though the manners of different nations require different degrees of the same quality, in the character which they think worthy of esteem, yet the worst that can be said to happen even here, is that the duties of one virtue are sometimes extended so as to encroach a little upon the precincts of some other. The rustic hospitality that is in fashion among the Poles encroaches, perhaps, a little upon œconomy and good order; and the frugality that is esteemed in Holland, upon generosity and good-fellowship. The hardiness demanded of savages diminishes their humanity; and, perhaps, the delicate sensibility required in civilized nations, sometimes destroys the masculine firmness of the character. In general, the style of manners which takes place in any nation, may commonly upon the whole be said to be that which is most suitable to its situation. Hardiness is the character most suitable to the circumstances of a savage; sensibility to those of one who lives in a very civilized country. Even here, therefore, we cannot complain that the moral sentiments of men, as displayed by them, are very grossly perverted.

It is not therefore in the general style of conduct or behaviour that

13

custom authorises the widest departure from what is the natural propriety of action.   With regard to particular usages, its influence is often
much more destructive of good morals, and it is capable of establishing,
as lawful and blámeless, particular actions, which shock the very
plainest principles of right and wrong.

Can there be greater barbarity, for example, than to hurt an infant?
Its helplessness, its innocence, its amiableness, call forth the compassion, even of an enemy, and not to spare that tender age is regarded as
the most furious effort of an enraged and cruel conqueror.   What then
should we imagine must be the heart of a parent who could injure that
weakness which even a furious enemy is afraid to violate?   Yet the ex-
position, that is, the murder of new-born infants, was a practice allowed
of in almost all the states of Greece, even among the polite and civilized Athenians ; and whenever the circumstances of the parent rendered
it inconvenient to bring up the child, to abandon it to hunger or to wild
beasts was regarded without blame or censure.   This practice had
probably begun in times of the most savage barbarity.   The imaginations of men had been first made familiar with it in that earliest period
of society, and the uniform continuance of the custom had hindered
them afterwards from perceiving its enormity.   We find, at this day,
that this practice prevails among all savage nations ; and in that rudest
and lowest state of society it is undoubtedly more pardonable than in
any other.   The extreme indigence of a savage is often such that he
himself is frequently exposed to the greatest extremity of hunger, he
often dies of pure want, and it is frequently impossible for him to support both himself and his child.   We cannot wonder, therefore, that in
this case he should abandon it.   One who, in flying from an enemy,
whom it was impossible to resist, should throw down his infant, because
it retarded his flight, would surely be excusable; since, by attempting
to save it, he could only hope for the consolation of dying with it.   That
in this state of society, therefore, a parent should be allowed to judge
whether he can bring up his child, ought not to surprise us so greatly.
In the latter ages of Greece, however, the same thing was permitted
from views of remote interest or conveniency, which could by no means
excuse it.   Uninterrupted custom had by this time so thoroughly author-
ised the practice, that not only the loose maxims of the world tolerated
this barbarous prerogative, but even the doctrine of philosophers, which
ought to have been more just and accurate, was led away by the established custom, and upon this, as upon many other occasions, instead
of censuring, supported the horrible abuse, by far-fetched considerations
of public utility.   Aristotle talks of it as of what the magistrate ought
upon many occasions to encourage.   The humane Plato is of the same
opinion, and, with all that love of mankind which seems to animate all
his writings, no where marks this practice with disapprobation.   When
custom can·give sanction to so dreadful a violation of humanity, we

may well imagine that there is scarce any particular practice so gross which it cannot authorise.   Such a thing, we hear men every day saying, is commonly done, and they seem to think this a sufficient apology for what, in itself, is the most unjust and unreasonable conduct.

There is an obvious reason why custom should never pervert our sentiments with regard to the general style and character of conduct and behaviour, in the same degree as with regard to the propriety or unlawfulness of particular usages.   There never can be any such custom.   No society could subsist a moment, in which the usual strain of men's conduct and behaviour was of a piece with the horrible practice I have just now mentioned.

Part VI.—Of the Character of Virtue.

INTRODUCTION.—When we consider the character of any individual, we naturally view it under two different aspects ; first, as it may affect his own happiness ; and secondly, as it may affect that of other people.

SEC. I.—OF THE CHARACTER OF THE INDIVIDUAL, SO FAR AS IT AFFECTS HIS OWN HAPPINESS ; OR OF PRUDENCE.

THE preservation and healthful state of the body seem to be the objects which Nature first recommends to the care of every individual.   The appetites of hunger and thirst, the agreeable or disagreeable sensations of pleasure and pain, of heat and cold, &c., may be considered as lessons delivered by the voice of Nature herself, directing him what he ought to choose, and what he ought to avoid, for this purpose.   The first lessons which he is taught by those to whom his childhood is entrusted, tend, the greater part of them, to the *same* purpose.   Their principal object is to teach him how to keep out of harm's way..

As he grows up, he soon learns that some care and foresight are necessary for providing the means of gratifying those natural appetites, of procuring pleasure and avoiding pain, of procuring the agreeable and avoiding the disagreeable temperature of heat and cold.   In the proper direction of this care and foresight consists the art of preserving and increasing what is called his external fortune.

Though it is in order to supply the necessities and conveniencies of the body, that the advantages of external fortune are originally recommended to us, yet we cannot live long in the world without perceiving that the respect of our equals, our credit and rank in the society we live in, depend very much upon the degree in which we possess, or are supposed to possess, those advantages.   The desire of becoming the

* 13

proper objects of this respect, of deserving and obtaining this credit and rank among our equals, is, perhaps, the strongest of all our desires, and our anxiety to obtain the advantages of fortune is accordingly much more excited and irritated by this desire, than by that of supplying all the necessities and conveniencies of the body, which are always very easily supplied to us.

Our rank and credit among our equals, too, depend very much upon, what, perhaps, a virtuous man would wish them to depend entirely, our character and conduct, or upon the confidence, esteem, and good-will, which these naturally excite in the people we live with.

The care of the health, of the fortune, of the rank and reputation of the individual, the objects upon which his comfort and happiness in this life are supposed principally to depend, is considered as the proper business of that virtue which is commonly called Prudence.

We suffer more, it has already been observed, when we fall from a better to a worse situation, than we ever enjoy when we rise from a worse to a better. Security, therefore, is the first and the principal object of prudence. It is averse to expose our health, our fortune, our rank, or reputation, to any sort of hazard. It is rather cautious than enterprising, and more anxious to preserve the advantages which we already possess, than forward to prompt us to the acquisition of still greater advantages. The methods of improving our fortune, which it principally recommends to us, are those which expose to no loss or hazard ; real knowledge and skill in our trade or profession, assiduity and industry in the exercise of it, frugality, and even some degree of parsimony, in all our expenses.

The prudent man always studies seriously and earnestly to understand whatever he professes to understand, and not merely to persuade other people that he understands it ; and though his talents may not always be very brilliant, they are always perfectly genuine. He neither endeavours to impose upon you by the cunning devices of an artful impostor, nor by the arrogant airs of an assuming pedant, nor by the confident assertions of a superficial and impudent pretender. He is not ostentatious even of the abilities which he really possesses. His conversation is simple and modest, and he is averse to all the quackish arts by which other people so frequently thrust themselves into public notice and reputation. For reputation in his profession he is naturally disposed to rely a good deal upon the solidity of his knowledge and abilities ; and he does not always think of cultivating the favour of those little clubs and cabals, who, in the superior arts and sciences, so often erect themselves into the supreme judges of merit ; and who make it their business to celebrate the talents and virtues of one another, and to decry whatever can come into competition with them. If he ever connects himself with any society of this kind, it is merely in self-defence, not with a view to impose upon the public, but to hinder the public from being imposed upon, to his disadvantage, by the clamours, the whispers, or the intrigues, either of that particular society, or of some other of the same kind.

The prudent man is always sincere, and feels horror at the very thought of exposing himself to the disgrace which attends upon the detection of falsehood. But though always sincere, he is not always frank and open ; and though he never tells any thing but the truth, he does not always think himself bound, when not properly called upon, to tell the whole truth. As he is cautious in his actions, so he is reserved in his speech ; and never rashly or unnecessarily obtrudes his opinion concerning either things or persons.

The prudent man, though not always distinguished by the most exquisite sensibility, is always very capable of friendship. But his friendship is not that ardent and passionate, but too often transitory affection, which appears so delicious to the generosity of youth and inexperience. It is a sedate, but steady and faithful attachment to a few well-tried and well-chosen companions; in the choice of whom he is not guided by the giddy admiration of shining accomplishments, but by the sober esteem of modesty, discretion, and good conduct. But though capable of friendship, he is not always much disposed to general sociality. He rarely frequents, and more rarely figures in those convivial societies which are distinguished for the jollity and gaiety of their conversation. Their way of life might too often interfere with the regularity of his temperance, might interrupt the steadiness of his industry, or break in upon the strictness of his frugality.

But though his conversation may not always be very sprightly or diverting, it is always perfectly inoffensive. He hates the thought of being guilty of any petulance or rudeness. He never assumes impertinently over any body, and, upon all common occasions, is willing to place himself rather below than above his equals. Both in his conduct and conversation, he is an exact observer of decency, and respects with an almost religious scrupulosity, all the established decorums and ceremonials of society. And, in this respect, he sets a much better example than has frequently been done by men of much more splendid talents and virtues, who, in all ages, from that of Socrates and Aristippus, down to that of Dr. Swift and Voltaire, and from that of Philip and Alexander the Great, down to that of the great Czar Peter of Muscovy, have too often distinguished themselves by the most improper and even insolent contempt of all the ordinary decorums of life and conversation, and who have thereby set the most pernicious example to those who wish to resemble them, and who too often content themselves with imitating their follies, without even attempting to attain their perfections.

In the steadiness of his industry and frugality, in his steadily sacrificing the ease and enjoyment of the present moment for the probable expectation of the still greater ease and enjoyment of a more distant but more lasting period of time, the prudent man is always both supported and rewarded by the entire approbation of the impartial spectator, and of the representative of the impartial spectator, the man within the breast. The impartial spectator does not feel himself worn out by the present labour of those whose conduct he surveys; nor does he feel himself solicited by the importunate calls of their present appetites. To him their present, and what is likely to be their future, situation, are very nearly the same : he sees them nearly at the same distance, and is affected by them very nearly in the same manner. He knows, however, that to the persons principally concerned, they are very far from being the same, and that they naturally affect *them* in a very different manner. He cannot therefore but approve, and even applaud, that proper exertion of self-command, which enables them to act as if their present and their future situation affected them nearly in the same manner in which they affect him.

The man who lives within his income, is naturally contented with his situation, which, by continual, though small accumulations, is growing better and better every day. He is enabled gradually to relax, both in the rigour of his parsimony and in the severity of his application ; and he feels with double satisfaction this gradual increase of ease and enjoyment, from having felt before the hardship which attended the want of them. He has no anxiety to change so comfortable a situation and does not go in quest of new enterprises and adventures, which might endanger, but could not well increase the secure tranquillity which he actually enjoys. If he enters into any new projects or enterprises, they are likely to be well concerted and well prepared. He can never be hurried or driven into them by any necessity, but has always time and leisure to deliberate soberly and coolly concerning what are likely to be their consequences.

The prudent man is not willing to subject himself to any responsibility which his duty does not impose upon him. He is not a bustler in business where he has no concern ; is not a meddler in other people's affairs ; is not a professed counsellor or adviser, who obtrudes his advice where nobody is asking it. He confines himself, as much as his duty will permit, to his own affairs, and has no taste for that foolish importance which many people wish to derive from appearing to have some influence in the management of those of other people. He is averse to enter into any party disputes, hates faction, and is not always very forward to listen to the voice even of noble and great ambition. When distinctly called upon, he will not decline the service of his country, but he will not cabal in order to force himself into it, and would be much better pleased that the public business were well managed by some other person, than that he himself should have the trouble, and incur the resposibility, of managing it. In the bottom of his heart he would prefer the undisturbed enjoyment of secure tranquillity, not only to all the vain splendour of successful ambition, but to the real and solid glory of performing the greatest and most magnanimous actions.

Prudence, in short, when directed merely to the care of the health, of the fortune, and the rank and reputation of the individual, though it is regarded as a most respectable, and even in some degree, as an amiable and agreeable quality, yet it never is considered as one, either of the most endearing, or of the most ennobling of the virtues. It commands a certain cold esteem, but does not seem entitled to any very ardent love or admiration.

Wise and judicious conduct, when directed to greater and nobler purposes than the care of the health, the fortune, the rank and reputation of the individual, is frequently and very properly called prudence. We talk of the prudence of the great general, of the great statesman, of the great legislator. Prudence is, in all these cases, combined with many greater and more splendid virtues, with valour, with extensive and strong benevolence, with a sacred regard to the rules of justice, and all these supported by a proper degree of self-command. This superior prudence, when carried to the highest degree of perfection, necessarily supposes the art, the talent, and the habit or disposition of acting with the most perfect propriety in every possible circumstance and situation. It necessarily supposes the utmost perfection of all the intellectual and of all the moral virtues. It is the best head joined to the best heart. It is the most perfect wisdom combined with the most perfect virtue. It constitutes very nearly the character of the Academical or Peripatetic sage, as the superior prudence does that of the Epicurean.

Mere imprudence, or the mere want of the capacity to take care of one's-self, is, with the generous and humane, the object of compassion ; with those of less delicate sentiments, of neglect, or, at worst, of contempt, but never of hatred or indignation. When combined with other vices, however, it aggravates in the highest degree the infamy and disgrace which would otherwise attend them. The artful knave, whose dexterity and address exempt him, though not from strong suspicions, yet from punishment or distinct detection, is too often received in the world with an indulgence which he by no means deserves. The awkward and foolish one, who, for want of this dexterity and address, is convicted and brought to punishment, is the object of universal hatred, contempt, and derision. In countries where great crimes frequently pass unpunished, the most atrocious actions become almost familiar, and cease to impress the people with that horror which is universally felt in countries where an exact administration of justice takes place. The injustice is the same in both countries ; but the imprudence is often very different. In the latter, great crimes are evidently great follies. In the former, they are not always considered as such. In Italy, during the greater part of the sixteenth century, assassinations, murders, and even murders under trust, seem to have been almost familiar among the superior ranks of people. Cæsar Borgia invited four of the little princes in his neighbourhood, who all possessed little sovereignties, and commanded little armies of their own, to a friendly conference at Senigaglia, where, as soon as they arrived, he put them all to death. This infamous action, though certainly not approved of even in that age of crimes, seems to have contributed very little to the discredit, and not in the least to the ruin of the perpetrator. That ruin happened a few years after from causes altogether disconnected with this crime. Machiavel, not indeed a man of the nicest morality even for his own times, was resident, as minister from the republic of Florence, at the court of Cæsar Borgia when this crime was committed. He gives a very particular account of it, and in that pure, elegant, and simple language which distinguishes all his writings. He talks of it very coolly; is pleased with the address with which Cæsar Borgia conducted it ; has much contempt for the dupery and weakness of the sufferers ; but no compassion for their miserable and untimely death, and no sort of indignation at the cruelty and falsehood of their murderer. The violence and injustice of great conquerors are often regarded with foolish wonder and admiration ; those of petty thieves, robbers, and murderers, with contempt, hatred, and even horror upon all occasions. The former, though they are a hundred times more mischievous and destructive, yet when successful, they often pass for deeds of the most heroic magnanimity. The latter are always viewed with hatred and aversion, as the follies, as well as the crimes, of the lowest and most worthless of mankind. The injustice of the former is certainly, at least, as great as that of the latter ; but the folly and imprudence are not near so great. A wicked and worthless man of parts often goes through the world with much more credit than he deserves. A wicked and worthless fool appears always, of all mortals, the most hateful, as well as the most contemptible. As prudence combined with other virtues, constitutes the noblest; so imprudence combined with other vices, constitutes the vilest of all characters.

SECT. II.—OF THE CHARACTER OF THE INDIVIDUAL, SO FAR AS IT CAN AFFECT THE HAPPINESS OF OTHER PEOPLE.

INTRODUCTION.—The character of every individual, so far as it can affect the happiness of other people, must do so by its disposition either to hurt or to benefit them.

Proper resentment for injustice attempted, or actually committed, is the only motive which, in the eyes of the impartial spectator, can justify our hurting or disturbing in any respect the happiness of our neighbour.

To do so from any other motive is itself a violation of the laws of justice, which force ought to be employed either to restrain or to punish. The wisdom of every state or commonwealth endeavours, as well as it can, to employ the force of the society to restrain those who are subject to its authority from hurting or disturbing the happiness of one another. The rules which it establishes for this purpose, constitute the civil and criminal law of each particular state or country. The principles upon which those rules either are, or ought to be founded, are the subject of a particular science, of all sciences by far the most important, but hitherto, perhaps, the least cultivated, that of natural jurisprudence; concerning which it belongs not to our present subject to enter into any detail. A sacred and religious regard not to hurt or disturb in any respect the happiness of our neighbour, even in those cases where no law can properly protect him, constitutes the character of the perfectly innocent and just man; a character which, when carried to a certain delicacy of attention, is always highly respectable and even venerable for its own sake, and can scarce ever fail to be accompanied with many other virtues, with great feeling for other people, with great humanity and great benevolence. It is a character sufficiently understood, and requires no further explanation. In the present section I shall only endeavour to explain the foundation of that order which nature seems to have traced out for the distribution of our good offices, or for the direction and employment of our very limited powers of beneficence: first, towards individuals; and secondly, towards societies.

The same unerring wisdom, it will be found, which regulates every other part of her conduct, directs, in this respect too, the order of her recommendations; which are always stronger or weaker in proportion as our beneficence is more or less necessary, or can be more or less useful.

CHAP. I.—*Of the Order in which Individuals are recommended by Nature to our Care and Attention.*

EVERY man, as the Stoics used to say, is first and principally recommended to his own care; and every man is certainly, in every respect, fitter and abler to take care of himself than of any other person. Every man feels his own pleasures and his own pains more sensibly than those of other people. The former are the original sensations; the latter the reflected or sympathetic images of those sensations. The former may be said to be the substance; the latter the shadow.

After himself, the members of his own family, those who usually live in the same house with him, his parents, his children, his brothers and sisters, are naturally the objects of his warmest affections. They are naturally and usually the persons upon whose happiness or misery his conduct must have the greatest influence. He is more habituated to sympathize with them. He knows better how every thing is likely to affect them, and his sympathy with them is more precise and determinate, than it can be with the greater part of other people. It approaches nearer, in short, to what he feels for himself.

This sympathy too, and the affections which are founded on it, are by nature more strongly directed towards his children than towards his parents, and his tenderness for the former seems generally a more active principle, than his reverence and gratitude towards the latter. In the natural state of things, it has already been observed, the existence of the child, for some time after it comes into the world, depends altogether upon the care of the parent; that of the parent does not naturally depend upon the care of the child. In the eye of nature, it would seem, a child is a more important object than an old man; and excites a much more lively, as well as a much more universal sympathy. It ought to do so. Every thing may be expected, or at least hoped, from the child. In ordinary cases, very little can be either expected or hoped from the old man. The weakness of childhood interests the affections of the most brutal and hard-hearted. It is only to the virtuous and humane, that the infirmities of old age are not the objects of contempt and aversion. In ordinary cases, an old man dies without being much regretted by any body. Scarce a child can die without rending asunder the heart of somebody.

The earliest friendships, the friendships which are naturally contracted when the heart is most susceptible of that feeling, are those among brothers and sisters. Their good agreement, while they remain in the same family, is necessary for its tranquillity and happiness. They are capable of giving more pleasure or pain to one another than to the greater part of other people. Their situation renders their mutual sympathy of the utmost importance to their common happiness; and, by the wisdom of nature, the same situation, by obliging them to accommodate to one another, renders that sympathy more habitual, and thereby more lively, more distinct, and more determinate.

The children of brothers and sisters are naturally connected by the friendship which, after separating into different families, continues to take place between their parents. Their good agreement improves the enjoyment of that friendship; their discord would disturb it. As they seldom live in the same family, however, though of more importance to one another than to the greater part of other people, they are of much less than brothers and sisters. As their mutual sympathy is less necessary, so it is less habitual, and therefore proportionably weaker.

The children of cousins, being still less connected, are of still less importance to one another; and the affection gradually diminishes as the relation grows more and more remote.

What is called affection, is in reality nothing but habitual sympathy. Our concern in the happiness or misery of those who are the objects of

what we call our affections; our desire to promote the one, and to prevent the other; are either the actual feeling of that habitual sympathy,
or the necessary consequences of that feeling.   Relations being usually
placed in situations which naturally create this habitual sympathy, it is
expected that a suitable degree of affection should take place among
them. We generally find that it actually does take place; we therefore
naturally expect that it should; and we are, upon that account, more
shocked when, upon any occasion, we find that it does not.   The
general rule is established, that persons related to one another in a
certain degree, ought always to be affected towards one another in a
certain manner, and that there is always the highest impropriety, and
sometimes even a sort of impiety, in their being affected in a different
manner. A parent without parental tenderness, a child devoid of all
filial reverence, appear monsters, the objects, not of hatred only, but of
horror to their neighbours.

Though in a particular instance, the circumstances which usually
produce those natural affections, as they are called, may, by some
accident, not have taken place, yet respect for the general rule will
frequently, in some measure, supply their place, and produce something
which, though not altogether the same, may bear, however, a very considerable resemblance to those affections. A father is apt to be less
attached to a child, who, by some accident, has been separated from
him in its infancy, and who does not return to him till it is grown up to
manhood. The father is apt to feel less paternal tenderness for the
child; the child, less filial reverence for the father. Brothers and
sisters, when they have been educated in distant countries, are apt to
feel a similar diminution of affection. With the dutiful and the virtuous, however, respect for the general rule will frequently produce something which, though by no means the same, yet may very much
resemble those natural affections. Even during the separation, the
father and the child, the brothers or the sisters, are by no means
indifferent to one another. They all consider one another as persons
to and from whom certain affections are due, and they live in the hopes
of being some time or another in a situation to enjoy that friendship
which ought naturally to have taken place among persons so nearly
connected. Till they meet, the absent son, the absent brother, are
frequently the favourite son, the favourite brother. They have never
offended, or, if they have, it is so long ago, that the offence is forgotten,
as some childish trick not worth the remembering. Every account they
have heard of one another, if conveyed by people of any tolerable good
nature, has been, in the highest degree, flattering and favourable. The
absent son, the absent brother, is not like other ordinary sons and
brothers; but an all-perfect son, an all-perfect brother; and the most
romantic hopes are entertained of the happiness to be enjoyed in the
friendship and conversation of such persons. When they meet, it is

often with so strong a disposition to conceive that habitual sympathy which constitutes the family affection, that they are very apt to fancy they have actually conceived it, and to behave to one another as if they had.   Time and experience, however, I am afraid, too frequently undeceive them.   Upon a more familiar acquaintance, they frequently discover in one another habits, humours, and inclinations, different from what they expected, to which, from want of habitual sympathy, from want of the real principle and foundation of what is properly called family-affection, they cannot now easily accommodate themselves. They have never lived in the situation which almost necessarily forces that easy accommodation, and though they may now be sincerely desirous to assume it, they have really become incapable of doing so. Their familiar conversation and intercourse soon become less pleasing to them, and, upon that account, less frequent.   They may continue to live with one another in the mutual exchange of all essential good offices, and with every other external appearance of decent regard. But that cordial satisfaction, that delicious sympathy, that confidential openness and ease, which naturally take place in the conversation of those who have lived long and familiarly with one another, it seldom happens that they can completely enjoy.

It is only, however, with the dutiful and the virtuous, that the general rule has even this slender authority.   With the dissipated, the profligate, and the vain, it is entirely disregarded.   They are so far from respecting it, that they seldom talk of it but with the most indecent derision ; and an early and long separation of this kind never fails to estrange them most completely from one another.   With such persons, respect for the general rule can at best produce only a cold and affected civility (a very slender semblance of real regard) ; and even this, the slightest offence, the smallest opposition of interest, commonly puts an end to altogether.

The education of boys at distant great schools, of young men at distant colleges, of young ladies in distant nunneries and boarding-schools, seems, in the higher ranks of life, to have hurt most essentially the domestic morals, and consequently the domestic happiness, both of France and England.   Do you wish to educate your children to be dutiful to their parents, to be kind and affectionate to their brothers and sisters? put them under the necessity of being dutiful children, of being kind and affectionate brothers and sisters : educate them in your own house.   From their parent's house, they may, with propriety and advantage, go out every day to attend public schools : but let their dwelling be always at home.   Respect for you must always impose a very useful restraint upon their conduct; and respect for them may frequently impose no useless restraint upon your own. Surely no acquirement, which can possibly be derived from what is called a public education, can make any sort of compensation for what is almost certainly and necessarily lost by it.   Domestic education is the institution of nature; public education, the contrivance of man. It is surely unnecessary to say, which is likely to be the wisest.

In some tragedies and romances, we meet with many beautiful and interesting scenes, founded upon what is called, the force of blood, or upon the wonderful affection which near relations are supposed to conceive for one another, even before they know that they have any such connection.   This force of blood, however, I am afraid, exists no where but in tragedies and romances.   Even in tragedies and romances, it is never supposed to take place between any relations, but those who are naturally bred up in the same house; between parents and children, between brothers and sisters.   To imagine any such mysterious affection between cousins, or even between aunts or uncles, and nephews or nieces, would be too ridiculous.

In pastoral countries, and in all countries where the authority of law is not alone sufficient to give perfect security to every member of the state, all the different branches of the same family commonly choose to live in the neighbourhood of one another.   Their association is frequently necessary for their common defence.   They are all, from the highest to the lowest, of more or less importance to one another. Their concord strengthens their necessary association: their discord always weakens, and might destroy it.   They have more intercourse with one another, than with the members of any other tribe.   The remotest members of the same tribe claim some connection with one another; and, where all other circumstances are equal, expect to be treated with more distinguished attention than is due to those who have no such pretensions.   It is not many years ago that, in the Highlands of Scotland, the chieftain used to consider the poorest man of his clan, as his cousin and relation.   The same extensive regard to kindred is said to take place among the Tartars, the Arabs, the Turkomans, and, I believe, among all other nations who are nearly in the same state of society in which the Scots Highlanders were about the beginning of the present century.

In commercial countries, where the authority of law is always perfectly sufficient to protect the meanest man in the state, the descendants of the same family, having no such motive for keeping together, naturally separate and disperse, as interest or inclination may direct. They soon cease to be of importance to one another; and, in a few generations, not only lose all care about one another, but all remembrance of their common origin, and of the connection which took place among their ancestors.   Regard for remote relations becomes, in every country, less and less, according as this state of civilization has been longer and more completely established.   It has been longer and more completely established in England than in Scotland; and remote relations are, accordingly, more considered in the latter country than in the

former, though, in this respect, the difference between the two
countries is growing less and less every day. Great lords, indeed,
are, in every country, proud of remembering and acknowledging their
connection with one another, however remote. The remembrance of
such illustrious relations flatters not a little the family pride of them
all; and it is neither from affection, nor from any thing which resembles
affection, but from the most frivolous and childish of all vanities, that
this remembrance is so carefully kept up. Should some more humble,
though, perhaps, much nearer kinsman, presume to put such great men
in mind of his relation to their family, they seldom fail to tell him that
they are bad genealogists, and miserably ill-informed concerning their
own family history. It is not in that order that we are to expect any
extraordinary extension of, what is called, natural affection.

I consider what is called natural affection as more the effect of the
moral than of the supposed physical connection between the parent
and the child. A jealous husband, indeed, notwithstanding the moral
connection, notwithstanding the child's having been educated in his
own house, often regards, with hatred and aversion, that unhappy child
which he supposes to be the offspring of his wife's infidelity. It is the
lasting monument of a most disagreeable adventure ; of his own dishonour, and of the disgrace of his family.

Among well-disposed people, the necessity or conveniency of mutual
accommodation, very frequently produces a friendship not unlike that
which takes place among those who are born to live in the same
family. Colleagues in office, partners in trade, call one another brothers ; and frequently feel towards one another as if they really were
so. Their good agreement is an advantage to all ; and, if they are
tolerably reasonable people, they are naturally disposed to agree. We
expect that they should do so ; and their disagreement is a sort of a
small scandal. The Romans expressed this sort of attachment by the
word *necessitudo*, which, from the etymology, seems to denote that it
was imposed by the necessity of the situation.

Even the trifling circumstance of living in the same neighbourhood,
has some effect of the same kind. We respect the face of a man whom
we see every day, provided he has never offended us. Neighbours can
be very convenient, and they can be very troublesome, to one another.
If they are good sort of people, they are naturally disposed to agree.
We expect their good agreement ; and to be a bad neighbour is a very
bad character. There are certain small good offices, accordingly, which
are universally allowed to be due to a neighbour in preference to any
other person who has no such connection.

This natural disposition to accommodate and to assimilate, as much
as we can, our own sentiments, principles, and feelings, to those which
we see fixed and rooted in the persons whom we are obliged to live and
converse a great deal with, is the cause of the contagious effects of both

good and bad company. The man who associates chiefly with the wise and the virtuous, though he may not himself become either wise or virtuous, cannot help conceiving a certain respect at least for wisdom and virtue ; and the man who associates chiefly with the profligate and the dissolute, though he may not himself become profligate and dissolute, must soon lose, at least, all his original abhorrence of profligacy and dissolution of manners. The similarity of family characters, which we so frequently see transmitted through several successive generations, may, perhaps, be partly owing to this disposition to assimilate ourselves to those whom we are obliged to live and converse a great deal with. The family character, however, like the family countenance, seems to be owing, not altogether to the moral, but partly too to the physical connection. The family countenance is certainly altogether owing to the latter.

But of all attachments to an individual, that which is founded altogether upon esteem and approbation of his good conduct and behaviour, confirmed by much experience and long acquaintance, is, by far, the most respectable. Such friendships, arising not from a constrained sympathy, not from a sympathy which has been assumed and rendered habitual for the sake of convenience and accommodation; but from a natural sympathy, from an involuntary feeling that the persons to whom we attach ourselves are the natural and proper objects of esteem and approbation ; can exist only among men of virtue. Men of virtue only can feel that entire confidence in the conduct and behaviour of one another, which can, at all times, assure them that they can never either offend or be offended by one another. Vice is always capricious : virtue only is regular and orderly. The attachment which is founded upon the love of virtue, as it is certainly, of all attachments, the most virtuous ; so it is likewise the happiest, as well as the most permanent and secure. Such friendships need not be confined to a single person, but may safely embrace all the wise and virtuous, with whom we have been long and intimately acquainted, and upon whose wisdom and virtue we can, upon that account, entirely depend. They who would confine friendship to two persons, seem to confound the wise security of friendship with the jealousy and folly of love. The hasty, fond, and foolish intimacies of young people, founded, commonly, upon some slight similarity of character, altogether unconnected with good conduct, upon a taste, perhaps, for the same studies, the same amusements, the same diversions, or upon their agreement in some singular principle or opinion, not commonly adopted ; those intimacies which a freak begins, and which a freak puts an end to, how agreeable soever they may appear while they last, can by no means deserve the sacred and the venerable name of friendship.

Of all the persons, however, whom nature points out for our peculiar beneficence, there are none to whom it seems more properly directed than to those whose beneficence we have ourselves already experienced. Nature, which formed men for that mutual kindness so necessary for their happiness, renders every man the peculiar object of kindness to the persons to whom he himself has been kind. Though their gratitude should not always correspond to his beneficence, yet the sense of his merit, the sympathetic gratitude of the impartial spectator, will always correspond to it. The general indignation of other people against the baseness of their ingratitude will even, sometimes, increase the general sense of his merit. No benevolent man ever lost altogether the fruits of his benevolence. If he does not always gather them from the persons from whom he ought to have gathered them, he seldom fails to gather them, and with a tenfold increase, from other people. Kindness is the parent of kindness ; and if to be beloved by our brethren be the great object of our ambition, the surest way of obtaining it is, by our conduct to show that we really love them.

After the persons who are recommended to our beneficence, either their connection with ourselves, by their personal qualities, or by their past services, come those who are pointed out, not indeed to, what is called, our friendship, but to our benevolent attention and good offices ; those who are distinguished by their extraordinary situation ; the greatly fortunate and the greatly unfortunate, the rich and the powerful, the poor and the wretched. The distinction of ranks, the peace and order of society, are, in a great measure, founded upon the respect which we naturally conceive for the former. The relief and consolation of human misery depend altogether upon our compassion for the latter. The peace and order of society, is of more importance than even the relief of the miserable. Our respect for the great, accordingly, is most apt to offend by its excess ; our fellow-feeling for the miserable, by its defect. Moralists exhort us to charity and compassion. They warn us against the fascination of greatness. This fascination, indeed, is so powerful, that the rich and the great are too often preferred to the wise and the virtuous. Nature has wisely judged that the distinction of ranks, the peace and order of society, would rest more securely upon the plain and palpable difference of birth and fortune, than upon the invisible and often uncertain difference of wisdom and virtue. The undistinguishing eyes of the great mob of mankind can well enough perceive the former : it is with difficulty that the nice discernment of the wise and the virtuous can sometimes distinguish the latter. In the order of all those recommendations to virtue, the benevolent wisdom of nature is equally evident.

It may, perhaps, be unnecessary to observe, that the combination of two or more of those exciting causes of kindness, increases the kindness. The favour and partiality which, when there is no envy in the case, we naturally bear to greatness, are much increased when it is joined with wisdom and virtue. If, notwithstanding that wisdom and virtue, the great man should fall into those misfortunes, those dangers and distresses, to which the most exalted stations are often the most exposed, we are much more deeply interested in his fortune than we should be in that of a person equally virtuous, but in a more humble situation. The most interesting subjects of tragedies and romances are the misfortunes of virtuous and magnanimous kings and princes. If, by the wisdom and manhood of their exertions, they should extricate themselves from those misfortunes, and recover completely their former superiority and security, we cannot help viewing them with the most enthusiastic and even extravagant admiration. The grief which we felt for their distress, the joy which we feel for their prosperity, seem to combine together in enhancing that partial admiration which we naturally conceive both for the station and the character.

When those different beneficent affections happen to draw different ways, to determine by any precise rules in what cases we ought to comply with the one, and in what with the other, is, perhaps, altogether impossible. In what cases friendship ought to yield to gratitude, or gratitude to friendship ; in what cases the strongest of all natural affections ought to yield to a regard for the safety of those superiors upon whose safety often depends that of the whole society ; and in what cases natural affection may, without impropriety, prevail over that regard ; must be left altogether to the decision of the man within the breast, the supposed impartial spectator, the great judge and arbiter of our conduct. If we place ourselves completely in his situation, if we really view ourselves with his eyes, and as he views us, and listen with diligent and reverential attention to what he suggests to us, his voice will never deceive us. We shall stand in need of no casuistic rules to direct our conduct. These it is often impossible to accommodate to all the different shades and gradations of circumstance, character, and situation, to differences and distinctions which, though not imperceptible, are, by their nicety and delicacy, often altogether undefinable. In that beautiful tragedy of Voltaire, the Orphan of China, while we admire the magnanimity of Zamti, who is willing to sacrifice the life of his own child, in order to preserve that of the only feeble remnant of his ancient sovereigns and masters ; we not only pardon, but love the maternal tenderness of Idame, who, at the risk of discovering the important secret of her husband, reclaims her infant from the cruel hands of the Tartars, into which it had been delivered.

CHAP. II.—*Of the Order in which Societies are by Nature recommended to our Beneficence.*

THE same principles that direct the order in which individuals are recommended to our beneficence, direct that likewise in which societies are recommended to it. Those to which it is, or may be of most importance, are first and principally recommended to it.

The state or sovereignty in which we have been born and educated, and under the protection of which we continue to live, is, in ordinary cases, the greatest society upon whose happiness or misery our good or bad conduct can have much influence. It is accordingly, by nature, most strongly recommended to us. Not only we ourselves, but all the objects of our kindest affections, our children, our parents, our relations, our friends, our benefactors, all those whom we naturally love and revere the most, are commonly comprehended within it ; and their prosperity and safety depend in some measure upon its prosperity and safety. It is by nature, therefore, endeared to us, not only by all our selfish, but by all our private benevolent affections. Upon account of our own connexion with it, its prosperity and glory seem to reflect some sort of honour upon ourselves. When we compare it with other societies of the same kind, we are proud of its superiority, and mortified in some degree if it appears in any respect below them. All the illustrious characters which it has produced in former times (for against those of our own times envy may sometimes prejudice us a little), its warriors its statesmen, its poets, its philosophers, and men of letters of all kinds ; we are disposed to view with the most partial admiration, and to rank them (sometimes most unjustly) above those of all other nations. The patriot who lays down his life for the safety, or even for the vain-glory of this society, appears to act with the most exact propriety. He appears to view himself in the light in which the impartial spectator naturally and necessarily views him, as but one of the multitude, in the eye of that equitable judge, of no more consequence than any other in it, but bound at all times to sacrifice and devote himself to the safety, to the service, and even to the glory of the greater number. But though this sacrifice appears to be perfectly just and proper, we know how difficult it is to make it, and how few people are capable of making it. His conduct, therefore, excites not only our entire approbation, but our highest wonder and admiration, and seems to merit all the applause which can be due to the most heroic virtue. The traitor, on the contrary, who, in some peculiar situation, fancies he can promote his own little interest by betraying to the public enemy that of his native country ; who, regardless of the judgment of the man within the breast, prefers himself, in this respect so shamefully and so basely, to all those with whom he has any connexion; appears to be of all villains the most detestable.

The love of our own nation often disposes us to view, with the most malignant jealousy and envy, the prosperity and aggrandisement of any other neighbouring nation. Independent and neighbouring nations, having no common superior to decide their disputes, all live in continual dread and suspicion of one another. Each sovereign, expecting little justice from his neighbours, is disposed to treat them with as little as he expects from them. The regard for the laws of nations, or for those rules which independent states profess or pretend to think themselves bound to observe in their dealings with one another, is often very little more than mere pretence and profession. From the smallest interest, upon the slightest provocation, we see those rules every day, either evaded or directly violated without shame or remorse. Each nation foresees, or imagines it foresees, its own subjugation in the increasing power and aggrandisement of any of its neighbours; and the mean principle of national prejudice is often founded upon the noble one of the love of our own country. The sentence with which the elder Cato is said to have concluded every speech which he made in the senate, whatever might be the subject, '*It is my opinion like-* '*wise that Carthage ought to be destroyed,*' was the natural expression of the savage patriotism of a strong but coarse mind, enraged almost to madness against a foreign nation from which his own had suffered so much. The more humane sentence with which Scipio Nasica is said to have concluded all his speeches, '*It is my opinion like-* '*wise that Carthage ought not to be destroyed,*' was the liberal expression of a more enlarged and enlightened mind, who felt no aversion to the prosperity even of an old enemy, when reduced to a state which could no longer be formidable to Rome. France and England may each of them have some reason to dread the increase of the naval and military power of the other; but for either of them to envy the internal happiness and prosperity of the other, the cultivation of its lands, the advancement of its manufactures, the increase of its commerce, the security and number of its ports and harbours, its proficiency in all the liberal arts and sciences, is surely beneath the dignity of two such great nations. These are all real improvements of the world we live in. Mankind are benefited, human nature is ennobled by them. In such improvements each nation ought, not only to endeavour itself to excel, but from the love of mankind, to promote, instead of obstructing the excellence of its neighbours. These are all proper objects of national emulation, not of national prejudice or envy.

The love of our own country seems not to be derived from the love of mankind. The former sentiment is altogether independent of the latter, and seems sometimes even to dispose us to act inconsistently with it. France may contain, perhaps, near three times the number of inhabitants which Great Britain contains. In the great society of mankind, therefore, the prosperity of France should appear to be an object of much greater importance than that of Great Britain. The British subject, however, who, upon that account, should prefer upon all occasions the prosperity of the former to that of the latter country, would not be thought a good citizen of Great Britain. We do not love our country merely as a part of the great society of mankind: we love

14 *

it for its own sake, and independently of any such consideration. That wisdom which contrived the system of human affections, as well as that of every other part of nature, seems to have judged that the interest of the great society of mankind would be best promoted by directing the principal attention of each individual to that particular portion of it, which was most within the sphere both of his abilities and of his understanding.

National prejudices and hatreds seldom extend beyond neighbouring nations. We very weakly and foolishly, perhaps, call the French our natural enemies; and they perhaps, as weakly and foolishly, consider us in the same manner. Neither they nor we bear any sort of envy to the prosperity of China or Japan. It very rarely happens, however, that our good-will towards such distant countries can be exerted with much effect.

The most extensive public benevolence which can commonly be exerted with any considerable effect, is that of the statesmen, who project and form alliances among neighbouring or not very distant nations, for the preservation either of, what is called, the balance of power, or of the general peace and tranquillity of the states within the circle of their negotiations. The statesmen, however, who plan and execute such treaties, have seldom anything in view, but the interest of their respective countries. Sometimes, indeed, their views are more extensive. The Count d'Avaux, the plenipotentiary of France, at the treaty of Munster, would have been willing to sacrifice his life (according to the Cardinal de Retz, a man not over-credulous in the virtue of other people) in order to have restored, by that treaty, the general tranquillity of Europe. King William seems to have had a zeal for the liberty and independency of the greater part of the sovereign states of Europe; which, perhaps, might be a good deal stimulated by his particular aversion to France, the state from which, during his time, that liberty and independency were principally in danger. Some share of the same spirit seems to have descended to the first ministry of Queen Anne.

Every independent state is divided into many different orders and societies, each of which has its own particular powers, privileges, and immunities. Every individual is naturally more attached to his own particular order or society, than to any other. His own interest, his own vanity, the interest and vanity of many of his friends and companions, are commonly a good deal connected with it.' He is ambitious to extend its privileges and immunities. He is zealous to defend them against the encroachments of every other order of society.

Upon the manner in which any state is divided into the different orders and societies which compose it, and upon the particular distribution which has been made of their respective powers, privileges, and immunities, depends, what is called, the constitution of that particular state.

Upon the ability of each particular order or society to maintain its own powers, privileges, and immunities, against the encroachments of every other, depends the stability of that particular constitution. That particular constitution is necessarily more or less altered, whenever any of its subordinate parts is either raised above or depressed below whatever had been its former rank and condition.

All those different orders and societies are dependent upon the state to which they owe their security and protection. That they are all subordinate to that state, and established only in subserviency to its prosperity and preservation, is a truth acknowledged by the most partial member of every one of them. It may often, however, be hard to convince him that the prosperity and preservation of the state requires any diminution of the powers, privileges, and immunities of his own particular order of society. This partiality, though it may sometimes be unjust, may not, upon that account, be useless. It checks the spirit of innovation. It tends to preserve whatever is the established balance among the different orders and societies into which the state is divided ; and while it sometimes appears to obstruct some alterations of government which may be fashionable and popular at the time, it contributes in reality to the stability and permanency of the whole system.

The love of our country seems, in ordinary cases, to involve in it two different principles ; first, a certain respect and reverence for that constitution or form of government which is actually established ; and secondly, an earnest desire to render the condition of our fellow-citizens as safe, respectable, and happy as we can. He is not a citizen who is not disposed to respect the laws and to obey the civil magistrate ; and he is certainly not a good citizen who does not wish to promote, by every means in his power, the welfare of the whole society of his fellow citizens.

In peaceable and quiet times, those two principles generally coincide and lead to the same conduct. The support of the established government seems evidently the best expedient for maintaining the safe, respectable, and happy situation of our fellow-citizens ; when we see that this government actually maintains them in that situation. But in times of public discontent, faction, and disorder, those two different principles may draw different ways, and even a wise man may be disposed to think some alteration necessary in that constitution or form of government, which, in its actual condition, appears plainly unable to maintain the public tranquillity. In such cases, however, it often requires, perhaps, the highest effort of political wisdom to determine when a real patriot ought to support and endeavour to re-establish the authority of the old system, and when we ought to give way to the more daring, but often dangerous, spirit of innovation.

Foreign war and civil faction are the two situations which afford the most splendid opportunities for the display of public spirit. The hero who serves his country successfully in foreign war gratifies the wishes of the whole nation, and is, upon that account, the object of universal gratitude and admiration. In times of civil discord, the leaders of the contending parties, though they may be admired by one half of their fellow-citizens, are commonly execrated by the other. Their characters and the merit of their respective services appear commonly more doubtful. The glory which is acquired by foreign war is, upon this account, almost always more pure and more splendid than that which can be acquired in civil faction.

The leader of the successful party, however, if he has authority enough to prevail upon his own friends to act with proper temper and moderation (which he frequently has not), may sometimes render to his country a service much more essential and important than the greatest victories and the most extensive conquests. He may re-establish and improve the constitution, and from the very doubtful and ambiguous character of the leader of a party, he may assume the greatest and noblest of all characters, that of the reformer and legislator of a great state ; and, by the wisdom of his institutions, secure the internal tranquillity and happiness of his fellow-citizens for many succeeding generations.

Amidst the turbulence and disorder of faction, a certain spirit of system is apt to mix itself with that public spirit which is founded upon the love of humanity, upon a real fellow-feeling with the inconveniencies and distresses to which some of our fellow-citizens may be exposed. This spirit of system commonly takes the direction of that more gentle public spirit, always animates it, and often inflames it even to the madness of fanaticism. The leaders of the discontented party seldom fail to hold out some plausible plan of reformation which, they pretend, will not only remove the inconveniencies and relieve the distresses immediately complained of, but will prevent, in all time coming, any return of the like inconveniencies and distresses. They often propose, upon this account, to new model the constitution, and to alter, in some of its most essential parts, that system of government under which the subjects of a great empire have enjoyed, perhaps, peace, security, and even glory, during the course of several centuries together. The great body of the party are commonly intoxicated with the imaginary beauty of this ideal system, of which they have no experience, but which has been represented to them in all the most dazzling colours in which the eloquence of their leaders could paint it. Those leaders themselves, though they originally may have meant nothing but their own aggrandisement, become many of them in time the dupes of their own sophistry, and are as eager for this great reformation as the weakest and most foolish of their followers. Even though the leaders should have preserved their own heads, as indeed they commonly do, free from this fanaticism, yet they dare not always disappoint the expectation of their followers ; bnt are often obliged, though contrary to their principle and their conscience, to act as if they were under the common delusion. The violence of the party, refusing all palliatives, all temperaments, all reasonable accommodations, by requiring too much frequently obtains nothing ; and those inconveniencies and distresses which, with a little moderation, might in a great measure have been removed and relieved, are left altogether without the hope of a remedy.

The man whose public spirit is prompted altogether by humanity and benevolence, will respect the established powers and privileges even of individuals, and still more those of the great orders and societies, into which the state is divided. Though he should consider some of them as in some measure abusive, he will content himself with moderating what he often cannot annihilate without great violence. When he cannot conquer the rooted prejudices of the people by reason and persuasion, he will not attempt to subdue them by force ; but will religiously observe what, by Cicero, is justly called the divine maxim of Plato, never to use violence to his country no more than to his parents. He will accommodate, as well as he can, his public arrangements to the confirmed habits and prejudices of the people ; and will remedy, as well as he can, the inconveniencies which may flow from the want of those regulations which the people are averse to submit to. When he cannot establish the right, he will not disdain to ameliorate the wrong ; but like Solon, when he cannot establish the best system of laws, he will try to establish the best that the people can bear.

The man of system, on the contrary, is apt to be very wise in his own conceit : and is often so enamoured with the supposed beauty of his own ideal plan of government, that he cannot suffer the smallest deviation from any part of it. He goes on to establish it completely and in all its parts, without any regard either to the great interests, or to the strong prejudices which may oppose it. He seems to imagine that he can arrange the different members of a great society with as much ease as the hand arranges the different pieces upon a chess-board. He does not consider that the pieces upon the chess-board have no other principle of motion besides that which the hand impresses upon them; but that, in the great chess-board of human society, every single piece has a principle of motion of its own, altogether different from that which the legislature might choose to impress upon it. If those two principles coincide and act in the same direction, the game of human society will go on easily and harmoniously, and is very likely to be happy and successful. If they are opposite or different, the game will go on miserably, and human society must be at all times in the highest degree of disorder.

Some general, and even systematical, idea of the perfection of policy and law, may no doubt be necessary for directing the views of the statesman. But to insist upon establishing, and upon establishing all at once, and in spite of all opposition, every thing which that idea may seem to require, must often be the highest degree of arrogance. It is to erect his own judgment into the supreme standard of right and wrong. It is to fancy himself the only wise and worthy man in the commonwealth, and that his fellow-citizens should accommodate themselves to him and not he to them. 'It is upon this account, that of all political speculators, sovereign princes are by far the most dangerous. This arrogance is perfectly familiar to them. They entertain no doubt of the immense superiority of their own judgment. When such imperial and royal reformers, therefore, condescend to contemplate the constitution of the country which is committed to their government, they seldom see any thing so wrong in it as the obstructions which it may sometimes oppose to the execution of their own will. They hold in contempt the divine maxim of Plato, and consider the state as made for themselves, not themselves for the state. The great object of their reformation, therefore, is to remove those obstructions; to reduce the authority of the nobility; to take away the privileges of cities and provinces, and to render both the greatest individuals and the greatest orders of the state, as incapable of opposing their commands, as the weakest and most insignificant.

CHAP. III.—*Of Universal Benevolence.*

THOUGH our effectual good offices can very seldom be extended to any wider society than that of our country; our good-will is circumscribed by no boundary, but may embrace the immensity of the universe. We cannot form the idea of any innocent and sensible being, whose happiness we should not desire, or to whose misery, when distinctly brought home to the imagination, we should not have some degree of aversion. The idea of a mischievous, though sensible, being, indeed, naturally provokes our hatred: but the ill-will which, in this case, we bear to it, is really the effect of our universal benevolence. It is the effect of the sympathy which we feel with the misery and resentment of those other innocent and sensible beings, whose happiness is disturbed by its malice.

This universal benevolence, how noble and generous soever, can be the source of no solid happiness to any man who is not thoroughly convinced that all the inhabitants of the universe, the meanest as well as the greatest, are under the immediate care and protection of that great, benevolent, and all-wise Being, who directs all the movements of nature; and who is determined, by his own unalterable perfections, to maintain in it, at all times, the greatest possible quantity of happiness. To this universal benevolence, on the contrary, the very suspicion of a fatherless world, must be the most melancholy of all reflections; from the thought that all the unknown regions of infinite and incomprehensible space may be filled with nothing but endless misery and wretchedness. All the splendour of the highest prosperity can never enlighten the gloom with which so dreadful an idea must necessarily overshadow the imagination; nor, in a wise and virtuous man, can all the sorrow of the most afflicting adversity ever dry up the joy which necessarily springs from the habitual and thorough conviction of the truth of the contrary system.

The wise and virtuous man is at all times willing that his own private interest should be sacrificed to the public interest of his own particular order or society. He is at all times willing, too, that the interest of this order or society should be sacrificed to the greater interest of the state or sovereignty, of which it is only a subordinate part. He should, therefore, be equally willing that all those inferior interests should be sacrificed to the greater interest of the universe, to the interest of that great society of all sensible and intelligent beings, of which God himself is the immediate administrator and director. If he is deeply impressed with the habitual and thorough conviction that this benevolent and all-wise Being can admit into the system of his government, no partial evil which is not necessary for the universal good, he must consider all the misfortunes which may befal himself, his friends, his society, or his country, as necessary for the prosperity of the universe, and therefore as what he ought, not only to submit to with resignation, but as what he himself, if he had known all the connexions and dependencies of things, ought sincerely and devoutly to have wished for.

Nor does this magnanimous resignation to the will of the great Director of the universe, seem in any respect beyond the reach of human nature. Good soldiers, who both love and trust their general, frequently march with more gaiety and alacrity to the forlorn station, from which they never expect to return, than they would to one where there was neither difficulty nor danger. In marching to the latter, they could feel no other sentiment than that of the dulness of ordinary duty; in marching to the former, they feel that they are making the noblest exertion which it is possible for man to make. They know that their general would not have ordered them upon this station, had it not been necessary for the safety of the army, for the success of the war. They cheerfully sacrifice their own little systems to the prosperity of a greater system. They take an affectionate leave of their comrades, to whom they wish all happiness and success; and march out, not only with submissive obedience, but often with shouts of the most joyful exultation, to that fatal, but splendid and honourable station to which they are appointed. No conductor of an army can deserve more unlimited trust, more ardent and zealous affection, than the great Conductor of the universe. In the greatest public as well as private disasters, a wise man ought to consider that he himself, his friends and countrymen, have only been ordered upon the forlorn station of the universe; that had it not been necessary for the good of the whole, they would not have been so ordered; and that it is their duty, not only with humble resignation to submit to this allotment, but to endeavour to embrace it with alacrity and joy. A wise man should surely be capable of doing what a good soldier holds himself at all times in readiness to do.

The idea of that divine Being, whose benevolence and wisdom have, from all eternity, contrived and conducted the immense machine of the universe, so as at all times to produce the greatest possible quantity of happiness, is certainly of all the objects of human contemplation by far the most sublime. Every other thought necessarily appears mean in the comparison. The man whom we believe to be principally occupied in this sublime contemplation, seldom fails to be the object of our highest veneration; and though his life should be altogether contemplative, we often regard him with a sort of religious respect much superior to that with which we look upon the most active and useful servant of the commonwealth. The Meditations of Marcus Antoninus, which turn principally upon this subject, have contributed more, perhaps, to the general admiration of his character, than all the different trans- actions of his just, merciful, and beneficent reign.

The administration of the great system of the universe, however, the care of the universal happiness of all rational and sensible beings, is the business of God and not of man. To man is allotted a much humbler department, but one much more suitable to the weakness of his powers, and to the narrowness of his comprehension; the care of his own happiness, of that of his family, his friends, his country: that he is occupied in contemplating the more sublime, can never be an excuse for his neglecting the more humble department; and he must not expose himself to the charge which Avidius Cassius is said to have brought, perhaps unjustly, against Marcus Antoninus; that while he employed himself in philosophical speculations, and contemplated the prosperity of the universe, he neglected that of the Roman empire. The most sublime speculation of the contemplative philosopher can scarce compensate the neglect of the smallest active duty.

SEC. III.—OF SELF-COMMAND.

THE man who acts according to the rules of perfect prudence, of strict justice, and of proper benevolence, may be said to be perfectly virtuous. But the most perfect knowledge of those rules will not alone enable him to act in this manner: his own passions are very apt to mislead him: sometimes to drive him and sometimes to seduce him to violate all the rules which he himself, in all his sober and cool hours, approves of. The most perfect knowledge, if it is not supported by the most perfect self-command, will not always enable him to do his duty.

Some of the best of the ancient moralists seem to have considered those passions as divided into two different classes : first, into those which it requires a considerable exertion of self-command to restrain even for a single moment ; and secondly, into those which it is easy to restrain for a single moment, or even for a short period of time ; but which, by their continual and almost incessant solicitations, are, in the course of a life, very apt to mislead into great deviations.

Fear and anger, together with some other passions which are mixed or connected with them, constitute the first class.   The love of ease, of pleasure, of applause, and of many other selfish gratifications, constitute the second.   Extravagant fear and furious anger, it is often difficult to restrain even for a single moment.   The love of ease, of pleasure, of applause, and other selfish gratifications, it is always easy to restrain for a single moment, or even for a short period of time ; but, by their continual solicitations, they often mislead us into many weaknesses which we have afterwards much reason to be ashamed of. The former set of passions may often be said to drive, the latter to seduce us, from our duty.   The command of the former was, by the ancient moralists above alluded to, denominated fortitude, manhood, and strength of mind ; that of the latter, temperance, decency, modesty, and moderation.

The command of each of those two sets of passions, independent of the beauty which it derives from its utility ; from its enabling us upon all occasions to act according to the dictates of prudence, of justice, and of proper benevolence ; has a beauty of its own, and seems to deserve for its own sake a certain degree of esteem and admiration. In the one case, the strength and greatness of the exertion excites some degree of that esteem and admiration.   In the other, the uniformity, the equality and unremitting steadiness of that exertion.

The man who, in danger, in torture, upon the approach of death, preserves his tranquillity unaltered, and suffers no word, no gesture to escape him which does not perfectly accord with the feelings of the most indifferent spectator, necessarily commands a very high degree of admiration.   If he suffers in the cause of liberty and justice, for the sake of humanity and the love of his country, the most tender compassion for his sufferings, the strongest indignation against the injustice of his persecutors, the warmest sympathetic gratitude for his beneficent intentions, the highest sense of his merit, all join and mix themselves with the admiration of his magnanimity, and often inflame that sentiment into the most enthusiastic and rapturous veneration.   The heroes of ancient and modern history, who are remembered with the most peculiar favour and affection, are many of them those who, in the cause of truth, liberty, and justice, have perished upon the scaffold, and who behaved there with that ease and dignity which became them. Had the enemies of Socrates suffered him to die quietly in his bed, the glory even of that great philosopher might possibly never have acquired that dazzling splendour in which it has been beheld in all succeeding ages. In the English history, when we look over the illustrious heads which have been engraven by Vertue and Howbraken, there is scarce any body, I imagine, who does not feel that the axe, the emblem of having been beheaded, which is engraved under some of the most illustrious of them, under those of the Sir Thomas Mores, of the Raleighs, the Russels, the Sydneys, &c., sheds a real dignity and depth of interest over the characters to which it is affixed, much superior to what they can derive from all the futile ornaments of heraldry, with which they are sometimes accompanied.

Nor does this magnanimity give lustre only to the characters of innocent and virtuous men. It draws some degree of favourable regard even upon those of the greatest criminals; and when a robber or highwayman is brought to the scaffold, and behaves there with decency and firmness, though we perfectly approve of his punishment, we often cannot help regretting that a man who possessed such great and noble powers should have been capable of such mean enormities.

War is the great school both for acquiring and exercising this species of magnanimity. Death, as we say, is the king of terrors; and the man who has conquered the fear of death, is not likely to lose his presence of mind at the approach of any other natural evil. In war, men become familiar with death, and are thereby necessarily cured of that superstitious horror with which it is viewed by the weak and inexperienced. They consider it merely as the loss of life, and as no further the object of aversion than as life may happen to be that of desire. They learn from experience, too, that many seemingly great dangers are not so great as they appear; and that, with courage, activity, and presence of mind, there is often a good probability of extricating themselves with honour from situations where at first they could see no hope. The dread of death is thus greatly diminished; and the confidence or hope of escaping it, augmented. They learn to expose themselves to danger with less reluctance. They are less anxious to get out of it, and less apt to lose their presence of mind while they are in it. It is this habitual contempt of danger and death which ennobles the profession of a soldier, and bestows upon it, in the natural apprehensions of mankind, a rank and dignity superior to that of any other profession; and the skilful and successful exercise of this profession, in the service of their country, seems to have constituted the most distinguishing feature in the character of the favourite heroes of all ages.

Great warlike exploit, though undertaken contrary to every principle of justice, and carried on without any regard to humanity, sometimes interests us, and commands even some degree of a certain sort of esteem for the very worthless characters which conduct it. We are interested even in the exploits of the buccaneers ; and read with some sort of esteem and admiration, the history of the most worthless men, who, in pursuit of the most criminal purposes, endured greater hardships, surmounted greater difficulties, and encountered greater dangers, than perhaps any which the course of history gives an account of.

The command of anger appears upon many occasions not less generous and noble than that of fear. The proper expression of just indignation composes many of the most splendid and admired passages both of ancient and modern eloquence. The Philippics of Demosthenes, the Catalinarians of Cicero, derive their whole beauty from the noble propriety with which this passion is expressed. But this just indignation is nothing but anger restrained and properly attempered to what the impartial spectator can enter into. The blustering and noisy passion which goes beyond this, is always odious and offensive, and interests us, not for the angry man, but for the man with whom he is angry. The nobleness of pardoning appears, upon many occasions, superior even to the most perfect propriety of resenting. When either proper acknowledgments have been made by the offending party, or even without any such acknowledgments, when the public interest requires that the most mortal enemies should unite for the discharge of some important duty, the man who can cast away all animosity, and act with confidence and cordiality towards the person who had most grievously offended him, does seem most justly to merit our highest admiration.

The command of anger, however, does not always appear in such splendid colours. Fear is contrary to anger, and is often the motive which restrains it ; and in such cases the meanness of the motive takes away all the nobleness of the restraint. Anger prompts to attack, and the indulgence of it seems sometimes to show a sort of courage and superiority to fear. The indulgence of anger is sometimes an object of vanity. That of fear never is. Vain and weak men, among their inferiors, or those who dare not resist them, often affect to be ostentatiously passionate, and fancy that they show, what is called, spirit in being so. A bully tells many stories of his own insolence, which are not true, and imagines that he thereby renders himself, if not more amiable and respectable, at least more formidable to his audience. Modern manners, which, by favouring the practice of duelling, may be said, in some cases, to encourage private revenge, contribute, perhaps, a good deal to render, in modern times, the restraint of anger by fear still more contemptible than it might otherwise appear to be. There is always something dignified in the command of fear, whatever may be the motive upon which it is founded. It is not so with the command of anger. Unless it is founded altogether in the sense of decency, of dignity, and propriety, it never is perfectly agreeable.

To act according to the dictates of prudence, of justice, and proper beneficence, seems to have no great merit where there is no temptation to do otherwise. But to act with cool deliberation in the midst of the greatest dangers and difficulties ; to observe religiously the sacred rules of justice in spite both of the greatest interests which might tempt, and the greatest injuries which might provoke us to violate them ; never to suffer the benevolence of our temper to be damped or discouraged by the malignity and ingratitude of the individuals towards whom it may have been exercised ; is the character of the most exalted wisdom and virtue. Self-command is not only itself a great virtue, but from it all the other virtues seem to derive their principal lustre.

The command of fear, the command of anger, are always great and noble powers. When they are directed by justice and benevolence, they are not only great virtues, but increase the splendour of those other virtues. They may, however, sometimes be directed by very different motives ; and in this case, though still great and respectable, they may be excessively dangerous. The most intrepid valour may be employed in the cause of the greatest injustice. Amidst great provocations, apparent tranquillity and good humour may sometimes conceal the most determined and cruel resolution to revenge. The strength of mind requisite for such dissimulation, though always and necessarily contaminated by the baseness of falsehood, has, however, been often much admired by many people of no contemptible judgment. The dissimulation of Catherine of Medicis is often celebrated by the profound historian Davila ; that of Lord Digby, afterwards Earl of Bristol, by the grave and conscientious Lord Clarendon ; that of the first Ashley Earl of Shaftesbury, by the judicious Mr. Locke. Even Cicero seems to consider this deceitful character, not indeed as of the highest dignity, but as not unsuitable to a certain flexibility of manners, which, he thinks may, notwithstanding, be, upon the whole, both agreeable and respectable. He exemplifies it by the characters of Homer's Ulysses, of the Athenian Themistocles, of the Spartan Lysander, and of the Roman Marcus Crassus. This character of dark and deep dissimulation occurs most commonly in times of great public disorder ; amidst the violence of faction and civil war. When law has become in a great measure impotent, when the most perfect innocence cannot alone insure safety, regard to self-defence obliges the greatest part of men to have recourse to dexterity, to address, and to apparent accommodation to whatever happens to be, at the moment, the prevailing party. This false character, too, is frequently accompanied with the coolest and most determined courage. The proper exercise of it supposes that courage, as death is commonly the certain consequence of detection. It may be employed indifferently, either to exasperate or to allay those furious animosities of adverse factions which impose the necessity of assuming it ; and though it may sometimes be useful, it is at least equally liable to be excessively pernicious.

The command of the less violent and turbulent passions seems much less liable to be abused to any pernicious purpose. Temperance, decency, modesty, and moderation, are always amiable, and can seldom be directed to any bad end. It is from the unremitting steadiness of those gentler exertions' of self-command, that the amiable virtue of chastity, that the respectable virtues of industry and frugality, derive all that sober lustre which attends them. The conduct of all those who are contented to walk in the humble paths of private and peaceable life, derives from the same principle the greater part of the beauty and grace which belong to it ; a beauty and grace, which, though much less dazzling, is not always less pleasing than those which accompany the more splendid actions of the hero, the statesman, or the legislator.

After what has already been said, in several different parts of this discourse, concerning the nature of self-command, I judge it unnecessary to enter into any further detail concerning those virtues. I shall only observe at present, that the point of propriety, the degree of any passion which the impartial spectator approves of, is differently situated in different passions. In some passions the excess is less disagreeable than the defect ; and in such passions the point of propriety seems to stand high, or nearer to the excess than to the defect. In other passions, the defect is less disagreeable than the excess ; and in such passions the point of propriety seems to stand low, or nearer to the defect than to the excess. The former are the passions which the spectator is most, the latter, those which he is least disposed to sympathize with. The former, too, are the passions of which the immediate feeling or sensation is agreeable to the person principally concerned ; the latter, those of which it is disagreeable. It may be laid down as a general rule, that the passions which the spectator is most disposed to sympathize with, and in which, upon that account, the point of propriety may be said to stand high, are those of which the immediate feeling or sensation is more or less agreeable to the person principally concerned : and that, on the contrary, the passions which the spectator is least disposed to sympathize with, and in which, upon that account, the point of propriety may be said to stand low, are those of which the immediate feeling or sensation is more or less disagreeable, or even painful, to the person principally concerned. This general rule, so far as I have been able to observe, admits not of a single exception. A few examples will at once both sufficiently explain it and demonstrate the truth of it.

The disposition to the affections which tend to unite men in society to humanity, kindness, natural affection, friendship, esteem, may sometimes be excessive. Even the excess of this disposition, however, renders a man interesting to every body. Though we blame it, we still regard it with compassion, and even with kindness, and never with dislike. We are more sorry for it than angry at it. To the person himself, the indulgence even of such excessive affections is, upon many occasions, not only agreeable, but delicious. Upon some occasions, indeed, especially when directed, as is too often the case, towards unworthy objects, it exposes him to much real and heartfelt distress. Even upon such occasions, however, a well-disposed mind regards him with the most exquisite pity, and feels the highest indignation against those who affect to despise him for his weakness and imprudence. The defect of this disposition, on the contrary, what is called hardness of heart, while it renders a man insensible to the feelings and distresses of other people, renders other people equally insensible to his ; and, by excluding him from the friendship of all the world, excludes him from the best and most comfortable of all social enjoyments.

The disposition to the affections which drive men from one another, and which tend, as it were, to break the bands of human society; the disposition to anger, hatred, envy, malice, revenge; is, on the contrary, much more apt to offend by its excess than by its defect. The excess renders a man wretched and miserable in his own mind, and the object of hatred, and sometimes even of horror, to other people. The defect is very seldom complained of. It may, however, be defective. The want of proper indignation is a most essential defect in the manly character, and, upon many occasions, renders a man incapable of protecting either himself or his friends from insult and injustice. Even that principle, in the excess and improper direction of which consists the odious and detestable passion of envy, may be defective. Envy is that passion which views with malignant dislike the superiority of those who are really entitled to all the superiority they possess. The man, however, who, in matters of consequence, tamely suffers other people, who are entitled to no such superiority, to rise above him or get before him, is justly condemned as mean-spirited. This weakness is commonly founded in indolence, sometimes in good nature, in an aversion to opposition, to bustle and solicitation, and sometimes, too, in a sort of ill-judged magnanimity, which fancies that it can always continue to despise the advantage which it then despises, and, therefore, so easily gives up. Such weakness, however, is commonly followed by much regret and repentance ; and what had some appearance of magnanimity in the beginning frequently gives place to a most malignant envy in the end, and to a hatred of that superiority, which those who have once attained it, may often become really entitled to, by the very circumstance of having attained it. In order to live comfortably in the world, it is, upon all occasions, as necessary to defend our dignity and rank, as it is to defend our life or our fortune.

Our sensibility to personal danger and distress, like that to personal provocation, is much more apt to offend by its excess than by its defect. No character is more contemptible than that of a coward ; no character is more admired than that of the man who faces death with intrepidity, and maintains his tranquillity and presence of mind amidst the most dreadful dangers. We esteem the man who supports pain and even torture with manhood and firmness; and we can have little regard for him who sinks under them, and abandons himself to useless outcries and womanish lamentations. A fretful temper, which feels, with too much sensibility, every little cross accident, renders a man miserable in himself and offensive to other people. A calm one, which does not allow its tranquillity to be disturbed, either by the small injuries, or by the little disasters incident to the usual course of human affairs; but which, amidst the natural and moral evils infesting the world, lays its account and is contented to suffer a little from both, is a blessing to the man himself, and gives ease and security to all his companions.

Our sensibility, however, both to our own injuries and to our own misfortunes, though generally too strong, may likewise be too weak. The man who feels little for his own misfortunes, must always feel less for those of other people, and be less disposed to relieve them. The man who has little resentment for the injuries which are done to himself, must always have less for those which are done to other people, and be less disposed either to protect or to avenge them. A stupid insensibility to the events of human life necessarily extinguishes all that keen and earnest attention to the propriety of our own conduct, which constitutes the real essence of virtue. We can feel little anxiety about the propriety of our own actions, when we are indifferent about the events which may result from them. The man who feels the full distress of the calamity which has befallen him, who feels the whole baseness of the injustice which has been done to him, but who feels still more strongly what the dignity of his own character requires; who does not abandon himself to the guidance of the undisciplined passions which his situation might naturally inspire; but who governs his whole behaviour and conduct according to those restrained and corrected emotions which the great inmate, the great demi-god within the breast prescribes and approves of; is alone the real man of virtue, the only real and proper object of love, respect, and admiration. Insensibility and that noble firmness, that exalted self-command, which is founded in the sense of dignity and propriety, are so far from being altogether the same, that in proportion as the former takes place, the merit of the latter is, in many cases, entirely taken away.

But though the total want of sensibility to personal injury, to personal danger and distress, would, in such situations, take away the whole merit of self-command, that sensibility, however, may very easily be too exquisite, and it frequently is so. When the sense of propriety, when the authority of the judge within the breast, can control this extreme sensibility, that authority must no doubt appear very noble and very great. But the exertion of it may be too fatiguing; it may have too much to do. The individual, by a great effort, may behave perfectly

15

well. But the contest between the two principles, the warfare within the breast, may be too violent to be at all consistent with internal tranquillity and happiness. The wise man whom Nature has endowed with this too exquisite sensibility, and whose too lively feelings have not been sufficiently blunted and hardened by early education and proper exercise, will avoid, as much as duty and propriety will permit, the situations for which he is not perfectly fitted. The man whose feeble and delicate constitution renders him too sensible to pain, to hardship, and to every sort of bodily distress, should not wantonly embrace the profession of a soldier. The man of too much sensibility to injury, should not rashly engage in the contests of faction. Though the sense of propriety should be strong enough to command all those sensibilities, the composure of the mind must always be disturbed in the struggle. In this disorder the judgment cannot always maintain its ordinary acuteness and precision; and though he may always mean to act properly, he may often act rashly and imprudently, and in a manner which he himself will, in the succeeding part of his life, be for ever ashamed of. A certain intrepidity, a certain firmness of nerves and hardiness of constitution, whether natural or acquired, are undoubtedly the best preparatives for all the great exertions of self-command.

Though war and faction are certainly the best schools for forming every man to this hardiness and firmness of temper, though they are the best remedies for curing him of the opposite weaknesses, yet, if the day of trial should happen to come before he has completely learned his lesson, before the remedy has had time to produce its proper effect, the consequences might not be agreeable.

Our sensibility to the pleasures, to the amusements, and enjoyments of human life, may offend, in the same manner, either by its excess or by its defect. Of the two, however, the excess seems less disagreeable than the defect. Both to the spectator and to the person principally concerned, a strong propensity to joy is certainly more pleasing than a dull insensibility to the objects of amusement and diversion. We are charmed with the gaiety of youth, and even with the playfulness of childhood: but we soon grow weary of the flat and tasteless gravity which too frequently accompanies old age. When this propensity, indeed, is not restrained by the sense of propriety, when it is unsuitable to the time or to the place, to the age or to the situation of the person, when, to indulge it, he neglects either his interest or his duty; it is justly blamed as excessive, and as hurtful both to the individual and to the society. In the greater part of such cases, however, what is chiefly to be found fault with is, not so much the strength of the propensity to joy, as the weakness of the sense of propriety and duty. A young man who has no relish for the diversions and amusements that are natural and suitable to his age, who talks of nothing but his book or his business, is disliked as formal and pedantic; and we give him no credit for his abstinence even from improper indulgences, to which he seems to have so little inclination.

The principle of self-estimation may be too high, and it may likewise be too low. It is so very agreeable to think highly, and so very disagreeable to think meanly of ourselves, that, to the person himself, it cannot well be doubted, but that some degree of excess must be much less disagreeable than any degree of defect. But to the impartial spectator, it may perhaps be thought, things must appear quite differently, and that to him, the defect must always be less disagreeable than the excess. And in our companions, no doubt, we much more frequently complain of the latter than of the former. When they assume upon us, or set themselves before us, their self-estimation mortifies our own. Our own pride and vanity prompt us to accuse them of pride and vanity, and we cease to be the impartial spectators of their conduct. When the same companions, however, suffer any other man to assume over them a superiority which does not belong to him, we not only blame them, but often despise them as mean-spirited. When, on the contrary, among other people, they push themselves a little more forward, and scramble to an elevation disproportioned, as we think, to their merit, though we may not perfectly approve of their conduct, we are often, upon the whole, diverted with it ; and, where there is no envy in the case, we are almost always much less displeased with them, than we should have been, had they only suffered themselves to sink below their proper station.

In estimating our own merit, in judging of our own character and conduct, there are two different standards to which we naturally compare them. The one is the idea of exact propriety and perfection, so far as we are each of us capable of comprehending that idea. The other is that degree of approximation to this idea which is commonly attained in the world, and which the greater part of our friends and companions, of our rivals and competitors, may have actually arrived at. We very seldom (I am disposed to think, we never) attempt to judge of ourselves without giving more or less attention to both these different standards. But the attention of different men, and even of the same man at different times, is often very unequally divided between them ; and is sometimes principally directed towards the one, and sometimes towards the other.

So far as our attention is directed towards the first standard, the wisest and best of us all, can, in his own character and conduct, see nothing but weakness and imperfection ; can discover no ground for arrogance and presumption, but a great deal for humility, regret, and repentance. So far as our attention is directed towards the second, we may be affected either in the one way or in the other, and feel ourselves, either really above, or really below, the standard with which we seek to compare ourselves.

15 *

The wise and virtuous man directs his principal attention to the first standard ; the idea of exact propriety and perfection. There exists in the mind of every man, an idea of this kind, gradually formed from his observations upon the character and conduct both of himself and of other people.   It is the slow, gradual, and progressive work of the great demigod within the breast, the great judge and arbiter of conduct.   This idea is in every man more or less accurately drawn, its colouring is more or less just, its outlines are more or less exactly designed, according to the delicacy and acuteness of that sensibility, with which those observations were made, and according to the care and attention employed in making them.   In the wise and virtuous man they have been made with the most acute and delicate sensibility, and the utmost care and attention have been employed in making them. Every day some feature is improved ; every day some blemish is corrected.   He has studied this idea more than other people, he comprehends it more distinctly, he has formed a much more correct image of it, and is much more deeply enamoured of its exquisite and divine beauty.   He endeavours, as well as he can, to assimilate his own character to this archetype of perfection.   But he imitates the work of a divine artist, which can never be equalled.   He feels the imperfect success of all his best endeavours, and sees, with grief and affliction, in how many different features the mortal copy falls short of the immortal original. He remembers, with concern and humiliation, how often, from want of attention, from want of judgment, from want of temper, he has, both in words and actions, both in conduct and conversation, violated the exact rules of perfect propriety ; and has so far departed from that model, according to which he wished to fashion his own character and conduct.   When he directs his attention towards the second standard, indeed, that degree of excellence which his friends and acquaintances have commonly arrived at, he may be sensible of his own superiority.   But, as his principal attention is always directed towards the first standard, he is necessarily much more humbled by the one comparison, than he ever can be elevated by the other.   He is never so elated as to look down with insolence even upon those who are really below him.   He feels so well his own imperfection, he knows so well the difficulty with which he attained his own distant approximation to rectitude, that he cannot regard with contempt the still greater imperfections of other people.   Far from insulting over their inferiority, he views it with the most indulgent commiseration, and, by his advice as well as example, is at all times willing to promote their further advancement.   If, in any particular qualification, they happen to be superior to him (for who is so perfect as not to have many superiors in many different qualifications ?), far from envying their superiority, he, who knows how difficult it is to excel, esteems and honours their excellence, and never fails to bestow upon it the full measure of applause which it deserves. His whole mind, in short, is deeply impressed, his whole behaviour and deportment are distinctly stamped with the character of real modesty; with that of a very moderate estimation of his own merit, and, at the same time, with a very full sense of the merit of other people.

In all the liberal and ingenious arts, in painting, in poetry, in music, in eloquence, in philosophy, the great artist feels always the real imperfection of his own best works, and is more sensible than any man how much they fall short of that ideal perfection of which he has formed some conception, which he imitates as well as he can, but which he despairs of ever equalling. It is the inferior artist only, who is ever perfectly satisfied with his own performances. He has little conception of this ideal perfection, about which he has little employed his thoughts ; and it is chiefly to the works of other artists, of, perhaps, a still lower order, that he deigns to compare his own works. Boileau, the great French poet (in some of his works, perhaps not inferior to the greatest poet of the same kind, either ancient or modern), used to say, that no great man was ever completely satisfied with his own works. His acquaintance Santeuil (a writer of Latin verses, and who, on account of that school-boy accomplishment, had the weakness to fancy himself a poet), assured him that he himself was always completely satisfied with *his* own. Boileau replied, with, perhaps, an arch ambiguity, that he certainly was the only great man that ever was so. Boileau, in judging of his own works, compared them with the standard of ideal perfection, which, in his own particular branch of the poetic art, he had, I presume, meditated as deeply, and conceived as distinctly, as it is possible for man to conceive it. Santeuil, in judging of *his* own works, compared them, I suppose, chiefly to those of the other Latin poets of his own time, to the great part of whom he was certainly very far from being inferior. But to support and finish off, if I may say so, the conduct and conversation of a whole life to some resemblance of this ideal perfection, is surely much more difficult than to work up to an equal resemblance any of the productions of any of the ingenious arts. The artist sits down to his work undisturbed, at leisure, in the full possession and recollection of all his skill, experience, and knowledge. The wise man must support the propriety of his own conduct in health and sickness, in success and in disappointment, in the hour of fatigue and drowsy indolence, as well as in that of the most awakened attention. The most sudden and unexpected assaults of difficulty and distress must never surprise him. The injustice of other people must never provoke him to injustice. The violence of faction must never confound him. All the hardships and hazards of war must never either dishearten or appal him.

Of the persons who, in estimating their own merit, in judging of their own character and conduct, direct by far the greater part of their attention to the second standard, to that ordinary degree of excellence which is commonly attained by other people, there are some who really and justly feel themselves very much above it, and who, by every intelligent and impartial spectator, are acknowledged to be so. The attention of such persons, however, being always principally directed, not to the standard of ideal, but to that of ordinary perfection, they have little sense of their own weaknesses and imperfections ; they have little modesty; and are often assuming, arrogant, and presumptuous; great admirers of themselves, and great contemners of other people. Though their characters are in general much less correct, and their merit much inferior to that of the man of real and modest virtue ; yet their excessive presumption, founded upon their own excessive self-admiration, dazzles the multitude, and often imposes even upon those who are much superior to the multitude. The frequent, and often wonderful, success of the most ignorant quacks and impostors, both civil and religious, sufficiently demonstrate how easily the multitude are imposed upon by the most extravagant and groundless pretensions. But when those pretensions are supported by a very high degree of real and solid merit, when they are displayed with all the splendour which ostentation can bestow upon them, when they are supported by high rank and great power, when they have often been successfully exerted, and are, upon that account, attended by the loud acclamations of the multitude ; even the man of sober judgment often abandons himself to the general admiration. The very noise of those foolish acclamations often contributes to confound his understanding, and while he sees those great men only at a certain distance, he is often disposed to worship them with a sincere admiration, superior even to that with which they appear to worship themselves. When there is no envy in the case, we all take pleasure in admiring, and are, upon that account, naturally disposed, in our own fancies, to render complete and perfect in every respect the characters which, in many respects, are so very worthy of admiration. The excessive self-admiration of those great men is well understood, perhaps, and even seen through, with some degree of derision, by those wise men who are much in their familiarity, and who secretly smile at those lofty pretensions, which, by people at a distance, are often regarded with reverence, and almost with adoration. Such, however, have been, in all ages, the greater part of those men who have procured to themselves the most noisy fame, the most extensive reputation ; a fame and reputation, too, which have too often descended to the remotest posterity.

Great success in the world, great authority over the sentiments and opinions of mankind, have very seldom been acquired without some degree of this excessive self-admiration. The most splendid characters, the men who have performed the most illustrious actions, who have brought about the greatest revolutions, both in the situations and opinions of mankind ; the most successful warriors, the greatest statesmen and legislators, the eloquent founders and leaders of the most numerous and most successful sects and parties ; have many of them been, not more distinguished for their very great merit, than for a degree of presumption and self-admiration altogether disproportioned even to that very great merit. This presumption was, perhaps, necessary, not only to prompt them to undertakings which a more sober mind would never have thought of, but to command the submission and obedience of their followers to support them in such undertakings. When crowned with success, accordingly, this presumption has often betrayed them into a vanity that approached almost to insanity and folly. Alexander the Great appears, not only to have wished that other people should think him a god, but to have been at least very well-disposed to fancy himself such. Upon his deathbed, the most ungodlike of all situations, he requested of his friends that, to the respectable list of deities, into which himself had long before been inserted, his old mother Olympia might likewise have the honour of being added. Amidst the respectful admiration of his followers and disciples, amidst the universal applause of the public, after the oracle, which probably had followed the voice of that applause, had pronounced him the wisest of men, the great wisdom of Socrates, though it did not suffer him to fancy himself a god, yet was not great enough to hinder him from fancying that he had secret and frequent intimations from some invisible and divine being. The sound head of Cæsar was not so perfectly sound as to hinder him from being much pleased with his divine genealogy from the goddess Venus ; and, before the temple of this pretended great-grandmother, to receive, without rising from his seat, the Roman senate, when that illustrious body came to present him with some decrees conferring upon him the most extravagant honours. This insolence, joined to some other acts of an almost childish vanity, little to be expected from an understanding at once so very acute and comprehensive, seems, by exasperating the public jealousy, to have emboldened his assassins, and to have hastened the execution of their conspiracy. The religion and manners of modern times give our great men little encouragement to fancy themselves either gods or even prophets. Success, however, joined to great popular favour, has often so far turned the heads of the greatest of them, as to make them ascribe to themselves both an importance and an ability much beyond what they really possessed ; and, by this presumption, to precipitate themselves into many rash and sometimes ruinous adventures. It is a characteristic almost peculiar to the great Duke of Marlborough, that ten years of such uninterrupted and such splendid success as scarce any other general could boast of, never betrayed him into a a single rash action, scarce into a single rash word or expression. The same temperate coolness and self-command cannot, I think, be ascribed to any other great warrior of later times ; not to Prince Eugene, not to the late King of Prussia, not the the great Prince of Condé, not even to Gustavus Adolphus. Turenne seems to have approached the nearest to it ; but several different transactions of his life sufficiently demonstrate that it was in him by no means so perfect as it was in the great Duke of Marlborough.

In the humble projects of private life, as well as in the ambitious and proud pursuits of high stations, great abilities and successful enterprise, in the beginning, have frequently encouraged to undertakings which necessarily led to bankruptcy and ruin in the end.

The esteem and admiration which every impartial spectator conceives for the real merit of those spirited, magnanimous, and high-minded persons, as it is a just and well-founded sentiment, so it is a steady and permanent one, and altogether independent of their good or bad fortune. It is otherwise with that admiration which he is apt to conceive for their excessive self-estimation and presumption. While they are successful, indeed, he is often perfectly conquered and over-borne by them. Success covers from his eyes, not only the great imprudence, but frequently the great injustice of their enterprises ; and far from blaming this defective part of their character, he often views it with the most enthusiastic admiration. When they are unfortunate, however, things change their colours and their names. What was before heroic magnanimity, resumes its proper appellation of extravagant rashness and folly ; and the blackness of that avidity and injustice, which was before hid under the splendour of prosperity, comes full into view, and blots the whole lustre of their enterprise. Had Cæsar, instead of gaining, lost the battle of Pharsalia, his character would, at this hour, have ranked a little above that of Cataline, and the weakest man would have viewed his enterprise against the laws of his country in blacker colours, than, perhaps even Cato, with all the animosity of a partyman, ever viewed it at the time. His real merit, the justness of his taste, the simplicity and elegance of his writings, the propriety of his eloquence, his skill in war, his resources in distress, his cool and sedate judgment in danger, his faithful attachment to his friends, his unexampled generosity to his enemies, would all have been acknowledged ; as the real merit of Cataline, who had many great qualities, is acknowledged at this day. But the insolence and injustice of his all-grasping ambition would have darkened and extinguished the glory of all that real merit. Fortune has in this, as well as in some other respects already mentioned, great influence over the moral sentiments of mankind, and, according as she is either favourable or adverse, can render the same character the object, either of general love and admiration, or of universal hatred and contempt. This great disorder in our moral sentiments is by no means, however, without its utility ; and we may on this, as well as on many other occasions, admire the wisdom of God even in the weakness and folly of man. Our admiration of success is founded upon the same principle with our respect for wealth and greatness, and is equally necessary for establishing the distinction of ranks and the order of society.   By this admiration of success we are taught to submit more easily to those superiors, whom the course of human affairs may assign to us ; to regard with reverence, and sometimes even with a sort of respectful affection, that fortunate violence which we are no longer capable of resisting ; not only the violence of such splendid characters as those of a Cæsar or an Alexander, but often that of the most brutal and savage barbarians, of an Attila, a Gengis, or a Tamerlane. To all such mighty conquerors the great mob of mankind are naturally disposed to look up with a wondering, though, no doubt, with a very weak and foolish admiration.   By this admiration, however, they are taught to acquiesce with less reluctance under that government which an irresistible force imposes upon them, and from which no reluctance could deliver them.

Though in prosperity, however, the man of excessive self-estimation may sometimes appear to have some advantage over the man of correct and modest virtue ; though the applause of the multitude, and of those who see them both only at a distance, is often much louder in favour of the one than it ever is in favour of the other ; yet, all things fairly computed, the real balance of advantage is, perhaps in all cases, greatly in favour of the latter and against the former.   The man who neither ascribes to himself, nor wishes that other people should ascribe to him, any other merit besides that which really belongs to him, fears no humiliation, dreads no detection ; but rests contented and secure upon the genuine truth and solidity of his own character. His admirers may neither be very numerous nor very loud in their applauses ; but the wisest man who sees him the nearest and who knows him the best, admires him the most.   To a real wise man the judicious and well-weighed approbation of a single wise man, gives more heartfelt satisfaction than all the noisy applauses of ten thousand ignorant though enthusiastic admirers.   He may say with Parmenides, who, upon reading a philosophical discourse before a public assembly at Athens, and observing, that, except Plato, the whole company had left him, continued, notwithstanding, to read on, and said that Plato alone was audience sufficient for him.

It is otherwise with the man of excessive self-estimation.   The wise men who see him the nearest, admire him the least.   Amidst the intoxication of prosperity, their sober and just esteem falls so far short of the extravagance of his own self-admiration, that he regards it as mere malignity and envy.   He suspects his best friends.   Their company becomes offensive to him.   He drives them from his presence, and often rewards their services, not only with ingratitude, but with cruelty and injustice.   He abandons his confidence to flatterers and traitors, who pretend to idolize his vanity and presumption ; and that character which in the beginning, though in some respects defective, was, upon the whole, both amiable and respectable, becomes contemptible and odious in the end. Amidst the intoxication of prosperity, Alexander killed Clytus, for having preferred the exploits of his father Philip to his own ; put Calisthenes to death in torture, for having refused to adore him in the Persian manner ; and murdered the great friend of his father, the venerable Parmenio, after having, upon the most groundless suspicions, sent first to the torture and afterwards to the scaffold the only remaining son of that old man, the rest having all before died in his own service. This was that Parmenio of whom Philip used to say, that the Athenians were very fortunate who could find ten generals every year, while he himself, in the whole course of his life, could never find one but Parmenio. It was upon the vigilance and attention of this Parmenio that he reposed at all times with confidence and security, and, in his hours of mirth and jollity, used to say, ' Let us drink, my friends : we may do it with safety, for Parmenio ' never drinks.' It was this same Parmenio, with whose presence and counsel, it had been said, Alexander had gained all his victories ; and without his presence and counsel, he had never gained a single victory. The humble, admiring, and flattering friends, whom Alexander left in power and authority behind him, divided his empire among themselves, and after having thus robbed his family and kindred of their inheritance, put, one after another, every single surviving individual of them, whether male or female, to death.

We frequently, not only pardon, but thoroughly enter into and sympathize with the excessive self-estimation of those splendid characters in which we observe a great and distinguished superiority above the common level of mankind. We call them spirited, magnanimous, and high-minded ; words which all involve in their meaning a considerable degree of praise and admiration. But we cannot enter into and sympathize with the excessive self-estimation of those characters in which we can discern no such distinguished superiority. We are disgusted and revolted by it ; and it is with some difficulty that we can either pardon or suffer it. We call it pride or vanity ; two words, of which the latter always, and the former for the most part, involve in their meaning a considerable degree of blame.

Those two vices, however, though resembling, in some respects, as being both modifications of excessive self-estimation, are yet, in many respects, very different from one another.

The proud man is sincere, and, in the bottom of his heart, is convinced of his own superiority ; though it may sometimes be difficult to guess upon what that conviction is founded. He wishes you to view him in no other light than that in which, when he places himself in your situation, he really views himself. He demands no more of you than, what he thinks, justice. If you appear not to respect him as he-respects himself, he is more offended than mortified, and feels the same indignant resentment as if he had suffered a real injury. He does not even then, however, deign to explain the grounds of his own pretensions. He disdains to court your esteem. He affects even to despise it, and endeavours to maintain his assumed station, not so much by making you sensible of his superiority, as of your own meanness. He seems to wish not so much to excite your esteem for *himself*, as to mortify *that* for *yourself*.

The vain man is not sincere, and, in the bottom of his heart, is very seldom convinced of that superiority which he wishes you to ascribe to him. He wishes you to view him in much more splendid colours than those in which, when he places himself in your situation, and supposes you to know all that he knows, he can really view himself. When you appear to view him, therefore, in different colours, perhaps in his proper colours, he is much more mortified than offended. The grounds of his claim to that character which he wishes you to ascribe to him, he takes every opportunity of displaying, both by the most ostentatious and unnecessary exhibition of the good qualities and accomplishments which he possesses in some tolerable degree, and sometimes even by false pretensions to those which he either possesses in no degree, or in so very slender a degree that he may well enough be said to possess them in no degree. Far from despising your esteem, he courts it with the most anxious assiduity. Far from wishing to mortify your self-estimation, he is happy to cherish it, in hopes that in return you will cherish his own. He flatters in order to be flattered. He studies to please, and endeavours to bribe you into a good opinion of him by politeness and complaisance, and sometimes even by real and essential good offices, though often displayed, perhaps, with unnecessary ostentation.

The vain man sees the respect which is paid to rank and fortune, and wishes to usurp this respect, as well as that for talents and virtues. His dress, his equipage, his way of living, accordingly, all announce both a higher rank and a greater fortune than really belong to him; and in order to support this foolish imposition for a few years in the beginning of his life, he often reduces himself to poverty and distress long before the end of it. As long as he can continue his expense, however, his vanity is delighted with viewing himself, not in the light in which you would view him if you knew all that he knows; but in that in which, he imagines, he has, by his own address, induced you actually to view him. Of all the illusions of vanity that is, perhaps, the most common. Obscure strangers who visit foreign countries, or who, from a remote province, come to visit, for a short time, the capital of their own country, most frequently attempt to practise it. The folly of the attempt, though always very great and most unworthy of a man of sense, may not be altogether so great upon such as upon most other occasions. If their stay is short, they may escape any disgraceful detection ; and, after indulging their vanity for a few months or a few years, they may return to their own homes, and repair, by future parsimony, the waste of their past profusion.

The proud man can very seldom be accused of this folly. His sense of his own dignity renders him careful to preserve his independency, and, when his fortune happens not to be large, though he wishes to be decent, he studies to be frugal and attentive in all his expenses. The ostentatious expense of the vain man is highly offensive to him. It outshines, perhaps, his own. It provokes his indignation as an insolent assumption of a rank which is by no means due ; and he never talks of it without loading it with the harshest and severest reproaches.

The proud man does not always feel himself at his ease in the company of his equals, and still less in that of his superiors. He cannot lay down his lofty pretensions, and the countenance and conversation of such company overawe him so much that he dare not display them. He has recourse to humbler company, for which he has little respect, which he would not willingly choose, and which is by no means agreeable to him ; that of his inferiors, his flatterers, and dependants. He seldom visits his superiors, or, if he does, it is rather to show that he is entitled to live in such company, than for any real satisfaction that he enjoys in it. It is as Lord Clarendon says of the Earl of Arundel, that he sometimes went to court, because he could there only find a greater man than himself ; but that he went very seldom, because he found there a greater man than himself.

It is quite otherwise with the vain man. He courts the company of his superiors as much as the proud man shuns it. Their splendour, he seems to think, reflects a splendour upon those who are much about them. He haunts the courts of kings and the levees of ministers, and gives himself the air of being a candidate for fortune and preferment, when in reality he possesses the much more precious happiness, if he knew how to enjoy it, of not being one. He is fond of being admitted to the tables of the great, and still more fond of magnifying to other people the familiarity with which he is honoured there. He associates himself, as much as he can, with fashionable people, with those who are supposed to direct the public opinion, with the witty, with the learned, with the popular ; and he shuns the company of his best friends whenever the very uncertain current of public favour happens to run in any respect against them. With the people to whom he wishes to recommend himself, he is not always very delicate about the means which he employs for that purpose ; unnecessary ostentation, groundless pretensions, constant assentation, frequently flattery, though for the most part a pleasant and sprightly flattery, and very seldom the gross and fulsome flattery of a parasite. The proud man, on the contrary, never flatters, and is frequently scarce civil to any body.

Notwithstanding all its groundless pretensions, however, vanity is almost always a sprightly and a gay, and very often a good-natured passion. Pride is always a grave, a sullen, and a severe one. Even the falsehoods of the vain man are all innocent falsehoods, meant to raise himself, not to lower other people. To do the proud man justice he very seldom stoops to the baseness of falsehood. When he does, however, his falsehoods are by no means so innocent. They are all mischievous, and meant to lower other people. He is full of indignation at the unjust superiority, as he thinks it, which is given to them. He views them with malignity and envy, and, in talking of them, often endeavours, as much as he can, to extenuate and lessen whatever are the grounds upon which their superiority is supposed to be founded. Whatever tales are circulated to their disadvantage, though he seldom forges them himself, yet he often takes pleasure in believing them, is by no means unwilling to repeat them, and even sometimes with some degree of exaggeration. The worst falsehoods of vanity are what we call white lies: those of pride, whenever it condescends to falsehood, are all of the opposite complexion.

Our dislike to pride and vanity generally disposes us to rank the persons whom we accuse of those vices rather below than above the common level. In this judgment however, I think, we are most frequently in the wrong, and that both the proud and the vain man are often (perhaps for the most part) a good deal above it; though not near so much as either the one really thinks himself, or as the other wishes you to think him. If we compare them with their own pretensions, they may appear the just objects of contempt. But when we compare them with what the greater part of their rivals and competitors really are, they may appear quite otherwise, and very much above the common level. Where there is this real superiority, pride is frequently attended with many respectable virtues; with truth, with integrity, with a high sense of honour, with cordial and steady friendship, with the most inflexible firmness and resolution. Vanity, with many amiable ones; with humanity, with politeness, with a desire to oblige in all little matters, and sometimes with a real generosity in great ones; a generosity, however, which it often wishes to display in the most splendid colours that it can. By their rivals and enemies, the French, in the last century, were accused of vanity; the Spaniards, of pride; and foreign nations were disposed to consider the one as the more amiable; the other, as the more respectable people.

The words *vain* and *vanity* are never taken in a good sense. We sometimes say of a man, when we are talking of him in good humour, that he is the better for his vanity, or that his vanity is more diverting than offensive; but we still consider it as a foible and a ridiculous feature in his character.

The words *proud* and *pride*, on the contrary, are sometimes taken in a good sense. We frequently say of a man, that he is too proud, or that he has too much noble pride, ever to suffer himself to do a mean thing. Pride is, in this case, confounded with magnanimity. Aristotle, a philosopher who certainly knew the world, in drawing the character of the magnanimous man, paints him with many features which, in the two last centuries, were commonly ascribed to the Spanish character: that he was deliberate in all his resolutions; slow, and even tardy, in all his actions; that his voice was grave, his speech deliberate, his step and motion slow; that he appeared indolent and even slothful, not at all disposed to bustle about little matters, but to act with the most determined and vigorous resolution upon all great and illustrious occasions: that he was not a lover of danger, or forward to expose himself to little dangers, but to great dangers; and that, when he exposed himself to danger, he was altogether regardless of his life.

The proud man is commonly too well contented with himself to think that his character requires any amendment. The man who feels himself all-perfect, naturally enough despises all further improvement. His self-sufficiency and absurd conceit of his own superiority, commonly attend him from his youth to his most advanced age; and he dies, as Hamlet says, 'with all his sins upon his head, unanointed, unanealed.'

It is frequently quite otherwise with the vain man. The desire of the esteem and admiration of other people, when for qualities and talents which are the natural and proper objects of esteem and admiration, is the real love of true glory; a passion which, if not the very best passion of human nature, is certainly one of the best. Vanity is very frequently no more than an attempt prematurely to usurp that glory before it is due. Though your son, under five-and-twenty years of age, should be but a coxcomb; do not, upon that account, despair of his becoming, before he is forty, a very wise and worthy man, and a real proficient in all those talents and virtues to which, at present, he may only be an ostentatious and empty pretender. The great secret of education is to direct vanity to proper objects. Never suffer him to value himself upon trivial accomplishments. But do not always discourage his pretensions to those that are of real importance. He would not pretend to them if he did not earnestly desire to possess them. Encourage this desire; afford him every means to facilitate the acquisition; and do not take too much offence, although he should sometimes assume the air of having attained it a little before the time.

Such, I say, are the distinguishing characteristics of pride and vanity, when each of them acts according to its proper character. But the proud man is often vain; and the vain man is often proud. Nothing can be more natural than that the man, who thinks much more highly of himself than he deserves, should wish that other people should think still more highly of him: or that the man, who wishes that other people should think more highly of him than he thinks of himself, should, at the same time, think much more highly of himself than he deserves. Those two vices being frequently blended in the same character, the characteristics of both are necessarily confounded; and we sometimes find the superficial and impertinent ostentation of vanity joined to the most malignant and derisive insolence of pride. We are sometimes, upon that account, at a loss how to rank a particular character, or whether to place it among the proud or among the vain.

Men of merit considerably above the common level, sometimes under-rate as well as over-rate themselves. Such characters, though not very dignified, are often, in private society, far from being disagreeable. His companions all feel themselves much at their ease in the society of a man so perfectly modest and unassuming. If those companions, how-ever, have not both more discernment and more generosity than ordi-nary, though they may have some kindness for him, they have seldom much respect; and the warmth of their kindness is very seldom suffi-cient to compensate the coldness of their respect. Men of no more than ordinary discernment never rate any person higher than he appears to rate himself. He seems doubtful himself, they say, whether he is perfectly fit for such a situation or such an office; and imme-diately give the preference to some impudent blockhead who entertains no doubt about his own qualifications. Though they should have dis-cernment, yet, if they want generosity, they never fail to take advantage of his simplicity, and to assume over him an impertinent superiority which they are by no means entitled to. His good nature may enable him to bear this for some time; but he grows weary at last, and fre-quently when it is too late, and when that rank, which he ought to have assumed, is lost irrecoverably, and usurped, in consequence of his own backwardness, by some of his more forward, though much less meritorious companions. A man of this character must have been very fortunate in the early choice of his companions, if, in going through the world, he meets always with fair justice, even from those whom, from his own past kindness, he might have some reason to consider as his best friends; and a youth, who may be too unassuming and too unambitious, is frequently followed by an insignificant, complaining, and discontented old age.

Those unfortunate persons whom nature has formed a good deal below the common level, seem oftentimes to rate themselves still more below it than they really are. This humility appears sometimes to sink them into idiotism. Whoever has taken the trouble to examine idiots with attention, will find that, in many of them, the faculties of the understanding are by no means weaker than in several other people, who, though acknowledged to be dull and stupid, are not, by any body, accounted idiots. Many idiots, with no more than ordinary education, have been taught to read, write, and account tolerably well. Many persons, never accounted idiots, notwithstanding the most careful education, and notwithstanding that, in their advanced age, they have had spirit enough to attempt to learn what their early education had not taught them, have never been able to acquire, in any tolerable degree, any one of those three accomplishments.   By an instinct of pride, however, they set themselves upon a level with their equals in age and situation; and, with courage and firmness, maintain their proper station among their companions.   By an opposite instinct, the idiot feels himself below every company into which you can introduce him.   Ill-usage, to which he is extremely liable, is capable of throwing him into the most violent fits of rage and fury.   But no good usage, no kindness or indulgence, can ever raise him to converse with you as your equal.   If you can bring him to converse with you at all, however, you will frequently find his answers sufficiently pertinent, and even sensible.   But they are always stamped with a distinct consciousness of his own great inferiority.   He seems to shrink and, as it were, to retire from your look and conversation; and to feel, when he places himself in your situation, that, notwithstanding your apparent condescension, you cannot help considering him as immensely below you.   Some idiots, perhaps the greater part, seem to be so, chiefly or altogether, from a certain numbness or torpidity in the faculties of the understanding. But there are others, in whom those faculties do not appear more torpid or benumbed than in many other people who are not accounted idiots.   But that instinct of pride, necessary to support them upon an equality with their brethren, seems to be totally wanting in the former and not in the latter.

That degree of self-estimation, therefore, which contributes most to the happiness and contentment of the person himself, seems likewise most agreeable to the impartial spectator.

The man who esteems himself as he ought, and no more than he ought, seldom fails to obtain from other people all the esteem that he himself thinks due.   He desires no more than is due to him, and he rests upon it with complete satisfaction.

The proud and the vain man, on the contrary, are constantly dissatisfied.   The one is tormented with indignation at the unjust superiority, as he thinks it, of other people.   The other is in continual dread of the shame, which, he foresees, would attend upon the detection of his groundless pretensions.   Even the extravagant pretensions of the man of real magnanimity, though, when supported by splendid abilities and virtues, and, above all, by good fortune, they impose upon the multitude, whose applauses he little regards, do not impose upon those wise men whose approbation he can only value, and whose esteem he is most anxious to acquire.   He feels that they see through, and suspects that they despise his excessive presumption; and he often suffers the cruel misfortune of becoming, first the jealous and secret, and at last the open, furious, and vindictive enemy of those very persons, whose friendship it would have given him the greatest happiness to enjoy with unsuspicious security.   .

Though our dislike to the proud and the vain often disposes us to rank them rather below than above their proper station, yet, unless we are provoked by some particular and personal impertinence, we very seldom venture to use them ill. In common cases, we endeavour, for our own ease, rather to acquiesce, and, as well as we can, to accommodate ourselves to their folly. But, to the man who under-rates himself, unless we have both more discernment and more generosity than belong to the greater part of men, we seldom fail to do, at least, all the injustice which he does to himself, and frequently a great deal more. He is not only more unhappy in his own feelings than either the proud or the vain, but he is much more liable to every sort of ill-usage from other people. In almost all cases, it is better to be a little too proud, than, in any respect, too humble; and, in the sentiment of self-estimation, some degree of excess seems, both to the person himself and to the impartial spectator, to be less disagreeable than any degree of defect of that feeling.

In this, therefore, as well as in every other emotion, passion, and habit, the degree that is most agreeable to the impartial spectator is likewise most agreeable to the person himself ; and according as either the excess or the defect is least offensive to the former, so, either the one or the other is in proportion least disagreeable to the latter.

CONCLUSION OF THE SIXTH PART.

CONCERN for our own happiness recommends to us the virtue of prudence : concern for that of other people, the virtues of justice and beneficence; of which, the one restrains us from hurting, the other prompts us to promote that happiness. Independent of any regard either to what are, or to what ought to be, or to what upon a certain condition would be, the sentiments of other people, the first of those three virtues is originally recommended to us by our selfish, the other two by our benevolent affections. Regard to the sentiments of other people, however, comes afterwards both to enforce and to direct the practice of all those virtues; and no man during, either the whole course of his life, or that of any considerable part of it, ever trod steadily and uniformly in the paths of prudence, of justice, or of proper beneficence, whose conduct was not principally directed by a regard to the sentiments of the supposed impartial spectator, of the great inmate of the breast, the great judge and arbiter of conduct. If in the course of the day we have swerved in any respect from the rules which he prescribes to us; if we have either exceeded or relaxed in our frugality;

if we have either exceeded or relaxed in our industry; if through passion or inadvertency, we have hurt in any respect the interest or happiness of our neighbour; if we have neglected a plain and proper opportunity of promoting that interest and happiness; it is this inmate who, in the evening, calls us to an account for all those omissions and violations, and his reproaches often make us blush inwardly both for our folly and inattention to our own happiness, and for our still greater indifference and inattention, perhaps, to that of other people.

But though the virtues of prudence, justice, and beneficence, may, upon different occasions, be recommended to us almost equally by two different principles; those of self-command are, upon most occasions, principally and almost entirely recommended to us by one; by the sense of propriety, by regard to the sentiments of the supposed impartial spectator. Without the restraint which this principle imposes, every passion would, upon most occasions, rush headlong, if I may say so, to its own gratification. Anger would follow the suggestions of its own fury; fear those of its own violent agitations. Regard to no time or place would induce vanity to refrain from the loudest and most impertinent ostentation; or voluptuousness from the most open, indecent, and scandalous indulgence. Respect for what are, or for what ought to be, or for what upon a certain condition would be, the sentiments of other people, is the sole principle which, upon most occasions, over-awes all those mutinous and turbulent passions into that tone and temper which the impartial spectator can enter into and cordially sympathize with.

Upon some occasions, indeed, those passions are restrained, not so much by a sense of their impropriety, as by prudential considerations of the bad consequences which might follow from their indulgence. In such cases, the passions, though restrained, are not always subdued, but often remain lurking in the breast with all their original fury. The man whose anger is restrained by fear, does not always lay aside his anger, but only reserves its gratification for a more safe opportunity. But the man who, in relating to some other person the injury which has been done to him, feels at once the fury of his passion cooled and becalmed by sympathy with the more moderate sentiments of his companion, who at once adopts those more moderate sentiments, and comes to view that injury, not in the black and atrocious colours in which he had originally beheld it, but in the much milder and fairer light in which his companion naturally views it; not only restrains, but in some measure subdues, his anger. The passion becomes really less than it was before, and less capable of exciting him to the violent and bloody revenge which at first, perhaps, he might have thought of inflicting on his enemy.

Those passions which are restrained by the sense of propriety, are all in some degree moderated and subdued by it. But those which are restrained only by prudential considerations of any kind, are, on the contrary, frequently inflamed by the restraint, and sometimes (long after the provocation given, and when nobody is thinking about it) burst out absurdly and unexpectedly, and that with tenfold fury and violence.

Anger, however, as well as every other passion, may, upon many occasions, be very properly restrained by prudential considerations. Some exertion of manhood and self-command is even necessary for this sort of restraint; and the impartial spectator may sometimes view it with that sort of cold esteem due to that species of conduct which he considers as a mere matter of vulgar prudence; but never with that affectionate admiration with which he surveys the same passions, when, by the sense of propriety, they are moderated and subdued to what he himself can readily enter into. In the former species of restraint, he may frequently discern some degree of propriety, and, if you will, even of virtue; but it is a propriety and virtue of a much inferior order to those which he always feels with transport and admiration in the latter.

The virtues of prudence, justice, and beneficence, have no tendency to produce any but the most agreeable effects. Regard to those effects, as it originally recommends them to the actor, so does it afterwards to the impartial spectator. In our approbation of the character of the prudent man, we feel, with peculiar complacency, the security which he must enjoy while he walks under the safeguard of that sedate and deliberate virtue. In our approbation of the character of the just man, we feel, with equal complacency, the security which all those connected with him, whether in neighbourhood, society, or business must derive from his scrupulous anxiety never either to hurt or offend. In our approbation of the character of the beneficent man, we enter into the gratitude of all those who are within the sphere of his good offices, and conceive with them the highest sense of his merit. In our approbation of all those virtues, our sense of their agreeable effects, of their utility, either to the person who exercises them, or to some other persons, joins with our sense of their propriety, and constitutes always a considerable, frequently the greater part of that approbation.

But in our approbation of the virtues of self-command, complacency with their effects sometimes constitutes no part, and frequently but a small part, of that approbation. Those effects may sometimes be agreeable, and sometimes disagreeable; and though our approbation is no doubt stronger in the former case, it is by no means altogether destroyed in the latter. The most heroic valour may be employed indifferently in the cause either of justice or of injustice; and though it is no doubt much more loved and admired in the former case, it still appears a great and respectable quality even in the latter. In that, and in all the other virtues of self-command, the splendid and dazzling

16 *

236 THE TWO QUESTIONS ON THE PRINCIPLES OF MORALS.

quality seems always to be the greatness and steadiness of the exertion, and the strong sense of propriety which is necessary in order to make and to maintain that exertion. The effects are too often but too little regarded.

Part VII.—Of Systems of Moral Philosophy.

SEC. I.—OF THE QUESTIONS WHICH OUGHT TO BE EXAMINED IN A THEORY OF MORAL SENTIMENTS.

IF we examine the most celebrated and remarkable of the different theories which have been given concerning the nature and origin of our moral sentiments, we shall find that almost all of them coincide with some part or other of that which I have been endeavouring to give an account of; and that if every thing which has already been said be fully considered, we shall be at no loss to explain what was the view or aspect of nature which led each particular author to form his particular system. From some one or other of those principles which I have been endeavouring to unfold, every system of morality that ever had any reputation in the world has, perhaps, ultimately been derived. As they are all of them, in this respect, founded upon natural principles, they are all of them in some measure in the right. But as many of them are derived from a partial and imperfect view of nature, there are many of them too in some respects in the wrong.

In treating of the principles of morals there are two questions to be considered. First, wherein does virtue consist? Or what is the tone of temper, and tenor of conduct, which constitutes the excellent and praise-worthy character, the character which is the natural object of esteem, honour, and approbation? And, secondly, by what power or faculty in the mind is it, that this character, whatever it be, is recommended to us? Or in other words, how and by what means does it come to pass, that the mind prefers one tenor of conduct to another, denominates the one right and the other wrong; considers the one as the object of approbation, honour, and reward, and the other of blame, censure, and punishment?

We examine the first question when we consider whether virtue consists in benevolence, as Dr. Hutcheson imagines; or in acting suitably to the different relations we stand in, as Dr. Clark supposes; or in the wise and prudent pursuit of our own real and solid happiness, as has been the opinion of others.

We examine the second question, when we consider, whether the virtuous character, whatever it consists in, be recommended to us by self-love, which makes us perceive that this character, both in ourselves and others, tends most to promote our own private interest; or by reason, which points out to us the difference between one character and

another, in the same manner as it does that between truth and falsehood ; or by a peculiar power of perception, called a moral sense, which
this virtuous character gratifies and pleases, as the contrary disgusts
and displeases it ; or last of all, by some other principle in human
nature, such as a modification of sympathy, or the like.

I shall begin with considering the systems which have been formed
concerning the first of these questions, and shall proceed afterwards to
examine those concerning the second.

Sec. II.—Of the different Accounts which have been given of the Nature of Virtue.

INTRODUCTION.—The different accounts which have been given of the
nature of virtue, or of the temper of mind which constitutes the excellent
and praise-worthy character, may be reduced to three different classes.
According to some, the virtuous temper of mind does not consist in any
one species of affections, but in the proper government and direction
of all our affections, which may be either virtuous or vicious according
to the objects which they pursue, and the degree of vehemence with
which they pursue them.   According to these authors, therefore, virtue
consists in propriety.

According to others, virtue consists in the judicious pursuit of our
own private interest and happiness, or in the proper government and
direction of those selfish affections which aim solely at this end.   In
the opinion of these, therefore, virtue consists in prudence.

Another set of authors make virtue consist in those affections only
which aim at the happiness of others, not in those which aim at our
own.   According to them, therefore, disinterested benevolence is the
only motive which can stamp upon actions the character of virtue.

The character of virtue, it is evident, must either be ascribed indifferently to all our affections, when under proper government and
direction ; or be confined to some one class or division of them.

The great division of our affections is into the selfish and the benevolent.   If the character of virtue, therefore, cannot be ascribed indifferently to all our affections, when under proper government and direction, it must be confined either to those which aim directly at our
own private happiness, or to those which aim directly at that of
others.   If virtue, therefore, does not consist in propriety, it must consist either in prudence or in benevolence.   Besides these three, it is
scarce possible to imagine that any other account can be given of the
nature of virtue.   I shall endeavour to show hereafter how all the other
accounts, which are seemingly different from any of these, coincide at
bottom with some one or other of them.

CHAP. I.—*Of those Systems which make Virtue consist in Propriety.*

ACCORDING to Plato, to Aristotle, and to Zeno, virtue consists in the propriety of conduct, or in the suitableness of the affection from which we act to the object which excites it.

I. In the system of Plato (See Plato de Rep. lib. iv.) the soul is considered as something like a little state or republic, composed of three different faculties or orders.

The first is the judging faculty, the faculty which determines not only what are the proper means for attaining any end, but also what ends are fit to be pursued, and what degree of relative value we ought to put upon each. This faculty Plato called, as it is very properly called, reason, and considered it as what had a right to be the governing principle of the whole. Under this appellation, it is evident, he comprehended not only that faculty by which we judge of truth and falsehood, but that by which we judge of the propriety or the impropriety of our desires and affections.

The different passions and appetites, the natural subjects of this ruling principle, but which are so apt to rebel against their master, he reduced to two different classes or orders. The first consisted of those passions, which are founded in pride and resentment, or in what the schoolmen called the irascible part of the soul; ambition, animosity, the love of honour, and the dread of shame, the desire of victory, superiority, and revenge; all those passions, in short, which are supposed either to rise from, or to denote what, by a metaphor in our language, we commonly call spirit or natural fire. The second consisted of those passions which are founded in the love of pleasure, or in what the schoolmen called the concupiscible part of the soul. It comprehended all the appetites of the body, the love of ease and of security, and of all the sensual gratifications.

It rarely happens that we break in upon that plan of conduct, which the governing principle prescribes, and which in all our cool hours we had laid down to ourselves as what was most proper for us to pursue, but when prompted by one or other of those two different sets of passions; either by ungovernable ambition and resentment, or by the importunate solicitations of present ease and pleasure. But though these two orders of passions are so apt to mislead us, they are still considered as necessary parts of human nature: the first having been given to defend us against injuries, to assert our rank and dignity in the world, to make us aim at what is noble and honourable, and to make us distinguish those who act in the same manner; the second, to provide for the support and necessities of the body.

In the strength, acuteness, and perfection of the governing principle was placed the essential virtue of prudence, which, according to Plato, consisted in a just and clear discernment, founded upon general and scientific ideas, of the ends which were proper to be pursued, and of the means which were proper for attaining them.

When the first set of passions, those of the irascible part of the soul, had that degree of strength and firmness, which enabled them, under the direction of reason, to despise all dangers in the pursuit of what was honourable and noble ; it constituted the virtue of fortitude and magnanimity. This order of passions, according to this system, was of a more generous and noble nature than the other. They were considered upon many occasions as the auxiliaries of reason, to check and restrain the inferior and brutal appetites. We are often angry at ourselves, it was observed, we often become the objects of our own resentment and indignation, when the love of pleasure prompts to do what we disapprove of ; and the irascible part of our nature is in this manner called in to assist the rational against the concupiscible.

When all those three different parts of our nature were in perfect concord with one another, when neither the irascible nor concupiscible passions ever aimed at any gratification which reason did not approve of, and when reason never commanded any thing, but what these of their own accord were willing to perform : this happy composure, this perfect and complete harmony of soul, constituted that virtue which in their language is expressed by a word which we commonly translate temperance, but which might more properly be translated good temper, or sobriety and moderation of mind.

Justice, the last and greatest of the four cardinal virtues, took place, according to this system, when each of those three faculties of the mind confined itself to its proper office, without attempting to encroach upon that of any other ; when reason directed and passion obeyed, and when each passion performed its proper duty, and exerted itself towards its proper object easily and without reluctance, and with that degree of force and energy, which was suitable to the value of what it pursued. In this consisted that complete virtue, that perfect propriety of conduct, which Plato, after some of the ancient Pythagoreans, has well denominated Justice.

The word, it is to be observed, which expresses justice in the Greek language, has several different meanings ; and as the correspondent word in all other languages, so far as I know, has the same, there must be some natural affinity among those various significations. In one sense we are said to do justice to our neighbour when we abstain from doing him any positive harm, and do not directly hurt him, either in his person, or in his estate, or in his reputation. This is that justice which I have treated of above, the observance of which may be extorted by force, and the violation of which exposes to punishment. In another sense we are said not to do justice to our neighbour unless we conceive for him all that love, respect, and esteem, which his character, his situation, and his connexion with ourselves, render suitable and proper for us to feel, and unless we act accordingly. It is in this sense that we are said to do injustice to a man of merit who is connected with us, though we abstain from hurting him in every respect, if we do not exert ourselves to serve him and to place him in that situation in which the impartial spectator would be pleased to see him. The first sense of the word coincides with what Aristotle and the Schoolmen call commutative justice, and with what Grotius calls the *justitia expletrix*, which consists in abstaining from what is another's, and in doing voluntarily whatever we can with propriety be forced to do. The second sense of the word coincides with what some have called distributive justice,° and with the *justitia attributrix* of Grotius, which consists in proper beneficence, in the becoming use of what is our own, and in the applying it to those purposes, either of charity or generosity, to which it is most suitable, in our situation, that it should be applied. In this sense justice comprehends all the social virtues. There is yet another sense in which the word justice is sometimes taken, still more extensive than either of the former, though very much akin to the last; and which runs too, so far as I know, through all languages. It is in this last sense that we are said to be unjust, when we do not seem to value any particular object with that degree of esteem, or to pursue it with that degree of ardour which to the impartial spectator it may appear to deserve or to be naturally fitted for exciting. Thus we are said to do injustice to a poem or a picture, when we do not admire them enough, and we are said to do them more than justice when we admire them too much. In the same manner we are said to do injustice to ourselves when we appear not to give sufficient attention to any particular object of self-interest. In this last sense, what is called justice means the same thing with exact and perfect propriety of conduct and behaviour, and comprehends in it, not only the offices of both commutative and distributive justice, but of every other virtue, of prudence, of fortitude, of temperance. It is in this last sense that Plato evidently understands what he calls justice, and which, therefore, according to him, comprehends in it the perfection of every sort of virtue.

Such is the account given by Plato of the nature of virtue, or of that temper of mind which is the proper object of praise and approbation. It consists, according to him, in that state of mind in which every faculty confines itself within its proper sphere without encroaching upon that of any other, and performs its proper office with that precise degree of strength and vigour which belongs to it. His account, it is evident, coincides in every respect with what we have said above concerning the propriety of conduct.

II. Virtue, according to Aristotle (Ethic. Nic. l. 2. c. 5. et seq. et l. 3.

° The distributive justice of Aristotle is somewhat different. It consists in the proper distribution of rewards from the public stock of a community. See Aristotle Ethic. Nic. l. 5. c. 2.

c. 4. et seq.), consists in the habit of mediocrity according to right reason.   Every particular virtue, according to him, lies in a kind of middle between two opposite vices, of which the one offends from being too much, the other from being too little affected by a particular species of object.   Thus the virtue of fortitude or courage lies in the middle between the opposite vices of cowardice and of presumptuous rashness, of which the one offends from being too much, and the other from being too little affected by the objects of fear.   Thus too the virtue of frugality lies in a middle between avarice and profusion, of which the one consists in an excess, the other in a defect of the proper attention to the objects of self-interest.   Magnanimity, in the same manner, lies in a middle between the excess of arrogance and the defect of pusillanimity, of which the one consists in too extravagant, the other in too weak a sentiment of our own worth and dignity.   It is unnecessary to observe that this account of virtue corresponds, too, pretty exactly with what has been said above concerning the propriety and impropriety of conduct.

According to Aristotle (Ethic. Nic. lib. ii. ch. 1, 2, 3, and 4.), indeed, virtue did not so much consist in those moderate and right affections, as in the habit of this moderation.   In order to understand this, it is to be observed, that virtue may be considered either as the quality of an action, or the quality of a person.   Considered as the quality of an action, it consists, even according to Aristotle, in the reasonable moderation of the affection from which the action proceeds, whether this disposition be habitual to the person or not.   Considered as the quality of a person, it consists in the habit of this reasonable moderation, in its having become the customary and usual disposition of the mind. Thus the action which proceeds from an occasional fit of generosity is undoubtedly a generous action, but the man who performs it, is not necessarily a generous person, because it may be the single action of the kind which he ever performed.   The motive and disposition of heart, from which this action was performed, may have been quite just and proper: but as this happy mood seems to have been the effect rather of accidental humour than of any thing steady or permanent in the character, it can reflect no great honour on the performer.   When we denominate a character generous or charitable, or virtuous in any respect, we mean to signify that the disposition expressed by each of those appellations is the usual and customary disposition of the person. But single actions of any kind, how proper and suitable soever, are of little consequence to show that this is the case.   If a single action was sufficient to stamp the character of any virtue upon the person who performed it, the most worthless of mankind might lay claim to all the virtues ; since there is no man who has not, upon some occasions, acted with prudence, justice, temperance, and fortitude.   But though single actions, how laudable soever, reflect very little praise upon the person who performs them, a single vicious action performed by one whose conduct is usually pretty regular, greatly diminishes and sometimes destroys altogether our opinion of his virtue. A single action of this kind sufficiently shows that his habits are not perfect, and that he is less to be depended upon, than, from the usual train of his behaviour, we might have been apt to imagine.

Aristotle too (Mag. Mor. lib. i. ch. 1.) when he made virtue to consist in practical habits, had it probably in his view to oppose the doctrine of Plato, who seems to have been of opinion that just sentiments and reasonable judgments concerning what was fit to be done or to be avoided, were alone sufficient to constitute the most perfect virtue. Virtue, according to Plato, might be considered as a species of science, and no man, he thought, could see clearly and demonstratively what was right and what was wrong, and not act accordingly. Passion might make us act contrary to doubtful and uncertain opinions, not to plain and evident judgments. Aristotle, on the contrary, was of opinion that no conviction of the understanding was capable of getting the better of inveterate habits, and that our good morals arose not from knowledge but from action.

III. According to Zeno,* the founder of the Stoical doctrine, every animal was by nature recommended to its own care, and was endowed with the principle of self-love, that it might endeavour to preserve, not only its existence, but all the different parts of its nature, in the best and most perfect state of which they were capable.

The self-love of man embraced, if I may say so, his body and all its different members, his mind and all its different faculties and powers, and desired the preservation and maintenance of them all in their best and most perfect condition. Whatever tended to support this state of existence was, therefore, by nature pointed out to him as fit to be chosen ; and whatever tended to destroy it, as fit to be rejected. Thus health, strength, agility, and ease of body as well as the external conveniences which could promote these ; wealth, power, honours, the respect and esteem of those we live with ; were naturally pointed out to us as things eligible, and of which the possession was preferable to the want. On the other hand, sickness, infirmity, unwieldiness, pain of body, as well as all the external inconveniences which tend to occasion or bring on any of them ; poverty, the want of authority, the contempt or hatred of those we live with; were, in the same manner, pointed out to us as things to be shunned and avoided. In each of those two opposite classes of objects, there were some which appeared to be more the objects either of choice or rejection, than others in the same class. Thus, in the first class, health appeared evidently preferable to strength, and strength to agility; reputation to power, and power to riches. And thus too, in the second class, sickness was more to be avoided than

* See Cicero de finibus, lib. iii. ; also Diogenes Laertius in Zenone, lib. vii. segment 84.

unwieldiness of body, ignominy than poverty, and poverty than the loss of power.   Virtue and the propriety of conduct consisted in choosing and rejecting all different objects and circumstances according as they were by nature rendered more or less the objects of choice or rejection; in selecting always from among the several objects of choice presented to us, that which must be chosen, when we could not obtain them all; and in selecting, too, out of the several objects of rejection offered to us, that which was least to be avoided, when it was not in our power to avoid them all.   By choosing and rejecting with this just and accurate discernment, by thus bestowing upon every object the precise degree of attention it deserved, according to the place which it held in this natural scale of things, we maintained, acccording to the Stoics, that perfect rectitude of conduct which constituted the essence of virtue.   This was what they called to live consistently, to live according to nature, and to obey those laws and directions which nature, or the Author of nature, had prescribed for our conduct.

So far the Stoical idea of propriety and virtue is not very different from that of Aristotle and the ancient Peripatetics.

Among those primary objects which nature had recommended to us as eligible, was the prosperity of our family, of our relations, of our friends, of our country, of mankind, and of the universe in general. Nature too, had taught us, that as the prosperity of two was preferable to that of one, that of many, or of all, must be infinitely more so. That we ourselves were but one, and that consequently wherever our prosperity was inconsistent with that, either of the whole, or of any considerable part of the whole, it ought, even in our own choice, to yield to what was so vastly preferable.   As all the events in this world were conducted by the providence of a wise, powerful, and good God, we might be assured that whatever happened tended to the prosperity and perfection of the whole.   If we ourselves, therefore, were in poverty, in sickness, or in any other calamity, we ought, first of all, to use our utmost endeavours, so far as justice and our duty to others will allow, to rescue ourselves from this disagreeable circumstance.   But if, after all we could do, we found this impossible, we ought to rest satisfied that the order and perfection of the universe required that we should in the mean time continue in this situation.   And as the prosperity of the whole should, even to us, appear preferable to so insignificant a part as ourselves, our situation, whatever it was, ought from that moment to become the object of our liking, if we would maintain that complete propriety and rectitude of sentiment and conduct in which consisted the perfection of our nature.   If, indeed, any opportunity of extricating ourselves should offer, it became our duty to embrace it.   The order of the universe, it was evident, no longer required our continuance in this situation, and the great Director of the world plainly called upon us to leave it, by so clearly pointing out the road which we were to follow. It was the same case with the adversity of our relations, our friends, our country. If, without violating any more sacred obligation, it was in our power to prevent or put an end to their calamity, it undoubtedly was our duty to do so. The propriety of action, the rule which Jupiter had given us for the direction of our conduct, evidently required this of us. But if it was altogether out of our power to do either, we ought then to consider this event as the most fortunate which could possibly have happened : because we might be assured that it tended most to the prosperity and order of the whole, which was that we ourselves, if we were wise and equitable, ought most of all to desire. It was our own final interest considered as a part of that whole, of which the prosperity ought to be, not only the principal, but the sole object of our desire.

‘ In what sense,’ says Epictetus, ‘ are some things said to be accord-
‘ ing to our nature, and others contrary to it ? It is in that sense in
‘ which we consider ourselves as separated and detached from all other
‘ things. For thus it may be said to be according to the nature of the
‘ foot to be always clean. But if you consider it as a foot, and not as
‘ something detached from the rest of the body, it must behove it some-
‘ times to trample in the dirt, and sometimes to tread upon thorns, and
‘ sometimes, too, to be cut off for the sake of the whole body ; and if it
‘ refuses this, it is no longer a foot. Thus, too, ought we to conceive
‘ with regard to ourselves. What are you ? A man. If you consider
‘ yourself as something separated and detached, it is agreeable to your
‘ nature to live to old age, to be rich, to be in health. But if you con-
‘ sider yourself as a man, and as a part of a whole, upon account of that
‘ whole, it will behove you sometimes to be in sickness, sometimes to be
‘ exposed to the inconveniency of a sea voyage, sometimes to be in
‘ want, and at last perhaps to die before your time. Why then do you
‘ complain ? Do not you know that by doing so, as the foot ceases to
‘ be a foot, so you cease to be man ?’

A wise man never complains of the destiny of Providence, nor thinks the universe in confusion when he is out of order. He does not look upon himself as a whole, separated and detached from every other part of nature, to be taken care of by itself and for itself. He regards himself in the light in which he imagines the great genius of human nature, and of the world, regards him. He enters, if I may say so, into the sentiments of that divine Being, and considers himself as an atom, a particle, of an immense and infinite system, which must and ought to be disposed of according to the conveniency of the whole. Assured of the wisdom which directs all the events of human life, whatever lot befalls him, he accepts it with joy, satisfied that, if he had known all the connections and dependencies of the different parts of the universe, it is the very lot which he himself would have wished for. If it is life, he is contented to live ; and if it is death, as nature must have no further occasion for his presence here, he willingly goes where he is appointed. I accept, said a cynical philosopher, whose doctrines were in this respect the same as those of the Stoics, I accept, with equal joy and satisfaction, whatever fortune can befall me. Riches or poverty, pleasure or pain, health or sickness, all is alike : nor would I desire that the gods should in any respect change my destination. If I was to ask of them any thing beyond what their bounty has already bestowed, it should be that they would inform me beforehand what it was their pleasure should be done with me, that I might of my own accord place myself in this situation, and demonstrate the cheerfulness with which I embraced their allotment. If I am going to sail, says Epictetus, I choose the best ship and the best pilot, and I wait for the fairest weather that my circumstances and duty will allow. Prudence and propriety, the principles which the gods have given me for the direction of my conduct, require this of me ; but they require no more : and if, notwithstanding, a storm arises, which neither the strength of the vessel nor the skill of the pilot are likely to withstand, I give myself no trouble about the consequence. All that I had to do is done already. The directors of my conduct never command me to be miserable, to be anxious, desponding, or afraid. Whether we are to be drowned, or to come to a harbour, is the business of Jupiter, not mine. I leave it entirely to his determination, nor ever break my rest with considering which way he is likely to decide it, but receive whatever may come with equal indifference and security.

From this perfect confidence in that benevolent wisdom which governs the universe, and from this entire resignation to whatever order that wisdom might think proper to establish, it necessarily followed, that to the Stoical wise man, all the events of human life must be in a great measure indifferent. His happiness consisted altogether, first, in the contemplation of the happiness and perfection of the great system of the universe, of the good government of the great republic of gods and men, of all rational and sensible beings ; and, secondly, in discharging his duty, in acting properly in the affairs of this great republic whatever little part that wisdom had assigned to him. The propriety or impropriety of his endeavours might be of great consequence to him. Their success or disappointment could be of none at all ; could excite no passionate joy or sorrow, no passionate desire or aversion. If he preferred some events to others, if some situations were the objects of his choice and others of his rejection, it was not because he regarded the one as in themselves in any respect better than the other, or thought that his own happiness would be more complete in what is called the fortunate than in what is regarded as the distressful situation ; but because the propriety of action, the rule which the gods had given him for the direction of his conduct, required him to choose and reject in this manner. All his affections were absorbed and swallowed up in two great affections ; in that for the discharge of his own duty, and in that for the greatest possible happiness of all rational and sensible beings. For the gratification of this latter affection, he rested with the most perfect security upon the wisdom and power of the great Superintendent of the universe. His sole anxiety was about the gratification of the former ; not about the event, but about the propriety of his own endeavours. Whatever the event might be, he trusted to a superior power and wisdom for turning it to promote that great end which he himself was most desirous of promoting.

This propriety of choosing and rejecting, though originally pointed out to us, and as it were recommended and introduced to our acquaintance by the things, and for the sake of the things, chosen and rejected ; yet when we had once become thoroughly acquainted with it, the order, the grace, the beauty which we discerned in this conduct, the happiness which we felt resulted from it, necessarily appeared to us of much greater value than the actual obtaining of all the different objects of choice, or the actual avoiding of all those of rejection. From the observation of this propriety arose the happiness and the glory ; from the neglect of it, the misery and the disgrace of human nature.

But to a wise man, to one whose passions were brought under perfect subjection to the ruling principles of his nature, the exact observation of this propriety was equally easy upon all occasions. Was he in prosperity, he returned thanks to Jupiter for having joined him with circumstances which were easily mastered, and in which there was little temptation to do wrong. Was he in adversity, he equally returned thanks to the director of this spectacle of human life, for having opposed to him a vigorous athlete, over whom, though the contest was likely to be more violent, the victory was more glorious, and equally certain. Can there be any shame in that distress which is brought upon us without any fault of our own, and in which we behave with perfect propriety ? There can, therefore, be no evil, but, on the contrary, the greatest good and advantage. A brave man exults in those dangers in which, from no rashness of his own, his fortune has involved him. They afford an opportunity of exercising that heroic intrepidity, whose exertion gives the exalted delight which flows from the consciousness of superior propriety and deserved admiration. One who is master of all his exercises has no aversion to measure his strength and activity with the strongest. And, in the same manner, one who is master of all his passions, does not dread any circumstance in which the Superintendent of the universe may think proper to place him. The bounty of that divine Being has provided him with virtues which render him superior to every situation. If it is pleasure, he has temperance to refrain from it ; if it is pain, he has constancy to bear it ; if it is danger or death, he has magnanimity and fortitude to despise it. The events of human life can never find him unprepared, or at a loss how to maintain that propriety of sentiment and conduct which, in his own apprehension, constitutes at once his glory and his happiness.

Human life the Stoics appear to have considered as a game of great skill; in which, however, there was a mixture of chance, or of what is vulgarly understood to be chance. In such games the stake is commonly a trifle, and the whole pleasure of the game arises from playing well, from playing fairly, and playing skilfully. If notwithstanding all his skill, however, the good player should, by the influence of chance, happen to lose, the loss ought to be a matter, rather of merriment, than of serious sorrow. He has made no false stroke; he has done nothing which he ought to be ashamed of; he has enjoyed completely the whole pleasure of the game. If, on the contrary, the bad player notwithstanding all his blunders, should, in the same manner, happen to win, his success can give him but little satisfaction. He is mortified by the remembrance of all the faults which he committed. Even during the play he can enjoy no part of the pleasure which it is capable of affording. From ignorance of the rules of the game, fear and doubt and hesitation are the disagreeable sentiments that precede almost every stroke which he plays; and when he has played it, the mortification of finding it a gross blunder, commonly completes the unpleasing circle of his sensations. Human life, with all the advantages which can possibly attend it, ought, according to the Stoics, to be regarded but as a mere twopenny stake; a matter by far too insignificant to merit any anxious concern. Our only anxious concern ought to be, not about the stake, but about the proper method of playing. If we placed our happiness in winning the stake, we placed it in what depended upon causes beyond our power and out of our direction. We necessarily exposed ourselves to perpetual fear and uneasiness, and frequently to grievous and mortifying disappointments. If we placed it in playing well, in playing fairly, in playing wisely and skilfully; in the propriety of our own conduct in short; we placed it in what, by proper discipline, education, and attention, might be altogether in our own power, and under our own direction. Our happiness was perfectly secure, and beyond the reach of fortune. The event of our actions, if it was out of our power, was equally out of our concern, and we could never feel either fear or anxiety about it; nor ever suffer any grievous, or even any serious disappointment.

Human life itself, as well as every different advantage or disadvantage which can attend it, might, they said, according to different circumstances, be the proper object either of our choice or of our rejection. If, in our actual situation, there were more circumstances agreeable to nature than contrary to it; more circumstances which were the objects of choice than of rejection; life, in this case, was, upon the whole, the proper object of choice, and the propriety of conduct required that we should remain in it. If, on the other hand, there were, in our actual situation, without any probable hope of amendment, more circumstances contrary to nature than agreeable to it; more circumstances which were the objects of rejection than of choice; life itself, in this case, became, to a wise man, the object of rejection, and he was not only at liberty to remove out of it, but the propriety of conduct, the rule which the gods had given him for the direction of his conduct, required him to do so. I am ordered, says Epictetus, not to dwell at Nicopolis. I do not dwell there. I am ordered not to dwell at Athens. I do not dwell at Athens. I am ordered not to dwell in Rome. I do not dwell in Rome. I am ordered to dwell in the little and rocky island of Gyaræ. I go and dwell there. But the house smokes in Gyaræ. If the smoke is moderate, I will bear it, and stay there. If it is excessive, I will go to a house from whence no tyrant can remove me. I keep in mind always that the door is open, that I can walk out when I please, and retire to that hospitable house which is at all times open to all the world; for beyond my undermost garment, beyond my body, no man living has any power over me. If your situation is upon the whole disagreeable; if your house smokes too much for you, said the Stoics, walk forth by all means. But walk forth without repining; without murmuring or complaining. Walk forth calm, contented, rejoicing, returning thanks to the gods, who, from their infinite bounty, have opened the safe and quiet harbour of death, at all times ready to receive us from the stormy ocean of human life; who have prepared this sacred, this inviolable, this great asylum, always open, always accessible; altogether beyond the reach of human rage and injustice; and large enough to contain both all those who wish, and all those who do not wish to retire to it: an asylum which takes away from every man every pretence of complaining, or even of fancying that there can be any evil in human life, except such as he may suffer from his own folly and weakness.

The Stoics, in the few fragments of their philosophy which have come down to us, sometimes talk of leaving life with a gaiety, and even with a levity, which, were we to consider those passages by themselves, might induce us to believe that they imagined we could with propriety leave it whenever we had a mind, wantonly and capriciously, upon the slightest disgust or uneasiness. 'When you sup with such a person, says Epictetus, 'you complain of the long stories which he tells you 'about his Mysian wars. "Now my friend," says he, "having told you '"how I took possession of an eminence at such a place, I will tell you '"how I was besieged in such another place." But if you have a mind 'not to be troubled with his long stories, do not accept of his supper. 'If you accept of his supper, you have not the least pretence to com- 'plain of his long stories. It is the same case with what you call the 'evils of human life. Never complain of that of which it is at all times 'in your power to rid yourself.' Notwithstanding this gaiety and even levity of expression, however, the alternative of leaving life, or of remaining in it, was, according to the Stoics, a matter of the most serious and important deliberation. We ought never to leave it till we were distinctly called upon to do so by that superintending Power which had originally placed us in it. But we were to consider ourselves as called upon to do so, not merely at the appointed and unavoidable term of human life. Whenever the providence of that superintending Power had rendered our condition in life upon the whole the proper object rather of rejection than of choice; the great rule which he had given us for the direction of our conduct, then required us to leave it. We might then be said to hear the awful and benevolent voice of that divine Being distinctly calling upon us to do so.

It was upon this account that, according to the Stoics, it might be the duty of a wise man to remove out of life though he was perfectly happy; while, on the contrary, it might be the duty of a weak man to remain in it, though he was necessarily miserable. If, in the situation of the wise man, there were more circumstances which were the natural objects of rejection than of choice, the whole situation became the object of rejection, and the rule which the gods had given him for the direction of his conduct, required that he should remove out of it as speedily as particular circumstances might render convenient. He was, however, perfectly happy even during the time that he might think proper to remain in it. He had placed his happiness, not in obtaining the objects of his choice, or in avoiding those of his rejection; but in always choosing and rejecting with exact propriety; not in the success, but in the fitness of his endeavours and exertions. If, in the situation of the weak man, on the contrary, there were more circumstances which were the natural objects of choice than of rejection; his whole situation became the proper object of choice, and it was his duty to remain in it. He was unhappy, however, from not knowing how to use those circumstances. Let his cards be ever so good, he did not know how to play them, and could enjoy no sort of real satisfaction, either in the progress, or in the event of the game, in whatever manner it might happen to turn out. (Cicero de finibus, lib. 3. c. 13.)

The propriety, upon some occasions, of voluntary death, though it was, perhaps, more insisted upon by the Stoics, than by any other sect of ancient philosophers, was, however, a doctrine common to them all, even to the peaceable and indolent Epicureans. During the age in which flourished the founders of all the principal sects of ancient philosophy; during the Peloponnesian war and for many years after its conclusion, all the different republics of Greece were, at home, almost always distracted by the most furious factions; and abroad, involved in the most sanguinary wars, in which each fought, not merely for superiority or dominion, but either completely to extirpate all its enemies, or, what was not less cruel, to reduce them into the vilest of all states, that of domestic slavery, and to sell them, man, woman, and child, like so many herds of cattle, to the highest bidder in the market. The smallness of the greater part of those states, too, rendered it, to each of them, no very improbable event, that it might itself fall into that very calamity which it had so frequently, 'either, perhaps, actually inflicted, or at least attempted to inflict upon some of its neighbours. In this disorderly state of things, the most perfect innocence, joined to both the highest rank and the greatest public services, could give no security to any man that, even at home and among his own relations and fellow-citizens, he was not, at some time or another, from the prevalence of some hostile and furious faction, to be condemned to the most cruel and ignominious punishment. If he was taken prisoner in war, or if the city of which he was a member was conquered, he was exposed, if possible, to still greater injuries and insults. But every man naturally, or rather necessarily, familiarizes his imagination with the distresses to which he foresees that his situation may frequently expose him. It is impossible that a sailor should not frequently think of storms and shipwrecks and foundering at sea, and of how he himself is likely both to feel and to act upon such occasions. It was impossible, in the same manner, that a Grecian patriot or hero should not familiarize his imagination with all the different calamities to which he was sensible his situation must frequently, or rather constantly, expose him. As an American savage prepares his death-song, and considers how he should act when he has fallen into the hands of his enemies, and is by them put to death in the most lingering tortures, and amidst the insults and derision of all the spectators; so a Grecian patriot or hero could not avoid frequently employing his thoughts in considering what he ought both to suffer and to do in banishment, in captivity, when reduced to slavery, when put to the torture, when brought to the scaffold. But the philosophers of all the different sects very justly represented virtue; that is, wise, just, firm and temperate conduct; not only as the most probable, but as the certain and infallible road to happiness even in this life. This conduct, however, could not always exempt, and might even sometimes expose the person who followed it to all the calamities which were incident to that unsettled situation of public affairs. They endeavoured, therefore, to show that happiness was either altogether, or at least in a great measure, independent of fortune; the Stoics, that it was so altogether; the Academic and Peripatetic philosophers, that it was so in a great measure. Wise, prudent, and good conduct was, in the first place, the conduct most likely to ensure success in every species of undertaking; and secondly, though it should fail of success, yet the mind was not left without consolation. The virtuous man might still enjoy the complete approbation of his own breast; and might still feel that, how untoward soever things might be without, all was calm and peace and

concord within. He might generally comfort himself, too, with the
assurance that he possessed the love and esteem of every intelligent
and impartial spectator, who could not fail both to admire his conduct,
and to regret his misfortune.

Those philosophers endeavoured, at the same time, to show, that
the greatest misfortunes to which human life was liable, might be supported more easily than was commonly imagined. They endeavoured
to point out the comforts which a man might still enjoy when reduced
to poverty, when driven into banishment, when exposed to the injustice
of popular clamour, when labouring under blindness, under deafness,
in the extremity of old age, upon the approach of death. They pointed
out, too, the considerations which might contribute to support his constancy under the agonies of pain and even of torture, in sickness, in
sorrow for the loss of children, for the death of friends and relations,
etc. The few fragments which have come down to us of what the
ancient philosophers had written upon these subjects, form, perhaps,
one of the most instructive, as well as one of the most interesting
remains of antiquity. The spirit and manhood of their doctrines make
a wonderful contrast with the desponding, plaintive, and whining tone
of some modern systems.

But while those ancient philosophers endeavoured in this manner to
suggest every consideration which could, as Milton says, arm the
obdured breast with stubborn patience, as with triple steel; they, at
the same time, laboured above all to convince their followers that there
neither was nor could be any evil in death; and that, if their situation
became at any time too hard for their constancy to support, the remedy
was at hand, the door was open, and they might, without fear, walk out
when they pleased. If there was no world beyond the present, death,
they said, could be no evil; and if there was another world, the gods
must likewise be in that other, and a just man could fear no evil while
under their protection. Those philosophers, in short, prepared a death-
song, if I may say so, which the Grecian patriots and heroes might
make use of upon the proper occasions; and, of all the different sects,
the Stoics, I think it must be acknowledged, had prepared by far the
most animated and most spirited song.

Suicide, however, never seems to have been very common among the
Greeks. Excepting Cleomenes, I cannot at present recollect any very
illustrious either patriot or hero of Greece, who died by his own hand.
The death of Aristomenes is as much beyond the period of true history
as that of Ajax. The common story of the death of Themistocles,
though within that period, bears upon its face all the marks of a most
romantic fable. Of all the Greek heroes whose lives have been written
by Plutarch, Cleomenes appears to have been the only one who perished
in this manner. Theramines, Socrates, and Phocion, who certainly did
not want courage, suffered themselves to be sent to prison, and sub-

mitted patiently to that death to which the injustice of their fellow-citizens had condemned them.   The brave Eumenes allowed himself to be delivered up, by his own mutinous soldiers, to his enemy Antigonus, and was starved to death, without attempting any violence.   The gallant Philopœmen suffered himself to be taken prisoner by the Messenians, was thrown into a dungeon, and was supposed to have been privately poisoned.   Several of the philosophers, indeed, are said to have died in this manner; but their lives have been so very foolishly written, that very little credit is due to the greater part of the tales which are told of them.   Three different accounts have been given of the death of Zeno the Stoic.   One is, that after enjoying, for ninety-eight years, the most perfect state of health, he happened, in going out of his school, to fall; and though he suffered no other damage than that of breaking or dislocating one of his fingers, he struck the ground with his hand, and, in the words of the Niobe of Euripides, said, *I come, why doest thou call me?* and immediately went home and hanged himself.   At that great age, one should think, he might have had a little more patience.   Another account is, that, at the same age, and in consequence of a like accident, he starved himself to death.   The third account is, that, at seventy-two years of age, he died in the natural way; by far the most probable account of the three, and supported too by the authority of a cotemporary, who must have had every opportunity of being well-informed; of Persæus, originally the slave, and afterwards the friend and disciple of Zeno.   The first account is given by Apollonius of Tyre, who flourished about the time of Augustus Cæsar, between two and three hundred years after the death of Zeno.   I know not who is the author of the second account.   Apollonius, who was himself a Stoic, had probably thought it would do honour to the founder of a sect which talked so much about voluntary death, to die in this manner by his own hand.   Men of letters, though, after their death, they are frequently more talked of than the greatest princes or statesmen of their times, are generally, during their life, so obscure and insignificant that their adventures are seldom recorded by cotemporary historians.   Those of after-ages, in order to satisfy the public curiosity, and having no authentic documents either to support or to contradict their narratives, seem frequently to have fashioned them according to their own fancy; and almost always with a great mixture of the marvellous.   In this particular case the marvellous, though supported by no authority, seems to have prevailed over the probable, though supported by the best.   Diogenes Laertius plainly gives the preference to the story of Apollonius.   Lucian and Lactantius appear both to have given credit to that of the great age and of the violent death.

This fashion of voluntary death appears to have been much more prevalent among the proud Romans, than it ever was among the lively, ingenious, and accommodating Greeks.   Even among the Romans, the fashion seems not to have been established in the early and, what are called, the virtuous ages of the republic. The common story of the death of Regulus, though probably a fable, could never have been invented, had it been supposed that any dishonour could fall upon that hero, from patiently submitting to the tortures which the Carthaginians are said to have inflicted upon him.   In the later ages of the republic, some dishonour, I apprehend, would have attended this submission. In the different civil wars which preceded the fall of the commonwealth, many of the eminent men of all the contending parties chose rather to perish by their own hands, than to fall into those of their enemies. The death of Cato, celebrated by Cicero, and censured by Cæsar, and become the subject of a very serious controversy between, perhaps, the two most illustrious advocates that the world had ever beheld, stamped a character of splendour upon this method of dying which it seems to have retained for several ages after.   The eloquence of Cicero was superior to that of Cæsar.   The admiring prevailed greatly over the censuring party, and the lovers of liberty, for many ages afterwards, looked up to Cato as to the most venerable martyr of the republican party.   The head of a party, the Cardinal de Retz observes, may do what he pleases; as long as he retains the confidence of his own friends, he can never do wrong; a maxim of which his eminence had himself, upon several occasions, an opportunity of experiencing the truth.   Cato, it seems, joined to his other virtues that of an excellent bottle companion.   His enemies accused him of drunkenness, but, says Seneca, whoever objected this vice to Cato, will find it easier to prove that drunkenness is a virtue, than that Cato could be addicted to any vice.

Under the Emperors this method of dying seems to have been, for a long time, perfectly fashionable.   In the epistles of Pliny we find an account of several persons who chose to die in this manner, rather from vanity and ostentation, it would seem, than from what would appear, even to a sober and judicious Stoic, any proper or necessary reason. Even the ladies, who are seldom behind in following the fashion, seem frequently to have chosen, most unnecessarily, to die in this manner; and, like the ladies in Bengal, to accompany, upon some occasions, their husbands to the tomb.   The prevalence of this fashion certainly occasioned many deaths which would not otherwise have happened. All the havoc, however, which this, perhaps the highest exertion of human vanity and impertinence, could occasion, would, probably, at no time, be very great.

The principle of suicide, the principle which would teach us, upon some occasions, to consider that violent action as an object of applause and approbation, seems to be altogether a refinement of philosophy. Nature, in her sound and healthful state, seems never to prompt us to suicide.   There is, indeed, a species of melancholy (a disease to which human nature, among its other calamities, is unhappily subject) which seems to be accompanied with, what one may call, an irresistible appetite for self-destruction. In circumstances often of the highest external prosperity, and sometimes too, in spite even of the most serious and deeply impressed sentiments of religion, this disease has frequently been known to drive its wretched victims to this fatal extremity. The unfortunate persons who perish in this miserable manner, are the proper objects, not of censure, but of commiseration. To attempt to punish them, when they are beyond the reach of all human punishment, is not more absurd than it is unjust. That punishment can fall only on their surviving friends and relations, who are always perfectly innocent, and to whom the loss of their friend, in this disgraceful manner, must always be alone a very heavy calamity. Nature, in her sound and healthful state, prompts us to avoid distress upon all occasions; upon many occasions to defend ourselves against it, though at the hazard, or even with the certainty of perishing in that defence. But, when we have neither been able to defend ourselves from it, nor have perished in that defence, no natural principle, no regard to the approbation of the supposed impartial spectator, to the judgment of the man within the breast, seems to call upon us to escape from it by destroying ourselves. It is only the consciousness of our own weakness, of our own incapacity to support the calamity with proper manhood and firmness, which can drive us to this resolution. I do not remember to have either read or heard of any American savage, who, upon being taken prisoner by some hostile tribe, put himself to death, in order to avoid being afterwards put to death in torture, and amidst the insults and mockery of his enemies. He places his glory in supporting those torments with manhood, and in retorting those insults with tenfold contempt and derision.

This contempt of life and death, however, and, at the same time, the most entire submission to the order of Providence; the most complete contentment with every event which the current of human affairs could possibly cast up, may be considered as the two fundamental doctrines upon which rested the whole fabric of Stoical morality. The independent and spirited, but often harsh Epictetus, may be considered as the great apostle of the first of those doctrines : the mild, the humane, the benevolent Antoninus, of the second.

The emancipated slave of Epaphroditus, who, in his youth, had been subjected to the insolence of a brutal master, who, in his riper years, was, by the jealousy and caprice of Domitian, banished from Rome and Athens, and obliged to dwell at Nicopolis, and who, by the same tyrant, might expect every moment to be sent to Gyaræ, or, perhaps, to be put to death; could preserve his own tranquillity only by fostering in his mind the most sovereign contempt of human life. He never exults so much, accordingly; his eloquence is never so animated as when he represents the futility and nothingness of all its pleasures and all its pains.

The good-natured emperor, the absolute sovereign of the whole civilized part of the world, who certainly had no peculiar reason to complain of his own allotment, delights in expressing his contentment with the ordinary course of things, and in pointing out beauties even in those parts of it where vulgar observers are not apt to see any. There is a propriety and even an engaging grace, he observes, in old age as well as in youth ; and the weakness and decrepitude of the one state are as suitable to nature as the bloom and vigour of the other. Death, too, is just as proper a termination of old age, as youth is of childhood, or manhood of youth. 'As we frequently say,' he remarks upon another occasion, 'that the physician has ordered to such a man to ride on 'horseback, or to use the cold bath, or to walk barefooted ; so ought 'we to say, that Nature, the great conductor and physician of the uni'verse, has ordered to such a man a disease, or the amputation of a 'limb, or the loss of a child.' By the prescriptions of ordinary physicians the patient swallows many a bitter potion, undergoes many a painful operation. From the very uncertain hope, however, that health may be the consequence, he gladly submits to all. The harshest prescriptions of the great Physician of nature, the patient may, in the same manner, hope will contribute to his own health, to his own final prosperity and happiness : and he may be perfectly assured that they not only contribute, but are indispensably necessary to the health, to the prosperity and happiness of the universe, to the furtherance and advancement of the great plan of Jupiter. Had they not been so, the universe would never have produced them ; its all-wise Architect and Conductor would never have suffered them to happen. As all, even the smallest of the co-existent parts of the universe, are exactly fitted to one another, and all contribute to compose one immense and connected system, so all, even apparently the most insignificant of the successive events which follow one another, make parts, and necessary parts, of that great chain of causes and effects which had no beginning, and which will have no end ; and which, as they all necessarily result from the original arrangement and contrivance of the whole ; so they are all essentially necessary, not only to its prosperity, but to its continuance and preservation. Whoever does not cordially embrace whatever befalls him, whoever is sorry that it has befallen him, whoever wishes that it had not befallen him, wishes, so far as in him lies, to stop the motion of the universe, to break that great chain of succession, by the progress of which that system can alone be continued and preserved, and, for some little conveniency of his own, to disorder and discompose the whole machine of the world. 'O world,' says he, in another place, 'all things are suitable to me which are suitable to thee. 'Nothing is too early or too late to me which is seasonable for thee. 'All is fruit to me which thy seasons bring forth. From thee are all 'things ; in thee are all things ; for thee are all things. One man

'says, O beloved city of Cecrops. Wilt not thou say, O beloved
' city of God?'

From these very sublime doctrines the Stoics, or at least some of the
Stoics, attempted to deduce all their paradoxes.

The Stoical wise man endeavoured to enter into the views of the
great Superintendent of the universe, and to see things in the same
light in which that divine Being beheld them. But, to the great
Superintendent of the universe, all the different events which the
course of his providence may bring forth, what to us appear the
smallest and the greatest, the bursting of a bubble, as Mr. Pope says,
and that of a world, for example, were perfectly equal, were equally
parts of that great chain which he had predestined from all eternity,
were equally the effects of the same unerring wisdom, of the same
universal and boundless benevolence. To the Stoical wise man, in the
same manner, all those different events were perfectly equal. In the
course of those events, indeed, a little department, in which he had
himself some little management and direction, had been assigned to
him. In this department he endeavoured to act as properly as he
could, and to conduct himself according to those orders which, he
understood, had been prescribed to him. But he took no anxious or
passionate concern either in the success, or in the disappointment of
his own most faithful endeavours. The highest prosperity and the
total destruction of that little department, of that little system which
had been in some measure committed to his charge, were perfectly
indifferent to him. If those events had depended upon him, he would
have chosen the one, and he would have rejected the other. But as
they did not depend upon him, he trusted to a superior wisdom, and
was perfectly satisfied that the event which happened, whatever it
might be, was the very event which he himself, had he known all the
connections and dependencies of things, would most earnestly and
devoutly have wished for. Whatever he did under the influence and
direction of those principles was equally perfect ; and when he stretched
out his finger, to give the example which they commonly made use of,
he performed an action in every respect as meritorious, as worthy of
praise and admiration, as when he laid down his life for the service of
his country. As, to the great Superintendent of the universe, the
greatest and the smallest exertions of his power, the formation and
dissolution of a world, the formation and dissolution of a bubble, were
equally easy, were equally admirable, and equally the effects of the
same divine wisdom and benevolence ; so, to the Stoical wise man,
what we would call the great action required no more exertion than the
little one, was equally easy, proceeded from exactly the same principles,
was in no respect more meritorious, nor worthy of any higher degree of
praise and admiration.

As all those who had arrived at this state of perfection were equally happy, so all those who fell in the smallest degree short of it, how nearly soever they might approach to it, were equally miserable. As the man, they said, who was but an inch below the surface of the water, could no more breathe than he who was an hundred yards below it ; so the man who had not completely subdued all his private, partial, and selfish passions, who had any other earnest desire but that for the universal happiness, who had not completely emerged from that abyss of misery and disorder into which his anxiety for the gratification of those private, partial, and selfish passions had involved him, could no more breathe the free air of liberty and independency, could no more enjoy the security and happiness of the wise man, than he who was most remote from that situation. As all the actions of the wise man were perfect and equally perfect ; so all those of the man who had not arrived at this supreme wisdom were faulty, and, as some Stoics pretended, equally faulty. As one truth, they said, could not be more true, nor one falsehood more false than another ; so an honourable action could not be more honourable, nor a shameful one more shameful than another. As in shooting at a mark, the man who missed it by an inch had equally missed it with him who had done so by a hundred yards ; so the man who, in what to us appears the most insignificant action, had acted improperly and without a sufficient reason, was equally faulty with him who had done so in, what to us appears, the most important ; the man who has killed a cock, for example, improperly and without a sufficient reason, was as criminal as he who had murdered his father.

If the first of those two paradoxes should appear sufficiently violent, the second is evidently too absurd to deserve any serious consideration. It is, indeed, so very absurd that one can scarce help suspecting that it must have been in some measure misunderstood or misrepresented. At any rate, I cannot allow myself to believe that such men as Zeno or Cleanthes, men, it is said, of the most simple as well as of the most sublime eloquence, could be the authors, either of these, or of the greater part of the other Stoical paradoxes, which are in general mere impertinent quibbles, and do so little honour to their system that I shall give no further account of them. I am disposed to impute them rather to Chrysippus, the disciple and follower, indeed, of Zeno and Cleanthes, but who, from all that has been delivered down to us concerning him, seems to have been a mere dialectical pedant, without taste or elegance of any kind. He may have been the first who reduced their doctrines into a scholastic or technical system of artificial definitions, divisions, and subdivisions ; one of the most effectual expedients, perhaps, for extinguishing whatever degree of good sense there may be in any moral or metaphysical doctrine. Such a man may very easily be supposed to have understood too literally some animated expressions of his masters in describing the happiness of the man of perfect virtue, and the unhappiness of whoever might fall short of that character.

The Stoics in general seem to have admitted that there might be a degree of proficiency in those who had not advanced to perfect virtue and happiness. They distributed those proficients into different classes, according to the degree of their advancement ; and they called the imperfect virtues which they supposed them capable of exercising, not rectitudes, but proprieties, fitnesses, decent and becoming actions, for which a plausible or probable reason could be assigned, what Cicero expresses by the Latin word *officia*, and Seneca, I think more exactly, by that of *convenientia*. The doctrine of those imperfect, but attainable virtues, seems to have constituted what we may call the practical morality of the Stoics. It is the subject of Cicero's Offices ; and is said to have been that of another book written by Marcus Brutus, but which is now lost.

The plan and system which Nature has sketched out for our conduct, seems to us to be altogether different from that of the Stoical philosophy.

By Nature the events which immediately affect that little department in which we ourselves have some little management and direction, which immediately affect ourselves, our friends, our country, are the events which interest us the most, and which chiefly excite our desires and aversions, our hopes and fears, our joys and sorrows. Should those passions be, what they are very apt to be, too vehement, Nature has provided a proper remedy and correction. The real or even the imaginary presence of the impartial spectator, the authority of the man within the breast, is always at hand to overawe them into the proper tone and temper of moderation.

If, notwithstanding our most faithful exertions, all the events which can affect this little department, should turn out the most unfortunate and disastrous, Nature has by no means left us without consolation. That consolation may be drawn, not only from the complete approbation of the man within the breast, but, if possible, from a still nobler and more generous principle, from a firm reliance upon, and a reverential submission to, that benevolent wisdom which directs all the events of human life, and which, we may be assured, would never have suffered those misfortunes to happen, had they not been indispensably necessary for the good of the whole.

Nature has not prescribed to us this sublime contemplation as the great business and occupation of our lives. She only points it out to us as the consolation of our misfortunes. The Stoical philosophy prescribes it as the great business and occupation of our lives. That philosophy teaches us to interest ourselves earnestly and anxiously in no events, external to the good order of our own minds, to the propriety of our own choosing and rejecting, except in those which concern a department where we neither have nor ought to have any sort of management or direction, the department of the great Superintendent of the universe.   By the perfect apathy which it prescribes to us, by endeavouring, not merely to moderate, but to eradicate all our private, partial, and selfish affections, by suffering us to feel for whatever can befall ourselves, our friends, our country, not even the sympathetic and reduced passions of the impartial spectator, it endeavours to render us altogether indifferent and unconcerned in the success or miscarriage of every thing which Nature has prescribed to us as the proper business and occupation of our lives.

The reasonings of philosophy, it may be said, though they may confound and perplex the understanding, can never break down the necessary connection which Nature has established between causes and their effects.   The causes which naturally excite our desires and aversions, our hopes and fears, our joys and sorrows, would no doubt, notwithstanding all the reasonings of Stoicism, produce upon each individual, according to the degree of his actual sensibility, their proper and necessary effects.   The judgments of the man within the breast, however, might be a good deal affected by those reasonings, and that great inmate might be taught by them to attempt to overawe all our private, partial, and selfish affections into a more or less perfect tranquillity.   To direct the judgments of this inmate is the great purpose of all systems of morality.   That the Stoical philosophy had very great influence upon the character and conduct of its followers, cannot be doubted ; and that, though it might sometimes incite them to unnecessary violence, its general tendency was to animate them to actions of the most heroic magnanimity and most extensive benevolence.

IV. Besides these ancient, there are some modern systems, according to which virtue consists in propriety ; or in the suitableness of the affection from which we act, to the cause or object which excites it.   The system of Dr. Clark, which places virtue in acting according to the relation of things, in regulating our conduct according to the fitness or incongruity which there may be in the application of certain actions to certain things, or to certain relations : that of Mr. Wollaston, which places it in acting according to the truth of things, according to their proper nature and essence, or in treating them as what they really are, and not as what they are not : that of my Lord Shaftesbury, which places it in maintaining a proper balance of the affections, and in allowing no passion to go beyond its proper sphere ; are all of them more or less inaccurate descriptions of the same fundamental idea.

None of those systems either give, or even pretend to give, any precise or distinct measure by which this fitness or propriety of affection can be ascertained or judged of.   That precise and distinct measure can be found no where but in the sympathetic feelings of the impartial and well-informed spectator.

The description of virtue, besides, which is either given, or at least meant and intended to be given in each of those systems, for some of the modern authors are not very fortunate in their manner of expressing themselves, is no doubt quite just, so far as it goes. There is no virtue without propriety, and wherever there is propriety some degree of approbation is due. But still this description is imperfect. For though propriety is an essential ingredient in every virtuous action, it is not always the sole ingredient. Beneficent actions have in them another quality by which they appear not only to deserve approbation but recompense. None of those systems account either easily or sufficiently for that superior degree of esteem which seems due to such actions, or for that diversity of sentiment which they naturally excite. Neither is the description of vice more complete. For, in the same manner, though impropriety is a necessary ingredient in every vicious action, it is not always the sole ingredient; and there is often the highest degree of absurdity and impropriety in very harmless and insignificant actions. Deliberate actions, of a pernicious tendency to those we live with, have, besides their impropriety, a peculiar quality of their own by which they appear to deserve, not only disapprobation, but punishment; and to be the objects, not of dislike merely, but of resentment and revenge: and none of those systems easily and sufficiently account for that superior degree of detestation which we feel for such actions.

CHAP. II.—*Of those Systems which make Virtue consist in Prudence.*

THE most ancient of those systems which make virtue consist in prudence, and of which any considerable remains have come down to us, is that of Epicurus, who is said, however, to have borrowed all the leading principles of his philosophy from some of those who had gone before him, particularly from Aristippus; though it is very probable, notwithstanding this allegation of his enemies, that at least his manner of applying those principles was altogether his own.

According to Epicurus (Cicero de finibus, lib. i. Diogenes Laert. l. x.) bodily pleasure and pain were the sole ultimate objects of natural desire and aversion. That they were always the natural objects of those passions, he thought required no proof. Pleasure might, indeed, appear sometimes to be avoided; not, however, because it was pleasure, but because, by the enjoyment of it, we should either forfeit some greater pleasure, or expose ourselves to some pain that was more to be avoided than this pleasure was to be desired. Pain, in the same manner, might appear sometimes to be eligible; not, however, because it was pain, but because by enduring it we might either avoid a still greater pain, or acquire some pleasure of much more importance. That bodily pain and pleasure, therefore, were always the natural objects of desire and aversion, was, he thought, abundantly evident. Nor was it less so, he imagined, that they were the sole ultimate objects of those passions. Whatever else was either desired or avoided, was so, according to him, upon account of its tendency to produce one or other of those sensations. The tendency to procure pleasure rendered power and riches desirable, as the contrary tendency to produce pain made poverty and insignificancy the objects of aversion. Honour and reputation were valued, because the esteem and love of those we live with were of the greatest consequence both to procure pleasure and to defend us from pain. Ignominy and bad fame, on the contrary, were to be avoided, because the hatred, contempt, and resentment of those we lived with, destroyed all security, and necessarily exposed us to the greatest bodily evils.

All the pleasures and pains of the mind were, according to Epicurus, ultimately derived from those of the body. The mind was happy when it thought of the past pleasures of the body, and hoped for others to come : and it was miserable when it thought of the pains which the body had formerly endured, and dreaded the same or greater thereafter.

But the pleasures and pains of the mind, though ultimately derived from those of the body, were vastly greater than their originals. The body felt only the sensation of the present instant, whereas the mind felt also the past and the future, the one by remembrance, the other by anticipation, and consequently both suffered and enjoyed much more. When we are under the greatest bodily pain, he observed, we shall always find, if we attend to it, that it is not the suffering of the present instant which chiefly torments us, but either the agonizing remembrance of the past, or the yet more horrible dread of the future. The pain of each instant, considered by itself, and cut off from all that goes before and all that comes after it, is a trifle, not worth the regarding. Yet this is all which the body can ever be said to suffer. In the same manner, when we enjoy the greatest pleasure, we shall always find that the bodily sensation, the sensation of the present instant, makes but a small part of our happiness, that our enjoyment chiefly arises either from the cheerful recollection of the past, or the still more joyous anticipation of the future, and that the mind always contributes by much the largest share of the entertainment.

Since our happiness and misery, therefore, depended chiefly on the mind, if this part of our nature was well disposed, if our thoughts and opinions were as they should be, it was of little importance in what manner our body was affected. Though under great bodily pain, we might still enjoy a considerable share of happiness, if our reason and judgment maintained their superiority. We might entertain ourselves with the remembrance of past, and with the hopes of future pleasure ; we might soften the rigour of our pains, by recollecting what it was which, even in this situation, we were under any necessity of suffering. That this was merely the bodily sensation, the pain of the present instant, which by itself could never be very great. That whatever agony we suffered from the dread of its continuance, was the effect of an opinion of the mind, which might be corrected by juster sentiments ; by considering that, if our pains were violent, they would probably be of short duration ; and that if they were of long continuance, they would probably be moderate, and admit of many intervals of ease ; and that, at any rate, death was always at hand and within call to deliver us, which as, according to him, it put an end to all sensation, either of pain or pleasure, could not be regarded as an evil. When we are, said he, death is not ; and when death is, we are not ; death therefore can be nothing to us.

If the actual sensation of positive pain was in itself so little to be feared, that of pleasure was still less to be desired. Naturally the sensation of pleasure was much less pungent than that of pain. If, therefore, this last could take so very little from the happiness of a well-disposed mind, the other could add scarce any thing to it. When the body was free from pain and the mind from fear and anxiety, the super-added sensation of bodily pleasure could be of very little importance ; and though it might diversify, could not properly be said to increase the happiness of this situation.

In ease of body, therefore, and in security of tranquillity of mind, consisted, according to Epicurus, the most perfect state of human nature, the most complete happiness which man was capable of enjoying. To obtain this great end of natural desire was the sole object of all the virtues, which, according to him, were not desirable upon their own account, but chiefly upon account of their tendency to bring about this situation.

Prudence, for example, though, according to this philosophy, the source and principle of all the virtues, was not desirable upon its own account. That careful and laborious and circumspect state of mind, ever watchful and ever attentive to the most distant consequences of every action, could not be a thing pleasant or agreeable for its own sake, but upon account of its tendency to procure the greatest goods and to keep off the greatest evils.

To abstain from pleasure too, to curb and restrain our natural passions for enjoyment, which was the office of temperance, could never be desirable for its own sake. The whole value of this virtue arose from its utility, from its enabling us to postpone the present enjoyment for the sake of a greater to come, or to avoid a greater pain that might ensue from it. Temperance, in short, was, according to the Epicureans, nothing but prudence with regard to pleasure.

To support labour, to endure pain, to be exposed to danger or to death, the situations which fortitude would often lead us into, were surely still less the objects of natural desire. They were chosen only to avoid greater evils. We submitted to labour, in order to avoid the greater shame and pain of poverty, and we exposed ourselves to danger and to death in defence of our liberty and property, the means and instruments of pleasure and happiness; or in defence of our country, in the safety of which our own was necessarily comprehended. Fortitude enabled us to do all this cheerfully, as the best which, in our present situation, could possibly be done, and was in reality no more than prudence, good judgment, and presence of mind in properly appreciating pain, labour, and danger, always choosing the less in order to avoid the greater evil.

It is the same case with justice. To abstain from what is another's was not desirable on its own account, and it could not surely be better for you, that I should possess what is my own, than that you should possess it. You ought, however, to abstain from whatever belongs to me, because by doing otherwise you will provoke the resentment and indignation of mankind. The security and tranquillity of your mind will be entirely destroyed. You will be filled with fear and consternation at the thought of that punishment which you will imagine that men are at all times ready to inflict upon you, and from which no power, no art, no concealment, will ever, in your own fancy, be sufficient to protect you. The other species of justice which consists in doing proper good offices to different persons, according to the various relations of neighbours, kinsmen, friends, benefactors, superiors, or equals, which they may stand in to us, is recommended by the same reasons. To act properly in all these different relations procures us the esteem and love of those we live with; as to do otherwise excites their contempt and hatred. By the one we naturally secure, by the other we necessarily endanger our own ease and tranquillity, the great and ultimate objects of all our desires. The whole virtue of justice, therefore, the most important of all the virtues, is no more than discreet and prudent conduct with regard to our neighbours.

Such is the doctrine of Epicurus concerning the nature of virtue. It may seem extraordinary that this philosopher, who is described as a person of the most amiable manners, should never have observed, that, whatever may be the tendency of those virtues, or of the contrary vices, with regard to our bodily ease and security, the sentiments which they naturally excite in others are the objects of a much more passionate desire or aversion than all their other consequences; that to be amiable, to be respectable, to be the proper object of esteem, is by every well-disposed mind more valued than all the ease and security which love, respect, and esteem can procure us; that, on the contrary, to be odious, to be contemptible, to be the proper object of indignation, is more dreadful than all that we can suffer in our body from hatred, contempt, or indignation; and that consequently our desire of the one character, and our aversion to the other, cannot arise from any regard to the effects which either of them may produce upon the body.

This system is, no doubt, altogether inconsistent with that which I have been endeavouring to establish. It is not difficult, however, to discover from what phasis, if I may say so, from what particular view or aspect of nature, this account of things derives its probability. By the wise contrivance of the Author of nature, virtue is upon all ordinary occasions, even with regard to this life, real wisdom, and the surest and readiest means of obtaining both safety and advantage. Our success or disappointment in our undertakings must very much depend upon the good or bad opinion which is commonly entertained of us, and upon the general disposition of those we live with, either to assist or to oppose us. But the best, the surest, the easiest, and the readiest way of obtaining the advantageous, and of avoiding the unfavourable judgments of others, is undoubtedly to render ourselves the proper objects of the former and not of the latter. ' Do you desire,' said Socrates, 'the reputation of a good musician? The only sure way of obtaining 'it, is to become a good musician. Would you desire in the same 'manner to be thought capable of serving your country either as a 'general or as a statesman? The best way in this case too is really to 'acquire the art and experience of war and government, and to become 'really fit to be a general or a statesman. And in the same manner if 'you would be reckoned sober, temperate, just, and equitable, the best 'way of acquiring this reputation is to become sober, temperate, just, 'and equitable. If you can really render yourself amiable, respectable, 'and the proper object of esteem, there is no fear of your not soon 'acquiring the love, the respect, and esteem of those you live with.' Since the practice of virtue, therefore, is in general so advantageous, and that of vice so contrary to our interest, the consideration of those opposite tendencies undoubtedly stamps an additional beauty and propriety upon the one, and a new deformity and impropriety upon the other. Temperance, magnanimity, justice, and beneficence, come thus to be approved of, not only under their proper characters, but under the additional character of the highest wisdom and most real prudence. And in the same manner, the contrary vices of intemperance, pusillanimity, injustice, and either malevolence or sordid selfishness, come to be disapproved of, not only under their proper characters, but under the additional character of the most short-sighted folly and weakness. Epicurus appears in every virtue to have attended to this species of propriety only. It is that which is most apt to occur to those who are endeavouring to persuade others to regularity of conduct. When men by their practice, and perhaps too by their maxims, manifestly show that the natural beauty of virtue is not like to have much effect upon them, how is it possible to move them but by representing the folly of their conduct, and how much they themselves are in the end likely to suffer by it?

By running up all the different virtues too to this one species of propriety, Epicurus indulged a propensity, which is natural to all men, but which philosophers in particular are apt to cultivate with a peculiar fondness, as the great means of displaying their ingenuity, the propensity to account for all appearances from as few principles as possible. And he, no doubt, indulged this propensity still further, when he referred all the primary objects of natural desire and aversion to the pleasures and pains of the body. The great patron of the atomical philosophy, who took so much pleasure in deducing all the powers and qualities of bodies from the most obvious and familiar, the figure, motion, and arrangement of the small parts of matter, felt no doubt a similar satisfaction, when he accounted, in the same manner, for all the sentiments and passions of the mind from those which are most obvious and familiar.

The system of Epicurus agreed with those of Plato, Aristotle, and Zeno, in making virtue consist in acting in the most suitable manner to obtain (Prima naturæ) primary objects of natural desire. It differed from all of them in two other respects; first, in the account which it gave of those primary objects of natural desire; and secondly, in the account which it gave of the excellence of virtue, or of the reason why that quality ought to be esteemed.

The primary objects of natural desire consisted, according to Epicurus, in bodily pleasure and pain, and in nothing else: whereas, according to the other three philosophers, there were many other objects, such as knowledge, such as the happiness of our relations, of our friends, and of our country, which were ultimately desirable for their own sakes.

Virtue too, according to Epicurus, did not deserve to be pursued for its own sake, nor was itself one of the ultimate objects of natural appetite, but was eligible only upon account of its tendency to prevent pain and to procure ease and pleasure. In the opinion of the other three, on the contrary, it was desirable, not merely as the means of procuring the other primary objects of natural desire, but as something which was in itself more valuable than them all. Man, they thought, being born for action, his happiness must consist, not merely in the agreeableness of his passive sensations, but also in the propriety of his active exertions.

CHAP. III.—*Of those Systems which make Virtue consist in Benevolence.*

THE system which makes virtue consist in benevolence, though I think not so ancient as all those which I have already given an account of, is, however, of very great antiquity. It seems to have been the doctrine of the greater part of those philosophers who, about and after the age of Augustus, called themselves Eclectics, who pretended to follow chiefly the opinions of Plato and Pythagoras, and who upon that account are commonly known by the name of the later Platonists.

In the divine nature, according to these authors, benevolence or love was the sole principle of action, and directed the exertion of all the other attributes. The wisdom of the Deity was employed in finding out the means for bringing about those ends which his goodness suggested, and his infinite power was exerted to execute them. Benevolence, however, was still the supreme and governing attribute, to which the others were subservient, and from which the whole excellency, or the whole morality, if I may be allowed such an expression, of the divine operations, was ultimately derived. The whole perfection and virtue of the human mind consisted in some resemblance or participation of the divine perfections, and, consequently, in being filled with the same principle of benevolence and love which influenced all the actions of the Deity. The actions of men which flowed from this motive were alone truly praise-worthy, or could claim any merit in the sight of the Deity. It was by actions of charity and love only that we could imitate, as became us, the conduct of God, that we could express our humble and devout admiration of his infinite perfections, that by fostering in our own minds the same divine principle, we could bring our own affections to a greater resemblance with his holy attributes, and thereby become more proper objects of his love and esteem ; till we arrived at that immediate converse and communication with the Deity to which it was the great object of this philosophy to raise us.

This system, as it was much esteemed by many ancient fathers of the Christian church, so after the Reformation it was adopted by several divines of the most eminent piety and learning and of the most amiable manners; particularly, by Dr. Ralph Cudworth, by Dr. Henry More, and by Mr. John Smith of Cambridge. But of all the patrons of this system, ancient or modern, the late Dr. Hutcheson was undoubtedly, beyond all comparison, the most acute, the most distinct, the most philosophical, and what is of the greatest consequence of all, the soberest and most judicious.

That virtue consists in benevolence is a notion supported by many appearances in human nature. It has been observed already, that proper benevolence is the most graceful and agreeable of all the affections, that it is recommended to us by a double sympathy, that as its tendency is necessarily beneficent, it is the proper object of gratitude and reward, and that upon all these accounts it appears to our natural sentiments to possess a merit superior to any other. It has been observed, too, that even the weaknesses of benevolence are not very disagreeable to us, whereas those of every other passion are always extremely disgusting. Who does not abhor excessive malice, excessive selfishness, or excessive resentment? But the most excessive indulgence even of partial friendship is not so offensive. It is the benevolent passions only which can exert themselves without any regard or attention to propriety, and yet retain something about them which is engaging. There is something pleasing even in mere instinctive goodwill, which goes on to do good offices without once reflecting whether by this conduct it is the proper object either of blame or approbation. It is not so with the other passions. The moment they are deserted, the moment they are unaccompanied by the sense of propriety, they cease to be agreeable.

As benevolence bestows upon those actions which proceed from it, a beauty superior to all others, so the want of it, and much more the contrary inclination, communicates a peculiar deformity to whatever evidences such a disposition. Pernicious actions are often punishable for no other reason than because they show a want of sufficient attention to the happiness of our neighbour.

Besides all this, Dr. Hutcheson (Inquiry concerning Virtue, sect. 1. and 2.) observed, that whenever in any action, supposed to proceed from benevolent affections, some other motive had been discovered, our sense of the merit of this action was just so far diminished as this motive was believed to have influenced it. If an action, supposed to proceed from gratitude, should be discovered to have arisen from an expectation of some new favour, or if what was apprehended to proceed from public spirit, should be found out to have taken its origin from the hope of a pecuniary reward, such a discovery would entirely destroy, all notion of merit or praise-worthiness in either of these actions. Since, therefore, the mixture of any selfish motive, like that of a baser alloy, diminished or took away altogether the merit which would otherwise have belonged to any action, it was evident, he imagined, that virtue must consist in pure and disinterested benevolence alone.

When those actions, on the contrary, which are commonly supposed to proceed from a selfish motive, are discovered to have arisen from a benevolent one, it greatly enhances our sense of their merit. If we believed of any person that he endeavoured to advance his fortune from no other view but that of doing friendly offices, and of making proper returns to his benefactors, we should only love and esteem him the more. And this observation seemed still more to confirm the conclusion, that it was benevolence only which could stamp upon any action the character of virtue.

Last of all, what, he imagined, was an evident proof of the justness of this account of virtue, in all the disputes of casuists concerning the rectitude of conduct, the public good, he observed, was the standard to which they constantly referred; thereby universally acknowledging

18 *

that whatever tended to promote the happiness of mankind was right and laudable and virtuous, and the contrary, wrong, blamable, and vicious. In the late debates about passive obedience and the right of resistance, the sole point in controversy among men of sense was whether universal submission would probably be attended with greater evils than temporary insurrections when privileges were invaded. Whether what, upon the whole, tended most to the happiness of mankind, was not also morally good, was never once, he said, made a question by them.

Since benevolence, therefore, was the only motive which could bestow upon any action the character of virtue, the greater the benevolence which was evidenced by any action, the greater the praise which must belong to it.

Those actions which aimed at the happiness of a great community, as they demonstrated a more enlarged benevolence than those which aimed only at that of a smaller system, so were they, likewise, proportionally the more virtuous. The most virtuous of all affections, therefore, was that which embraced as its object the happiness of all intelligent beings. The least virtuous, on the contrary, of those to which the character of virtue could in any respect belong, was that which aimed no further than at the happiness of an individual, such as a son, a brother, a friend.

In directing all our actions to promote the greatest possible good, in submitting all inferior affections to the desire of the general happiness of mankind, in regarding one's self but as one of the many, whose prosperity was to be pursued no further than it was consistent with, or conducive to that of the whole, consisted the perfection of virtue.

Self-love was a principle which could never be virtuous in any degree or in any direction. It was vicious whenever it obstructed the general good. When it had no other effect than to make the individual take care of his own happiness, it was merely innocent, and though it deserved no praise, neither ought it to incur any blame. Those benevolent actions which were performed, notwithstanding some strong motive from self-interest, were the more virtuous upon that account. They demonstrated the strength and vigour of the benevolent principle.

Dr. Hutcheson * was so far from allowing self-love to be in any case a motive of virtuous actions, that even a regard to the pleasure of self-approbation, to the comfortable applause of our own consciences, according to him, diminished the merit of a benevolent action. This was a selfish motive, he thought, which, so far as it contributed to any action, demonstrated the weakness of that pure and disinterested benevolence which could alone stamp upon the conduct of man the character of virtue. In the common judgments of mankind, however, this regard

---

* Inquiry concerning Virtue, sect. 2. art. 4. ; also Illustrations on the Moral Sense, sect. 5, last paragraph.

to the approbation of our own minds is so far from being considered as what can in any respect diminish the virtue of any action, that it is often rather looked upon as the sole motive which deserves the appellation of virtuous.

Such is the account given of the nature of virtue in this amiable system, a system which has a peculiar tendency to nourish and support in the human heart the noblest and the most agreeable of all affections, and not only to check the injustice of self-love, but in some measure to discourage that principle altogether, by representing it as what could never reflect any honour upon those who were influenced by it.

As some of the other systems which I have already given an account of, do not sufficiently explain from whence arises the peculiar excellency of the supreme virtue of beneficence, so this system seems to have the contrary defect, of not sufficiently explaining from whence arises our approbation of the inferior virtues of prudence, vigilance, circumspection, temperance, constancy, firmness. The view and aim of our affections, the beneficent and hurtful effects which they tend to produce, are the only qualities at all attended to in this system. Their propriety and impropriety, their suitableness and unsuitableness, to the cause which excites them, are disregarded altogether.

Regard to our own private happiness and interest, too, appear upon many occasions very laudable principles of action. The habits of œconomy, industry, discretion, attention, and application of thought, are generally supposed to be cultivated from self-interested motives, and at the same time are apprehended to be very praise-worthy qualities, which deserve the esteem and approbation of every body. The mixture of a selfish motive, it is true, seems often to sully the beauty of those actions which ought to arise from a benevolent affection. The cause of this, however, is not that self-love can never be the motive of a virtuous action, but that the benevolent principle appears in this particular case to want its due degree of strength, and to be altogether unsuitable to its object. The character, therefore, seems evidently imperfect, and upon the whole to deserve blame rather than praise. The mixture of a benevolent motive in an action to which self-love alone ought to be sufficient to prompt us, is not so apt indeed to diminish our sense of its propriety, or of the virtue of the person who performs it. We are not ready to suspect any person of being defective in selfishness. This is by no means the weak side of human nature, or the failing of which we are apt to be suspicious. If we could really believe, however, of any man, that, was it not from a regard to his family and friends, he would not take that proper care of his health, his life, or his fortune, to which self-preservation alone ought to be sufficient to prompt him, it would undoubtedly be a failing, though one of those amiable failings which render a person rather the object of pity than of contempt or hatred. It would still, however, somewhat diminish the dignity and respectableness of his character. Carelessness and want of œconomy are universally disapproved of, not, however, as proceeding from a want of benevolence, but from a want of proper attention to the objects of self-interest.

Though the standard by which casuists frequently determine what is right or wrong in human conduct, be its tendency to the welfare or disorder of society, it does not follow that a regard to the welfare of society should be the sole virtuous motive of action, but only that, in competition, it ought to cast the balance against all other motives.

Benevolence may, perhaps, be the sole principle of action in the Deity, and there are several not improbable arguments which tend to persuade us that it is so. It is not easy to conceive what other motive an independent and all-perfect Being, who stands in need of nothing external, and whose happiness is complete in himself, can act from. But whatever may be the case with the Deity, so imperfect a creature as man, the support of whose existence requires so many things external to him, must often act from many other motives. The condition of human nature were peculiarly hard, if those affections, which, by the very nature of our being, ought frequently to influence our conduct, could upon no occasion appear virtuous, or deserve esteem and commendation from any body.

Those three systems, that which places virtue in propriety, that which places it in prudence, and that which makes it consist in benevolence, are the principal accounts which have been given of the nature of virtue. To one or other of them, all the other descriptions of virtue, how different soever they may appear, are easily reducible.

That system which places virtue in obedience to the will of the Deity, may be accounted either among those which make it consist in prudence, or among those which make it consist in propriety. When it is asked, why we ought to obey the will of the Deity, this question, which would be impious and absurd in the highest degree, if asked from any doubt that we ought to obey him, can admit but of two different answers. It must either be said that we ought to obey the will of the Deity because he is a Being of infinite power, who will reward us eternally if we do so, and punish us eternally if we do otherwise : or it must be said, that independent of any regard to our own happiness, or to rewards and punishments of any kind, there is a congruity and fitness that a creature should obey its creator, that a limited and imperfect being should submit to one of infinite and incomprehensible perfections. Besides one or other of these two, it is impossible to conceive that any other answer can be given to this question. If the first answer be the proper one, virtue consists in prudence, or in the proper pursuit of our own final interest and happiness ; since it is upon this account that we are obliged to obey the will of the Deity. If the second answer be the proper one, virtue must consist in propriety, since the ground of our obligation to obedience is the suitableness or congruity of the sentiments of humility and submission to the superiority of the object which excites them.

That system which places virtue in utility, coincides too with that which makes it consist in propriety. According to this system, all those qualities of the mind which are agreeable or advantageous, either to the person himself or to others, are approved of as virtuous, and the contrary are disapproved of as vicious. But the agreeableness or utility of any affection depends upon the degree which it is allowed to subsist in. Every affection is useful when it is confined to a certain degree of moderation ; and every affection is disadvantageous when it exceeds the proper bounds. According to this system therefore, virtue consists not in any one affection, but in the proper degree of all the affections. The only difference between it and that which I have been endeavouring to establish, is, that it makes utility, and not sympathy, or the correspondent affection of the spectator, the natural and original measure of this proper degree.

CHAP. IV.—*Of Licentious Systems.*

ALL those systems, which I have hitherto given an account of, suppose that that there is a real and essential distinction between vice and virtue, whatever these qualities may consist in. There is a real and essential difference between the propriety and impropriety of any affection, between benevolence and any other principle of action, between real prudence and short-sighted folly or precipitate rashness. In the main, too, all of them contribute to encourage the praiseworthy, and to discourage the blameable disposition.

It may be true, perhaps, of some of them, that they tend, in some measure, to break the balance of the affections, and to give the mind a particular bias to some principles of action, beyond the proportion that is due to them. The ancient systems, which place virtue in propriety, seem chiefly to recommend the great, the awful, and the respectable virtues, the virtues of self-government and self-command ; fortitude, magnanimity, independency upon fortune, the contempt of all outward accidents, of pain, poverty, exile and death. It is in these great exertions that the noblest propriety of conduct is displayed. The soft, the amiable, the gentle virtues, all the virtues of indulgent humanity are, in comparison, but little insisted upon, and seem, on the contrary, by the Stoics in particular, to have been often regarded as weaknesses, which it behoved a wise man not to harbour in his breast.

The benevolent system, on the other hand, while it fosters and encourages all those milder virtues in the highest degree, seems entirely to neglect the more awful and respectable qualities of the mind. It even denies them the appellation of virtues. It calls them moral abilities, and treats them as qualities which do not deserve the same sort of esteem and approbation, that is due to what is properly denominated virtue. All those principles of action which aim only at our own interest, it treats, if that be possible, still worse. So far from having any merit of their own, they diminish, it pretends, the merit of benevolence, when they co-operate with it ; and prudence, it is asserted, when employed only in promoting private interest, can never even be imagined a virtue.

That system, again, which makes virtue consist in prudence only, while it gives the highest encouragement to the habits of caution, vigilance, sobriety, and judicious moderation, seems to degrade equally both the amiable and respectable virtues, and to strip the former of all their beauty, and the latter of all their grandeur.

But notwithstanding these defects, the general tendency of each of those three systems is to encourage the best and most laudable habits of the human mind, and it were well for society, if, either mankind in general, or even those few who pretend to live according to any philosophical rule, were to regulate their conduct by the precepts of any one of them. We may learn from each of them something that is both valuable and peculiar. If it was possible, by precept and exhortation, to inspire the mind with fortitude and magnanimity, the ancient systems of propriety would seem sufficient to do this. Or if it was possible, by the same means, to soften it into humanity, and to awaken the affections of kindness and general love towards those we live with, some of the pictures which the benevolent system presents us, might seem capable of producing this effect. We may learn from the system of Epicurus, though undoubtedly the most imperfect of all the three, how much the practice of both the amiable and respectable virtues is conducive to our own interest, to our own ease and safety and quiet even in this life. As Epicurus placed happiness in the attainment of ease and security, he exerted himself in a particular manner to show that virtue was, not merely the best and the surest, but the only means of acquiring those invaluable possessions. The good effects of virtue upon our inward tranquillity and peace of mind, are what other philosophers have chiefly celebrated. Epicurus, without neglecting this topic, has chiefly insisted unpon the influence of that amiable quality on our outward prosperity and safety. It was upon this account that his writings were so much studied in the ancient world by men of all different philosophical parties. It is from him that Cicero, the great enemy of the Epicurean system, borrows his most agreeable proofs that virtue alone is sufficient to secure happiness. Seneca, though a Stoic, the sect most opposite to that of Epicurus, yet quotes this philosopher more frequently than any other.

There is, however, another system which seems to take away altogether the distinction between vice and virtue, and of which the tendency is, upon that account, wholly pernicious : I mean the system of Dr. Mandeville. Though the notions of this author are in almost every respect erroneous, there are, however, some appearances in human nature, which, when viewed in a certain manner, seem at first sight to favour them.   These described and exaggerated by the lively and humorous, though coarse and rustic eloquence of Dr. Mandeville, have thrown upon his doctrines an air of truth and probability which is very apt to impose upon the unskilful.

Dr. Mandeville considers whatever is done from a sense of propriety, from a regard to what is commendable and praiseworthy, as being done from a love of praise and commendation, or as he calls it from vanity.   Man, he observes, is naturally much more interested in his own happiness than in that of others, and it is impossible that in his heart he can ever really prefer their prosperity to his own.   Whenever he appears to do so, we may be assured that he imposes upon us, and that he is then acting from the same selfish motives as at all other times. Among his other selfish passions, vanity is one of the strongest, and he is always easily flattered and greatly delighted with the applauses of those about him.   When he appears to sacrifice his own interest to that of his companions, he knows that this conduct will be highly agreeable to their self-love, and that they will not fail to express their satisfaction by bestowing upon him the most extravagant praises. The pleasure which he expects from this, over-balances, in his opinion, the interest which he abandons in order to procure it.   His conduct, therefore, upon this occasion, is in reality just as selfish, and arises from just as mean a motive as upon any other.   He is flattered, however, and he flatters himself with the belief that it is entirely disinterested ; since, unless this was supposed, it would not seem to merit any commendation either in his own eyes or in those of others.   All public spirit, therefore, all preference of public to private interest, is, according to him, a mere cheat and imposition upon mankind; and that human virtue which is so much boasted of, and which is the occasion of so much emulation among men, is the mere offspring of flattery begot upon pride.

Whether the most generous and public-spirited actions may not, in some sense, be regarded as proceeding from self-love, I shall not at present examine.   The decision of this question is not, I apprehend, of any importance towards establishing the reality of virtue, since self-love may frequently be a virtuous motive of action.   I shall only endeavour to show that the desire of doing what is honourable and noble, of rendering ourselves the proper objects of esteem and approbation, cannot with any propriety be called vanity.   Even the love of well-grounded fame and reputation, the desire of acquiring esteem by what is really estimable, does not deserve that name. The first is the love of virtue, the noblest and the best passion of human nature.   The second is the love of true glory, a passion inferior no doubt to the former, but which in dignity appears to come immediately after it. He is guilty of vanity who desires praise for qualities which are either not praise-worthy in any degree, or not in that degree in which he expects to be praised for them; who sets his character upon the frivolous ornaments of dress and equipage, or upon the equally frivolous accomplishments of ordinary behaviour. He is guilty of vanity who desires praise for what indeed very well deserves it, but what he perfectly knows does not belong to him. The empty coxcomb who gives himself airs of importance which he has no title to, the silly liar who assumes the merit of adventures which never happened, the foolish plagiary who gives himself out for the author of what he has no pretensions to, are properly accused of this passion. He too is said to be guilty of vanity who is not contented with the silent sentiments of esteem and approbation, who seems to be fonder of their noisy expressions and acclamations than of the sentiments themselves, who is never satisfied but when his own praises are ringing in his ears, and who solicits with the most anxious importunity all external marks of respect, is fond of titles, of compliments, of being visited, of being attended, of being taken notice of in public places with the appearance of deference and attention. This frivolous passion is altogether different from either of the two former, and is the passion of the lowest and the least of mankind, as they are of the noblest and the greatest.

But though these three passions, the desire of rendering ourselves the proper objects of honour and esteem, or of becoming what is honourable and estimable; the desire of acquiring honour and esteem by really deserving those sentiments; and the frivolous desire of praise at any rate, are widely different; though the two former are always approved of, while the latter never fails to be despised; there is, however, a certain remote affinity among them, which, exaggerated by the humorous and diverting eloquence of this lively author, has enabled him to impose upon his readers. There is an affinity between vanity and the love of true glory, as both these passions aim at acquiring esteem and approbation. But they are different in this, that the one is a just, reasonable, and equitable passion, while the other is unjust, absurd, and ridiculous. The man who desires esteem for what is really estimable, desires nothing but what he is justly entitled to, and what cannot be refused him without some sort of injury. He, on the contrary, who desires it upon any other terms, demands what he has no just claim to. The first is easily satisfied, is not apt to be jealous or suspicious that we do not esteem him enough, and is seldom solicitous about receiving many external marks of our regard. The other, on the contrary, is never to be satisfied, is full of jealousy and suspicion that we do not esteem him so much as he desires, because he has some secret consciousness that he desires more than he deserves. The least neglect of ceremony, he considers as a mortal affront, and as an expression of the most determined contempt. He is restless and impatient, and perpetually afraid that we have lost all respect for him, and is upon this account always anxious to obtain new expressions of our esteem, and cannot be kept in temper but by continual attendance and adulation.

There is an affinity, too, between the desire of becoming what is honourable and estimable and the desire of honour and esteem, between the love of virtue and the love of true glory. They resemble one another not only in this respect, that both aim at really being what is honourable and noble, but even in that respect in which the love of true glory resembles what is properly called vanity, some reference to the sentiments of others. The man of the greatest magnanimity, who desires virtue for its own sake, and is most indifferent about what actually are the opinions of mankind with regard to him, is still, however, delighted with the thoughts of what they should be, with the consciousness that though he may neither be honoured nor applauded, he is still the proper object of honour and applause, and that if mankind were cool and candid and consistent with themselves, and properly informed of the motives and circumstances of his conduct, they would not fail to honour and applaud him. Though he despises the opinions which are actually entertained of him, he has the highest value for those which ought to be entertained of him. That he might think himself worthy of those honourable sentiments, and, whatever was the idea which other men might conceive of his character, that when he should put himself in their situation, and consider, not what was, but what ought to be their opinion, he should always have the highest idea of it himself, was the great and exalted motive of his conduct. As even in the love of virtue, therefore, there is still some reference, though not to what is, yet to what in reason and propriety ought to be, the opinion of others, there is even in this respect some affinity between it and the love of true glory. There is, however, at the same time, a very great difference between them. The man who acts solely from a regard to what is right and fit to be done, from a regard to what is the proper object of esteem and approbation, though these sentiments should never be bestowed upon him, acts from the most sublime and godlike motive which human nature is even capable of conceiving. The man, on the other hand, who while he desires to mérit approbation, is at the same time anxious to obtain it, though he, too, is laudable in the main, yet his motives have a greater mixture of human infirmity. He is in danger of being mortified by the ignorance and injustice of mankind, and his happiness is exposed to the envy of his rivals and the folly of the public. The happiness of the other, on the contrary, is altogether secure and independent of fortune, and of the caprice of those he lives with. The contempt and hatred which may be thrown upon him by the ignorance of mankind, he considers as not belonging to him, and is not at all mortified by it. Mankind despise and hate him from a false notion of his character and conduct. If they knew him better, they would esteem and love him. It is not him whom, properly speaking, they hate and despise, but another person whom they mistake him to be. Our friend, whom we should meet at a masquerade in the garb of our enemy, would be more diverted than mortified, if under that disguise we should vent our indignation against him. Such are the sentiments of a man of real magnanimity, when exposed to unjust censure. It seldom happens, however, that human nature arrives at this degree of firmness. Though none but the weakest and most worthless of mankind are much delighted with false glory, yet, by a strange inconsistency, false ignominy is capable of mortifying those who appear the most resolute and determined.

Dr. Mandeville is not satisfied with representing the frivolous motive of vanity, as the source of all those actions which are commonly accounted virtuous. He endeavours to point out the imperfection of human virtue in many other respects. In every case, he pretends, it falls short of that complete self-denial which it pretends to, and, instead of a conquest, is commonly no more than a concealed indulgence of our passions. Wherever our reserve with regard to pleasure falls short of the most ascetic abstinence, he treats it as gross luxury and sensuality. Every thing, according to him, is luxury which exceeds what is absolutely necessary for the support of human nature, so that there is vice even in the use of a clean shirt or of a convenient habitation. The indulgence of the inclination to sex, in the most lawful union, he considers as the same sensuality with the most hurtful gratification of that passion, and derides that temperance and that chastity which can be practised at so cheap a rate. The ingenious sophistry of his reasoning, is here, as upon many other occasions, covered by the ambiguity of language. There are some of our passions which have no other names except those which mark the disagreeable and offensive degree. The spectator is more apt to take notice of them in this degree than in any other. When they shock his own sentiments, when they give him some sort of antipathy and uneasiness, he is necessarily obliged to attend to them, and is from thence naturally led to give them a name. When they fall in with the natural state of his own mind, he is very apt to overlook them altogether, and either gives them no name at all, or, if he gives them any, it is one which marks rather the subjection and restraint of the passion, than the degree which it still is allowed to subsist in, after it is so subjected and restrained. Thus the common names (luxury and lust) of the love of pleasure, and of the love of sex, denote a vicious and offensive degree of those passions. The words temperance and chastity, on the other hand, seem to mark rather the restraint and subjection which they are kept under, than the degree which they are still allowed to subsist in. When he can show, therefore, that they still subsist in some degree, he imagines, he has entirely demolished the reality of the virtues of temperance and chastity, and shown them to be mere impositions upon the inattention and simplicity of mankind. Those virtues, however, do not require an entire insensibility to the objects of the passions which they mean to govern. They only aim at restraining the violence of those passions so far as not to hurt the individual, and neither disturb nor offend society.

It is the great fallacy of Dr. Mandeville's book (Fable of the Bees) to represent every passion as wholly vicious, which is so in any degree and in any direction. It is thus that he treats every thing as vanity which has any reference, either to what are, or to what ought to be the sentiments of others ; and it is by means of this sophistry, that he establishes his favourite conclusion, that private vices are public benefits. If the love of magnificence, a taste for the elegant arts and improvements of human life, for whatever is agreeable in dress, furniture, or equipage, for architecture, statuary, painting, and music, is to be regarded as luxury, sensuality, and ostentation, even in those whose situation allows, without any inconveniency, the indulgence of those passions, it is certain that luxury, sensuality, and ostentation are public benefits : since without the qualities upon which he thinks proper to bestow such opprobrious names, the arts of refinement could never find encouragement, and must languish for want of employment. Some popular ascetic doctrines which had been current before his time, and which placed virtue in the entire extirpation and annihilation of all our passions, were the real foundation of this licentious system. It was easy for Dr. Mandeville to prove, first, that this entire conquest never actually took place among men ; and secondly, that if it was to take place universally, it would be pernicious to society, by putting an end to all industry and commerce, and in a manner to the whole business of human life. By the first of these propositions, he seemed to prove that there was no real virtue, and that what pretended to be such, was a mere cheat and imposition upon mankind ; and by the second, that our private vices were public benefits, since without them no society could prosper or flourish.

Such is the system of Dr. Mandeville, which once made so much noise in the world, and which, though, perhaps, it never gave occasion to more vice than what would have been without it, at least taught that vice, which arose from other causes, to appear with more effrontery, and to avow the corruption of its motives with a profligate audaciousness which had never been heard of before.

But how destructive soever this system may appear, it could never have imposed upon so great a number of persons, nor have occasioned so general an alarm among those who are the friends of better principles, had it not in some respects bordered upon the truth. A system of natural philosophy may appear very plausible, and be for a long time very generally received in the world, and yet have no foundation in nature, nor any sort of resemblance to the truth. The vortices of Des Cartes were regarded by a very ingenious nation, for near a century together, as a most satisfactory account of the revolutions of the heavenly bodies. Yet it has been demonstrated, to the conviction of all mankind, that these pretended causes of those wonderful effects, not only do not actually exist, but are utterly impossible, and if they did exist, could produce no such effects as are ascribed to them. But it is otherwise with systems of moral philosophy, and an author who pretends to account for the origin of our moral sentiments, cannot deceive us so grossly, nor depart so very far from all resemblance to the truth. When a traveller gives an account of some distant country, he may impose upon our credulity, the most groundless and absurd fictions as the most certain matters of fact. But when a person pretends to inform us of what passes in our neighbourhood, and of the affairs of the very parish which we live in, though here too, if we are so careless as not to examine things with our own eyes, he may deceive us in many respects, yet the greatest falsehoods which he imposes upon us must bear some resemblance to the truth, and must even have a considerable mixture of truth in them. An author who treats of natural philosophy, and pretends to assign the causes of the great phenomena of the universe, pretends to give an account of the affairs of a very distant country, concerning which he may tell us what he pleases, and as long as his narration keeps within the bounds of seeming possibility, he need not despair of gaining of belief. But when he proposes to explain the origin of our desires and affections, of our sentiments of approbation and disapprobation, he pretends to give an account, not only of the affairs of the very parish that we live in, but of our own domestic concerns. Though here too, like indolent masters who put their trust in a steward who deceives them, we are very liable to be imposed upon, yet we are incapable of passing any account which does not preserve some little regard to the truth. Some of the articles, at least, must be just, and even those which are most overcharged must have had some foundation, otherwise the fraud would be detected even by that careless inspection which we are disposed to give. The author who should assign, as the cause of any natural sentiment, some principle which neither had any connection with it, nor resembled any other principle which had some such connection, would appear absurd and ridiculous to the most injudicious and unexperienced reader.

SEC. III.—OF THE DIFFERENT SYSTEMS WHICH HAVE BEEN FORMED CONCERNING THE PRINCIPLE OF APPROBATION.

INTRODUCTION.—After the inquiry concerning the nature of virtue, the next question of importance in Moral Philosophy, is concerning the principle of approbation, concerning the power or faculty of the mind which renders certain characters agreeable or disagreeable to us, makes us prefer one tenor of conduct to another, denominate the one right and the other wrong, and consider the one as the object of approbation, honour, and reward, or the other as that of blame, censure, and punishment.

Three different accounts have been given of this principle of approbation. According to some, we approve and disapprove both of our own actions and of those of others, from self-love only, or from some view of their tendency to our own happiness or disadvantage : according to others, reason, the same faculty by which we distinguish between truth and falsehood, enables us to distinguish between what is fit and unfit both in actions and affections : according to others, this distinction is altogether the effect of immediate sentiment and feeling, and arises from the satisfaction or disgust with which the view of certain actions or affections inspires us. Self-love, reason and sentiment, therefore, are the three different sources which have been assigned for the principle of approbation.

Before I proceed to give an account of those different systems, I must observe, that the determination of this second question, though of the greatest importance in speculation, is of none in practice. The question concerning the nature of virtue necessarily has some influence upon our notions of right and wrong in many particular cases. That concerning the principle of approbation can possibly have no such effect. To examine from what contrivance or mechanism within, those different notions or sentiments arise, is a mere matter of philosophical curiosity.

CHAP. I.—*Of those Systems which deduce the Principle of Approbation from Self-love.*

THOSE who account for the principle of approbation from self-love, do not all account for it in the same manner, and there is a good deal of confusion and inaccuracy in all their different systems. According to Mr. Hobbes, and many of his followers (Puffendorff, Mandeville), man is driven to take refuge in society, not by any natural love which he bears to his own kind, but because without the assistance of others he is incapable of subsisting with ease or safety. Society, upon this account, becomes necessary to him, and whatever tends to its support and welfare, he considers as having a remote tendency to his own interest ; and, on the contrary, whatever is likely to disturb or destroy it, he regards as in some measure hurtful or pernicious to himself. Virtue is the great support, and vice the great disturber of human society. The former, therefore, is agreeable, and the latter offensive to every man ; as from the one he foresees the prosperity, and from the other the ruin and disorder of what is so necessary for the comfort and the security of his existence.

That the tendency of virtue to promote, and of vice to disturb the order of society, when we consider it coolly and philosophically, reflects a very great beauty upon the one, and a very great deformity upon the other, cannot, as I have observed upon a former occasion, be called in question. Human society, when we contemplate it in a certain abstract and philosophical light, appears like a great, an immense machine, whose regular and harmonious movements produce a thousand agreeable effects. As in any other beautiful and noble machine that was the production of human art, whatever tended to render its movements more smooth and easy, would derive a beauty from this effect, and, on the contrary, whatever tended to obstruct them would displease upon that account : so virtue, which is, as it were, the fine polish to the wheels of society, necessarily pleases ; while vice, like the vile rust, which makes them jar and grate upon one another, is as necessarily offensive. This account, therefore, of the origin of approbation and disapprobation, so far as it derives them from a regard to the order of society, runs into that principle which gives beauty to utility, and which I have explained upon a former occasion ; and it is from thence that this system derives all that appearance of probability which it possesses. When those authors describe the innumerable advantages of a cultivated and social, above a savage and solitary life ; when they expatiate upon the necessity of virtue and good order for the maintenance of the one, and demonstrate how infallibly the prevalence of vice and disobedience to the laws tend to bring back the other, the reader is charmed with the novelty and grandeur of those views which they open to him : he sees plainly a new beauty in virtue, and a new deformity in vice, which he had never taken notice of before, and is commonly so delighted with the discovery, that he seldom takes time to reflect, that this political view having never occurred to him in his life before, cannot possibly be the ground of that approbation and disapprobation with which he has been accustomed to consider those different qualities.

When those authors, on the other hand, deduce from self-love the interest which we take in the welfare of society, and the esteem which upon that account we bestow upon virtue, they do not mean, that when we in this age applaud the virtue of Cato, and detest the villany of Cataline, our sentiments are influenced by the notion of any benefit we receive from the one, or of any detriment we suffer from the other. It was not because the prosperity or subversion of society, in those remote

ages and nations, was apprehended to have any influence upon our
happiness or misery in the present times; that according to those
philosophers, we esteemed the virtuous and blamed the disorderly
character.   They never imagined that our sentiments were influenced
by any benefit or damage which we suppposed actually to redound to
us, from either; but by that which might have redounded to us, had
we lived in those distant ages and countries; or by that which might
still redound to us, if in our own times we should meet with characters
of the same kind.   The idea, in short, which those authors were grop-
ing about, but which they were never able to unfold distinctly, was that
indirect sympathy which we feel with the gratitude or resentment of
those who received the benefit or suffered the damage resulting from
such opposite characters : and it was this which they were indistinctly
pointing at, when they said, that it was not the thought of what we had
gained or suffered which prompted our applause or indignation, but the
conception or imagination of what we might gain or suffer if we were to
act in society with such associates.

    Sympathy, however, cannot, in any sense, be regarded as a selfish
principle.   When I sympathize with your sorrow or your indignation,
it may be pretended, indeed, that my emotion is founded in self-love,
because it arises from bringing your case home to myself, from putting
myself in your situation, and thence conceiving what I should feel in
the like circumstances.   But though sympathy is very properly said to
arise from an imaginary change of situations with the person principally
concerned, yet this imaginary change is not supposed to happen to me
in my own person and character, but in that of the person with whom
I sympathize.   When I condole with you for the loss of your only son,
in order to enter into your grief I do not consider what I, a person of
such a character and profession, should suffer, if I had a son, and if
that son was unfortunately to die; but I consider what I should suffer
if I was really you, and I not only change circumstances with you, but
I change persons and characters.   My grief, therefore, is entirely upon
your account, and not in the least upon my own.   It is not, therefore
in the least selfish.   How can that be regarded as a selfish passion,
which does not arise even from the imagination of any thing that has
befallen, or that relates to myself, in my own proper person and
character, but which is entirely occupied about what relates to you?   A
man may sympathize with a woman in child-bed; though it is impossible that he should conceive himself as suffering her pains in his own
proper person and character.   That whole account of human nature,
however, which deduces all sentiments and affections from self-love,
which has made so much noise in the world, but which, so far as I
know, has never yet been fully and distinctly explained, seems to me to
have arisen from some confused misapprehension of the system of
sympathy.

CHAP. II.—*Of those Systems which make Reason the Principle of Approbation.*

IT is well known to have been the doctrine of Mr. Hobbes, that a state of nature is a state of war; and that antecedent to the institution of civil government, there could be no safe or peaceable society among men. To preserve society, therefore, according to him, was to support civil government, and to destroy civil government was the same thing as to put an end to society. But the existence of civil government depends upon the obedience that is paid to the supreme magistrate. The moment he loses his authority, all government is at an end. As self-preservation, therefore, teaches men to applaud whatever tends to promote the welfare of society, and to blame whatever is likely to hurt it; so the same principle, if they would think and speak consistently, ·ought to teach them to applaud upon all occasions obedience to the civil magistrate, and to blame all disobedience and rebellion. The very ideas of laudable and blamable, ought to be the same with those of obedience and disobedience. The laws of the civil magistrate, therefore, ought to be regarded as the sole ultimate standards of what was just and unjust, of what was right and wrong.

It was the avowed intention of Mr. Hobbes, by propagating these notions, to subject the consciences of men immediately to the civil, and not to the ecclesiastical powers, whose turbulence and ambition, he had been taught, by the example of his own times, to regard as the principal source of the disorders of society. His doctrine, upon this account, was peculiarly offensive to theologians, who accordingly did not fail to vent their indignation against him with great asperity and bitterness. It was likewise offensive to all sound moralists, as it supposed that there was no natural distinction between right and wrong, that these were mutable and changeable, and depended upon the mere arbitrary will of the civil magistrate. This account of things, therefore, was attacked from all quarters, and by all sorts of weapons, by sober reason as well as by furious declamation.

In order to confute so odious a doctrine, it was necessary to prove, that antecedent to all law or positive institution, the mind was naturally endowed with a faculty, by which it distinguished in certain actions and affections, the qualities of right, laudable, and virtuous, and in others those of wrong, blamable, and vicious.

Law, it was justly observed by Dr. Cudworth (Immutable Morality, l. i), could not be the original source of those distinctions; since upon the supposition of such a law, it must either be right to obey it, and wrong to disobey it, or indifferent whether we obeyed it or disobeyed it. That law which it was indifferent whether we obeyed or disobeyed, could not, it was evident, be the source of those distinctions; neither could that which it was right to obey and wrong to disobey, since even this still supposed the antecedent notions or ideas of right and wrong, and that obedience to the law was conformable to the idea of right, and disobedience to that of wrong.

Since the mind, therefore, had a notion of those distinctions antecedent to all law, it seemed necessarily to follow, that it derived this notion from reason, which pointed out the difference between right and wrong, in the same manner in which it did that between truth and falsehood: and this conclusion, which, though true in some respects, is rather hasty in others, was more easily received at a time when the abstract science of human nature was but in its infancy, and before the distinct offices and powers of the different faculties of the human mind had been carefully examined and distinguished from one another. When this controversy with Mr. Hobbes was carried on with the greatest warmth and keenness, no other faculty had been thought of from which any such ideas could possibly be supposed to arise. It became at this time, therefore, the popular doctrine, that the essence of virtue and vice did not consist in the conformity or disagreement of human actions with the law of a superior, but in their conformity or disagreement with reason, which was thus considered as the original source and principle of approbation and disapprobation.

That virtue consists in conformity to reason, is true in some respects, and this faculty may very justly be considered as, in some sense, the source and principle of approbation and disapprobation, and of all solid judgments concerning right and wrong. It is by reason that we discover those general rules of justice by which we ought to regulate our actions: and it is by the same faculty that we form those more vague and indeterminate ideas of what is prudent, of what is decent, of what is generous or noble, which we carry constantly about with us, and according to which we endeavour, as well as we can, to model the tenor of our conduct. The general maxims of morality are formed, like all other general maxims, from experience and induction. We observe in a great variety of particular cases what pleases or displeases our moral faculties, what these approve or disapprove of, and, by induction from this experience, we establish those general rules. But induction is always regarded as one of the operations of reason. From reason, therefore, we are very properly said to derive all those general maxims and ideas. It is by these, however, that we regulate the greater part of our moral judgments, which would be extremely uncertain and precarious if they depended altogether upon what is liable to so many variations as immediate sentiment and feeling, which the different states of health and humour are capable of altering so essentially. As our most solid judgments, therefore, with regard to right and wrong, are regulated by maxims and ideas derived from an induction of reason, virtue may very properly be said to consist in a conformity to

19 *

reason, and so far this faculty may be considered as the source and principle of approbation and disapprobation.

But though reason is undoubtedly the source of the general rules of morality, and of all the moral judgments which we form by means of them; it is altogether absurd and unintelligible to suppose that the first perceptions of right and wrong can be derived from reason, even in those particular cases upon the experience of which the general rules are formed. These first perceptions, as well as all other experiments upon which any general rules are founded, cannot be the object of reason, but of immediate sense and feeling. It is by finding in a vast variety of instances that one tenor of conduct constantly pleases in a certain manner, and that another as constantly displeases the mind, that we form the general rules of morality. But reason cannot render any particular object either agreeable or disagreeable to the mind for its own sake. Reason may show that this object is the means of obtaining some other which is naturally either pleasing or displeasing, and in this manner may render it either agreeable or disagreeable for the sake of something else. But nothing can be agreeable or disagreeable for its own sake, which is not rendered such by immediate sense and feeling. If virtue, therefore, in every particular instance, necessarily pleases for its own sake, and if vice as certainly displeases the mind, it cannot be reason, but immediate sense and feeling, which thus reconciles us to the one, and alienates us from the other.

Pleasure and pain are the great objects of desire and aversion: but these are distinguished, not by reason, but by immediate sense and feeling. If virtue, therefore, be desirable for its own sake, and if vice be, in the same manner, the object of aversion, it cannot be reason which originally distinguishes those different qualities, but immediate sense and feeling.

As reason, however, in a certain sense, may justly be considered as the principle of approbation and disapprobation, these sentiments were, through inattention, long regarded as originally flowing from the operations of this faculty. Dr. Hutcheson had the merit of being the first who distinguished with any degree of precision in what respect all moral distinctions may be said to arise from reason, and in what respect they are founded upon immediate sense and feeling. In his illustrations upon the moral sense he has explained this so fully, and, in my opinion, so unanswerably, that, if any controversy is still kept up about this subject, I can impute it to nothing, but either to inattention to what that gentleman has written, or to a superstitious attachment to certain forms of expression, a weakness not very uncommon among the learned, especially in subjects so deeply interesting as the present, in which a man of virtue is often loath to abandon even the propriety of a single phrase which he has been accustomed to.

CHAP. III.—*Of those Systems which make Sentiment the Principle of Approbation.*

THOSE systems which make sentiment the principle of approbation may be divided into two different classes.

I. According to some the principle of approbation is founded upon a sentiment of a peculiar nature, upon a particular power of perception exerted by the mind at the view of certain actions or affections; some of which affecting this faculty in an agreeable and others in a disagreeable manner, the former are stamped with the characters of right, laudable, and virtuous; the latter with those of wrong, blamable, and vicious. This sentiment being of a peculiar nature distinct from every other, and the effect of a particular power of perception, they give it a particular name, and call it a moral sense.

II. According to others, in order to account for the principle of approbation, there is no occasion for supposing any new power of perception which had never been heard of before. Nature, they imagine acts here, as in all other cases, with the strictest œconomy, and produces a multitude of effects from one and the same cause; and sympathy, a power which has always been taken notice of, and with which the mind is manifestly endowed, is, they think, sufficient to account for all the effects ascribed to this peculiar faculty.

I. Dr. Hutcheson (Inquiry concerning Virtue) had been at great pains to prove that the principle of approbation was not founded on self-love. He had demonstrated, too, that it could not arise from any operation of reason. Nothing remained, he thought, but to suppose it a faculty of a peculiar kind, with which Nature had endowed the human mind, in order to produce this one particular and important effect. When self-love and reason were both excluded, it did not occur to him that there was any other known faculty of the mind which could in any respect answer this purpose.

This new power of perception he called a moral sense, and supposed it to be somewhat analogous to the external senses. As the bodies around us, by affecting these in a certain manner, appear to possess the different qualities of sound, taste, odour, colour; so the various affections of the human mind, by touching this particular faculty in a certain manner, appear to possess the different qualities of amiable and odious, of virtuous and vicious, of right and wrong.

The various senses or powers of perception (Treatise of the Passions) from which the human mind derives all its simple ideas, were, according to this system, of two different kinds, of which the one were called the direct or antecedent, the other, the reflex or consequent senses. The direct senses were those faculties from which the mind derived the perception of such species of things as did not presuppose the antecedent perception of any other. Thus sounds and colours were objects of the direct senses. To hear a sound or to see a colour does not presuppose the antecedent perception of any other quality or object. The reflex or consequent senses, on the other hand, were those faculties from which the mind derived the perception of such species of things as presupposed the antecedent perception of some other. Thus harmony and beauty were objects of the reflex senses. In order to perceive the harmony of a sound, or the beauty of a colour, we must first perceive the sound or the colour. The moral sense was considered as a faculty of this kind. That faculty, which Mr. Locke calls reflection, and from which he derived the simple ideas of the different passions and emotions of the human mind, was, according to Dr. Hutcheson, a direct internal sense. That faculty again by which we perceived the beauty or deformity, the virtue or vice, of those different passions and emotions, was a reflex, internal sense.

Dr. Hutcheson endeavoured still further to support this doctrine, by showing that it was agreeable to the analogy of nature, and that the mind was endowed with a variety of other reflex senses exactly similar to the moral sense; such as a sense of beauty and deformity in external objects; a public sense, by which we sympathize with the happiness or misery of our fellow-creatures; a sense of shame and honour, and a sense of ridicule.

But notwithstanding all the pains which this ingenious philosopher has taken to prove that the principle of approbation is founded in a peculiar power of perception, somewhat analogous to the external senses, there are some consequences, which he acknowledges to follow from this doctrine, that will, perhaps, be regarded by many as a sufficient confutation of it. The qualities, he allows,* which belong to the objects of any sense, cannot, without the greatest absurdity, be ascribed to the sense itself. Who ever thought of calling the sense of seeing black or white, the sense of hearing loud or low, or the sense of tasting sweet or bitter? And, according to him, it is equally absurd to call our moral faculties virtuous or vicious, morally good or evil. These qualities belong to the objects of those faculties, not to the faculties themselves. If any man, therefore, was so absurdly constituted as to approve of cruelty and injustice as the highest virtues, and to disapprove of equity and humanity as the most pitiful vices, such a constitution of mind might indeed be regarded as inconvenient both to the individual and to the society, and likewise as strange, surprising, and unnatural in itself; but it could not, without the greatest absurdity, be denominated vicious or morally evil.

Yet surely if we saw any man shouting with admiration and applause at a barbarous and unmerited execution, which some insolent tyrant had ordered, we should not think we were guilty of any great absurdity

* Illustrations upon the Moral Sense, sect. 1. p. 237, et seq.; third edition.

in denominating this behaviour vicious and morally evil in the highest degree, though it expressed nothing but depraved moral faculties, or an absurd approbation of this horrid action, as of what was noble, magnanimous, and great.   Our heart, I imagine, at the sight of such a spectator, would forget for a while its sympathy with the sufferer, and feel nothing but horror and detestation, at the thought of so execrable a wretch.   We should abominate him even more than the tyrant who might be goaded on by the strong passions of jealousy, fear, and resentment, and upon that account be more excusable.   But the sentiments of the spectator would appear altogether without cause or motive, and therefore most perfectly and completely detestable.   There is no perversion of sentiment or affection which our heart would be more averse to enter into, or which it would reject with greater hatred and indignation than one of this kind ; and so far from regarding such a constitution of mind as being merely something strange or inconvenient, and not in any respect vicious or morally evil, we should rather consider it as the very last and most dreadful stage of depravity.

Correct moral sentiments, on the contrary, naturally appear in some degree laudable and morally good.   The man, whose censure and applause are upon all occasions suited with the greatest accuracy to the value or unworthiness of the object, seems to deserve a degree even of moral approbation.   We admire the delicate precision of his moral sentiments : they lead our own judgments, and, upon account of their uncommon and surprising justness, they even excite our wonder and applause.   We cannot indeed be always sure that the conduct of such a person would be in any respect correspondent to the precision and accuracy of his judgment concerning the conduct of others.   Virtue requires habit and resolution of mind, as well as delicacy of sentiment ; and unfortunately the former qualities are sometimes wanting, where the latter is in the greatest perfection.   This disposition of mind. however, though it may sometimes be attended with imperfections, is incompatible with any thing that is grossly criminal, and is the happiest foundation upon which the superstructure of perfect virtue can be built.   There are many men who mean very well, and seriously purpose to do what they think their duty, who notwithstanding are disagreeable because of the coarseness of their moral sentiments.

It may be said, perhaps, that though the principle of approbation is not founded upon any perception that is in any respect analogous to the external senses, it may still be founded upon a peculiar sentiment which answers this one particular purpose and no other.   Approbation and disapprobation, it may be pretended, are certain feelings or emotions which arise in the mind upon the view of different characters and actions ; and as resentment might be called a sense of injuries, or gratitude a sense of benefits, so these may very properly receive the name of a sense of right and wrong, or of a moral sense.

But this account of things, though it may not be liable to the same objections with the foregoing, is exposed to others which may be equally unanswerable.

First of all, whatever variations any particular emotion may undergo, it still preserves the general features which distinguish it to be an emotion of such a kind, and these general features are always more striking and remarkable than any variation which it may undergo in particular cases. Thus anger is an emotion of a particular kind : and accordingly its general features are always more distinguishable than all the variations it undergoes in particular cases. Anger against a man is, no doubt, somewhat different from anger against a woman, and that again from anger against a child. In each of those three cases, the general passion of anger receives a different modification from the particular character of its object, as may easily be observed by the attentive. But still the general features of the passion predominate in all these cases. To distinguish these, requires no nice observation : a very delicate attention, on the contrary, is necessary to discover their variations : every body takes notice of the former ; scarce any body observes the latter. If approbation and disapprobation, therefore, were, like gratitude and resentment, emotions of a particular kind, distinct from every other, we should expect that in all the variations which either of them might undergo, it would still retain the general features which mark it to be an emotion of such a particular kind, clear, plain and easily distinguishable. But in fact it happens quite otherwise. If we attend to what we really feel when upon different occasions we either approve or disapprove, we shall find that our emotion in one case is often totally different from that in another, and that no common features can possibly be discovered between them. Thus the approbation with which we view a tender, delicate, and humane sentiment, is quite different from that with which we are struck by one that appears great, daring, and magnanimous. Our approbation of both may, upon different occasions, be perfect and entire ; but we are softened by the one, and we are elevated by the other, and there is no sort of resemblance between the emotions which they excite in us. But, according to that system which I have been endeavouring to establish, this must necessarily be the case. As the emotions of the person whom we approve of, are, in those two cases, quite opposite to one another, and as our approbation arises from sympathy with those opposite emotions, what we feel upon the one occasion, can have no sort of resemblance to what we feel upon the other. But this could not happen if approbation consisted in a peculiar emotion which had nothing in common with the sentiments we approved of, but which arose at the view of those sentiments, like any other passion at the view of its proper object. The same thing holds true with regard to disapprobation. Our horror for cruelty has no sort of resemblance to our contempt for mean-

spiritedness.   It is quite a different species of discord which we feel at
the view of those two different vices, between our own minds and those
of the person whose sentiments and behaviour we consider.

Secondly, I have already observed, that not only the different
passions or affections of the human mind which are approved or disapproved of, appear morally good or evil, but that proper and improper
approbation appear, to our natural sentiments, to be stamped with the
same characters.   I would ask, therefore, how it is, that, according to
this system, we approve or disapprove of proper or improper approbation?   To this question there is, I imagine, but one reasonable answer
which can possibly be given.   It must be said, that when the approbation with which our neighbour regards the conduct of a third person
coincides with our own, we approve of his approbation, and consider it
as, in some measure, morally good ; and that, on the contrary, when it
does not coincide with our own sentiments, we disapprove of it, and
consider it as, in some measure, morally evil.   It must be allowed,
therefore, that, at least in this one case, the coincidence or opposition
of sentiment, between the observer and the person observed, constitutes
moral approbation or disapprobation.   And if it does so in this one
case, I would ask, why not in every other? to what purpose imagine a
new power of perception in order to account for those sentiments ?

Against every account of the principle of approbation, which makes
it depend upon a peculiar sentiment, distinct from every other, I would
object that it is strange that this sentiment, which Providence undoubtedly intended to be the governing principle of human nature,
should hitherto have been so little taken notice of, as not to have got a
name in any language.   The word Moral Sense is of very late formation, and cannot yet be considered as making part of the English
tongue.   The word Approbation has but within these few years been
appropriated to denote peculiarly any thing of this kind.   In propriety
of language we approve of whatever is entirely to our satisfaction, of
the form of a building, of the contrivance of a machine, of the flavour
of a dish of meat.   The word Conscience does not immediately denote
any moral faculty by which we approve or disapprove.   Conscience
supposes, indeed, the existence of some such faculty, and properly signifies our consciousness of having acted agreeably or contrary to its
directions.   When love, hatred, joy, sorrow, gratitude, resentment,
with so many other passions which are all supposed to be the subjects
of this principle, have made themselves considerable enough to get
titles to know them by, is it not surprising that the sovereign of them
all should hitherto have been so little heeded, that, a few philosophers
excepted, nobody has yet thought it worth while to bestow a name
upon that principle.

When we approve of any character or action, the sentiments which
we feel, are, according to the foregoing system, derived from four

sources, which are in some respects different from one another. First, we sympathize with the motives of the agent; secondly, we enter into the gratitude of those who receive the benefit of his actions; thirdly, we observe that his conduct has been agreeable to the general rules by which those two sympathies generally act; and, last of all, when we consider such actions as making a part of a system of behaviour which tends to promote the happiness either of the individual or of the society, they appear to derive a beauty from this utility, not unlike that which we ascribe to any well-contrived machine. After deducting, in any one particular case, all that must be acknowledged to proceed from some one or other of these four principles, I should be glad to know what remains, and I shall freely allow this overplus to be ascribed to a moral sense, or to any other peculiar faculty, provided any body will ascertain precisely what this overplus is. It might be expected, perhaps, that if there was any such peculiar principle, such as this moral sense is supposed to be, we should feel it, in some particular cases, separated and detached from every other, as we often feel joy, sorrow, hope, and fear, pure and unmixed with any other emotion. This, however, I imagine, cannot even be pretended. I have never heard any instance alleged in which this principle could be said to exert itself alone and unmixed with sympathy or antipathy, with gratitude or resentment, with the perception of the agreement or disagreement of any action to an established rule, or last of all, with that general taste for beauty and order which is excited by inanimated as well as by animated objects.

II. There is another system which attempts to account for the origin of our moral sentiments from sympathy, distinct from that which I have been endeavouring to establish. It is that which places virtue in utility, and accounts for the pleasure with which the spectator surveys the utility of any quality from sympathy with the happiness of those who are affected by it. This sympathy is different both from that by which we enter into the motives of the agent, and from that by which we go along with the gratitude of the persons who are benefited by his actions. It is the same principle with that by which we approve of a well-contrived machine. But no machine can be the object of either of those two last-mentioned sympathies. I have already, in the fourth part of this discourse, given some account of this system.

SEC. IV.—OF THE MANNER IN WHICH DIFFERENT AUTHORS HAVE
TREATED OF THE PRACTICAL RULES OF MORALITY.

IT was observed in the third part of this discourse, that the rules of justice are the only rules of morality which are precise and accurate; that those of all the other virtues are loose, vague, and indeterminate;

that the first may be compared to the rules of grammar ; the others to those which critics lay down for the attainment of what is sublime and elegant in composition, and which present us rather with a general idea of the perfection we ought to aim at, than afford us any certain and infallible directions for acquiring it.

As the different rules of morality admit such different degrees of accuracy, those authors who have endeavoured to collect and digest them into systems have done it in two different manners ; and one set has followed through the whole that loose method to which they were naturally directed by the consideration of one species of virtues; while another has as universally endeavoured to introduce into their precepts that sort of accuracy of which only some of them are susceptible. The first have written like critics, the second like grammarians.

I. The first, among whom we may count all the ancient moralists, have contented themselves with describing in a general manner the different vices and virtues, and with pointing out the deformity and misery of the one disposition, as well as the propriety and happiness of the other, but have not affected to lay down many precise rules that are to hold good unexceptionally in all particular cases. They have only endeavoured to ascertain, as far as language is capable of ascertaining, first, wherein consists the sentiment of the heart, upon which each particular virtue is founded, what sort of internal feeling or emotion it is which constitutes the essence of friendship, of humanity, of generosity, of justice, of magnanimity, and of all the other virtues, as well as of the vices which are opposed to them : and, secondly, what is the general way of acting, the ordinary tone and tenor of conduct to which each of those sentiments would direct us, or how it is that a friendly, a generous, a brave, a just, and a humane man, would upon ordinary occasions, choose to act.

To characterize the sentiment of the heart, upon which each particular virtue is founded, though it requires both a delicate and an accurate pencil, is a task, however, which may be executed with some degree of exactness. It is impossible, indeed, to express all the variations which each sentiment either does or ought to undergo, according to every possible variation of circumstances. They are endless, and language wants names to mark them by. The sentiment of friendship, for example, which we feel for an old man is different from that which we feel for a young : that which we entertain for an austere man different from that which we feel for one of softer and gentler manners : and that again from what we feel for one of gay vivacity and spirit. The friendship which we conceive for a man is different from that with which a woman affects us, even where there is no mixture of any grosser passion. What author could enumerate and ascertain these and all the other infinite varieties which this sentiment is capable of undergoing ? But still the general sentiment of friendship and familiar attachment which is common to them all, may be ascertained with a sufficient degree of accuracy. The picture which is drawn of it, though it will always be in many respects incomplete, may, however, have such a resemblance as to make us know the original when we meet with it, and even distinguish it from other sentiments to which it has a considerable resemblance, such as good-will, respect, admiration.

To describe, in a general manner, what is the ordinary way of acting to which each virtue would prompt us, is still more easy. It is, indeed, scarce possible to describe the internal sentiment or emotion upon which it is founded, without doing something of this kind. It is impossible by language to express, if I may say so, the invisible features of all the different modifications of passion as they show themselves within. There is no other way of marking and distinguishing them from one another, but by describing the effects which they produce without, the alterations which they occasion in the countenance, in the air and external behaviour, the resolutions they suggest, the actions they prompt to. It is thus that Cicero, in the first book of his Offices, endeavours to direct us to the practice of the four cardinal virtues, and that Aristotle in the practical parts of his Ethics, points out to us the different habits by which he would have us regulate our behaviour, such as liberality, magnificence, magnanimity, and even jocularity and good humour, qualities which that indulgent philosopher has thought worthy of a place in the catalogue of the virtues, though the lightness of that approbation which we naturally bestow upon them, should not seem to entitle them to so venerable a name.

Such works present us with agreeable and lively pictures of manners. By the vivacity of their descriptions they inflame our natural love of virtue, and increase our abhorrence of vice: by the justness as well as delicacy of their observations they may often help both to correct and to ascertain our natural sentiments with regard to the propriety of conduct, and suggesting many nice and delicate attentions, form us to a more exact justness of behaviour, than what, without such instruction, we should have been apt to think of. In treating of the rules of morality, in this manner, consists the science which is properly called Ethics, a science which, though like criticism, it does not admit of the most accurate precision, is, however, both highly useful and agreeable. It is of all others the most susceptible of the embellishments of eloquence, and by means of them of bestowing, if that be possible, a new importance upon the smallest rules of duty. Its precepts, when thus dressed and adorned, are capable of producing upon the flexibility of youth, the noblest and most lasting impressions, and as they fall in with the natural magnanimity of that generous age, they are able to inspire, for a time at least, the most heroic resolutions, and thus tend both to establish and confirm the best and most useful habits of which the mind of man is susceptible. Whatever precept and exhortation can do to animate us to the practice of virtue, is done by this science delivered in this manner.

II. The second set of moralists, among whom we may count all the casuists of the middle and latter ages of the Christian church, as well as all those who in this and in the preceding century have treated of what is called natural jurisprudence, do not content themselves with characterizing in this general manner that tenor of conduct which they would recommend to us, but endeavour to lay down exact and precise rules for the direction of every circumstance of our behaviour. As justice is the only virtue with regard to which such exact rules can properly be given; it is this virtue, that has chiefly fallen under the consideration of those two different sets of writers. They treat of it, however, in a very different manner.

Those who write upon the principles of jurisprudence, consider only what the person to whom the obligation is due, ought to think himself entitled to exact by force; what every impartial spectator would approve of him for exacting, or what a judge or arbiter, to whom he had submitted his case, and who had undertaken to do him justice, ought to oblige the other person to suffer or to perform. The casuists, on the other hand, do not so much examine what it is, that might properly be exacted by force, as what it is, that the person who owes the obligation ought to think himself bound to perform from the most sacred and scrupulous regard to the general rules of justice, and from the most conscientious dread, either of wronging his neighbour, or of violating the integrity of his own character. It is the end of jurisprudence to prescribe rules for the decisions of judges and arbiters. It is the end of casuistry to prescribe rules for the conduct of a good man. By observing all the rules of jurisprudence, supposing them ever so perfect, we should deserve nothing but to be free from external punishment. By observing those of casuistry, supposing them such as they ought to be, we should be entitled to considerable praise by the exact and scrupulous delicacy of our behaviour.

It may frequently happen that a good man ought to think himself bound, from a sacred and conscientious regard to the general rules of justice, to perform many things which it would be the highest injustice to extort from him, or for any judge or arbiter to impose upon him by force. To give a trite example; a highwayman, by the fear of death, obliges a traveller to promise him a certain sum money. Whether such a promise, extorted in this manner by force, ought to be regarded as obligatory, is a question that has been much debated.

If we consider it merely as a question of jurisprudence, the decision can admit of no doubt. It would be absurd to suppose that the highwayman can be entitled to use force to constrain the other to perform. To extort the promise was a crime which deserved the highest punishment, and to extort the performance would only be adding a new crime to the former. He can complain of no injury who has been only deceived by the person by whom he might justly have been killed. To suppose that a judge ought to enforce the obligation of such promises, or that the magistrate ought to allow them to sustain action at law, would be the most ridiculous of all absurdities. If we consider this question, therefore, as a question of jurisprudence, we can be at no loss about the decision.

But if we consider it as a question of casuistry, it will not be so easily determined. Whether a good man, from a conscientious regard to that most sacred rule of justice, which commands the observance of all serious promises, would not think himself bound to perform, is at least much more doubtful. That no regard is due to the disappointment of the wretch who brings him into this situation, that no injury is done to the robber, and consequently that nothing can be extorted by force, will admit of no sort of dispute. But whether some regard is not, in this case, due to his own dignity and honour, to the inviolable sacredness of that part of his character which makes him reverence the law of truth and abhor every thing that approaches to treachery and false-hood, may, perhaps, more reasonably be made a question. The casuists accordingly are greatly divided about it. One party, with whom we may count Cicero among the ancients, among the moderns, Puffendorf, Barbeyrac his commentator, and above all the late Dr. Hutcheson, one who in most cases was by no means a loose casuist, determine, without any hesitation, that no sort of regard is due to any such promise, and that to think otherwise is mere weakness and superstition. Another party, among whom we may reckon (St. Augustine, La Placette) some of the ancient fathers of the church, as well as some very eminent modern casuists, have been of another opinion, and have judged all such promises obligatory.

If we consider the matter according to the common sentiments of mankind, we shall find that some regard would be thought due even to a promise of this kind; but that it is impossible to determine how much, by any general rule that will apply to all cases without exception. The man who was quite frank and easy in making promises of this kind, and who violated them with as little ceremony, we should not choose for our friend and companion. A gentleman who should promise a highwayman five pounds and not perform, would incur some blame. If the sum promised, however, was very great, it might be more doubtful what was proper to be done. If it was such, for example, that the payment of it would entirely ruin the family of the promiser, if it was so great as to be sufficient for promoting the most useful purposes, it would appear in some measure criminal, at least extremely improper, to throw it for the sake of a punctilio into such worthless hands. The man who should beggar himself, or who should throw away an hundred thousand pounds, though he could afford that vast sum, for the sake of observing such a parole with a thief, would appear to the common sense of mankind, absurd and extravagant in the highest degree.   Such profusion would seem inconsistent with his duty, with what he owed both to himself and others, and what, therefore, regard to a promise extorted in this manner, could by no means authorise.   To fix, however, by any precise rule, what degree of regard ought to be paid to it, or what might be the greatest sum which could be due from it, is evidently impossible.   This would vary according to the characters of the persons, according to their circumstances, according to the solemnity of the promise, and even according to the incidents of the rencounter: and if the promiser had been treated with a great deal of that sort of gallantry, which is sometimes to be met with in persons of the most abandoned characters, more would seem due than upon other occasions.   It may be said in general, that exact propriety requires the observance of all such promises, wherever it is not inconsistent with some other duties that are more sacred; such as regard to the public interest, to those whom gratitude, whom natural affection, or whom the laws of proper beneficence should prompt us to provide for.   But, as was formerly taken notice of, we have no precise rules to determine what external actions are due from a regard to such motives, nor, consequently, when it is that those virtues are inconsistent with the observance of such promises.

It is to be observed, however, that whenever such promises are violated, though for the most necessary reasons, it is always with some degree of dishonour to the person who made them.   After they are made, we may be convinced of the impropriety of observing them.   But still there is some fault in having made them.   It is at least a departure from the highest and noblest maxims of magnanimity and honour.   A brave man ought to die, rather than make a promise which he can neither keep without folly, nor violate without ignominy.   For some degree of ignominy always attends a situation of this kind.   Treachery and falsehood are vices so dangerous, so dreadful, and, at the same time, such as may so easily, and, upon many occasions, so safely be indulged, that we are more jealous of them than of almost any other.   Our imagination therefore attaches the idea of shame to all violations of faith, in every circumstance and in every situation.   They resemble, in this respect, the violations of chastity in the fair sex, a virtue of which, for the like reasons, we are excessively jealous; and our sentiments are not more delicate with regard to the one, than with regard to the other.   Breach of chastity dishonours irretrievably.   No circumstances, no solicitation can excuse it; no sorrow, no repentance atone for it.   We are so nice in this respect that even a rape dishonours, and the innocence of the mind cannot, in our imagination, wash out the pollution of the body.   It is the same case with the violation of faith, when it has been solemnly pledged, even to the most worthless of mankind. Fidelity is so necessary a virtue, that we apprehend it in general to be due even to those to whom nothing else is due, and whom we think it lawful to kill and destroy. It is to no purpose that the person who has been guilty of the breach of it, urges that he promised in order to save his life, and that he broke his promise because it was inconsistent with some other respectable duty to keep it. These circumstances may alleviate, but cannot entirely wipe out his dishonour. He appears to have been guilty of an action with which, in the imaginations of men, some degree of shame is inseparably connected. He has broken a promise which he had solemnly averred he would maintain; and his character, if not irretrievably stained and polluted, has at least a ridicule affixed to it, which it will be very difficult entirely to efface; and no man, I imagine, who had gone through an adventure of this kind would be fond of telling the story.

This instance may serve to show wherein consists the difference between casuistry and jurisprudence, even when both of them consider the obligations of the general rules of justice.

But though this difference be real and essential, though those two sciences propose quite different ends, the sameness of the subject has made such a similarity between them, that the greater part of authors whose professed design was to treat of jurisprudence, have determined the different questions they examine, sometimes according to the principles of that science, and sometimes according to those of casuistry, without distinguishing, and, perhaps, without being themselves aware, when they did the one, and when the other.

The doctrine of the casuists, however, is by no means confined to the consideration of what a conscientious regard to the general rules of justice would demand of us. It embraces many other parts of Christian and moral duty. What seems principally to have given occasion to the cultivation of this species of science was the custom of auricular confession, introduced by the Roman Catholic superstition, in times of barbarism and ignorance. By that institution, the most secret actions, and even the thoughts of every person, which could be suspected of receding in the smallest degree from the rules of Christian purity, were to be revealed to the confessor. The confessor informed his penitents whether, and in what respect, they had violated their duty, and what penance it behoved them to undergo, before he could absolve them in the name of the offended Deity.

The consciousness, or even the suspicion of having done wrong, is a load upon every mind, and is accompanied with anxiety and terror in all those who are not hardened by long habits of iniquity. Men, in this, as in all other distresses, are naturally eager to disburthen themselves of the oppression which they feel upon their thoughts, by unbosoming the agony of their mind to some person whose secrecy and discretion they can confide in. The shame, which they suffer from this acknowledgment, is fully compensated by that alleviation of their uneasiness which the sympathy of their confidence seldom fails to occasion. It relieves them to find that they are not altogether unworthy of regard, and that however their past conduct may be censured, their present disposition is at least approved of, and is perhaps sufficient to compensate the other, at least to maintain them in some degree of esteem with their friend. A numerous and artful clergy had, in those times of superstition, insinuated themselves into the confidence of almost every private family. They possessed all the little learning which the times could afford, and their manners, though in many respects rude and disorderly, were polished and regular compared with those of the age they lived in. They were regarded, therefore, not only as the great directors of all religious, but of all moral duties. Their familiarity gave reputation to whoever was so happy as to possess it, and every mark of their disapprobation stamped the deepest ignominy upon all who had the misfortune to fall under it. Being considered as the great judges of right and wrong, they were naturally consulted about all scruples that occurred, and it was reputable for any person to have it known that he made those holy men the confidants of all such secrets, and took no important or delicate step in his conduct without their advice and approbation. It was not difficult for the clergy, therefore, to get it established as a general rule, that they should be entrusted with what it had already become fashionable to entrust them, and with what they generally would have been entrusted, though no such rule had been established. To qualify themselves for confessors became thus a necessary part of the study of churchmen and divines, and they were thence led to collect what are called cases of conscience, nice and delicate situations in which it is hard to determine whereabouts the propriety of conduct may lie. Such works, they imagined, might be of use both to the directors of consciences and to those who were to be directed; and hence the origin of books of casuistry.

The moral duties which fell under the consideration of the casuists were chiefly those which can, in some measure at least, be circumscribed within general rules, and of which the violation is naturally attended with some degree of remorse and some dread of suffering punishment. The design of that institution which gave occasion to their works, was to appease those terrors of conscience which attend upon the infringement of such duties. But it is not every virtue of which the defect is accompanied with any very severe compunctions of this kind, and no man applies to his confessor for absolution, because he did not perform the most generous, the most friendly, or the most magnanimous action which, in his circumstances, it was possible to perform. In failures of this kind, the rule that is violated is commonly not very determinate, and is generally of such a nature too, that though the observance of it might entitle to honour and reward, the violation seems to expose to no positive blame, censure, or punishment. The exercise of such virtues the casuists seem to have regarded as a sort of works of supererogation, which could not be very strictly exacted, and which it was therefore unnecessary for them to treat of.

The breaches of moral duty, therefore, which came before the tribunal of the confessor, and upon that account fell under the cognisance of the casuists, were chiefly of three different kinds.

First and principally, breaches of the rules of justice. The rules here are all express and positive, and the violation of them is naturally attended with the consciousness of deserving, and the dread of suffering punishment both from God and man.

Secondly, breaches of the rules of chastity. These in all grosser instances are real breaches of the rules of justice, and no person can be guilty of them without doing the most unpardonable injury to some other. In smaller instances, when they amount only to a violation of those exact decorums which ought to be observed in the conversation of the two sexes, they cannot indeed justly be considered as violations of the rules of justice. They are generally, however, violations of a pretty plain rule, and, at least in one of the sexes, tend to bring ignominy upon the person who has been guilty of them, and consequently to be attended in the scrupulous with some degree of shame and contrition of mind.

Thirdly, breaches of the rules of veracity. The violation of truth, it is to be observed, is not always a breach of justice, though it is so upon many occasions, and consequently cannot always expose to any external punishment. The vice of common lying, though a most miserable meanness, may frequently do hurt to nobody, and in this case no claim of vengeance or satisfaction can be due either to the persons imposed upon, or to others. But though the violation of truth is not always a breach of justice, it is always a breach of a very plain rule, and what does naturally tend to cover with shame the person who has been guilty of it.

There seems to be in young children an instinctive disposition to believe whatever they are told. Nature seems to have judged it necessary for their preservation that they should, for some time at least, put implicit confidence in those to whom the care of their childhood, and of the earliest and most necessary parts of their education, is intrusted. Their credulity, accordingly, is excessive, and it requires long and much experience of the falsehood of mankind to reduce them to a reasonable degree of diffidence and distrust. In grown-up people the degrees of credulity are, no doubt, very different. The wisest and most experienced are generally the least credulous. But the man scarce lives who is not more credulous than he ought to be, and who does not, upon many occasions, give credit to tales, which not only turn out to be perfectly false, but which a very moderate degree of reflection and attention might have taught him could not well be true. The natural disposition is always to believe. It is acquired wisdom and experience only that teach incredulity, and they very seldom teach it enough. The wisest and most cautious of us all frequently gives credit to stories which he himself is afterwards both ashamed and astonished that he could possibly think of believing.

The man whom we believe is necessarily, in the things concerning which we believe him, our leader and director, and we look up to him with a certain degree of esteem and respect. But as from admiring other people we come to wish to be admired ourselves ; so from being led and directed by other people we learn to wish to become ourselves leaders and directors. And as we cannot always be satisfied merely with being admired, unless we can at the same time persuade ourselves that we are in some degree really worthy of admiration; so we cannot always be satisfied merely with being believed, unless we are at the same time conscious that we are really worthy of belief. As the desire of praise and that of praise-worthiness, though very much akin, are yet distinct and separate desires ; so the desire of being believed and that of being worthy of belief, though very much akin too, are equally distinct and separate desires.

The desire of being believed, the desire of persuading, of leading and directing other people, seems to be one of the strongest of all our natural desires. It is, perhaps, the instinct upon which is founded the faculty of speech, the characteristical faculty of human nature. No other animal possesses this faculty, and we cannot discover in any other animal any desire to lead and direct the judgment and conduct of its fellows. Great ambition, the desire of real superiority, of leading and directing, seems to be altogether peculiar to man, and speech is the great instrument of ambition, of real superiority, of leading and directing the judgments and conduct of other people.

It is always mortifying not to be believed, and it is doubly so when we suspect that it is because we are supposed to be unworthy of belief and capable of seriously and wilfully deceiving. To tell a man that he lies, is of all affronts the most mortal. But whoever seriously and wilfully deceives is necessarily conscious to himself that he merits this affront, that he does not deserve to be believed, and that he forfeits all title to that sort of credit from which alone he can derive any sort of ease, comfort, or satisfaction in the society of his equals. The man who had the misfortune to imagine that nobody believed a single word he said, would feel himself the outcast of human society, would dread the very thought of going into it, or of presenting himself before it, and could scarce fail, I think, to die of despair. It is probable, however, that no man ever had just reason to entertain this humiliating opinion of himself. The most notorious liar, I am disposed to believe, tells the fair truth at least twenty times for once that he seriously and deliberately lies ; and, as in the most cautious the disposition to believe is apt to prevail over that to doubt and distrust ; so in those who are the most regardless of truth, the natural disposition to tell it prevails upon most occasions over that to deceive, or in any respect to alter or to disguise it.

We are mortified when we happen to deceive other people, though unintentionally, and from having been ourselves deceived. Though this involuntary falsehood may frequently be no mark of any want of veracity, of any want of the most perfect love of truth, it is always in some degree a mark of want of judgment, of want of memory, of improper credulity, of some degree of precipitancy and rashness. It always diminishes our authority to persuade, and always brings some degree of suspicion upon our fitness to lead and direct. The man who sometimes misleads from mistake, however, is widely different from him who is capable of wilfully deceiving. The former may be trusted upon many occasions ; the latter very seldom upon any.

Frankness and openness conciliate confidence. We trust the man, who seems willing to trust us. We see clearly, we think, the road by which he means to conduct us, and we abandon ourselves with pleasure to his guidance and direction. Reserve and concealment, on the contrary, call forth diffidence. We are afraid to follow the man who is going we do not know where. The great pleasure of conversation and society, besides, arises from a certain correspondence of sentiments and opinions, from a certain harmony of minds, which like so many musical instruments coincide and keep time with one another. But this most delightful harmony cannot be obtained unless there is a free communication of sentiments and opinions. We all desire, upon this account, to feel how each other is affected, to penetrate into each other's bosoms, and to observe the sentiments and affections which really subsist there. The man who indulges us in this natural passion, who invites us into his heart, who, as it were, sets open the gates of his breast to us, seems to exercise a species of hospitality more delightful than any other. No man, who is in ordinary good temper, can fail of pleasing, if he has the courage to utter his real sentiments as he feels them, and because he feels them. It is this unreserved sincerity which renders even the prattle of a child agreeable. How weak and imperfect soever the views of the open-hearted, we take pleasure to enter into them, and endeavour, as much as we can, to bring down our own understanding to the level of their capacities, and to regard every subject in the particular light in which they appear to have considered it. This passion to discover the real sentiments of others is naturally so strong, that it often degenerates into a troublesome and impertinent curiosity to pry into those secrets of our neighbours which they have very justifiable reasons for concealing ; and, upon many occasions, it requires prudence and a strong sense of propriety to govern this, as well as all the other passions of human nature, and to reduce it to that pitch which any impartial spectator can approve of. To disappoint this curiosity, however, when it is kept within proper bounds, and aims at nothing which there can be any just reason for concealing, is equally disagreeable in its turn. The man who eludes our most innocent questions, who gives no satisfaction to our most inoffensive inquiries, who plainly wraps himself up in impenetrable obscurity, seems, as it were, to build a wall about his breast. We run forward to get within it, with all the eagerness of harmless curiosity ; and feel ourselves all at once pushed back with rude and offensive violence.

The man of reserve and concealment, though seldom a very amiable character, is not disrespected or despised. He seems to feel coldly towards us, and we feel as coldly towards him. He is not much praised or beloved, but he is as little hated or blamed. He very seldom, however, has occasion to repent of his caution, and is generally disposed rather to value himself upon the prudence of his reserve. Though his conduct, therefore, may have been very faulty, and sometimes even hurtful, he can very seldom be disposed to lay his case before the casuists, or to fancy that he has any occasion for their acquittal or for their approbation.

It is not always so with the man, who, from false information, from inadvertency, from precipitancy and rashness, has involuntarily deceived. Though it should be in a matter of little consequence, in telling a piece of common news, for example, if he is a real lover of truth, he is ashamed of his own carelessness, and never fails to embrace the first opportunity of making the fullest acknowledgments. If it is in a matter of some consequence, his contrition is still greater; and if any unlucky or fatal consequence has followed from his misinformation, he can scarce ever forgive himself. Though not guilty, he feels himself to be in the highest degree, what the ancients called, piacular, and is anxious and eager to make every sort of atonement in his power. Such a person might frequently be disposed to lay his case before the casuists, who have in general been very favourable to him, and though they have sometimes justly condemned him for rashness, they have universally acquitted him of the ignominy of falsehood.

But the man who had the most frequent occasion to consult them, was the man of equivocation and mental reservation, the man who seriously and deliberately meant to deceive, but who, at the same time, wished to flatter himself that he had really told the truth. With him they have dealt variously. When they approved very much of the motives of his deceit, they have sometimes acquitted him, though, to do the casuists justice, they have in general and much more frequently condemned him.

The chief subjects of the works of the casuists, therefore, were the conscientious regard that is due to the rules of justice; how far we ought to respect the life and property of our neighbour; the duty of restitution; the laws of chastity and modesty, and wherein consisted what, in the language of the casuists, were called the sins of concupiscence; the rules of veracity, and the obligation of oaths, promises, and contracts of all kinds.

It may be said in general of the works of the casuists that they attempted, to no purpose, to direct by precise rules what it belongs to feeling and sentiment only to judge of. How is it possible to ascertain by rules the exact point at which, in every case, a delicate sense of justice begins to run into a frivolous and weak scrupulosity of conscience? When is it that secrecy and reserve begin to grow into dissimulation? How far may an agreeable irony be carried, and at what precise point it begins to degenerate into a detestable lie? What is the highest pitch of freedom and ease of behaviour which can be regarded as graceful and becoming, and when is it that it first begins to run into a negligent and thoughtless licentiousness? With regard to all such matters, what would hold good in any one case would scarce do so exactly in any other, and what constitutes the propriety and happiness of behaviour varies in every case with the smallest variety of situation. Books of casuistry, therefore, are generally as useless as they are commonly tiresome. They could be of little use to one who should consult them upon occasion, even supposing their decisions to be just; because, notwithstanding the multitude of cases collected in them, yet upon account of the still greater variety of possible circumstances, it is a chance, if among all those cases there be found one exactly parallel to that under consideration. One, who is really anxious to do his duty, must be very weak, if he can imagine that he has much occasion for them; and with regard to one who is negligent of it, the very style of those writings is not such as is likely to awaken him to more attention. None of them tend to animate us to what is generous and noble. None of them do tend to soften us to what is gentle and humane. Many of them, on the contrary, tend rather to teach us to chicane with our own consciences, and by their vain subtilties serve to authorise innumerable evasive refinements with regard to the most essential articles of our duty. That frivolous accuracy which they attempted to introduce into subjects which do not admit of it, almost necessarily betrayed them into those dangerous errors, and at the same time rendered their works dry and disagreeable, abounding in abstruse and metaphysical distinctions, but incapable of exciting in the heart any of those emotions which it is the principal use of books of morality to excite in the readers.

The two useful parts of moral philosophy, therefore, are Ethics and Jurisprudence: casuistry ought to be rejected altogether; and the ancient moralists appear to have judged much better, who, in treating of the same subjects, did not affect any such nice exactness, but contented themselves with describing, in a general manner, what is the sentiment upon which justice, modesty, and veracity are founded, and what is the ordinary way of acting to which those great virtues would commonly prompt us.

Something indeed, not unlike the doctrine of the casuists, seems to have been attempted by several philosophers. There is something of this kind in the third book of Cicero's Offices, where he endeavours like a casuist, to give rules for our conduct in many nice cases, in which it is difficult to determine whereabouts the point of propriety may lie. It appears too, from many passages in the same book, that several other philosophers had attempted something of the same kind before him. Neither he nor they, however, appear to have aimed at giving a complete system of this sort, but only meant to show how situations may occur, in which it is doubtful, whether the highest propriety of conduct consists in observing or in receding from what, in ordinary cases, are the rules of our duty.

Every system of positive law may be regarded as a more or less imperfect attempt towards a system of natural jurisprudence, or towards an enumeration of the particular rules of justice. As the violation of justice is what men will never submit to from one another, the public magistrate is under a necessity of employing the power of the commonwealth to enforce the practice of this virtue. Without this precaution, civil society would become a scene of bloodshed and disorder, every man revenging himself at his own hand whenever he fancied he was injured. To prevent the confusion which would attend upon every man's doing justice to himself, the magistrate, in all governments that have acquired any considerable authority, undertakes to do justice to all, and promises to hear and to redress every complaint of injury. In all well-governed states, too, not only judges are appointed for determining the controversies of individuals, but rules are prescribed for regulating the decisions of those judges ; and these rules are, in general, intended to coincide with those of natural justice. It does not, indeed, always happen that they do so in every instance. Sometimes what is called the constitution of the state, that is, the interest of the government ; sometimes the interest of particular orders of men who tyrannize the government, warp the positive laws of the country from what natural justice would prescribe. In some countries, the rudeness and barbarism of the people hinder the natural sentiments of justice from arriving at that accuracy and precision which, in more civilized nations, they naturally attain to. Their laws are, like their manners, gross and rude and undistinguishing. In other countries the unfortunate constitution of their courts of judicature hinders any regular system of jurisprudence from ever establishing itself among them, though the improved manners of the people may be such as would admit of the most accurate. In no country do the decisions of positive law coincide exactly, in every case, with the rules which the natural sense of justice would dictate. Systems of positive law, therefore, though they deserve the greatest authority, as the records of the sentiments of mankind in different ages and nations, yet can never be regarded as accurate systems of the rules of natural justice.

It might have been expected that the reasonings of lawyers, upon the different imperfections and improvements of the laws of different countries, should have given occasion to an inquiry into what were the natural rules of justice independent of all positive institution. It might have been expected that these reasonings should have led them to aim at establishing a system of what might properly be called natural jurisprudence, or a theory of the general principles which ought to run through and be the foundation of the laws of all nations. But though the reasonings of lawyers did produce something of this kind, and though no man has treated systematically of the laws of any particular country, without intermixing in his work many observations of this sort ; it was very late in the world before any such general system was thought of, or before the philosophy of law was treated of by itself, and without regard to the particular institutions of any one nation. In none of the ancient moralists, do we find any attempt towards a particular enumeration of the rules of justice. Cicero in his Offices, and Aristotle in his Ethics, treat of justice in the same general manner in which they treat of all the other virtues. In the laws of Cicero and Plato, where we might naturally have expected some attempts towards an enumeration of those rules of natural equity, which ought to be enforced by the positive laws of every country, there is, however. nothing of this kind. Their laws are laws of police, not of justice. Grotius seems to have been the first who attempted to give the world any thing like a system of those principles which ought to run through, and be the foundation of the laws of all nations ; and his treatise of the laws of war and peace, with all its imperfections, is perhaps at this day the most complete work that has yet been given upon this subject. I shall in another discourse endeavour to give an account of the general principles of law and government, and of the different revolutions they have undergone in the different ages and periods of society, not only in what concerns justice, but in what concerns police, revenue, and arms, and whatever else is the object of law. I shall not, therefore, at present, enter into any further detail concerning the history of jurisprudence.

CONSIDERATIONS

CONCERNING THE FIRST

FORMATION OF LANGUAGES, Etc., Etc.

THE assignation of particular names to denote particular objects, that is, the institution of nouns substantive, would, probably be one of the first steps towards the formation of language. Two savages, who had never been taught to speak, but had been bred up remote from the societies of men, would naturally begin to form that language by which they would endeavour to make their mutual wants intelligible to each other, by uttering certain sounds, whenever they meant to denote certain objects. Those objects only which were most familiar to them, and which they had most frequent occasion to mention would have particular names assigned to them. The particular cave whose covering sheltered them from the weather, the particular tree whose fruit relieved their hunger, the particular fountain whose water allayed their thirst, would first be denominated by the words *cave, tree, fountain*, or by whatever other appellations they might think proper, in that primitive jargon, to mark them. Afterwards, when the more enlarged experience of these savages had led them to observe, and their necessary occasions obliged them to make mention of other caves, and other trees, and other fountains, they would naturally bestow, upon each of those new objects, the same name, by which they had been accustomed to express the similar objects they were first acquainted with. The new objects had none of them any name of its own, but each of them exactly resembled another object, which had such an appellation. It was impossible that those savages could behold the new objects, without recollecting the old ones ; and the name of the old ones, to which the new bore so close a resemblance. When they had occasion, therefore, to mention or to point out to each other, any of the new objects, they would naturally utter the name of the correspondent old one, of which the idea could not fail, at that instant, to present itself to their memory in the strongest and liveliest manner. And thus, those words, which were originally the proper names of individuals, would each of them insensibly become the common name of a multitude. A child that is just learning to speak, calls every person who comes to the house its papa or its mamma ; and thus bestows upon the whole species those names which it had been taught to apply to two individuals. I have known a clown, who did not know the proper name of the river which ran by his own door.   It was *the river*, he said, and he never heard any other name for it.   His experience, it seems, had not led him to observe any other river.   The general word *river*, therefore, was, it is evident, in his acceptance of it, a proper name, signifying an individual object. If this person had been carried to another river, would he not readily have called it a river?   Could we suppose any person living on the banks of the Thames so ignorant as not to know the general word *river* but to be acquainted only with the particular word *Thames*, if he was brought to any other river, would he not readily call it *a Thames?* This, in reality, is no more than what they, who are well acquainted with the general word, are very apt to do.   An Englishman, describing any great river which he may have seen in some foreign country, naturally says, that it is another Thames.   The Spaniards, when they first arrived upon the coast of Mexico, and observed the wealth, populousness, and habitations of that fine country, so much superior to the savage nations which they had been visiting for some time before, cried out, that it was another Spain.   Hence it was called New Spain ; and this name has stuck to that unfortunate country ever since.   We say, in the same manner, of a hero, that he is an Alexander ; of an orator, that he is a Cicero ; of a philosopher, that he is a Newton.   This way of speaking, which the grammarians call an Antonomasia, and which is still extremely common, though now not at all necessary, demonstrates how mankind are disposed to give to one object the name of any other, which nearly resembles it, and thus to denominate a multitude, by what originally was intended to express an individual.

It is this application of the name of an individual to a great multitude of objects, whose resemblance naturally recalls the idea of that individual, and of the name which expresses it, that seems originally to have given occasion to the formation of those classes and assortments, which, in the schools, are called genera and species, and of which the ingenious and eloquent M. Rousseau of Geneva finds himself so much at a loss to account for the origin.   What constitutes a species is merely a number of objects, bearing a certain degree of resemblance to one another, and on that account denominated by a single appellation, which may be applied to express any one of them.

When the greater part of objects had thus been arranged under their proper classes and assortments, distinguished by such general names, it was impossible that the greater part of that almost infinite number of individuals, comprehended under each particular assortment or species, could have any peculiar or proper names of their own, distinct from the general name of the species.   When there was occasion, therefore, to mention any particular object, it often became necessary to distinguish it from the other objects comprehended under the same general name, either, first, by its peculiar qualities ; or, secondly, by the pecu-

liar relation which it stood in to some other things.   Hence the necessary origin of two other sets of words, of which the one should express
quality ; the other, relation.

Nouns adjective are the words which express quality considered as
qualifying, or, as the schoolmen say, in concrete with, some particular
subject.   Thus the word *green* expresses a certain quality considered
as qualifying, or as in concrete with, the particular subject to which it
may be applied.   Words of this kind, it is evident, may serve to distinguish particular objects from others comprehended under the same
general appellation.   The words *green tree*, for example, might serve
to distinguish a particular tree from others that were withered or that
were blasted.

Prepositions are the words which express relation considered, in the
same manner, in concrete with the co-relative object.   Thus the prepositions *of, to, for, with, by, above, below*, &c., denote some relation
subsisting between the objects expressed by the words between which
the prepositions are placed ; and they denote that this relation is considered in concrete with the co-relative object.   Words of this kind
serve to distinguish particular objects from others of the same species,
when those particular objects cannot be so properly marked out by any
peculiar qualities of their own.   When we say, *the green tree of the
meadow*, for example, we distinguish a particular tree, not only by the
quality which belongs to it, but by the relation which it stands in to
another object.

As neither quality nor relation can exist in abstract, it is natural to
suppose that the words which denote them considered in concrete, the
way in which we always see them subsist, would be of much earlier invention than those which express them considered in abstract, the way
in which we never see them subsist.   The words *green* and *blue* would,
in all probability, be sooner invented than the words *greenness* and *blue-
ness* ; the words *above* and *below*, than the words *superiority* and *inferiority*.   To invent words of the latter kind requires a much greater
effort of abstraction than to invent those of the former.   It is probable
therefore, that such abstract terms would be of much later institution.
Accordingly, their etymologies generally show that they are so, they
being generally derived from others that are concrete.

But though the invention of nouns adjective be much more natural
than that of the abstract nouns substantive derived from them, it would
still, however, require a considerable degree of abstraction and generalization.   Those, for example, who first invented the words *green,
blue, red*, and the other names of colours, must have observed and
compared together a great number of objects, must have remarked
their resemblances and dissimilitudes in respect of the quality of
colour, and must have arranged them, in their own minds, into different
classes and assortments, according to those resemblances and dissimili-

tudes. An adjective is by nature a general, and in some measure an abstract word, and necessarily pre-supposes the idea of a certain species or assortment of things, to all of which it is equally applicable. The word *green* could not, as we were supposing might be the case of the word *cave*, have been originally the name of an individual, and afterwards have become, by what grammarians call an Antonomasia, the name of a species. The word *green* denoting, not the name of a substance, but the peculiar quality of a substance, must from the very first have been a general word, and considered as equally applicable to any other substance possessed of the same quality. The man who first distinguished a particular object by the epithet of *green*, must have observed other objects that were not *green*, from which he meant to separate it by this appellation. The institution of this name, therefore, supposes comparison. It likewise supposes some degree of abstraction. The person who first invented this appellation must have distinguished the quality from the object to which it belonged, and must have conceived the object as capable of subsisting without the quality. The invention, therefore, even of the simplest nouns adjective must have required more metaphysics than we are apt to be aware of. The different mental operations, of arrangement or classing, of comparison, and of abstraction, must all have been employed, before even the names of the different colours, the least metaphysical of all nouns adjective, could be instituted. From all which I infer, that when languages were beginning to be formed, nouns adjective would by no means be the words of the earliest invention.

There is nothing expedient for denoting the different qualities of different substance, which as it requires no abstraction, nor any conceived separation of the quality from the subject, seems more natural than the invention of nouns adjective, and which, upon this account, could hardly fail, in the first formation of language, to be thought of before them. This expedient is to make some variation upon the noun substantive itself, according to the different qualities which it is endowed with. Thus in many languages, the qualities both of sex and of the want of sex, are expressed by different terminations in the nouns substantive, which denote objects so qualified. In Latin, for example, *lupus, lupa; equus, equa; juvencus, juvenca; Julius, Julia; Lucretius, Lucretia*, &c., denote the qualities of male and female in the animals and persons to whom such appellations belong, without needing the addition of any adjective for this purpose. On the other hand, the words *forum, pratum, plaustrum*, denote by their peculiar termination the total absence of sex in the different substances which they stand for. Both sex, and the want of all sex, being naturally considered as qualities modifying and inseparable from the particular substances to which they belong, it was natural to express them rather by a modification in the noun substantive, than by any general and abstract word expressive of this particular species of quality. The expression bears, it is evident, in this way, a much more exact analogy to the idea or object which it denotes than in the other. The quality appears, in nature, as a modification of the substance, and as it is thus expressed in language, by a modification of the noun substantive, which denotes that substance, the quality and the subject are, in this case, blended together, if I may say so, in the expression, in the same manner as they appear to be in the object and in the idea. Hence the origin of the masculine, feminine, and neutral genders, in all the ancient languages. By means of these, the most important of all distinctions, that of substances into animated and inanimated, and that of animals into male and female, seem to have been sufficiently marked without the assistance of adjectives, or of any general names denoting this most extensive species of qualifications.

There are no more than these three genders in any of the languages with which I am acquainted; that is to say, the formation of nouns substantive can, by itself, and without the accompaniment of adjectives, express no other qualities but those three above mentioned, the qualities of male, of female, of neither male nor female. I should not, however, be surprised, if, in other languages with which I am unacquainted, the different formations of nouns substantive should be capable of expressing many other different qualities. The different diminutives of the Italian, and of some other languages, do, in reality, sometimes express a great variety of different modifications in the substances denoted by those nouns which undergo such variations.

It was impossible, however, that nouns substantive could, without losing altogether their original form, undergo so great a number of variations, as would be sufficient to express that almost infinite variety of qualities, by which it might, upon different occasions, be necessary to specify and distinguish them. Though the different formation of nouns substantive, therefore, might, for some time, forestall the necessity of inventing nouns adjective, it was impossible that this necessity could be forestalled altogether. When nouns adjective came to be invented, it was natural that they should be formed with some similarity to the substantives to which they were to serve as epithets or qualifications. Men would naturally give them the same terminations with the substantives to which they were first applied, and from that love of similarity of sound, from that delight in the returns of the same syllables, which is the foundation of analogy in all languages, they would be apt to vary the termination of the same adjective, according as they had occasion to apply it to a masculine, to a feminine, or to a neutral substantive. They would say, *magnus lupus, magna lupa, magnum pratum*, when they meant to express a great *he wolf*, a great *she wolf*, or a great *meadow*.

This variation, in the termination of the noun adjective, according to the gender of the substantive, which takes place in all the ancient languages, seems to have been introduced. chiefly for the sake of a certain similarity of sound, of a certain species of rhyme, which is naturally so very agreeable to the human ear. Gender, it is to observed, cannot properly belong to a noun adjective, the signification of which is always precisely the same, to whatever species of substantives it is applied. When we say, *a great man, a great woman*, the word *great* has precisely the same meaning in both cases, and the difference of the sex in the subjects to which it may be applied, makes no sort of difference in its signification. *Magnus, magna, magnum*, in the same manner, are words which express precisely the same quality, and the change of the termination is accompanied with no sort of variation in the meaning. Sex and gender are qualities which belong to substances, but cannot belong to the qualities of substances. In general, no quality, when considered in concrete, or as qualifying some particular subject, can itself be conceived as the subject of any other quality ; though when considered in abstract it may. No adjective therefore can qualify any other adjective. A *great good man*, means a man who is both *great* and *good*. Both the adjectives qualify the substantive ; they do not qualify one another. On the other hand, when we say, the *great goodness* of the man, the word *goodness* denoting a quality considered in abstract, which may itself be the subject of other qualities, is upon that account capable of being qualified by the word *great*.

If the original invention of nouns adjective would be attended with so much difficulty, that of prepositions would be accompanied with yet more. Every preposition, as I have already observed, denotes some relation considered in concrete with the co-relative object. The preposition *above*, for example, denotes the relation of superiority, not in abstract, as it is expressed by the word *superiority*, but in concrete with some co-relative object. In this phrase, for example, *the tree above the cave*, the word *above* expresses a certain relation between the *tree* and the *cave*, and it expresses this relation in concrete with the co-relative object, *the cave*. A preposition always requires, in order to complete the sense, some other word to come after it; as may be observed in this particular instance. Now, I say, the original invention of such words would require a yet greater effort of abstraction and generalization, than that of nouns adjective. First of all, the relation is, in itself, a more metaphysical object than a quality. Nobody can be at a loss to explain what is meant by a quality; but few people will find themselves able to express, very distinctly, what is understood by a relation. Qualities are almost always the objects of our external senses; relations never are. No wonder therefore, that the one set of objects should be so much more comprehensible than the other. Secondly, though prepositions always express the relation which they stand for, in concrete with the co-relative object, they could not have originally been formed without a considerable effort of abstraction. 'A preposition denotes a relation, and nothing but a relation. But before men could institute a word, which signified a relation, and nothing but a relation, they must have been able, in some measure, to consider this relation abstractedly from the related objects; since the idea of those objects does not, in any respect, enter into the signification of the preposition. The invention of such a word, therefore, must have required a considerable degree of abstraction. Thirdly, a preposition is from its nature a general word, which, from its very first institution, must have been considered as equally applicable to denote any other similar relation. The man who first invented the word *above*, must not only have distinguished, in some measure, the relation of *superiority* from the objects which were so related, but he must also have distinguished this relation from other relations, such as, from the relation of *inferiority* denoted by the word *below*, from the relation of *juxta-position*, expressed by the word *beside*, and the like. He must have conceived this word, therefore, as expressive of a particular sort or species of relation distinct from every other, which could not be done without a considerable effort of comparison and generalization.

Whatever were the difficulties, therefore, which embarrassed the first invention of nouns adjective, the same, and many more, must have embarrassed that of prepositions. If mankind, therefore, in the first formation of languages, seem to have, for some time, evaded the necessity of nouns adjective, by varying the termination of the names of substances, according as these varied in some of their most important qualities, they would much more find themselves under the necessity of evading, by some similar contrivance, the yet more difficult invention of prepositions. The different cases in the ancient languages is a contrivance of precisely the same kind. The genitive and dative cases, in Greek and Latin, evidently supply the place of the prepositions; and by a variation in the noun substantive, which stands for the co-relative term, express the relation which subsists between what is denoted by that noun substantive, and what is expressed by some other word in the sentence. In these expressions, for example, *fructus arboris, the fruit of the tree; sacer Herculi, sacred to Hercules;* the variations made in the co-relative words, *arbor* and *Hercules*, express the same relations which are expressed in English by the prepositions *of* and *to*.

To express a relation in this manner, did not require any effort of abstraction. It was not here expressed by a peculiar word denoting relation and nothing but relation, but by a variation upon the co-relative term. It was expressed here, as it appears in nature, not as something separated and detached, but as thoroughly mixed and blended with the co-relative object.

To express relation in this manner, did not require any effort of generalization. The words *arboris* and *Herculi*, while they involve in

their signification the same relation expressed by the English prepositions *of* and *to*, are not, like those prepositions, general words, which
can be applied to express the same relation between whatever other
objects it might be observed to subsist.

To express relation in this manner did not require any effort of
comparison. The words *arboris* and *Herculi* are not general words
intended to denote a particular species of relations which the inventors
of those expressions meant, in consequence of some sort of comparison,
to separate and distinguish from every other sort of relation. The
example, indeed, of this contrivance would soon probably be followed,
and whoever had occasion to express a similar relation between any
other objects would be very apt to do it by making a similar variation
on the name of the co-relative object. This, I say, would probably, or
rather certainly happen; but it would happen without any intention or
foresight in those who first set the example, and who never meant to
establish any general rule. The general rule would establish itself
insensibly, and by slow degrees, in consequence of that love of analogy
and similarity of sound, which is the foundation of by far the greater
part of the rules of grammar.

To express relation, therefore, by a variation in the name of the co-
relative object, requiring neither abstraction, nor generalization, nor
comparison of any kind, would, at first, be much more natural and
easy, than to express it by those general words called prepositions, of
of which the first invention must have demanded some degree of all
those operations.

The number of cases is different in different languages. There are
five in the Greek, six in the Latin, and there are said to be ten in the
Armenian language. It must have naturally happened that there
should be a greater or a smaller number of cases, according as in the
terminations of nouns substantive the first formers of any language
happened to have established a greater or a smaller number of variations, in order to express the different relations they had occasion to
take notice of, before the invention of those more general and abstract
prepositions which could supply their place.

It is, perhaps, worth while to observe that those prepositions, which
in modern languages hold the place of the ancient cases, are, of all
others, the most general, and abstract, and metaphysical; and of consequence, would probably be the last invented. Ask any man of common acuteness, What relation is expressed by the preposition *above?*
He will readily answer, that of *superiority*. By the preposition *below?*
He will as quickly reply that of *inferiority*. But ask him, what relation
is expressed by the preposition *of*, and, if he has not beforehand employed his thoughts a good deal upon these subjects, you may safely
allow him a week to consider of his answer. The prepositions *above* and
below do not denote any of the relations expressed by the cases in the

ancient languages. But the preposition *of*, denotes the same relation, which is in them expressed by the genitive case; and which, it is easy to observe, is of a very metaphysical nature. The preposition *of*, denotes relation in general, considered in concrete with the co-relative object. It marks that the noun substantive which goes before it, is somehow or other related to that which comes after it, but without in any respect ascertaining, as is done by the preposition *above*, what is the peculiar nature of that relation. We often apply it, therefore, to express the most opposite relations; because, the most opposite relations agree so far that each of them comprehends in it the general idea or nature of a relation. We say, *the father of the son*, and *the son of the father; the fir-trees of the forest*, and the *forest of the fir-trees*. The relation in which the father stands to the son is, it is evident, a quite opposite relation to that in which the son stands to the father; that in which the parts stand to the whole, is quite opposite to that in which the whole stands to the parts. The word *of*, however, serves very well to denote all those relations, because in itself it denotes no particular relation, but only relation in general; and so far as any particular relation is collected from such expressions, it is inferred by the mind, not from the preposition itself, but from the nature and arrangement of the substantives, between which the preposition is placed.

What I have said concerning the preposition *of*, may in some measure be applied to the prepositions *to, for, with, by*, and to whatever other prepositions are made use of in modern languages, to supply the place of the ancient cases. They all of them express very abstract and metaphysical relations, which any man, who takes the trouble to try it, will find it extremely difficult to express by nouns substantive, in the same manner as we may express the relation denoted by the preposition *above*, by the noun substantive *superiority*. They all of them, however, express some specific relation, and are, consequently, none of them so abstract as the preposition *of*, which may be regarded as by far the most metaphysical of all prepositions. The prepositions, therefore, which are capable of supplying the place of the ancient cases, being more abstract than the other prepositions, would naturally be of more difficult invention. The relations at the same time which those prepositions express, are, of all others, those which we have most frequent occasion to mention. The prepositions *above, below, near, within, without, against*, &c., are much more rarely made use of, in modern languages, than the prepositions *of, to, for, with, from, by*. A preposition of the former kind will not occur twice in a page; we can scarce compose a single sentence without the assistance of one or two of the latter. If these latter prepositions, therefore, which supply the place of the cases, would be of such difficult invention on account of their abstractedness, some expedient to supply their place must have been of indispensable necessity, on account of the frequent occasion which men have to take notice of the relations which they denote. But there is no expedient so obvious, as that of varying the termination of one of the principal words.

It is, perhaps, unnecessary to observe, that there are some of the cases in the ancient languages, which, for particular reasons, cannot be represented by any prepositions. These are the nominative, accusative, and vocative cases. In those modern languages, which do not admit of any such variety in the terminations of their nouns substantive, the correspondent relations are expressed by the place of the words, and by the order and construction of the sentence.

As men have frequently occasion to make mention of multitudes as well as of single objects, it became necessary that they should have some method of expressing number. Number may be expressed either by a particular word, expressing number in general, such as the words *many*, *more*, &c., or by some variation upon the words which express the things numbered. It is this last expedient which mankind would probably have recourse to, in the infancy of language. Number, considered in general, without relation to any particular set of objects numbered, is one of the most abstract and metaphysical ideas, which the mind of man is capable of forming; and, consequently, is not an idea, which would readily occur to rude mortals, who were just beginning to form a language. They would naturally, therefore, distinguish when they talked of a single, and when they talked of a multitude of objects, not by any metaphysical adjectives, such as the English *a*, *an*, *many*, but by a variation upon the termination of the word which signified the objects numbered. Hence the origin of the singular and plural numbers, in all the ancient languages; and the same distinction has likewise been retained in all the modern languages, at least, in the greater part of the words.

All primitive and uncompounded languages seem to have a dual, as well as a plural number. This is the case of the Greek, and I am told of the Hebrew, of the Gothic, and of many other languages. In the rude beginnings of society, *one*, *two*, and *more*, might possibly be all the numeral distinctions which mankind would have any occasion to take notice of. These they would find it more natural to express, by a variation upon every particular noun substantive, than by such general and abstract words as *one*, *two*, *three*, *four*, &c. These words, though custom has rendered them familiar to us, express, perhaps, the most subtile and refined abstractions, which the mind of man is capable of forming. Let any one consider within himself, for example, what he means by the word *three*, which signifies neither three shillings, nor three pence, nor three men, nor three horses, but three in general; and he will easily satisfy himself that a word, which denotes so very metaphysical an abstraction, could not be either a very obvious or a very early invention. I have read of some savage nations, whose language was capable of expressing no more than the three first numeral distinctions. But whether it expressed those distinctions by three general words, or by variations upon the nouns substantive, denoting the things numbered, I do not remember to have met with any thing which could clearly determine.

As all the same relations which subsist between single, may likewise subsist between numerous objects, it is evident there would be occasion for the same number of cases in the dual and in the plural, as in the singular number. Hence the intricacy and complexness of the declensions in all the ancient languages. In the Greek there are five cases in each of the three numbers, consequently fifteen in all.

As nouns adjective, in the ancient languages, varied their terminations according to the gender of the substantive to which they were applied, so did they likewise according to the case and the number. Every noun adjective in the Greek language, therefore, having three genders, and three numbers, and five cases in each number, may be considered as having five and forty different variations. The first formers of language seem to have varied the termination of the adjective, according to the case and the number of the substantive, for the same reason which made them vary it according to the gender; the love of analogy, and of a certain regularity of sound. In the signification of adjectives there is neither case nor number, and the meaning of such words is always precisely the same, notwithstanding all the variety of termination under which they appear. *Magnus vir, magni viri, magnorum virorum; a great man, of a great man, of great men;* in all these expressions the words, *magnus, magni, magnorum,* as well as the word *great,* have precisely one and the same signification, though the substantives to which they are applied have not. The difference of termination in the noun adjective is accompanied with no sort of difference in the meaning. An adjective denotes the qualification of a noun substantive. But the different relations in which that noun substantive may occasionally stand, can make no sort of difference upon its qualification. If the declensions of the ancient languages are so very complex, their conjugations are infinitely more so. And the complexness of the one is founded upon the same principle with that of the other, the difficulty of forming, in the beginnings of language, abstract and general terms.

Verbs must necessarily have been coëval with the very first attempts towards the formation of language. No affirmation can be expressed without the assistance of some verb. We never speak but in order to express our opinion that something either is or is not. But the word denoting this event, or this matter of fact, which is the subject of our affirmation, must always be a verb.

Impersonal verbs, which express in one word a complete event, which preserve in the expression that perfect simplicity and unity, which there always is in the object and in the idea, and which suppose no abstraction, or metaphysical division of the event into its several constituent members of subject and attribute, would, in all probability, be the species of verbs first invented. The verbs *pluit, it rains; ningit, it snows; tonat, it thunders; lucet, it is day; turbatur, there is a confusion,* &c., each of them express a complete affirmation, the whole of an event, with that perfect simplicity and unity with which the mind conceives it in nature. On the contrary, the phrases, *Alexander ambulat, Alexander walks; Petrus sedet, Peter sits,* divide the event, as it were, into two parts, the person or subject, and the attribute, or matter of fact, affirmed of that subject. But in nature, the idea or conception of Alexander walking, is as perfectly and completely one simple conception, as that of Alexander not walking. The division of this event, therefore, into two parts, is altogether artificial, and is the effect of the imperfection of language, which, upon this, as upon many other occasions, supplies, by a number of words, the want of one, which could express at once the whole matter of fact that was meant to be affirmed. Every body must observe how much more simplicity there is in the natural expression, *pluit,* than in the more artificial expressions, *imber decidit, the rain falls;* or *tempestas est pluvia, the weather is rainy.* In these two last expressions, the simple event, or matter of fact, is artificially split and divided in the one, into two ; in the other, into three parts. In each of them it is expressed by a sort of grammatical circumlocution, of which the significancy is founded upon a certain metaphysical analysis of the component parts of the idea expressed by the word *pluit.* The first verbs, therefore, perhaps even the first words, made use of in the beginnings of language, would in all probability be such impersonal verbs. It is observed accordingly, I am told, by the Hebrew grammarians, that the radical words of their language, from which all the others are derived, are all of them verbs, and impersonal verbs.

It is easy to conceive how, in the progress of language, those impersonal verbs should become personal. Let us suppose, for example, that the word *venit, it comes,* was originally an impersonal verb, and that it denoted, not the coming of something in general, as at present, but the coming of a particular object, such as *the lion.* The first savage inventors of language, we shall suppose, when they observed the approach of this terrible animal, were accustomed to cry out to one another, *venit,* that is, *the lion comes;* and that this word thus expressed a complete event, without the assistance of any other. Afterwards, when, on the further progress of language, they had begun to give names to particular substances, whenever they observed the approach of any other terrible object, they would naturally join the name of that object to the word *venit,* and cry out, *venit ursus, venit lupus.* By degrees the word *venit* would thus come to signify the coming of any terrible object, and not merely the coming of the lion. It would, now, therefore, express, not the coming of a particular object, but the coming of an object of a particular kind. Having become more general in its signification, it could no longer represent any particular distinct event by itself, and without the assistance of a noun substantive, which might serve to ascertain and determine its signification. It would now, therefore, have become a personal, instead of an impersonal verb. We may easily conceive how, in the further progress of society, it might still grow more general in its signification, and come to signify, as at present, the approach of any thing whatever, whether it were good, bad, or indifferent.

It is probably in some such manner as this, that almost all verbs have become personal, and that mankind have learned by degrees to split and divide almost every event into a great number of metaphysical parts, expressed by the different parts of speech, variously combined in the different members of every phrase and sentence.* The same sort of progress seems to have been made in the art of speaking as in the art of writing. When mankind first began to attempt to express their ideas by writing, every character represented a whole word. But the number of words being almost infinite, the memory found itself quite loaded and oppressed by the multitude of characters which it was obliged to retain. Necessity taught them, therefore, to divide words into their elements, and to invent characters which should represent, not the words themselves, but the elements of which they were composed. In consequence of this invention, every particular word came to be represented, not by one character, but by a multitude of characters; and the expression of it in writing became much more intricate and complex than before. But though particular words were thus represented by a greater number of characters, the whole language was expressed by a much smaller, and about four and twenty letters were found capable of supplying the place of that immense multitude of characters, which were requisite before. In the same manner, in the beginnings of language, men seem to have attempted to express every particular event, which they had occasion to take notice of, by a particular word, which expressed at once the whole of that event. But as the number of words must, in this case, have become really infinite in consequence of the really infinite variety of events, men found themselves partly compelled by necessity, and partly conducted by nature, to divide

---

* As the far greater part of verbs express, at present, not an event, but the attribute of an event, and, consequently, require a subject, or nominative case, to complete their signification, some grammarians, not having attended to this progress of nature, and being desirous to make their common rules quite universal, and without any exception, have insisted that all verbs required a nominative, either expressed or understood ; and have, accordingly, put themselves to the torture to find some awkward nominatives to those 'few verbs which still expressing a complete event, plainly admit of none. *Pluit*, for example, according to *Sanctius*, means *pluvia pluit*, in English, *the rain rains*. See Sancti Minerva, l. 3. c. 1.

every event into what may be called its metaphysical elements, and to institute words, which should denote not so much the events, as the elements of which they were composed. The expression of every particular event, became in this manner more intricate and complex, but the whole system of the language became more coherent, more connected, more easily retained and comprehended.

When verbs, from being originally impersonal, had thus, by the division of the event into its metaphysical elements, become personal it is natural to suppose that they would first be made use of in the third person singular. No verb is ever used impersonally in our language nor, so far as I know, in any other modern tongue. But in the ancient languages, whenever any verb is used impersonally, it is always in the third person singular. The termination of those verbs, which are still always impersonal, is constantly the same with that of the third person singular of personal verbs. The consideration of these circumstances, joined to the naturalness of the thing itself, may therefore serve to convince us that verbs first became personal in what is now called the third person singular.

But as the event, or matter of fact, which is expressed by a verb, may be affirmed either of the person who speaks, or of the person who is spoken to, as well as of some third person or object, it becomes necessary to fall upon some method of expressing these two peculiar relations of the event. In the English language this is commonly done, by prefixing, what are called the personal pronouns, to the general word which expresses the event affirmed. *I came, you came, he* or *it came;* in these phrases the event of having come is, in the first, affirmed of the speaker; in the second, of the person spoken to; in the third, of some other person or object. The first formers of language, it may be imagined, might have done the same thing, and prefixing in the same manner the two first personal pronouns, to the same termination of the verb, which expressed the third person singular, might have said *ego venit, tu venit,* as well as *ille* or *illud venit.* And I make no doubt but they would have done so, if at the time when they had first occasion to express these relations of the verb there had been any such words as either *ego* or *tu* in their language. But in this early period of the language, which we are now endeavouring to describe, it is extremely improbable that any such words would be known. Though custom has now rendered them familiar to us, they, both of them, express ideas extremely metaphysical and abstract. The word *I,* for example, is a word of a very particular species. Whatever speaks may denote itself by this personal pronoun. The word *I,* therefore, is a general word, capable of being predicated, as the logicians say, of an infinite variety of objects. It differs, however, from all other general words in this respect; that the object of which it may be predicated, do not form any particular species of objects distinguished from all others. The word *I*, does not, like the word *man*, denote a particular class of objects separated from all others by peculiar qualities of their own. It is far from being the name of a species, but, on the contrary, whenever it is made use of, it always denotes a precise individual, the particular person who then speaks. It may be said to be, at once, both what the logicians call, a singular, and what they call, a common term ; and to join, in its signification the seemingly opposite qualities of the most precise individuality and the most extensive generalization. This word, therefore, expressing so very abstract and metaphysical an idea, would not easily or readily occur to the first formers of language. What are called the personal pronouns, it may be observed, are among the last words of which children learn to make use. A child, speaking of itself, says, *Billy walks, Billy sits*, insteads of *I walk, I sit*. As in the beginnings of language, therefore, mankind seem to have evaded the invention of at least the more abstract prepositions, and to have expressed the same relations which these *now* stand for, by varying the termination of the co-relative term, so they likewise would naturally attempt to evade the necessity of inventing those more abstract pronouns by varying the termination of the verb, according as the event which it expressed was intended to be affirmed of the first, second, or third person. This seems, accordingly, to be the universal practice of all the ancient languages. In Latin, *veni, venisti, venit*, sufficiently denote, without any other addition, the different events expressed by the English phrases, *I came, you came, he* or *it came*. The verb would, for the same reason, vary its termination, according as the event was intended to be affirmed of the first, second, or third persons plural ; and what is expressed by the English phrases, *we came, ye came, they came*, would be denoted by the Latin words, *venimus, venisitis, veneunt*. Those primitive languages, too, which upon account of the difficulty of inventing numeral names, had introduced a dual, as well as a plural number, into the declension of their nouns substantive, would probably, from analogy, do the same thing in the conjugations of their verbs. And thus in all original languages, we might expect to find, at least six, if not eight or nine variations, in the termination of every verb, according as the event which it denoted was meant to be affirmed of the first, second, or third persons singular, dual, or plural. These variations again being repeated, along with others, through all its different tenses, through all its different modes, and through all its different voices, must necessarily have rendered their conjugations still more intricate and complex than their declensions.

Language would probably have continued upon this footing in all countries, nor would ever have grown more simple in its declensions and conjugations, had it not become more complex in its composition, in consequence of the mixture of several languages with one another, occasioned by the mixture of different nations. As long as any language was spoke by those only who learned it in their infancy, the intricacy of its declensions and conjugations could occasion no great embarrassment. The far greater part of those who had occasion to speak it, had acquired it at so very early a period of their lives, so insensibly and by such slow degrees, that they were scarce ever sensible of the difficulty. But when two nations came to be mixed with one another, either by conquest or migration, the case would be very different. Each nation, in order to make itself intelligible to those with whom it was under the necessity of conversing, would be obliged to learn the language of the other. The greater part of individuals too, learning the new language, not by art, or by remounting to its rudiments and first principle, but by rote, and by what they commonly heard in conversation, would be extremely perplexed by the intricacy of its declensions and conjugations. They would endeavour, therefore, to supply their ignorance of these, by whatever shift the language could afford them. Their ignorance of the declensions they would naturally supply by the use of prepositions ; and a Lombard, who was attempting to speak Latin, and wanted to express that such a person was a citizen of Rome, or a benefactor to Rome, if he happened not to be acquainted with the genitive and dative cases of the word *Roma*, would naturally express himself by prefixing the prepositions *ad* and *de* to the nominative ; and instead of *Romæ*, would say, *ad Roma*, and *de Roma*. *Al Roma* and *di Roma*, accordingly, is the manner in which the present Italians, the descendants of the ancient Lombards and Romans, express this and all other similar relations. And in this manner prepositions seem to have been introduced, in the room of the ancient declensions. The same alteration has, I am informed, been produced upon the Greek language, since the taking of Constantinople by the Turks. The words are, in a great measure, the same as before ; but the grammar is entirely lost, prepositions having come in the place of the old declensions. This change is undoubtedly a simplification of the language, in point of rudiments and principle. It introduces, instead of a great variety of declensions, one universal declension, which is the same in every word, of whatever gender, number, or termination.

A similar expedient enables men, in the situation above mentioned, to get rid of almost the whole intricacy of their conjugations. There is in every language a verb, known by the name of the substantive verb ; in Latin, *sum;* in English, *I am*. This verb denotes not the existence of any particular event, but existence in general. It is, upon that account, the most abstract and metaphysical of all verbs ; and, consequently, could by no means be a word of early invention. When it came to be invented, however, as it had all the tenses and modes of any other verb, by being joined with the passive participle, it was capable of supplying the place of the whole passive voice, and of rendering this part of their conjugations as simple and uniform as the use of prepositions had rendered their declensions. A Lombard, who wanted to say, *I am loved*, but could not recollect the word *amor*, naturally endeavoured to supply his ignorance, by saying *ego sum amatus*. *Io sono amato*, is at this day the Italian expression, which corresponds to the English phrase above mentioned.

There is another verb, which, in the same [manner, runs through all languages, and which is distinguished by the name of the possessive verb; in Latin, *habeo;* in English, *I have.* This verb, likewise, denotes an event of an extremely abstract and metaphysical nature, and, consequently, cannot be supposed to have been a word of the earliest invention. When it came to be invented, however, by being applied to the passive participle, it was capable of supplying a great part of the active voice, as the substantive verb had supplied the whole of the passive. A Lombard, who wanted to say, *I had loved,* but could not recollect the word *amaveram*, would endeavour to supply the place of it, by saying either *ego habebam amatum* or *ego habui amatum. Io avevá amato,* or *Io ebbi amato*, are the correspondent Italian expressions at this day. And thus upon the intermixture of different nations with one another, the conjugations, by means of different auxiliary verbs, were made to approach the simplicity and uniformity of the declensions.

In general it may be laid down for a maxim, that the more simple any language is in its composition, the more complex it must be in its declensions and its conjugations; and on the contrary, the more simple it is in its declensions and its conjugations, the more complex it must be in its composition.

The Greek seems to be, in a great measure, a simple, uncompounded language, formed from the primitive jargon of those wandering savages, the ancient Hellenians and Pelasgians, from whom the Greek nation is said to have been descended. All the words in the Greek language are derived from about three hundred primitives, a plain evidence that the Greeks formed their language almost entirely among themselves, and that when they had occasion for a new word, they were not accustomed, as we are, to borrow it from some foreign language, but to form it, either by composition or derivation, from some other word or words, in their own. The declensions and conjugations, therefore, of the Greek are much more complex than those of any other European language with which I am acquainted.

The Latin is a composition of the Greek and of the ancient Tuscan languages. Its declensions and conjugations accordingly are much less complex than those of the Greek; it has dropped the dual number in both. Its verbs have no optative mood distinguished by any peculiar termination. They have but one future. They have no aorist distinct from the preterit-perfect; they have no middle voice; and even many of their tenses in the passive voice are eked out, in the same manner as in the modern languages, by the help of the substantive verb joined to the passive participle. In both the voices, the number of infinitives and participles is much smaller in the Latin than in the Greek.

The French and Italian languages are each of them compounded, the one of the Latin and the language of the ancient Franks, the other of the same Latin and the language of the ancient Lombards. As they are both of them, therefore, more complex in their composition than the Latin, so are they likewise more simple in their declensions and conjugations. With regard to their declensions, they have both of them lost their cases altogether; and with regard to their conjugations, they have both of them lost the whole of the passive, and some part of the active voices of their verbs. The want of the passive voice they supply entirely by the substantive verb joined to the passive participle; and they make out part of the active, in the same manner, by the help of the possessive verb and the same passive participle.

The English is compounded of the French and the ancient Saxon languages. The French was introduced into Britain by the Norman conquest, and continued, till the time of Edward III. to be the sole language of the law as well as the principal language of the court. The English, which came to be spoken afterwards, and which continues to be spoken now, is a mixture of the ancient Saxon and this Norman French. As the English language, therefore, is more complex in its composition than either the French or the Italian, so is it likewise more simple in its declensions and conjugations. Those two languages retain, at least, a part of the distinction of genders, and their adjectives vary their termination according as they are applied to a masculine or to a feminine substantive. But there is no such distinction in the English language, whose adjectives admit of no variety of termination. The French and Italian languages have, both of them, the remains of a conjugation; and all those tenses of the active voice, which cannot be expressed by the possessive verb joined to the passive participle, as well as many of those which can, are, in those languages, marked by varying the termination of the principal verb. But almost all those other tenses are in the English eked out by other auxiliary verbs, so that there is in this language scarce even the remains of a conjugation. *I love, I loved, loving*, are all the varieties of termination which the greater part of the English verbs admit of. All the different modifications of meaning, which cannot be expressed by any of those three terminations, must be made out by different auxiliary verbs joined to some one or other of them. Two auxiliary verbs supply all the deficiencies of the French and Italian conjugations; it requires more than half a dozen to supply those of the English, which, besides the substantive and possessive verbs, makes use of *do, did; will, would; shall, should; can, could; may, might.*

It is in this manner that language becomes more simple in its rudiments and principles, just in proportion as it grows more complex in its composition, and the same thing has happened in it, which commonly happens with regard to mechanical engines. All machines are generally, when first invented, extremely complex in their principles, and there is often a particular principle of motion for every particular movement which it is intended they should perform. Succeeding improvers observe, that one principle may be so applied as to produce several of those movements; and thus the machine becomes gradually more and more simple, and produces its effects with fewer wheels, and fewer principles of motion. In language, in the same manner, every case of every noun, and every tense of every verb, was originally expressed by a particular distinct word, which served for this purpose and for no other. But succeeding observations discovered, that one set of words was capable of supplying the place of all that infinite number, and that four or five prepositions, and half a dozen auxiliary verbs, were capable of answering the end of all the declensions, and of all the conjugations in the ancient languages.

But this simplification of languages, though it arises, perhaps, from similar causes, has by no means similar effects with the correspondent simplification of machines. The simplification of machines renders them more and more perfect, but this simplification of the rudiments of languages renders them more and more imperfect, and less proper for many of the purposes of language; and this for the following reasons.

First of all, languages are by this simplification rendered more prolix, several words having become necessary to express what could have been expressed by a single word before. Thus the words, *Dei* and *Deo*, in the Latin, sufficiently shew, without any addition, what relation the object signified is understood to stand in to the objects expressed by the other words in the sentence. But to express the same relation in English, and in all other modern languages, we must make use of, at least, two words, and say, *of God, to God*. So far as the declensions are concerned, therefore, the modern languages are much more prolix than the ancient. The difference is still greater with regard to the conjugations. What a Roman expressed by the single word *amavissem*, an Englishman is obliged to express by four different words, *I should have loved*. It is unnecessary to take any pains to show how much this prolixness must enervate the eloquence of all modern languages. How much the beauty of any expression depends upon its conciseness, is well known to those who have any experience in composition.

Secondly, this simplification of the principles of languages renders them less agreeable to the ear. The variety of termination in the Greek and Latin, occasioned by their declensions and conjugations, gives a sweetness to their language altogether unknown to ours, and a variety unknown to any other modern language. In point of sweetness, the Italian, perhaps, may surpass the Latin, and almost equal the Greek; but in point of variety, it is greatly inferior to both.

324 ANCIENT AND MODERN CONSTRUCTION CONTRASTED.

Thirdly, this simplification, not only renders the sounds of our language less agreeable to the ear, but it also restrains us from disposing such sounds as we have, in the manner that might be most agreeable. It ties down many words to a particular situation, though they might often be placed in another with much more beauty. In the Greek and Latin, though the adjective and substantive were separated from one another, the correspondence of their terminations still showed their mutual reference, and the separation did not necessarily occasion any sort of confusion. Thus in the first line of Virgil,

Tityre tu patulæ recubans sub tegmine fagi ;

we easily see that *tu* refers to *recubans*, and *patulæ* to *fagi;* though the related words are separated from one another by the intervention of several others ; because the terminations, showing the correspondence of their cases, determine their mutual reference. But if we were to translate this line literally into English, and say, *Tityrus, thou of spreading reclining under the shade beech,* Œdipus himself could not make sense of it ; because there is here no difference of termination, to determine which substantive each adjective belongs to. It is the same case with regard to verbs. In Latin the verb may often be placed, without any inconveniency or ambiguity, in any part of the sentence. But in English its place is almost always precisely determined. It must follow the subjective and precede the objective member of the phrase in almost all cases. Thus in Latin whether you say, *Joannem verberavit Robertus,* or *Robertus verberavit Joannem,* the meaning is precisely the same, and the termination fixes John to be the sufferer in both cases. But in English *John beat Robert,* and *Robert beat John,* have by no means the same signification. The place therefore of the three principal members of the phrase is in the English, and for the same reason in the French and Italian languages, almost always precisely determined ; whereas in the ancient languages a greater latitude is allowed, and the place of those members is often, in a great measure, indifferent. We must have recourse to Horace, in order to interpret some parts of Milton's literal translation ;

Who now enjoys thee credulous all gold,
Who always vacant, always amiable
Hopes thee ; of flattering gales
Unmindful—

are verses which it is impossible to interpret by any rules of our language. There are no rules in our language, by which any man could discover, that, in the first line, *credulous* referred to *who,* and not to *thee;* or that *all gold* referred to any thing ; or, that in the fourth line, *unmindful,* referred to *who,* in the second, and not to *thee* in the third ; or, on the contrary, that, in the second line, *always vacant, always amiable,* referred to *thee* in the third, and not to *who* in the same line with it. In the Latin, indeed, all this is abundantly plain.

Qui nunc te fruitur credulus aureâ,
Qui semper vacuam, semper amabilem
Sperat te ; nescius auræ fallacis.

Because the terminations in the Latin determine the reference of each adjective to its proper substantive, which it is impossible for any thing in the English to do.   How much this power of transposing the order of their words must have facilitated the compositions of the ancients, both in verse and prose, can hardly be imagined.   That it must greatly have facilitated their versification it is needless to observe ; and in prose, whatever beauty depends upon the arrangement and construction of the several members of the period, must to them have been acquirable with much more ease, and to much greater perfection than it can be to those whose expression is constantly confined by the prolixness, constraint, and monotony of modern languages.

THE PRINCIPLES

WHICH LEAD AND DIRECT

PHILOSOPHICAL ENQUIRIES;

AS ILLUSTRATED BY

THE HISTORY OF ASTRONOMY.

WONDER, surprise, and admiration, are words which, though often confounded, denote, in our language, sentiments that are indeed allied, but that are in some respects different also, and distinct from one another. What is new and singular, excites that sentiment which, in strict propriety, is called Wonder ; what is unexpected, Surprise ; and what is great or beautiful, Admiration.

We wonder at all extraordinary and uncommon objects, at all the rarer phenomena of nature, at meteors, comets, eclipses, at singular plants and animals, and at every thing, in short, with which we have before been either little or not at all acquainted ; and we still wonder, though forewarned of what we are to see.

We are surprised at those things which we have seen often, but which we least of all expected to meet with in the place where we find them ; we are surprised at the sudden appearance of a friend, whom we have seen a thousand times, but whom we did not at all imagine we were to see then.

We admire the beauty of a plain or the greatness of a mountain, though we have seen both often before, and though nothing appears to us in either, but what we had expected with certainty to see.

Whether this criticism upon the precise meaning of these words be just, is of little importance. I imagine it is just, though I acknowledge, that the best writers in our language have not always made use of them according to it. Milton, upon the appearance of Death to Satan, says, that

> The Fiend what this might be admir'd,
> Admir'd, not fear'd.——

But if this criticism be just, the proper expression should have been *wonder'd.*—Dryden, upon the discovery of Iphigenia sleeping, says that

> The fool of nature stood with stupid eyes,
> And gaping mouth, that testified surprise.

But what Cimon must have felt upon this occasion could not so much be Surprise, as Wonder and Admiration. All that I contend for is, that the sentiments excited by what is new, by what is unexpected, and by what is great and beautiful are really different, however the words made use of to express them may sometimes be confounded. Even the admiration which is excited by beauty, is quite different (as will appear more fully hereafter) from that which is inspired by greatness, though we have but one word to denote them.

These sentiments, like all others when inspired by one and the same object, mutually support and enliven one another: an object with which we are quite familiar, and which we see every day, produces, though both great and beautiful, but a small effect upon us ; because our admiration is not supported either by Wonder or by Surprise : and if we have heard a very accurate description of a monster, our Wonder will be the less when we see it ; because our previous knowledge of it will in a great measure prevent our Surprise.

It is the design of this essay to consider particularly the nature and causes of each of these sentiments, whose influence is of far wider extent than we should be apt upon a careless view to imagine. I shall begin with Surprise.

———

SEC. I.—*Of the Effect of Unexpectedness, or of Surprise.*

WHEN an object of any kind, which has been for some time expected and foreseen, presents itself, whatever be the emotion which it is by nature fitted to excite, the mind must have been prepared for it, and must even in some measure have conceived it before-hand ; because the idea of the object having been so long present to it, must have before-hand excited some degree of the same emotion which the object itself would excite : the change, therefore, which its presence produces comes thus to be less considerable, and the emotion or passion which it excites glides gradually and easily into the heart, without violence, pain or difficulty.

But the contrary of all this happens when the object is unexpected ; the passion is then poured in all at once upon the heart, which is thrown, if it is a strong passion, into the most violent and convulsive emotions, such as sometimes cause immediate death ; sometimes, by the suddenness of the ecstacy, so entirely disjoint the whole frame of the imagination, that it never after returns to its former tone and composure, but falls either into a frenzy or habitual lunacy ; and such as almost always occasion a momentary loss of reason, or of that attention to other things which our situation or our duty requires.

How much we dread the effects of the more violent passions, when they come suddenly upon the mind, appears from those preparations which all men think necessary when going to inform any one of what is capable of exciting them. Who would choose all at once to inform his friend of an extraordinary calamity that had befallen him, without taking care before-hand, by alarming him with an uncertain fear, to announce, if one may say so, his misfortune, and thereby prepare and dispose him for receiving the tidings ?

Those panic terrors which sometimes seize armies in the field, or great cities, when an enemy is in the neighbourhood, and which deprive for a time the most determined of all deliberate judgments, are never excited but by the sudden apprehension of unexpected danger. Such violent consternations, which at once confound whole multitudes, benumb their understandings, and agitate their hearts, with all the agony of extravagant fear, can never be produced by any foreseen danger, how great soever. Fear, though naturally a very strong passion, never rises to such excesses, unless exasperated both by wonder, from the uncertain nature of the danger, and by surprise, from the suddenness of the apprehension.

Surprise, therefore, is not to be regarded as an original emotion of a species distinct from all others. The violent and sudden change produced upon the mind, when an emotion of any kind is brought suddenly upon it, constitutes the whole nature of Surprise.

But when not only a passion and a great passion comes all at once upon the mind, but when it comes upon it while the mind is in the mood most unfit for conceiving it, the Surprise is then the greatest. Surprises of joy when the mind is sunk into grief, or of grief when it is elated with joy, are therefore the most unsupportable. The change is in this case the greatest possible. Not only a strong passion is conceived all at once, but a strong passion the direct opposite of that which was before in possession of the soul. When a load of sorrow comes down upon the heart that is expanded and elated with gaiety and joy, it seems not only to damp and oppress it, but almost to crush and bruise it, as a real weight would crush and bruise the body. On the contrary, when from an unexpected change of fortune, a tide of gladness seems, if I may say so, to spring up all at once within it, when depressed and contracted with grief and sorrow, it feels as if suddenly extended and heaved up with violent and irresistible force, and is torn with pangs of all others most exquisite, and which almost always occasion faintings, deliriums, and sometimes instant death. For it may be worth while to observe, that though grief be a more violent passion than joy, as indeed all uneasy sensations seem naturally more pungent than the opposite agreeable ones, yet of the two, Surprises of joy are still more insupportable than Surprises of grief. We are told that after the battle of Thrasimenus, while a Roman lady, who had been informed that her son was slain in the action, was sitting alone bemoaning her misfortunes, the young man who escaped came suddenly into the room to her, and that she cried out and expired instantly in a transport of joy. Let us suppose the contrary of this to have happened, and that in the midst of domestic festivity and mirth, he had suddenly fallen down dead at her feet, is it likely that the effects would have been equally violent? I imagine not. The heart springs to joy with a sort of natural elasticity, it abandons itself to so agreeable an emotion, as soon as the object is presented ; it seems to pant and leap forward to meet it, and the passion in its full force takes at once entire and complete possession of the soul. But it is otherwise with grief; the heart recoils from, and resists the first approaches of that disagreeable passion, and it requires some time before the melancholy object can produce its full effect. Grief comes on slowly and gradually, nor ever rises at once to that height of agony to which it is increased after a little time. But joy comes rushing upon us all at once like a torrent. The change produced, therefore, by a surprise of joy is more sudden, and upon that account more violent and apt to have more fatal effects, than that which is occasioned by a surprise of grief ; there seems, too, to be something in the nature of surprise, which makes it unite more easily with the brisk and quick motion of joy, than with the slower and heavier movement of grief. Most men who can take the trouble to recollect, will find that they have heard of more people who died or became distracted with sudden joy, than with sudden grief. Yet from the nature of human affairs, the latter must be much more frequent than the former. A man may break his leg, or lose his son, though he has had no warning of either of these events, but he can hardly meet with an extraordinary piece of good fortune, without having had some foresight of what was to happen.

Not only grief and joy, but all the other passions, are more violent, when opposite extremes succeed each other. Is any resentment so keen as what follows the quarrels of lovers, or any love so passionate as what attends their reconcilement ?

Even the objects of the external senses affect us in a more lively manner, when opposite extremes succeed to or are placed beside each other. Moderate warmth seems intolerable heat if felt after extreme cold.   What is bitter will seem more so when tasted after what is very sweet; a dirty white will seem bright and pure when placed by a jet black.   The vivacity in short of every sensation, as well as of every sentiment, seems to be greater or less in proportion to the change made by the impression of either upon the situation of the mind or organ; but this change must necessarily be the greatest when opposite sentiments and sensations are contrasted, or succeed immediately to one another.   Both sentiments and sensations are then the liveliest; and this superior vivacity proceeds from nothing but their being brought upon the mind or organ when in a state most unfit for conceiving them.

As the opposition of contrasted sentiments heightens their vivacity, so the resemblance of those which immediately succeed each other renders them more faint and languid.   A parent who has lost several children immediately after one another, will be less affected with the death of the last than with that of the first, though the loss in itself be, in this case, undoubtedly greater; but his mind being already sunk into sorrow, the new misfortune seems to produce no other effect than a continuance of the same melancholy, and is by no means apt to occasion such transports of grief as are ordinarily excited by the first calamity of the kind; he receives it, though with great dejection, yet with some degree of calmness and composure, and without anything of that anguish and agitation of mind which the novelty of the misfortune is apt to occasion.   Those who have been unfortunate through the whole course of their lives are often indeed habitually melancholy, and sometimes peevish and splenetic, yet upon any fresh disappointment, though they are vexed and complain a little, they seldom fly out into any more violent passion, and never fall into those transports of rage or grief which often, upon like occasions, distract the fortunate and successful.

Upon this are founded, in a great measure, some of the effects of habit and custom.   It is well known that custom deadens the vivacity of both pain and pleasure, abates the grief we should feel for the one, and weakens the joy we should derive from the other.   The pain is supported without agony, and the pleasure enjoyed without rapture: because custom and the frequent repetition of any object comes at last to form and bend the mind or organ to that habitual mood and disposition which fits them to receive its impression, without undergoing any very violent change.

SEC. II.--*Of Wonder, or of the Effects of Novelty.*

IT is evident that the mind takes pleasure in observing the resemblances that are discoverable betwixt different objects.   It is by means of such observations that it endeavours to arrange and methodise all its ideas, and to reduce them into proper classes and assortments.   Where it can observe but one single quality that is common to a great variety of otherwise widely different objects, that single circumstance will be sufficient for it to connect them all together, to reduce them to one common class, and to call them by one general name. It is thus that all things endowed with a power of self-motion, beasts, birds, fishes, insects, are classed under the general name of Animal; and that these again, along with those which want that power, are arranged under the still more general word, Substance: and this is the origin of those assortments of objects and ideas which in the schools are called Genera and Species, and of those abstract and general names, which in all languages are made use of to express them.

The further we advance in knowledge and experience, the greater number of divisions and subdivisions of those Genera and Species we are both inclined and obliged to make. We observe a greater variety of particularities amongst those things which have a gross resemblance; and having made new divisions of them, according to those newly-observed particularities, we are then no longer to be satisfied with being able to refer an object to a remote genus, or very general class of things, to many of which it has but a loose and imperfect resemblance. A person, indeed, unacquainted with botany may expect to satisfy your curiosity, by telling you, that such a vegetable is a weed, or, perhaps in still more general terms, that it is a plant. But a botanist will neither give nor accept of such an answer. He has broke and divided that great class of objects into a number of inferior assortments, accord to those varieties which his experience has discovered among them; and he wants to refer each individual plant to some tribe of vegetables, with all of which it may have a more exact resemblance, than with many things comprehended under the extensive genus of plants. A child imagines that it gives a satisfactory answer when it tells you, that an object whose name it knows not is a thing, and fancies that it informs you of something, when it thus ascertains to which of the two most obvious and comprehensive classes of objects a particular impression ought to be referred; to the class of realities or solid substances which it calls *things*, or to that of appearances which it calls *nothings*.

Whatever, in short, occurs to us we are fond of referring to some species or class of things, with all of which it has a nearly exact resemblance: and though we often know no more about them than about it, yet we are apt to fancy that by being able to do so, we show ourselves to be better acquainted with it, and to have a more thorough insight into its nature. But when something quite new and singular is presented, we feel ourselves incapable of doing this. The memory cannot, from all its stores, cast up any image that nearly resembles this strange appearance. If by some of its qualities it seems to resemble, and to be connected with a species which we have before been acquainted with, it is by others separated and detached from that, and from all the other assortments of things we have hitherto been able to make. It stands alone and by itself in the imagination, and refuses to be grouped or confounded with any set of objects whatever. The imagination and memory exert themselves to no purpose, and in vain look around all their classes of ideas in order to find one under which it may be arranged. They fluctuate to no purpose from thought to thought, and we remain still uncertain and undetermined where to place it, or what to think of it. It is this fluctuation and vain recollection, together with the emotion or movement of the spirits that they excite, which constitute the sentiment properly called *Wonder*, and which occasion that staring, and sometimes that rolling of the eyes, that suspension of the breath, and that swelling of the heart, which we may all observe, both in ourselves and others, when wondering at some new object, and which are the natural symptoms of uncertain and undetermined thought. What sort of a thing can that be? What is that like? are the questions which, upon such an occasion, we are all naturally disposed to ask. If we can recollect many such objects which exactly resemble this new appearance, and which present themselves to the imagination naturally, and as it were of their own accord, our Wonder is entirely at an end. If we can recollect but a few, and which it requires too some trouble to be able to call up, our Wonder is indeed diminished, but not quite destroyed. If we can recollect none, but are quite at a loss, it is the greatest possible.

With what curious attention does a naturalist examine a singular plant, or a singular fossil, that is presented to him? He is at no loss to refer it to the general genus of plants or fossils; but this does not satisfy him, and when he considers all the different tribes or species of either with which he has hitherto been acquainted, they all, he thinks, refuse to admit the new object among them. It stands alone in his imagination, and as it were detached from all the other species of that genus to which it belongs. He labours, however, to connect it with some one or other of them. Sometimes he thinks it may be placed in this, and sometimes in that other assortment; nor is he ever satisfied, till he has fallen upon one which, in most of its qualities, it resembles. When he cannot do this, rather than it should stand quite by itself, he will enlarge the precincts, if I may say so, of some species, in order to make room for it; or he will create a new species on purpose to receive it, and call it a Play of Nature, or give it some other appellation, under which he arranges all the oddities that he knows not what else to do with. But to some class or other of known objects he must refer it, and betwixt it and them he must find out some resemblance or other, before he can get rid of that Wonder, that uncertainty and anxious curiosity excited by its singular appearance, and by its dissimilitude with all the objects he had hitherto observed.

As single and individual objects thus excite our Wonder when, by

their uncommon qualities and singular appearance, they make us uncertain to what species of things we ought to refer them; so a succession of objects which follow one another in an uncommon train or
order, will produce the same effect, though there be nothing particular
in any one of them taken by itself.

When one accustomed object appears after another, which it does
not usually follow, it first excites, by its unexpectedness, the sentiment
properly called Surprise, and afterwards, by the singularity of the succession, or order of its appearance, the sentiment properly called
Wonder. We start and are surprised at seeing it there, and then
wonder how it came there. The motion of a small piece of iron along
a plain table is in itself no extraordinary object, yet the person who
first saw it begin, without any visible impulse, in consequence of the
motion of a loadstone at some little distance from it, could not behold
it without the most extreme Surprise; and when that momentary
emotion was over, he would still wonder how it came to be conjoined
to an event with which, according to the ordinary train of things, he
could have so little suspected it to have any connection.

When two objects, however unlike, have often been observed to follow
each other, and have constantly presented themselves to the senses in
that order, they come to be connected together in the fancy, that the
idea of the one seems, of its own accord, to call up and introduce that
of the other. If the objects are still observed to succeed each other as
before, this connection, or, as it has been called, this association of
their ideas, becomes stricter and stricter, and the habit of the imagination to pass from the conception of the one to that of the other, grows
more and more rivetted and confirmed. As its ideas move more rapidly
than external objects, it is continually running before them, and therefore anticipates, before it happens, every event which falls out according to this ordinary course of things. When objects succeed each other
in the same train in which the ideas of the imagination have thus been
accustomed to move, and in which, though not conducted by that chain
of events presented to the senses, they have acquired a tendency to go
on of their own accord, such objects appear all closely connected with
one another, and the thought glides easily along them, without effort
and without interruption. They fall in with the natural career of the
imagination; and as the ideas which represented such a train of things
would seem all mutually to introduce each other, every last thought to
be called up by the foregoing, and to call up the succeeding; so when
the objects themselves occur, every last event seems, in the same manner, to be introduced by the foregoing, and to introduce the succeeding.
There is no break, no stop, no gap, no interval. The ideas excited by
so coherent a chain of things seem, as it were, to float through the
mind of their own accord, without obliging it to exert itself, or to make
any effort in order to pass from one of them to another.

But if this customary connection be interrupted, if one or more objects appear in an order quite different from that to which the imagination has been accustomed, and for which it is prepared, the contrary of all this happens. We are at first surprised by the unexpectedness of the new appearance, and when that momentary emotion is over, we still wonder how it came to occur in that place. The imagination no longer feels the usual facility of passing from the event which goes before to that which comes after. It is an order or law of succession to which it has not been accustomed, and which it therefore finds some difficulty in following, or in attending to. The fancy is stopped and interrupted in that natural movement or career, according to which it was proceeding. Those two events seem to stand at a distance from each other; it endeavours to bring them together, but they refuse to unite; and it feels, or imagines it feels, something like a gap or interval betwixt them. It naturally hesitates, and, as it were, pauses upon the brink of this interval; it endeavours to find out something which may fill up the gap, which, like a bridge, may so far at least unite those seemingly distant objects, as to render the passage of the thought betwixt them smooth, and natural, and easy. The supposition of a chain of intermediate, though invisible, events, which succeed each other in a train similar to that in which the imagination has been accustomed to move, and which links together those two disjointed appearances, is the only means by which the imagination can fill up this interval, is the only bridge which, if one may say so, can smooth its passage from the one object to the other. Thus, when we observe the motion of the iron, in consequence of that of the loadstone, we gaze and hesitate, and feel a want of connection betwixt two events which follow one another in so unusual a train. But when, with Des Cartes, we imagine certain invisible effluvia to circulate round one of them, and by their repeated impulses to impel the other, both to move towards it, and to follow its motion, we fill up the interval betwixt them, we join them together by a sort of bridge, and thus take off that hesitation and difficulty which the imagination felt in passing from the one to the other. That the iron should move after the loadstone seems, upon this hypothesis, in some measure according to the ordinary course of things. Motion after impulse is an order of succession with which of all things we are the most familiar. Two objects which are so connected seem, to our mind, no longer to be disjointed, and the imagination flows smoothly and easily along them.

Such is the nature of this second species of Wonder, which arises from an unusual succession of things. The stop which is thereby given to the career of the imagination, the difficulty which it finds in passing along such disjointed objects, and the feeling of something like a gap or interval betwixt them, constitute the whole essence of this emotion. Upon the clear discovery of a connecting chain of intermediate events, it vanishes altogether. What obstructed the movement of the imagination is then removed. Who wonders at the machinery of the opera-house who has once been admitted behind the scenes? In the wonders of nature, however, it rarely happens that we can discover so clearly this connecting chain. With regard to a few even of them, indeed, we seem to have been really admitted behind the scenes, and our wonder accordingly is entirely at an end. Thus the eclipses of the sun and moon, which once, more than all the other appearances in the heavens, excited the terror and amazement of mankind, seem now no longer to be wonderful, since the connecting chain has been found out which joins them to the ordinary course of things. Nay, in those cases in which we have been less successful, even the vague hypothesis of Des Cartes, and the yet more indetermined notions of Aristotle, have, with their followers, contributed to give some coherence to the appearances of nature, and might diminish, though they could not destroy, their wonder. If they did not completely fill up the interval betwixt the two disjointed objects, they bestowed upon them, however, some sort of loose connection which they wanted before.

That the imagination feels a real difficulty in passing along two events which follow one another in an uncommon order, may be confirmed by many obvious observations. If it attempts to attend beyond a certain time to a long series of this kind, the continual efforts it is obliged to make, in order to pass from one object to another, and thus follow the progress of the succession, soon fatigue it, and if repeated too often, disorder and disjoint its whole frame. It is thus that too severe an application to study sometimes brings on lunacy and frenzy, in those especially who are somewhat advanced in life, but whose imaginations, from being too late in applying, have not got those habits which dispose them to follow easily the reasonings in the abstract sciences. Every step of a demonstration, which to an old practitioner is quite natural and easy, requires from them the most intense application of thought.

Spurred on, however, either by ambition or by admiration for the subject, they still continue till they become, first confused, then giddy, and at last distracted. Could we conceive a person of the soundest judgment, who had grown up to maturity, and whose imagination had acquired those habits, and that mould, which the constitution of things in this world necessarily impresses upon it, to be all at once transported alive to some other planet, where nature was governed by laws quite different from those which take place here; as he would be continually obliged to attend to events, which must to him appear in the highest degree jarring, irregular, and discordant, he would soon feel the same confusion and giddiness begin to come upon him, which would at last end in the same manner, in lunacy and distraction. Neither, to produce this effect, is it necessary that the objects should be either great or interesting, or even uncommon, in themselves. It is sufficient that they follow one another in an uncommon order. Let any one attempt to look over even a game of cards, and to attend particularly to every single stroke, and if he is unacquainted with the nature and rules of the games ; that is, with the laws which regulate the succession of the cards; he will soon feel the same confusion and giddiness begin to come upon him, which, were it to be continued for days and months, would end in the same manner, in lunacy and distraction. But if the mind be thus thrown into the most violent disorder, when it attends to a long series of events which follow one another in an uncommon train, it must feel some degree of the same disorder, when it observes even a single event fall out in this unusual manner : for the violent disorder can arise from nothing but the too frequent repetition of this smaller uneasiness.

That it is the unusualness alone of the succession which occasions this stop and interruption in the progress of the imagination as well as the notion of an interval betwixt the two immediately succeeding objects, to be filled up by some chain of intermediate events, is not less evident. The same orders of succession, which to one set of men seem quite according to the natural course of things, and such as require no intermediate events to join them, shall to another appear altogether incoherent and disjointed, unless some such events be supposed : and this for no other reason, but because such orders of succession are familiar to the one, and strange to the other. When we enter the work-houses of the most common artizans; such as dyers, brewers, distillers; we observe a number of appearances, which present themselves in an order that seems to us very strange and wonderful. Our thought cannot easily follow it, we feel an interval betwixt every two of them, and require some chain of intermediate events, to fill it up, and link them together. But the artizan himself, who has been for many years familiar with the consequences of all the operations of his art, feels no such interval. They fall in with what custom has made the natural movement of his imagination : they no longer excite his Wonder, and if he is not a genius superior to his profession, so as to be capable of making the very easy reflection, that those things, though familiar to him, may be strange to us, he will be disposed rather to laugh at, than sympathize with our Wonder. He cannot conceive what occasion there is for any connecting events to unite those appearances, which seem to him to succeed each other very naturally. It is their nature, he tells us, to follow one another in this order, and that accordingly they always do so. In the same manner bread has, since the world begun been the common nourishment of the human body, and men have so long seen it, every day, converted into flesh and bones, substances in all respects so unlike it, that they have seldom had the curiosity to inquire by what process of interme-

336 THE MIND CONFUSED BY CONTEMPLATING STRANGE EVENTS

diate events this change is brought about. Because the passage of the thought from the one object to the other is by custom become quite smooth and easy, almost without the supposition of any such process. Philosophers, indeed, who often look for a chain of invisible objects to join together two events that occur in an order familiar to all the world, have endeavoured to find out a chain of this kind betwixt the two events I have just now mentioned ; in the same manner as they have endeavoured, by a like intermediate chain, to connect the gravity, the elasticity, and even the cohesion of natural bodies, with some of their other qualities. These, however, are all of them such combinations of events as give no stop to the imaginations of the bulk of mankind, as excite no Wonder, nor any apprehension that there is wanting the strictest connection between them. But as in those sounds, which to the greater part of men seem perfectly agreeable to measure and harmony, the nicer ear of a musician will discover a want, both of the most exact time, and of the most perfect coincidence ; so the more practised thought of a philosopher, who has spent his whole life in the study of the connecting principles of nature, will often feel an interval betwixt two objects, which, to more careless observers, seem very strictly conjoined. By long attention to all the connections which have ever been presented to his observation, by having often compared them with one another, he has, like the musician, acquired, if one may so, a nicer ear, and a more delicate feeling with regard to things of this nature. And as to the one, that music seems dissonance which falls short of the most perfect harmony ; so to the other, those events seem altogether separated and disjoined, which may fall short of the strictest and most perfect connection.

Philosophy is the science of the connecting principles of nature Nature, after the largest experience that common observation can acquire, seems to abound with events which appear solitary and incoherent with all that go before them, which therefore disturb the easy movement of the imagination; which makes its ideas succeed each other, if one may say so, by irregular starts and sallies; and which thus tend, in some measure, to introduce those confusions and distractions we formerly mentioned. Philosophy, by representing the invisible chains which bind together all these disjointed objects, endeavours to introduce order into this chaos of jarring and discordant appearances, to allay this tumult of the imagination, and to restore it, when it surveys the great revolutions of the universe, to that tone of tranquillity and composure, which is both most agreeable in itself, and most suitable to its nature. Philosophy, therefore, may be regarded as one of those arts which address themselves to the imagination; and whose theory and history, upon that account, fall properly within the circumference of our subject. Let us endeavour to trace it, from its first origin, up to that summit of perfection to which it is at present supposed to have arrived, and to which, indeed, it has equally been supposed to have arrived in almost all former times.   It is the most sublime of all the agreeable arts, and its revolutions have been the greatest, the most frequent, and the most distinguished of all those that have happened in the literary world.   Its history, therefore, must, upon all accounts, be the most entertaining and the most instructive. Let us examine, therefore, all the different systems of nature, which, in these western parts of the world, the only parts of whose history we know anything, have successively been adopted by the learned and ingenious; and, without regarding their absurdity or probability, their agreement or inconsistency with truth and reality, let us consider them only in that particular point of view which belongs to our subject; and content ourselves with inquiring how far each of them was fitted to soothe the imagination, and to render the theatre of nature a more co-herent, and therefore a more magnificent spectacle, than otherwise it would have appeared to be.   According as they have failed or succeeded in this, they have constantly failed or succeeded in gaining reputation and renown to their authors; and this will be found to be the clue that is most capable of conducting us through all the labyrinths of philoso-phical history: for in the mean time, it will serve to confirm what has gone before, and to throw light upon what is to come after, that we observe, in general, that no system, how well soever in other respects supported, has ever been able to gain any general credit on the world, whose connecting principles were not such as were familiar to all man-kind.   Why has the chemical philosophy in all ages crept along in ob-scurity, and been so disregarded by the generality of mankind, while other systems, less useful, and not more agreeable to experience, have possessed universal admiration for whole centuries together?   The connecting principles of the chemical philosophy are such as the gene-rality of mankind know nothing about, have rarely seen, and have never been acquainted with; and which to them, therefore, are in-capable of smoothing the passage of the imagination betwixt any two seemingly disjointed objects.   Salts, sulphurs, and mercuries, acids and alkalis, are principles which can smooth things to those only who live about the furnace; but whose most common operations seem, to the bulk of mankind, as disjointed as any two events which the che-mists would connect together by them.   Those artists, however, natu-rally explained things to themselves by principles that were familiar to themselves.   As Aristotle observes, that the early Pythagoreans, who first studied arithmetic, explained all things by the properties of num-bers; and Cicero tells us, that Aristoxenus, the musician, found the nature of the soul to consist in harmony.   In the same manner, a learned physician lately gave a system of moral philosophy upon the principles of his own art, in which wisdom and virtue were the health-ful state of the soul; the different vices and follies, the different diseases to which it was subject; in which the causes and symptoms of those diseases were ascertained; and, in the same medical strain, a proper method of cure prescribed. In the same manner also, others have written parallels of painting and poetry, of poetry and music, of music and architecture, of beauty and virtue, of all the fine arts; systems which have universally owed their origin to the lucubrations of those who were acquainted with the one art, but ignorant of the other; who therefore explained to themselves the phenomena, in that which was strange to them, by those in that which was familiar; and with whom, upon that account, the analogy, which in other writers gives occasion to a few ingenious similitudes, became the great hinge upon which every thing turned.

SECT. III.—*Of the Origin of Philosophy.*

MANKIND, in the first ages of society, before the establishment of law, order, and security, have little curiosity to find out those hidden chains of events which bind together the seemingly disjointed appearances of nature. A savage, whose subsistence is precarious, whose life is every day exposed to the rudest dangers, has no inclination to amuse himself with searching out what, when discovered, seems to serve no other purpose than to render the theatre of nature a more connected spectacle to his imagination. Many of these smaller incoherences, which in the course of things perplex philosophers, entirely escape his attention. Those more magnificent irregularities, whose grandeur he cannot overlook, call forth his amazement. Comets, eclipses, thunder, lightning, and other meteors, by their greatness, naturally overawe him, and he views them with a reverence that approaches to fear. His inexperience and uncertainty with regard to every thing about them, how they came, how they are to go, what went before, what is to come after them, exasperate his sentiment into terror and consternation. But our passions, as Father Malbranche observes, all justify themselves; that is, suggest to us opinions which justify them. As those appearances terrify him, therefore, he is disposed to believe every thing about them which can render them still more the objects of his terror. That they proceed from some intelligent, though invisible causes, of whose vengeance and displeasure they are either the signs or the effects, is the notion of all others most capable of enhancing this passion, and is that, therefore, which he is most apt to entertain. To this, too, that cowardice and pusillanimity, so natural to man in his uncivilized state, still more disposes him; unprotected by the laws of society, exposed, defenceless, he feels his weakness upon all occasions; his strength and security upon none.

But all the irregularities of nature are not of this awful or terrible kind. Some of them are perfectly beautiful and agreeable. These, therefore, from the same impotence of mind, would be beheld with love and complacency, and even with transports of gratitude; for whatever is the cause of pleasure naturally excites our gratitude. A child caresses the fruit that is agreeable to it, as it beats the stone that hurts it. The notions of a savage are not very different. The ancient Athenians, who solemnly punished the axe which had accidentally been the cause of the death of a man, erected altars, and offered sacrifices to the rainbow. Sentiments not unlike these, may sometimes, upon such occasions, begin to be felt even in the breasts of the most civilized, but are presently checked by the reflection, that the things are not their proper objects. But a savage, whose notions are guided altogether by wild nature and passion, waits for no other proof that a thing is the proper object of any sentiment, than that it excites it. The reverence and gratitude, with which some of the appearances of nature inspire him, convince him that they are the proper objects of reverence and gratitude, and therefore proceed from some intelligent beings, who take pleasure in the expressions of those sentiments. With him, therefore, every object of nature, which by its beauty or greatness, its utility or hurtfulness, is considerable enough to attract his attention, and whose operations are not perfectly regular, is supposed to act by the direction of some invisible and designing power. The sea is spread out into a calm, or heaved into a storm, according to the good pleasure of Neptune. Does the earth pour forth an exuberant harvest? It is owing to the indulgence of Ceres. Does the vine yield a plentiful vintage? It flows from the bounty of Bacchus. Do either refuse their presents? It is ascribed to the displeasure of those offended deities. The tree which now flourishes and now decays, is inhabited by a Dryad, upon whose health or sickness its various appearances depend. The fountain, which sometimes flows in a copious, and sometimes in a scanty stream, which appears sometimes clear and limpid, and at other times muddy and disturbed, is affected in all its changes by the Naiad who dwells within it. Hence the origin of Polytheism, and of that vulgar superstition which ascribes all the irregular events of nature to the favour or displeasure of intelligent, though invisible beings, to gods, demons, witches, genii, fairies. For it may be observed, that in all polytheistic religions, among savages, as well as in the early ages of heathen antiquity, it is the irregular events of nature only that are ascribed to the agency and power of their gods. Fire burns, and water refreshes; heavy bodies descend, and lighter substances fly upwards, by the necessity of their own nature; nor was the invisible hand of Jupiter ever apprehended to be employed in those matters. But thunder and lightning, storms and sunshine, those more irregular events, were ascribed to his favour, or his anger. Man, the only designing power with which they were acquainted, never acts but either to stop or to alter the course which natural events would take, if left to themselves.

Those other intelligent beings, whom they imagined, but knew not, were naturally supposed to act in the same manner; not to employ themselves in supporting the ordinary course of things, which went on of its own accord, but to stop, to thwart, and to disturb it. And thus, in the first ages of the world, the lowest and most pusillanimous superstition supplied the place of philosophy.

But when law has established order and security, and subsistence ceases to be precarious, the curiosity of mankind is increased, and their fears are diminished. The leisure which they then enjoy renders them more attentive to the appearances of nature, more observant of her smallest irregularities, and more desirous to know what is the chain which links them together. That some such chain subsists betwixt all her seemingly disjointed phenomena, they are necessarily led to conceive; and that magnanimity and cheerfulness which all generous natures acquire who are bred in civilized societies, where they have so few occasions to feel their weakness, and so many to be conscious of their strength and security, renders them less disposed to employ, for this connecting chain, those invisible beings whom the fear and ignorance of their rude forefathers had engendered. Those of liberal fortunes, whose attention is not much occupied either with business or with pleasure, can fill up the void of their imagination, which is thus disengaged from the ordinary affairs of life, no other way than by attending to that train of events which passes around them. While the great objects of nature thus pass in review before them, many things occur in an order to which they have not been accustomed. Their imagination, which accompanies with ease and delight the regular progress of nature, is stopped and embarrassed by those seeming incoherences; they excite their wonder, and seem to require some chain of intermediate events, which, by connecting them with something that has gone before, may thus render the whole course of the universe consistent and of a piece. Wonder, therefore, and not any expectation of advantage from its discoveries, is the first principle which prompts mankind to the study of Philosophy, of that science which pretends to lay open the concealed connections that unite the various appearances of nature; and they pursue this study for its own sake, as an original pleasure or good in itself, without regarding its tendency to procure them the means of many other pleasures.

Greece, and the Greek colonies in Sicily, Italy, and the Lesser Asia, were the first countries which, in these western parts of the world, arrived at a state of civilized society. It was in them, therefore, that the first philosophers, of whose doctrine we have any distinct account, appeared. Law and order seem indeed to have been established in the great monarchies of Asia and Egypt, long before they had any footing in Greece: yet, after all that has been said concerning the learning of the Chaldeans and Egyptians, whether there ever was in those nations any thing which deserved the name of science, or whether that despotism which is more destructive of security and leisure than anarchy itself, and which prevailed over all the East, prevented the growth of Philosophy, is a question which, for want of monuments, cannot be determined with any degree of precision.

The Greek colonies having been settled amid nations either altogether barbarous, or altogether unwarlike, over whom, therefore, they soon acquired a very great authority, seem, upon that account, to have arrived at a considerable degree of empire and opulence before any state in the parent country had surmounted that extreme poverty, which, by leaving no room for any evident distinction of ranks, is necessarily attended with the confusion and misrule which flows from a want of all regular subordination.   The Greek islands being secure from the invasion of land armies, or from naval forces, which were in those days but little known, seem, upon that account too, to have got before the continent in all sorts of civility and improvement.   The first philosophers, therefore, as well as the first poets, seem all to have been natives, either of their colonies, or of their islands.   It was from thence that Homer, Archilochus, Stesichorus, Simonides, Sappho, Anacreon, derived their birth.   Thales and Pythagoras, the founders of the two earliest sects of philosophy, arose, the one in an Asiatic colony, the other in an island; and neither of them established his school in the mother country.

What was the particular system of either of those two philosophers, or whether their doctrine was so methodized as to deserve the name of a system, the imperfection, as well as the uncertainty of all the traditions that have come down to us concerning them, make it impossible to determine.   The school of Pythagoras, however, seems to have advanced further in the study of the connecting principles of nature, than that of the Ionian philosopher.   The accounts which are given of Anaximander, Anaximenes, Anaxagoras, Archelaus, the successors of Thales, represent the doctrines of those sages as full of the most inextricable confusion.   Something, however, that approaches to a composed and orderly system, may be traced in what is delivered down to us concerning the doctrine of Empedocles, of Archytas, of Timæus, and of Ocellus the Lucanian, the most renowned philosophers of the Italian school.   The opinions of the two last coincide pretty much; the one, with those of Plato; the other, with those of Aristotle; nor do those of the two first seem to have been very different, of whom the one was the author of the doctrine of the Four Elements, the other the inventor of the Categories; who, therefore, may be regarded as the founders, the one, of the ancient Physics; the other, of the ancient Dialectic; and, how closely these were connected will appear hereafter. It was in the school of Socrates, however, from Plato and Aristotle, that Philosophy first received that form, which introduced her, if one may say so, to the general acquaintance of the world. It is from them, therefore, that we shall begin to give her history in any detail. Whatever was valuable in the former systems, which was at all consistent with their general principles, they seem to have consolidated into their own. From the Ionian philosophy, I have not been able to discover that they derived anything. From the Pythagorean school, both Plato and Aristotle seem to have derived the fundamental principles of almost all their doctrines. Plato, too, appears to have borrowed something from two other sects of philosophers, whose extreme obscurity seems to have prevented them from acquiring themselves any extensive reputation; the one was that of Cratylus and Heraclitus; the other was Xenophanes, Parmenides, Melissus, and Zeno. To pretend to rescue the system of any of those ante-Socratic sages, from that oblivion which at present covers them all, would be a vain and useless attempt. What seems, however, to have been borrowed from them, shall sometimes be marked as we go along.

There was still another school of philosophy, earlier than Plato, from which, however, he was so far from borrowing any thing, that he seems to have bent the whole force of his reason to discredit and expose its principles. This was the philosophy of Leucippus, Democratus, and Protagoras, which accordingly seems to have submitted to his eloquence, to have lain dormant, and to have been almost forgotten for some generations, till it was afterwards more successfully revived by Epicurus.

Sec. IV.—*The History of Astronomy.*

OF all the phenomena of nature, the celestial appearances are, by their greatness and beauty, the most universal objects of the curiosity of mankind. Those who surveyed the heavens with the most careless attention, necessarily distinguished in them three different sorts of objects; the Sun, the Moon, and the Stars. These last, appearing always in the same situation, and at the same distance with regard to one another, and seeming to revolve every day round the earth in parallel circles, which widened gradually from the poles to the equator, were naturally thought to have all the marks of being fixed, like so many gems, in the concave side of the firmament, and of being carried round by the diurnal revolutions of that solid body: for the azure sky, in which the stars seem to float, was readily apprehended, upon account of the uniformity of their apparent motions, to be a solid body, the roof or outer wall of the universe, to whose inside all those little sparkling objects were attached.

The Sun and Moon, often changing their distance and situation, in regard to the other heavenly bodies, could not be apprehended to be attached to the same sphere with them. They assigned, therefore, to each of them, a sphere of its own; that is, supposed each of them to be attached to the concave side of a solid and transparent body, by whose revolutions they were carried round the earth.   There was not, indeed, in this case, the same ground for the supposition of such sphere as in that of the Fixed Stars; for neither the Sun nor the Moon appear to keep always at the same distance with regard to any one of the other heavenly bodies.   But as the motion of the Stars had been accounted for by an hypothesis of this kind, it rendered the theory of the heavens more uniform, to account for that of the Sun and Moon in the same manner.   The sphere of the sun they placed above that of the Moon; as the Moon was evidently seen in eclipses to pass betwixt the Sun and the Earth.   Each of them was supposed to revolve by a motion of its own, and at the same time to be affected by the motion of the Fixed Stars.   Thus, the Sun was carried round from east to west by the communicated movement of this outer sphere, which produced his diurnal revolutions, and the vicissitudes of day and night; but at the same time he had a motion of his own, contrary to this, from west to east, which occasioned his annual revolution, and the continual shifting of his place with regard to the Fixed Stars.   This motion was more easy, they thought, when carried on edgeways, and not in direct opposition to the motion of the outer sphere, which occasioned the inclination of the axis of the sphere of the Sun, to that of the sphere of the Fixed Stars; this again produced the obliquity of the ecliptic, and the consequent changes of the seasons.   The moon, being placed below the sphere of the Sun, had both a shorter course to finish, and was less obstructed by the contrary movement of the sphere of the Fixed Stars, from which she was farther removed.   She finished her period, therefore, in a shorter time, and required but a month, instead of a year, to complete it.

The Stars, when more attentively surveyed, were some of them observed to be less constant and uniform in their motions than the rest, and to change their situations with regard to the other heavenly bodies; moving generally eastward, yet appearing sometimes to stand still, and sometimes even to move westwards.   These, to the number of five, were distinguished by the name of Planets, or Wandering Stars, and marked with the particular appellations of Saturn, Jupiter, Mars, Venus, and Mercury.   As, like the Sun and Moon, they seem to accompany the motion of the Fixed Stars from east to west, but at the same time to have a motion of their own, which is generally from west to east; they were each of them, as well as those two great lamps of heaven, apprehended to be attached to the inside of a solid concave and transparent sphere, which had a revolution of its own, that was almost directly contrary to the revolution of the outer heaven, but which, at the same time, was hurried along by the superior violence and greater rapidity of this last.

This is the system of concentric Spheres, the first regular system of

Astronomy, which the world beheld, as it was taught in the Italian school before Aristotle, and his two contemporary philosophers, Eudoxus and Callippus, had given it all the perfection which it is capable of receiving. Though rude and inartificial, it is capable of connecting together, in the imagination, the grandest and the most seemingly disjointed appearances in the heavens. The motions of the most remarkable objects in the celestial regions, the Sun, the Moon, the Fixed Stars, are sufficiently connected with one another by this hypothesis. The eclipses of these two great luminaries are, though not so easily calculated, as easily explained, upon this ancient, as upon the modern system. When these early philosophers explained to their disciples the very simple causes of those dreadful phenomena, it was under the seal of the most sacred secrecy, that they might avoid the fury of the people, and not incur the imputation of impiety, when they thus took from the gods the direction of those events, which were apprehended to be the most terrible tokens of their impending vengeance. The obliquity of the ecliptic, the consequent changes of the seasons, the vicissitudes of day and night, and the different lengths of both days and nights in the different seasons, correspond too, pretty exactly, with this ancient doctrine. And if there had been no other bodies discoverable in the heavens, besides the Sun, the Moon, and the Fixed Stars, this hypothesis might have stood the examinations of all ages and gone down triumphant to the remotest posterity.

If it gained the belief of mankind by its plausibility, it attracted their wonder and admiration; sentiments that still more confirmed their belief, by the novelty and beauty of that view of nature which it presented to the imagination. Before this system was taught in the world, the earth was regarded as, what it appears to the eye, a vast, rough, and irregular plain, the basis and foundation of the universe, surrounded on all sides by the ocean, and whose roots extended themselves through the whole of that infinite depth which is below it. The sky was considered as a solid hemisphere, which covered the earth, and united with the ocean at the extremity of the horizon. The Sun, the Moon, and all the heavenly bodies rose out of the eastern, climbed up the convex side of the heavens, and descended again into the western ocean, and from thence, by some subterraneous passages, returned to their first chambers in the east. Nor was this notion confined to the people, or to the poets who painted the opinions of the people; it was held by Xenophanes, founder of the Eleatic philosophy, after that of the Ionian and Italian schools, the earliest that appeared in Greece. Thales of Miletus too, who, according to Aristotle, represented the Earth as floating upon an immense ocean of water, may have been nearly of the same opinion; notwithstanding what we are told by Plutarch and Apuleius concerning his astronomical discoveries, all of which must plainly have been of a much later date. To those who had no other idea of nature, besides what they derived from so confused an account of things, how agreeable must that system have appeared, which represented the Earth as distinguished into land and water, self-balanced and suspended in the centre of the universe, surrounded by the elements of Air and Ether, and covered by eight polished and crystalline Spheres, each of which was distinguished by one or more beautiful and luminous bodies, and all of which revolved round their common centre, by varied, but by equable and proportionable motions. It seems to have been the beauty of this system that gave Plato the notion of something like an harmonic proportion, to be discovered in the motions and distances of the heavenly bodies ; and which suggested to the earlier Pythagoreans, the celebrated fancy of the Music of the Spheres ; a wild and romantic idea, yet such as does not ill correspond with that admiration, which so beautiful a system, recommended too by the graces of novelty, is apt to inspire.

Whatever are the defects which this account of things labours under, they are such, as to the first observers of the heavens could not readily occur. If all the motions of the Five Planets cannot, the greater part of them may, be easily connected by it ; they and all their motions are the least remarkable objects in the heavens ; the greater part of mankind take no notice of them at all ; and a system, whose only defect lies in the account which it gives of them, cannot thereby be much disgraced in their opinion. If some of the appearances too of the Sun and Moon, the sometimes accelerated and again retarded motions of those luminaries but ill correspond with it ; these, too, are such as cannot be discovered but by the most attentive observation, and such as we cannot wonder that the imaginations of the first enquirers should slur over, if one may say so, and take little notice of.

It was, however, to remedy those defects, that Eudoxus, the friend and auditor of Plato, found it necessary to increase the number of the Celestial Spheres. Each Planet is sometimes observed to advance forward in that eastern course which is peculiar to itself, sometimes to retire backwards, and sometimes again to stand still. To suppose that the sphere of the planet should by its own motion, if one may say so, sometimes roll forwards, sometimes roll backwards, and sometimes do neither the one nor the other, is contrary to all the natural propensities of the imagination, which accompanies with ease and delight any regular and orderly motion, but feels itself perpetually stopped and interrupted, when it endeavours to attend to one so desultory and uncertain. It would pursue, naturally and of its own accord, the direct or progressive movement of the Sphere, but is every now and then shocked, if one may say so, and turned violently out of its natural career by the retrograde and stationary appearances of the Planet, betwixt which and its more usual motion, the fancy feels a want of connection, a gap or interval, which it cannot fill up, but by supposing

23

some chain of intermediate events to join them. The hypothesis of a number of other spheres revolving in the heavens, besides those in which the luminous bodies themselves were infixed, was the chain with which Eudoxus endeavoured to supply it. He bestowed four of these Spheres upon each of the five Planets; one in which the luminous body itself revolved, and three others above it. Each of these had a regular and constant, but a peculiar movement of its own, which it communicated to what was properly the Sphere of the Planet, and thus occasioned that diversity of motions observable in those bodies. One of these Spheres, for example, had an oscillatory motion, like the circular pendulum of a watch. As when you turn round a watch, like a Sphere upon its axis, the pendulum will, while turned round along with it, still continue to oscillate, and communicate to whatever body is comprehended within it, both its own oscillations and the circular motion of the watch; so this oscillating Sphere, being itself turned round by the motion of the Sphere above it, communicated to the Sphere below it, that circular, as well as its own oscillatory motions; produced by the one, the daily revolutions: by the other, the direct, stationary, and retrograde appearances of the Planet, which derived from a third Sphere that revolution by which it performed its annual period. The motions of all these Spheres were in themselves constant and equable, such as the imagination could easily attend to and pursue, and which connected together that otherwise incoherent diversity of movements observable in the Sphere of the Planet. The motions of the Sun and Moon being more regular than those of the Five Planets, by assigning three Spheres to each of them, Eudoxus imagined he could connect together all the diversity of movements discoverable in either. The motion of the Fixed Stars being perfectly regular, one Sphere he judged sufficient for them all. So that, according to this account, the whole number of Celestial Spheres amounted to twenty-seven. Callippus, though somewhat younger, the contemporary of Eudoxus, found that even this number was not enough to connect together the vast variety of movements which he discovered in those bodies, and therefore increased it to thirty-four. Aristotle, upon a yet more attentive observation, found that even all these Spheres would not be sufficient, and therefore added twenty-two more, which increased their number to fifty-six. Later observers discovered still new motions, and new inequalities, in the heavens. New Spheres were therefore still to be added to the system, and some of them to be placed even above that of the Fixed Stars. So that in the sixteenth century, when Fracostorio, smit with the eloquence of Plato and Aristotle, and with the regularity and harmony of their system, in itself perfectly beautiful, though it corresponds but inaccurately with the phenomena, endeavoured to revive this ancient Astronomy, which had long given place to that of Ptolemy and Hipparchus, he found it necessary to multiply the number of Celestial Spheres to seventy-two ; neither were all these found to be enough.

This system had now become as intricate and complex as those appearances themselves, which it had been invented to render uniform and coherent.   The imagination, therefore, found itself but little re- lieved from that embarrassment, into which those appearances had thrown it, by so perplexed an account of things.   Another system, for this reason, not long after the days of Aristotle, was invented by Apol- lonius, which was afterwards perfected by Hipparchus, and has since been delivered down to us by Ptolemy, the more artificial system of Eccentric Spheres and Epicycles.

In this system, they first distinguished between the real and apparent motion of the heavenly bodies.   These, they observed, upon account of their immense distance, must necessarily appear to revolve in circles concentric with the globe of the Earth, and with one another : but that we cannot, therefore, be certain that they really revolve in such circles, since, though they did not, they would still have the same appearance. By supposing, therefore, that the Sun and the other Planets revolved in circles, whose centres were very distant from the centre of the Earth ; that consequently, in the progress of their revolution, they must sometimes approach nearer, and sometimes recede further from it, and must to its inhabitants appear to move faster in the one case, and slower in the other, those philosophers imagined they could ac- count for the apparently unequal velocities of all those bodies.

By supposing, that in the solidity of the Sphere of each of the Five Planets there was formed another little Sphere, called an Epicycle, which revolved round its own centre, at the same time that it was carried round the centre of the Earth by the revolution of the great Sphere, betwixt whose concave and convex sides it was inclosed ; in the same manner as we might suppose a little wheel inclosed within the outer circle of a great wheel, and which whirled about several times upon its own axis, while its centre was carried round the axis of the great wheel, they imagined they could account for the retrograde and stationary appearances of those most irregular objects in the heavens. The Planet, they supposed, was attached to the circumference, and whirled round the centre of this little Sphere, at the same time that it was carried round the earth by the movement of the great Sphere. The revolution of this little Sphere, or Epicycle, was such, that the Planet, when in the upper part of it ; that is, when furthest off and least sensible to the eye ; was carried round in the same direction with the centre of the Epicycle, or with the Sphere in which the Epicycle was inclosed : but when in the lower part, that is, when nearest and most sensible to the eye ; it was carried round a direction contrary to that of the centre of the Epicycle : in the same manner as every point in the upper part of the outer circle of a coach-wheel revolves forward in the same direction with the axis, while every point, in the lower part, revolves backwards in a contrary direction to the axis. The motions of the Planet, therefore, surveyed from the Earth, appeared direct, when in the upper part of the Epicycle, and retrograde, when in the lower. When again it either descended from the upper part to the lower, or ascended from the lower to the upper, it appeared stationary.

But, though, by the eccentricity of the great Sphere, they were thus able, in some measure, to connect together the unequal velocities of the heavenly bodies, and by the revolutions of the little Sphere, the direct, stationary, and retrograde appearances of the Planets, there was another difficulty that still remained., Neither the Moon, nor the three superior Planets, appear always in the same part of the heavens, when at their periods of most retarded motion, or when they are supposed to be at the greatest distance from the Earth. The apogeum therefore, or the point of greatest distance from the Earth, in the Spheres of each of those bodies, must have a movement of its own, which may carry it successively through all the different points of the Ecliptic. They supposed, therefore, that while the great eccentric Sphere revolved eastwards round its centre, that its centre too revolved westwards in a circle of its own, round the centre of the Earth, and thus carried its apogeum through all the different points of the Ecliptic.

But with all those combined and perplexed circles; though the patrons of this system were able to give some degree of uniformity to the real directions of the Planets, they found it impossible so to adjust the velocities of those supposed Spheres to the phenomena, as that the revolution of any one of them, when surveyed from its own centre, should appear perfectly equable and uniform. From that point, the only point in which the velocity of what moves in a circle can be truly judged of, they would still appear irregular and inconstant, and such as tended to embarrass and confound the imagination. They invented, therefore, for each of them, a new Circle, called the Equalizing Circle, from whose centre they should all appear perfectly equable: that is, they so adjusted the velocities of these Spheres, as that, though the revolution of each of them would appear irregular when surveyed from its own centre, there should, however, be a point comprehended within its circumference, from whence its motions should appear to cut off, in equal times, equal portions of the Circle, of which that point was supposed to be the centre.

Nothing can more evidently show how much the repose and tranquillity of the imagination is the ultimate end of philosophy, than the invention of this Equalizing Circle. The motions of the heavenly bodies had appeared inconstant and irregular, both in their velocities and in their directions. They were such, therefore, as tended to embarrass and confound the imagination, whenever it attempted to trace them. The invention of Eccentric Spheres, of Epicycles, and of the

revolution of the centres of the Eccentric Spheres, tended to allay this
confusion, to connect together those disjointed appearances, and to
introduce harmony and order into the mind's conception of the movements of those bodies.   It did this, however, but imperfectly; it introduced uniformity and coherence into their real directions.   But their
velocities, when surveyed from the only point in which the velocity of
what moves in a Circle can be truly judged of, the centre of that Circle,
still remained, in some measure, inconstant as before; and still, therefore, embarrassed the imagination.   The mind found itself somewhat
relieved from this embarrassment, when it conceived, that how irregular
soever the motions of each of those Circles might appear, when surveyed from its own centre, there was, however, in each of them, a point,
from whence its revolution would appear perfectly equable and uniform,
and such as the imagination could easily follow.   Those philosophers
transported themselves, in fancy, to the centres of these imaginary
Circles, and took pleasure in surveying from thence, all those fantastical motions, arranged, according to that harmony and order, which
it had been the end of all their researches to bestow upon them.   Here,
at last, they enjoyed that tranquillity and repose which they had pursued through all the mazes of this intricate hypothesis; and here they
beheld this, the most beautiful and magnificent part of the great theatre
of nature, so disposed and constructed, that they could attend, with
delight, to all the revolutions and changes that occurred in it.

These, the System of Concentric, and that of Eccentric Spheres,
seem to have been the two Systems of Astronomy, that had most credit
and reputation with that part of the ancient world, who applied themselves particularly to the study of the heavens.   Cleanthes, however,
and the other philosophers of the Stoical sect who came after him,
appear to have had a system of their own, quite different from either.
But though justly renowned for their skill in dialectic, and for the
security and sublimity of their moral doctrines, those sages seem never
to have had any high reputation for their knowledge of the heavens;
neither is the name of any one of them ever counted in the catalogue
of the great astronomers, and studious observers of the Stars among
the ancients.   They rejected the doctrine of the Solid Spheres ; and
maintained, that the celestial regions were filled with a fluid ether, of
too yielding a nature to carry along with it, by any motion of its own,
bodies so immensely great as the Sun, Moon, and Five Planets.   These,
therefore, as well as the Fixed Stars, did not derive their motion from
the circumambient body, but had each of them, in itself, and peculiar
to itself, a vital principle of motion, which directed it to move with its
own peculiar velocity, and its own peculiar direction.   It was by this
internal principle that the Fixed Stars revolved directly from east to
west in circles parallel to the Equator, greater or less, according to their
distance or nearness to the Poles, and with velocities so proportioned,

that each of them finished its diurnal period in the same time, in something less than twenty-three hours and fifty-six minutes. It was, by a
principle of the same kind, that the Sun moved westward, for they
allowed of no eastward motion in the heavens, but with less velocity
than the Fixed Stars, so as to finish his diurnal period in twenty-four
hours, and, consequently, to fall every day behind them, by a space of
the heavens nearly equal to that which he passes over in four minutes;
that is, nearly equal to a degree. This revolution of the Sun, too, was
neither directly westwards, nor exactly circular ; but after the Summer
Solstice, his motion began gradually to decline a little southwards,
appearing in his meridian to-day, further south than yesterday ; and
to-morrow still further south than to-day ; and thus continuing every
day to describe a spiral line round the Earth, which carried him gradually further and further southwards, till he arrived at the Winter
Solstice. Here this spiral line began to change its direction, and to
bring him gradually, every day, further and further northwards, till it
again restored him to the Summer Solstice. In the same manner they
accounted for the motion of the Moon, and that of the Five Planets,
by supposing that each of them revolved westwards, but with directions
and velocities, that were both different from one another, and continually varying; generally, however, in spherical lines, and somewhat inclined to the Equator.

This system seems never to have had the vogue. The system of
Concentric as well as that of Eccentric Spheres gives some sort of
reason, both for the constancy and equability of the motion of the
Fixed Stars, and for the variety and uncertainty of that of the Planets.
Each of them bestows some sort of coherence upon those apparently
disjointed phenomena. But this other system seems to leave them
pretty much as it found them. Ask a Stoic, why all the Fixed Stars
perform their daily revolutions in circles parallel to each other, though
of very different diameters, and with velocities so proportioned that
they all finish their period at the same time, and through the whole
course of it preserve the same distance and situation with regard to one
another ? He can give no other answer, but that the peculiar nature,
or if one may say so, the caprice of each Star directs it to move in
that peculiar manner. His system affords him no principle of connection, by which he can join together, in his imagination, so great a
number of harmonious revolutions. But either of the other two
systems, by the supposition of the solid firmament, affords this easily.
He is equally at a loss to connect together the peculiarities that are
observed in the motions of the other heavenly bodies ; the spiral
motion of them all ; their alternate progression from north to south,
and from south to north; the sometimes accelerated, and again retarded motions of the Sun and Moon ; the direct retrograde and
stationary appearances of the Planets. All these have, in his system,

no bond of union, but remain as loose and incoherent in the fancy, as they at first appeared to the senses, before philosophy had attempted, by giving them a new arrangement, by placing them at different distances, by assigning to each some peculiar but regular principle of motion, to methodize and dispose them into an order that should enable the imagination to pass as smoothly, and with as little embarrassment, along them, as along the most regular, most familiar, and most coherent appearances of nature.

Such were the systems of Astronomy that, in the ancient world, appear to have been adopted by any considerable party. Of all of them, the system of Eccentric Spheres was that which corresponded most exactly with the appearances of the heavens. It was not invented till after those appearances had been observed, with some accuracy, for more than a century together; and it was not completely digested by Ptolemy till the reign of Antoninus, after a much longer course of observations. We cannot wonder, therefore, that it was adapted to a much greater number of the phenomena, than either of the other two systems, which had been formed before those phenomena were observed with any degree of attention, which, therefore, could connect them together only while they were thus regarded in the gross, but which, it could not be expected, should apply to them when they came to be considered in the detail. From the time of Hipparchus, therefore, this system seems to have been pretty generally received by all those who attended particularly to the study of the heavens. That astronomer first made a catalogue of the Fixed Stars; calculated, for six hundred years, the revolutions of the Sun, Moon, and Five Planets; marked the places in the heavens, in which, during all that period, each of those bodies should appear; ascertained the times of the eclipses of the Sun and Moon, and the particular places of the Earth in which they should be visible. His calculations were founded upon this system, and as the events corresponded to his predictions, with a degree of accuracy which, though inferior to what Astronomy has since arrived at, was greatly superior to any thing which the world had then known, they ascertained, to all astronomers and mathematicians, the preference of his system, above all those which had been current before.

It was, however, to astronomers and mathematicians, only, that they ascertained this; for, notwithstanding the evident superiority of this system, to all those with which the world was then acquainted, it was never adopted by one sect of philosophers.

Philosophers, long before the days of Hipparchus, seem to have abandoned the study of nature, to employ themselves chiefly in ethical, rhetorical, and dialectical questions. Each party of them too, had by this time completed their peculiar system or theory of the universe, and no human consideration could then have induced them to give up any part of it. That supercilious and ignorant contempt too, with which at this time they regarded all mathematicians, among whom they counted astronomers, seems even to have hindered them from enquiring so far into their doctrines as to know what opinions they held.   Neither Cicero nor Seneca, who have so often occasion to mention the ancient systems of Astronomy, takes any notice of that of Hipparchus.   His name is not to be found in the writings of Seneca. It is mentioned but once in those of Cicero, in a letter to Atticus, but without any note of approbation, as a geographer, and not as an astronomer.   Plutarch, when he counts up, in his second book, concerning the opinions of philosophers, all the ancient systems of Astronomy, never mentions this, the only tolerable one which was known in his time.   Those three authors, it seems, conversed only with the writings of philosophers.   The elder Pliny, indeed, a man whose curiosity extended itself equally to every part of learning, describes the system of Hipparchus, and never mentions its author, which he has occasion to do often, without some note of that high admiration which he had so justly conceived for his merit.   Such profound ignorance in those professed instructors of mankind, with regard to so important a part of the learning of their own times, is so very remarkable, that I thought it deserved to be taken notice of, even in this short account of the revolutions of the philosophy of the ancients.

Systems in many respects resemble machines.   A machine is a little system, created to perform, as well as to connect together, in reality, those different movements and effects which the artist has occasion for.   A system is an imaginary machine invented to connect together in the fancy those different movements and effects which are already in reality performed.   The machines that are first invented to perform any particular movement are always the most complex, and succeeding artists generally discover that, with fewer wheels, with fewer principles of motion, than had originally been employed, the same effects may be more easily produced.   The first systems, in the same manner, are always the most complex, and a particular connecting chain, or principle, is generally thought necessary to unite every two seemingly disjointed appearances : but it often happens, that one great connecting principle is afterwards found to be sufficient to bind together all the discordant phenomena that occur in a whole species of things.   How many wheels are necessary to carry on the movements of this imaginary machine, the system of Eccentric Spheres !   The westward diurnal revolution of the Firmament, whose rapidity carries all the other heavenly bodies along with it, requires one.   The periodical eastward revolutions of the Sun, Moon, and Five Planets, require, for each of those bodies, another.   Their differently accelerated and retarded motions require, that those wheels, or circles, should neither be concentric with the Firmament, nor with one another ; which, more than any thing, seems to disturb the harmony of the universe.   The retrograde and stationary appearance of the Five Planets, as well as the extreme inconstancy of the Moon's motion, require, for each of them, an Epicycle, another little wheel attached to the circumference of the great wheel, which still more interrupts the uniformity of the system. The motion of the apogeum of each of those bodies requires, in each of them, still another wheel, to carry the centres of their Eccentric Spheres round the centre of the Earth. And thus, this imaginary machine, though, perhaps, more simple, and certainly better adapted to the phenomena than the Fifty-six Planetary Spheres of Aristotle, was still too intricate and complex for the imagination to rest in it with complete tranquillity and satisfaction.

It maintained its authority, however, without any diminution of reputation, as long as science was at all regarded in the ancient world. After the reign of Antoninus, and, indeed, after the age of Hipparchus, who lived almost three hundred years before Antoninus, the great reputation which the earlier philosophers had acquired, so imposed upon the imaginations of mankind, that they seem to have despaired of ever equalling their renown. All human wisdom, they supposed, was comprehended in the writings of those elder sages. To abridge, to explain, and to comment upon them, and thus show themselves, at least, capable of understanding some of their sublime mysteries, became now the only road to reputation. Proclus and Theon wrote commentaries upon the system of Ptolemy; but, to have attempted to invent a new one, would then have been regarded, not only as presumption, but as impiety to the memory of their so much revered predecessors.

The ruin of the empire of the Romans, and, along with it, the subversion of all law and order, which happened a few centuries afterwards, produced the entire neglect of that study of the connecting principles of nature, to which leisure and security can alone give occasion. After the fall of those great conquerors and civilizers of mankind, the empire of the Caliphs seems to have been the first state under which the world enjoyed that degree of tranquillity which the cultivation of the sciences requires. It was under the protection of those generous and magnificent princes, that the ancient philosophy and astronomy of the Greeks were restored and established in the East; that tranquillity, which their mild, just, and religious government diffused over their vast empire, revived the curiosity of mankind, to inquire into the connecting principles of nature. The same of the Greek and Roman learning, which was then recent in the memories of men, made them desire to know, concerning these abstruse subjects, what were the doctrines of the so much renowned sages of those two nations.

They translated, therefore, into the Arabian language, and studied, with great eagerness, the works of many Greek philosophers, particularly of Aristotle, Ptolemy, Hippocrates, and Galen. The superiority which they easily discovered in them, above the rude essays which their own nation had yet had time to produce, and which were such, we may suppose, as arise every where in the first infancy of science, necessarily determined them to embrace their systems, particularly that of Astronomy : neither were they ever afterwards able to throw off their authority. For, though the munificence of the Abassides, the second race of the Caliphs, is said to have supplied the Arabian astronomers with larger and better instruments than any that were known to Ptolemy and Hipparchus, the study of the sciences seems, in that mighty empire, to have been either of too short, or too interrupted a continuance, to allow them to make any considerable correction in the doctrines of those old mathematicians. The imaginations of mankind had not yet got time to grow so familiar with the ancient systems, as to regard them without some degree of that astonishment which their grandeur and novelty excited ; a novelty of a peculiar kind, which had at once the grace of what was new, and the authority of what was ancient. They were still, therefore, too much enslaved to those systems, to dare to depart from them, when those confusions which shook, and at last overturned the peaceful throne of the Caliphs, banished the study of the sciences from that empire. They had, however, before this, made some considerable improvements : they had measured the obliquity of the Ecliptic, with more accuracy than had been done before. The tables of Ptolemy had, by the length of time, and by the inaccuracy of the observations upon which they were founded, become altogether wide of what was the real situation of the heavenly bodies, as he himself indeed had foretold they would do. It became necessary, therefore, to form new ones, which was accordingly executed by the orders of the Caliph Almamon, under whom, too, was made the first mensuration of the Earth that we know off, after the commencement of the Christian era, by two Arabian astronomers, who, in the plain of Sennaar, measured two degrees of its circumference.

The victorious arms of the Saracens carried into Spain the learning, as well as the gallantry, of the East ; and along with it, the tables of Almamon, and the Arabian translations of Ptolemy and Aristotle ; and thus Europe received a second time, from Babylon, the rudiments of the science of the heavens. The writings of Ptolemy were translated from Arabic into Latin ; and the Peripatetic philosophy was studied in Averroes and Avicenna with as much eagerness and as much submission to its doctrines in the West, as it had been in the East.

The doctrine of the Solid Spheres had, originally, been invented, in order to give a physical account of the revolutions of the heavenly bodies, according to the system of Concentric Circles, to which that doctrine was very easily accommodated. Those mathematicians who invented the doctrine of Eccentric Circles and Epicycles, contented themselves with showing, how, by supposing the heavenly bodies to revolve in such orbits, the phenomena might be connected together, and some sort of uniformity and coherence be bestowed upon their real motions. The physical causes of those motions they left to the consideration of the philosophers; though, as appears from some passages of Ptolemy, they had some general apprehension, that they were to be explained by a like hypothesis. But, though the system of Hipparchus was adopted by all astronomers and mathematicians, it never was received, as we have already observed, by any one sect of philosophers among the ancients. No attempt, therefore, seems to have been made amongst them, to accommodate to it any such hypothesis.

The schoolmen, who received, at once, from the Arabians, the philosophy of Aristotle, and the astronomy of Hipparchus, were necessarily obliged to reconcile them to one another, and to connect together the revolutions of the Eccentric Circles and Epicycles of the one, by the solid Spheres of the other. Many different attempts of this kind were made by many different philosophers : but, of them all, that of Purbach, in the fifteenth century, was the happiest and the most esteemed. Though his hypothesis is the simplest of any of them, it would be in vain to describe it without a scheme ; neither is it easily intelligible with one ; for, if the system of Eccentric Circles and Epicycles was before too perplexed and intricate for the imagination to rest in it with complete tranquillity and satisfaction, it became much more so, when this addition had been made to it. The world, justly indeed, applauded the ingenuity of that philosopher, who could unite, so happily, two such seemingly inconsistent systems. His labours, however, seem rather to have increased than to have diminished the causes of that dissatisfaction, which the learned soon began to feel with the system of Ptolemy. He, as well as all those who had worked upon the same plan before, by rendering this account of things more complex, rendered it more embarrassing than it had been before.

Neither was the complexness of this system the sole cause of the dissatisfaction, which the world in general began, soon after the days of Purbach, to express for it. The tables of Ptolemy having, upon account of the inaccuracy of the observations on which they were founded, become altogether wide of the real situation of the heavenly bodies, those of Almamon, in the ninth century, were, upon the same hypothesis, composed to correct their deviations. These again, a few ages afterwards, became, for the same reason, equally useless. In the thirteenth century, Alphonsus, the philosophical King of Castile, found it necessary to give orders for the composition of those tables, which bear his name. It is he, who is so well known for the whimsical impiety of using to say, that, had he been consulted at the creation of the universe, he could have given good advice ; an apophthegm which is supposed to have proceeded from his dislike to the intricate system of Ptolemy. In the fifteenth century, the deviation of the Alphonsine tables began to be as sensible, as those of Ptolemy and

Almamon had been before. It appeared evident, therefore, that, though the system of Ptolemy might, in the main, be true, certain corrections were necessary to be made in it before it could be brought to correspond with exact precision to the phenomena. For the revolution of his Eccentric Circles and Epicycles, supposing them to exist, could not, it was evident, be precisely such as he represented them ; since the revolutions of the heavenly bodies deviated, in a short time, so widely from what the most exact calculations, that were founded upon his hypothesis, represented them. It had plainly, therefore, become necessary to correct, by more accurate observations, both the velocities and directions of all the wheels and circles of which his hypothesis is composed. This, accordingly, was begun by Purbach, and carried on by Regiomontanus, the disciple, the continuator, and the perfector of the system of Purbach ; and one, whose untimely death, amidst innumerable projects for the recovery of old, and the invention and advancement of new sciences, is, even at this day, to be regretted.

When you have convinced the world, that an established system ought to be corrected, it is not very difficult to persuade them that it should be destroyed. Not long, therefore, after the death of Regiomontanus, Copernicus began to meditate a new system, which should connect together the new appearances, in a more simple as well as a more accurate manner, than that of Ptolemy.

The confusion, in which the old hypothesis represented the motions of the heavenly bodies, was, he tells us, what first suggested to him the design of forming a new system, that these, the noblest works of nature, might no longer appear devoid of that harmony and proportion which discover themselves in her meanest productions. What most of all dissatisfied him, was the notion of the Equalizing Circle, which, by representing the revolutions of the Celestial Spheres, as equable only, when surveyed from a point that was different from their centres, introduced a real inequality into their motions ; contrary to that most natural, and indeed fundamental idea, with which all the authors of astronomical systems, Plato, Eudoxus, Aristotle, even Hipparchus and Ptolemy themselves, had hitherto set out, that the real motions of such beautiful and divine objects must necessarily be perfectly regular, and go on, in a manner, as agreeable to the imagination, as the objects themselves are to the senses. He began to consider, therefore, whether, by supposing the heavenly bodies to be arranged in a different order from that in which Aristotle and Hipparchus has placed them, this so much sought for uniformity might not be bestowed upon their motions. To discover this arrangement, he examined all the obscure traditions delivered down to us, concerning every other hypothesis which the ancients had invented, for the same purpose. He found, in Plutarch, that some old Pythagoreans had represented the Earth as revolving in the centre of the universe, like a wheel round its own axis ; and that others, of the same sect, had removed it from the centre, and represented it as revolving in the Ecliptic like a star round the central fire. By this central fire, he supposed they meant the Sun; and though in this he was very widely mistaken, it was, it seems, upon this interpretation, that he began to consider how such an hypothesis might be made to correspond to the appearances. The supposed authority of these old philosophers, if it did not originally suggest to him his system, seems, at least, to have confirmed him in an opinion, which, it is not improbable, that he had beforehand other reasons for embracing, notwithstanding what he himself would affirm to the contrary.

It then occurred to him, that, if the Earth was supposed to revolve every day round its axis, from west to east, all the heavenly bodies would appear to revolve, in a contrary direction, from east to west. The diurnal revolution of the heavens, upon this hypothesis, might be only apparent; the firmament, which has no other sensible motion, might be perfectly at rest; while the Sun, the Moon, and the Five Planets, might have no other movement beside that eastward revolution, which is peculiar to themselves. That, by supposing the Earth to revolve with the Planets, round the Sun, in an orbit, which comprehended within it the orbits of Venus and Mercury, but was comprehended within those of Mars, Jupiter, and Saturn, he could, without the embarrassment of Epicycles, connect together the apparent annual revolutions of the Sun, and the direct, retrograde, and stationary appearances of the Planets: that while the Earth really revolved round the Sun on one side of the heavens, the Sun would appear to revolve round the Earth on the other; that while she really advanced in her annual course, he would appear to advance eastward in that movement which is peculiar to himself. That, by supposing the axis of the Earth to be always parallel to itself, not to be quite perpendicular, but somewhat inclined to the plane of her orbit, and consequently to present to the Sun, the one pole when on the one side of him, and the other when on the other, he would account for the obliquity of the Ecliptic; the Sun's seemingly alternate progression from north to south, and from south to north, the consequent change of the seasons, and different lengths of the days and nights in the different seasons.

If this new hypothesis thus connected together all these appearances as happily as that of Ptolemy, there were others which it connected together much better. The three superior Planets, when nearly in conjunction with the Sun, appear always at the greatest distance from the Earth, are smallest, and least sensible to the eye, and seem to revolve forward in their direct motion with the greatest rapidity. On the contrary, when in opposition to the Sun, that is, when in their meridian about midnight, they appear nearest the Earth, are largest, and most sensible to the eye, and seem to revolve backwards in their retrograde motion. To explain these appearances, the system of Ptolemy supposed each of these Planets to be at the upper part of their several Epicycles, in the one case; and at the lower, in the other. But it afforded no satisfactory principle of connection, which could lead the mind easily to conceive how the Epicycles of those Planets, whose spheres were so distant from the sphere of the Sun, should thus, if one may say so, keep time to his motion. The system of Copernicus afforded this easily, and like a more simple machine, without the assistance of Epicycles, connected together, by fewer movements, the complex appearances of the heavens. When the superior Planets appear nearly in conjunction with the Sun, they are then in the side of their orbits, which is almost opposite to, and most distant from the Earth, and therefore appear smallest, and least sensible to the eye. But, as they then revolve in a direction which is almost contrary to that of the Earth, they appear to advance forward with double velocity; as a ship, that sails in a contrary direction to another, appears from that other, to sail both with its own velocity, and the velocity of that from which it is seen. On the contrary, when those Planets are in opposition to the Sun, they are on the same side of the Sun with the Earth, are nearest it, most sensible to the eye, and revolve in the same direction with it; but, as their revolutions round the Sun are slower than that of the Earth, they are necessarily left behind by it, and therefore seem to revolve backwards; as a ship which sails slower than another, though it sails in the same direction, appears from that other to sail backwards. After the same manner, by the same annual revolution of the Earth, he connected together the direct and retrograde motions of the two inferior Planets, as well as the stationary appearances of all the Five.

There are some other particular phenomena of the two inferior Planets, which correspond still better to this system, and still worse to that of Ptolemy. Venus and Mercury seem to attend constantly upon the motion of the Sun, appearing, sometimes on the one side, and sometimes on the other, of that great luminary; Mercury being almost always buried in his rays, and Venus never receding above forty-eight degrees from him, contrary to what is observed in the other three Planets, which are often seen in the opposite side of the heavens, at the greatest possible distance from the Sun. The system of Ptolemy accounted for this, by supposing that the centres of the Epicycles of these two Planets were always in the same line with those of the Sun and the Earth; that they appeared therefore in conjunction with the Sun, when either in the upper or lower part of their Epicycles, and at the greatest distance from him, when in the sides of them. It assigned, however, no reason why the Epicycles of these two Planets should observe so different a rule from that which takes place in those of the other three, nor for the enormous Epicycle of Venus, whose sides must have been forty-eight degrees distant from the Sun, while its centre was in conjunction with him, and whose diameter must have covered more than a quadrant of the Great Circle. But how easily all these appearances coincide with the hypothesis, which represents those two inferior Planets revolving round the Sun in orbits comprehended within the orbit of the Earth, is too obvious to require an explanation.

Thus far did this new account of things render the appearances of the heavens more completely coherent than had been done by any of the former systems. It did this, too, by a more simple and intelligible, as well as more beautiful machinery. It represented the Sun, the great enlightener of the universe, whose body was alone larger than all the Planets taken together, as established immovable in the centre, shedding light and heat on all the worlds that circulated around him in one uniform direction, but in longer or shorter periods, according to their different distances. It took away the diurnal revolution of the firmament, whose rapidity, upon the old hypothesis, was beyond what even thought could conceive. It not only delivered the imagination from the embarrassment of Epicycles, but from the difficulty of conceiving these two opposite motions going on at the same time, which the system of Ptolemy and Aristotle bestowed upon all the Planets; I mean, their diurnal westward, and periodical eastward revolutions. The Earth's revolution round its own axis took away the necessity for supposing the first, and the second was easily conceived when by itself. The Five Planets, which seem, upon all other systems, to be objects of a species by themselves, unlike to every thing to which the imagination has been accustomed, when supposed to revolve along with the Earth round the Sun, were naturally apprehended to be objects of the same kind with the Earth, habitable, opaque, and enlightened only by the rays of the Sun. And thus this hypothesis, by classing them in the same species of things, with an object that is of all others the most familiar to us, took off that wonder and that uncertainty which the strangeness and singularity of their appearance had excited; and thus far, too, better answered the great end of Philosophy.

Neither did the beauty and simplicity of this system alone recommend it to the imagination ; the novelty and unexpectedness of that view of nature, which it opened to the fancy, excited more wonder and surprise than the strangest of those appearances, which it had been invented to render natural and familiar, and these sentiments still more endeared it. For, though it is the end of Philosophy, to allay that wonder, which either the unusual or seemingly disjointed appearances of nature excite, yet she never triumphs so much, as when, in order to connect together a few, in themselves, perhaps, inconsiderable objects, she has, if I may say so, created another constitution of things, more natural, indeed, and such as the imagination can more easily attend to, but more new, more contrary to common opinion and expectation, than any of those appearances themselves. As, in the instance before us, in order to connect together some seeming irregularities in the motions of the Planets, the most inconsiderable objects in the heavens, and of which the greater part of mankind have no occasion to take any notice during the whole course of their lives, she has, to talk in the hyperbolical language of Tycho-Brahe, moved the Earth from its foundations, stopped the revolution of the Firmament, made the Sun stand still, and subverted the whole order of the Universe.

Such were the advantages of this new hypothesis, as they appeared to its author, when he first invented it. But, though that love of paradox, so natural to the learned, and that pleasure, which they are so apt to take in exciting, by the novelties of their supposed discoveries, the amazement of mankind, may, notwithstanding what one of his disciples tells us to the contrary, have had its weight in prompting Copernicus to adopt this system ; yet, when he had completed his Treatise of Revolutions, and began coolly to consider what a strange doctrine he was about to offer to the world, he so much dreaded the prejudice of mankind against it, that, by a species of continence, of all others the most difficult to a philosopher, he detained it in his closet for thirty years together. At last, in the extremity of old age, he allowed it to be extorted from him, but he died as soon as it was printed, and before it was published to the world.

When it appeared in the world, it was almost universally disapproved of, by the learned as well as by the ignorant. The natural prejudices of sense, confirmed by education, prevailed too much with both, to allow them to give it a fair examination. A few disciples only, whom he himself had instructed in his doctrine, received it with esteem and admiration. One of them, Reinholdus, formed, upon this hypothesis, larger and more accurate astronomical tables, than what accompanied the Treatise of Revolutions, in which Copernicus had been guilty of some errors in calculation. It soon appeared, that these Prutenic Tables, as they were called, corresponded more exactly with the heavens, than the Tables of Alphonsus. This ought naturally to have formed a prejudice in favour of the diligence and accuracy of Copernicus in observing the heavens. But it ought to have formed none in favour of his hypothesis; since the same observations, and the result of the same calculations, might have been accommodated to the system of Ptolemy, without making any greater alteration in that system than what Ptolemy had foreseen, and had even foretold should be made. It formed, however, a prejudice in favour of both, and the learned began to examine, with some attention, an hypothesis which afforded the easiest methods of calculation, and upon which the most exact predictions had been made. The superior degree of coherence, which it bestowed upon the celestial appearances, the simplicity and uniformity which it introduced into the real directions and velocities of the Planets, soon disposed many astronomers, first to favour, and at last to embrace a system, which thus connected together so happily, the most disjointed of those objects that chiefly occupied their thoughts. Nor can any thing more evidently demonstrate, how easily the learned give up the evidence of their senses to preserve the coherence of the ideas of their imagination, than the readiness with which this, the most violent paradox in all philosophy, was adopted by many ingenious astronomers, notwithstanding its inconsistency with every system of physics then known in the world, and notwithstanding the great number of other more real objections, to which, as Copernicus left it, this account of things was most justly exposed.

It was adopted, however, nor can this be wondered at, by astronomers only. The learned in all other sciences, continued to regard it with the same contempt as the vulgar. Even astronomers were divided about its merit; and many of them rejected a doctrine, which not only contradicted the established system of Natural Philosophy, but which, considered astronomically only, seemed, to them, to labour under several difficulties.

Some of the objections against the motion of the Earth, that were drawn from the prejudices of sense, the patrons of this system, indeed, easily enough got over. They represented, that the Earth might really be in motion, though, to its inhabitants, it seemed to be at rest; and that the Sun and Fixed Stars might really be at rest, though from the Earth they seemed to be in motion; in the same manner as a ship, which sails through a smooth sea, seems to those who are in it, to be at rest, though really in motion; while the objects which she passes along, seem to be in motion, though really at rest.

But there were some other objections, which, though grounded upon the same natural prejudices, they found it more difficult to get over. The earth had always presented itself to the senses, not only as at rest, but as inert, ponderous, and even averse to motion. The imagination had always been accustomed to conceive it as such, and suffered the greatest violence, when obliged to pursue, and attend it, in that rapid motion which the system of Copernicus bestowed upon it. To enforce their objection, the adversaries of this hypothesis were at pains to calculate the extreme rapidity of this motion. They represented, that the circumference of the Earth had been computed to be above twenty-thousand miles: if the Earth, therefore, was supposed to revolve every day round its axis, every point of it near the equator would pass over above twenty-three thousand miles in a day; and consequently, near a thousand miles in an hour, and about sixteen miles in a minute; a motion more rapid than that of a cannon ball, or even than the swifter progress of sound. The rapidity of its periodical revolution was yet more violent than that of its diurnal rotation. How, therefore, could the imagination ever conceive so ponderous a body to be naturally endowed with so dreadful a movement? The Peripatetic Philosophy, the only philosophy then known in the world, still further confirmed this prejudice. That philosophy, by a very natural, though, perhaps, groundless distinction, divided all motion into Natural and Violent. Natural motion was that which flowed from an innate tendency in the body, as when a stone fell downwards: Violent motion, that which arose from external force, and which was, in some measure, contrary to the natural tendency of the body, as when a stone was thrown upwards, or horizontally. No violent motion could be lasting; for, being constantly weakened by the natural tendency of the body, it would soon be destroyed. The natural motion of the Earth, as was evident in all its parts, was downwards, in a straight line to the centre; as that of fire and air was upwards, in a straight line from the centre. It was the heavens only that revolved naturally in a circle. Neither, therefore, the supposed revolution of the Earth round its own centre, nor that round the Sun, could be natural motions; they must therefore be violent, and consequently could be of no long continuance. It was in vain that Copernicus replied, that gravity was, probably, nothing else besides a tendency in the different parts of the same Planet, to unite themselves to one another; that this tendency took place, probably, in the parts of the other Planets, as well as in those of the Earth; that it could very well be united with a circular motion; that it might be equally natural to the whole body of the Planet, and to every part of it; that his adversaries themselves allowed, that a circular motion was natural to the heavens, whose diurnal revolution was infinitely more rapid than even that motion which he had bestowed upon the Earth; that though a like motion was natural to the Earth, it would still appear to be at rest to its inhabitants, and all the parts of it to tend in a straight line to the centre, in the same manner as at present. But this answer, how satisfactory soever it may appear to be now, neither did nor could appear to be satisfactory then. By admitting the distinction betwixt natural and violent motions, it was founded upon the same ignorance of mechanical principles with the objection. The systems of Aristotle and Hipparchus supposed, indeed, the diurnal motion of the heavenly bodies to be infinitely more rapid than even that dreadful movement which Copernicus bestowed upon the Earth. But they supposed, at the same time, that those bodies were objects of a quite different species, from any we are acquainted with, near the surface of the Earth, and to which, therefore, it was less difficult to conceive that any sort of motion might be natural. Those objects, besides, had never presented themselves to the senses, as moving otherwise, or with less rapidity, than these systems represented them. The imagination, therefore, could feel no difficulty in following a representation which the senses had rendered quite familiar to it. But when the Planets came to be regarded as so many Earths, the case was quite altered. The imagination had been accustomed to conceive such objects as tending rather to rest than motion; and this idea of their natural inertness, encumbered, if one may say so, and clogged its flight whenever it endeavoured to pursue them in their periodical courses, and to conceive them as continually rushing through the celestial spaces, with such violent and unremitting rapidity.

Nor were the first followers of Copernicus more fortunate in their answers to some other objections, which were founded indeed in the same ignorance of the laws of motion, but which, at the same time, were necessarily connected with that way of conceiving things, which then prevailed universally in the learned world.

If the earth, it was said, revolved so rapidly from west to east, a perpetual wind would set in from east to west, more violent than what blows in the greatest hurricanes ; a stone, thrown westwards would fly to a much greater distance than one thrown with the same force eastwards ; as what moved in a direction, contrary to the motion of the Earth, would necessarily pass over a greater portion of its surface, than what, with the same velocity, moved along with it.   A ball, it was said, dropped from the mast of a ship under sail, does not fall precisely at the foot of the mast, but behind it ; and in the same manner, a stone dropped from a high tower would not, upon the supposition of the Earth's motion, fall precisely at the bottom of the tower, but west of it, the Earth being, in the mean time, carried away eastward from below it.   It is amusing to observe, by what subtile and metaphysical evasions the followers of Copernicus endeavoured to elude this objection, which before the doctrine of the Composition of Motion had been explained by Galileo, was altogether unanswerable.   They allowed, that a ball dropped from the mast of a ship under sail would not fall at the foot of the mast, but behind it ; because the ball, they said, was no part of the ship, and because the motion of the ship was natural neither to itself nor to the ball.   But the stone was a part of the earth, and the diurnal and annual revolutions of the Earth were natural to the whole, and to every part of it, and therefore to the stone.   The stone, therefore, having naturally the same motion with the Earth, fell precisely at the bottom of the tower.   But this answer could not satisfy the imagination, which still found it difficult to conceive how these motions could be natural to the earth ; or how a body, which had always presented itself to the senses as inert, ponderous, and averse to motion, should naturally be continually wheeling about both its own axis and the Sun, with such violent rapidity.   It was, besides, argued by Tycho Brahe, upon the principles of the same philosophy which had afforded both the objection and the answer, that even upon the supposition, that any such motion was natural to the whole body of the Earth, yet the stone, which was separated from it, could no longer be actuated by that motion.   The limb, which is cut off from an animal, loses those animal motions which were natural to the whole. The branch, which is cut off from the trunk, loses that vegetative

24 *

motion which is natural to the whole tree. Even the metals, minerals, and stones, which were dug out from the bosom of the Earth, lose those motions which occasioned their production and increase, and which were natural to them in their original state. Though the diurnal and annual motion of the Earth, therefore, had been natural to them while they were contained in its bosom, it could no longer be so when they were separated from it.

Tycho Brahe, the great restorer of the science of the heavens, who had spent his life, and wasted his fortune upon the advancement of Astronomy, whose observations were both more numerous and more accurate than those of all the astronomers who had gone before him, was himself so much affected by the force of this objection, that, though he had never mentioned the system of Copernicus without some note of high admiration he had conceived for its author, he could never himself be induced to embrace it ; yet all his astronomical observations tended to confirm it. They demonstrated, that Venus and Mercury were sometimes above, and sometimes below the Sun ; and that, consequently, the Sun, and not the Earth, was the centre of their periodical revolutions. They showed, that Mars, when in his meridian at midnight, was nearer to the Earth than the Earth is to the Sun ; though, when in conjunction with the Sun, he was much more remote from the Earth than that luminary ; a discovery which was absolutely inconsistent with the system of Ptolemy, which proved, that the Sun, and not the Earth, was the centre of the periodical revolutions of Mars, as well as of Venus and Mercury; and which demonstrated that the Earth was placed betwixt the orbits of Mars and Venus. They made the same thing probable with regard to Jupiter and Saturn ; that they, too, revolved round the Sun ; and that, therefore, the Sun, if not the centre of the universe, was at least, that of the planetary system. They proved that Comets were superior to the Moon, and moved through the heavens in all possible directions ; an observation incompatible with the Solid Spheres of Aristotle and Purbach, and which, therefore, overturned the physical part, at least, of the established systems of Astronomy.

All these observations, joined to his aversion to the system, and perhaps, notwithstanding the generosity of his character, some little jealousy for the fame of Copernicus, suggested to Tycho the idea of a new hypothesis, in which the Earth continued to be, as in the old account, the immovable centre of the universe, round which the firmament revolved every day from east to west, and, by some secret virtue, carried the Sun, the Moon, and the Five Planets along with it, notwithstanding their immense distance, and notwithstanding that there was nothing betwixt it and them but the most fluid ether. But, although all these seven bodies thus obeyed the diurnal revolution of the Firmament, they had each of them, as in the old system, too, a contrary periodical eastward revolution of their own, which made them appear to be every day, more or less, left behind by the Firmament. The Sun was the centre of the periodical revolutions of the Five Planets; the Earth, that of the Sun and Moon. The Five Planets followed the Sun in his periodical revolution round the Earth, as they did the Firmament in its diurnal rotation. The three superior Planets comprehended the Earth within the orbit in which they revolved round the Sun, and had each of them an Epicycle to connect together, in the same manner as in the system of Ptolemy, their direct, retrograde, and stationary appearances. As, notwithstanding their immense distance, they followed the Sun in his periodical revolution round the Earth, keeping always at an equal distance from him, they were necessarily brought much nearer to the Earth when in opposition to the Sun, than than when in conjunction with him. Mars, the nearest of them, when in his meridian at midnight, came within the orbit which the Sun described round the Earth, and consequently was then nearer to the Earth than the Earth was to the Sun. The appearances of the two inferior Planets were explained, in the same manner, as in the system of Copernicus, and consequently required no Epicycle to connect them. The circles in which the Five Planets performed their periodical revolutions round the Sun, as well as those in which the Sun and Moon performed theirs round the Earth, were, as both in the old and new hypothesis, Eccentric Circles, to connect together their differently accelerated and retarded motions.

Such was the system of Tycho Brahe, compounded, as is evident, out of these of Ptolemy and Copernicus; happier than that of Ptolemy, in the account which it gives of the motions of the two inferior Planets; more complex, by supposing the different revolutions of all the Five to be performed round two different centres; the diurnal round the Earth, the periodical round the Sun, but, in every respect, more complex and more incoherent than that of Copernicus. Such, however, was the difficulty that mankind felt in conceiving the motion of the Earth, that it long balanced the reputation of that otherwise more beautiful system. It may be said, that those who considered the heavens only, favoured the system of Copernicus, which connected so happily all the appearances which presented themselves there; but that those who looked upon the Earth, adopted the account of Tycho Brahe, which, leaving it at rest in the centre of the universe, did less violence to the usual habits of the imagination. The learned were, indeed, sensible of the intricacy, and of the many incoherences of that system; that it gave no account why the Sun, Moon, and Five Planets, should follow the revolution of the Firmament; or why the Five Planets, notwithstanding the immense distance of the three superior ones, should obey the periodical motion of the Sun; or why the Earth, though placed between the orbits of Mars and Venus, should remain immovable in the centre of the Firmament, and constantly resist the influence of whatever it was, which carried bodies that were so much larger than itself, and that were placed on all sides of it, periodically round the Sun. Tycho Brahe died before he had fully explained his system. His great and merited renown disposed many of the learned to believe, that, had his life been longer, he would have connected together many of these incoherences, and knew methods of adapting his system to some other appearances, with which none of his followers could connect it.

The objection to the system of Copernicus, which was drawn from the nature of motion, and that was most insisted on by Tycho Brahe, was at last fully answered by Galileo; not, however, till about thirty years after the death of Tycho, and about a hundred after that of Copernicus. It was then that Galileo, by explaining the nature of the composition of motion, by showing, both from reason and experience, that a ball dropped from the mast of a ship under sail would fall precisely at the foot of the mast, and by rendering this doctrine, from a great number of other instances, quite familiar to the imagination, took off, perhaps, the principal objection which had been made to this hypothesis of the astronomers.

Several other astronomical difficulties, which encumbered this account of things, were removed by the same philosopher. Copernicus, after altering the centre of the world, and making the Earth, and all the Planets revolve round the Sun, was obliged to leave the Moon to revolve round the Earth as before. But no example of any such secondary Planet having then been discovered in the heavens, there seemed still to be this irregularity remaining in the system. Galileo, who first applied telescopes to Astronomy, discovered, by their assistance, the Satellites of Jupiter, which, revolving round that Planet, at the same time that they were carried along with it in its revolution, round either the Earth, or the Sun, made it seem less contrary to the analogy of nature, that the Moon should both revolve round the Earth, and accompany her in her revolution round the Sun.

It had been objected to Copernicus, that, if Venus and Mercury revolved round the Sun in an orbit comprehended within the orbit of the Earth, they would show all the same phases with the Moon; present, sometimes their darkened, and sometimes their enlightened sides to the Earth, and sometimes part of the one, and part of the other. He answered, that they undoubtedly did all this; but that their smallness and distance hindered us from perceiving it. This very bold assertion of Copernicus was confirmed by Galileo. His telescopes rendered the phases of Venus quite sensible, and thus demonstrated, more evidently than had been done, even by the observations of Tycho Brahe, the revolutions of these two Planets round the Sun, as well as so far destroyed the system of Ptolemy.

The mountains and seas, which, by the help of the same instrument, he discovered, or imagined he had discovered in the Moon, rendering that Planet, in every respect, similar to the Earth, made it seem less contrary to the analogy of nature, that, as the Moon revolved round the Earth, the Earth should revolve round the Sun.

The spots which, in the same manner, he discovered in the Sun, demonstrating, by their motion, the revolution of the Sun round his axis, made it seem less improbable that the Earth, a body so much smaller than the Sun, should likewise revolve round her axis in the same manner.

Succeeding telescopical observations, discovered, in each of the Five Planets, spots not unlike those which Galileo had observed in the Moon, and thereby seemed to demonstrate what Copernicus had only conjectured, that the Planets were naturally opaque, enlightened only by the rays of the Sun, habitable, diversified by seas and mountains, and, in every respect, bodies of the same kind with the earth ; and thus added one other probability to this system. By discovering, too, that each of the Planets revolved round its own axis, at the same time that it was carried round either the Earth or the Sun, they made it seem quite agreeable to the analogy of nature, that the Earth, which, in every other respect, resembled the Planets, should, like them too, revolve round its own axis, and at the same time perform its periodical motion round the Sun.

While, in Italy, the unfortunate Galileo was adding so many probabilities to the system of Copernicus, there was another philosopher employing himself in Germany, to ascertain, correct, and improve it ; Kepler, with great genius, but without the taste, or the order and method of Galileo, possessed, like all his other countrymen, the most laborious industry, joined to that passion for discovering proportions and resemblances betwixt the different parts of nature, which, though common to all philosophers, seems, in him, to have been excessive. He had been instructed, by Mæstlinus, in the system of Copernicus ; and his first curiosity was, as he tells us, to find out, why the Planets, the Earth being counted for one, were Six in number ; why they were placed at such irregular distances from the Sun ; and whether there was any uniform proportion betwixt their several distances, and the times employed in their periodical revolutions. Till some reason, or proportion of this kind, could be discovered, the system did not appear to him to be completely coherent. He endeavoured, first, to find it in the proportions of numbers, and plain figures ; afterwards, in those of the regular solids ; and, last of all, in those of the musical divisions of the Octave. Whatever was the science which Kepler was studying, he seems constantly to have pleased himself with finding some analogy betwixt it and the system of the universe ; and thus, arithmetic and music, plane and solid geometry, came all of them by turns to illustrate the doctrine of the Sphere, in the explaining of which he was, by his

profession, principally employed.   Tycho Brahe, to whom he had presented one of his books, though he could not but disapprove of his
system, was pleased, however, with his genius, and with his indefatigable
diligence in making the most laborious calculations.   That generous
and magnificent Dane invited the obscure and indigent Kepler to come
and live with him, and communicated to him, as soon as he arrived,
his observations upon Mars, in the arranging and methodizing of which
his disciples were at that time employed.   Kepler, upon comparing
them with one another, found, that the orbit of Mars was not a perfect
circle; that one of its diameters was somewhat longer than the other;
and that it approached to an oval, or an ellipse, which had the Sun
placed in one of its foci.   He found, too, that the motion of the Planet
was not equable; that it was swiftest when nearest the Sun, and slowest
when furthest from him; and that its velocity gradually increased, or
diminished, according as it approached or receded from him.   The
observations of the same astronomer discovered to him, though not so
evidently, that the same things were true of all the other Planets; that
their orbits were elliptical, and that their motions were swiftest when
nearest the Sun, and slowest when furthest from him.   They showed
the same things, too, of the Sun, if supposed to revolve round the
Earth; and consequently of the Earth, if it also was supposed to
revolve round the Sun.

That the motions of all the heavenly bodies were perfectly circular,
had been the fundamental idea upon which every astronomical hypothesis, except the irregular one of the Stoics, had been built.   A circle,
as the degree of its curvature is every where the same, is of all curve
lines the simplest and the most easily conceived.   Since it was evident,
therefore, that the heavenly bodies did not move in straight lines, the
indolent imagination found, that it could most easily attend to their
motions if they were supposed to revolve in perfect circles.   It had,
upon this account, determined that a circular motion was the most
perfect of all motions, and that none but the most perfect motion could
be worthy of such beautiful and divine objects; and it had upon this
account, so often, in vain, endeavoured to adjust to the appearances, so
many different systems, which all supposed them to revolve in this
perfect manner.

The equality of their motions was another fundamental idea, which,
in the same manner, and for the same reason, was supposed by all the
founders of astronomical systems.   For an equal motion can be more
easily attended to, than one that is continually either accelerated or
retarded.   All inconsistency, therefore, was declared to be unworthy
those bodies which revolved in the celestial regions, and to be fit only
for inferior and sublunary things.   The calculations of Kepler overturned, with regard to the Planets, both these natural prejudices of the
imagination; destroyed their circular orbits; and introduced into their

real motions, such an equality as no equalizing circle would remedy. It was, however, to render their motion perfectly equable, without even the assistance of a equalizing circle, that Copernicus, as he himself assures us, had originally invented his system. Since the calculations of Kepler, therefore, overturned what Copernicus had principally in view in establishing his system, we cannot wonder that they should at first seem rather to embarrass than improve it.

It is true, by these elliptical orbits and unequal motions, Kepler disengaged the system from the embarrassment of those small Epicycles, which Copernicus, in order to connect the seemingly accelerated and retarded movements of the Planets, with their supposed real equality, had been obliged to leave in it. For it is remarkable, that though Copernicus had delivered the orbits of the Planets from the enormous Epicycles of Hipparchus, that though in this consisted the great superiority of his system above that of the ancient astronomers, he was yet obliged, himself, to abandon, in some measure, this advantage, and to make use of some small Epicycles, to join together those seeming irregularities. His Epicycles indeed, like the irregularities for whose sake they were introduced, were but small ones, and the imaginations of his first followers seem, accordingly, either to have slurred them over altogether, or scarcely to have observed them. Neither Galileo, nor Gassendi, the two most eloquent of his defenders, take any notice of them. Nor does it seem to have been generally attended to, that there was any such thing as Epicycles in the system of Copernicus, till Kepler, in order to vindicate his own elliptical orbits, insisted, that even, according to Copernicus, the body of the Planet was to be found but at two different places in the circumference of that circle which the centre of its Epicycle described.

It is true, too, that an ellipse is, of all curve lines after a circle, the simplest and most easily conceived ; and it is true, besides all this, that, while Kepler took from the motion of the Planets the easiest of all proportions, that of equality, he did not leave them absolutely without one, but ascertained the rule by which their velocities continually varied ; for a genius so fond of analogies, when he had taken away one, would be sure to substitute another in its room. Notwithstanding all this, notwithstanding that his system was better supported by observations than any system had ever been before, yet, such was the attachment to the equal motions and circular orbits of the Planets, that it seems, for some time, to have been in general but little attended to by the learned, to have been altogether neglected by philosophers, and not much regarded even by astronomers.

Gassendi, who began to figure in the world about the latter days of Kepler, and who was himself no mean astronomer, seems indeed to have conceived a good deal of esteem for his diligence and accuracy in accommodating the observations of Tycho Brahe to the system of

Copernicus. But Gassendi appears to have had no comprehension of the importance of those alterations which Kepler had made in that system, as is evident from his scarcely ever mentioning them in the whole course of his voluminous writings upon Astronomy. Des Cartes, the contemporary and rival of Gassendi, seems to have paid no attention to them at all, but to have built his Theory of the Heavens, without any regard to them. Even those astronomers, whom a serious attention had convinced of the justness of his corrections, were still so enamoured with the circular orbits and equal motion, that they endeavoured to compound his system with those ancient but natural prejudices. Thus, Ward endeavoured to show that, though the Planets moved in elliptical orbits, which had the Sun in one of their foci, and though their velocities in the elliptical line were continually varying, yet, if a ray was supposed to be extended from the centre of any one of them to the other focus, and to be carried along by the periodical motion of the Planet, it would make equal angles in equal times, and consequently cut off equal portions of the circle of which that other focus was the centre. To one, therefore, placed in that focus, the motion of the Planet would appear to be perfectly circular and perfectly equable, in the same manner as in the Equalizing Circles of Ptolemy and Hipparchus. Thus Bouillaud, who censured this hypothesis of Ward, invented another of the same kind, infinitely more whimsical and capricious. The Planets, according to that astronomer, always revolve in circles ; for that being the most perfect figure, it is impossible they should revolve in any other. No one of them, however, continues to move in any one circle, but is perpetually passing from one to another, through an infinite number of circles, in the course of each revolution ; for an ellipse, said he, is an oblique section of a cone, and in a cone, betwixt the two vortices of the ellipse there is an infinite number of circles, out of the infinitely small portions of which the elliptical line is compounded. The Planet, therefore which moves in this line, is, in every point of it, moving in an infinitely small portion of a certain circle. The motion of each Planet, too, according to him, was necessarily, for the same reason, perfectly equable. An equable motion being the most perfect of all motions. It was not, however, in the elliptical line, that it was equable, but in any one of the circles that were parallel to the base of that cone, by whose section this elliptical line had been formed : for, if a ray was extended from the Planet to any one of those circles, and carried along by its periodical motion, it would cut off equal portions of that circle in equal times ; another most fantastical equalising circle, supported by no other foundation besides the frivolous connection between a cone and an ellipse, and recommended by nothing but the natural passion for circular orbits and equable motions. It may be regarded as the last effort of this passion, and may serve to show the force of that principle which could thus oblige this accurate observer, and great improver of the Theory of the Heavens, to adopt so strange an hypothesis.   Such was the difficulty and hesitation with which the followers of Copernicus adopted the corrections of Kepler.

The rule, indeed, which Kepler ascertained for determining the gradual acceleration or retardation in the movement of the Planets, was intricate, and difficult to be comprehended ; it could therefore but little facilitate the progress of the imagination in tracing those revolutions which were supposed to be conducted by it.   According to that astronomer, if a straight line was drawn from the centre of each Planet to the Sun, and carried along by the periodical motion of the Planet, it would describe equal areas in equal times, though the Planet did not pass over equal spaces ; and the same rule he found, took place nearly with regard to the Moon.   The imagination, when acquainted with the law by which any motion is accelerated or retarded, can follow and attend to it more easily, than when at a loss, and, as it were, wandering in uncertainty with regard to the proportion which regulates its varieties ; the discovery of this analogy therefore, no doubt, rendered the system of Kepler more agreeable to the natural taste of mankind : it, was, however, an analogy too difficult to be followed, or comprehended, to render it completely so.

Kepler, besides this, introduced another new analogy into the system, and first discovered, that there was one uniform relation observed betwixt the distances of the Planets from the Sun, and the times employed in their periodical motions.   He found, that their periodical times were greater than in proportion to their distances, and less than in proportion to the squares of those distances; but, that they were nearly as the mean proportionals betwixt their distances and the squares of their distances; or, in other words, that the squares of their periodical times were nearly as the cubes of their distances; an analogy, which, though, like all others, it no doubt rendered the system somewhat more distinct and comprehensible, was, however, as well as the former, of too intricate a nature to facilitate very much the effort of the imagination in conceiving it.

The truth of both these analogies, intricate as they were, was at last fully established by the observations of Cassini.   That astronomer first discovered, that the secondary Planets of Jupiter and Saturn revolved round their primary ones, according to the same laws which Kepler had observed in the revolutions of the primary ones round the Sun, and that of the Moon round the earth ; that each of them described equal areas in equal times, and that the squares of their periodic times were as the cubes of their distances.   When these two last abstruse analogies, which, when Kepler at first observed them, were but little regarded, had been thus found to take place in the revolutions of the Four Satellites of Jupiter, and in those of the Five of Saturn, they were now thought not only to confirm the doctrine of Kepler, but to add a new probability to the Copernican hypothesis. The observations of Cassini seem to establish it as a law of the system, that, when one body revolved round another, it described equal areas in equal times; and that, when several revolved round the same body, the squares of their periodic times were as the cubes of their distances. If the Earth and the Five Planets were supposed to revolve round the Sun, these laws, it was said, would take place universally. But if, according to the system of Ptolemy, the Sun, Moon, and Five Planets were supposed to revolve round the Earth, the periodical motions of the Sun and Moon, would, indeed, observe the first of these laws, would each of them describe equal areas in equal times; but they would not observe the second, the squares of their periodic times would not be as the cubes of their distances: and the revolutions of the Five Planets would observe neither the one law nor the other. Or if, according to the system of Tycho Brahe, the Five Planets were supposed to revolve round the Sun, while the Sun and Moon revolved round the Earth, the revolutions of the Five Planets round the Sun, would, indeed, observe both these laws; but those of the Sun and Moon round the Earth would observe only the first of them. The analogy of nature, therefore, could be preserved completely, according to no other system but that of Copernicus, which, upon that account, must be the true one. This argument is regarded by Voltaire, and the Cardinal of Polignac, as an irrefragable demonstration; even M'Laurin, who was more capable of judging, nay, Newton himself, seems to mention it as one of the principal evidences for the truth of that hypothesis. Yet, an analogy of this kind, it would seem, far from a demonstration, could afford, at most, but the shadow of a probability.

It is true, that though Cassini supposed the Planets to revolve in an oblong curve, it was in a curve somewhat different from that of Kepler. In the ellipse, the sum of the two lines which are drawn from any one point in the circumference to the two foci, is always equal to that of those which are drawn from any other point in the circumference to the same foci. In the curve of Cassini, it is not the sum of the lines, but the rectangles which are contained under the lines, that are always equal. As this, however, was a proportion more difficult to be comprehended by astronomers than the other, the curve of Cassini has never had the vogue.

Nothing now embarrassed the system of Copernicus, but the difficulty which the imagination felt in conceiving bodies so immensely ponderous as the Earth and the other Planets revolving round the Sun with such incredible rapidity. It was in vain that Copernicus pretended, that, notwithstanding the prejudices of sense, this circular motion might be as natural to the Planets, as it is to a stone to fall to the ground. The imagination had been accustomed to conceive such objects as tending rather to rest than motion. This habitual idea of their natural inertness was incompatible with that of their natural motion. It was in vain that Kepler, in order to assist the fancy in connecting together this natural inertness with their astonishing velocities, talked of some vital and immaterial virtue, which was shed by the Sun into the surrounding spaces, which was whirled about with his revolution round his own axis, and which, taking hold of the Planets, forced them, in spite of their ponderousness and strong propensity to rest, thus to whirl about the centre of the system. The imagination had no hold of this immaterial virtue, and could form no determinate idea of what it consisted in. The imagination, indeed, felt a gap, or interval, betwixt the constant motion and the supposed inertness of the Planets, and had in this, as in all other cases, some general idea or apprehension that there must be a connecting chain of intermediate objects to link together these discordant qualities. Wherein this connecting chain consisted, it was, indeed, at a loss to conceive; nor did the doctrine of Kepler lend it any assistance in this respect. That doctrine, like almost all those of the philosophy in fashion during his time, bestowed a name upon this invisible chain, called it an immaterial virtue, but afforded no determinate idea of what was its nature.

Des Cartes was the first who attempted to ascertain, precisely, wherein this invisible chain consisted, and to afford the imagination a train of intermediate events, which, succeeding each other in an order that was of all others the most familiar to it, should unite those incoherent qualities, the rapid motion, and the natural inertness of the Planets. Des Cartes was the first who explained wherein consisted the real inertness of matter; that it was not in an aversion to motion, or in a propensity to rest, but in a power of continuing indifferently either at rest or in motion, and of resisting, with a certain force, whatever endeavoured to change its state from the one to the other. According to that ingenious and fanciful philosopher, the whole of infinite space was full of matter, for with him matter and extension were the same, and consequently there could be no void. This immensity of matter, he supposed to be divided into an infinite number of very small cubes; all of which, being whirled about upon their own centres, necessarily gave occasion to the production of two different elements. The first consisted of those angular parts, which, having been necessarily rubbed off, and grinded yet smaller by their mutual friction, constituted the most subtle and movable part of matter. The second consisted of those little globules that were formed by the rubbing off of the first. The interstices betwixt these globules of the second element was filled up by the particles of the first. But in the infinite collisions, which must occur in an infinite space filled with matter, and all in motion, it must necessarily happen that many of the globules of the second element should be broken and grinded down into the first. The quantity

of the first element having been thus increased beyond what was sufficient to fill up the interstices of the second, it must, in many places,
have been heaped up together, without any mixture of the second along
with it. Such, according to Des Cartes, was the original division of
matter. Upon this infinitude of matter thus divided, a certain quantity
of motion was originally impressed by the Creator of all things, and
the laws of motion were so adjusted as always to preserve the same
quantity in it, without increase, and without diminution. Whatever
motion was lost by one part of matter, was communicated to some
other; and whatever was acquired by one part of matter, was derived
from some other: and thus, through an eternal revolution, from rest
to motion, and from motion to rest, in every part of the universe, the
quantity of motion in the whole was always the same.

But, as there was no void, no one part of matter could be moved
without thrusting some other out of its place, nor that without thrusting
some other, and so on. To avoid, therefore, an infinite progress, he
supposed that the matter which any body pushed before it, rolled immediately backwards, to supply the place of that matter which flowed
in behind it; and as we may observe in the swimming of a fish, that
the water which it pushes before it, immediately rolls backward, to
supply the place of what flows in behind it, and thus forms a small
circle or vortex round the body of the fish. It was, in the same manner, that the motion originally impressed by the Creator upon the
infinitude of matter, necessarily produced in it an infinity of greater
and smaller vortices, or circular streams: and the law of motion being
so adjusted as always to preserve the same quantity of motion in the
universe, those vortices either continued for ever, or by their dissolution gave birth to others of the same kind. There was, thus, at all
times, an infinite number of greater and smaller vortices, or circular
streams, revolving in the universe.

But, whatever moves in a circle, is constantly endeavouring to fly off
from the centre of its revolution. For the natural motion of all bodies
is in a straight line. All the particles of matter, therefore, in each of
those greater vortices, were continually pressing from the centre to the
circumference, with more or less force, according to the different degrees
of their bulk and solidity. The larger and more solid globules of the
second element forced themselves upwards to the circumference, while
the smaller, more yielding, and more active particles of the first, which
could flow, even through the interstices of the second, were forced
downwards to the centre. They were forced downwards to the centre,
notwithstanding their natural tendency was upwards to the circumference; for the same reason that a piece of wood, when plunged in
water, is forced upwards to the surface, notwithstanding its natural
tendency is downwards to the bottom; because its tendency downwards is less strong than that of the particles of water, which, therefore,

if one may say so, press in before it, and thus force it upwards. But there being a greater quantity of the first element than what was necessary to fill up the interstices of the second, it was necessarily accumulated in the centre of each of these great circular streams, and formed there the fiery and active substance of the Sun. For, according to that philosopher, the Solar Systems were infinite in number, each Fixed Star being the centre of one: and he is among the first of the moderns, who thus took away the boundaries of the Universe; even Copernicus and Kepler, themselves, having confined it within, what they supposed, to be the vault of the Firmament.

The centre of each vortex being thus occupied by the most active and movable parts of matter, there was necessarily among them, a more violent agitation than in any other part of the vortex, and this violent agitation of the centre cherished and supported the movement of the whole. But, among the particles of the first element, which fill up the interstices of the second, there are many, which, from the pressure of the globules on all sides of them, necessarily receive an angular form, and thus constitute a third element of particles less fit for motion than those of the other two. As the particles, however, of this third element were formed in the interstices of the second, they are necessarily smaller than those of the second, and are, therefore, along with those of the first, urged down towards the centre, where, when a number of them happen to take hold of one another, they form such spots upon the surface of the accumulated particles of the first element, as are often discovered by telescopes upon the face of that Sun which enlightens and animates our particular system. Those spots are often broken and dispelled, by the violent agitation of the particles of the first element, as has hitherto happily been the case with those which have successively been formed upon the face of our Sun. Sometimes, however, they encrust the whole surface of that fire which is accumulated in the centre; and the communication betwixt the most active and the most inert parts of the vortex being thus interrupted, the rapidity of its motion immediately begins to languish, and can no longer defend it from being swallowed up and carried away by the superior violence of some other like circular stream; and in this manner, what was once a Sun, becomes a Planet. Thus, the time was, according to this system, when the Moon was a body of the same kind with the Sun, the fiery centre of a circular stream of ether, which flowed continually round her; but her face having been crusted over by a congeries of angular particles, the motion of this circular stream began to languish, and could no longer defend itself from being absorbed by the more violent vortex of the Earth, which was then, too, a Sun, and which chanced to be placed in its neighbourhood. The Moon, therefore, became a Planet, and revolved round the Earth. In process of time, the same fortune, which had thus befallen the Moon, befell also the Earth; its face was encrusted by a gross and inactive substance; the motion of its vortex began to languish, and it was absorbed by the greater vortex of the Sun: but though the vortex of the Earth had thus become languid, it still had force enough to occasion both the diurnal revolution of the Earth, and the monthly motion of the Moon. For a small circular stream may easily be conceived as flowing round the body of the Earth, at the same time that it is carried along by that great ocean of ether which is continually revolving round the Sun; in the same manner, as in a great whirlpool of water, one may often see several small whirlpools, which revolve round centres of their own, and at the same time are carried round the centre of the great one. Such was the cause of the original formation and consequent motions of the Planetary System. When a solid body is turned round its centre, those parts of it, which are nearest, and those which are remotest from the centre, complete their revolutions in one and the same time. But it is otherwise with the revolutions of a fluid; the parts of it which are nearest the centre complete their revolutions in a shorter time, than those which are remoter. The Planets, therefore, all floating, in that immense tide of ether which is continually setting in from west to east round the body of the Sun, complete their revolutions in a longer or a shorter time, according to their nearness or distance from him. There was, however, according to Des Cartes, no very exact proportion observed betwixt the times of their revolutions and their distances from the centre. For that nice analogy, which Kepler had discovered betwixt them, having not yet been confirmed by the observations of Cassini, was, as I before took notice, entirely disregarded by Des Cartes. According to him, too, their orbits might not be perfectly circular, but be longer the one way than the other, and thus approach to an Ellipse. Nor yet was it necessary to suppose, that they described this figure with geometrical accuracy, or even that they described always precisely the same figure. It rarely happens, that nature can be mathematically exact with regard to the figure of the objects she produces, upon account of the infinite combinations of impulses, which must conspire to the production of each of her effects. No two Planets, no two animals of the same kind, have exactly the same figure, nor is that of any one of them perfectly regular. It was in vain, therefore, that astronomers laboured to find that perfect constancy and regularity in the motions of the heavenly bodies, which is to be found in no other parts of nature. These motions, like all others, must either languish or be accelerated, according as the cause which produces them, the revolution of the vortex of the Sun, either languishes, or is accelerated; and there are innumerable events which may occasion either the one or the other of those changes.

It was thus, that Des Cartes endeavoured to render familiar to the imagination, the greatest difficulty in the Copernican system, the rapid motion of the enormous bodies of the Planets. When the fancy had thus been taught to conceive them as floating in an immense ocean of ether, it was quite agreeable to its usual habits to conceive, that they should follow the stream of this ocean, how rapid soever. This was an order of succession to which it had been long accustomed, and with which it was, therefore, quite familiar. This account, too, of the motions of the Heavens, was connected with a vast, an immense system, which joined together a greater number of the most discordant phenomena of nature, than had been united by any other hypothesis; a system in which the principles of connection, though perhaps equally imaginary, were, however, more distinct and determinate, than any that had been known before; and which attempted to trace to the imagination, not only the order of succession by which the heavenly bodies were moved, but that by which they, and almost all other natural objects, had originally been produced.—The Cartesian philosophy begins now to be almost universally rejected, whilst the Copernican system continues to be universally received. Yet it is not easy to imagine, how much probability and coherence this admired system was long supposed to derive from that exploded hypothesis. Till Des Cartes had published his principles, the disjointed and incoherent system of Tycho Brahe, though it was embraced heartily and completely by scarce any body, was yet constantly talked of by all the learned, as, in point of probability, upon a level with Copernicus. They took notice, indeed, of its inferiority with regard to coherence and connection, expressing hopes, however, that these defects might be remedied by some future improvements. But when the world beheld that complete, and almost perfect coherence, which the philosophy of Des Cartes bestowed upon the system of Copernicus, the imaginations of mankind could no longer refuse themselves the pleasure of going along with so harmonious an account of things. The system of Tycho Brahe was every day less and less talked of, till at last it was forgotten altogether.

The system of Des Cartes, however, though it connected together the real motions of the heavenly bodies according to the system of Copernicus, more happily than had been done before, did so only when they were considered in the gross; but did not apply to them, when they were regarded in the detail. Des Cartes, as was said before, had never himself observed the Heavens with any particular application. Though he was not ignorant, therefore, of any of the observations which had been made before his time, he seems to have paid them no great degree of attention; which, probably, proceeded from his own inexperience in the study of Astronomy. So far, therefore, from accommodating his system to all the minute irregularities, which Kepler had ascertained in the movements of the Planets; or from showing, particularly, how these irregularities, and no other, should arise from it, he contented himself with observing, that perfect uniformity could not

25

be expected in their motions, from the nature of the causes which produced them ; that certain irregularities might take place in them, for a
great number of successive revolutions, and afterwards gave way to
others of a different kind : a remark which, happily, relieved him from
the necessity of applying his system to the observations of Kepler, and
the other Astronomers.

But when the observations of Cassini had established the authority
of those laws, which Kepler had first discovered in the system, the
philosophy of Des Cartes, which could afford no reason why such particular laws should be observed, might continue to amuse the learned
in other sciences, but could no longer satisfy those that were skilled in
Astronomy. Sir Isaac Newton first attempted to give a physical
account of the motions of the Planets, which should accommodate
itself to all the constant irregularities which astronomers had ever observed in their motions. The physical connection, by which Des
Cartes had endeavoured to bind together the movements of the Planets,
was the laws of impulse ; of all the orders of succession, those which
are most familiar to the imagination ; as they all flow from the inertness of matter. After this quality, there is no other with which we
are so well acquainted as that of gravity. We never act upon matter,
but we have occasion to observe it. The superior genius and sagacity
of Sir Isaac Newton, therefore, made the most happy, and, we may
now say, the greatest and most admirable improvement that was ever
made in philosophy, when he discovered, that he could join together
the movements of the Planets by so familiar a principle of connection,
which completely removed all the difficulties the imagination had
hitherto felt in attending to them. He demonstrated, that, if the
Planets were supposed to gravitate towards the Sun, and to one another,
and at the same time to have had a projecting force originally impressed upon them, the primary ones might all describe ellipses in one
of the foci of which that great luminary was placed ; and the secondary ones might describe figures of the same kind round their respective primaries, without being disturbed by the continual motion of the
centres of their revolutions. That if the force, which retained each of
them in their orbits, was like that of gravity, and directed towards the
Sun, they would, each of them, describe equal areas in equal times.
That if this attractive power of the Sun, like all other qualities which
are diffused in rays from a centre, diminished in the same proportion as
the squares of the distances increased, their motions would be swiftest
when nearest the Sun, and slowest when farthest off from him, in the
same proportion in which, by observation, they are discovered to be ;
and that upon the same supposition, of this gradual diminution of their
respective gravities, their periodic times would bear the same proportion to their distances, which Kepler and Cassini had established
betwixt them. Having thus shown, that gravity might be the connect-

ing principle which joined together the movements of the Planets, he endeavoured next to prove that it really was so. Experience shows us, what is the power of gravity near the surface of the Earth. That it is such as to make a body fall, in the first second of its descent, through about fifteen Parisian feet. The Moon is about sixty semidiameters of the Earth distant from its surface. If gravity, therefore, was supposed to diminish, as the squares of the distance increase, a body, at the Moon, would fall towards the Earth in a minute ; that is, in sixty seconds, through the same space, which it falls near its surface in one second. But the arch which the Moon describes in a minute, falls, by observation, about fifteen Parisian feet below the tangent drawn at the beginning of it. So far, therefore, the Moon may be conceived as constantly falling towards the Earth.

The system of Sir Isaac Newton corresponded to many other irregularities which Astronomers had observed in the Heavens. It assigned a reason, why the centres of the revolutions of the Planets were not precisely in the centre of the Sun, but in the common centre of gravity of the Sun and the Planets. From the mutual attraction of the Planets, it gave a reason for some other irregularities in their motions ; irregularities, which are quite sensible in those of Jupiter and Saturn, when those Planets are nearly in conjunction with one another. But of all the irregularities in the Heavens, those of the Moon had hitherto given the greatest perplexity to Astronomers ; and the system of Sir Isaac Newton corresponded, if possible, yet more accurately with them than with any of the other Planets. The Moon, when either in conjunction, or in opposition to the Sun, appears furthest from the Earth, and nearest to it when in her quarters. According to the system of that philosopher, when she is in conjunction with the Sun, she is nearer the Sun than the Earth is ; consequently, more attracted to him, and, therefore, more separated from the Earth. On the contrary, when in opposition to the Sun, she is further from the Sun than the Earth. The Earth, therefore, is more attracted to the Sun : and consequently, in this case, too, further separated from the Moon. But, on the other hand, when the Moon is in her quarters, the Earth and the Moon, being both at equal distance from the Sun, are equally attracted to him. They would not, upon this account alone, therefore, be brought nearer to one another. As it is not in parallel lines however that they are attracted towards the Sun, but in lines which meet in his centre, they are, thereby, still further approached to one another. Sir Isaac Newton computed the difference of the forces with which the Moon and the Earth ought, in all those different situations, according to his theory, to be impelled towards one another ; and found, that the different degrees of their approaches, as they had been observed by Astronomers, corresponded exactly to his computations. As the attraction of the Sun, in the conjunctions and oppositions, diminishes the gravity of

25. *

the Moon towards the Earth, and, consequently, makes her necessarily extend her orbit, and, therefore, require a longer periodical time to finish it. But, when the Moon and the Earth are in that part of the orbit which is nearest the Sun, this attraction of the Sun will be the greatest; consequently, the gravity of the Moon towards the Earth will there be most diminished; her orbit be most extended; and her periodic time be, therefore, the longest. This is, also, agreeable to experience, and in the very same proportion, in which, by computation, from these principles, it might be expected.

The orbit of the Moon is not precisely in the same Plane with that of the Earth; but makes a very small angle with it. The points of intersection with those two Planes, are called, the Nodes of the Moon. These Nodes of the Moon are in continual motion, and in eighteen or nineteen years, revolve backwards, from east to west, through all the different points of the Ecliptic. For the Moon, after having finished her periodical revolution, generally intersects the orbit of the Earth somewhat behind the point where she had intersected it before. But, though the motion of the Nodes is thus generally retrograde, it is not always so, but is sometimes direct, and sometimes they appear even stationary; the Moon generally intersects the Plane of the Earth's orbit behind the point where she had intersected it in her former revolution; but she sometimes intersects it before that point, and sometimes in the very same point. It is the situation of those Nodes which determines the times of Eclipses, and their motions had, upon this account, at all times, been particularly attended to by Astronomers. Nothing, however, had perplexed them more, than to account for these so inconsistent motions, and, at the same time, preserve their so much sought-for regularity in the revolutions of the Moon. For they had no other means of connecting the appearances together than by supposing the motions which produced them, to be, in reality, perfectly regular and equable. The history of Astronomy, therefore, gives an account of a greater number of theories invented for connecting together the motions of the Moon, than for connecting together those of all the other heavenly bodies taken together. The theory of gravity, connected together, in the most accurate manner, by the different actions of the Sun and the Earth, all those irregular motions; and it appears, by calculation, that the time, the quantity, and the duration of those direct and retrograde motions of the Nodes, as well as of their stationary appearances, might be expected to be exactly such, as the observations of Astronomers have determined them.

The same principle, the attraction of the Sun, which thus accounts for the motions of the Nodes, connects, too, another very perplexing irregularity in the appearances of the Moon; the perpetual variation in the inclination of her orbit to that of the Earth.

As the Moon revolves in an ellipse, which has the centre of the

Earth in one of its foci, the longer axis of its orbit is called the Line of its Apsides. This line is found, by observation, not to be always directed towards the same points of the Firmament, but to revolve forwards from west to east, so as to pass through all the points of the Ecliptic, and to complete its period in about nine years ; another irregularity, which had very much perplexed Astronomers, but which the theory of gravity sufficiently accounted for.

The Earth had hitherto been regarded as perfectly globular, probably for the same reason which had made men imagine, that the orbits of the Planets must necessarily be perfectly circular. But Sir Isaac Newton, from mechanical principles, concluded, that, as the parts of the Earth must be more agitated by her diurnal revolution at the Equator, than at the Poles, they must necessarily be somewhat elevated at the first, and flattened at the second. The observation, that the oscillations of pendulums were slower at the Equator than at the Poles, seeming to demonstrate, that gravity was stronger at the Poles, and weaker at the Equator, proved, he thought, that the Equator was further from the centre than the Poles. All the measures, however, which had hitherto been made of the Earth, seemed to show the contrary, that it was drawn out towards the Poles, and flattened towards the Equator. Newton, however, preferred his mechanical computations to the former measures of Geographers and Astronomers ; and in this he was confirmed by the observations of Astronomers on the figure of Jupiter, whose diameter at the Pole seems to be to his diameter at the Equator, as twelve to thirteen ; a much greater inequality than could be supposed to take place betwixt the correspondent diameters of the Earth, but which was exactly proportioned to the superior bulk of Jupiter, and the superior rapidity with which he performs his diurnal revolutions. The observations of Astronomers at Lapland and Peru have fully confirmed Sir Isaac's system, and have not only demonstrated, that the figure of the Earth is, in general, such as he supposed it ; but that the proportion of its axis to the diameter of its Equator is almost precisely such as he had computed it. And of all the proofs that have ever been adduced of the diurnal revolution of the Earth, this perhaps is the most solid and most satisfactory.

Hipparchus, by comparing his own observations with those of some former Astronomers, had found that the equinoctial points were not always opposite to the same part of the Heavens, but that they advanced gradually eastward by so slow a motion, as to be scarce sensible in one hundred years, and which would require thirty-six thousand to make a complete revolution of the Equinoxes, and to carry them successively through all the different points of the Ecliptic. More accurate observations discovered that this procession of the Equinoxes was not so slow as Hipparchus had imagined it, and that it required somewhat less than twenty-six thousand years to give them a complete

revolution. While the ancient system of Astronomy, which represented
the Earth as the immovable centre of the universe, took place, this
appearance was necessarily accounted for, by supposing that the Firmament, besides its rapid diurnal revolution round the poles of the Equator, had likewise a slow periodical one round those of the Ecliptic.
And when the system of Hipparchus was by the schoolmen united
with the solid Spheres of Aristotle, they placed a new crystalline
Sphere above the Firmament, in order to join this motion to the rest.
In the Copernican system, this appearance had hitherto been connected with the other parts of that hypothesis, by supposing a small
revolution in the Earth's axis from east to west. Sir Isaac Newton
connected this motion by the same principle of gravity, by which he
had united all the others, and showed, how the elevation of the parts
of the Earth at the Equator must, by the attraction of the Sun, produce the same retrograde motion of the Nodes of the Ecliptic, which
it produced of the Nodes of the Moon. He computed the quantity of
motion which could arise from this action of the Sun, and his calculations
here too corresponded with the observations of Astronomers.

Comets have hitherto, of all the appearances in the Heavens, been
the least attended to by Astronomers. The rarity and inconstancy of
their appearance, seemed to separate them entirely from the constant,
regular, and uniform objects in the Heavens, and to make them
resemble more the inconstant, transitory, and accidental phenomena of
those regions that are in the neighbourhood of the Earth. Aristotle,
Eudoxus, Hipparchus, Ptolemy, and Purbach, therefore, had all degraded them below the Moon, and ranked them among the meteors of
the upper regions of the air. The observations of Tycho Brahe
demonstrated, that they ascended into the celestial regions, and were
often higher than Venus or the Sun. Des Cartes, at random, supposed
them to be always higher than even the orbit of Saturn ; and seems,
by the superior elevation he thus bestowed upon them, to have been
willing to compensate that unjust degradation which they had suffered
for so many ages before. The observations of some later Astronomers
demonstrated, that they too revolved about the Sun, and might therefore be parts of the Solar System. Newton accordingly applied his
mechanical principle of gravity to explain the motions of these bodies.
That they described equal areas in equal times, had been discovered
by the observations of some later Astronomers ; and Newton endeavoured to show how from this principle, and those observations, the
nature and position of their several orbits might be ascertained, and
their periodic times determined. His followers have, from his principles,
ventured even to predict the returns of several of them, particularly of one
which is to make its appearance in 1758.* We must wait for that time

* It must be observed, that the whole of this Essay was written previous to the date here
mentioned ; and that the return of the comet happened agreeably to the prediction.

before we can determine, whether his philosophy corresponds as happily to this part of the system as to all the others. In the meantime, however, the ductility of this principle, which applied itself so happily to these, the most irregular of all the celestial appearances, and which has introduced such complete coherence into the motions of all the Heavenly Bodies, has served not a little to recommend it to the imaginations of mankind.

But of all the attempts of the Newtonian philosophy, that which would appear to be the most above the reach of human reason and experience, is the attempt to compute the weights and densities of the Sun, and of the several Planets. An attempt, however, which was indispensably necessary to complete the coherence of the Newtonian system. The power of attraction which, according to the theory of gravity, each body possesses, is in proportion to the quantity of matter contained in that body. But the periodic time in which one body, at a given distance, revolves round another that attracts it, is shorter in proportion as this power is greater, and consequently as the quantity of matter in the attracting body. If the densities of Jupiter and Saturn were the same with that of the Earth, the periodic times of their several Satellites would be shorter than by observation they are found to be. Because the quantity of matter, and consequently the attracting power of each of them, would be as the cubes of their diameters. By comparing the bulks of those Planets, and the periodic times of their Satellites, it is found that, upon the hypothesis of gravity, the density of Jupiter must be greater than that of Saturn, and the density of the Earth greater than that of Jupiter. This seems to establish it as a law in the system, that the nearer the several Planets approach to the Sun, the density of their matter is the greater: a constitution of things which seems to be the most advantageous of any that could have been established; as water of the same density with that of our Earth, would freeze under the Equator of Saturn, and boil under that of Mercury.

Such is the system of Sir Isaac Newton, a system whose parts are all more strictly connected together, than those of any other philosophical hypothesis. Allow his principle, the universality of gravity, and that it decreases as the squares of the distance increase, and all the appearances, which he joins together by it, necessarily follow. Neither is their connection merely a general and loose connection, as that of most other systems, in which either these appearances, or some such like appearances, might indifferently have been expected. It is everywhere the most precise and particular that can be imagined, and ascertains the time, the place, the quantity, the duration of each individual phenomenon, to be exactly such as, by observation, they have been determined to be. Neither are the principles of union, which it employs, such as the imagination can find any difficulty in going along with. The gravity of matter is, of all its qualities, after its inertness, that which is most familiar to us. We never act upon it without having occasion to observe this property. The law too, by which it is supposed to diminish as it recedes from its centre, is the same which takes place in all other qualities which are propagated in rays from a centre, in light, and in every thing else of the same kind. It is such, that we not only find that it does take place in all such qualities, but we are necessarily determined to conceive that, from the nature of the thing, it must take place. The opposition which was made in France, and in some other foreign nations, to the prevalence of this system, did not arise from any difficulty which mankind naturally felt in conceiving gravity as an original and primary mover in the constitution of the universe. The Cartesian system, which had prevailed so generally before it, had accustomed mankind to conceive motion as never beginning, but in consequence of impulse, and had connected the descent of heavy bodies, near the surface of the Earth, and the other Planets, by this more general bond of union; and it was the attachment the world had conceived for this account of things, which indisposed them to that of Sir Isaac Newton. His system, however, now prevails over all opposition, and has advanced to the acquisition of the most universal empire that was ever established in philosophy. His principles, it must be acknowledged, have a degree of firmness and solidity that we should in vain look for in any other system. The most sceptical cannot avoid feeling this. They not only connect together most perfectly all the phenomena of the Heavens, which had been observed before his time; but those also which the persevering industry and more perfect instruments of later Astronomers have made known to us have been either easily and immediately explained by the application of his principles, or have been explained in consequence of more laborious and accurate calculations from these principles, than had been instituted before. And even we, while we have been endeavouring to represent all philosophical systems as mere inventions of the imagination, to connect together the otherwise disjointed and discordant phenomena of Nature, have insensibly been drawn in, to make use of language expressing the connecting principles of this one, as if they were the real chains which Nature makes use of to bind together her several operations. Can we wonder then, that it should have gained the general and complete approbation of mankind, and that it should now be considered, not as an attempt to connect in the imagination the phenomena of the Heavens, but as the greatest discovery that ever was made by man, the discovery of an immense chain of the most important and sublime truths, all closely connected together, by one capital fact, of the reality of which we have daily experience.

* * * * * * * *
* * * * * * * *

Note by the Editors.

The Author, at the end of this Essay, left some Notes and Memorandums, from which it appears, that he considered this last part of his History of Astronomy as imperfect, and needing several additions. The Editors, however, chose rather to publish than suppress it. It must be viewed, not as a History or Account of Sir Isaac Newton's Astronomy, but chiefly as an additional illustration of those Principles in the Human Mind which Mr. Smith has pointed out to be the universal motives of Philosophical Researches.

THE PRINCIPLES

WHICH LEAD AND DIRECT

PHILOSOPHICAL ENQUIRIES;

ILLUSTRATED BY THE

HISTORY OF THE ANCIENT PHYSICS.

FROM arranging and methodizing the System of the Heavens, Philosophy descended to the consideration of the inferior parts of Nature, of the Earth, and of the bodies which immediately surround it. If the objects, which were here presented to its view, were inferior in greatness or beauty, and therefore less apt to attract the attention of the mind, they were more apt, when they came to be attended to, to embarrass and perplex it, by the variety of their species, and by the intricacy and seeming irregularity of the laws or orders of their succession. The species of objects in the Heavens are few in number; the Sun, the Moon, the Planets, and the Fixed Stars, are all which those philosophers could distinguish. All the changes too, which are ever observed in these bodies, evidently arise from some difference in the velocity and direction of their several motions; but the variety of meteors in the air, of clouds, rainbows, thunder, lightning, winds, rain, hail, snow, is vastly greater; and the order of their succession seems to be still more irregular and inconstant. The species of fossils, minerals, plants, animals, which are found in the Waters, and near the surface of the Earth, are still more intricately diversified; and if we regard the different manners of their production, their mutual influence in altering, destroying, supporting one another, the orders of their succession seem to admit of an almost infinite variety. If the imagination, therefore, when it considered the appearances in the Heavens, was often perplexed, and driven out of its natural career, it would be much more exposed to the same embarrassment, when it directed its attention to the objects which the Earth presented to it, and when it endeavoured to trace their progress and successive revolutions.

To introduce order and coherence into the mind's conception of this seeming chaos of dissimilar and disjointed appearances, it was necessary to deduce all their qualities, operations, and laws of succession, from those of some particular things, with which it was perfectly acquainted and familiar, and along which its imagination could glide smoothly and easily, and without interruption. But as we would in vain attempt to deduce the heat of a stove from that of an open chimney, unless we could show that the same fire which was exposed in the one, lay concealed in the other; so it was impossible to deduce the qualities and laws of succession, observed in the more uncommon appearances of Nature, from those of such as were more familiar, if those customary objects were not supposed, however disguised in their appearance, to enter into the composition of those rarer and more singular phenomena. To render, therefore, this lower part of the great theatre of nature a coherent spectacle to the imagination, it became necessary to suppose, first, That all the strange objects of which it consisted were made up out of a few, with which the mind was extremely familiar: and secondly, That all their qualities, operations and rules of succession, were no more than different diversifications of those to which it had long been accustomed, in these primary and elementary objects.

Of all the bodies of which these inferior parts of the universe seem to be composed, those with which we are most familiar, are the Earth, which we tread upon; the Water, which we every day use; the Air, which we constantly breathe; and the Fire, whose benign influence is not only required for preparing the common necessaries of life, but for the continual support of that vital principle which actuates both plants and animals. These therefore, were by Empedocles, and the other philosophers of the Italian school, supposed to be the elements, out of which, at least, all the inferior parts of nature were composed. The familiarity of those bodies to the mind, naturally disposed it to look for some resemblance to them in whatever else was presented to its consideration. The discovery of some such resemblance united the new object to an assortment of things, with which the imagination was perfectly acquainted. And if any analogy could be observed betwixt the operations and laws of succession of the compound, and those of the simple objects, the movement of the fancy, in tracing their progress, became quite smooth, and natural, and easy. This natural anticipation, too, was still more confirmed by such a slight and inaccurate analysis of things, as could be expected in the infancy of science, when the curiosity of mankind, grasping at an account of all things before it had got full satisfaction with regard to any one, hurried on to build, in imagination, the immense fabric of the universe. The heat, observed in both plants and animals, seemed to demonstrate, that Fire made a part of their composition. Air was not less necessary for the subsistence of both, and seemed, too, to enter into the fabric of animals by respiration, and into that of plants by some other means. The juices which circulated through them showed how much of their texture was owing to Water. And their resolution into Earth by putrefaction discovered that this element had not been left out in their original formation. A similar analysis seemed to show the same principles in most of the other compound bodies.

The vast extent of those bodies seemed to render them, upon another account, proper to be the great stores out of which nature compounded all the other species of things. Earth and Water divide almost the whole of the terrestrial globe between them. The thin transparent covering of the Air surrounds it to an immense height upon all sides. Fire, with its attendant, light, seems to descend from the celestial regions, and might, therefore, either be supposed to be diffused through the whole of those etherial spaces, as well as to be condensed and conglobated in those luminous bodies, which sparkle across them, as by the Stoics; or, to be placed immediately under the sphere of the Moon, in the region next below them, as by the Peripatetics, who could not reconcile the devouring nature of Fire with the supposed unchangeable essence of their solid and crystalline spheres.

The qualities, too, by which we are chiefly accustomed to characterize and distinguish natural bodies, are all of them found, in the highest degree in those Four Elements. The great divisions of the objects, near the surface of the Earth, are those into hot and cold, moist and dry, light and heavy. These are the most remarkable properties of bodies ; and it is upon them that many of their other most sensible qualities and powers seem to depend. Of these, heat and cold were naturally enough regarded by those first enquirers into nature, as the active, moisture and dryness, as the passive qualities of matter. It was the temperature of heat and cold which seemed to occasion the growth and dissolution of plants and animals ; as appeared evident from the effects of the change of the seasons upon both. A proper degree of moisture and dryness was not less necessary for these purposes ; as was evident from the different effects and productions of wet and dry seasons and soils. It was the heat and cold, however, which actuated and determined those two otherwise inert qualities of things, to a state either of rest or motion. Gravity and levity were regarded

as the two principles of motion, which directed all sublunary things to
their proper place : and all those six qualities, taken together, were,
upon such an inattentive view of nature, as must be expected in the
beginnings of philosophy, readily enough apprehended to be capable of
connecting together the most remarkable revolutions, which occur in
these inferior parts of the universe.   Heat and dryness were the qualities which characterized the element of Fire; heat and moisture that
of Air ; moisture and cold that of Water ; cold and dryness that of
Earth.   The natural motion of two of these elements, Earth and Water,
was downwards, upon account of their gravity.   This tendency, however, was stronger in the one than in the other, upon account of the
superior gravity of Earth.   The natural motion of the two other elements, Fire and Air, was upwards, upon account of their levity; and
this tendency, too, was stronger in the one than in the other, upon
account of the superior levity of Fire.   Let us not despise those ancient
philosophers, for thus supposing, that these two elements had a positive
levity, or a real tendency upwards.   Let us remember, that this notion
has an appearance of being confirmed by the most obvious observations ; that those facts and experiments, which demonstrate the weight
of the Air, and which no superior sagacity, but chance alone, presented
to the moderns, were altogether unknown to them ; and that, what
might, in some measure, have supplied the place of those experiments,
the reasonings concerning the causes of the ascent of bodies, in fluids
specifically heavier than themselves, seem to have been unknown in
the ancient world, till Archimedes discovered them, long after their
system of physics was completed, and had acquired an established
reputation : that those reasonings are far from being obvious, and that
by their inventor, they seem to have been thought applicable only to
the ascent of Solids in Water, and not even to that of Solids in Air,
much less to that of one fluid in another.   But it is this last only which
could explain the ascent of flame, vapours, and fiery exhalations, without the supposition of a specific levity.

Thus, each of those Four Elements had, in the system of the Universe, a place which was peculiarly allotted to it, and to which it naturally tended.   Earth and Water rolled down to the centre ; the Air
spread itself above them ; while the Fire soared aloft, either to the
celestial region, or to that which was immediately below it.   When
each of those simple bodies had thus obtained its proper sphere, there
was nothing in the nature of any one of them to make it pass into the
place of the other, to make the Fire descend into the Air, the Air into
the Water, or the Water into the Earth ; or, on the contrary, to bring
up the Earth into the place of the Water, the Water into that of the
Air, or the Air into that of the Fire.   All sublunary things, therefore,
if left to themselves, would have remained in an eternal repose.   The
revolution of the heavens, those of the Sun, Moon, and Five Planets,

by producing the vicissitudes of Day and Night, and of the Seasons, prevented this torpor and inactivity from reigning through the inferior parts of nature ; inflamed by the rapidity of their circumvolutions, the element of Fire, and forced it violently downwards into the Air, into the Water, and into the Earth, and thereby produced those mixtures of the different elements which kept up the motion and circulation of the lower parts of Nature ; occasioned, sometimes, the entire transmutation of one element into another, and sometimes the production of forms and species different from them all, and in which, though the qualities of them all might be found, they were so altered and attempered by the mixture, as scarce to be distinguishable.

Thus, if a small quantity of Fire was mixed with a great quantity of Air, the moisture and moderate warmth of the one entirely surmounted and changed into their own essence the intense heat and dryness of the other; and the whole aggregate became Air. The contrary of which happened, if a small quantity of Air was mixed with a great quantity of Fire: the whole, in this case, became Fire. In the same manner, if a small quantity of Fire was mixed with a great quantity of Water, then, either the moisture and cold of the Water might surmount the heat and dryness of the Fire, so that the whole should become Water ; or, the moisture of the Water might surmount the dryness of the Fire, while, in its turn, the heat of the Fire surmounted the coldness of the Water, so as that the whole aggregate, its qualities being heat and moisture, should become Air, which was regarded as the more natural and easy metamorphosis of the two. In the same manner they explained how like changes were produced by the different mixtures of Fire and Earth, Earth and Water, Water and Air, Air and Earth ; and thus they connected together the successive transmutations of the elements into one another.

Every mixture of the Elements, however, did not produce an entire transmutation. They were sometimes so blended together, that the qualities of the one, not being able to destroy, served only to attemper those of the other. Thus Fire, when mixed with Water, produced sometimes a watery vapour, whose qualities were heat and moisture ; which partook at once of the levity of the Fire, and of the gravity of the Water, and which was elevated by the first into the Air, but retained by the last from ascending into the region of Fire. The relative cold, which they supposed prevailed in the middle region of the Air, upon account of its equal distance, both from the region of Fire, and from the rays that are reflected by the surface of the Earth, condensed this vapour into Water ; the Fire escaped it, and flew upwards, and the Water fell down in rain, or, according to the different degrees of cold that prevailed in the different seasons, was sometimes congealed into snow, and sometimes into hail. In the same manner, Fire, when mixed with Earth, produced sometimes a fiery exhalation, whose qualities were heat and dryness, which being elevated by the levity of the first into the Air condensed by the cold, so as to take fire, and being at the same time surrounded by watery vapours, burst forth into thunder and lightning, and other fiery meteors. Thus they connected together the different appearances in the Air, by the qualities of their Four Elements; and from them, too, in the same manner, they endeavoured to deduce all the other qualities in the other homogeneous bodies, that are near the surface of the Earth. Thus, to give an example, with regard to the hardness and softness of bodies; heat and moisture, they observed, were the great softeners of matter. Whatever was hard, therefore, owed that quality either to the absence of heat, or to the absence of moisture. Ice, crystal, lead, gold, and almost all metals, owed their hardness to the absence of heat, and were, therefore, dissolvable by Fire. Rock-salt, nitre, alum, and hard clay, owed that quality to the absence of moisture, and were therefore, dissolvable in water. And, in the same manner, they endeavoured to connect together most of the other tangible qualities of matter. Their principles of union, indeed, were often such as had no real existence, and were always vague and undetermined in the highest degree; they were such, however, as might be expected in the beginnings of science, and such as, with all their imperfections, could enable mankind both to think and to talk, with more coherence, concerning those general subjects, than without them they would have been capable of doing. Neither was their system entirely devoid either of beauty or magnificence. Each of the Four Elements having a particular region allotted to it, had a place of rest, to which it naturally tended, by its motion, either up or down, in a straight line, and where, when it had arrived, it naturally ceased to move. Earth descended, till it arrived at the place of Earth; Water, till it arrived at that of Water; and Air, till it arrived at that of Air; and there each of them tended to a state of eternal repose and inaction. The Spheres consisted of a Fifth Element, which was neither light nor heavy, and whose natural motion made it tend, neither to the centre, nor from the centre, but revolve round it in a circle. As, by this motion, they could never change their situation with regard to the centre, they had no place of repose, no place to which they naturally tended more than to any other, but revolved round and round for ever. This Fifth Element was subject neither to generation nor corruption, nor alteration of any kind; for whatever changes may happen in the Heavens, the senses can scarce perceive them, and their appearance is the same in one age as in another. The beauty, too, of their supposed crystalline spheres seemed still more to entitle them to this distinction of unchangeable immortality. It was the motion of those Spheres, which occasioned the mixtures of the Elements, and from thence, the production of all the forms and species, that diversify the world. It was the approach of the Sun and of the other Planets, to the different parts of the Earth, which, by forcing down the element of Fire, occasioned the generation of those forms. It was the recess of those bodies, which, by allowing each Element to escape to its proper sphere, brought about, in an equal time, their corruption. It was the periods of those great lights of Heaven, which measured out to all sublunary things, the term of their duration, of their growth, and of their decay, either in one, or in a number of seasons, according as the Elements of which they were composed, were either imperfectly or accurately blended and mixed with one another. Immortality, they could bestow upon no individual form, because the principles out of which it was formed, all tending to disengage themselves, and to return to their proper spheres, necessarily, at last, brought about its dissolution. But, though all individuals were thus perishable, and constantly decaying, every species was immortal, because the subject-matter out of which they were made, and the revolution of the Heavens, the cause of their successive generations, continued to be always the same.

In the first ages of the world, the seeming incoherence of the appearances of nature, so confounded mankind, that they despaired of discovering in her operations any regular system. Their ignorance, and confusion of thought, necessarily gave birth to that pusillanimous superstition, which ascribes almost every unexpected event, to the arbitrary will of some designing, though invisible beings, who produced it for some private and particular purpose. The idea of an universal mind, of a God of all, who originally formed the whole, and who governs the whole by general laws, directed to the conservation and prosperity of the whole, without regard to that of any private individual, was a notion to which they were utterly strangers. Their gods, though they were apprehended to interpose, upon some particular occasions, were so far from being regarded as the creators of the world, that their origin was apprehended to be posterior to that of the world. The Earth, according to Hesiod, was the first production of the chaos. The Heavens arose out of the Earth, and from both together, all the gods, who afterwards inhabited them. Nor was this notion confined to the vulgar, and to those poets who seem to have recorded the vulgar theology. Of all the philosophers of the Ionian school, Anaxagoras, it is well known, was the first who supposed that mind and understanding were requisite to account for the first origin of the world, and who, therefore, compared with the other philosophers of his time, talked, as Aristotle observes, like a sober man among drunkards ; but whose opinion was, at the time, so remarkable, that he seems to have got a sirname from it. The same notion, of the spontaneous origin of the world, was embraced, too, as the same author tells, by the early Pythagoreans, a sect, which, in the ancient world, was never regarded as irreligious. Mind, and understanding, and consequently Deity, being the most perfect, were necessarily, according to them, the last productions of Nature. For in all other things, what was most perfect, they observed, always came last. As in plants and animals, it is not the seed that is most perfect, but the complete animal, with all its members, in the one ; and the complete plant, with all its branches, leaves, flowers, and fruits, in the other. This notion, which could take place only while Nature was still considered as, in some measure, disorderly and inconsistent in her operations, was necessarily renounced by those philosophers, when, upon a more attentive survey, they discovered, or imagined they had discovered, more distinctly, the chain which bound all her different parts to one another. As soon as the Universe was regarded as a complete machine, as a coherent system, governed by general laws, and directed to general ends, viz. its own preservation and prosperity, and that of all the species that are in it ; the resemblance which it evidently bore to those machines which are produced by human art, necessarily impressed those sages with a belief, that in the original formation of the world there must have been employed an art resembling the human art, but as much superior to it, as the world is superior to the machines which that art produces. The unity of the system, which, according to this ancient philosophy, is most perfect, suggested the idea of the unity of that principle, by whose art it was formed ; and thus, as ignorance begot superstition, science gave birth to the first theism that arose among those nations, who were not enlightened by divine Revelation. According to Timæus, who was followed by Plato, that intelligent Being who formed the world endowed it with a principle of life and understanding, which extends from its centre to its remotest circumference, which is conscious of all its changes, and which governs and directs all its motions to the great end of its formation. This soul of the world was itself a God, the greatest of all the inferior, and created deities ; of an essence that was indissoluble, by any power but by that of him who made it, and which was united to the body of the world, so as to be inseparable by every force, but his who joined them, from the exertion of which his goodness secured them. The beauty of the celestial spheres attracting the admiration of mankind, the constancy and regularity of their motions seeming to manifest peculiar wisdom and understanding, they were each of them supposed to be animated by an Intelligence of a nature that was, in the same manner, indissoluble and immortal, and inseparably united to that sphere which it inhabited. All the mortal and changeable beings which people the surface of the earth were formed by those inferior deities ; for the revolutions of the heavenly bodies seemed plainly to influence the generation and growth of both plants and animals, whose frail and fading forms bore the too evident marks of the weakness of those inferior causes, which joined their different parts to one another. According to Plato and Timæus, neither the

Universe, nor even those inferior deities who govern the Universe, were eternal, but were formed in time, by the great Author of all things, out of that matter which had existed from all eternity. This at least their words seemed to import, and thus they are understood by Cicero, and by all the other writers of earlier antiquity, though some of the later Platonists have interpreted them differently.

According to Aristotle, who seems to have followed the doctrine of Ocellus, the world was eternal ; the eternal effect of an eternal cause. He found it difficult, it would seem, to conceive what could hinder the First Cause from exerting his divine energy from all eternity. At whatever time he began to exert it, he must have been at rest during all the infinite ages of that eternity which had passed before it. To what obstruction, from within or from without, could this be owing ? or how could this obstruction, if it ever had subsisted, have ever been removed ? His idea of the nature and manner of existence of this First Cause, as it is expressed in the last book of his Physics, and the five last chapters of his Metaphysics, is indeed obscure and unintelligible in the highest degree, and has perplexed his commentators more than any other parts of his writings. Thus far, however, he seems to express himself plainly enough : that the First Heavens, that of the Fixed Stars, from which are derived the motions of all the rest, is revolved by an eternal, immovable, unchangeable, unextended being, whose essence consists in intelligence, as that of a body consists in solidity and extension ; and which is therefore necessarily and always intelligent, as a body is necessarily and always extended : that this Being was the first and supreme mover of the Universe : that the inferior Planetary Spheres derived each of them its peculiar revolution from an inferior being of the same kind ; eternal, immovable, unextended, and necessarily intelligent : that the sole object of the intelligences of those beings was their own essence, and the revolution of their own spheres ; all other inferior things being unworthy of their consideration ; and that therefore whatever was below the Moon was abandoned by the gods to the direction of Nature, and Chance, and Necessity. For though those celestial beings were, by the revolutions of their several Spheres, the original causes of the generation and corruption of all sublunary forms, they were causes who neither knew nor intended the effects which they produced. This renowned philosopher seems, in his theological notions, to have been directed by prejudices which, though extremely natural, are not very philosophical. The revolutions of the Heavens, by their grandeur and constancy, excited his admiration, and seemed, upon that account, to be effects not unworthy a Divine Intelligence. Whereas the meanness of many things, the disorder and confusion of all things below, exciting no such agreeable emotion, seemed to have no marks of being directed by that Supreme Understanding. Yet, though this opinion saps the foundations of human worship, and must have the same effects upon society as Atheism itself, one may easily trace, in the Metaphysics upon which it is grounded, the origin of many of the notions, or rather of many of the expressions, in the scholastic theology, to which no notions can be annexed.

The Stoics, the most religious of all the ancient sects of philosophers, seem in this, as in most other things, to have altered and refined upon the doctrine of Plato. The order, harmony, and coherence which this philosophy bestowed upon the Universal System, struck them with awe and veneration. As, in the rude ages of the world, whatever particular part of Nature excited the admiration of mankind, was apprehended to be animated by some particular divinity ; so the whole of Nature having, by their reasonings, become equally the object of admiration, was equally apprehended to be animated by a Universal Deity, to be itself a Divinity, an Animal ; a term which to our ears seems by no means synonymous with the foregoing; whose body was the solid and sensible parts of Nature, and whose soul was that etherial Fire, which penetrated and actuated the whole. For of all the four elements, out of which all things were composed, Fire or Ether seemed to be that which bore the greatest resemblance to the Vital Principle which informs both plants and animals, and therefore most likely to be the Vital Principle which animated the Universe. This infinite and unbounded Ether, which extended itself from the centre beyond the remotest circumference of Nature, and was endowed with the most consummate reason and intelligence, or rather was itself the very essence of reason and intelligence, had originally formed the world, and had communicated a portion, or ray, of its own essence to whatever was endowed with life and sensation, which, upon the dissolution of those forms, either immediately or some time after, was again absorbed into that ocean of Deity from whence it had originally been detached. In this system the Sun, the Moon, the Planets, and the Fixed Stars, were each of them also inferior divinities, animated by a detached portion of that etherial essence which was the soul of the world. In the system of Plato, the Intelligence which animated the world was different from that which originally formed it. Neither were these which animated the celestial spheres, nor those which informed inferior terrestrial animals, regarded as portions of this plastic soul of the world. Upon the dissolution of animals, therefore, their souls were not absorbed in the soul of the world, but had a separate and eternal existence, which gave birth to the notion of the transmigration of souls. Neither did it seem unnatural, that, as the same matter which had composed one animal body might be employed to compose another, that the same intelligence which had animated one such being should again animate another. But in the system of the Stoics, the intelligence which originally formed, and that which animated the world, were one and the same, all inferior intelligences were detached portions of the great one ; and therefore, in a longer, or in a shorter time, were all of them, even the gods themselves, who animated the celestial bodies, to be at last resolved into the infinite essence of this almighty Jupiter, who, at a distant period, should, by an universal conflagration, wrap up all things, in that etherial and fiery nature, out of which they had originally been deduced, again to bring forth a new Heaven and a new Earth, new animals, new men, new deities ; all of which would again, at a fated time, be swallowed up in a like conflagration, again to be re-produced, and again to be re-destroyed, and so on without end.

THE PRINCIPLES

WHICH LEAD AND DIRECT

PHILOSOPHICAL ENQUIRIES;

ILLUSTRATED BY THE HISTORY OF THE

ANCIENT LOGICS AND METAPHYSICS.

IN every transmutation, either of one element into another, or of one compound body either into the elements out of which it was composed, or into another compound body, it seemed evident, that both in the old and in the new species, there was something that was the same, and something that was different. When Fire was changed into Air, or Water into Earth, the Stuff, or Subject-matter of this Air and this Earth, was evidently the same with that of the former Fire or Water ; but the Nature or Species of those new bodies was entirely different. When, in the same manner, a number of fresh, green, and odoriferous flowers were thrown together in a heap, they, in a short time, entirely changed their nature, became putrid and loathsome, and dissolved into a confused mass of ordure, which bore no resemblance, either in sensible qualities or in its effects, to their former beautiful appearance. But how different soever the species, the subject-matter of the flowers, and of the ordure, was, in this case too, evidently the same. In every body therefore, whether simple or mixed, there were evidently two principles, whose combination constituted the whole nature of that particular body. The first was the Stuff, or Subject-matter, out of which it was made ; the second was the Species, the Specific Essence, the Essential, or, as the schoolmen have called it, the Substantial Form of the Body.

26 *

The first seemed to be the same in all bodies, and to have neither qualities nor powers of any kind, but to be altogether inert and imperceptible by any of the senses, till it was qualified and rendered sensible by its union with some species or essential form. All the qualities and powers of bodies seemed to depend upon their species or essential forms. It was not the stuff or matter of Fire, or Air, or Earth, or Water, which enabled those elements to produce their several effects, but that essential form which was peculiar to each of them. For it seemed evident that Fire must produce the effects of Fire, by that which rendered it Fire ; Air, by that which rendered it Air ; and that in the same manner all other simple and mixed bodies must produce their several effects, by that which constituted them such or such bodies ; that is, by their Specific Essence or essential forms. But it is from the effects of bodies upon one another, that all the changes and revolutions in the material world arise. Since these, therefore, depend upon the specific essences of those bodies, it must be the business of philosophy, that science which endeavours to connect together all the different changes that occur in the world, to determine wherein the Specific Essence of each object consists, in order to foresee what changes or revolutions may be expected from it. But the Specific Essence of each individual object is not that which is peculiar to it as an individual, but that which is common to it, with all other objects of the same kind. Thus the Specific Essence of the Water, which now stands before me, does not consist in its being heated by the Fire, or cooled by the Air, in such a particular degree ; in its being contained in a vessel of such a form, or of such dimensions. These are all accidental circumstances, which are altogether extraneous to its general nature, and upon which none of its effects as Water depend. Philosophy, therefore, in considering the general nature of Water, takes no notice of those particularities which are peculiar to this water, but confines itself to those things which are common to all Water. If, in the progress of its inquiries, it should descend to consider the nature of Water that is modified by such particular accidents, it still would not confine its consideration to this water contained in this vessel, and thus heated at this fire, but would extend its views to Water in general contained in such kind of vessels, and heated to such a degree at such a fire. In every case, therefore, Species, or Universals, and not Individuals, are the objects of Philosophy. Because whatever effects are produced by individuals, whatever changes can flow from them, must all proceed from some universal nature that is contained in them. As it was the business of Physics, or Natural Philosophy, to determine wherein consisted the Nature and Essence of every particular Species of things, in order to connect together all the different events that occur in the material world ; so there were two other sciences, which, though they had originally arisen out of that system of Natural Philosophy I have just been describing, were, however, apprehended to go before it, in the order in which the knowledge of Nature ought to be communicated. The first of these, Metaphysics, considered the general nature of Universals, and the different sorts or species into which they might be divided. The second of these, Logics, was built upon this doctrine of Metaphysics ; and from the general nature of Universals, and of the sorts into which they were divided, endeavoured to ascertain the general rules by which we might distribute all particular objects into general classes, and determine to what class each individual object belonged ; for in this, they justly enough apprehended, consisted the whole art of philosophical reasoning. As the first of these two sciences, Metaphysics, is altogether subordinate to the second, Logic, they seem, before the time of Aristotle, to have been regarded as one, and to have made up between them that ancient Dialectic of which we hear so much, and of which we understand so little : neither does this separation seem to have been much attended to, either by his own followers, the ancient Peripatetics, or by any other of the old sects of philosophers. The later schoolmen, indeed, have distinguished between Ontology and Logic ; but their Ontology contains but a small part of what is the subject of the metaphysical books of Aristotle, the greater part of which, the doctrines of Universals, and everything that is preparatory to the arts of defining and dividing, has, since the days of Porphery, been inserted into their Logic.

According to Plato and Timæus, the principles out of which the Deity formed the World, and which were themselves eternal, were three in number. The Subject-matter of things, the Species, or Specific Essences of things, and what was made out of these, the sensible objects themselves. These last had no proper or durable existence, but were in perpetual flux and succession. For as Heraclitus had said that no man ever passed the same river twice, because the water which he had passed over once was gone before he could pass over it a second time ; so, in the same manner, no man ever saw, or heard, or touched the same sensible object twice. When I look at the window, for example, the visible species, which strikes my eyes this moment, though resembling, is different from that which struck my eyes the immediately preceding moment. When I ring the bell, the sound, or audible species, which I hear this moment, though resembling in the same manner, is different, however, from that which I heard the moment before. When I lay my hand on the table, the tangible species which I feel this moment, though resembling, in the same manner, is numerically different too from that which I felt the moment before. Our sensations, therefore, never properly exist or endure one moment ; but, in the very instant of their generation, perish and are annihilated for ever. Nor are the causes of those sensations more permanent. No corporeal substance is ever exactly the same, either in whole or in any assignable part, during two successive, moments, but by the perpetual addition of new parts, as well as loss of old ones, is in continual flux and succession. Things of so fleeting a nature can never be the objects of science, or of any steady or permanent judgment. While we look at them, in order to consider them, they are changed and gone, and annihilated for ever. The objects of science, and of all the steady judgments of the understanding, must be permanent, unchangeable, always existent, and liable neither to generation nor corruption, nor alteration of any kind. Such are the species or specific essences of things. Man is perpetually changing every particle of his body ; and every thought of his mind is in continual flux and succession. But humanity, or human nature, is always existent, is always the same, is never generated, and is never corrupted. This, therefore, is the object of science, reason, and understanding, as man is the object of sense, and of those inconstant opinions which are founded upon sense. As the objects of sense were apprehended to have an external existence, independent of the act of sensation, so these objects of the understanding were much more supposed to have an external existence independent of the act of understanding. Those external essences were, according to Plato, the exemplars, according to which the Deity formed the world, and all the sensible objects that are in it. The Deity comprehended within his infinite essence, all these species, or external exemplars, in the same manner as he comprehended all sensible objects.

Plato, however, seems to have regarded the first of those as equally distinct with the second from what we would now call the Ideas or Thoughts of the Divine Mind,* and even to have supposed, that they had a particular place of existence, beyond the sphere of the visible

* He calls them, indeed, Ideas, a word which, in him, in Aristotle, and all the other writers of earlier antiquity, signifies a Species, and is perfectly synonymous with that other word Εἶδος, more frequently made use of by Aristotle. As, by some of the later sects of philosophers, particularly by the Stoics, all species, or specific essences, were regarded as mere creatures of the mind, formed by abstraction, which had no real existence external to the thoughts that conceived them, the word Idea came, by degrees, to its present signification, to mean, first, an abstract thought or conception ; and afterwards, a thought or conception of any kind ; and thus became synonymous with that other Greek word, Εννοια, from which it had originally a very different meaning. When the later Platonists, who lived at a time when the notion of the separate existence of specific essences was universally exploded, began to comment upon the writings of Plato, and upon that strange fancy that, in his writings, there was a double doctrine ; and that they were intended to seem to mean one thing, while at bottom they meant a very different, which the writings of no man in his senses ever were, or ever could be intended to do ; they represented his doctrine as meaning no more, than that the Deity formed the world after what we would now call an Idea, or plan conceived in his own mind, in the same manner as any other artist. But, if Plato had meant to express no more than this most natural and simple of all notions, he might surely have expressed it more plainly, and would hardly, one would think, have talked of it with so much emphasis, as of something which it required the utmost reach of thought to comprehend. According to this representation, Plato's notion of Species, or Universals, was the same with that of Aristotle. Aristotle, however, does not seem to understand it as such ; he bestows a great part of his

corporeal world; though this has been much controverted, both by the
later Platonists, and by some very judicious modern critics, who have
followed the interpretation of the later Platonists, as what did most

Metaphysics upon confuting it, and opposes it in all his other works; nor does he, in any one
of them, give the least hint, or insinuation, as if it could be suspected that, by the Ideas of
Plato, was meant the thoughts or conceptions of the Divine Mind. Is it possible that he, who
was twenty years in his school, should, during all that time, have misunderstood him, especially when his meaning was so very plain and obvious? Neither is this notion of the separate
existence of Species, distinct both from the mind which conceives them, and from the sensible
objects which are made to resemble them, one of those doctrines which Plato would but seldom
have occasion to talk of. However it may be interpreted, it is the very basis of his philosophy;
neither is there a single dialogue in all his works which does not refer to it. Shall we suppose,
that that great philosopher, who appears to have been so much superior to his master in every
thing but eloquence, wilfully, and upon all occasions, misrepresented, not one of the deep and
mysterious doctrines of the philosophy of Plato, but the first and most fundamental principle
of all his reasonings; when the writings of Plato were in the hands of every body; when his
followers and disciples were spread all over Greece; when almost every Athenian of distinction,
that was nearly of the same age with Aristotle, must have been bred in his school; when
Speusippus, the nephew and successor of Plato, as well as Xenocrates, who continued the
school in the Academy, at the same time that Aristotle held his in the Lyceum, must have
been ready, at all times, to expose and affront him for such gross disingenuity. Does not
Cicero, does not Seneca understand this doctrine in the same manner as Aristotle has represented it? Is there any author in all antiquity who seems to understand it otherwise, earlier
than Plutarch, an author who seems to have been as bad a critic in philosophy as in history,
and to have taken every thing at second-hand in both, and who lived after the origin of that
eclectic philosophy, from whence the later Platonists arose, and who seems himself to have
been one of that sect? Is there any one passage in any Greek author, near the time of
Aristotle and Plato, in which the word Idea is used in its present meaning, to signify a thought
or conception? Are not the words, which in all languages express reality or existence, directly
opposed to those which express thought, or conception only? Or, is there any other difference
betwixt a thing that exists, and a thing that does not exist, except this, that the one is a mere
conception, and that the other is something more than a conception? With what propriety,
therefore, could Plato talk of those eternal species, as of the only things which had any real
existence, if they were no more than the conceptions of the Divine Mind? Had not the
Deity, according to Plato, as well as according to the Stoics, from all eternity, the idea of
every individual, as well as of every species, and of the state in which every individual was to
be, in each different instance of its existence? Were not all the divine ideas, therefore, of
each individual, or of all the different states, which each individual was to be in during the
course of its existence, equally eternal and unalterable with those of the species? With what
sense, therefore, could Plato say, that the first were eternal, because the Deity had conceived
them from all eternity, since he had conceived the others from all eternity too, and since his
ideas of the Species could, in this respect, have no advantage of those of the individual?
Does not Plato, in many different places, talk of the Ideas of Species or Universals as innate,
and having been impressed upon the mind in its state of pre-existence, when it had an opportunity of viewing these Species as they are in themselves, and not as they are expressed in
their copies, or representatives upon earth? But if the only place of the existence of those
Species was the Divine Mind, will not this suppose, that Plato either imagined, like Father
Malbranche, that in its state of pre-existence, the mind saw all things in God: or that it was
itself an emanation of the Divinity? That he maintained the first opinion, will not be pretended by any body who is at all versed in the history of science. That enthusiastic notion,
though it may seem to be favoured by some passages in the Fathers, was never, it is well
known, coolly and literally maintained by any body before that Cartesian philosopher. That
the human mind was itself an emanation of the Divine, though it was the doctrine of the
Stoics, was by no means that of Plato; though, upon the notion of a pretended double
doctrine, the contrary has lately been asserted. According to Plato, the Deity formed the
soul of the world out of that substance which is always the same, that is, out of Species or
Universals; out of that which is always different, that is, out of corporeal substances; and out
of a substance that was of a middle nature between these, which it is not easy to understand

honour to the judgment of that renowned philosopher. All the objects in this world, continued he, are particular and individual. Here, therefore, the human mind has no opportunity of seeing any Species, or Universal Nature. Whatever ideas it has, therefore, of such beings, for it plainly has them, it must derive from the memory of what it has seen, in some former period of its existence, when it had an opportunity of visiting the place or Sphere of Universals. For some time after it is immersed in the body, during its infancy, its childhood, and a great part of its youth, the violence of those passions which it derives from the body, and which are all directed to the particular and individual objects of this world, hinder it from turning its attention to those Universal Natures, with which it had been conversant in the world from whence it came. The Ideas, of these, therefore, seem, in this first period of its existence here, to be overwhelmed in the confusion of those turbulent emotions, and to be almost entirely wiped out of its remembrance. During the continuance of this state, it is incapable of Reasoning, Science and Philosophy, which are conversant about Universals. Its whole attention is turned towards particular objects, concerning which, being directed by no general notions, it forms many vain and false opinions, and is filled with error, perplexity, and confusion. But, when age has abated the violence of its passions, and composed the confusion of its thoughts, it then becomes more capable of reflection, and of turning its attention to those almost forgotten ideas of things with which it had been conversant in the former state of its existence. All the particular objects in this sensible world, being formed after the eternal exemplars in that intellectual world, awaken, upon account of their resemblance, insensibly, and by slow degrees, the almost obliterated ideas of these last. The beauty, which is shared in different degrees among terrestrial objects, revives the same idea of that Universal Nature of beauty which exists in the intellectual world : particular acts of justice, of the universal nature of justice ; particular reasonings, and particular sciences, of the universal nature of science and reasoning ; particular roundnesses, of the universal nature of roundness ; particular squares, of the universal nature of squareness. Thus science, which is conversant about Universals, is derived from memory ; and to instruct any person concerning the general nature of any subject, is no more than to awaken in him the remembrance of what he formerly knew about it. This both Plato and Socrates imagined they could still further confirm, by the fallacious experiment,

what he meant by. Out of a part of the same composition, he made those inferior intelligences who animated the celestial spheres, to whom he delivered the remaining part of it, to form from thence the souls of men and animals. The souls of those inferior deities, though made out of a similar substance or composition, were not regarded as parts or emanations of that of the world : nor were those of animals, in the same manner, regarded as parts or emanations of those inferior deities : much less were any of them regarded as parts, or emanations of the great Author of all things.

which showed, that a person might be led to discover himself, without any information, any general truth, of which he was before ignorant, merely by being asked a number of properly arranged and connected questions concerning it.

The more the soul was accustomed to the consideration of those Universal Natures, the less it was attached to any particular and individual objects; it approached the nearer to the original perfection of its nature, from which, according to this philosophy, it had fallen. Philosophy, which accustoms it to consider the general Essence of things only, and to abstract from all their particular and sensible circumstances, was, upon this account, regarded as the great purifier of the soul. As death separated the soul from the body, and from the bodily senses and passions, it restored it to that intellectual world, from whence it had originally descended, where no sensible Species called off its attention from those general Essences of things. Philosophy, in this life, habituating it to the same considerations, brings it, in some degree, to that state of happiness and perfection, to which death restores the souls of just men in a life to come.

Such was the doctrine of Plato concerning the Species or Specific Essence of things. This, at least, is what his words seem to import, and thus he is understood by Aristotle, the most intelligent and the most renowned of all his disciples. It is a doctrine, which, like many of the other doctrines of abstract Philosophy, is more coherent in the expression than in the idea; and which seems to have arisen, more from the nature of language, than from the nature of things. With all its imperfections it was excusable, in the beginnings of philosophy, and is not a great deal more remote from the truth, than many others which have since been substituted in its room by some of the greatest pretenders to accuracy and precision. Mankind have had, at all times, a strong propensity to realize their own abstractions, of which we shall immediately see an example, in the notions of that very philosopher who first exposed the ill-grounded foundation of those Ideas, or Universals, of Plato and Timæus. To explain the nature, and to account for the origin of general Ideas, is, even at this day, the greatest difficulty in abstract philosophy. How the human mind, when it reasons concerning the general nature of triangles, should either conceive, as Mr. Locke imagines it does, the idea of a triangle, which is neither obtusangular, nor rectangular, nor acutangular; but which was at once both none and of all those together; or should, as Malbranche thinks necessary for this purpose, comprehend at once, within its finite capacity, all possible triangles of all possible forms and dimensions, which are infinite in number, is a question, to which it is surely not easy to give a satisfactory answer. Malbranche, to solve it, had recourse to the enthusiastic and unintelligible notion of the intimate union of the human mind with the divine, in whose infinite essence the immensity of such species could alone be comprehended; and in which alone, therefore, all finite intelligences could have an opportunity of viewing them. If, after more than two thousand years reasoning about this subject, this ingenious and sublime philosopher was forced to have recourse to so strange a fancy, in order to explain it, can we wonder that Plato, in the very first dawnings of science, should, for the same purpose, adopt an hypothesis, which has been thought, without much reason, indeed, to have some affinity to that of Malbranche, and which is not more out of the way?

What seems to have misled those early philosophers, was, the notion, which appears, at first, natural enough, that those things, out of which any object is composed, must exist antecedent to that object. But the things out of which all particular objects seem to be composed, are the stuff or matter of those objects, and the form or specific Essence, which determines them to be of this or that class of things. These, therefore, it was thought, must have existed antecedent to the object which was made up between them. Plato, who held, that the sensible world, which, according to him, is the world of individuals, was made in time, necessarily conceived, that both the universal matter, the object of spurious reason, and the specific essence, the object of proper reason and philosophy out of which it was composed, must have had a separate existence from all eternity. This intellectual world, very different from the intellectual world of Cudworth, though much of the language of the one has been borrowed from that of the other, was necessarily and always existent; whereas the sensible world owed its origin to the free will and bounty of its author.

A notion of this kind, as long as it is expressed in very general language; as long as it is not much rested upon, nor attempted to be very particularly and distinctly explained, passes easily enough, through the indolent imagination, accustomed to substitute words in the room of ideas; and if the words seem to hang easily together, requiring no great precision in the ideas. It vanishes, indeed; is discovered to be altogether incomprehensible, and eludes the grasp of the imagination, upon an attentive consideration. It requires, however, an attentive consideration; and if it had been as fortunate as many other opinions of the same kind, and about the same subject, it might, without exami-nation, have continued to be the current philosophy for a century or two. Aristotle, however, seems immediately to have discovered, that it was impossible to conceive, as actually existent, either that general matter, which was not determined by any particular species, or those species which were not embodied, if one may say so, in some particular portion of matter. Aristotle, too, held, as we have already observed the eternity of the sensible world. Though he held, therefore, that all sensible objects were made up of two principles, both of which, he calls, equally, substances, the matter and the specific essence, he was not obliged to hold, like Plato, that those principles existed prior in the order of time to the objects which they afterwards composed. They were prior, he said, in nature, but not in time, according to a distinction which was of use to him upon some other occasion. He distinguished, too, betwixt actual and potential existence. By the first, he seems to have understood what is commonly meant by existence or reality; by the second, the bare possibility of existence. His meaning, I say, seems to amount to this; though he does not explain it precisely in this manner. Neither the material Essence of body could, according to him, exist actually without being determined by some Specific Essence, to some particular class of things, nor any Specific Essence without being embodied in some particular portion of matter. Each of these two principles, however, could exist potentially in this separate state. That matter existed potentially, which, being endowed with a particular form, could be brought into actual existence; and that form, which, by being embodied in a particular portion of matter, could, in the same manner, be called forth into the class of complete realities. This potential existence of matter and form, he sometimes talks of, in expressions which resemble those of Plato, to whose notion of separate Essence it bears a very great affinity.

Aristotle, who seems in many things original, and who endeavoured to seem to be so in all things, added the principle of privation to those of matter and form, which he had derived from the ancient Pythagorean school. When Water is changed into Air, the transmutation is brought about by the material principle of those two elements being deprived of the form of Water, and then assuming the form of Air. Privation, therefore, was a third principle opposite to form, which entered into the generation of every Species, which was always from some other Species. It was a principle of generation, but not of composition, as is most obvious.

The Stoics, whose opinions were, in all the different parts of philosophy, either the same with, or very nearly allied to those of Aristotle and Plato, though often disguised in very different language, held, that all things, even the elements themselves, were compounded of two principles, upon one of which depended all the active, and upon the other all the passive, powers of these bodies. The last of these, they called Matter; the first, the Cause, by which they meant the very same thing which Aristotle and Plato understood, by their specific Essences. Matter, according to the Stoics, could have no existence separate from the cause or efficient principle which determined it to some particular class of things. Neither could the efficient principle exist separately from the material, in which it was always necessarily embodied. Their opinion, therefore, so far coincided with that of the old Peripatetics. The efficient principle, they said, was the Deity. By which they meant, that it was a detached portion of the etherial and divine nature, which penetrated all things, that constituted what Plato would have called the Specific Essence of each individual object; and so far their opinion coincides pretty nearly with that of the latter Platonists, who held, that the Specific Essences of all things were detached portions of their created deity, the soul of the world; and with that of some of the Arabian and Scholastic Commentators of Aristotle, who held that the substantial forms of all things descended from those Divine Essences which animated the Celestial Spheres. Such was the doctrine of the four principal Sects of the ancient Philosophers, concerning the Specific Essences of things, of the old Pythagoreans, of the Academical, the Peripatetic, and the Stoical Sects.

As this doctrine of Specific Essences seems naturally enough to have arisen from that ancient system of Physics, which I have above described, and which is, by no means, devoid of probability, so many of the doctrines of that system, which seems to us, who have been long accustomed to another, the most incomprehensible, necessarily flow from this metaphysical notion. Such are those of generation, corruption, and alteration; of mixture, condensation, and rarefaction. A body was generated or corrupted, when it changed its Specific Essence, and passed from one denomination to another. It was altered when it changed only some of its qualities, but still retained the same Specific Essence, and the same denomination. Thus, when a flower was withered, it was not corrupted; though some of its qualities were changed, it still retained the Specific Essence, and therefore justly passed under the denomination of a flower. But, when, in the further progress of its decay, it crumbled into earth, it was corrupted; it lost the Specific Essence, or substantial form of the flower, and assumed that of the earth, and therefore justly changed its denomination.

The Specific Essence, or universal nature that was lodged in each particular class of bodies, was not itself the object of any of our senses, but could be perceived only by the understanding. It was by the sensible qualities, however, that we judged of the Specific Essence of each object. Some of these sensible qualities, therefore, we regarded as essential, or such as showed, by their presence or absence, the presence or absence of that essential form from which they necessarily flowed. Others were accidental, or such whose presence or absence had no such necessary consequences. The first of these two sorts of qualities was called Properties; the second, Accidents.

In the Specific Essence of each object itself, they distinguished two parts; one of which was peculiar and characteristical of the one class of things of which that particular object was an individual, the other was common to it with some other higher classes of things. These two parts were, to the Specific Essence, pretty much what the Matter and the Specific Essence were to each individual body. The one, which was called the Genus, was modified and determined by the other, which was called the Specific Difference, pretty much in the same manner as the universal matter contained in each body was modified and determined by the Specific Essence of that particular class of bodies. These four, with the Specific Essence or Species itself, made up the number of the Five Universals, so well known in the schools by the names of Genus, Species, Differentia, Proprium, and Accidens.

*   *   *   *   *   *   *   *

OF THE

NATURE OF THAT IMITATION

WHICH TAKES PLACE IN WHAT ARE CALLED

THE IMITATIVE ARTS.

PART I.

THE most perfect imitation of an object of any kind must in all cases, it is evident, be another object of the same kind, made as exactly as possible after the same model. What, for example, would be the most perfect imitation of the carpet which now lies before me?—Another carpet, certainly, wrought as exactly as possible after the same pattern. But, whatever might be the merit or beauty of this second carpet, it would not be supposed to derive any from the circumstance of its having been made in imitation of the first. This circumstance of its being not an original, but a copy, would even be considered as some diminution of that merit; a greater or smaller, in proportion as the object was of a nature to lay claim to a greater or smaller degree of admiration. It would not much diminish the merit of a common carpet, because in such trifling objects, which at best can lay claim to so little beauty or merit of any kind, we do not always think it worth while to affect originality: it would diminish a good deal that of a carpet of very exquisite workmanship. In objects of still greater importance, this exact, or, as it would be called, this servile imitation, would be considered as the most unpardonable blemish. To build another St. Peter's or St. Paul's church, of exactly the same dimensions, proportions, and ornaments with the present buildings at Rome or London, would be supposed to argue such a miserable barrenness of genius and invention in the architect as would disgrace the most expensive magnificence.

The exact resemblance of the correspondent parts of the same object is frequently considered as a beauty, and the want of it as a deformity; as in the correspondent members of the human body, in the opposite wings of the same building, in the opposite trees of the same alley, in the correspondent compartments of the same piece of carpet-work, or of the same flower-garden, in the chairs or tables which stand in the correspondent parts of the same room, etc. But in objects of the same kind, which in other respects are regarded as altogether separate and unconnected, this exact resemblance is seldom considered as a beauty, nor the want of it as a deformity. A man, and in the same manner a horse, is handsome or ugly, each of them, on account of his own intrinsic beauty or deformity, without any regard to their resembling or not resembling, the one, another man, or the other, another horse. A set of coach-horses, indeed, is supposed to be handsomer when they are all exactly matched; but each horse is, in this case, considered not as a separated and unconnected object, or as a whole by himself, but as a part of another whole, to the other parts of which he ought to bear a certain correspondence: separated from the set, he derives neither beauty from his resemblance, nor deformity from his unlikeness to the other horses which compose it.

Even in the correspondent parts of the same object, we frequently require no more than a resemblance in the general outline. If the inferior members of those correspondent parts are too minute to be seen distinctly, without a separate and distinct examination of each part by itself, as a separate and unconnected object, we should sometimes even be displeased if the resemblance was carried beyond this general outline. In the correspondent parts of a room we frequently hang pictures of the same size; those pictures, however, resemble one another in nothing but the frame, or, perhaps, in the general character of the subject; if the one is a landscape, the other is a landscape too; if the one represents a religious or a bacchanalian subject, its companion represents another of the same kind. Nobody ever thought of repeating the same picture in each correspondent frame. The frame, and the general character of two or three pictures, is as much as the eye can comprehend at one view, or from one station. Each picture, in order to be seen distinctly, and understood thoroughly, must be viewed from a particular station, and examined by itself as a separate and unconnected object. In a hall or portico, adorned with statues, the niches, or perhaps the pedestals, may exactly resemble one another, but the statues are always different. Even the masks which are sometimes carried upon the different key-stones of the same arcade, or of the correspondent doors and windows of the same front, though they may all resemble one another in the general outline, yet each of them has always its own peculiar features, and a grimace of its own. There are some Gothic buildings in which the correspondent windows resemble one another only in the general outline, and not in the smaller ornaments and subdivisions. These are different in each, and the architect had considered them as too minute to be seen distinctly, without a particular and separate examination of each window by itself, as a separate and unconnected object. A variety of this sort, however, I think, is not agreeable. In objects which are susceptible only of a certain inferior order of beauty, such as the frames of pictures, the niches or the pedestals of statues, &c., there seems frequently to be affectation in the study of variety, of which the merit is scarcely ever sufficient to compensate the want of that perspicuity and distinctness, of that easiness to be comprehended and remembered, which is the natural effect of exact uniformity. In a portico of the Corinthian or Ionic order, each column resembles every other, not only in the general outline, but in all the minutest ornaments; though some of them, in order to be seen distinctly, may require a separate and distinct examination in each column, and in the entablature of each intercolumnation. In the inlaid tables, which, according to the present fashion, are sometimes fixed in the correspondent parts of the same room, the pictures only are different in each. All the other more frivolous and fanciful ornaments are commonly, so far at least as I have observed the fashion, the same in them all. Those ornaments, however, in order to be seen distinctly, require a distinct examination of each table.

The extraordinary resemblance of two natural objects, of twins, for example, is regarded as a curious circumstance; which, though it does not increase, yet does not diminish the beauty of either, considered as a separate and unconnected object. But the exact resemblance of two productions of art, seems to be always considered as some diminution of the merit of at least one of them; as it seems to prove, that one of them, at least, is a copy either of the other, or of some other original. One may say, even of the copy of a picture, that it derives its merit, not so much from its resemblance to the original, as from its resemblance to the object which the original was meant to resemble. The owner of the copy, so far from setting any high value upon its resemblance to the original, is often anxious to destroy any value or merit which it might derive from this circumstance. He is often anxious to persuade both himself and other people that it is not a copy, but an original, of which what passes for the original is only a copy. But, whatever merit a copy may derive from its resemblance to the original, an original can derive none from the resemblance of its copy.

But though a production of art seldom derives any merit from its resemblance to another object of the same kind, it frequently derives a great deal from its resemblance to an object of a different kind, whether that object be a production of art or of nature. A painted cloth, the work of some laborious Dutch artist, so curiously shaded and coloured as to represent the pile and softness of a woollen one, might derive some merit from its resemblance even to the sorry carpet which now lies before me. The copy might, and probably would, in this case, be of much greater value than the original. But if this carpet was represented as spread, either upon a floor or upon a table, and projecting from the background of the picture, with exact observation of perspective, and of light and shade, the merit of the imitation would be still even greater.

In Painting, a plain surface of one kind is made to resemble, not only a plain surface of another, but all the three dimensions of a solid substance. In Statuary and Sculpture, a solid substance of one kind, is made to resemble a solid substance of another. The disparity between the object imitating, and the object imitated, is much greater in the one art than in the other; and the pleasure arising from the imitation seems greater in proportion as this disparity is greater.

In Painting, the imitation frequently pleases, though the original object be indifferent, or even offensive. In Statuary and Sculpture it is otherwise. The imitation seldom pleases, unless the original object be in a very high degree either great, or beautiful, or interesting. A butcher's-stall, or a kitchen-dresser, with the objects which they commonly present, are not certainly the happiest subjects, even for Painting. They have, however, been represented with so much care and success by some Dutch masters, that it is impossible to view the pictures without some degree of pleasure. They would be most absurd subjects for Statuary or Sculpture, which are, however, capable of representing them. The picture of a very ugly or deformed man, such as Æsop, or Scarron, might not make a disagreeable piece of furniture. The statue certainly would. Even a vulgar ordinary man or woman, engaged in a vulgar ordinary action, like what we see with so much pleasure in the pictures of Rembrandt, would be too mean a subject for Statuary. Jupiter, Hercules, and Apollo, Venus and Diana, the Nymphs and the Graces, Bacchus, Mercury, Antinous, and Meleager, the miserable death of Laocoon, the melancholy fate of the children of Niobe, the Wrestlers, the fighting, the dying gladiator, the figures of gods and goddesses, of heroes and heroines, the most perfect forms of the human body, placed either in the noblest attitudes, or in the most interesting situations which the human imagination is capable of conceiving, are the proper, and therefore have always been the favourite, subjects of Statuary: that art cannot, without degrading itself, stoop to represent any thing that is offensive, or mean, or even indifferent. Painting is not so disdainful; and, though capable of representing the noblest objects, it can, without forfeiting its title to please, submit to imitate those of a much more humble nature. The merit of the imitation alone, and without any merit in the imitated object, is capable of supporting the dignity of Painting: it cannot support that of Statuary. There would seem, therefore, to be more merit in the one species of imitation than in the other.

In Statuary, scarcely any drapery is agreeable. The best of the ancient statues were either altogether naked or almost naked ; and those of which any considerable part of the body is covered, are represented as clothed in wet linen—a species of clothing which most certainly never was agreeable to the fashion of any country. This drapery too is drawn so tight, as to express beneath its narrow foldings the exact form and outline of any limb, and almost of every muscle of the body. The clothing which thus approached the nearest to no clothing at all, had, it seems, in the judgment of the great artists of antiquity, been that which was most suitable to Statuary. A great painter of the Roman school, who had formed his manner almost entirely upon the study of the ancient statues, imitated at first their drapery in his pictures ; but he soon found that in Painting it had the air of meanness and poverty, as if the persons who wore it could scarce afford clothes enough to cover them ; and that larger folds, and a looser and more flowing drapery, were more suitable to the nature of his art. In Painting, the imitation of so very inferior an object as a suit of clothes is capable of pleasing ; and, in order to give this object all the magnificence of which it is capable, it is necessary that the folds should be large, loose, and flowing. It is not necessary in Painting that the exact form and outline of every limb, and almost of every muscle of the body, should be expressed beneath the folds of the drapery ; it is sufficient if these are so disposed as to indicate in general the situation and attitude of the principal limbs. Painting, by the mere force and merit of its imitation, can venture, without the hazard of displeasing, to substitute, upon many occasions, the inferior in the room of the superior object, by making the one, in this manner, cover and entirely conceal a great part of the other. Statuary can seldom venture to do this, but with the utmost reserve and caution ; and the same drapery, which is noble and magnificent in the one art, appears clumsy and awkward in the other. Some modern artists, however, have attempted to introduce into Statuary the drapery which is peculiar to Painting. It may not, perhaps, upon every occasion, be quite so ridiculous as the marble periwigs in Westminster Abbey : but if it does not always appear clumsy and awkward, it is at best always insipid and uninteresting.

It is not the want of colouring which hinders many things from pleasing in Statuary which please in Painting ; it is the want of that degree of disparity between the imitating and the imitated object, which is necessary, in order to render interesting the imitation of an object which is itself not interesting. Colouring, when added to Statuary, so far from increasing, destroys almost entirely the pleasure which we receive from the imitation ; because it takes away the great source of that pleasure, the disparity between the imitating and the imitated object. That one solid and coloured object should exactly resemble another solid and coloured object, seems to be a matter of no great wonder or admiration. A painted statue, though it may resemble a human figure much more exactly than any statue which is not painted, is generally acknowledged to be a disagreeable and even an offensive object; and so far are we from being pleased with this superior likeness, that we are never satisfied with it; and, after viewing it again and again, we always find that it is not equal to what we are disposed to imagine it might have been: though it should seem to want scarce any thing but the life, we could not pardon it for thus wanting what it is altogether impossible it should have. The works of Mrs. Wright, a self-taught artist of great merit, are perhaps more perfect in this way than any thing I have ever seen. They do admirably well to be seen now and then as a show; but the best of them we shall find, if brought home to our own house, and placed in a situation where it was to come often into view, would make, instead of an ornamental, a most offensive piece of household furniture. Painted statues, accordingly, are universally reprobated, and we scarce ever meet with them. To colour the eyes of statues is not altogether so uncommon: even this, however, is disapproved by all good judges. 'I cannot bear it,' (a gentleman used to say, of great knowledge and judgment in this art), 'I cannot bear it; I always want them to speak to me.'

Artificial fruits and flowers sometimes imitate so exactly the natural objects which they represent, that they frequently deceive us. We soon grow weary of them, however; and, though they seem to want nothing but the freshness and the flavour of natural fruits and flowers, we cannot pardon them, in the same manner, for thus wanting what it is altogether impossible they should have. But we do not grow weary of a good flower and fruit painting. We do not grow weary of the foliage of the Corinthian capital, or of the flowers which sometimes ornament the frieze of that order. Such imitations, however, never deceive us; their resemblance to the original objects is always much inferior to that of artificial fruits and flowers. Such as it is, however, we are contented with it; and, where there is such disparity between the imitating and the imitated objects, we find that it is as great as it can be, or as we expect that it should be. Paint that foliage and those flowers with the natural colours, and, instead of pleasing more, they will please much less. The resemblance, however, will be much greater; but the disparity between the imitating and the imitated objects will be so much less, that even this superior resemblance will not satisfy us. Where the disparity is so very great, on the contrary, we are often contented with the most imperfect resemblance; with the very imperfect resemblance, for example, both as to the figure and the colour, of fruits and flowers in shell-work.

It may be observed, however, that, though in Sculpture the imitation of flowers and foliage pleases as an ornament of architecture, as a part of the dress which is to set off the beauty of a different and a more important object, it would not please alone, or as a separate and unconnected object, in the same manner as a fruit and flower painting pleases. Flowers and foliage, how elegant and beautiful soever, are not sufficiently interesting ; they have not dignity enough, if I may say so, to be proper subjects for a piece of Sculpture, which is to please alone, and not to appear as the ornamental appendage of some other object.

In Tapestry and Needle-work, in the same manner as in Painting, a plain surface is sometimes made to represent all the three dimensions of a solid substance. But both the shuttle' of the weaver, and the needle of the embroiderer, are instruments of imitation so much inferior to the pencil of the painter, that we are not surprised to find a proportionable inferiority in their productions. We have all more or less experience that they usually are much inferior : and, in appreciating a piece of Tapestry or Needle-work, we never compare the imitation of either with that of a good picture, for it never could stand that comparison, but with that of other pieces of Tapestry or Needle-work. We take into consideration, not only the disparity between the imitating and the imitated object, but the awkwardness of the instruments of imitation ; and if it is as well as any thing that can be expected from these, if it is better than the greater part of what actually comes from them, we are often not only contented but highly pleased.

A good painter will often execute in a few days a subject which would employ the best tapestry-weaver for many years ; though, in proportion to his time, therefore, the latter is always much worse paid than the former, yet his work in the end comes commonly much dearer to market. The great expense of good Tapestry, the circumstance which confines it to the palaces of princes and of great lords, gives it, in the eyes of the greater part of the people, an air of riches and magnificence, which contributes still further to compensate the imperfection of its imitation. In arts which address themselves, not to the prudent and the wise, but to the rich and the great, to the proud and the vain, we ought not to wonder if the appearances of great expense, of being what few people can purchase, of being one of the surest characteristics of great fortune, should often stand in the place of exquisite beauty, and contribute equally to recommend their productions. As the idea of expense seems often to embellish, so that of cheapness seems as frequently to tarnish the lustre even of very agreeable objects. The difference between real and false jewels is what even the experienced eye of a jeweller can sometimes with difficulty distinguish. Let an unknown lady, however, come into a public assembly, with a head-dress which appears to be very richly adorned with diamonds, and let a jeweller only whisper in our ear that they are' false stones, not only the lady will immediately sink in our imagination from the rank of a princess to that of a very ordinary woman, but the head-dress, from being an object of the most splendid magnificence, will at once become an impertinent piece of tawdry and tinsel finery.

It was some years ago the fashion to ornament a garden with yew and holly trees, clipped into the artificial shapes of pyramids, and columns, and vases, and obelisks. It is now the fashion to ridicule this taste as unnatural. The figure of a pyramid or obelisk, however, is not more unnatural to a yew-tree than to a block of porphyry or marble. When the yew-tree is presented to the eye in this artificial shape, the gardener does not mean that it should be understood to have grown in that shape : he means, first, to give it the same beauty of regular figure, which pleases so much in porphyry and marble ; and, secondly, to imitate in a growing tree the ornaments of those precious materials : he means to make an object of one kind resembling another object of a very different kind ; and to the original beauty of figure to join the relative beauty of imitation : but the disparity between the imitating and the imitated object is the foundation of the beauty of imitation. It is because the one object does not naturally resemble the other, that we are so much pleased with it, when by art it is made to do so. The shears of the gardener, it may be said, indeed, are very clumsy instruments of Sculpture. They are so, no doubt, when employed to imitate the figures of men, or even of animals. But in the simple and regular forms of pyramids, vases, and obelisks, even the shears of the gardener do well enough. Some allowance, too, is naturally made for the necessary imperfection of the instrument, in the same manner as in Tapestry and Needle-work. In short, the next time you have an opportunity of surveying those out-of-fashion ornaments, endeavour only to let yourself alone, and to restrain for a few minutes the foolish passion for playing the critic, and you will be sensible that they are not without some degree of beauty ; that they give the air of neatness and correct culture at least to the whole garden ; and that they are not unlike what the 'retired leisure, that' (as Milton says) 'in trim gardens 'takes his pleasure,' might be amused with. What then, it may be said, has brought them into such universal disrepute among us? In a pyramid or obelisk of marble, we know that the materials are expensive, and that the labour which wrought them into that shape must have been still more so. In a pyramid or obelisk of yew, we know that the materials could cost very little, and the labour still less. The former are ennobled by their expense ; the latter degraded by their cheapness. In the cabbage-garden of a tallow-chandler we may sometimes perhaps have seen as many columns and vases and other ornaments in yew, as there are in marble and porphyry at Versailles : it is this vulgarity which has disgraced them. The rich and the great, the proud and the vain will not admit into their gardens an ornament which the meanest of the people can have as well as they. The taste for these ornaments came originally from France ; where, notwithstanding that inconstancy of fashion with which we sometimes reproach the natives of that country, it still continues in good repute. In France, the condition of the inferior ranks of people is seldom so happy as it frequently is in England; and you will there seldom find even pyramids and obelisks of yew in the garden of a tallow-chandler. Such ornaments, not having in that country been degraded by their vulgarity, have not yet been excluded from the gardens of princes and lords.

The works of the great masters in Statuary and Painting, it is to be observed, never produce their effect by deception. They never are, and it never is intended that they should be, mistaken for the real objects which they represent. Painted Statuary may sometimes deceive an inattentive eye : proper Statuary never does. The little pieces of perspective in Painting, which it is intended should please by deception, represent always some very simple, as well as insignificant, objects : a roll of paper, for example, or the steps of a staircase, in the dark corner of some passage or gallery. They are generally the works too of some very inferior artists. After being seen once, and producing the little surprise which it is meant they should excite, together with the mirth which commonly accompanies it, they never please more, but appear to be ever after insipid and tiresome.

The proper pleasure which we derive from those two imitative arts, so far from being the effect of deception, is altogether incompatible with it. That pleasure is founded altogether upon our wonder at seeing an object of one kind represent so well an object of a very different kind, and upon our admiration of the art which surmounts so happily that disparity which Nature had established between them. The nobler works of Statuary and Painting appear to us a sort of wonderful phenomena, differing in this respect from the wonderful phenomena of Nature, that they carry, as it were, their own explication along with them, and demonstrate, even to the eye, the way and manner in which they are produced. The eye, even of an unskilful spectator, immediately discerns, in some measure, how it is that a certain modification of figure in Statuary, and of brighter and darker colours in Painting, can represent, with so much truth and vivacity, the actions, passions, and behaviour of men, as well as a great variety of other objects. The pleasing wonder of ignorance is accompanied with the still more pleasing satisfaction of science. We wonder and are amazed at the effect ; and we are pleased ourselves, and happy to find that we can comprehend, in some measure, how that wonderful effect is produced upon us.

A good looking-glass represents the objects which are set before it with much more truth and vivacity than either Statuary or Painting. But, though the science of optics may explain to the understanding, the looking-glass itself does not at all demonstrate to the eye how this effect is brought about. It may excite the wonder of ignorance ; and in a clown, who had never beheld a looking-glass before, I have seen that wonder rise almost to rapture and extasy ; but it cannot give the satisfaction of science.   In all looking-glasses the effects are produced by the same means, applied exactly in the same manner.   In every different statue and picture the effects are produced, though by similar, yet not by the same means ; and those means too are applied in a different manner in each.   Every good statue and picture is a fresh wonder, which at the same time carries, in some measure, its own explication along with it.   After a little use and experience, all looking-glasses cease to be wonders altogether ; and even the ignorant become so familiar with them, as not to think that their effects require any explication. .A looking-glass, besides, can represent only present objects ; and, when the wonder is once fairly over, we choose, in all cases, rather to contemplate the substance than to gaze at the shadow. One's own face becomes then the most agreeable object which a look-ing-glass can represent to us, and the only object which we do not soon grow weary with looking at ; it is the only present object of which we can see only the shadow : whether handsome or ugly, whether old or young, it is the face of a friend always, of which the features correspond exactly with whatever sentiment, emotion, or passion we may happen at that moment to feel.

In Statuary, the means by which the wonderful effect is brought about appear more simple and obvious than in Painting ; where the disparity between the imitating and the imitated object being much greater, the art which can conquer that greater disparity appears evidently, and almost to the eye, to be founded upon a much deeper science, or upon principles much more abstruse and profound.   Even in the meanest subjects we can often trace with pleasure the ingenious means by which Painting surmounts this disparity.   But we cannot do this in Statuary, because the disparity not being so great, the means do not appear so ingenious.   And it is upon this account, that in Painting we are often delighted with the representation of many things, which in Statuary would appear insipid, and not worth the looking at.

It ought to be observed, however, that though in Statuary the art of imitation appears, in many respects, inferior to what it is in Painting, yet, in a room ornamented with both statues and pictures of nearly equal merit, we shall generally find that the statues draw off our eye from the pictures.   There is generally but one or little more than one, point of view from which a picture can be seen with advantage, and it always presents to the eye precisely the same object.   There are many different points of view from which a statue may be seen with equal advantage, and from each it presents a different object.   There is more variety in the pleasure which we receive from a good statue, than in that which we receive from a good picture ; and one statue may fre-quently be the subject of many good pictures or drawings, all different from one another. The shadowy relief and projection of a picture, besides, is much flattened, and seems almost to vanish away altogether, when brought into comparison with the real and solid body which stands by it. How nearly soever these two arts may seem to be akin, they accord so very ill with one another, that their different productions ought, perhaps, scarce ever to be seen together.

PART II.

AFTER the pleasures which arise from the gratification of the bodily appetites, there seem to be none more natural to man than Music and Dancing. In the progress of art and improvement they are, perhaps, the first and earliest pleasures of his own invention; for those which arise from the gratification of the bodily appetites cannot be said to be his own invention. No nation has yet been discovered so uncivilized as to be altogether without them. It seems even to be amongst the most barbarous nations that the use and practice of them is both most frequent and most universal, as among the negroes of Africa and the savage tribes of America. In civilized nations, the inferior ranks of people have very little leisure, and the superior ranks have many other amusements; neither the one nor the other, therefore, can spend much of their time in Music and Dancing. Among savage nations, the great body of the people have frequently great intervals of leisure, and they have scarce any other amusement; they naturally, therefore, spend a great part of their time in almost the only one they have.

What the ancients called Rhythmus, what we call Time or Measure, is the connecting principle of those two arts; Music consisting in a succession of a certain sort of sounds, and Dancing in a succession of a certain sort of steps, gestures, and motions, regulated according to time or measure, and thereby formed, into a sort of whole or system; which in the one art is called a song or tune, and in the other a dance; the time or measure of the dance corresponding always exactly with that of the song or tune which accompanies and directs it.[*]

The human voice, as it is always the best, so it would naturally be the first and earliest of all musical instruments: in singing, or in its first attempts towards singing, it would naturally employ sounds as similar as possible to those which it had been accustomed to; that is, it would employ words of some kind or other, pronouncing them only in time and measure, and generally with a more melodious tone than had been usual in common conversation. Those words, however, might not, and probably would not, for a long time have any meaning, but might resemble the syllables which we make use of in *fol-faing*, or the

[*] The Author's Observations on the Affinity between Music, Dancing, and Poetry, are annexed to the end of Part III. of this Essay.

derry-down-down of our common ballads; and serve only to assist the voice in forming sounds proper to be modulated into melody, and to be lengthened or shortened according to the time and measure of the tune. This rude form of vocal Music, as it is by far the most simple and obvious, so it naturally would be the first and earliest.

In the succession of ages it could not fail to occur, that in room of those unmeaning or musical words, if I may call them so, might be substituted words which expressed some sense or meaning, and of which the pronunciation might coincide as exactly with the time and measure of the tune, as that of the musical words had done before. Hence the origin of Verse or Poetry. The Verse would for a long time be rude and imperfect. When the meaning words fell short of the measure required, they would frequently be cked out with the unmeaning ones, as is sometimes done in our common ballads. When the public ear came to be so refined as to reject, in all serious Poetry, the unmeaning words altogether, there would still be a liberty assumed of altering and corrupting, upon many occasions, the pronunciation of the meaning ones, for the sake of accommodating them to the measure. The syllables which composed them would, for this purpose, sometimes be improperly lengthened, and sometimes improperly shortened; and though no unmeaning words were made use of, yet an unmeaning syllable would sometimes be stuck to the beginning, to the end, or into the middle of a word. All these expedients we find frequently employed in the verses even of Chaucer, the father of the English Poetry. Many ages might pass away before verse was commonly composed with such correctness, that the usual and proper pronunciation of the words alone, and without any other artifice, subjected the voice to the observation of a time and measure, of the same kind with the time and measure of the science of Music.

The Verse would naturally express some sense which suited the grave or gay, the joyous or melancholy humour of the tune which it was sung to; being as it were blended and united with that tune, it would seem to give sense and meaning to what otherwise might not appear to have any, or at least any which could be clearly understood, without the accompaniment of such an explication.

A pantomime dance may frequently answer the same purpose, and, by representing some adventure in love or war, may seem to give sense and meaning to a Music, which might not otherwise appear to have any. It is more natural to mimic, by gestures and motions, the adventures of common life, than to express them in Verse or Poetry. The thought itself is more obvious, and the execution is much more easy. If this mimicry was accompanied by Music, it would of its own accord, and almost without any intention of doing so, accommodate, in some measure, its different steps and movements to the time and measure of the tune; especially if the same person both sung the tune and performed the mimicry, as is said to be frequently the case among the savage nations of Africa and America. Pantomime Dancing might in this manner serve to give a distinct sense and meaning to Music many ages before the invention, or at least before the common use of Poetry. We hear little, accordingly, of the Poetry of the savage nations who inhabit Africa and America, but a great deal of their pantomime dances.

Poetry, however, is capable of expressing many things fully and distinctly, which Dancing either cannot represent at all, or can represent but obscurely and imperfectly; such as the reasonings and judgments of the understanding; the ideas, fancies, and suspicions of the imagination; the sentiments, emotions, and passions of the heart. In the power of expressing a meaning with clearness and distinctness, Dancing is superior to Music, and Poetry to Dancing.

Of those three Sister Arts, which originally, perhaps, went always together, and which at all times go frequently together, there are two which can subsist alone, and separate from their natural companions, and one which cannot. In the distinct observation of what the ancients called Rhythmus, of what we call Time and Measure, consists the essence both of Dancing and of Poetry or Verse; or the characteristical quality which distinguishes the former from all other motion and action, and the latter from all other discourse. But, concerning the proportion between those intervals and divisions of duration which constitute what is called time and measure, the ear, it would seem, can judge with much more precision than the eye; and Poetry, in the same manner as Music, addresses itself to the ear, whereas Dancing addresses itself to the eye. In Dancing, the rhythmus, the proper proportion, the time and measure of its motions, cannot distinctly be perceived, unless they are marked by the more distinct time and measure of Music. It is otherwise in Poetry; no accompaniment is necessary to mark the measure of good Verse. · Music and Poetry, therefore, can each of them subsist alone; Dancing always requires the accompaniment of Music.

It is Instrumental Music which can best subsist apart, and separate from both Poetry and Dancing. Vocal Music, though it may, and frequently does, consist of notes which have no distinct sense or meaning, yet naturally calls for the support of Poetry.. But, 'Music, married 'to immortal Verse,' as Milton says, or even to words of any kind which have a distinct sense or meaning, is necessarily and essentially imitative. Whatever be the meaning of those words, though, like many of the songs of ancient Greece, as well as some of those of more modern times, they may express merely some maxims of prudence and morality, or may contain merely the simple narrative of some important event, yet even in such didactic and historical songs there will still be imitation; there will still be a thing of one kind, which by art is made to resemble a thing of a very different kind; there will still be Music imitating discourse; there will still be Rhythmus and Melody, shaped and fashioned into the form either of a good moral counsel, or of an amusing and interesting story.

In this first species of imitation, which being essential to, is therefore inseparable from, all such Vocal Music, there may be, and there commonly is, added a second. The words may, and commonly do, express the situation of some particular person, and all the sentiments and passions which he feels from that situation. It is a joyous companion who gives vent to the gaiety and mirth with which wine, festivity, and good company inspire him. It is a lover who complains, or hopes, or fears, or despairs. It is a generous man who expresses either his gratitude for the favours, or his indignation at the injuries, which may have been done to him. It is a warrior who prepares himself to confront danger, and who provokes or desires his enemy. It is a person in prosperity who humbly returns thanks for the goodness, or one in affliction who with contrition implores the mercy and forgiveness of that invisible Power to whom he looks up as the Director of all the events of human life. The situation may comprehend, not only one, but two, three, or more persons; it may excite in them all either similar or opposite sentiments; what is a subject of sorrow to one, being an occasion of joy and triumph to another; and they may all express, sometimes separately and sometimes together, the particular way in which each of them is affected, as in a duo, trio, or a chorus.

All this it may, and it frequently has been said is unnatural; nothing being more so, than to sing when we are anxious to persuade, or in earnest to express any very serious purpose. But it should be remembered, that to make a thing of one kind resemble another thing of a very different kind, is the very circumstance which, in all the Imitative Arts, constitutes the merits of imitation; and that to shape, and as it were to bend, the measure and the melody of Music, so as to imitate the tone and the language of counsel and conversation, the accent and the style of emotion and passion, is to make a thing of one kind resemble another thing of a very different kind.

The tone and the movements of Music, though naturally very different from those of conversation and passion, may, however, be so managed as to seem to resemble them. On account of the great disparity between the imitating and the imitated object, the mind in this, as in the other cases, cannot only be contented, but delighted, and even charmed and transported, with such an imperfect resemblance as can be had. Such imitative Music, therefore, when sung to words which explain and determine its meaning, may frequently appear to be a very perfect imitation. It is upon this account, that even the incomplete Music of a recitative seems to express sometimes all the sedateness and composure of serious but calm discourse, and sometimes all the exquisite sensibility of the most interesting passion. The more complete Music of an air is still superior, and, in the imitation of the more animated passions, has one great advantage over every sort of discourse, whether Prose or Poetry, which is not sung to Music. In a person who is either much depressed by grief or enlivened by joy, who is strongly affected either with love or hatred, with gratitude or resentment, with admiration or contempt, there is commonly one thought or idea which dwells upon his mind, which continually haunts him, which, when he has chased it away, immediately returns upon him, and which in company makes him absent and inattentive. He can think but of one object, and he cannot repeat to them that object so frequently as it recurs upon him. He takes refuge in solitude, where he can with freedom either indulge the extasy or give way to the agony of the agreeable or disagreeable passion which agitates him; and where he can repeat to himself, which he does sometimes mentally, and sometimes even aloud, and almost always in the same words, the particular thought which either delights or distresses him. Neither Prose nor Poetry can venture to imitate those almost endless repetitions of passion. They may describe them as I do now, but they dare not imitate them; they would become most insufferably tiresome if they did. The Music of a passionate air, not only may, but frequently does, imitate them; and it never makes its way so directly or so irresistibly to the heart as when it does so. It is upon this account that the words of an air, especially of a passionate one, though they are seldom very long, yet are scarce ever sung straight on to the end, like those of a recitative; but are almost always broken into parts, which are transposed and repeated again and again, according to the fancy or judgment of the composer. It is by means of such repetitions only, that Music can exert those peculiar powers of imitation which distinguish it, and in which it excels all the other Imitative Arts. Poetry and Eloquence, it has accordingly been often observed, produce their effect always by a connected variety and succession of different thoughts and ideas: but Music frequently produces its effects by a repetition of the same idea; and the same sense expressed in the same, or nearly the same, combination of sounds, though at first perhaps it may make scarce any impression upon us, yet, by being repeated again and again, it comes at last gradually, and by little and little, to move, to agitate, and to transport us.

To these powers of imitating, Music naturally, or rather necessarily, joins the happiest choice in the objects of its imitation. The sentiments and passions which Music can best imitate are those which unite and bind men together in society; the social, the decent, the virtuous, the interesting and affecting, the amiable and agreeable, the awful and respectable, the noble, elevating, and commanding passions. Grief and distress are interesting and affecting; humanity and compassion, joy and admiration, are amiable and agreeable; devotion is awful and respectable; the generous contempt of danger, the honourable indignation at injustice, are noble, elevating, and commanding. But it is these and such like passions which Music is fittest for imitating, and which it in fact most frequently imitates. They are, if I may say so, all Musical Passions; their natural tones are all clear, distinct, and almost melodious; and they naturally express themselves in a language which is distinguished by pauses at regular, and almost equal, intervals; and which, upon that account, can more easily be adapted to the regular returns of the correspondent periods of a tune. The passions, on the contrary, which drive men from one another, the unsocial, the hateful, the indecent, the vicious passions, cannot easily be imitated by Music. The voice of furious anger, for example, is harsh and discordant; its periods are all irregular, sometimes very long and sometimes very short, and distinguished by no regular pauses. The obscure and almost inarticulate grumblings of black malice and envy, the screaming outcries of dastardly fear, the hideous growlings of brutal and implacable revenge, are all equally discordant. It is with difficulty that Music can imitate any of those passions, and the Music which does imitate them is not the most agreeable. A whole entertainment may consist, without any impropriety, of the imitation of the social and amiable passions. It would be a strange entertainment which consisted altogether in the imitation of the odious and the vicious. A single song expresses almost always some social, agreeable, or interesting passion. In an opera the unsocial and disagreeable are sometimes introduced, but it is rarely, and as discords are introduced into harmony, to set off by their contrast the superior beauty of the opposite passions. What Plato said of Virtue, that it was of all beauties the brightest, may with some sort of truth be said of the proper and natural objects of musical imitation. They are either the sentiments and passions, in the exercise of which consist both the glory and the happiness of human life, or they are those from which it derives its most delicious pleasures, and most enlivening joys; or, at the worst and the lowest, they are those by which it calls upon our indulgence and compassionate assistance to its unavoidable weaknesses, distresses, and misfortunes.

To the merit of its imitation and to that of its happy choice in the objects which it imitates, the great merits of Statuary and Painting, Music joins another peculiar and exquisite merit of its own. Statuary and Painting cannot be said to add any new beauties of their own to the beauties of Nature which they imitate; they may assemble a greater number of those beauties, and group them in a more agreeable manner than they are commonly, or perhaps ever, to be found in Nature. It may perhaps be true, what the artists are so very fond of telling us, that no woman ever equalled, in all the parts of her body, the beauty of the Venus of Medicis, nor any man that of the Apollo of Belvidere. But they must allow, surely, that there is no particular beauty in any part or feature of those two famous statues, which is not at least equalled, if not much excelled, by what is to be found in many living subjects. But Music, by arranging, and as it were bending to its own time and measure, whatever sentiments and passions it expresses, not only assembles and groups, as well as Statuary and Painting, the different beauties of Nature which it imitates, but it clothes them, besides, with a new and an exquisite beauty of its own; it clothes them with melody and harmony, which, like a transparent mantle, far from concealing any beauty, serve only to give a brighter colour, a more enlivening lustre and a more engaging grace to every beauty which they infold.

To these two different sorts of imitation,—to that general one, by which Music is made to resemble discourse, and to that particular one, by which it is made to express the sentiments and feelings with which a particular situation inspires a particular person,—there is frequently joined a third. The person who sings may join to this double imitation of the singer the additional imitation of the actor; and express, not only by the modulation and cadence of his voice, but by his countenance, by his attitudes, by his gestures, and by his motions, the sentiments and feelings of the person whose situation is painted in the song. Even in private company, though a song may sometimes perhaps be said to be well sung, it can never be said to be well performed, unless the singer does something of this kind; and there is no comparison between the effect of what is sung coldly from a music-book at the end of a harpsichord, and of what is not only sung, but acted with proper freedom, animation, and boldness. An opera actor does no more than this; and an imitation which is so pleasing, and which appears even so natural, in private society, ought not to appear forced, unnatural, or disagreeable upon the stage.

In a good opera actor, not only the modulations and pauses of his voice, but every motion and gesture, every variation, either in the air of his head, or in the attitude of his body, correspond to the time and measure of Music: they correspond to the expression of the sentiment or passion which the Music imitates, and that expression necessarily corresponds to this time and measure. Music is as it were the soul which animates him, which informs every feature of his countenance, and even directs every movement of his eyes. Like the musical expression of a song, his action adds to the natural grace of the sentiment or action which it imitates, a new and peculiar grace of its own; the exquisite and engaging grace of those gestures and motions, of those airs and attitudes which are directed by the movement, by the time and measure of Music; this grace heightens and enlivens that expression. Nothing can be more deeply affecting than the interesting scenes of the serious opera, when to good Poetry and good Music, to the Poetry of Metastasio and the Music of Pergolese, is added the execution of a good actor. In the serious opera, indeed, the action is too often sacrificed to the Music; the castrati, who perform the principal parts, being always the most insipid and miserable actors. The sprightly airs of the comic opera are, in the same manner, in the highest degree enlivening and diverting. Though they do not make us laugh so loud as we sometimes do at the scenes of the common comedy, they make us smile more frequently; and the agreeable gaiety, the temperate joy, if I may call it so, with which they inspire us, is not only an elegant, but a most delicious pleasure. The deep distress and the great passions of tragedy are capable of producing some effect, though it should be but indifferently acted. It is not so with the lighter misfortunes and less affecting situations of comedy: unless it is at least tolerably acted, it is altogether insupportable. But the castrati are scarce ever tolerable actors; they are accordingly seldom admitted to play in the comic opera; which, being upon that account commonly better performed than the serious, appears to many people the better entertainment of the two.

The imitative powers of Instrumental are much inferior to those of Vocal Music; its melodious but unmeaning and inarticulated sounds cannot, like the articulations of the human voice, relate distinctly the circumstances of any particular story, or describe the different situations which those circumstances produced; or even express clearly, and so as to be understood by every hearer, the various sentiments and passions which the parties concerned felt from these situations : even its imitation of other sounds, the objects which it can certainly best imitate, is commonly so indistinct, that alone, and without any explication, it might not readily suggest to us what was the imitated object. The rocking of a cradle is supposed to be imitated in that concerto of Correlli, which is said to have been composed for the Nativity : but unless we were told beforehand, it might not readily occur to us what it meant to imitate, or whether it meant to imitate any thing at all ; and this imitation (which, though perhaps as successful as any other, is by no means the distinguished beauty of that admired composition) might only appear to us a singular and odd passage in Music. The ringing of bells and the singing of the lark and nightingale are imitated in the symphony of Instrumental Music which Mr. Handel has composed for the Allegro and Penseroso of Milton : these are not only sounds but musical sounds, and may therefore be supposed to be more within the compass of the powers of musical imitation. It is accordingly universally acknowledged, that in these imitations this great master has been remarkably successful ; and yet, unless the verses of Milton explained the meaning of the Music, it might not even in this case readily occur to us what it meant to imitate, or whether it meant to imitate any thing at all. With the explication of the words, indeed, the imitation appears, what it certainly is, a very fine one ; but without

ADAM SMITH ON THE IMITATIVE ARTS.

that explication it might perhaps appear only a singular passage, which had less connexion either with what went before or with what came after it, than any other in the Music.

Instrumental Music is said sometimes to imitate motion ; but in reality it only either imitates the particular sounds which accompany certain motions, or it produces sounds of which the time and measure bear some correspondence to the variations, to the pauses and inter-ruptions, to the successive accelerations and retardations of the motion which it means to imitate : it is in this way that it sometimes attempts to express the march and array of an army, the confusion and hurry of a battle, &c. In all these cases, however, its imitation is so very indistinct, that without the accompaniment of some other art, to explain and interpret its meaning, it would be almost always unintelligible ; and we could scarce ever know with certainty, either what it meant to imitate, or whether it meant to imitate any thing at all.

In the imitative arts, though it is by no means necessary that the imitating should so exactly resemble the imitated object, that the one should sometimes be mistaken for the other, it is, however, necessary that they should resemble at least so far, that the one should always readily suggest the other. It would be a strange picture which required an inscription at the foot to tell us, not only what particular person it meant to represent, but whether it meant to represent a man or a horse, or whether it meant to be a picture at all, and to represent any thing. The imitations of instrumental Music may, in some respects, be said to resemble such pictures. There is, however, this very essential differ-ence between them, that the picture would not be much mended by the inscription ; whereas, by what may be considered as very little more than such an inscription, instrumental Music, though it cannot always even then, perhaps, be said properly to imitate, may, however, produce all the effects of the finest and most perfect imitation. In order to explain how this is brought about, it will not be necessary to descend into any great depth of philosophical speculation.

That train of thoughts and ideas which is continually passing through the mind does not always move on with the same pace, if I may say so, or with the same order and connection. When we are gay and cheerful, its motion is brisker and more lively, our thoughts succeed one another more rapidly, and those which immediately follow one another seem frequently either to have but little connection, or to be connected rather by their opposition than by their mutual resemblance. As in this wanton and playful disposition of mind we hate to dwell long upon the same thought, so we do not much care to pursue resem-bling thoughts ; and the variety of contrast is more agreeable to us than the sameness of resemblance. It is quite otherwise when we are melancholy and desponding ; we then frequently find ourselves haunted, as it were, by some thought which we would gladly chase away, but which constantly pursues us, and which admits no followers, attendants, or companions, but such as are of its own kindred and complexion. A slow succession of resembling or closely connected thoughts is the characteristic of this disposition of mind; a quick succession of thoughts, frequently contrasted and in general very slightly connected, is the characteristic of the other. What may be called the natural state of the mind, the state in which we are neither elated nor dejected, the state of sedateness, tranquillity, and composure, holds a sort of middle place between those two opposite extremes; our thoughts may succeed one another more slowly, and with a more distinct connection, than in the one; but more quickly and with a greater variety, than in the other.

Acute sounds are naturally gay, sprightly, and enlivening; grave sounds solemn, awful, and melancholy. There seems too to be some natural connection between acuteness in tune and quickness in time or succession, as well as between gravity and slowness: an acute sound seems to fly off more quickly than a grave one: the treble is more cheerful than the bass; its notes likewise commonly succeed one another more rapidly. But instrumental Music, by a proper arrangement, by a quicker or slower succession of acute and grave, of resembling and contrasted sounds, can not only accommodate itself to the gay, the sedate, or the melancholy mood; but if the mind is so far vacant as not to be disturbed by any disorderly passion, it can, at least for the moment, and to a certain degree, produce every possible modification of each of those moods or dispositions. We all readily distinguish the cheerful, the gay, and the sprightly Music, from the melancholy, the plaintive, and the affecting; and both these from what holds a sort of middle place between them, the sedate, the tranquil, and the composing. And we are all sensible that, in the natural and ordinary state of the mind, Music can, by a sort of incantation, sooth and charm us into some degree of that particular mood or disposition which accords with its own character and temper. In a concert of instrumental Music the attention is engaged, with pleasure and delight, to listen to a combination of the most agreeable and melodious sounds, which follow one another, sometimes with a quicker, and sometimes with a slower succession; and in which those that immediately follow one another sometimes exactly or nearly resemble, and sometimes contrast with one another in tune, in time, and in order of arrangement. The mind being thus successively occupied by a train of objects, of which the nature, succession, and connection correspond, sometimes to the gay, sometimes to the tranquil, and sometimes to the melancholy mood or disposition, it is itself successively led into each of those moods or dispositions; and is thus brought into a sort of harmony or concord with the Music which so agreeably engages its attention.

It is not, however, by imitation properly, that instrumental Music produces this effect: instrumental Music does not imitate, as vocal Music, as Painting, or as Dancing would imitate, a gay, a sedate, or a melancholy person; it does not tell us, as any of those other arts could tell us, a pleasant, a serious, or a melancholy story. It is not, as in vocal Music, in Painting, or in Dancing, by sympathy with the gaiety, the sedateness, or the melancholy and distress of some other person, that instrumental Music soothes us into each of these dispositions: it becomes itself a gay, a sedate, or a melancholy object; and the mind naturally assumes the mood or disposition which at the time corresponds to the object which engages its attention. Whatever we feel from instrumental Music is an original, and not a sympathetic feeling: it is our own gaiety, sedateness, or melancholy; not the the reflected disposition of another person.

When we follow the winding alleys of some happily situated and well laid out garden, we are presented with a succession of landscapes, which are sometimes gay, sometimes gloomy, and sometimes calm and serene; if the mind is in its natural state, it suits itself to the objects which successively present themselves, and varies in some degree its mood and present humour with every variation of the scene. It would be improper, however, to say that those scenes imitated the gay, the calm, or the melancholy mood of the mind; they may produce in their turn each of those moods, but they cannot imitate any of them. Instrumental Music, in the same manner, though it can excite all those different dispositions, cannot imitate any of them. There are no two things in nature more perfectly disparate than sound and sentiment; and it is impossible by any human power to fashion the one into any thing that bears any real resemblance to the other.

This power of exciting and varying the different moods and dispositions of the mind, which instrumental Music really possesses to a very considerable degree, has been the principal source of its reputation for those great imitative powers which have been ascribed to it. 'Paint-'ing,' says an author, more capable of feeling strongly than of analysing accurately, Mr. Rousseau of Geneva, 'Painting, which presents its 'imitations, not to the imagination, but to the senses, and to only one 'of the senses, can represent nothing besides the objects of sight. 'Music, one might imagine, should be equally confined to those of 'hearing. It imitates, however, every thing, even those objects which 'are perceivable by sight only. By a delusion that seems almost in-'conceivable, it can, as it were, put the eye into the ear; and the 'greatest wonder, of an art which acts only by motion and succession, 'is, that it can imitate rest and repose. Night, Sleep, Solitude, and 'Silence are all within the compass of musical imitation. Though all 'Nature should be asleep, the person who contemplates it is awake; 'and the art of the musician consists in substituting, in the room of an

'image of what is not the object of hearing, that of the movements
'which its presence would excite in the mind of the spectator.'—That
is, of the effects which it would produce upon his mood and disposition.
'The musician (continues the same author) will sometimes, not only
'agitate the waves of the sea, blow up the flames of a conflagration,
'make the rain fall, the rivulets flow and swell the torrents, but he will
'paint the horrors of a hideous desert, darken the walls of a subter-
'raneous dungeon, calm the tempest, restore serenity and tranquillity
'to the air and the sky, and shed from the orchestra a new freshness
'over the groves and the fields.   He will not directly represent any of
'these objects, but he will excite in the mind the same movements
'which it would feel from seeing them.'

Upon this very eloquent description of Mr. Rousseau I must observe,
that without the accompaniment of the scenery and action of the opera,
without the assistance either of the scene-painter or of the poet, or of
both, the instrumental Music of the orchestra could produce none of
the effects which are here ascribed to it; and we could never know, we
could never even guess, which of the gay, melancholy, or tranquil objects above mentioned it meant to represent to us; or whether it meant
to represent any of them, and not merely to entertain us with a concert
of gay, melancholy, or tranquil Music; or, as the ancients called them,
of the Diastaltic, of the Systaltic, or of the Middle Music.   With that
accompaniment, indeed, though it cannot always even then, perhaps, be
said properly to imitate, yet by supporting the imitation of some other
art, it may produce all the same effects upon us as if itself had imitated
in the finest and most perfect manner.   Whatever be the object or
situation which the scene-painter represents upon the theatre, the
Music of the orchestra, by disposing the mind to the same sort of
mood and temper which it would feel from the presence of that object,
or from sympathy with the person who was placed in that situation,
can greatly enhance the effect of that imitation: it can accommodate
itself to every diversity of scene.   The melancholy of the man who,
upon some great occasion, only finds himself alone in the darkness, the
silence and solitude of the night, is very different from that of one who,
upon a like occasion, finds himself in the midst of some dreary and
inhospitable desert; and even in this situation his feelings would not
be the same as if he was shut up in a subterraneous dungeon.   The
different degrees of precision with which the Music of the orchestra
can accommodate itself to each of those diversities, must depend upon
the taste, the sensibility, the fancy and imagination of the composer:
it may sometimes, perhaps, contribute to this precision, that it should
imitate, as well as it can, the sounds which either naturally accompany,
or which might be supposed to accompany, the particular objects represented.   The symphony in the French opera of Alcyone, which
imitated the violence of the winds and the dashing of the waves, in the

tempest which was to drown Coix, is much commended by cotemporary writers. That in the opera of Isse, which imitated that murmuring in the leaves of the oaks of Dodona, which might be supposed to precede the miraculous pronunciation of the oracle: and that in the opera of Amadis, of which the dismal accents imitated the sounds which might be supposed to accompany the opening of the tomb of Ardan, before the apparition of the ghost of that warrior, are still more celebrated. Instrumental Music, however, without violating too much its own melody and harmony, can imitate but imperfectly the sounds of natural objects, of which the greater part have neither melody nor harmony. Great reserve, great discretion, and a very nice discernment are requisite, in order to introduce with propriety such imperfect imitations, either into Poetry or Music; when repeated too often, when continued too long, they appear to be what they really are, mere tricks, in which a very inferior artist, if he will only give himself the trouble to attend to them, can easily equal the greatest. I have seen a Latin translation of Mr. Pope's Ode on St. Cecilia's Day, which in this respect very much excelled the original. Such imitations are still easier in Music. Both in the one art and in the other, the difficulty is not in making them as well as they are capable of being made, but in knowing when and how far to make them at all: but to be able to accommodate the temper and character of the Music to every peculiarity of the scene and situation with such exact precision, that the one shall produce the very same effect upon the mind as the other, is not one of those tricks in which an inferior artist can easily equal the greatest; it is an art which requires all the judgment, knowledge, and invention of the most consummate master. It is upon this art, and not upon its imperfect imitation, either of real or imaginary sounds, that the great effects of instrumental Music depend; such imitations ought perhaps to be admitted only so far as they may sometimes contribute to ascertain the meaning, and thereby to enhance the effects of this art.

By endeavouring to extend the effects of scenery beyond what the nature of the thing will admit of, it has been much abused; and in the common, as well as in the musical drama, many imitations have been attempted, which, after the first and second time we have seen them, necessarily appear ridiculous: such are, the Thunder rumbling from the Mustard-bowl, and the Snow of Paper and thick Hail of Pease, so finely exposed by Mr. Pope. Such imitations resemble those of painted Statuary; they may surprise at first, but they disgust ever after, and appear evidently such simple and easy tricks as are fit only for the amusement of children and their nurses at a puppet-show. The thunder of either theatre ought certainly never to be louder than that which the orchestra is capable of producing; and their most dreadful tempests ought never to exceed what the scene painter is capable of representing. In such imitations there may be an art which merits some degree of esteem and admiration. In the other there can be none which merits any.

This abuse of scenery has both subsisted much longer, and been carried to a much greater degree of extravagance, in the musical than in the common drama. In France it has been long banished from the latter; but it still continues, not only to be tolerated, but to be admired and applauded in the former. In the French operas, not only thunder and lightning, storms and tempests, are commonly represented in the ridiculous manner above mentioned, but all the marvellous, all the supernatural of Epic Poetry, all the metamorphoses of Mythology, all the wonders of Witchcraft and Magic, every thing that is most unfit to be represented upon the stage, are every day exhibited with the most complete approbation and applause of that ingenious nation. The music of the orchestra producing upon the audience nearly the same effect which a better and more artful imitation would produce, hinders them from feeling, at least in its full force, the ridicule of those childish and awkward imitations which necessarily abound in that extravagant scenery. And in reality such imitations, though no doubt ridiculous every where, yet certainly appear somewhat less so in the musical than they would in the common drama. The Italian opera, before it was reformed by Apostolo, Zeno, and Metastasio, was in this respect equally extravagant, and was upon that account the subject of the agreeable raillery of Mr. Addison in several different papers of the Spectator. Even since that reformation it still continues to be a rule, that the scene should change at least with every act; and the unity of place never was a more sacred law in the common drama, than the violation of it has become in the musical: the latter seems in reality to require both a more picturesque and a more varied scenery, than is at all necessary for the former. In an opera, as the Music supports the effect of the scenery, so the scenery often serves to determine the character, and to explain the meaning of the Music; it ought to vary therefore as that character varies. The pleasure of an opera, besides, is in its nature more a sensual pleasure, than that of a common comedy or tragedy; the latter produce their effect principally by means of the imagination: in the closet, accordingly, their effect is not much inferior to what it is upon the stage. But the effect of an opera is seldom very great in the closet; it addresses itself more to the external senses, and as it soothes the ear by its melody and harmony, so we feel that it ought to dazzle the eye with the splendour of its scenery.

In an opera the instrumental Music of the orchestra supports the imitation both of the poet and of the actor, as well as of the scene-painter. The overture disposes the mind to that mood which fits it for the opening of the piece. The Music between the acts keeps up the impression which the foregoing had made, and prepares us for that which the following is to make. When the orchestra interrupts, as it frequently does, either the recitative or the air, it is in order either to enforce the effect of what had gone before, or to put the mind in the mood which fits it for hearing what is to come after. Both in the recitatives and in the airs it accompanies and directs the voice, and often brings it back to the proper tone and modulation, when it is upon the point of wandering away from them ; and the correctness of the best vocal Music is owing in a great measure to the guidance of instrumental ; though in all these cases it supports the imitation of another art, yet in all of them it may be said rather to diminish than to increase the resemblance between the imitating and the imitated object. Nothing can be more unlike to what really passes in the world, than that persons engaged in the most interesting situations, both of public and private life, in sorrow, in disappointment, in distress, in despair, should, in all that they say and do, be constantly accompanied with a fine concert of instrumental Music. Were we to reflect upon it, such accompaniment must in all cases diminish the probability of the action, and render the representation still less like nature than it otherwise would be. It is not by imitation, therefore, that instrumental Music supports and enforces the imitations of the other arts ; but it is by producing upon the mind, in consequence of other powers, the same sort of effect which the most exact imitation of nature, which the most perfect observation of probability, could produce. To produce this effect is, in such entertainments, the sole end and purpose of that imitation and observation. If it can be equally well produced by other means, this end and purpose may be equally well answered.

But if instrumental Music can seldom be said to be properly imitative, even when it is employed to support the imitation of some other art, it is commonly still less so when it is employed alone. Why should it embarrass its melody and harmony, or constrain its time and measure, by attempting an imitation which, without the accompaniment of some other art to explain and interpret its meaning, nobody is likely to understand? In the most approved instrumental Music, accordingly, in the overtures of Handel and the concertos of Correlli, there is little or no imitation, and where there is any, it is the source of but a very small part of the merit of those compositions. Without any imitation, instrumental Music can produce very considerable effects ; though its powers over the heart and affections are, no doubt, much inferior to those of vocal Music, it has, however, considerable powers: by the sweetness of its sounds it awakens agreeably, and calls upon the attention ; by their connection and affinity it naturally detains that attention, which follows easily a series of agreeable sounds, which have all a certain relation both to a common, fundamental, or leading note, called the key note ; and to a certain succession or combination of notes, called the song or composition. By means of this relation each foregoing sound seems to introduce, and as it were prepare the mind for the following : by its rhythmus, by its time and measure, it disposes that succession of sounds into a certain arrangement, which renders the whole more easy to be comprehended and remembered. Time and measure are to instrumental Music what order and method are to discourse; they break it into proper parts and divisions, by which we are enabled both to remember better what is gone before, and frequently to foresee somewhat of what is to come after; we frequently foresee the return of a period which we know must correspond to another which we remember to have gone before ; and, according to the saying of an ancient philosopher and musician, the enjoyment of Music arises partly from memory and partly from foresight. When the measure, after having been continued so long as to satisfy us, changes to another, that variety, which thus disappoints, becomes more agreeable to us than the uniformity which would have gratified our expectation : but without this order and method we could remember very little of what had gone before, and we could foresee still less of what was to come after ; and the whole enjoyment of Music would be equal to little more than the effect of the particular sounds which rung in our ears at every particular instant. By means of this order and method it is, during the progress of the entertainment, equal to the effect of all that we remember, and of all that we foresee ; and at the conclusion of the entertainment, to the combined and accumulated effect of all the different parts of which the whole was composed.

A well-composed concerto of instrumental Music, by the number and variety of the instruments, by the variety of the parts which are performed by them, and the perfect concord or correspondence of all these different parts ; by the exact harmony or coincidence of all the different sounds which are heard at the same time, and by that happy variety of measure which regulates the succession of those which are heard at different times, presents an object so agreeable, so great, so various, and so interesting, that alone, and without suggesting any other object, either by imitation or otherwise, it can occupy, and as it were fill up, completely the whole capacity of the mind, so as to leave no part of its attention vacant for thinking of any thing else. In the contemplation of that immense variety of agreeable and melodious sounds, arranged and digested, both in their coincidence and in their succession, into so complete and regular a system, the mind in reality enjoys not only a very great sensual, but a very high intellectual pleasure, not unlike that which it derives from the contemplation of a great system in any other science. A full concerto of such instrumental Music, not only does not require, but it does not admit of any accompaniment. A song or a dance, by demanding an attention which we have not to spare, would disturb, instead of heightening, the effect of the Music ; they may often very properly succeed, but they cannot accompany it. That music seldom means to tell any particular story, or to imitate any particular event, or in general to suggest any particular object, distinct from that combination of sounds of which itself is composed. Its meaning, therefore, may be said to be complete in itself, and to require no interpreters to explain it. What is called the subject of such Music is merely, as has already been said, a certain leading combination of notes, to which it frequently returns, and to which all its digressions and variations bear a certain affinity. It is altogether different from what is called the subject of a poem or a picture, which is always something which is not either in the poem or in the picture, or something distinct from that combination, either of words on the one hand or of colours on the other, of which they are respectively composed. The subject of a composition of instrumental Music is part of that composition: the subject of a poem or picture is part of neither.

The effect of instrumental Music upon the mind has been called its expression. In the feeling it is frequently not unlike the effect of what is called the expression of Painting, and is sometimes equally interesting. But the effect of the expression of Painting arises always from the thought of something which, though distinctly and clearly suggested by the drawing and colouring of the picture, is altogether different from that drawing and colouring. It arises sometimes from sympathy with, sometimes from antipathy and aversion to, the sentiments, emotions, and passions which the countenance, the action, the air and attitude of the persons represented suggest. The melody and harmony of instrumental Music, on the contrary, do not distinctly and clearly suggest any thing that is different from that melody and harmony. Whatever effect it produces is the immediate effect of that melody and harmony, and not of something else which is signified and suggested by them: they in fact signify and suggest nothing. It may be proper to say that the complete art of painting, the complete merit of a picture, is composed of three distinct arts or merits; that of drawing, that of colouring, and that of expression. But to say, as Mr. Addison does, that the complete art of a musician, the complete merit of a piece of Music, is composed or made up of three distinct arts or merits, that of melody, that of harmony, and that of expression, is to say, that it is made up of melody and harmony, and of the immediate and necessary effect of melody and harmony: the division is by no means logical; expression in painting is not the necessary effect either of good drawing or of good colouring, or of both together; a picture may be both finely drawn and finely coloured, and yet have very little expression: but that effect upon the mind which is called expression in Music, is the immediate and necessary effect of good melody. In the power of producing this effect consists the essential characteristic which distinguishes such melody from what is bad or indifferent. Harmony may enforce the effect of good melody, but without good melody the most skilful harmony can produce no effect which deserves the name of expression ; it can do little more than fatigue and confound the ear. A painter may possess, in a very eminent degree, the talents of drawing and colouring, and yet possess that of expression in a very inferior degree. Such a painter, too, may have great merit. In the judgment of Du Piles, even the celebrated Titian was a painter of this kind. But to say that a musician possessed the talents of melody and harmony in a very eminent degree, and that of expression in a very inferior one, would be to say, that in his works the cause was not followed by its necessary and proportionable effect. A musician may be a very skilful harmonist, and yet be defective in the talents of melody, air, and expression ; his songs may be dull and without effect. Such a musician too may have a certain degree of merit, not unlike that of a man of great learning, who wants fancy, taste, and invention.

Instrumental Music, therefore, though it may, no doubt, be considered in some respects as an imitative art, is certainly less so than any other which merits that appellation ; it can imitate but a few objects, and even these so imperfectly, that without the accompaniment of some other art, its imitation is scarce ever intelligible : imitation is by no means essential to it, and the principal effect it is capable of producing arises from powers altogether different from those of imitation.

PART III.

THE imitative powers of Dancing are much superior to those of instrumental Music, and are at least equal, perhaps superior, to those of any other art. Like instrumental Music, however, it is not necessarily or essentially imitative, and it can produce very agreeable effects, without imitating any thing. In the greater part of our common dances there is little or no imitation, and they consist almost entirely of a succession of such steps, gestures, and motions, regulated by the time and measure of Music, as either display extraordinary grace or require extraordinary agility. Even some of our dances, which are said to have been originally imitative, have, in the way in which we practise them, almost ceased to be so. The minuet, in which the woman, after passing and repassing the man several times, first gives him up one hand, then the other, and then both hands, is said to have been originally a Moorish dance, which emblematically represented the passion of love. Many of my readers may have frequently danced this dance, and, in the opinion of all who saw them, with great grace and propriety, though neither they nor the spectators once thought of the allegorical meaning which it originally intended to express.

A certain measured, cadenced step, commonly called a dancing step, which keeps time with, and as it were beats the measure of, the Music which accompanies and directs it, is the essential characteristic which distinguishes a dance from every other sort of motion. When the dancer, moving with a step of this kind, and observing this time and measure, imitates either the ordinary or the more important actions of human life, he shapes and fashions, as it were, a thing of one kind, into the resemblance of another thing of a very different kind : his art conquers the disparity which Nature has placed between the imitating and the imitated object, and has upon that account some degree of that sort of merit which belongs to all the imitative arts. This disparity, indeed, is not so great as in some other of those arts, nor consequently the merit of the imitation which conquers it. Nobody would compare the merit of a good imitative dancer to that of a good painter or statuary. The dancer, however, may have a very considerable degree of merit, and his imitation perhaps may sometimes be capable of giving us as much pleasure as that of either of the other two artists. All the subjects, either of Statuary or of History Painting, are within the compass of his imitative powers ; and in representing them, his art has even some advantage over both the other two. Statuary and History Painting can represent but a single instant of the action which they mean to imitate : the causes which prepared, the consequences which followed, the situation of that single instant are altogether beyond the compass of their imitation. A pantomime dance can represent distinctly those causes and consequences ; it is not confined to the situation of a single instant ; but, like Epic Poetry, it can represent all the events of a long story, and exhibit a long train and succession of connected and interesting situations. It is capable therefore of affecting us much more than either Statuary or Painting. The ancient Romans used to shed tears at the representations of their pantomimes, as we do at that of the most interesting tragedies ; an effect which is altogether beyond the powers of Statuary or Painting. ·

The ancient Greeks appear to have been a nation of dancers, and both their common and their stage dances seem to have been all imitative. The stage dances of the ancient Romans appear to have been equally so. Among that grave people it was reckoned indecent to dance in private societies ; and they could therefore have no common dances ; and among both nations imitation seems to have been considered as essential to dancing.

It is quite otherwise in modern times : though we have pantomime dances upon the stage, yet the greater part even of our stage dances are not pantomime, and cannot well be said to imitate any thing. The greater part of our common dances either never were pantomime, or, with a very few exceptions, have almost all ceased to be so.

This remarkable difference of character between the ancient and the modern dances seems to be the natural effect of a correspondent difference in that of the music, which has accompanied and directed both the one and the other.

In modern times we almost always dance to instrumental music, which being itself not imitative, the greater part of the dances which it directs, and as it were inspires, have ceased to be so. In ancient times, on the contrary, they seem to have danced almost always to vocal music; which being necessarily and essentially imitative, their dances became so too. The ancients seem to have had little or nothing of what is properly called instrumental music, or of music composed not to be sung by the voice, but to be played upon instruments, and both their wind and stringed instruments seem to have served only as an accompaniment and direction to the voice.

In the country it frequently happens, that a company of young people take a fancy to dance, though they have neither fiddler nor piper to dance to. A lady undertakes to sing while the rest of the company dance: in most cases she sings the notes only, without the words, and then the voice being little more than a musical instrument, the dance is performed in the usual way, without any imitation. But if she sings the words, and if in those words there happens to be somewhat more than ordinary spirit and humour, immediately all the company, especially all the best dancers, and all those who dance most at their ease, become more or less pantomimes, and by their gestures and motions express, as well as they can, the meaning and story of the song. This would be still more the case, if the same person both danced and sung; a practice very common among the ancients: it requires good lungs and a vigorous constitution; but with these advantages and long practice, the very highest dances may be performed in this manner. I have seen a Negro dance to his own song, the war-dance of his own country, with such vehemence of action and expression, that the whole company, gentlemen as well as ladies, got up upon chairs and tables, to be as much as possible out of the way of his fury. In the Greek language there are two verbs which both signify to dance; each of which has its proper derivatives, signifying a dance and a dancer. In the greater part of Greek authors, these two sets of words, like all others which are nearly synonymous, are frequently confounded, and used promiscuously. According to the best critics, however, in strict propriety, one of these verbs signifies to dance and sing at the same time, or to dance to one's own music. The other to dance without singing, or to dance to the music of other people. There is said too to be a correspondent difference in the signification of their respective derivatives. In the choruses of the ancient Greek tragedies, consisting sometimes of more than fifty persons, some piped and some sung, but all danced, and danced to their own music.

*   *   *   *   *   *   *

*   *   *   *   *   *   *

*** [*The following Observations were found among Mr.* SMITH'S
*Manuscripts, without any intimation whether they were intended
as part of this, or of a different Essay. As they appeared too
valuable to be suppressed, the Editors have annexed them to
this Essay.*]

Of the Affinity between Music, Dancing, and Poetry.

IN the second part of the preceding Essay I have mentioned the
connection between the two arts of *Music* and *Dancing*, formed by
the *Rhythmus*, as the ancients termed it, or, as we call it, the tune
or measure that equally regulates both.

It is not, however, every sort of step, gesture, or motion, of which the
correspondence with the tune or measure of Music will constitute a
Dance. It must be a step, gesture, or motion of a particular sort. In
a good opera-actor, not only the modulations and pauses of his voice,
but every motion and gesture, every variation, either in the air of his head
or in the attitude of his body, correspond to the time and measure of
Music. The best opera-actor, however, is not, according to the language of any country in Europe, understood to dance, yet in the performance of his part, he makes use of what is called the stage step; but
even this step is not understood to be a dancing step.

Though the eye of the most ordinary spectator readily distinguishes
between what is called a dancing step and any other step, gesture, or
motion, yet it may not perhaps be very easy to express what it is which
constitutes this distinction. To ascertain exactly the precise limits at
which the one species begins, and the other ends, or to give an accurate
definition of this very frivolous matter, might perhaps require more
thought and attention than the very small importance of the subject
may seem to deserve. Were I, however, to attempt to do this, I should
observe, that though in performing any ordinary action—in walking,
for example—from the one end of the room to the other, a person may
show both grace and agility, yet if he betrays the least intention of
showing either, he is sure of offending more or less, and we never fail
to accuse him of some degree of vanity and affectation. In the performance of any such ordinary action, every person wishes to appear
to be solely occupied about the proper purpose of the action: if he
means to show either grace or agility, he is careful to conceal that
meaning, and he is very seldom successful in doing so: he offends,
however, just in proportion as he betrays it, and he almost always
betrays it. In Dancing, on the contrary, every person professes, and
avows, as it were, the intention of displaying some degree either of
grace or of agility, or of both. The display of one, or other, or both
of these qualities, is in reality the proper purpose of the action; and
there can never be any disagreeable vanity or affectation in following

out the proper purpose of any action. When we say of any particular
person, that he gives himself many affected airs and graces in Dancing,
we mean either that he gives himself airs and graces which are unsuitable to the nature of the Dance, or that he executes awkwardly, perhaps
exaggerates too much, (the most common fault in Dancing,) the airs
and graces which are suitable to it. Every Dance is in reality a succession of airs and graces of some kind or other, and of airs and graces
which, if I may say so, profess themselves to be such. The steps,
gestures, and motions which, as it were, avow the intention of exhibiting a succession of such airs and graces, are the steps, the gestures,
and the motions which are peculiar to Dancing, and when these are
performed to the time and the measure of Music, they constitute what
is properly called a Dance.

But though every sort of step, gesture, or motion, even though performed to the time and measure of Music, will not alone make a
Dance, yet almost any sort of sound, provided it is repeated with a
distinct rhythmus, or according to a distinct time and measure, though
without any variation as to gravity or acuteness, will make a sort of
Music, no doubt indeed, an imperfect one. Drums, cymbals, and, so
far as I have observed, all other instruments of percussion, have only
one note ; this note, however, when repeated with a certain rhythmus,
or according to a certain time and measure, and sometimes, in order to
mark more distinctly that time and measure, with some little variation
as to loudness and lowness, though without any as to acuteness and
gravity, does certainly make a sort of Music, which is frequently far
from being disagreeable, and which even sometimes produces considerable effects. The simple note of such instruments, it is true, is generally a very clear, or what is called a melodious, sound. It does not
however seem indispensably necessary that it should be so. The
sound of the muffled drum, when it beats the dead march, is far from
being either clear or melodious, and yet it certainly produces a species
of Music which is sometimes affecting. Even in the performance of
the most humble of all artists, of the man who drums upon the table
with his fingers, we may sometimes distinguish the measure, and perhaps a little of the humour, of some favourite song ; and we must allow
that even he makes some sort of Music. Without a proper step and
motion, the observation of tune alone will not make a Dance ; time
alone, without tune, will make some sort of Music.

That exact observation of tune, or of the proper intervals of gravity
and acuteness, which constitutes the great beauty of all perfect Music,
constitutes likewise its great difficulty. The time, or measure of a song
are simple matters, which even a coarse and unpractised ear is capable
of distinguishing and comprehending : but to distinguish and comprehend all the variations of the tune, and to conceive with precision the
exact proportion of every note, is what the finest and most cultivated

ear is frequently no more than capable of performing. In the singing of the common people we may generally remark a distinct enough observation of time, but a very imperfect one of tune. To discover and to distinguish with precision the proper intervals of tune, must have been a work of long experience and much observation. In the theoretical treatises upon Music, what the authors have to say upon time is commonly discussed in a single chapter of no great length or difficulty. The theory of tune fills commonly all the rest of the volume, and has long ago become both an extensive and an abstruse science, which is often but imperfectly comprehended, even by intelligent artists. In the first rude efforts of uncivilized nations towards singing, the niceties of tune could be but little attended to : I have, upon this account, been frequently disposed to doubt of the great antiquity of those national songs, which it is pretended have been delivered down from age to age by a sort of oral tradition, without having been ever noted or distinctly recorded for many successive generations. The measure, the humour of the song, might perhaps have been delivered down in this manner, but it seems scarcely possible that the precise notes of the tune should have been so preserved. The method of singing some of what we reckon our old Scotch songs, has undergone great alterations within the compass of my memory, and it may have undergone still greater before.

The distinction between the sounds or tones of singing and those of speaking seems to be of the same kind with that between the steps, gestures, and motions of Dancing, and those of any other ordinary action ; though in speaking, a person may show a very agreeable tone of voice, yet if he seems to intend to show it, if he appears to listen to the sound of his own voice, and as it were to tune it into a pleasing modulation, he never fails to offend, as guilty of a most disagreeable affectation. In speaking, as in every other ordinary action, we expect and require that the speaker should attend only to the proper purpose of the action, the clear and distinct expression of what he has to say. In singing, on the contrary, every person professes the intention to please by the tone and cadence of his voice ; and he not only appears to be guilty of no disagreeable affectation in doing so, but we expect and require that he should do so. To please by the choice and arrangement of agreeable sounds is the proper purpose of all Music, vocal as well as instrumental ; and we always expect and require, that every person should attend to the proper purpose of whatever action he is performing. A person may appear to sing, as well as to dance, affectedly ; he may endeavour to please by sounds and tones which are unsuitable to the nature of the song, or he may dwell too much on those which are suitable to it, or in some other way he may show an overweening conceit of his own abilities, beyond what seems to be warranted by his performance. The disagreeable affectation appears to consist always, not in attempting to please by a proper, but by some improper modulation of the voice. It was early discovered that the vibrations of chords or strings, which either in their lengths, or in their densities, or in their degrees of tension, bear a certain proportion to one another, produce sounds which correspond exactly, or, as the musicians say, are the unisons of those sounds or tones of the human voice which the ear approves of in singing. This discovery has enabled musicians to speak with distinctness and precision concerning the musical sounds or tones of the human voice; they can always precisely ascertain what are the particular sounds or tones which they mean, by ascertaining what are the proportions of the strings of which the vibrations produce the unisons of those sounds or tones. What are called the intervals; that is, the differences, in point of gravity and acuteness, between the sounds or tones of a singing voice, are much greater and more distinct than those of the speaking voice. Though the former, therefore, can be measured and appreciated by the proportions of chords or strings, the latter cannot. The nicest instruments cannot express the extreme minuteness of these intervals. The heptamerede of Mr. *Sauveur* could express an interval so small as the seventh part of what is called a comma, the smallest interval that is admitted in modern Music. Yet even this instrument, we are informed by Mr. *Duclos*, could not express the minuteness of the intervals in the pronunciation of the Chinese language; of all the languages in the world, that of which the pronunciation is said to approach the nearest to singing, or in which the intervals are said to be the greatest.

As the sounds or tones of the singing voice, therefore, can be ascertained or appropriated, while those of the speaking voice cannot; the former are capable of being noted or recorded, while the latter are not.

ADAM SMITH

ON THE

EXTERNAL SENSES.

THE Senses, by which we perceive external objects, are commonly reckoned Five in Number; viz. Seeing, Hearing, Smelling, Tasting, and Touching.

Of these, the four first mentioned are each of them confined to particular parts or organs of the body; the Sense of Seeing is confined to the Eyes; that of Hearing to the Ears; that of Smelling to the Nostrils; and that of Tasting to the Palate. The Sense of Touching alone seems not to be confined to any particular organ, but to be diffused through almost every part of the body; if we except the hair and the nails of the fingers and toes, I believe through every part of it. I shall say a few words concerning each of these Senses; beginning with the last, proceeding backwards in the opposite order to that in which they are commonly enumerated.

Of the Sense of TOUCHING.

The objects of Touch always present themselves as pressing upon, or as resisting the particular part of the body which perceives them, or by which we perceive them. When I lay my hand upon the table, the table presses upon my hand, or resists the further motion of my hand, in the same manner as my hand presses upon the table. But pressure or resistance necessarily supposes externality in the thing which presses or resists. The table could not press upon, or resist the further motion of my hand, if it was not external to my hand. I feel it accordingly as something which is not merely an affection of the hand, but altogether external to and independent of my hand. The agreeable, indifferent, or painful sensation of pressure, accordingly as I happen to press hardly or softly, I feel, no doubt, as affections of my hand; but the thing which presses and which resists I feel as something altogether different from those affections, as external to my hand, and as being altogether independent of it.

In moving my hand along the table it soon comes, in every direction, to a place where this pressure or resistance ceases. This place we call the boundary, or end of the table; of which the extent and figure are determined by the extent and direction of the lines or surfaces which constitute this boundary or end.

It is in this manner that a man born blind, or who has lost his sight so early that he has no remembrance of visible objects, may form the most distinct idea of the extent and figure of all the different parts of his own body, and of every other tangible object which he has an opportunity of handling and examining. When he lays his hand upon his foot, as his hand feels the pressure or resistance of his foot, so his foot feels that of his hand. They are both external to one another, but they are, neither of them, altogether so external to him. He feels in both, and he naturally considers them as parts of himself, or at least as something which belongs to him, and which, for his own comfort, it is necessary that he should take some care of.

When he lays his hand upon the table, though his hand feels the pressure of the table, the table does not feel, at least he does not know that it feels, the pressure of his hand. He feels it therefore as something external, not only to his hand, but to himself, as something which makes no part of himself, and in the state and condition of which he has not necessarily any concern.

When he lays his hand upon the body either of another man, or of any other animal, though he knows, or at least may know, that they feel the pressure of his hand as much as he feels that of their body: yet as this feeling is altogether external to him, he frequently gives no attention to it, and at no time takes any further concern in it than he is obliged to do by that fellow-feeling which Nature has, for the wisest purposes, implanted in man, not only towards all other men, but (though no doubt in a much weaker degree) towards all other animals. Having destined him to be the governing animal in this world, it seems to have been her benevolent intention to inspire him with some degree of respect, even for the meanest and weakest of his subjects.

This power or quality of resistance we call Solidity; and the thing which possesses it, the Solid Body or Thing. As we feel it as something altogether external to us, so we necessarily conceive it as something altogether independent of us. We consider it, therefore, as what we call a Substance, or as a thing that subsists by itself, and independent of any other thing. Solid and substantial, accordingly, are two words which, in common language, are considered either as altogether or as nearly synonymous.

Solidity necessarily supposes some degree of extension, and that in all the three directions of length, breadth, and thickness. All the solid bodies, of which we have any experience, have some degree of such bulk or magnitude. It seems to be essential to their nature, and without it, we cannot even conceive how they should be capable of pressure or resistance; are are the powers by which they are made known to us, and by which alone they are capable of acting upon our own, and upon all other bodies.

Extension, at least any sensible extension, supposes divisibility. The body may be so hard, that our strength is not sufficient to break it; we still suppose, however, that if a sufficient force were applied, it might be so broken; and, at any rate, we can always, in fancy at least, imagine it to be divided into two or more parts.

Every solid and extended body, if it be not infinite, (as the universe may be conceived to be,) must have some shape or figure, or be bounded by certain lines and surfaces.

Every such body must likewise be conceived as capable both of motion and of rest; both of altering its situation with regard to other surrounding bodies, and of remaining in the same situation. That bodies of small or moderate bulk, are capable of both motion and rest we have constant experience. Great masses, perhaps, are according to the ordinary habits of the imagination, supposed to be more fitted for rest than for motion. Provided a sufficient force could be applied, however, we have no difficulty in conceiving that the greatest and most unwieldy masses might be made capable of motion. Philosophy teaches us, (and by reasons too to which it is scarcely possible to refuse our assent,) that the earth itself, and bodies much larger than the earth, are not only movable, but are at all times actually in motion, and continually altering their situation, in respect to other surrounding bodies, with a rapidity that almost passes all human comprehension. In the system of the universe, at least according to the imperfect notions which we have hitherto been able to attain concerning it, the great difficulty seems to be, not to find the most enormous masses in motion, but to find the smallest particle of matter that is perfectly at rest with regard to all other surrounding bodies.

These four qualities, or attributes of extension, divisibility, figure, and mobility, or the capacity of motion or rest, seem necessarily involved in the idea or conception of a solid substance. They are, in reality, inseparable from that idea or conception, and the solid substance cannot possibly be conceived to exist without them. No other qualities or attributes seem to be involved, in the same manner, in this our idea or conception of solidity. It would, however, be rash from thence to conclude that the solid substance can, as such, possess no other qualities or attributes. This rash conclusion, notwithstanding, has been not only drawn, but insisted upon, as an axiom of indubitable certainty, by philosophers of very eminent reputation.

Of these external and resisting substances, some yield easily, and change their figure, at least in some degree, in consequence of the pressure of our hand: others neither yield nor change their figure, in any respect, in consequence of the utmost pressure which our hand alone is capable of giving them. The former we call soft, the latter hard, bodies. In some bodies the parts are so very easily separable, that they not only yield to a very moderate pressure, but easily receive the pressing body within them, and without much resistance allow it to traverse their extent in every possible direction. These are called Fluid, in contradistinction to those of which the parts not being so easily separable, are upon that account peculiarly called Solid Bodies; as if they possessed, in a more distinct and perceptible manner, the characteristical quality of solidity or the power of resistance. Water, however (one of the fluids with which we are most familiar), when confined on all sides (as in a hollow globe of metal, which is first filled with it, and then sealed hermetically), has been found to resist pressure as much as the very hardest, or what we commonly call the most solid bodies.

Some fluids yield so very easily to the slightest pressure, that upon ordinary occasions we are scarcely sensible of their resistance; and are upon that account little disposed to conceive them as bodies, or as things capable of pressure and resistance. There was a time, as we may learn from Aristotle and Lucretius, when it was supposed to require some degree of philosophy to demonstrate that air was a real solid body, or capable of pressure and resistance. What, in ancient

29

times, and in vulgar apprehensions, was supposed to be doubtful with regard to air, still continues to be so with regard to light, of which the rays, however condensed or concentrated, have never appeared capable of making the smallest resistance to the motion of other bodies, the characteristical power or quality of what are called bodies, or solid substances. Some philosophers accordingly doubt, and some even deny, that light is a material or corporeal substance.

Though all bodies or solid substances resist, yet all those with which we are acquainted appear to be more or less compressible, or capable of having, without any diminution in the quantity of their matter, their bulk more or less reduced within a smaller space than that which they usually occupy. An experiment of the Florentine academy was supposed to have fully demonstrated that water was absolutely incompressible. The same experiment, however, having been repeated with more care and accuracy, it appears, that water, though it strongly resists compression, is, however, when a sufficient force is applied, like all other bodies, in some degree liable to it. Air, on the contrary, by the application of a very moderate force, is easily reducible within a much smaller portion of space than that which it usually occupies. The condensing engine, and what is founded upon it, the wind-gun, sufficiently demonstrate this: and even without the help of such ingenious and expensive machines, we may easily satisfy ourselves of the truth of this proportion, by squeezing a full-blown bladder of which the neck is well tied.

The hardness or softness of bodies, or the greater or smaller force with which they resist any change of shape, seems to depend altogether upon the stronger or weaker degree of cohesion with which their parts are mutually attracted to one another. The greater or smaller force with which they resist compression may, upon many occasions, be owing partly to the same cause: but it may likewise be owing to the greater or smaller proportion of empty space comprehended within their dimensions, or intermixed with the solid parts which compose them. A body which comprehended no empty space within its dimensions, which, through all its parts, was completely filled with the resisting substance, we are naturally disposed to conceive as something which would be absolutely incompressible, and which would resist, with unconquerable force, every attempt to reduce it within narrower dimensions. If the solid and resisting substance, without moving out of its place, should admit into the same place another solid and resisting substance, it would from that moment, in our apprehension, cease to be a solid and resisting substance, and would no longer appear to possess that quality, by which alone it is made known to us, and which we therefore consider as constituting its nature and essence, and as altogether inseparable from it. Hence our notion of what has been called impenetrability of matter; or of the absolute impossibility that two solid resisting substances should occupy the same place at the same time.

This doctrine, which is as old as Leucippus, Democritus, and Epicurus, was in the last century revived by Gassendi, and has since been adopted by Newton and the far greater part of his followers. It may at present be considered as the established system, or as the system that is most in fashion, and most approved of by the greater part of the philosophers of Europe. Though it has been opposed by several puzzling arguments, drawn from that species of metaphysics which confounds every thing and explains nothing, it seems upon the whole to be the most simple, the most distinct, and the most comprehensible account that has yet been given of the phenomena which are meant to be explained by it. I shall only observe, that whatever system may be adopted concerning the hardness or softness, the fluidity or solidity, the compressibility or incompressibility of the resisting substance, the certainty of our distinct sense and feeling of its Externality, or of its entire independency upon the organ which perceives it, or by which we perceive it, cannot in the smallest degree be affected by any such system. I shall not therefore attempt to give any further account of such systems.

Heat and cold being felt by almost every part of the human body, have commonly been ranked along with solidity and resistance, among the qualities which are the objects of Touch. It is not, however, I think, in our language proper to say that we touch, but that we feel the qualities of heat and cold. The word *feeling*, though in many cases we use it as synonymous to *touching*, has, however, a much more extensive signification, and is frequently employed to denote our internal, as well as our external, affections. We feel hunger and thirst, we feel joy and sorrow, we feel love and hatred.

Heat and cold, in reality, though they may frequently be perceived by the same parts of the human body, constitute an order of sensations altogether different from those which are the proper objects of Touch. They are naturally felt, not as pressing upon the organ, but as in the organ. What we feel while we stand in the sunshine during a hot, or in the shade during a frosty, day, is evidently felt, not as pressing upon the body, but as in the body. It does not necessarily suggest the presence of any external object, nor could we from thence alone infer the existence of any such object. It is a sensation which neither does nor can exist any where but either in the organ which feels it, or in the unknown principle of perception, whatever that may be, which feels in that organ, or by means of that organ. When we lay our hand upon a table, which is either heated or cooled a good deal beyond the actual temperature of our hand, we have two distinct perceptions: first, that of the solid or resisting table, which is necessarily felt as something external to, and independent of, the hand which feels it; and secondly,

29 °

that of the heat or cold, which by the contact of the table is excited in our hand, and which is naturally felt as nowhere but in our hand, or in the principle of perception which feels in our hand.

But though the sensations of heat and cold do not necessarily suggest the presence of any external object, we soon learn from experience that they are commonly excited by some such object: sometimes by the temperature of some external body immediately in contact with our own body, and sometimes by some body at either a moderate or a great distance from us; as by the fire in a chamber, or by the sun in a summer's day. By the frequency and uniformity of this experience, by the custom and habit of thought which that frequency and uniformity necessarily occasion, the Internal Sensation, and the External Cause of that Sensation, come in our conception to be so strictly connected, that in our ordinary and careless way of thinking, we are apt to consider them as almost one and the same thing, and therefore denote them by one and the same word. The confusion, however, is in this case more in the word than in the thought; for in reality we still retain some notion of the distinction, though we do not always evolve it with that accuracy which a very slight degree of attention might enable us to do. When we move our hand, for example, along the surface of a very hot or of a very cold table, though we say that the table is hot or cold in every part of it, we never mean that, in any part of it, it feels the sensations either of heat or of cold, but that in every part of it, it possesses the power of exciting one or other of those sensations in our bodies. The philosophers who have taken so much pains to prove that there is no heat in the fire, meaning that the sensation or feeling of heat is not in the fire, have laboured to refute an opinion which the most ignorant of mankind never entertained. But the same word being, in common language, employed to signify both the sensation and the power of exciting that sensation, they, without knowing it perhaps, or intending it, have taken advantage of this ambiguity, and have triumphed in their own superiority, when by irresistible arguments they establish an opinion which, in words indeed, is diametrically opposite to the most obvious judgments of mankind, but which in reality is perfectly agreeable to those judgments.

Of the Sense of TASTING.

WHEN we taste any solid or liquid substance, we have always two distinct perceptions: first, that of the solid or liquid body, which is naturally felt as pressing upon, and therefore as external to, and independent of, the organ which feels it; and secondly, that of particular taste, relish, or savour which it excites in the palate or organ of Tasting, and which is naturally felt, not as pressing upon, as external to, or as independent of, that organ; but as altogether in the organ, and nowhere but in the organ, or in the principle of perception which feels in that organ. When we say that the food which we eat has an agreeable or disagreeable taste in every part of it, we do not thereby mean that it has the feeling or sensation of taste in any part of it, but that in every part of it, it has the power of exciting that feeling or sensation in our palates. Though in this case we denote by the same word (in the same manner, and for the same reason, as in the case of heat and cold) both the sensation and the power of exciting that sensation, this ambiguity of language misleads the natural judgments of mankind in the one case as little as in the other. Nobody ever fancies that our food feels its own agreeable or disagreeable taste.

Of the Sense of SMELLING.

EVERY smell or odour is naturally felt as in the nostrils; not as pressing upon or resisting the organ, not as in any respect external to, or independent of, the organ, but as altogether in the organ, and nowhere else but in the organ, or in the principle of perception which feels in that organ. We soon learn from experience, however, that this sensation is commonly excited by some external body; by a flower, for example, of which the absence removes, and the presence brings back, the sensation. This external body we consider as the cause of this sensation, and we denominate by the same words both the sensation and the power by which the external body produces this sensation. But when we say that the smell is in the flower, we do not thereby mean that the flower itself has any feeling of the sensation which we feel; but that it has the power of exciting this sensation in our nostrils, or in the principle of perception which feels in our nostrils. Though this sensation, and the power by which it is excited, are thus denoted by the same word, this ambiguity of language misleads, in this case, the natural judgments of mankind as little as in the two preceding.

Of the Sense of HEARING.

EVERY sound is naturally felt as in the Ear, the organ of Hearing. Sound is not naturally felt as resisting or pressing upon the organ, or as in any respect external to, or independent of, the organ. We naturally feel it as an affection of our Ear, as something which is altogether in our Ear, and nowhere but in our Ear, or in the principle of perception which feels in our Ear. We soon learn from experience, indeed, that the sensation is frequently excited by bodies at a considerable distance from us; often at a much greater distance, than those ever are which excite the sensation of Smelling. We learn too from experience that this sound or sensation in our Ears receives different modifications, according to the distance and direction of the body which originally causes it. The sensation is stronger, the sound is louder, when that body is near. The sensation is weaker, the sound is lower, when that body is at a distance. The sound, or sensation, too undergoes some variation according as the body is placed on the right hand or on the left, before or behind us. In common language we frequently say, that the sound seems to come from a great or from a small distance, from the right hand or from the left, from before or from behind us. We frequently say too that we hear a sound at a great or small distance, on our right hand or on our left. The real sound, however, the sensation in our ear, can never be heard or felt any where but in our ear, it can never change its place, it is incapable of motion, and can come, therefore, neither from the right nor from the left, neither from before nor from behind us. The Ear can feel or hear nowhere but where it is, and cannot stretch out its powers of perception, either to a great or to a small distance, either to the right or to the left. By all such phrases we in reality mean nothing but to express our opinion concerning either the distance or the direction of the body which excites the sensation of sound. When we say that the sound is in the bell, we do not mean that the bell hears its own sound, or that any thing like our sensation is in the bell, but that it possesses the power of exciting that sensation in our organ of Hearing. Though in this, as well as in some other cases, we express by the same word, both the Sensation, and the Power of exciting that Sensation; this ambiguity of language occasions scarce any confusion in the thought, and when the different meanings of the word are properly distinguished, the opinions of the vulgar, and those of the philosopher, though apparently opposite, on examination turn out to be exactly the same.

These four classes of secondary qualities, as philosophers have called them, or to speak more properly, these four classes of Sensations; Heat and Cold, Taste, Smell, and Sound; being felt, not as resisting or pressing upon the organ, but as in the organ, are not naturally perceived as external and independent substances; or even as qualities of such substances; but as mere affections of the organ, and what can exist nowhere but in the organ.

They do not possess, nor can we even conceive them as capable of possessing, any one of the qualities, which we consider as essential to, and inseparable from, external solid and independent substances.

First, They have no extension. They are neither long nor short; they are neither broad nor narrow; they are neither deep nor shallow. The bodies which excite them, the spaces within which they may be perceived, may possess any of those dimensions; but the Sensations themselves can possess none of them. When we say of a Note in Music, that it is long or short, we mean that it is so in point of duration. In point of extension we cannot even conceive, that it should be either the one or the other.

Secondly, Those Sensations have no figure. They are neither round nor square, though the bodies which excite them, though the spaces within which they may be perceived, may be either the one or the other.

Thirdly, Those Sensations are incapable of motion. The bodies which excite them may be moved to a greater or to a smaller distance. The Sensations become fainter in the one case, and stronger in the other. Those bodies may change their direction with regard to the organ of Sensation. If the change be considerable, the Sensations undergo some sensible variation in consequence of it. But still we never ascribe motion to the Sensations. Even when the person who feels any of those Sensations, and consequently the organ by which he feels them, changes his situation, we never, even in this case, say, that the Sensation moves, or is moved. It seems to exist always, where alone it is capable of existing, in the organ which feels it. We never even ascribe to those Sensations the attribute of rest; because we never say that any thing is at rest, unless we suppose it capable of motion. We never say that any thing does not change its situation with regard to other things, unless we can suppose it to be capable of changing that situation.

Fourthly, Those Sensations, as they have no extension, so they can have no divisibility. We cannot even conceive that a degree of Heat or Cold, that a Smell, a Taste, or a Sound, should be divided (in the same manner as the solid and extended substance may be divided) into two halves, or into four quarters, or into any number of parts.

But though all these Sensations are equally incapable of division; there are three of them, Taste, Smell, and Sound; which seem capable of a certain composition and decomposition. A skilful cook will, by his taste, perhaps, sometimes distinguish the different ingredients, which enter into the composition of a new sauce, and of which the simple tastes make up the compound one of the sauce. A skilful perfumer may, perhaps, sometimes be able to do the same thing with regard to a new scent. In a concert of vocal and instrumental music, an acute and experienced Ear readily distinguishes all the different sounds which strike upon it at the same time, and which may, therefore, be considered as making up one compound sound.

Is it by nature, or by experience, that we learn to distinguish between simple and compound Sensations of this kind? I am disposed to believe that it is altogether by experience; and that naturally all Tastes, Smells, and Sounds, which affect the organ of Sensation at the same time, are felt as simple and uncompounded Sensations. It is altogether by experience, I think, that we learn to observe the different affinities and resemblances which the compound Sensation bears to the different simple ones, which compose it, and to judge that the different causes, which excite those different simple Sensations, enter into the composition of that cause which excites the compounded one.

It is sufficiently evident that this composition and decomposition is altogether different from that union and separation of parts, which constitutes the divisibility of solid extension.

The Sensations of Heat and Cold seem incapable even of this species of composition and decomposition. The Sensations of Heat and Cold may be stronger at one time and weaker at another. They may differ in degree, but they cannot differ in kind. The Sensations of Taste, Smell, and Sound, frequently differ, not only in degree, but in kind. They are not only stronger and weaker, but some Tastes are sweet and some bitter; some Smells are agreeable, and some offensive; some Sounds are acute, and some grave; and each of these different kinds or qualities, too, is capable of an immense variety of modifications. It is the combination of such simple Sensations, as differ not only in degree but in kind, which constitutes the compounded Sensation.

These four classes of Sensations, therefore, having none of the qualities which are essential to, and inseparable from, the solid, external, and independent substances which excite them, cannot be qualities or modifications of those substances. In reality we do not naturally consider them as such; though in the way in which we express ourselves on the subject, there is frequently a good deal of ambiguity and confusion. When the different meanings of words, however, are fairly distinguished, these Sensations are, even by the most ignorant and illiterate, understood to be, not the qualities, but merely the effects of the solid, external, and independent substances upon the sensible and living organ, or upon the principle of perception which feels in that organ.

Philosophers, however, have not in general supposed that those exciting bodies produce those Sensations immediately, but by the intervention of one, two, or more intermediate causes.

In the Sensation of Taste, for example, though the exciting body presses upon the organ of Sensation, this pressure is not supposed to be the immediate cause of the Sensation of Taste. Certain juices of the exciting body are supposed to enter the pores of the palate, and to excite, in the irritable and sensible fibres of that organ, certain motions or vibrations, which produce there the Sensation of Taste. But how those juices should excite such motions, or how such motions should produce, either in the organ, or in the principle of perception which feels in the organ, the Sensation of Taste; or a Sensation, which not only does not bear the smallest resemblance to any motion, but which itself seems incapable of all motion, no philosopher has yet attempted, nor probably ever will attempt, to explain to us.

The Sensations of Heat and Cold, of Smell and Sound, are frequently excited by bodies at a distance, sometimes at a great distance, from the organ which feels them. But it is a very ancient and well-established axiom in metaphysics, that nothing can act where it is not; and this axiom, it must, I think, be acknowledged, is at least perfectly agreeable to our natural and usual habits of thinking.

The Sun, the great source of both Heat and Light, is at an immense distance from us. His rays, however (traversing, with inconceivable rapidity, the immensity of the intervening regions), as they convey the Sensation of Light to our eyes, so they convey that of Heat to all the sensible parts of our body. They even convey the power of exciting that Sensation to all the other bodies that surround us. They warm the earth and air, we say; that is, they convey to the earth and the air the power of exciting that Sensation in our bodies. A common fire produces, in the same manner, all the same effects ; though the sphere of its action is confined within much narrower limits.

The odoriferous body, which is generally too at some distance from us, is supposed to act upon our organs by means of certain small particles of matter, called Effluvia, which being sent forth in all possible directions, and drawn into our nostrils by the inspiration of breathing, produce there the Sensation of Smell. The minuteness of those small particles of matter, however, must surpass all human comprehension. Inclose in a gold box, for a few hours, a small quantity of musk. Take out the musk, and clean the box with soap and water as carefully as it is possible. Nothing can be supposed to remain in the box, but such effluvia as, having penetrated into its interior pores, may have escaped the effects of this cleansing. The box, however, will retain the smell of musk for many, I do not know for how many years; and these effluvia, how minute soever we may suppose them, must have had the powers of subdividing themselves, and of emitting other effluvia of the same kind, continually, and without any interruption, during so long a period. The nicest balance, however, which human art has ever been able to invent, will not show the smallest increase of weight in the gold box immediately after it has been thus carefully cleaned.

The Sensation of Sound is frequently felt at a much greater distance from the sounding, than that of Smell ever is from the odoriferous body. The vibrations of the sounding body, however, are supposed to produce certain correspondent vibrations and pulses in the surrounding atmosphere, which being propagated in all directions, reach our organ of Hearing, and produce there the Sensation of Sound. There are not many philosophical doctrines, perhaps, established upon a more probable foundation, than that of the propagation of Sound by means of the pulses or vibrations of the air. The experiment of the bell, which, in an exhausted receiver, produces no sensible Sound, would alone render this doctrine somewhat more than probable. But this great probability is still further confirmed by the computations of Sir Isaac Newton, who has shown that, what is called the velocity of Sound, or the time which passes between the commencement of the action of the sounding body, and that of the Sensation in our ear, is perfectly suitable to the velocity with which the pulses and vibrations of an elastic fluid of the same density with the air, are naturally propagated. Dr.

Benjamin Franklin has made objections to this doctrine, but, I think, without success.

Such are the intermediate causes by which philosophers have endeavoured to connect the Sensation in our organs, with the distant bodies which excite them. How those intermediate causes, by the different motions and vibrations which they may be supposed to excite on our organs, produce there those different Sensations, none of which bear the smallest resemblance to vibration or motion of any kind, no philosopher has yet attempted to explain to us.

Of the Sense of SEEING.

DR. BERKLEY, in his New Theory of Vision, one of the finest examples of philosophical analysis that is to be found, either in our own, or in any other language, has explained, so very distinctly, the nature of the objects of Sight : their dissimilitude to, as well as their correspondence and connection with those of Touch, that I have scarcely any thing to add to what he has already done. It is only in order to render some things, which I shall have occasion to say hereafter, intelligible to such readers as may not have had an opportunity of studying his book, that I have presumed to treat of the same subject, after so great a master. Whatever I shall say upon it, if not directly borrowed from Dr. Berkley, has at least been suggested by what he has already said.

That the objects of Sight are not perceived as resisting or pressing upon the organ which perceives them, is sufficiently obvious. They cannot therefore suggest, at least in the same manner as the objects of Touch, their externality and independency of existence.

We are apt, however, to imagine that we see objects at a distance from us, and that consequently the externality of their existence is immediately perceived by our sight. But if we consider that the distance of any object from the eye, is a line turned endways to it; and that this line must consequently appear to it, but as one point ; we shall be sensible that distance from the eye cannot be the immediate object of Sight, but that all visible objects must naturally be perceived as close upon the organ, or more properly, perhaps, like all other Sensations, as in the organ which perceives them. That the objects of Sight are all painted in the bottom of the eye, upon a membrane called the *retina*, pretty much in the same manner as the like objects are painted in a Camera Obscura, is well known to whoever has the slightest tincture of the science of Optics : and the principle of perception, it is probable, originally perceives them, as existing in that part of the organ, and nowhere but in that part of the organ. No optician, accordingly, no person who has ever bestowed any moderate degree of attention upon the nature of Vision, has ever pretended that distance from the eye was the immediate object of Sight. How it is that, by means of our Sight we learn to judge of such distances Opticians have endeavoured to explain in several different ways. I shall not, however, at present, stop to examine their systems.

The objects of Touch are solidity, and those modifications of solidity which we consider as essential to it, and inseparable from it ; solid extension, figure, divisibility, and mobility.

The objects of Sight are colour, and those modifications of colour which, in the same manner, we consider as essential to it, and inseparable from it ; coloured extension, figure, divisibility, and mobility. When we open our eyes, the sensible coloured objects, which present themselves to us, must all have a certain extension, or must occupy a certain portion of the visible surface which appears before us. They must too have all a certain figure, or must be bounded by certain visible lines, which mark upon that surface the extent of their respective dimensions. Every sensible portion of this visible or coloured extension must be conceived as divisible, or as separable into two, three, or more parts. Every portion too of this visible or coloured surface must be conceived as moveable, or as capable of changing its situation, and of assuming a different arrangement with regard to the other portions of the same surface.

Colour, the visible, bears no resemblance to solidity, the tangible object. A man born blind, or who has lost his sight so early as to have no remembrance of visible objects, can form no idea or conception of colour. Touch alone can never help him to it. I have heard, indeed, of some persons who had lost their sight after the age of manhood, and who had learned to distinguish by the touch alone, the different colours of cloths or silks, the goods which it happened to be their business to deal in. The powers by which different bodies excite in the organs of Sight the Sensations of different colours, probably depend upon some difference in the nature, configuration, and arrangement of the parts which compose their respective surfaces. This difference may, to a very nice and delicate touch, make some difference in the feeling, sufficient to enable a person, much interested in the case, to make this distinction in some degree, though probably in a very imperfect and inaccurate one. A man born blind might possibly be taught to make the same distinctions. But though he might thus be able to name the different colours, which those different surfaces reflected, though he might thus have some imperfect notion of the remote causes of the Sensations, he could have no better idea of the Sensations themselves, than that other blind man, mentioned by Mr. Locke, had, who said that he imagined the Colour of Scarlet resembled the Sound of a Trumpet. A man born deaf may, in the same manner, be taught to speak articulately. He is taught how to shape and dispose of his organs, so as to pronounce each letter, syllable, and word. But still, though he may have some imperfect idea of the remote causes of the Sounds which he himself utters, of the remote causes of the Sensations which he himself excites in other people ; he can have none of those Sounds or Sensations themselves.

If it were possible, in the same manner, that a man could be born without the Sense of Touching, that of Seeing could never alone suggest to him the idea of Solidity, or enable him to form any notion of the external and resisting substance. It is probable, however, not only that no man, but that no animal was ever born without the Sense of Touching, which seems essential to, and inseparable from, the nature of animal life and existence. It is unnecessary, therefore, to throw away any reasoning, or to hazard any conjectures, about what might be the effects of what I look upon as altogether an impossible supposition. The eye when pressed upon by any external and solid substance, feels, no doubt, that pressure and resistance, and suggests to us (in the same manner as every other feeling part of the body) the external and independent existence of that solid substance. But in this case, the eye acts, not as the organ of Sight, but as an organ of Touch ; for the eye possesses the Sense of Touching in common with almost all the other parts of the body.

The extension, figure, divisibility, and mobility of Colour, the sole object of Sight, though, on account of their correspondence and connection with the extension, figure, divisibility, and mobility of Solidity, they are called by the same name, yet seem to bear no sort of resemblance to their namesakes. As Colour and Solidity bear no sort of resemblance to one another, so neither can their respective modifications. Dr. Berkley very justly observes, that though we can conceive either a coloured or a solid line to be prolonged indefinitely, yet we cannot conceive the one to be added to the other. We cannot, even in imagination, conceive an object of Touch to be prolonged into an object of Sight, or an object of Sight into an object of Touch. The objects of Sight and those of Touch constitute two worlds, which, though they have a most important correspondence and connection with one another, bear no sort of resemblance to one another. The tangible world, as well as all the different parts which compose it, has three dimensions, Length, Breadth, and Depth. The visible world, as well as all the different parts which compose it, has only two, Length and Breadth. It presents to us only a plain or surface, which, by certain shades and combinations of Colour, suggests and represents to us (in the same manner as a picture does) certain tangible objects which have no Colour, and which therefore can bear no resemblance to those shades and combinations of Colour. Those shades and combinations suggest those different tangible objects as at different distances, according to certain rules of Perspective, which it is, perhaps, not very easy to say how it is that we learn, whether by some particular instinct, or by some application of either reason or experience, which has become so perfectly habitual to us, that we are scarcely sensible when we make use of it.

The distinctness of this Perspective, the precision and accuracy with which, by means of it, we are capable of judging concerning the distance of different tangible objects, is greater or less, exactly in proportion as this distinctness, as this precision and accuracy, are of more or less importance to us. We can judge of the distance of near objects, of the chairs and tables for example, in the chamber where we are sitting, with the most perfect precision and accuracy; and if in broad daylight we ever stumble over any of them, it must be, not from any error in the Sight, but from some defect in the attention. The precision and accuracy of our judgment concerning such near objects are of the utmost importance to us, and constitute the great advantage which a man who sees has over one who is unfortunately blind. As the distance increases, the distinctness of this Perspective, the precision and accuracy of our judgment gradually diminish. Of the tangible objects which are even at the moderate distance of one, two, or three miles from the eye, we are frequently at a loss to determine which is nearest, and which remotest. It is seldom of much importance to us to judge with precision concerning the situation of the tangible objects which are even at this moderate distance. As the distance increases, our judgments become more and more uncertain; and at a very great distance, such as that of the fixed stars, it becomes altogether uncertain. The most precise knowledge of the relative situation of such objects could be of no other use to the enquirer than to satisfy the most unnecessary curiosity.

The distances at which different men can by Sight distinguish, with some degree of precision, the situation of the tangible objects which the visible ones represent, is very different; and this difference, though it, no doubt, may sometimes depend upon some difference in the original configuration of their eyes, yet seems frequently to arise altogether from the different customs and habits which their respective occupations have led them to contract. Men of letters, who live much in their closets, and have seldom occasion to look at very distant objects, are seldom far-sighted. Mariners, on the contrary, almost always are; those especially who have made many distant voyages, in which they have been the greater part of their time out of sight of land, and have in daylight been constantly looking out towards the horizon for the appearance of some ship, or of some distant shore. It often astonishes a landsman to observe with what precision a sailor can distinguish in the offing, not only the appearance of a ship which is altogether invisible to the landsman, but the number of her masts, the direction of her course, and the rate of her sailing. If she is a ship of his acquaintance, he frequently can tell her name, before the landsman has been able to discover even the appearance of a ship.

Visible objects, Colour, and all its different modifications, are in themselves mere shadows or pictures, which seem to float, as it were, before the organ of Sight. In themselves, and independent of their connection with the tangible objects which they represent, they are of no importance to us, and can essentially neither benefit us nor hurt us. Even while we see them we are seldom thinking of them. Even when we appear to be looking at them with the greatest earnestness, our whole attention is frequently employed, not upon them, but upon the tangible objects represented by them.

It is because almost our whole attention is employed, not upon the visible and representing, but upon the tangible and represented objects, that in our imaginations we are apt to ascribe to the former a degree of magnitude which does not belong to them, but which belongs altogether to the latter. If you shut one eye, and hold immediately before the other a small circle of plain glass, of not more than half an inch in diameter, you may see through that circle the most extensive prospects; lawns and woods, and arms of the sea, and distant mountains. You are apt to imagine that the Landscape which is thus presented to you, that the visible Picture which you thus see, is immensely great and extensive. The tangible objects which this visible Picture represents, undoubtedly are so. But the visible Picture which represents them can be no greater than the little visible circle through which you see it. If while you are looking through this circle, you could conceive a fairy hand and a fairy pencil to come between your eye and the glass, that pencil could delineate upon that little glass the outline of all those extensive lawns and woods, and arms of the sea, and distant mountains, in the full and the exact dimensions with which they are really seen by the naked eye.

Every visible object which covers from the eye any other visible object, must appear at least as large as that other visible object. It must occupy at least an equal portion of that visible plain or surface which is at that time presented to the eye. Opticians accordingly tell us, that all the visible objects which are seen under equal angles must to the eye appear equally large. But the visible object, which covers from the eye any other visible object, must necessarily be seen under angles at least equally large as those under which that other object is seen. When I hold up my finger, however, before my eye, it appears to cover the greater part of the visible chamber in which I am sitting. It should therefore appear as large as the greater part of that visible chamber. But because I know that the tangible finger bears but a very small proportion to the greater part of the tangible chamber, I am apt to fancy that the visible finger bears but a like proportion to the greater part of the visible chamber. My judgment corrects my eyesight, and, in my fancy, reduces the visible object, which represents the little tangible one, below its real visible dimensions; and, on the contrary, it augments the visible object which represents the great tangible one a good deal beyond those dimensions. My attention being generally altogether occupied about the tangible and represented, and not at all about the visible and representing objects, my careless fancy bestows upon the latter a proportion which does not in the least belong to them, but which belongs altogether to the former.

It is because the visible object which covers any other visible object must always appear at least as large as that other object, that opticians tell us that the sphere of our vision appears to the eye always equally large ; and that when we hold our hand before our eye in such a manner that we see nothing but the inside of the hand, we still see precisely the same number of visible points, the sphere of our vision is still as completely filled, the retina of the eye is as entirely covered with the object which is thus presented to it, as when we survey the most extensive horizon.

A young gentleman who was born with a cataract upon each of his eyes, was, in one thousand seven hundred and twenty-eight, couched by Mr. Cheselden, and by that means for the first time made to see distinctly. 'At first,' says the operator, 'he could bear but very little 'sight, and the things he saw he thought extremely large ; but upon 'seeing things larger, those first seen he conceived less, never being 'able to imagine any lines beyond the bounds he saw ; the room he 'was in, he said, he knew to be but part of the house, yet he could not 'conceive that the whole house would look bigger.' It was unavoidable that he should at first conceive, that no visible object could be greater, could present to his eye a greater number of visible points, or could more completely fill the comprehension of that organ, than the narrowest sphere of his vision. And when that sphere came to be enlarged, he still could not conceive that the visible objects which it presented could be larger than those which he had first seen. He must probably by this time have been in some degree habituated to the connection between visible and tangible objects, and enabled to conceive that visible object to be small which represented a small tangible object ; and that to be great, which represented a great one. The great objects did not appear to his sight greater than the small ones had done before ; but the small ones, which, having filled the whole sphere of his vision, had before appeared as large as possible, being now known to represent much smaller tangible objects, seemed in his conception to grow smaller. He had begun now to employ his attention more about the tangible and represented, than about the visible and representing objects ; and he was beginning to ascribe to the latter the proportions and dimensions which properly belonged altogether to the former.

As we frequently ascribe to the objects of Sight a magnitude and proportion which does not really belong to them, but to the objects of

Touch which they represent, so we likewise ascribe to them a steadiness of appearance, which as little belongs to them, but which they derive altogether from their connection with the same objects of Touch. The chair which now stands at the farther end of the room, I am apt to imagine, appears to my eye as large as it did when it stood close by me, when it was seen under angles at least four times larger than those under which it is seen at present, and when it must have occupied, at least, sixteen times that portion which it occupies at present, of the visible plain or surface which is now before my eyes. But as I know that the magnitude of the tangible and represented chair, the principal object of my attention, is the same in both situations, I ascribe to the visible and representing chair (though now reduced to less than the sixteenth part of its former dimensions) a steadiness of appearance, which certainly belongs not in any respect to it, but altogether to the tangible and represented one. As we approach to, or retire from, the tangible object which any visible one represents, the visible object gradually augments in the one case, and diminishes in the other. To speak accurately, it is not the same visible object which we see at different distances, but a succession of visible objects, which, though they all resemble one another, those especially which follow near after one another ; yet are all really different and distinct. But as we know that the tangible object which they represent remains always the same, we ascribe to them too a sameness which belongs altogether to it : and we fancy that we see the same tree at a mile, at half a mile, and at a few yards distance. At those different distances, however, the visible objects are so very widely different, that we are sensible of a change in their appearance. But still, as the tangible objects which they represent remain invariably the same, we ascribe a sort of sameness even to them too.

It has been said, that no man ever saw the same visible object twice ; and this, though, no doubt, an exaggeration, is, in reality, much less so than at first view it appears to be. Though I am apt to fancy that all the chairs and tables, and other little pieces of furniture in the room where I am sitting, appear to my eye always the same, yet their appearance is in reality continually varying, not only according to every variation in their situation and distance with regard to where I am sitting, but according to every, even the most insensible variation in the altitude of my body, in the movement of my head, or even in that of my eyes. The perspective necessarily varies according to all even the smallest of these variations ; and consequently the appearance of the objects which that perspective presents to me. Observe what difficulty a portrait painter finds, in getting the person who sits for his picture to present to him precisely that view of the countenance from which the first outline was drawn. The painter is scarce ever completely satisfied with the situation of the face which is presented to him, and finds that it is scarcely ever precisely the same with that from which he rapidly sketched the first outline. He endeavours, as well as he can, to correct the difference from memory, from fancy, and from a sort of art of approximation, by which he strives to express as nearly as he can, the ordinary effect of the look, air, and character of the person whose picture he is drawing. The person who draws from a statue, which is altogether immovable, feels a difficulty, though, no doubt, in a less degree, of the same kind. It arises altogether from the difficulty which he finds in placing his own eye precisely in the same situation during the whole time which he employs in completing his drawing. This difficulty is more than doubled upon the painter who draws from a living subject. The statue never is the cause of any variation or unsteadiness in its own appearance. The living subject frequently is.

The benevolent purpose of nature in bestowing upon us the sense of seeing, is evidently to inform us concerning the situation and distance of the tangible objects which surround us. Upon the knowledge of this distance and situation depends the whole conduct of human life, in the most trifling as well as in the most important transactions. Even animal motion depends upon it ; and without it we could neither move, nor even sit still, with complete security. The objects of sight, as Dr. Berkley finely observes, constitute a sort of language which the Author of Nature addresses to our eyes, and by which he informs us of many things, which it is of the utmost importance to us to know. As, in common language, the words or sounds bear no resemblance to the thing which they denote, so, in this other language, the visible objects bear no sort of resemblance to the tangible object which they represent, and of whose relative situation, with regard both to ourselves and to one another, they inform us.

He acknowledges, however, that though scarcely any word be by nature better fitted to express one meaning than any other meaning, yet that certain visible objects are better fitted than others to represent certain tangible objects. A visible square, for example, is better fitted than a visible circle to represent a tangible square. There is, perhaps, strictly speaking, no such thing as either a visible cube, or a visible globe, the objects of sight being all naturally presented to the eye as upon one surface. But still there are certain combinations of colours which are fitted to represent to the eye, both the near and the distant, both the advancing and the receding lines, angles, and surfaces of the tangible cube ; and there are others fitted to represent, in the same manner, both the near and the receding surface of the tangible globe. The combination which represents the tangible cube, would not be fit to represent the tangible globe ; and that which represents the tangible globe, would not be fit to represent the tangible cube. Though there may, therefore, be no resemblance between visible and tangible

30

objects, there seems to be some affinity or correspondence between them sufficient to make each visible object fitter to represent a certain precise tangible object than any other tangible object. But the greater part of words seem to have no sort of affinity or correspondence with the meanings or ideas which they express; and if custom had so ordered it, they might with equal propriety have been made use of to express any other meanings or ideas.

Dr. Berkley, with that happiness of illustration which scarcely ever deserts him, remarks, that this in reality is no more than what happens in common language; and that though letters bear no sort of resemblance to the words which they denote, yet that the same combination of letters which represents one word, would not always be fit to represent another; and that each word is always best represented by its own proper combination of letters. The comparison, however, it must be observed, is here totally changed. The connection between visible and tangible objects was first illustrated by comparing it with that between spoken language and the meanings or ideas which spoken language suggests to us; and it is now illustrated by the connection between written language and spoken language, which is altogether different. Even this second illustration, besides, will not apply perfectly to the case. When custom, indeed has perfectly ascertained the powers of each letter; when it has ascertained, for example, that the first letter of the alphabet shall always represent such a sound, and the second letter such another sound ; each word comes then to be more properly represented by one certain combination of written letters or characters, than it could be by any other combination. But still the characters themselves are altogether arbitrary, and have no sort of affinity or correspondence with the articulate sounds which they denote. The character which marks the first letter of the alphabet, for example, if custom had so ordered it, might, with perfect propriety, have been made use of to express the sound which we now annex to the second, and the character of the second to express that which we now annex to the first. But the visible characters which represent to our eyes the tangible globe, could not so well represent the tangible cube; nor could those which represent the tangible cube, so properly represent the tangible globe. There is evidently, therefore, a certain affinity and correspondence between each visible object and the precise tangible object represented by it, much superior to what takes place either between written and spoken language, or between spoken language and the ideas or meanings which it suggests. The language which nature addresses to our eyes, has evidently a fitness of representation, an aptitude for signifying the precise things which it denotes, much superior to that of any of the artificial languages which human art and ingenuity have ever been able to invent.

That this affinity and correspondence, however, between visible and tangible objects could not alone, and without the assistance of observation and experience, teach us, by any effort of reason, to infer what was the precise tangible object which each visible one represented, if it is not sufficiently evident from what has been already said, it must be completely so from the remarks of Mr. Cheselden upon the young gentleman above-mentioned, whom he had couched for a cataract. 'Though we say of this gentleman, that he was blind,' observes Mr. Cheselden, 'as we do of all people who have ripe 'cataracts; yet they are never so blind from that cause but that they 'can discern day from night; and for the most part, in a strong light, 'distinguish black, white, and scarlet; but they cannot perceive the 'shape of any thing; for the light by which these perceptions are 'made, being let in obliquely through aqueous humour, or the anterior 'surface of the crystalline, (by which the rays cannot be brought into 'a focus upon the retina,) they can discern in no other manner than a 'sound eye can through a glass of broken jelly, where a great variety 'of surfaces so differently refract the light, that the several distinct 'pencils of rays cannot be collected by the eye into their proper foci ; 'wherefore the shape of an object in such a case cannot be at all discerned 'though the colour may: and thus it was with this young gentleman, 'who, though he knew those colours asunder in a good light, yet when 'he saw them after he was couched, the faint ideas he had of them 'before were not sufficient for him to know them by afterwards; and 'therefore he did not think them the same which he had before known 'by those names.' This young gentleman, therefore, had some advantage over one who from a state of total blindness had been made for the first time to see. He had some imperfect notion of the distinction of colours; and he must have known that those colours had some sort of connection with the tangible objects which he had been accustomed to feel. But had he emerged from total blindness, he could have learnt this connection only from a very long course of observation and experience. How little this advantage availed him, however, we may learn partly from the passages of Mr. Cheselden's narrative, already quoted, and still more from the following :

'When he first saw,' says that ingenious operator, 'he was so far 'from making any judgment about distances, that he thought all 'objects whatever touched his eyes (as he expressed) as what he felt 'did his skin; and thought no objects so agreeable as those which 'were smooth and regular, though he could form no judgment of their 'shape, or guess what it was in any object that was pleasing to him. 'He knew not the shape of any thing, nor any one thing from another, 'however different in shape or magnitude; but upon being told what 'things were, whose form he before knew from feeling, he would care- 'fully observe, that he might know them again; but having too many

30 *

'objects to learn at once, he forgot many of them; and (as he said) at 'first learned to know, and again forgot a thousand things in a day. 'One particular only (though it may appear trifling) I will relate: 'Having often forgot which was the cat and which was the dog, he 'was ashamed to ask; but catching the cat (which he knew by feeling) 'he was observed to look at her steadfastly, and then setting her down, 'said, So, puss! I shall know you another time.'

When the young gentleman said, that the objects which he saw touched his eyes, he certainly could not mean that they pressed upon or resisted his eyes; for the objects of sight never act upon the organ in any way that resembles pressure or resistance. He could mean no more than that they were close upon his eyes, or, to speak more properly, perhaps, that they were in his eyes. A deaf man, who was made all at once to hear, might in the same manner naturally enough say, that the sounds which he heard touched his ears, meaning that he felt them as close upon his ears, or, to speak perhaps more properly, as in his ears.

Mr. Cheselden adds afterwards: 'We thought he soon knew what 'pictures represented which were showed to him, but we found after-'wards we were mistaken; for about two months after he was couched, 'he discovered at once they represented solid bodies, when to that 'time, he considered them only as party-coloured planes, or surfaces 'diversified with variety of paints; but even then he was no less sur-'prised, expecting the pictures would feel like the things they repre-'sented, and was amazed when he found those parts, which by their 'light and shadow appeared now round and uneven, felt only flat like 'the rest; and asked which was the lying sense, feeling or seeing?'

Painting, though, by combinations of light and shade, similar to those which Nature makes use of in the visible objects which she presents to our eyes, it endeavours to imitate those objects; yet it never has been able to equal the perspective of Nature, or to give to its productions that force and distinctness of relief and rejection which Nature bestows upon hers. When the young gentleman was just beginning to understand the strong and distinct perspective of Nature, the faint and feeble perspective of Painting made no impression upon him, and the picture appeared to him what it really was, a plain surface bedaubed with different colours. When he became more familiar with the perspective of Nature, the inferiority of that of Painting did not hinder him from discovering its resemblance to that of Nature. In the perspective of Nature, he had always found that the situation and distance of the tangible and represented objects, corresponded exactly to what the visible and representing ones suggested to him. He expected to find the same thing in the similar, though inferior perspective of Painting, and was disappointed when he found that the visible and tangible objects had not, in this case, their usual correspondence.

'In a year after seeing,' adds Mr. Cheselden, 'the young gentleman 'being carried upon Epsom-downs, and observing a large prospect, he 'was exceedingly delighted with it, and called it a new kind of seeing.' He had now, it is evident, come to understand completely the language of Vision. The visible objects which this noble prospect presented to him did not now appear as touching, or as close upon his eye. They did not now appear of the same magnitude with those small objects to which, for some time after the operation, he had been accustomed, in the little chamber where he was confined. Those new visible objects at once, and as it were of their own accord, assumed both the distance and the magnitude of the great tangible objects which they represented. He had now, therefore, it would seem, become completely master of the language of Vision, and he had become so in the course of a year; a much shorter period than that in which any person, arrived at the age of manhood, could completely acquire any foreign language. It would appear too, that he had made very considerable progress even in the two first months. He began at that early period to understand even the feeble perspective of Painting; and though at first he could not distinguish it from the strong perspective of Nature, yet he could not have been thus imposed upon by so imperfect an imitation, if the great principles of Vision had not beforehand been deeply impressed upon his mind, and if he had not, either by the association of ideas, or by some other unknown principle, been strongly determined to expect certain tangible objects in consequence of the visible ones which had been presented to him. This rapid progress, however, may, perhaps, be accounted for from that fitness of representation, which has already been taken notice of, between visible and tangible objects. In this language of Nature, it may be said, the analogies are more perfect; the etymologies, the declensions, and conjugations, if one may say so, are more regular than those of any human language. The rules are fewer, and those rules admit of no exceptions.

But though it may have been altogether by the slow paces of observation and experience that this young gentleman acquired the knowledge of the connection between visible and tangible objects; we cannot from thence with certainty infer, that young children have not some instinctive perception of the same kind. In him this instinctive power, not having been exerted at the proper season, may, from disuse, have gone gradually to decay, and at last have been completely obliterated. Or, perhaps (what seems likewise very possible), some feeble and unobserved remains of it may have somewhat facilitated his acquisition of what he might otherwise have found it much more difficult to acquire a knowledge of.

That, antecedent to all experience, the young of at least the greater part of animals possess some instinctive perception of this kind, seems abundantly evident. The hen never feeds her young by dropping the food into their bills, as the linnet and thrush feed theirs. Almost as soon as her chickens are hatched, she does not feed them, but carries them to the field to feed, where they walk about at their ease, it would seem, and appear to have the most distinct perception of all the tangible objects which surround them. We may often see them, accordingly, by the straightest road, run to and pick up any little grains which she shows them, even at the distance of several yards; and they no sooner come into the light than they seem to understand this language of Vision as well as they ever do afterwards. The young of the partridge and of the grouse seem to have, at the same early period, the most distinct perceptions of the same kind. The young partridge, almost as soon as it comes from the shell, runs about among long grass and corn; the young grouse among long heath, and would both most essentially hurt themselves if they had not the most acute, as well as distinct perception of the tangible objects which not only surround them but press upon them on all sides. This is the case too with the young of the goose, of the duck, and, so far as I have been able to observe, with those of at least the greater part of the birds which make their nests upon the ground, with the greater part of those which are ranked by Linnæus in the orders of the hen and the goose, and of many of those long-shanked and wading birds which he places in the order that he distinguishes by the name of Grallæ.

The young of those birds that build their nests in bushes, upon trees, in the holes and crevices of high walls, upon high rocks and precipices, and other places of difficult access; of the greater part of those ranked by Linnæus in the orders of the hawk, the magpie, and the sparrow, seem to come blind from the shell, and to continue so for at least some days thereafter. Till they are able to fly they are fed by the joint labour of both parents. As soon as that period arrives, however, and probably for some time before, they evidently enjoy all the powers of Vision in the most complete perfection, and can distinguish with most exact precision the shape and proportion of the tangible objects which every visible one represents. In so short a period they cannot be supposed to have acquired those powers from experience, and must therefore derive them from some instinctive suggestion. The sight of birds seems to be both more prompt and more acute than that of any other animals. Without hurting themselves they dart into the thickest and most thorny bushes, fly with the utmost rapidity through the most intricate forests, and while they are soaring aloft in the air, discover upon the ground the insects and grains upon which they feed.

The young of several sorts of quadrupeds seem, like those of the greater part of birds which make their nests upon the ground, to enjoy as soon as they come into the world the faculty of seeing as completely as they ever do afterwards. The day, or the day after they are dropped, the calf follows the cow, and the foal the mare, to the field; and though from timidity they seldom remove far from the mother, yet they seem to walk about at their ease; which they could not do unless they could distinguish, with some degree of precision, the shape and proportion of the tangible objects which each visible one represents. The degree of precision, however, with which the horse is capable of making this distinction, seems at no period of his life to be very complete. He is at all times apt to startle at many visible objects, which, if they distinctly suggested to him the real shape and proportion of the tangible objects which they represent, could not be the objects of fear; at the trunk or root of an old tree, for example, which happens to be laid by the roadside, at a great stone, or the fragment of a rock which happens to lie near the way where he is going. To reconcile him, even to a single object of this kind, which has once alarmed him, frequently requires some skill, as well as much patience and good temper in the rider. Such powers of sight, however, as Nature has thought proper to render him capable of acquiring, he seems to enjoy from the beginning, in as great perfection as he ever does afterwards.

The young of other quadrupeds, like those of the birds which make their nests in places of difficult access, come blind into the world. Their sight, however, soon opens, and as soon as it does so, they seem to enjoy it in the most complete perfection, as we may all observe in the puppy and the kitten. The same thing, I believe, may be said of all other beasts of prey, at least of all those concerning which I have been able to collect any distinct information. They come blind into the world; but as soon as their sight opens, they appear to enjoy it in the most complete perfection.

It seems difficult to suppose that man is the only animal of which the young are not endowed with some instinctive perception of this kind. The young of the human species, however, continue so long in a state of entire dependency, they must be so long carried about in the arms of their mothers or of their nurses, that such an instinctive perception may seem less necessary to them than to any other race of animals. Before it could be of any use to them, observation and experience may, by the known principle of the association of ideas, have sufficiently connected in their young minds each visible object with the corresponding tangible one which it is fitted to represent. Nature, it may be said, never bestows upon any animal any faculty which is not either necessary or useful, and an instinct of this kind would be altogether useless to an animal which must necessarily acquire the knowledge which the instinct is given to supply, long before that instinct could be of any use to it. Children, however, appear at so very early a period to know the distance, the shape, and magnitude of the different tangible objects which are presented to them, that I am disposed to believe that even they may have some instinctive perception of this kind; though possibly in a much weaker degree than the greater part of other animals. A child that is scarcely a month old, stretches out its hands to feel any little plaything that is presented to it. It distinguishes its nurse, and the other people who are much about it, from strangers. It clings to the former, and turns away from the latter. Hold a small looking-glass before a child of not more than two or three months old, and it will stretch out its little arms behind the glass, in order to feel the child which it sees, and which it imagines is at the back of the glass. It is deceived, no doubt; but even this sort of deception sufficiently demonstrates that it has a tolerably distinct apprehension of the ordinary perspective of Vision, which it cannot well have learnt from observation and experience.

Do any of our other senses, antecedently to such observation and experience, instinctively suggest to us some conception of the solid and resisting substances which excite their respective sensations, though these sensations bear no sort of resemblance to those substances?

The sense of Tasting certainly does not. Before we can feel the sensation, the solid and resisting substance which excites it must be pressed against the organs of Taste, and must consequently be perceived by them. Antecedently to observation and experience, therefore, the sense of Tasting can never be said instinctively to suggest some conception of that substance.

It may, perhaps, be otherwise with the sense of Smelling. The young of all suckling animals, (of the Mammalia of Linnæus,) whether they are born with sight or without it, yet as soon as they come into the world apply to the nipple of the mother in order to suck. In doing this they are evidently directed by the Smell. The Smell appears either to excite the appetite for the proper food, or at least to direct the new-born animal to the place where that food is to be found. It may perhaps do both the one and the other.

That when the stomach is empty, the Smell of agreeable food excites and irritates the appetite, is what we all must have frequently experienced. But the stomach of every new-born animal is necessarily empty. While in the womb it is nourished, not by the mouth, but by the navel-string. Children have been born apparently in the most perfect health and vigour, and have applied to suck in the usual manner; but immediately, or soon after, have thrown up the milk, and in the course of a few hours have died vomiting and in convulsions. Upon opening their bodies it has been found that the intestinal tube or canal had never been opened or pierced in the whole extent of its length; but, like a sack, admitted of no passage beyond a particular place. It could not have been in any respect by the mouth, therefore, but altogether by the navel-string, that such children had been nourished and fed up to the degree of health and vigour in which they were born. Every animal, while in the womb, seems to draw its nourishment, more like a vegetable, from the root, than like an animal from the mouth; and that nourishment seems to be conveyed to all the different parts of the body by tubes and canals in many respects different from those which afterwards perform the same function. As soon as it comes into the world, this new set of tubes and canals which the providential care of Nature had for a long time before been gradually preparing, is all at once and instantaneously opened. They are all empty, and they require to be filled. An uneasy sensation accompanies the one situation, and an agreeable one the other. The smell of the substance which is fitted for filling them, increases and irritates that uneasy sensation, and produces in the infant hunger, or the appetite for food.

But all the appetites which take their origin from a certain state of the body, seem to suggest the means of their own gratification; and, even long before experience, some anticipation or preconception of the pleasure which attends that gratification. In the appetite for sex, which frequently, I am disposed to believe almost always, comes a long time before the age of puberty, this is perfectly and distinctly evident. The appetite for food suggests to the new-born infant the operation of sucking, the only means by which it can possibly gratifying that appetite. It is continually sucking. It sucks whatever is presented to its mouth. It sucks even when there is nothing presented to its mouth, and some anticipation or preconception of the pleasure which it is to enjoy in sucking, seems to make it delight in putting its mouth into the shape and configuration by which it alone can enjoy that pleasure. There are other appetites in which the most unexperienced imagination produces a similar effect upon the organs which Nature has provided for their gratification.

The smell not only excites the appetite, but directs to the object which can alone gratify that appetite. But by suggesting the direction towards that object, the Smell must necessarily suggest some notion of distance and externality, which are necessarily involved in the idea of direction; in the idea of the line of motion by which the distance can best be overcome, and the mouth brought into contact with the unknown substance which is the object of the appetite. That the Smell should alone suggest any preconception of the shape or magnitude of the external body to which it directs, seems not very probable. The sensation of Smell seems to have no sort of affinity or correspondence with shape or magnitude; and whatever preconception the infant may have of these, (and it may very probably have some such preconception,) is likely to be suggested, not so much directly by the Smell, and indirectly by the appetite excited by that Smell; as by the principle which teaches the child to mould its mouth into the conformation and action of sucking, even before it reaches the object to which alone that conformation and action can be usefully applied.

The Smell, however, as it suggests the direction by which the external body must be approached, must suggest at least some vague idea or preconception of the existence of that body; of the thing to which it directs, though not perhaps of the precise shape and magnitude of that thing. The infant, too, feeling its mouth attracted and drawn as it were towards that external body, must conceive the Smell which thus draws and attracts it, as something belonging to or proceeding from that body, or what is afterwards denominated and obscurely understood to be as a sort of quality or attribute of that body.

The Smell, too, may very probably suggest some even tolerably distinct perception of the Taste of the food to which it directs. The respective objects of our different external senses seem, indeed, the greater part of them, to bear no sort of resemblance to one another. Colour bears no sort of resemblance to Solidity, nor to Heat, nor to Cold, nor to Sound, nor to Smell, nor to Taste. To this general rule, however, there seems to be one, and perhaps but one exception. The sensations of Smell and Taste seem evidently to bear some sort of resemblance to one another. Smell appears to have been given to us by Nature as the director of Taste. It announces, as it were, before trial, what is likely to be the Taste of the food which is set before us. Though perceived by a different organ, it seems in many cases to be but a weaker sensation nearly of the same kind with that of the Taste which that announces. It is very natural to suppose, therefore, that the Smell may suggest to the infant some tolerably distinct preconception of the Taste of the food which it announces, and may, even before experience, make its mouth, as we say, water for that food.

That numerous division of animals which Linnæus ranks under the class of *worms*, have, scarcely any of them, any head. They neither see nor hear, have neither eyes nor ears ; but many of them have the power of self-motion, and appear to move about in search of their food. They can be directed in this search by no other sense than that of Smelling. The most accurate microscopical observations, however, have never been able to discover in such animals any distinct organ of Smell. They have a mouth and a stomach, but no nostrils. The organ of Taste, it is probable, has in them a sensibility of the same kind with that which the olfactory nerves have in more perfect animals. They may, as it were, taste at a distance, and be attracted to their food by an affection of the same organ by which they afterwards enjoy it ; and Smell and Taste may in them be no otherwise distinguished than as weaker or stronger sensations derived from the same organ.

The sensations of Heat and Cold, when excited by the pressure of some body either heated or cooled beyond the actual temperature of our own organs, cannot be said, antecedently to observation and experience, instinctively to suggest any conception of the solid and resisting substance which excites them. What was said of the sense of Taste may very properly be said here. Before we can feel those sensations, the pressure of the external body which excites them must necessarily suggest, not only some conception, but the most distinct conviction of its own external and independent existence.

It may be otherwise, perhaps, when those sensations are either of them excited by the temperature of the external air. In a calm day when there is no wind, we scarcely perceive the external air as a solid body ; and the sensations of Heat and Cold, it may be thought, are then felt merely as affections of our own body, without any reference to any thing external. Several cases, however, may be conceived, in which it must be allowed, I imagine, that those sensations, even when excited in this manner, must suggest some vague notion of some external thing or substance which excites them. A new-born animal, which had the power of self-motion, and which felt its body, either agreeably or disagreeably, more heated or more cooled on the one side than on the other, would, I imagine, instinctively and antecedently to all observation and experience, endeavour to move towards the side in which it felt the agreeable, and to withdraw from that in which it felt the disagreeable sensation. But the very desire of motion supposes some notion or preconception of externality ; and the desire to move towards the side of the agreeable, or from that of the disagreeable sensation, supposes at least some vague notion of some external thing or place which is the cause of those respective sensations.

The degrees of Heat and Cold which are agreeable, it has been found from experience, are likewise healthful ; and those which are disagreeable, unwholesome. The degree of their unwholesomeness, too, seems to be pretty much in proportion to that of their disagreeableness. If either of them is so disagreeable as to be painful, it is generally destructive ; and, that, too, in a very short period of time. Those sensations appear to have been given us for the preservation of our own bodies. They necessarily excite the desire of changing our situation when it is unwholesome or destructive ; and when it is healthy, they allow us, or rather they entice us, to remain in it. But the desire of changing our situation necessarily supposes some idea of externality ; or of motion into a place different from that in which we actually are ; and even the desire of remaining in the same place supposes some idea of at least the possibility of changing. Those sensations could not well have answered the intention of Nature, had they not thus instinctively suggested some vague notion of external existence.

That Sound, the object of the sense of Hearing, though perceived itself as in the ear, and nowhere but in the ear, may likewise, instinctively, and antecedently to all observation and experience, obscurely suggest some vague notion of some external substance or thing which excites it, I am much disposed to believe. I acknowledge, however, that I have not been able to recollect any one instance in which this sense seems so distinctly to produce this effect, as that of Seeing, that of Smelling, and even that of Heat and Cold, appear to do in some particular cases. Unusual and unexpected Sound alarms always, and disposes us to look about for some external substance or thing as the cause which excites it, or from which it proceeds. Sound, however, considered merely as a sensation, or as an affection of the organ of Hearing, can in most cases neither benefit nor hurt us. It may be agreeable or disagreeable, but in its own nature it does not seem to announce any thing beyond the immediate feeling. It should not therefore excite any alarm. Alarm is always the fear of some uncertain evil beyond what is immediately felt, and from some unknown and external cause. But all animals, and men among the rest, feel some degree of this alarm, start, are roused and rendered circumspect and attentive by unusual and unexpected Sound. This effect, too, is produced so readily and so instantaneously that it bears every mark of an instinctive suggestion of an impression immediately struck by the hand of Nature, which does not wait for any recollection of past observation and experience. The hare, and all those other timid animals to whom flight is the only defence, are supposed to possess the sense of Hearing in the highest degree of activeness. It seems to be the sense in which cowards are very likely to excel.

The three senses of Seeing, Hearing, and Smelling, seem to be given to us by Nature, not so much in order to inform us concerning the actual situation of our bodies, as concerning that of those other external bodies, which, though at some distance from us, may sooner or later affect the actual situation, and eventually either benefit or hurt us.

OF THE AFFINITY

BETWEEN CERTAIN

ENGLISH AND ITALIAN VERSES.

THE measure of the verses, of which the octave of the Italians, their terzetti, and the greater part of their sonnets, are composed, seems to be as nearly the same with that of the English Heroic Rhyme, as the different genius and pronunciation of the two languages will permit.

The English Heroic Rhyme is supposed to consist sometimes of ten, and sometimes of eleven syllables: of ten, when the verse ends with a single, and of eleven, when it ends with a double rhyme.

The correspondent Italian verse is supposed to consist sometimes of ten, sometimes of eleven, and sometimes of twelve syllables, according as it happens to end with a single, a double, or a triple rhyme.

The rhyme ought naturally to fall upon the last syllable of the verse; it is proper likewise that it should fall upon an accented syllable, in order to render it more sensible. When, therefore, the accent happens to fall, not upon the last syllable, but upon that immediately before it, the rhyme must fall both upon the accented syllable and upon that which is not accented. It must be a double rhyme.

In the Italian language, when the accent falls neither upon the last syllable, nor upon that immediately before it, but upon the third syllable from the end, the rhyme must fall upon all the three. It must be a triple rhyme, and the verse is supposed to consist of twelve syllables:

Forsè era ver, non però credibile, &c.

Triple rhymes are not admitted into English Heroic Verse.

In the Italian language the accent falls much more rarely, either upon the third syllable from the end of a word, or upon the last syllable, than it does upon the one immediately before the last. In reality, this second syllable from the end seems, in that language, to be its most common and natural place. The Italian Heroic Poetry, therefore, is composed principally of double rhymes, or of verses supposed to consist of eleven syllables. Triple rhymes occur but seldom, and single rhymes still more seldom.

In the English language the accent falls frequently upon the last syllable of the word. Our language, besides, abounds in words of one syllable, the greater part of which do (for there are few which do not) admit of being accented. Words of one syllable are most frequently the concluding words of English rhymes. For both these reasons, English Heroic Rhyme is principally composed of single rhymes, or of verses supposed to consist of ten syllables. Double Rhymes occur almost as rarely in it, as either single or triple do in the Italian.

The rarity of double rhymes in English Heroic Verse makes them appear odd, and awkward, and even ludicrous, when they occur. By the best writers, therefore, they are reserved for light and ludicrous occasions; when, in order to humour their subject, they stoop to a more familiar style than usual. When Mr. Pope says;

Worth makes the man, and want of it the fellow;
The rest is all but leather or prunello;

he means, in compliance with his subject, to condescend a good deal below the stateliness of his diction on the Essay on Man. Double rhymes abound more in Dryden than in Pope, and in Butler's Hudibras more than in Dryden.

The rarity both of single and of triple rhyme in Italian Heroic Verse, gives them the same odd and ludicrous air which double rhymes have in English Verse. In Italian, triple rhymes occur more frequently than single rhymes. The slippery, or if I may be allowed to use a very low, but a very expressive word, the glib pronunciation of the triple rhyme (*verso sotrucciolo*) seems to depart less from the ordinary movement of the double rhyme, than the abrupt ending of the single rhyme (*verso tronco e cadente*), of the verse that appears to be cut off and to fall short of the usual measure. Single rhymes accordingly appear in Italian verse much more burlesque than triple rhymes. Single rhymes occur very rarely in Ariosto; but frequently in the more burlesque poem of Ricciardetto. Triple rhymes occur much oftener in all the best writers. It is thus, that what in English appears to be the verse of the greatest gravity and dignity, appears in Italian to be the most burlesque and ludicrous; for no other reason, I apprehend, but because in the one language it is the ordinary verse, whereas in the other it departs most from the movements of ordinary verse.

The common Italian Heroic Poetry being composed of double rhymes, it can admit both of single and of triple rhymes; which seem to recede from the common movement on opposite sides to nearly equal distances. The common English Heroic Poetry, consisting of single rhymes, it can admit of double ; but it cannot admit of triple rhymes, which would recede so far from the common movements as to appear perfectly burlesque and ridiculous. In English, when a word accented upon the third syllable from the end happens to make the last word of a verse, the rhyme falls upon the last syllable only. It is a single rhyme, and the verse consists of no more than ten syllables : but as the last syllable is not accented, it is an imperfect rhyme, which, however, when confined to the second verse of the couplet, and even there introduced but rarely, may have a very agreeable grace, and the line may even seem to run more easy and natural by means of it :

> Bùt of this fràme, the beàrings, and the tíes.
> The strict connèctions, nìce depèndencies, &c.

When by a well accented syllable in the end of the first line of a couplet, it has once been clearly ascertained what the rhyme is to be, a very slight allusion to it, such as can be made by a syllable of the same termination that is not accented, may often be sufficient to mark the coincidence in the second line ; a word of this kind in the end of the first line seldom succeeds so well :

> Th' inhabitants of old Jerusalem
> Were Jebusites ; the town so called from them.

A couplet in which both verses were terminated in this manner, would be extremely disagreeable and offensive.

In counting the syllables, even of verses which to the ear appear sufficiently correct, a considerable indulgence must frequently be given, before they can, in either language, be reduced to the precise number of ten, eleven, or twelve, according to the nature of the rhyme.   In the following couplet, for example, there are, strictly speaking, fourteen syllables in the first line, and twelve in the second.

> And many a hŭmoŭrous, many an amorous lay,
> Was sung by many a bard, on many a day.

By the rapidity, however, or, if I may use a very low word a second time, by the glibness of the pronunciation, those fourteen syllables in the first line, and those twelve in the second, appear to take up the time but of ten ordinary syllables.   The words *many a*, though they plainly consist of three distinct syllables, or sounds, which are all pronounced successively, or the one after the other, yet pass as but two syllables ; as do likewise these words, *hŭmoŭroŭs*, and *amorous*.   The words *heaven* and *given*, in the same manner, consist each of them of two syllables, which, how rapidly so ever they may be pronounced, cannot be pronounced but successively, or the one after the other.   In verse, however, they are considered as consisting but of one syllable.

In counting the syllables of the Italian Heroic Verse, still greater indulgences must be allowed : three vowels must there frequently be counted as making but one syllable, though they are all pronounced, rapidly indeed, but in succession, or the one after the other, and though no two of them are supposed to make a diphthong.   In these licenses too, the Italians seem not to be very regular, and the same concourse of vowels which in one place makes but one syllable, will in another sometimes make two.   There are even some words which in the end of a verse are constantly counted for two syllables, but which in any other part of it are never counted for more than one; such as the words *suo, tuo, suoi, tuoi.*

Ruscelli observes, that in the Italian Heroic Verse the accent ought to fall upon the fourth, the sixth, the eighth, and the tenth syllables ; and that if it falls upon the third, the fifth, the seventh, or the ninth syllables, it will spoil the verse.

In English, if the accent falls upon any of the above-mentioned odd syllables, it equally spoils the verse.

> Bow'd their stiff necks, loaden with stormy blasts,

though a line of Milton, has not the ordinary movement of an English Heroic Verse, the accent falls upon the third and sixth syllables.

In Italian frequently, and in English sometimes, an accent is with great grace thrown upon the first syllable, in which case it seldom happens that any other syllable is accented before the fourth : ,

> Cánto l'armé pietóse é'l capitáno.
> First in these fiélds I trý the sýlvan stráins.

Both in English and in Italian the second syllable may be accented

with great grace, and it generally is so when the first syllable is not
accented :

> *E in van l'inferno a' lui s' oppose; e in vano*
> *S' armò d' Asia, e di Libia il popol misto,* &c.
>
> Let us, since life can little more supply
> Than just to look about us, and to die, &c.

Both in English and in Italian Verse, an accent, though it must
never be misplaced, may sometimes be omitted with great grace. In
the last of the above-quoted English Verses there is no accent upon
the eighth syllable; the conjunction *and* not admitting of any. In the
following Italian Verse there is no accent upon the sixth syllable:

> *O Musa, tu, che di caduchi allori,* &c.

The preposition *di* will as little admit of an accent as the conjunction
and. In this case, however, when the even syllable is not accented,
neither of the odd syllables immediately before or behind it must be
accented.

Neither in English nor in Italian can two accents running be omitted.

It must be observed, that in Italian there are two accents, the grave
and the acute: the grave accent is always marked by a slight stroke
over the syllable to which it belongs ; the acute accent has no mark.

The English language knows no distinction between the grave and
the acute accents.

The same author observes, that in the Italian Verse the Pause, or
what the grammarians call the Cesura, may with propriety be introduced after either the third, the fourth, the fifth, the sixth, or the
seventh syllables. The like observations have been made by several
different writers upon the English Heroic Verse. Dobie admires particularly the verse in which there are two pauses ; one after the fifth,
and another after the ninth syllable. The example he gives is from
Petrarch :

> *Nel dolce tempo de la prima etade,* &c.

In this verse, the second pause, which he says comes after the ninth
syllable, in reality comes in between the two vowels, which, in the
Italian way of counting syllables, compose the ninth syllable. It may
be doubtful, therefore, whether this pause may not be considered as
coming after the eighth syllable. I do not recollect any good English
Verse in which the pause comes in after the ninth syllable. We have
many in which it comes in after the eighth :

> Yet oft, before his infant eyes, would run, &c.

In which verse there are two pauses ; one after the second, and the
other after the eighth syllable. I have observed many Italian Verses in
which the pause comes after the second syllable.

Both the English and the Italian Heroic Verse, perhaps, are not so properly composed of a certain number of syllables, which vary according to the nature of the rhyme ; as of a certain number of intervals, (of five invariably,) each of which is equal in length, or time, to two ordinary distinct syllables, though it may sometimes contain more, of which the extraordinary shortness compensates the extraordinary number.   The close frequently of each of those intervals, but always of every second interval, is marked by a distinct accent.   This accent may frequently, with great grace, fall upon the beginning of the first interval ; after which, it cannot, without spoiling the verse, fall any where but upon the close of an interval.   The syllable or syllables which come after the accent that closes the fifth interval are never accented.   They make no distinct interval, but are considered as a sort of excrescence of the verse, and are in a manner counted for nothing.

THE END.

BRADBURY, EVANS, AND CO., PRINTERS, WHITEFRIARS.

www.ingramcontent.com/pod-product-compliance
Lightning Source LLC
Chambersburg PA
CBHW052339110726
47901CB00005B/1288